THRILLING

LOST WORLDS

SHORT STORIES

ANTHOLOGY OF NEW & CLASSIC TALES

Foreword by Adam Roberts

FLAME TREE PUBLISHING

TALES

This is a FLAME TREE Book

Publisher & Creative Director: Nick Wells
Project Editor: Laura Bulbeck
Editorial Board: Gillian Whitaker, Josie Mitchell, Catherine Taylor

Publisher's Note: Due to the historical nature of the classic text, we're aware that there may be some language used which has the potential to cause offence to the modern reader. However, wishing overall to preserve the integrity of the text, rather than imposing contemporary sensibilities, we have left it unaltered.

FLAME TREE PUBLISHING
6 Melbray Mews, Fulham,
London SW6 3NS, United Kingdom
www.flametreepublishing.com

First published 2017

19 21 20 18
3 5 7 9 10 8 6 4 2

ISBN: 978-1-78664-181-6

The cover image is created by Flame Tree Studio based on artwork by Slava Gerj and Gabor Ruszkai.

A copy of the CIP data for this book is available from the British Library.

Printed in China

THRILLING

LOST WORLDS

SHORT STORIES

ANTHOLOGY OF NEW & CLASSIC TALES

Foreword by Adam Roberts

FLAME TREE PUBLISHING

TALES

Contents

GOTHIC FANTASY

Foreword: Lost Worlds Short Stories

IS IT THE WORLDS that are lost, or us? Readers have marvelled at travellers' tales for hundreds of years, but there comes a time when the actual world has been fully visited, marked out and mapped. Of course our hunger for the thrill of such explorers' tales doesn't go away when the globe is wholly explored. Indeed, if anything the appetite increases, as we sense that some special kind of glamour is ebbing from life. And so story-tellers take us to new realms, lost worlds and imaginary places, to supply the adventure, excitement and wonder we crave. It is not a coincidence that the great vogue for 'Lost World' stories coincided with the height of the imperial age. These are narratives that speak to a desire not only to know, but somehow to *possess* the wonders they describe.

This anthology collects together some of the most famous, and the best, of these tales. It's a testament, amongst other things, to the amazing variety of this kind of story. Some of them take us deeper into the only recently explored territories of what used to be called 'the third world': a South American volcanic plateau, upon which dinosaurs escaped extinction, in Arthur Conan Doyle's *The Lost World*; or to Antarctica in James De Mille's 'A Strange Manuscript Found in a Copper Cylinder' and H.P. Lovecraft's 'At the Mountains of Madness'; or into the heart of Africa in H. Rider Haggard's 'King Solomon's Mines'; or beyond Afghanistan in Rudyard Kipling's peerless 'The Man Who Would Be King'. Others, like H.G. Wells's 'In the Country of the Blind' and Charlotte Perkins Gilman's 'Herland', are set in more nebulously identified 'uncharted lands'. Other writers elected to repudiate merely horizontal exploration, and to move their imaginations vertically, or in stranger directions even than that. A. Merritt's 'The Face in the Abyss' and Jules Verne's *Journey to the Centre of the Earth* take us into the bowels of the earth, whilst Wells's 'In the Abyss' glimpses a strange civilization in the depths of the ocean. Howard's 'The Lost Race' takes us back in time *and* underground, and Fitz-James O'Brien imagines a new world so microscopic it can fit inside a single droplet of water. Some of the stories are satirical – Jonathan Swift casts a cold eye on the absurdity of society in his lost worlds, and Gilman wants to make us rethink our preconceptions about gender. But the best kind of 'Lost Worlds' story is always more than just a satirical reflection on the known. It is a gateway into the possibilities of the unknown, and a pledge that however comprehensively geography and science apprehend the world there are still new realms for us to seek out.

If we ask where this urge to explore comes from, we are not likely to be satisfied with a merely geographical answer. It's part of who we are, as individuals, as a species, not something easily satiated with any particular or material discovery. We are looking, like Tennyson's Ulysses, for that untravelled world whose margin fades for ever and for ever as we move. We call this genre 'Lost Worlds', not 'Found Worlds', after all; and the best of these kinds of tales intrigue and lead us on even as they supply our sensibilities with wonder and novelty. They are stories that disclose, rather than enclose, and that tells us something important about the human experience – that we are still drawn to the unknown, because it is the unknown that defines us.

Adam Roberts
www.adamroberts.com

Publisher's Note

This latest title in our deluxe Gothic Fantasy short story anthologies is packed with high adventure – from dark valleys and high mountain passes, to ancient creatures and mysterious races. Once again, in order to include some of the best examples of the classic fiction in the Lost Worlds genre, we have provided some tantalizing extracts from longer novels – but all come with a link at the end to download the full story. Featuring such iconic works as Arthur Conan Doyle's dinosaur epic *The Lost World* and H.P. Lovecraft's chilling tale *At The Mountains of Madness*, as well as some rarer finds like Fitz-James O'Brien's 'The Diamond Lens', you'll discover pockets of the unknown in the strangest of places.

Every year the response to our call for submissions seems to grow and grow, giving us a rich universe of stories to choose from, but making our job all the more difficult in narrowing down the final selection. We've loved delving into such a variety of worlds out of time and out of place, and ultimately chose a selection of stories we hope sit alongside each other and with the classic selection, to provide a fantastic *Lost Worlds* book for all to enjoy.

THRILLING

LOST WORLDS

SHORT STORIES

ANTHOLOGY OF NEW & CLASSIC TALES

Foreword by Adam Roberts

FLAME TREE PUBLISHING

TALES

An Echo of Gondwana

Mike Adamson

THE MOUNTAINS of eastern Australia are an ancient land, and their high, cool rainforests hold their secrets close. I could not have said what silent stirring drew me, my whole life through, to their mysterious glades, but a day came when I could face something grander and more terrifying than I ever imagined this world could hold.

These feelings first stirred in me as a youngster in Adelaide, a school trip to the Art Gallery on North Terrace, and I found myself looking up at Isaac Whitehead's 1859 painting *In the Sassafrass Valley, Victoria*. This canvas has bewitched me ever since with its infinitude of detail, the dark depths of the understory, the sunlit upperworks of treeferns and exotic giants, the rushing stream tumbling in its bed, the whole dwarfing the tiny figures of explorers who move before the titanic scale of nature as if among the feet of gods and colossi. I stared at the painting for a long time, unable to tear myself away, uncaring for the other masterworks around it, and looking back when my teacher drew me on with the party. I visited again many times over the years and the painting has never lost its spell. Now, perhaps, I understand why.

There is a spirit in this land, as there probably is in every land. I do not know if what I perceive is the same spirit the indigenous Australians have always known and understood, and I have not trespassed upon their sacred traditions in my own need to know, but I have felt the soul that dwells in the land, and sensed the frightening scale on which time and nature move. These are things one does not take lightly, and I let my instinctive respect for these mysteries guide me.

My workmates never understood my reluctance to include them in my bushwalks and camping expeditions – I wanted solitude, not mateship around a campfire. Long nights of drinking would undo the delicate tracery of interconnections I was seeking, and I wanted only to get as far from other human beings as I could. *Davy Evans is a loner*, they would say. *Just leave him be.* Not all national parks allow camping, yet to feel the spirit of the wild by night was a siren song, and I knew I must stand among the ancient woodlands, alone and undisturbed, to absorb anything of the strange power they held.

You see, these forests are called the *Gondwana Rainforests*, and are held to be the last islands of unbroken living continuity from the time of the dinosaurs. Australia, along with Antarctica, India and others formed the southern supercontinent, named for Gondwana, in India, which broke up into the present masses over many millions of years. Many ancient lineages are found in the scattered highland forests, now isolated by elevation and terrain from each other and many secrets lie undiscovered. The Wollemi Pine was found in my own lifetime, thought to date from the Jurassic, and such an ocean of time strikes one mute with awe.

Perhaps it was the depth of the ages I sought, some tangible contact with the truly ancient, but these forests drew me back many times over the years – Barrington Tops, Mt. Seaview, Dorrigo, Mt. Hyland and more, clear up from New South Wales to the Daintree on the Queensland coast. To place my bare palm upon the trunk of a giant of the woods, itself many centuries old, but whose genetic lineage ran back into the mists of prehistory, was to feel a shudder in my spine and hear a whisper at the edges of my mind, as if something great and more than a little frightening was trying to speak to me.

As I grow older I have become contemptuous of human society. The ever-increasing hurry and bluster, rank commercialism and corruption which sever us so completely from our natural origins, blocking out all notions of any reality before itself, repel me. Perhaps this disconnect from the time we live in is why I have no family to follow on, and while there is reason to lament in this, there is also a cold logic. The compulsion of my life has never failed to call, and each time I went back into the high country I felt I drew closer.

Closer to *what*, I did not know. Not until the night closed around me.

* * *

They say the moon affects the cycles of life in the ocean all over the world, both with the tides and its phases, and a full moon often makes people do crazy things – according to hospital ERs. Maybe it was the full moon that made me drive up into the highlands, looking for any way to even be close to the relic forests as spring turned toward summer, and my GPS found me a little-used graded track, maybe a forestry or fire service way. I followed it in my 4WD with a sense of trespass as afternoon turned to evening and the green of the Australian forest before the heat of summer arrives surrounded me with its wild randomness. Truly, eucalypts often seem frozen in the act of gesticulation, thrashing in some extremis upon a timescale to which we are not privy, and this gives the landscape a sense of both baroque complexity and the untamed.

I had approached these highlands by more usual routes in the past but sensed I was in familiar country. I could retrace my way easily enough, and was not lost. I had my hiking kit, tough boots, mobile phone, flashlight and camera, all the bits and pieces one collects to travel safely in the wild places, water bottle, first aid kit, bug repellent, emergency rations. Much of it was rarely needed, but better to have it than not.

I found a parking spot under cover of spreading branches late in the day and rested for a while before checking my maps and taking a GPS fix on my location. I had no idea quite where I would end up but navigating back to the vehicle in the dark was another matter. I was not foolhardy, I meant to take no risks, but the ephemeral call of the ancient land would not be denied, and as the sun dropped behind the trees and plunged the peaks into a maze of golden glow and shadows, I locked my car, hefted my light pack and set off toward the towering trees of the relic. I was not sure how close I would get, close *enough*, I hoped.

Night in the bush is truly dark as city folk cannot appreciate. Pure, sable darkness, unrelieved but for the light of the stars, can be frightening, as can the silence of the outback. Here there was breeze in the treetops and the thousand minute sounds of the night, and I closed up my tough jacket as the cool of evening built. The moon would rise in a while, a few nights past full. I found a sun-warmed rock to rest upon among the gigantic trees, the araucarias and Antarctic beech, the treeferns and podocarps, and simply closed my eyes to *listen* to the world.

This was what I had sought so long, to be in the right place at the right time, to *feel* the flowing currents in the earth, to almost *hear* the resonance of the songlines sacred to the First Australians. It occurred to me I really had no business being here, but the earth itself seemed accepting; the land told me I was welcome for the moment and that meant more than human permits. I tried to divorce my ego and view the world with a blank mental slate, let each sound and feeling provide its own meaning. I breathed deeply, concentrated on a smooth cycling of breath, and waited for the moonrise.

What did I smell? The forest was an amalgam of growth and decay, stirred by the fresh wind. When I listened beyond the rush of blood in my ears, past the tinitis of the modern age, I heard the minute scratchings of tiny feet as nocturnal animals appeared, the flutter of microbats hunting insects, the hiss and chitter of the latter; the surreal sounds of rare and exotic frogs in a watercourse not far away, and the tread of larger animals out there in the night.

How primal was this…? *Totally*, I judged, for here nature alone held sway. In these peaks life's pageant was unbroken for 150 million years, at least, there had always been a forest in this place since the days when reptiles ruled, and the depth of time seemed to drop away from me like a bottomless chasm as I tried to envision it. I felt giddy, suspended over an eternity and liable to plunge into its immensity if I lost my hold on the here and now.

Perhaps this was the real terror of the wild – not even untamed but utterly beyond even knowledge of the fiction of human reality. This world, this place, was oblivious of the doings of the human race, mankind was merely an abstraction. To come face to face with such a notion was profoundly satisfying, though I knew it was my own interpretation grafted upon nature. Yet it was pleasing, as if feeling my way to a fundamentality of existence, and I explored it silently, seeming more and more comfortable here.

Perhaps I began to fall into a shallow, shallow sleep, for it seemed my mind drifted in a warm, suggestible cocoon of impressions. That narrow band between waking and sleeping – still conscious enough for the mind to be aware yet enough asleep for the dream cortex to be engaged – was a rich hunting ground for the mind's self-reflexive property, the raising of memories, impressions and needs to the mirror of dream.

Some say dreams are a gateway to the unseen. Certainly the First Australians place great value on dream perception, as do other peoples around the world, and as I fell gently into a meditative regimen I felt nothing amiss, nothing jarred. The world was a microcosm of possibilities and I was open to them, come what may.

I had no preconceptions other than the lifelong calling which told me something waited here to be found, and as I slipped into the strange waking-dream state I remained aware of the cooling evening air, the sounds of the forest around me, but through my closed eyelids I began to perceive the world by the light of a great silver moon which seemed somehow different from the one I expected to clear the trees in a while.

The forest seemed to shimmer, to tremble with a life so pronounced it was an unseen current of vast potential. A waterfall in the distance, seen between the giant trunks, glimmered in its plummet, the moonlight making of it a shaft of quicksilver though its rumble was far removed. The night was filled with calls and cries in voices I could not recognise, strange hootings and ululations, screeches and distant, base resonances. What fluttered before the moon seemed bat-like but like no bat I had ever seen, and the sense of creeping life in every part of this woodland was overwhelming. The smell of the forest was strong, rich, earthy, yet the air was not the air of modern times, some quality of its content or ionic relationships was simply different.

I found no difficulty in these perceptions, no incongruity, and flowed with them. The night air on my face was overlaid with the impressions of the place into which I looked, and part of me was excited as I had never been before. Was this the sense of place I had sought all my life? The *genius loci* of the ancient highlands? If so, I was privileged to be given this glimpse into rampant life bereft of humankind.

The human condition styles all it does not understand, all beyond its control, as terrible, and nature has been the terror of the human race since the first moment someone was able to conceive of him or herself as somehow different from the living world. *How much more at peace*, I thought, *are peoples for whom nature is their lived reality, rather than the concrete streets through which no green can grow*. Which is the more monstrous, nature rampant or nature suppressed?

Some fascinating, almost addictive property of this new perception held my attention, kept me focused so I neither drifted into sleep nor back awake, but remained tightly attuned to this conduit into the unseen secrets of the peaks. So bound was I to the vision, nothing could jar me from it, and my amazement was an entirely personal wonder when the dinosaurs appeared from the black shadows before me.

They were small, dog-sized, swift-running bipeds in a large social pack which streamed through the silver-blue night in a cascade of pattering footfalls, pausing at times with bird-like grace to crop the ferns, their great binocular eyes bright as they scanned all about for danger. Now I understood the calls out there in the dark, the bellows and trombone-like notes of massive iguanodonts, and the guttural sounds of things more malevolent. The pack of ornithopods milled around me, oblivious, it seemed, and I observed them for some time, amazed at the dexterity of their grasping fore-paws; but eventually an alarm cry from a lookout sent the whole pack scurrying into the deep shadows of the denser woods in a few heartbeats and I waited with bated breath for what had startled them.

Heavy footfalls came softly on the breeze and before I was truly ready for the encounter a great shape moved, treeferns swayed and parted, and a brutal head was thrust into the glade, followed by a tremendous S-curve neck and barrel chest. Clawed feet carried the beast with the grace of a dancer, it paused on one foot to scent the air before moving on cautiously. This was a late-surviving polar allosaur – I reminded myself Australia lay at the south pole in Cretaceous times – and the top predator of these woodlands. *What a magnificent creature*, was my impression, my heart racing to see this lost giant, but it raced for different reasons when I realised this one was aware of me. It stood rock-still and stared, nostrils flared as it scented the night air, and those eyes, staring from under flared ridges of bony scales, looked right into me.

Can I die here? Was my sudden thought, a desperate flailing to remember this was first cousin to a dream, I sat on a rock in the 21st century and all I perceived was long gone. *Surely*, it must be so. Yet the allosaur looked across ten meters of moonlit glade with unerring accuracy, and let out a deep rumble from parted jaws, lowering its head as if to my own level. Then, one careful step at a time, the dinosaur came closer. I sat rigid with fear, feeling the earth tremble under me as tons of animal approached, and closed my nose to the beast's strong smell as the head, larger than a horse's, came town and the bird-like eyes looked into my soul.

How long this moment lasted I did not know, my fear at first costing me the nuances of the encounter. But at last I sensed the great predator was not viewing me as prey, and I relaxed. I took in the moonlight in the huge eyes, their pupils wide open, and the delicate traceries of fine scales around them. Bright colours patterned the hide of the neck arch and a dappled pattern, reminding me of tiger stripes, ran down the back; this was an ambush predator of the woodland, and perfectly adapted to its environment.

But after a while I realised I was not only seeing the beast, I was seeing *myself*, as if from the beast's perspective. This strange inversion let me see myself as a small and peculiar creature in this world, and I had pity for my own ineffectual nature. I could not survive here, and though the dinosaur had no intelligence of an order we would recognize, I was overwhelmed with the impression the creature understood me in strange, deep ways, and *judged* me – judged me irrelevant. To be dismissed was a salutary shock, but it is no denigration to feel small before time and life.

As if in explanation to my subconscious, I perceived a flurry, a cascade, of mental images, the days and nights, the epochs, of existence here, the pageant of life enacting the great dance of death. The seasons flowed by, the continents drifted and fractured, the beasts warred, migrated and brought forth the eggs of a million generations – endlessly, beneath the cooling sun as this land slid ever closer to the pole and these forests became frost-locked for the deepest months of winter. Then the ornithopod packs hibernated in the deepest woods, sharing body heat, the life of the rivers lay locked in stasis, and the greater beasts walked north along the shores and rivers. Treeferns and cycads were rimed with white cloaks of frost and all life bowed to the cold.

The sun crossed the sky through a billion days and nights, time passed in an avalanche that left me shaking, drenched with the mental impression of the uncountable lives expressed in this arena, and whose stamp, impression, signature, remained upon the land if one knew how to look, to listen, properly. It was too much for me to take in, a panorama too wide, an epic too vast, and I mentally flung up a hand to shield my eyes, but to no avail, the world spoke to my innermost being and would not be denied. *Here is your grail*, it seemed to say, *this is what you crave, feast upon the river of time and never forget...Never forget...*

The experience flowed through me, the ages passed like rushing rapids, my whole being was illuminated as if from within and I could only ride the sensations, uncomprehending, still studied inscrutably by the great allosaur that stood silently before me, head low to stare into my eyes.

And at last, when I felt I could take no more, my senses dulled, my nerve endings numbed by the dizzying vista revealed to me, the beast opened wide its jaws and bellowed, a sound to wake the dead, filling the highlands with reverberations, overlapping echoes, and shushing the small creatures of the night to silence.

I dare not open my eyes as I felt the hot, stinking breath in my face, but the sudden chill of night air replaced the feeling and my abused synapses found themselves resting in simple, quiet darkness. I sat upon a rock in a softly humming night, and smelled the ancient woods, and when I opened my eyes the familiar old moon rode over the trees, waning a few days beyond full.

But one thing remained to my wide-open senses, and I was neither surprised nor afraid when the outline of the allosaur moved before me, almost solid, almost transparent, those scales, scutes and glittering eyes so vividly outlined in the silver-blue night.

The beast stood a while, tail twitching, nostrils flaring, then turned and passed with silent grace into the trees and faded from my world.

* * *

I staggered back to my car through the moonlight more in shock than sobriety. My mind was still desperately trying to process the deluge of imagery, the exposure to the ancient past which seemed recorded in the living world, in the rock of the land, and it was all I could do to steady my breathing and follow my GPS on my phone back through the woodland. I fought for mental balance as I went, and at times leaned against a tree to pant, willing myself to stay conscious, as if I could go out in a dead faint at any time. My fear was losing all touch with the world as I knew it, being precipitated headlong into the bottomless gulf of the ages and never finding my way back.

For what it was worth, I returned to my 4WD by moonlight and flashlight without incident. I checked myself and my pack over for unwelcome bugs or spiders, then unlocked with a blip from the lights and sank into the comfort of the *artificial*. The door shut out the night and I drank from my water bottle, stilled my trembling hands, and at last scrubbed them hard over my face.

I had my answer, it seemed, and I must make sense of it, but abruptly my fear was that the memories would fade, and I knew I must write it all down as soon as possible. Driving while so preoccupied would be a challenge and I was in no hurry to go, but sat and stared off through the dark at the moon on the forest canopy, and knew I was deeply, profoundly changed. I left this mountain a different man – or perhaps having woken to the man I always was, or needed to be.

What did it mean, if the spirit of the land had whispered to me? Revealed to me the secrets it had always held so tightly from mortal gaze? Long meditation was needed to put any sense to the vista of titans which had passed my waking eyes, and I looked back for a long while at the dreaming forests. I did not know where this would take me, or if such communion would ever be granted me a second time, but I appreciated the gift down deep where the soul dwells and knew I was indelibly marked by it, to see through the human world as never before to nature beneath the surface… And never again will I look on Whitehead's classic painting without seeing the denizens of the Cretaceous woods race through the dappled shade, and remembering the ghostly allosaur in the moonlight.

Tears of the Gods

Sarah L. Byrne

LEGEND HAD IT that the blue rain was the tears of the gods, though just why gods would weep in blue no one could quite explain. Modern science said the odd meteorological phenomenon was simply a matter of copper sulphate, spores from the blue copper-feeding algae in the deep vents forced into the atmosphere by volcanic activity. Gita knew differently. Opening the door of her house at the patter of the heavy drops on the titanium roof – how did it manage to even sound so blue? – she held out a hand and let the liquid pool in her palm.

What the blue rain really meant was change.

Gita's hand started to itch. Back inside, she held it under the cold tap, washing off the residue of the rain before her skin began to blister from the contact with the irritant. The first time she'd seen the corrosive blue rain had been more than ten years since, when she first arrived. She and Silvia, assigned Survey work as a couple for the first time, and who cared if it was some backwater planet, not exactly a career-boosting move? It had come again the day the shuttle had arrived to take Silv away for the last time. The relentless blue rain beating futile on its impassive grey hull, and Gita's dreams trampled in the dust. When the blue rain had come for the third time, she'd made the decision to leave the city, with its bright lights and protective dome, and volunteered for this lonely post. Just her in a little house in the desert outside the city boundaries.

Change meant a number of things to a woman past forty, even aside from the obvious one. But one thing you knew about change by this age was that it was inevitable. It came like the blue rain whether you liked it or not or just hadn't made your mind up yet. So Gita wasn't surprised when her door buzzer sounded, though she jumped at the sudden noise all the same.

When did I get so used to silence?

Gita slid the door open to reveal a familiar figure, foot already tapping with impatience. Min. Standing there lithe and long-legged in her black leather-look protective gear, the usual energy was visibly humming through her every muscle. Min bounded into the porch, bringing the wet-sand smell of desert rain with her, then tugged off her soft helmet-hood so her short ash-blond hair stood up spikily, grinned at Gita and flashed her a wink.

"What's new, gorgeous?"

Min: Survey project manager, one-woman whirlwind of unstoppable energy, old friend.

Some things, at least, did not change.

"Don't flirt with me," Gita said sourly, as Min stripped off the rest of her outer layers and discarded them on the porch floor. "We both know you don't mean it."

"Might do," Min said, though she did at least look slightly shame-faced. In the soft light of the interior, she looked Gita up and down. Gita knew she was taking in every detail: the old flannel pyjamas, the streaks of grey in the unbrushed dark hair that tumbled to her shoulders. Min herself looked fantastic as always, even standing in her socks, all wiry grace and boyish charm.

"How've you been?" she asked at last.

"Fine," Gita said. "At least I am as long as people don't keep coming here bothering me."

Min raised an eyebrow.

"Might do you good to be bothered a bit more," she observed. "You're getting a bit...odd. Out here all on your own. People are starting to talk."

"I've always been odd," Gita said. "I just don't bother hiding it anymore."

"All the same." Min brushed this off. "I haven't forgotten you exist, and the Survey hasn't either. We've got a job for you."

Change. There it was, then. There was no avoiding it.

* * *

The sun blazed down hot on the desert trail, and Gita sweated in her weather-resistant trousers and jacket. She'd left off the headgear and filter-mask at least – she wasn't worried about rain any time soon, with a sky as clear as this – and the rest of the team had followed her lead and done the same. Gita paused to catch her breath for a moment, to push the damp strands of hair off her forehead. The trail was too steep and narrow now for wheeled transport. Where they were going, the only way was by foot.

"You want to stop for a break?" Ed asked, beside her. Kind young Ed. New-qualified and on the way up, and solicitous of her as if she was his own old grandma.

"Not at all."

Gita took a sip of water from her drink tube and forced herself onwards. She was awkwardly aware of being the oldest person on this trek, among all the keen young things, all temporary placements. No one came out here any more unless they needed a bit of exoplanet experience to advance their careers, and had to take what they could get. She felt heavy, and not just the way her muscles were softened from inactivity, or the couple of extra middle-aged pounds around her middle.

"You're the most senior microbiologist out here," Min had argued, as Gita resisted her efforts to prise her out of the comfortable hole her quiet little life had become. "You're wasted doing weather observations, that stuff should have been automated years ago, anyway. We need you on this."

Gita strongly suspected there was no such urgent need. Sure, the volcanic clefts were finally officially safe to access, now sufficient time had passed since any activity other than a bit of odd-coloured rain. And someone might as well have a look around, bring back some samples for analysis. But this had the flavour of one of Min's for-your-own-good social engineering moves. Especially when Gita had hesitated, and that little crease had appeared between Min's eyebrows, concern and sympathy and more than a little admonishment.

"She's been gone a long time, Gita. Life goes on, you know."

So it did. So here she was, heading for the mountains, the weird scooped-out shapes of them on the horizon, eroded by the abrasive rainfall, no sky-scraping peaks here.

But except for that, it could almost be back on Earth somewhere. Morocco maybe, the Atlas mountains. Silv would have liked it out here.

* * *

The first pioneers in this part of space, a hundred years back, had called it the planet of the gods. Since then it had acquired a serial number but no better name.

It was an ironic usage now, of course, because what a godforsaken place it was these days, now the Survey and the terraforming projects had moved onto the bigger and better worlds in the system. Even the bright-lights frontier-town city under the dome was fading, businesses leaving and families packing up. But people had seen things. The people who'd been here before the Survey with its safety protocols had come along and put restrictions on wandering into the remote places. They'd seen things, or said they had; things that became a kind of legend. You could still find their accounts cached somewhere on the old internet if you looked: accounts of ethereal things that materialised out of nowhere and drifted in the wind, and some had said the planet must have its own gods. Others said it was heatstroke or dehydration or whatever it was they were smoking back then, and that you-see-what-you-want-to-see. And they were probably right. But still.

Gita liked to think the gods wept for Silv. Someone had to. Gita was worn dry by the years, by solitude. Someone had to remember her; Gita struggled to picture her face sometimes. Like now, lying awake in her narrow single tent, as the chatter and giggles of her young companions finally quietened, giving way to the weight of the desert-silent night.

It had been cancer, and not one of the curable ones. Not one of the slow-moving chronic types, manageable if you didn't mind taking so many pills a day you rattled when you walked. It had been the kind that tore through you silent as a scream in space and by the time you suspected that niggling ache in your back, that odd nausea – not pregnant, are you? Hah, chance'd be a fine thing, spawn of the gods, hey? – might be anything more than one-of-those-things, it was too late, far too late to even talk about treatment.

Silv hadn't wanted to go off-planet. She'd loved this place, even though the medical facilities were basic. If there's nothing they can do anyway…

The transfer shuttle she'd finally agreed to had come too late for her, and the cold silent burden it carried away to the mainland – for freezing, for shipping back to her family, her legal next-of-kin – had not really even been Silv anymore. Gita could have made a fuss about the legal thing, about Silv's wishes, how she'd wanted to be buried – I was her family too, you know I was – but she had no stomach for that fight. She could have gone along, taken compassionate leave: Min had in fact stopped just short of ordering her onto the shuttle. But the real Silv was still here. The memory of her was right here, where the gods themselves wept their corrosive blue tears because she was gone. That funny, gentle, gorgeous woman who'd loved this place and wanted to grow old here. She was gone.

* * *

"I'll go in," Gita said, as they stood high above the desert, looking down into the crevice that opened up in the rock at their feet.

"You sure?" Ed frowned in concern.

"I've done quite a bit of climbing, you know." She was irritated by the dubious looks they gave her; that was enough to make her determined, despite her tiredness from the ascent. That, and if this was going to done, it should be done properly, taking the samples with minimum disturbance to the environment.

Gita clipped her descender device onto her harness, checked the rope and the spring-loaded anchor wedged in the rock. All in order. Here we go.

How many years had it been? Odd how your body remembered things. Her gloved hands slipped a little on the rope, her feet groping more clumsily for the wall than she would have liked. But the harness took her weight, she began to descend smoothly into the dark crevasse, the pale glow of her headtorch dimly lighting the way.

"All right down there?" someone shouted down from the blinding-bright sliver of light above.

"All good," Gita called back.

And then the rope slithered loose and she was falling.

She'd fallen before. There was never any life-before-your-eyes endless-seeming plunge. Just a brief panicked flail of your arms and legs then the ground slamming you hard in the back. Gita lay still for a moment, trying to catch her breath, letting her hammering heart slow. She moved her arms and legs tentatively: nothing broken, the protective gear had taken the worst of the impact. She wasn't sure how far she'd fallen. The rope had been good for ten metres; they hadn't expected the cave to go deeper than that. She didn't think the blue algae could survive too far from the warmth and oxygen of the surface.

Warmth, yes. It was warm down here, and there was a hot coppery tang in the air that Gita could taste even through her filter mask. She turned her head. Liquid bubbled blue in the pool inches from her face, from where she lay on a narrow rock ledge. She'd been lucky not to fall in that pool – deep and larger than she'd first realised, an underwater lagoon stretching into the shadows. Might have been an easier landing though. Gita winced with the sharp pain in her back as she started to ease herself up. And then the surface erupted. The god burst forth from the depths and rose up before her.

Sleek, blue-translucent, it breached the surface like the ethereal ghost of a dolphin, stretching, forming. Liquid fountained from the pore that took shape in its centre. Air was forced out in reed-like whistles and clicks. Turning towards her; reaching. Then splitting apart into a thousand glistening particles, as a panicked shout echoed down from above.

"Dr. G? Can you hear me? You all right?" "I'm all right," Gita called back. But she didn't move. She just watched.

Those shining droplets, raining back down into the pool of their birth: safe, contained, to reform again, reborn.

She understood then: the blue raindrops were not the tears of the gods, but their death. Unless, for them, the two things were the same.

* * *

They hauled her out strapped to a backboard, despite her protestations. She unstrapped herself and pulled off her face mask, blinking in the too-bright daylight, fending off the attentions of the slightly panicked young woman with the medical kit. Gita winced a little as she saw the crumbled rock where the anchor had pulled out of its crack. The rock must have been more fragile than it looked, eroded with the corrosive rainfall and vapour. Should have thought of that. Once upon a time she would have checked and double-checked everything.

You were supposed to get less reckless with age, weren't you, not more? That depended on your priorities, maybe. On what you had to lose. How much of a hurry you were in to meet your gods.

Ed and his young team had hitched the rescue rope around a sturdy outcrop, the most likely thing to hold. Good thinking there, and brave of them to risk themselves for her. They weren't bad people. They couldn't help being irritating, any more than she could help becoming more of a cranky old woman with every passing year. They'd grabbed some samples from the pool while they were down there. They'd done it hastily, in a hurry to get out, afraid of the rope corroding and trapping them. They'd done it before Gita'd had the chance to tell them not to, though they'd at least remembered to use the proper vials: temperature and acidity controlled.

The medic hovered over her with her handheld scanner. Gita barely noticed. Her mind was still spinning with it, with what she'd seen down there, liquid flowing and forming into a god-like thing. No, not liquid exactly, because if she had this right, that azure pool was teeming with the blue algae. Cells, tiny creatures. Millions, maybe billions of them, coming together like the cells that organised to form the pavement mosaic layers of her skin, or that pulsed through those blue veins so fragile along her wrists.

Gita looked up from where she'd been staring at her own hands.

"I saw it," she said slowly. "It was what people saw, what they wrote about. You know, the gods, the ones who cry the blue tears, I saw it..."

The young medic goggled at her briefly, then frowned, leaned in with the scanner again. "Dr. G, did you hit your head when you fell?"

Gita sighed. No one read old electronic media any more, did they? No one cared about the legends. But – if what they had in those little vials was what she thought it was – that was going to change.

* * *

"I don't want anyone messing around down there," she said to Min, back at the office. "I don't want anyone touching the site, or any of those volcanic shafts. I don't want anyone going near it without my supervision."

"Oh?" Min raised an eyebrow, from the other side of her desk. She had one foot drawn up onto her chair, chin resting on her knee – typical Min – and her eyes were keen. "Well, nice to see you taking an interest in something at last. Maybe the near-death experience was just what you needed to snap you out of it. Bit extreme though, don't you think?"

"It wasn't anything like that," Gita said. "It was just a few bruises. I've had worse." In truth she was stiff and sore all over; walking gingerly as an old woman in the morning and pressing her palms into her back when no one was looking. Now, though, she shrugged off the pain.

"You know the protocols for dealing with exospecies," she said.

"Of course I do," Min returned. "I wrote half of 'em, didn't I? But they're intended for higher species, not slimes and algaes or whatever."

"They're not algae like the stuff you get on a pond back home. They're protozoa, as far as I can tell from the samples we did get, single-celled organisms. But they're more than that, they're self-assembling into something bigger. Into a higher species. Like, you know, how an ant colony or a swarm of bees does. We need to get a linguist in, that's the protocol. Nothing about them without them, isn't that how you put it?"

Min clicked her tongue, frowned at her across the desk. "Bees are pretty amazing things," she admitted. "But, you know, they don't actually talk to people."

"It wasn't actually bees, that was a goddamn analogy." Gita crossed her arms, faced Min down. "We're doing this properly, or not at all."

"Since when were you, of all people, so bothered with protocol?" Min asked. "If this is what you say, there's going to be some big interest in it, this could be huge for you."

Gita just shrugged. She didn't know herself why she was doing this, didn't know how to name or define the feelings she had. She just knew that the god-creature she'd seen was something to be protected, guarded. That no one was going to touch it without her saying so, no one was going to take another being she loved from this place where it belonged, where it was supposed to be, where it was supposed to live out its life and pour its dying tears into the dry ground to begin the cycle over again.

Change, I don't want anything to change. Not yet. I'm not ready.

* * *

"So, hey," Min said, as Gita swung by the office on her way to check on her samples. "I got you that linguist you were asking for."

"Already?" Gita asked, a little dismayed. She'd hoped for more time – for what, she wasn't sure. More time to study, to understand. She'd come to like just spending time with the little blue creatures, hoarding them close to herself – these tiny things that migrated and clung to each other in their gel dish like raindrops on a leaf, some innate longing for each other in the very atoms of their chemistry.

Not like Silv, her cells refusing to cooperate, turning against each other, mutinying against their higher purpose. If only someone had seen it that way at the time. Could they have been persuaded, negotiated with? Could the errant cells have been gathered up and returned prodigal to start over? Gita sighed.

"You found someone pretty quick," she said. "For out here, anyway. They are actually qualified, aren't they?"

"She, not they," Min said with one of her wicked winks. "She's supposed to be pretty good."

She, not they. As if you could gather up the pieces of a shattered woman and put them back together with no more than a trick of language. She wasn't likely to be that good.

* * *

Anne was her name. A spare, scholarly-looking woman with her grey hair close-cropped, she came into Min's office with a tentative shyness odd for her age.

"Hi," Gita said tiredly, making the effort to lift her eyes and look at the newcomer properly. She should at least be polite.

"*Ap se milkar khushi huyee*," Anne said in Hindi, with a quick little smile. Pleased to meet you. Gita blinked. How long had it been, how did the words sound so strange and yet as familiar as the scent of magnolia in a long-ago garden and grazed knees from forbidden climbing.

Anne's smile became hesitant.

"I'm sorry, I thought…"

"No," Gita said. She felt a smile start to come to her face as well, the odd stretch of it stranger than the shape of those ancient words in her mouth. "No, it's all right. I was just surprised."

"Told you she was good," Min said, looking pleased with herself. "Anne worked on the cetacean language project, back in the day. Looking for the next challenge, apparently."

Is that what I am?

"It was a bit like a dolphin," Gita explained again for Anne's benefit, a bit tersely this time, fearing mockery or doubt. "The thing I saw. In the shape it made, the way it was using liquid and air to make sounds. And it was like bees, too, that's what I thought of afterwards. Like a swarm of them, all those little protozoa coming together to make a whole something, and I'd swear it was trying to talk to me. I mean, I know bee swarms don't talk…" – she trailed off self-consciously, aware of Min's sceptical gaze.

"Actually, they do." Anne flashed her a glance of startling blue eyes. "Split off into groups and communicate with each other, it's a kind of dance-based language. I mean, obviously we've known that for a while, but there's been some interesting work recently, starting to look like it's a lot more complicated than we thought. I'd be fascinated to take a look at this discovery of yours."

"Well," Gita said. She refrained from looking around at Min: what did I tell you? "I need to go out there to return the samples," she said to Anne instead. "You can come along, if you like."

"I'll put a team together," Min began, swivelling back towards her screen.

"No." Gita cut her off before she could get started. "Just the two of us. I don't want the site disturbed. Protocol, remember?"

Min quirked an eyebrow.

"Protocol. Of course."

* * *

Anne was a quiet companion on the trek, and that was a solace to Gita's silence-accustomed soul; a relief after Min's relentless tight-wound energy and a welcome change from boisterous young interns of her last trip. Anne had gazed out of the window of the vehicle as Gita drove, her eyes on the odd-shaped mountain range, alert but contemplative. When they'd gotten out to walk, she'd hefted her pack – heavy with her recording equipment – without complaint, declining Gita's offer of help.

"Thank you, it's fine." She smiled, self-deprecating. "I'm quite strong, actually."

She was, Gita was starting to realise. That fragile-looking build belied a wiry strength, a distance-runner's body. Not like Silv, with her tumbling amber curls and ready laugh and that softness, the generous roundedness of her. Anne couldn't have been more different. But she had a deep stillness about her that was like cool water in the desert. No rings on any of her fingers.

As they approached the place, they went quietly, walking with soft steps. No words. Anne watched while Gita anchored the ropes, carefully. A multi-point system based in the hard-packed sand not the crumble-prone rock. She was taking no chances this time.

Someday, if all went according to plan – Min and the Survey's plans, that was – there'd be permanent steps, safety-approved according to protocol, pulleys for getting equipment up and down. But not today.

Gita went first, no dramatic falls this time, just her feet touching lightly on the smooth-worn stone of the ledge. Anne followed quietly, competently, following Gita's instructions to the letter. They stood and contemplated the lagoon for a while, the surface shimmering blue-dark in the light of their torches.

"This is where the blue rain comes from?" Anne asked at length.

"Vents like this, yes. This one here's been dormant ten years, likely will be for a while yet. There was one a few kilometres from here blew the other week though, and we had the rain." And everything changed. "The volcanic eruptions denature the cell membranes; that's how I understand it, the copper-bound proteins dissolve into the water that gets forced up into the atmosphere, into the clouds."

"Tears of the gods," Anne said. She extended her hand towards the blue surface as if in sympathy. "I see why now."

Gita nodded, surprised, and yet not surprised somehow.

You understand.

Anne knelt down to unpack her recording equipment and set it up around the cavern. With respectful care, she slipped the wired probes into the blue water, drawing back gingerly as though she expected it to erupt before her.

No god rose up out of the depths. The surface breathed though, ripples spreading outwards, in response to the touch. Below there was movement. Low vocalisations echoed in the depths, trilling in and out of audible frequency, bouncing off the rock walls of the pools.

Anne knelt in rapt silence, glancing from the turbid waters to the screen on her recording device and back again, her gaze intent.

"That's amazing," she whispered at last, looking up at Gita with a grin of genuine delight that it tore at her not to return.

"You know what they're saying?"

"Not yet, there'll be a lot of analysis to do. But it's a language for sure. It's enough. We'll understand, don't worry. I can do this. Amazing though, it's like nothing else we've seen."

"This could be huge for you, then? Being lead researcher on a project like this?"

"Well, it's the same for you, surely, on the biology side? Your manager, Min, she was talking about the applications for cancer models. She said you had some ideas already?"

"Only tentative ones," Gita admitted. So tentative she hardly dared voice them. But a flood of ideas all the same, just from looking at the way those cells assembled, cooperated. There was a torrent of questions too: how did they deal with the cells that didn't cooperate, how could a being split apart and reorganise like that, recovering from the kind of catastrophe that would devastate any other organism? And was it the same being, afterwards, not some randomly composed other thing? Did it remember what it had been before?

Gita chewed her lip, biting back the longing for knowledge and understanding that used to drive her on. She'd thought that had died inside her ten years ago. That enthusiasm that wanted to rise up and respond to the call of this other woman's quiet excitement. She barely knew how to let that happen anymore, barely dared to try.

"That's far off," she said.

"Sure, but we'll get there."

Gita drew a breath, warm air through her mouth filter, spoke slowly.

"What if that isn't what they want?"

Anne turned to look at her through her filter mask, those bluest eyes deep and grave in the flickering blue of the light.

"If they want to stay hidden, right here, for as long as they live, and never see another soul?"

Gita nodded, wordlessly.

"Then we'll do that. There's protocol for it, and I'll back you every step of the way. If they want to be left alone, we'll make sure they are."

But what if they don't want that, what if this woman's gentle persistence coaxes words from them, draws them out of their long hiding in their deep safe places and then there's no going back?

"Such a huge opportunity, though," Gita said.

Anne shrugged, lightly. "There are other worlds than this."

"I know." Gita thought of them. The first long-ago one with the magnolia and the dusty lane behind the house. All the bright new worlds being discovered now, and more of them out there waiting to be found. And all the worlds she'd known over the years, the ones where she'd touched down so lightly she wouldn't have left footprints even if it hadn't been all terraformed fake anyway.

"This one's different," she said. She was tired of it now, of the clinging to a ten-year burden, wanting to lay it down at last. "For me, it is."

"I know," Anne said. Gita wondered just how much she did know, how much background Min had seen fit to feed her. It didn't seem to matter. There was knowing like that, and then there was knowing: one soul open to another, reaching to touch, to understand. And in this place of the gods, they were almost there.

Gita knelt down, popped open the lids of the vials, and carefully slid the contents into the pool. Letting the cells go, letting them merge into their…what? Mother, progenitor, society – home? The surface rippled again. But not spreading out this time, but drawing in, gathering up: surging.

The god rose out of the water again, blue and shimmering, vast. Gita heard Anne's startled gasp, even behind her mask, felt the other woman's gloved fingertips brush against hers – softly, shyly almost. She understood that need, that reaching for human contact in the face of this wonder, even as she dared to feel the hope of something more, dared to think of the possibilities.

Then she blinked, looking up at the god-creature as it dived and surged again: not the single cetacean shape she'd seen before, but splitting into two, merging and separating again, mimicking the vision it saw before it. There was a future to be made, Gita knew then: choices to be made in this place by two women and the closest thing to a god they'd likely ever see.

Tears would come again, blue and otherwise; there was no change for better or worse without them, that was the way of this world and every other. But that was far away. Gita let her fingers twine through Anne's, and even through the protective fabric she knew the warmth and shape of them.

This would not be a day for tears.

The Temple of the Cat

Thomas Canfield

THE JUNGLES of Bolivia and Brazil were extensive and remote, rich in plants which had not yet been fully investigated. They possessed enormous potential for medicinal applications. Already the expedition had collected several samples. But at the back of Gallagher's mind resided the dream of making a discovery of a different kind, of following in the footsteps of such explorers as Hiram Bingham. There were not any sites of the splendor and magnitude of Machu Picchu left undiscovered, of course. But there were still mysteries which remained unsolved, still stretches of jungle where few had ventured and where the unknown had yet to be investigated. The Temple of the Cat, however, had never once entered into Gallagher's thinking. Nor would it have had they not stumbled upon the slaughtered remains of a jaguar.

Gallagher poked at the carcass with a stick. A cloud of flies swarmed into the air and then, undisturbed, settled again. The arrow was lodged between the jaguar's ribs, where the heart should reside. It was an uncannily accurate shot. It would have to have been made at close range and the target – an animal legendary for its lightning reflexes and elusiveness – stationary. That, or it was the most extraordinary feat of marksmanship imaginable.

"How do you suppose anyone managed such a shot?" Gallagher looked at the surrounding jungle. The mass of plants and vines and creepers which compassed them on all sides was almost impenetrable. It was hard going merely making their way through such terrain. To hunt here, to track and locate game, seemed a pursuit only a madman would undertake. Stalking a jaguar, that was no less incomprehensible. The meat was not edible. The pelt, the beautiful, exotic pelt which allowed the cat to slip through the jungle undetected, had not been harvested. The only purpose behind the killing seemed to be just that: to kill.

Alejandro Gutierrez stepped forward, crouched over the carcass. He had joined the expedition in La Paz. He was affiliated with the University there and brought a wealth of knowledge to their ranks, though his exact title and duties eluded Gallagher's understanding. Now he rested one hand on the jaguar's pelt, felt along the ribcage and flanks. Flies buzzed around his face but Gutierrez seemed not to notice. He lifted the jaguar's head, drew the upper lip back to expose the teeth. He made a noise in his throat indicative of surprise or perhaps, of admiration. Then he gripped the haft of the arrow with one hand.

"Alex?" Gallagher interrupted more out of instinct than from conviction. "Do you think that's a good idea?" Gutierrez's eyes revealed nothing, only an acknowledgement that Gallagher had addressed him. "I mean, perhaps we ought just to let it go. It's none of our business, really."

"But it is our business." Gutierrez spoke softly, not so much disagreeing with Gallagher as correcting a flaw in his reasoning. "We must know who is engaged in such killing. And to what end." Gutierrez braced himself, pulled at the shaft. It held fast a long moment then, slowly, yielded. The arrow pulled free intact, followed by a gout of black blood. The flies swarmed. Gutierrez held the arrow aloft.

"Silver," he observed, pointing to the head. He handed the arrow to Gallagher.

The head had, indeed, been fashioned from silver. Not machine cast but crafted by hand. Gallagher looked at the jaguar again then at the dense tangle of jungle. Anything might be hiding out there, anything at all. Their expedition might pass within mere feet of it and never be the wiser.

"Why silver? Do you mean to tell me that you were expecting to find something like this?"

"I was not expecting it, no." Gutierrez's expression was impassive. "I thought it a possibility only because of the accuracy of the shot." Gutierrez noticed a streak of blood on his forearm, attempted to wipe it away with a tissue. It was not the jaguar's blood, however, but his own. He had cut himself removing the arrow.

Gutierrez sluiced the puncture with water, applied antiseptic from the first aid kit then covered it with a clean dressing. Gallagher had not thought Gutierrez the fussy sort but these precautions struck him as excessive – even here, in the jungle, where any wound was subject to infection.

"You do mean to explain to me the meaning of this, don't you?" Gallagher endeavored to keep the irritation out of his voice. "Whatever you know, whatever you suspect, you need to take me into your confidence."

Gutierrez shrugged. But behind the façade of indifference Gallagher thought that he detected genuine concern – along with some other, darker, emotion which he could not identify. "Nomadic tribes pass through this area, indigenous peoples. These Indians, the Kumari, are too remote and too few for the government to bother with. They are apolitical and so long as they do not pose any sort of threat or disturbance the government is content leaving them to their own devices. They brook no man's authority – and no government's. They ask only to be left alone. In this, their wishes have largely been respected. Most consider them to be harmless." Gutierrez paused, smiled. "I do not number myself amongst such people."

"You made no mention of them before." Gallagher was more upset than he let on. "Why is that?"

"I made no mention of the jaguars, either." Gutierrez's smile showed signs of strain. "They have been there all along, concealed from our notice. There was no reason to apprehend an attack. Why allow them to become a distraction?"

"These indigenous peoples," Gallagher's tone was sharp, "do you mean to imply that they have been there all along, too?"

"But of course!" Again Gutierrez smiled and again Gallagher sensed the insincerity of his smile. "From the very first. They have observed us from a distance, curious as to what we were doing. Why should they not be curious? Our conduct is no less a mystery to them than theirs is to us. I made no mention of their presence because to do so would serve no purpose."

It was this very fact – Gutierrez's omission – which troubled Gallagher more than anything. They were miles deep in the jungle, a three day hike minimum from the last straggling outpost of what might be called civilization. Gallagher could not risk alienating Gutierrez and dare not imply any loss of faith in his integrity or reliability. The expedition was too dependent upon his help. Best to let the matter rest until they returned to La Paz. Gallagher cleaned the arrow, wrapped it in a protective cloth and secured it in one of the backpacks.

"What are you doing?" Gutierrez's eyes were dark with concern.

"Preserving the arrow for further study. Why?"

"I should not do that, senhor." Gutierrez wet his lips. "The Kumari always return to retrieve their arrows. They are very particular about that. They left it behind only to make certain that the jaguar was dead."

Gallagher looked at the jaguar. Its pelt was matted with blood. Flies swarmed its head and flanks. "It's dead. I'm willing to go out on a limb and proclaim that for a fact. Anybody wants the arrow, they're welcome to come and claim it. If the Kumari are so adept at following our movements as you say, they'll know where to find us."

* * *

When they made camp that night, Gutierrez pitched his tent as far away from the fire, and from the others, as was possible. It was as though he were observing a kind of self-imposed quarantine. He disappeared into his tent early, was not seen again until the following morning.

Gallagher settled in next to the fire, shared a flask of whiskey with a fellow American named Blakeslee. They drank steadily and with purpose, listening to the night sounds of the jungle.

"What's got into Gutierrez, do you think?" Blakeslee scratched at a three day growth of beard. "Going off by himself like that, shunning the whiskey – that's not like him."

Gallagher stared out past the flickering glow of the fire into the shadows. "If I had to hazard a guess, I'd say it was the jaguar. Something about the carcass spooked him."

"Yeah?" Blakeslee was skeptical. "Don't know why that would upset him. Myself, I was more concerned when he started talking about the Indians. Them watching us – that's enough to give anyone the willies. You figure it's true?"

Gallagher pulled his eyes away from the shadows reluctantly. "Do I figure what's true?"

"The Indians! I don't know about you but that about freaked me out. Don't get me wrong, I got no problem with Indians. I do have a problem with being watched. That bugs me."

Gallagher poked at the fire with a stick. "Assuming that they're out there, assuming that they're watching us, there isn't a damn thing that we can do about it. They know the jungle and the terrain. They can come and go as they please. Unless they choose to reveal themselves, it's likely we aren't ever going to catch them at it."

"Yeah." Blakeslee's tone was morose. "All the same, I'm going to keep a sharp eye out. I don't want anybody sneaking up on me. I especially don't want anybody barging into my tent at night. Anyone who tries it," Blakeslee patted at his hip, "I got a surprise waiting for them."

Gallagher was unimpressed. "How good a shot are you with that thing? When's the last time that you fired at a moving target?"

"What?" Blakeslee was indignant. "You think I don't know how to use a handgun?"

"I'm sure you visit the range at least twice a year, along with the other members of the faculty. The question is: can you hit something?"

"Damn straight I can! Try coming into my tent at night and you won't have to ask a second time."

"That's good. I only ask because anybody who shows up at your tent, we already know that they can shoot. Took a jaguar out with a bow, a single shot to the heart, almost as though it had a bull's-eye painted on it. That's not bad marksmanship by my reckoning."

"No." Blakeslee sobered suddenly. "No, it isn't."

"Not only that, this same shooter fashions his arrowheads out of silver. I know a little Indian lore but I got to tell you – I never heard of that." Gallagher poked at the fire with savage vehemence. "Our friend Senhor Gutierrez, on the other hand, he didn't seem overly surprised. In fact, I don't think it would be an exaggeration to say he appeared almost to be expecting it. That's a little odd, don't you think?" Gallagher lapsed into silence a long moment. "Whatever the explanation, Gutierrez didn't seem inclined to share it with the rest of us. That alone is enough to give me pause."

"What are you saying?" Blakeslee shifted uneasily, drawing nearer to the fire. "You think he's hiding something?"

"Put it this way." Gallagher offered a taut smile. In the backwash from the fire his expression was indistinguishable from a grimace. "It isn't only the Indians we ought to be keeping an eye on. I'm placing Gutierrez under observation as well." Gallagher stood up, thrust the stick into the fire as though slaying an enemy. "You might want to do the same."

* * *

The following morning when Gutierrez stepped out of his tent, Gallagher was shocked at the change in his appearance. Overnight, Gutierrez had gone from being hale and hearty to looking deathly ill. His face was gaunt and drawn, the skin stretched tight over the underlying bone structure. His eyes were sunk deep in his skull, glittered with a harsh, feverish light. His left arm, the one he had cut with the arrowhead, was swathed in bandages almost to his armpit.

"Sweet Mother of God! What happened to you, Alex?"

"Happened?" Gutierrez's eyes darted around the camp. "What do you mean?"

"You look like you're at death's door! I never seen such a change. Yesterday you looked healthy enough to scale the summit of the world. Today...Here, let me get you some water." Gallagher grabbed one of the canteens, handed it to Gutierrez.

Gutierrez looked at the canteen and frowned. He shook it so that the water sloshed but did not drink. "I'm fine," he declared. "I've a little touch of fever, is all."

"You haven't seen yourself. That's more than a touch. We're going to have to get you to a doctor."

Gutierrez shook his head. "Whiskey. Give me a drink of whiskey, instead."

"Whiskey? You're sure?" Gallagher had never heard of treating a fever with whiskey. But Gutierrez was so emphatic that Gallagher decided to humor him. Gutierrez could hardly be any worse off, he reasoned. Gallagher dug out the remains of last night's whiskey, half a flask, and watched Gutierrez chug it at a single go. The liquor seemed to steady him. Color filtered back into his face. The cadaverous expression, near cousin to death, softened and loosened its grip. But the eyes remained as before: fierce and haunted, consumed by distrust.

"Better?" Gallagher asked.

"Yeah." Gutierrez wiped his mouth with the back of his hand.

"I've got to see what we can do about getting you to a doctor." Gallagher ran through their options and didn't like any of them. He could send Gutierrez back with one of the porters, a three day trek through the jungle. But that was chancy, to say the least. He could use the shortwave to radio for help. But there was no clearing where they could execute an evac and no assurance that anyone would respond, no matter how dire the emergency. Lastly, he could turn the expedition around and head back to civilization. None of these choices had a lot to recommend it.

"How fit are you for walking?" Gallagher asked. "It'll take three days, minimum, to reach a doctor."

"Three days?" Gutierrez offered a crooked smile. "Might as well be eternity. No, we push ahead. That's our only option."

"There's nothing but jungle in front of us," Gallagher pointed out. "We're near the frontier of Brazil. But that's only a line on a map. It isn't like there's going to be any help when we get there. It isn't like there's going to be anything."

"Listen to what I'm trying to tell you." Gutierrez seized Gallagher by his shoulders. "Jaguars are the bringers of fire, do you understand? In Indian legend, it was the jaguars that first brought fire to Man. That's why their blood brings the fever, brings heat. The only way to draw it off, to extinguish it, is to enter the Temple of the Cat."

The Temple of the Cat! There was not a scholar of any merit who had not heard of the Temple – nor any of any sense who thought it more than a fable. It was part of the lore of the Andes, stretching back for centuries. In some remote fastness unknown to the outside world resided an ancient temple whose adherents took an oath of fidelity to the jaguar – and accompanied it with a vow of silence unto death. The tale took many forms, adopted many guises. But always it retained the common thread that the jaguar was central to the cult. The ceremony and ritual, the Temple itself, were cloaked in obscurity, forbidden to outsiders. But it was only a legend, constructed out of wisps of gossamer. There was nothing solid or substantive behind it.

"There is no such temple." Gallagher's expression was almost hostile

"Ah! Have you forgotten the arrow fashioned from silver?" Gutierrez's eyes sparkled, whether from excitement or as a consequence of the fever, it was impossible to say. "Only the adherents of the Temple hunt in such a fashion. Only they posses such accuracy with a bow."

"And why would they slaughter a jaguar? Explain that to me."

"The acolytes of the Temple, so it is said, must slay a jaguar as part of their initiation. It is thus that they acquire some of the attributes of the cat: its stealth, its cunning, its gift of concealment. They draw nearer to the jaguar in spirit, emptying the contents of its heart into their own. All of these things I have heard."

"Nonsense!" Gallagher's lip curled with scorn. "You can't expect anyone seriously to believe that? Such rubbish adorns the pages of dime novels. It is not a subject for legitimate scientific inquiry." Gallagher noticed uneasiness amongst the porters. Their eyes darted at the surrounding jungle and they whispered amongst themselves.

"Perhaps." Gutierrez's forehead was beaded with perspiration. "Though your science is far from infallible. It, too, has its blind spots. Its range and reach are not so all encompassing as you imagine."

Gallagher frowned. Every man has his holy writ which he will not suffer to be challenged. Gallagher's allegiance to scientific principles was absolute, unassailable. "That it is the fever talking and not yourself. This Temple, as all the legends declare, cannot be discovered by outsiders. Hence its existence, or its non-existence, can never be definitively established. That is a very old formula – one that many a charlatan has been known to exploit."

"The skeptic and the man of faith." Gutierrez bobbed his head. "It is, indeed, a difficult divide to reconcile. But suppose I was to tell you," Gutierrez wet his lips, "suppose I was to assert that a man stricken by the fever, infected by the blood of the jaguar, will be drawn to the Temple, will find his way there whether he wishes it or not. The impulse, the instinct, is overwhelming. It cannot be suppressed or denied."

Gallagher stared at Gutierrez, unable to tell whether the man was lucid or not. "You mean to say that you can take us to the Temple, you can show us the way?"

"Oh no, senhor, I did not say that." The flicker of a smile washed across Gutierrez's face. "Of myself, I can do nothing. But the fever will guide us there unerringly. Blood calls out to blood. It is not a summons which can be ignored."

* * *

They stumbled down into the valley late on the second day, sweating and cursing, hacking their way through the jungle by hand. The humidity was oppressive, a low cloud cover overhead making the air seem even hotter. Their porters had abandoned them along the way, disappearing into the jungle one by one. They were convinced that Gutierrez was mad – and that Gallagher was madder still for following him. Gallagher was not certain that they were not right on both counts.

The fever, which had only just touched Gutierrez at the outset, had taken full possession of him now. He was a terrifying sight. His eyes glittered and shone. They emitted a steady stream of light even in the dark, like those of a jaguar stalking its prey. Gutierrez's flesh had drawn in tight to his bones. The fever seemed to be devouring his substance, consuming his muscle mass to fuel some driving urge. Sick as he was, Gutierrez pushed ahead at a blistering pace. He walked with a lithe, cat-like tread which was powerful yet seemed to conserve energy at the same time. His gestures had become swift and slashing. At rest, he remained absolutely still.

"He's deranged." Blakeslee was no less terrified by Gutierrez than the porters but had nowhere to run to. "Completely out of his mind. You only have to look at him to recognize it." Yet there was method to his madness. Gutierrez picked his way through the jungle with ease, never hesitating or in doubt as to which direction to follow.

He led the descent into the valley now, head thrust forward as though tracking some scent. The valley was a narrow cleft beneath a towering overstory of trees. It was choked with creepers and vines and dense clusters of ferns taller than any man. An aerial survey might have missed it altogether. But entering on foot, Gallagher was impressed by the steep drop-off and the untamed splendor of the place. A profusion of plant species he had never seen before dominated the land. It was a niche ecosystem, had developed along lines different from those which prevailed over the rest of the continent. Gallagher could not have said whether they were in Bolivia or Brazil. More importantly, he was no longer certain that he could find his way back to civilization again.

Gutierrez stopped abruptly, frozen in a posture not devoid of menace.

"What is it?" Gallagher kept his distance. They all gave Gutierrez a wide berth now, recognizing that his condition did not invite companionship. The fever did not appear to be contagious but none of them wished to put the matter to the test.

Gallagher drew closer, picking his way around a mass of vines with care. When he saw what had caught Gutierrez's attention he, too, froze.

"Sweet Jesus!" Gallagher protested. "I must be seeing things. Tell me that I'm seeing things." Foraging through the underbrush was a beast of large frame and immense power. It stood erect upon its hind haunches and feasted on the leaves of a eucalyptus tree: a giant ground sloth, extinct these ten thousand years past by common reckoning. The sloth appeared oblivious to their presence or perhaps, merely indifferent.

"This is off-the-charts crazy!" Blakeslee came up behind Gallagher. "That thing has no business being here. None! Neither do we, for that matter. Let's get out while the getting is good!"

Gallagher hardly heard these words. A rising excitement had taken possession of him, a sense of anticipation such as he had never experienced before. If such a creature as the sloth could exist, why not the Temple? Might it not be real as well?

"What about the Temple, Alex?" Gallagher's tone was urgent. "Is it possible that I was wrong and that it actually exists?"

Gutierrez turned toward Gallagher, eyes aflame with fever. His lips were twisted in an expression which seemed to convey both amusement and contempt. "Possible? Haven't I said as much? It's a wonder you took no heed from the porters." Gutierrez thrust his face forward. "Do you imagine their fear was based solely on superstition? They have not your erudition, to be sure. But they have something which you do not: an instinct toward self-preservation."

Gutierrez strode toward the sloth. To Gallagher's amazement, the beast moved out of his way. Gutierrez brushed aside a thick tangle of creepers, revealing a set of stone steps worn with age. At the top was a doorway giving way on to utter darkness. Gutierrez bounded up the steps and slipped inside. His eyes peered out from the dark, filled with an unspoken challenge. Then they, too, disappeared.

Gallagher hesitated. Should he follow Gutierrez, as he was tempted to do? Or should he turn and flee, run back to civilization and to safety, as an inner voice was screaming at him to do. He was torn in both directions at once, unable to make up his mind. His thought process had become muddled, disoriented. His throat felt scratchy and dry. When he touched his forehead, the skin radiated heat. As in a dream, Gallagher found himself mounting the stairs. He entered the Temple through the doorway, the words 'Blood calls out to blood' resonating through his skull.

In the dark, momentarily blinded, Gallagher heard the sound of feet padding along a stone corridor. A figure emerged out of the dark – an apparition which had once been a man. Its skin bore a pattern of black and tan rosettes, identical to those which distinguished the jaguar.

The stranger's muzzle probed Gallagher. The examination, so foreign to human behavior and norms, sought to confirm Gallagher's status, to determine whether his blood bore the signature of the jaguar. At length he was ushered toward the inner sanctum, untrod these many centuries by any not initiates of the Temple and of its ritual.

The Chief Priest stepped forward out of the darkness, a dagger balanced between his two hands. He held it aloft so that the assembled acolytes might view it, chanted words in a language Gallagher did not recognize. The cadence of his voice, the harsh inflection of his words, caused the hair along the back of Gallagher's neck to stand erect.

The Priest approached Gallagher. His eyes were deep gold in color, glittered with the predatory relish of a jaguar examining its prey.

The Lost World
Chapters VII–X
Arthur Conan Doyle

[Publisher's Note: At this point in the story, reporter Edward Malone, adventurer Lord John Roxton and biologist Professor Summerlee have volunteered to join famous zoologist Professor Challenger in South America, to find out whether his claims of having discovered dinosaurs there are really true.]

Chapter VII
'Tomorrow we Disappear into the Unknown'

I WILL NOT BORE those whom this narrative may reach by an account of our luxurious voyage upon the Booth liner, nor will I tell of our week's stay at Para (save that I should wish to acknowledge the great kindness of the Pereira da Pinta Company in helping us to get together our equipment). I will also allude very briefly to our river journey, up a wide, slow-moving, clay-tinted stream, in a steamer which was little smaller than that which had carried us across the Atlantic. Eventually we found ourselves through the narrows of Obidos and reached the town of Manaos. Here we were rescued from the limited attractions of the local inn by Mr. Shortman, the representative of the British and Brazilian Trading Company. In his hospital Fazenda we spent our time until the day when we were empowered to open the letter of instructions given to us by Professor Challenger. Before I reach the surprising events of that date I would desire to give a clearer sketch of my comrades in this enterprise, and of the associates whom we had already gathered together in South America. I speak freely, and I leave the use of my material to your own discretion, Mr. McArdle, since it is through your hands that this report must pass before it reaches the world.

The scientific attainments of Professor Summerlee are too well known for me to trouble to recapitulate them. He is better equipped for a rough expedition of this sort than one would imagine at first sight. His tall, gaunt, stringy figure is insensible to fatigue, and his dry, half-sarcastic, and often wholly unsympathetic manner is uninfluenced by any change in his surroundings. Though in his sixty-sixth year, I have never heard him express any dissatisfaction at the occasional hardships which we have had to encounter. I had regarded his presence as an encumbrance to the expedition, but, as a matter of fact, I am now well convinced that his power of endurance is as great as my own. In temper he is naturally acid and sceptical. From the beginning he has never concealed his belief that Professor Challenger is an absolute fraud, that we are all embarked upon an absurd wild-goose chase and that we are likely to reap nothing but disappointment and danger in South America, and corresponding ridicule in England. Such are the views which, with much passionate distortion of his thin features and wagging of his thin, goat-like beard, he poured into our ears all the way from Southampton to Manaos. Since landing from the boat he has obtained some consolation from the beauty and variety of the insect and bird life around him, for he is absolutely whole-hearted in his devotion to science. He spends his days flitting through the woods with his shot-gun and his butterfly-net, and his evenings in mounting the many specimens he has acquired. Among his minor peculiarities are that he is careless as to his attire, unclean in his person, exceedingly absent-minded in his habits, and addicted to smoking a short briar pipe, which is seldom out of his mouth. He has been upon several scientific expeditions in his youth (he was with Robertson in Papua), and the life of the camp and the canoe is nothing fresh to him.

Lord John Roxton has some points in common with Professor Summerlee, and others in which they are the very antithesis to each other. He is twenty years younger, but has something of the same spare, scraggy physique. As to his appearance, I have, as I recollect, described it in that portion of my narrative which I have left behind me in London. He is exceedingly neat and prim in his ways, dresses always with great care in white drill suits and high brown mosquito-boots, and shaves at least once a day. Like most men of action, he is laconic in speech, and sinks readily into his own thoughts, but he is always quick to answer a question or join in a conversation, talking in a queer, jerky, half-humorous fashion. His knowledge of the world, and very especially of South America, is surprising, and he has a whole-hearted belief in the possibilities of our journey which is not to be dashed by the sneers of Professor Summerlee. He has a gentle voice and a quiet manner, but behind his twinkling blue eyes there lurks a capacity for furious wrath and implacable resolution, the more dangerous because they are held in leash. He spoke little of his own exploits in Brazil and Peru, but it was a revelation to me to find the excitement which was caused by his presence among the riverine natives, who looked upon him as their champion and protector. The exploits of the Red Chief, as they called him, had become legends among them, but the real facts, as far as I could learn them, were amazing enough.

These were that Lord John had found himself some years before in that no-man's-land which is formed by the half-defined frontiers between Peru, Brazil, and Columbia. In this great district the wild rubber tree flourishes, and has become, as in the Congo, a curse to the natives which can only be compared to their forced labor under the Spaniards upon the old silver mines of Darien. A handful of villainous half-breeds dominated the country, armed such Indians as would support them, and turned the rest into slaves, terrorizing them with the most inhuman tortures in order to force them to gather the India-rubber, which was then floated down the river to Para. Lord John Roxton expostulated on behalf of the wretched victims, and received nothing but threats and insults for his pains. He then formally declared war against Pedro Lopez, the leader of the slave-drivers, enrolled a band of runaway slaves in his service, armed them, and conducted a campaign, which ended by his killing with his own hands the notorious half-breed and breaking down the system which he represented.

No wonder that the ginger-headed man with the silky voice and the free and easy manners was now looked upon with deep interest upon the banks of the great South American river, though the feelings he inspired were naturally mixed, since the gratitude of the natives was equaled by the resentment of those who desired to exploit them.

One useful result of his former experiences was that he could talk fluently in the Lingoa Geral, which is the peculiar talk, one-third Portuguese and two-thirds Indian, which is current all over Brazil.

I have said before that Lord John Roxton was a South Americomaniac. He could not speak of that great country without ardor, and this ardor was infectious, for, ignorant as I was, he fixed my attention and stimulated my curiosity. How I wish I could reproduce the glamour of his discourses, the peculiar mixture of accurate knowledge and of racy imagination which gave them their fascination, until even the Professor's cynical and sceptical smile would gradually vanish from his thin face as he listened. He would tell the history of the mighty river so rapidly explored (for some of the first conquerors of Peru actually crossed the entire continent upon its waters), and yet so unknown in regard to all that lay behind its ever-changing banks.

"What is there?" he would cry, pointing to the north. "Wood and marsh and unpenetrated jungle. Who knows what it may shelter? And there to the south? A wilderness of swampy forest, where no white man has ever been. The unknown is up against us on every side. Outside the narrow lines of the rivers what does anyone know? Who will say what is possible in such a country? Why should old man Challenger not be right?" At which direct defiance the stubborn sneer would reappear upon Professor Summerlee's face, and he would sit, shaking his sardonic head in unsympathetic silence, behind the cloud of his briar-root pipe.

* * *

So much, for the moment, for my two white companions, whose characters and limitations will be further exposed, as surely as my own, as this narrative proceeds. But already we have enrolled certain retainers who may play no small part in what is to come. The first is a gigantic negro named Zambo, who is a black Hercules, as willing as any horse, and about as intelligent. Him we enlisted at Para, on the recommendation of the steamship company, on whose vessels he had learned to speak a halting English.

It was at Para also that we engaged Gomez and Manuel, two half-breeds from up the river, just come down with a cargo of redwood. They were swarthy fellows, bearded and fierce, as active and wiry as panthers. Both of them had spent their lives in those upper waters of the Amazon which we were about to explore, and it was this recommendation which had caused Lord John to engage them. One of them, Gomez, had the further advantage that he could speak excellent English. These men were willing to act as our personal servants, to cook, to row, or to make themselves useful in any way at a payment of fifteen dollars a month. Besides these, we had engaged three Mojo Indians from Bolivia, who are the most skilful at fishing and boat work of all the river tribes. The chief of these we called Mojo, after his tribe, and the others are known as Jose and Fernando. Three white men, then, two half-breeds, one negro, and three Indians made up the personnel of the little expedition which lay waiting for its instructions at Manaos before starting upon its singular quest.

At last, after a weary week, the day had come and the hour. I ask you to picture the shaded sitting-room of the Fazenda St. Ignatio, two miles inland from the town of Manaos. Outside lay the yellow, brassy glare of the sunshine, with the shadows of the palm trees as black and definite as the trees themselves. The air was calm, full of the eternal hum of insects, a tropical chorus of many octaves, from the deep drone of the bee to the high, keen pipe of the mosquito. Beyond the veranda was a small cleared garden, bounded with cactus hedges and adorned with clumps of flowering shrubs, round which the great blue butterflies and the tiny humming-birds fluttered and darted in crescents of sparkling light. Within we were seated round the cane table, on which lay a sealed envelope. Inscribed upon it, in the jagged handwriting of Professor Challenger, were the words:

"Instructions to Lord John Roxton and party. To be opened at Manaos upon July 15th, at 12 o'clock precisely."

Lord John had placed his watch upon the table beside him.

"We have seven more minutes," said he. "The old dear is very precise."

Professor Summerlee gave an acid smile as he picked up the envelope in his gaunt hand.

"What can it possibly matter whether we open it now or in seven minutes?" said he. "It is all part and parcel of the same system of quackery and nonsense, for which I regret to say that the writer is notorious."

"Oh, come, we must play the game accordin' to rules," said Lord John. "It's old man Challenger's show and we are here by his good will, so it would be rotten bad form if we didn't follow his instructions to the letter."

"A pretty business it is!" cried the Professor, bitterly. "It struck me as preposterous in London, but I'm bound to say that it seems even more so upon closer acquaintance. I don't know what is inside this envelope, but, unless it is something pretty definite, I shall be much tempted to take the next down-river boat and catch the Bolivia at Para. After all, I have some more responsible work in the world than to run about disproving the assertions of a lunatic. Now, Roxton, surely it is time."

"Time it is," said Lord John. "You can blow the whistle." He took up the envelope and cut it with his penknife. From it he drew a folded sheet of paper. This he carefully opened out and flattened on the table. It was a blank sheet. He turned it over. Again it was blank. We looked at each other in a bewildered silence, which was broken by a discordant burst of derisive laughter from Professor Summerlee.

"It is an open admission," he cried. "What more do you want? The fellow is a self-confessed humbug. We have only to return home and report him as the brazen imposter that he is."

"Invisible ink!" I suggested.

"I don't think!" said Lord Roxton, holding the paper to the light. "No, young fellah my lad, there is no use deceiving yourself. I'll go bail for it that nothing has ever been written upon this paper."

"May I come in?" boomed a voice from the veranda.

The shadow of a squat figure had stolen across the patch of sunlight. That voice! That monstrous breadth of shoulder! We sprang to our feet with a gasp of astonishment as Challenger, in a round, boyish straw-hat with a coloured ribbon – Challenger, with his hands in his jacket-pockets and his canvas shoes daintily pointing as he walked – appeared in the open space before us. He threw back his head, and there he stood in the golden glow with all his old Assyrian luxuriance of beard, all his native insolence of drooping eyelids and intolerant eyes.

"I fear," said he, taking out his watch, "that I am a few minutes too late. When I gave you this envelope I must confess that I had never intended that you should open it, for it had been my fixed intention to be with you before the hour. The unfortunate delay can be apportioned between a blundering pilot and an intrusive sandbank. I fear that it has given my colleague, Professor Summerlee, occasion to blaspheme."

"I am bound to say, sir," said Lord John, with some sternness of voice, "that your turning up is a considerable relief to us, for our mission seemed to have come to a premature end. Even now I can't for the life of me understand why you should have worked it in so extraordinary a manner."

Instead of answering, Professor Challenger entered, shook hands with myself and Lord John, bowed with ponderous insolence to Professor Summerlee, and sank back into a basket-chair, which creaked and swayed beneath his weight.

"Is all ready for your journey?" he asked.

"We can start tomorrow."

"Then so you shall. You need no chart of directions now, since you will have the inestimable advantage of my own guidance. From the first I had determined that I would myself preside over your investigation. The most elaborate charts would, as you will readily admit, be a poor substitute for my own intelligence and advice. As to the small ruse which I played upon you in the matter of the envelope, it is clear that, had I told you all my intentions, I should have been forced to resist unwelcome pressure to travel out with you."

"Not from me, sir!" exclaimed Professor Summerlee, heartily. "So long as there was another ship upon the Atlantic."

Challenger waved him away with his great hairy hand.

"Your common sense will, I am sure, sustain my objection and realize that it was better that I should direct my own movements and appear only at the exact moment when my presence was needed. That moment has now arrived. You are in safe hands. You will not now fail to reach your destination. From henceforth I take command of this expedition, and I must ask you to complete your preparations tonight, so that we may be able to make an early start in the morning. My time is of value, and the same thing may be said, no doubt, in a lesser degree of your own. I propose, therefore, that we push on as rapidly as possible, until I have demonstrated what you have come to see."

Lord John Roxton has chartered a large steam launch, the Esmeralda, which was to carry us up the river. So far as climate goes, it was immaterial what time we chose for our expedition, as the temperature ranges from seventy-five to ninety degrees both summer and winter, with no appreciable difference in heat. In moisture, however, it is otherwise; from December to May is the period of the rains, and during this time the river slowly rises until it attains a height of nearly forty feet above its low-water mark. It floods the banks, extends in great lagoons over a monstrous waste of country, and forms a huge district, called locally the Gapo, which is for the most part too marshy for foot-travel and too shallow for boating. About June the waters begin to fall, and are at their lowest at October or November. Thus our expedition was at the time of the dry season, when the great river and its tributaries were more or less in a normal condition.

The current of the river is a slight one, the drop being not greater than eight inches in a mile. No stream could be more convenient for navigation, since the prevailing wind is south-east, and sailing boats may make a continuous progress to the Peruvian frontier, dropping down again with the current. In our own case the excellent engines of the Esmeralda could disregard the sluggish flow of the stream, and we made as rapid progress as if we were navigating a stagnant lake. For three days we steamed north-westwards up a stream which even here, a thousand miles from its mouth, was still so enormous that from its centre the two banks were mere shadows upon the distant skyline. On the fourth day after leaving Manaos we turned into a tributary which at its mouth was little smaller than the main stream. It narrowed rapidly, however, and after two more days' steaming we reached an Indian village, where the Professor insisted that we should land, and that the Esmeralda should be sent back to Manaos. We should soon come upon rapids, he explained, which would make its further use impossible. He added privately that we were now approaching the door of the unknown country, and that the fewer whom we took into our confidence the better it would be. To this end also he made each of us give our word of honour that we would publish or say nothing which would give any exact clue as to the whereabouts of our travels, while the servants were all solemnly sworn to the same effect. It is for this reason that I am compelled to be vague in my narrative, and I would warn my readers that in any map or diagram which I may give the relation of places to each other may be correct, but the points of the compass are carefully confused, so that in no way can it be taken as an actual guide to the country. Professor Challenger's reasons for secrecy may be valid or not, but we had no choice but to adopt them, for he was prepared to abandon the whole expedition rather than modify the conditions upon which he would guide us.

It was August 2nd when we snapped our last link with the outer world by bidding farewell to the Esmeralda. Since then four days have passed, during which we have engaged two large canoes from the Indians, made of so light a material (skins over a bamboo framework) that we should be able to carry them round any obstacle. These we have loaded with all our effects, and have engaged two additional Indians to help us in the navigation. I understand that they are the very two – Ataca and Ipetu by name – who accompanied Professor Challenger upon his previous journey. They appeared to be terrified at the prospect of repeating it, but the chief has patriarchal powers in these countries, and if the bargain is good in his eyes the clansman has little choice in the matter.

So tomorrow we disappear into the unknown. This account I am transmitting down the river by canoe, and it may be our last word to those who are interested in our fate. I have, according to our arrangement, addressed it to you, my dear Mr. McArdle, and I leave it to your discretion to delete, alter, or do what you like with it. From the assurance of Professor Challenger's manner – and in spite of the continued scepticism of Professor Summerlee – I have no doubt that our leader will make good his statement, and that we are really on the eve of some most remarkable experiences.

Chapter VIII
'The Outlying Pickets of the New World'

OUR FRIENDS AT HOME may well rejoice with us, for we are at our goal, and up to a point, at least, we have shown that the statement of Professor Challenger can be verified. We have not, it is true, ascended the plateau, but it lies before us, and even Professor Summerlee is in a more chastened mood. Not that he will for an instant admit that his rival could be right, but he is less persistent in his incessant objections, and has sunk for the most part into an observant silence. I must hark back, however, and continue my narrative from where I dropped it. We are sending home one of our local Indians who is injured, and I am committing this letter to his charge, with considerable doubts in my mind as to whether it will ever come to hand.

When I wrote last we were about to leave the Indian village where we had been deposited by the Esmeralda. I have to begin my report by bad news, for the first serious personal trouble (I pass over the incessant bickerings between the Professors) occurred this evening, and might have had a tragic ending. I have spoken of our English-speaking half-breed, Gomez – a fine worker and a willing fellow, but afflicted, I fancy, with the vice of curiosity, which is common enough among such men. On the last evening he seems to have hid himself near the hut in which we were discussing our plans, and, being observed by our huge negro Zambo, who is as faithful as a dog and has the hatred which all his race bear to the half-breeds, he was dragged out and carried into our presence. Gomez whipped out his knife, however, and but for the huge strength of his captor, which enabled him to disarm him with one hand, he would certainly have stabbed him. The matter has ended in reprimands, the opponents have been compelled to shake hands, and there is every hope that all will be well. As to the feuds of the two learned men, they are continuous and bitter. It must be admitted that Challenger is provocative in the last degree, but Summerlee has an acid tongue, which makes matters worse. Last night Challenger said that he never cared to walk on the Thames Embankment and look up the river, as it was always sad to see one's own eventual goal. He is convinced, of course, that he is destined for Westminster Abbey. Summerlee rejoined, however, with a sour smile, by saying that he understood that Millbank Prison had been pulled down. Challenger's conceit is too colossal to allow him to be really annoyed. He only smiled in his beard and repeated "Really! Really!" in the pitying tone one would use to a child. Indeed, they are children both – the one wizened and cantankerous, the other formidable and overbearing, yet each with a brain which has put him in the front rank of his scientific age. Brain, character, soul – only as one sees more of life does one understand how distinct is each.

The very next day we did actually make our start upon this remarkable expedition. We found that all our possessions fitted very easily into thc two canoes, and we divided our personnel, six in each, taking the obvious precaution in the interests of peace of putting one Professor into each canoe. Personally, I was with Challenger, who was in a beatific humor, moving about as one in a silent ecstasy and beaming benevolence from every feature. I have had some experience of him in other moods, however, and shall be the less surprised when the thunderstorms suddenly come up amidst the sunshine. If it is impossible to be at your ease, it is equally impossible to be dull in his company, for one is always in a state of half-tremulous doubt as to what sudden turn his formidable temper may take.

For two days we made our way up a good-sized river some hundreds of yards broad, and dark in colour, but transparent, so that one could usually see the bottom. The affluents of the Amazon are, half of them, of this nature, while the other half are whitish and opaque, the difference depending upon the class of country through which they have flowed. The dark indicate vegetable decay, while the others point to clayey soil. Twice we came across rapids, and in each case made a portage of half a mile or so to avoid them. The woods on either side were primeval, which are more easily penetrated than woods of the second growth, and we had no great difficulty in carrying our canoes through them. How shall I ever forget the solemn mystery of it? The height of the trees and the thickness of the boles exceeded anything which I in my town-bred life could have imagined, shooting upwards in magnificent columns until, at an enormous distance above our heads, we could dimly discern the spot where they threw out their side-branches into Gothic upward curves which coalesced to form one great matted roof of verdure, through which only an occasional golden ray of sunshine shot downwards to trace a thin dazzling line of light amidst the majestic obscurity. As we walked noiselessly amid the thick, soft carpet of decaying vegetation the hush fell upon our souls which comes upon us in the twilight of the Abbey, and even Professor Challenger's full-chested notes sank into a whisper. Alone, I should have been ignorant of the names of these giant growths, but our men of science pointed out the cedars, the great silk cotton trees, and the redwood trees, with all that profusion of various plants which has made this continent the chief supplier to the human race of those gifts of Nature which depend upon the vegetable world, while it is the most backward in those products which come from animal life. Vivid orchids and wonderful coloured lichens smoldered upon the swarthy tree-trunks and where a wandering shaft of light fell full upon the golden allamanda, the scarlet star-clusters of the tacsonia, or the rich deep blue of ipomaea, the effect was as a dream of fairyland. In these great wastes of forest, life, which abhors darkness, struggles ever upwards to the light. Every plant, even the smaller ones, curls and writhes to the green surface, twining itself round its stronger and taller brethren in the effort. Climbing plants are monstrous and luxuriant, but others which have never been known to climb elsewhere learn the art as an escape from that somber shadow, so that the common nettle, the jasmine, and even the jacitara palm tree can be seen circling the stems of the cedars and striving to reach their crowns. Of animal life there was no movement amid the majestic vaulted aisles which stretched from us as we walked, but a constant movement far above our heads told of that multitudinous world of snake and monkey, bird and sloth, which lived in the sunshine, and looked down in wonder at our tiny, dark, stumbling figures in the obscure depths immeasurably below them. At dawn and at sunset the howler monkeys screamed together and the parrakeets broke into shrill chatter, but during the hot hours of the day only the full drone of insects, like the beat of a distant surf, filled the ear, while nothing moved amid the solemn vistas of stupendous trunks, fading away into the darkness which held us in. Once some bandy-legged, lurching creature, an ant-eater or a bear, scuttled clumsily amid the shadows. It was the only sign of earth life which I saw in this great Amazonian forest.

And yet there were indications that even human life itself was not far from us in those mysterious recesses. On the third day out we were aware of a singular deep throbbing in the air, rhythmic and solemn, coming and going fitfully throughout the morning. The two boats were paddling within a few yards of each other when first we heard it, and our Indians remained motionless, as if they had been turned to bronze, listening intently with expressions of terror upon their faces.

"What is it, then?" I asked.

"Drums," said Lord John, carelessly; "war drums. I have heard them before."

"Yes, sir, war drums," said Gomez, the half-breed. "Wild Indians, bravos, not mansos; they watch us every mile of the way; kill us if they can."

"How can they watch us?" I asked, gazing into the dark, motionless void.

The half-breed shrugged his broad shoulders.

"The Indians know. They have their own way. They watch us. They talk the drum talk to each other. Kill us if they can."

By the afternoon of that day – my pocket diary shows me that it was Tuesday, August 18th – at least six or seven drums were throbbing from various points. Sometimes they beat quickly, sometimes slowly, sometimes in obvious question and answer, one far to the east breaking out in a high staccato rattle, and being followed after a pause by a deep roll from the north. There was something indescribably nerve-shaking and menacing in that constant mutter, which seemed to shape itself into the very syllables of the half-breed, endlessly repeated, "We will kill you if we can. We will kill you if we can." No one ever moved in the silent woods. All the peace and soothing of quiet Nature lay in that dark curtain of vegetation, but away from behind there came ever the one message from our fellow-man. "We will kill you if we can," said the men in the east. "We will kill you if we can," said the men in the north.

All day the drums rumbled and whispered, while their menace reflected itself in the faces of our coloured companions. Even the hardy, swaggering half-breed seemed cowed. I learned, however, that day once for all that both Summerlee and Challenger possessed that highest type of bravery, the bravery of the scientific mind. Theirs was the spirit which upheld Darwin among the gauchos of the Argentine or Wallace among the head-hunters of Malaya. It is decreed by a merciful Nature that the human brain cannot think of two things simultaneously, so that if it be steeped in curiosity as to science it has no room for merely personal considerations. All day amid that incessant and mysterious menace our two Professors watched every bird upon the wing, and every shrub upon the bank, with many a sharp wordy contention, when the snarl of Summerlee came quick upon the deep growl of Challenger, but with no more sense of danger and no more reference to drum-beating Indians than if they were seated together in the smoking-room of the Royal Society's Club in St. James's Street. Once only did they condescend to discuss them.

"Miranha or Amajuaca cannibals," said Challenger, jerking his thumb towards the reverberating wood.

"No doubt, sir," Summerlee answered. "Like all such tribes, I shall expect to find them of poly-synthetic speech and of Mongolian type."

"Polysynthetic certainly," said Challenger, indulgently. "I am not aware that any other type of language exists in this continent, and I have notes of more than a hundred. The Mongolian theory I regard with deep suspicion."

"I should have thought that even a limited knowledge of comparative anatomy would have helped to verify it," said Summerlee, bitterly.

Challenger thrust out his aggressive chin until he was all beard and hat-rim. "No doubt, sir, a limited knowledge would have that effect. When one's knowledge is exhaustive, one comes to other conclusions." They glared at each other in mutual defiance, while all round rose the distant whisper, "We will kill you – we will kill you if we can."

That night we moored our canoes with heavy stones for anchors in the centre of the stream, and made every preparation for a possible attack. Nothing came, however, and with the dawn we pushed upon our way, the drum-beating dying out behind us. About three o'clock in the afternoon we came to a very steep rapid, more than a mile long – the very one in which Professor Challenger had suffered disaster upon his first journey. I confess that the sight of it consoled me, for it was really the first direct corroboration, slight as it was, of the truth of his story. The Indians carried first our canoes and then our stores through the brushwood, which is very thick at this point, while we four whites, our rifles on our shoulders, walked between them and any danger coming from the woods. Before evening we had successfully passed the rapids, and made our way some ten miles above them, where we anchored for the night. At this point I reckoned that we had come not less than a hundred miles up the tributary from the main stream.

It was in the early forenoon of the next day that we made the great departure. Since dawn Professor Challenger had been acutely uneasy, continually scanning each bank of the river. Suddenly he gave an exclamation of satisfaction and pointed to a single tree, which projected at a peculiar angle over the side of the stream.

"What do you make of that?" he asked.

"It is surely an Assai palm," said Summerlee.

"Exactly. It was an Assai palm which I took for my landmark. The secret opening is half a mile onwards upon the other side of the river. There is no break in the trees. That is the wonder and the mystery of it. There where you see light-green rushes instead of dark-green undergrowth, there between the great cotton woods, that is my private gate into the unknown. Push through, and you will understand."

It was indeed a wonderful place. Having reached the spot marked by a line of light-green rushes, we poled out two canoes through them for some hundreds of yards, and eventually emerged into a placid and shallow stream, running clear and transparent over a sandy bottom. It may have been twenty yards across, and was banked in on each side by most luxuriant vegetation. No one who had not observed that for a short distance reeds had taken the place of shrubs, could possibly have guessed the existence of such a stream or dreamed of the fairyland beyond.

For a fairyland it was – the most wonderful that the imagination of man could conceive. The thick vegetation met overhead, interlacing into a natural pergola, and through this tunnel of verdure in a golden twilight flowed the green, pellucid river, beautiful in itself, but marvelous from the strange tints thrown by the vivid light from above filtered and tempered in its fall. Clear as crystal, motionless as a sheet of glass, green as the edge of an iceberg, it stretched in front of us under its leafy archway, every stroke of our paddles sending a thousand ripples across its shining surface. It was a fitting avenue to a land of wonders. All sign of the Indians had passed away, but animal life was more frequent, and the tameness of the creatures showed that they knew nothing of the hunter. Fuzzy little black-velvet monkeys, with snow-white teeth and gleaming, mocking eyes, chattered at us as we passed. With a dull, heavy splash an occasional cayman plunged in from the bank. Once a dark, clumsy tapir stared at us from a gap in the bushes, and then lumbered away through the forest; once, too, the yellow, sinuous form of a great puma whisked amid the brushwood, and its green, baleful eyes glared hatred at us over its tawny shoulder. Bird life was abundant, especially the wading birds, stork, heron, and ibis gathering in little groups, blue, scarlet, and white, upon every log which jutted from the bank, while beneath us the crystal water was alive with fish of every shape and colour.

For three days we made our way up this tunnel of hazy green sunshine. On the longer stretches one could hardly tell as one looked ahead where the distant green water ended and the distant green archway began. The deep peace of this strange waterway was unbroken by any sign of man.

"No Indian here. Too much afraid. Curupuri," said Gomez.

"Curupuri is the spirit of the woods," Lord John explained. "It's a name for any kind of devil. The poor beggars think that there is something fearsome in this direction, and therefore they avoid it."

On the third day it became evident that our journey in the canoes could not last much longer, for the stream was rapidly growing more shallow. Twice in as many hours we stuck upon the bottom. Finally we pulled the boats up among the brushwood and spent the night on the bank of the river. In the morning Lord John and I made our way for a couple of miles through the forest, keeping parallel with the stream; but as it grew ever shallower we returned and reported, what Professor Challenger had already suspected, that we had reached the highest point to which the canoes could be brought. We drew them up, therefore, and concealed them among the bushes, blazing a tree with our axes, so that we should find them again. Then we distributed the various burdens among us – guns, ammunition, food, a tent, blankets, and the rest – and, shouldering our packages, we set forth upon the more laborious stage of our journey.

An unfortunate quarrel between our pepper-pots marked the outset of our new stage. Challenger had from the moment of joining us issued directions to the whole party, much to the evident discontent of Summerlee. Now, upon his assigning some duty to his fellow-Professor (it was only the carrying of an aneroid barometer), the matter suddenly came to a head.

"May I ask, sir," said Summerlee, with vicious calm, "in what capacity you take it upon yourself to issue these orders?"

Challenger glared and bristled.

"I do it, Professor Summerlee, as leader of this expedition."

"I am compelled to tell you, sir, that I do not recognize you in that capacity."

"Indeed!" Challenger bowed with unwieldy sarcasm. "Perhaps you would define my exact position."

"Yes, sir. You are a man whose veracity is upon trial, and this committee is here to try it. You walk, sir, with your judges."

"Dear me!" said Challenger, seating himself on the side of one of the canoes. "In that case you will, of course, go on your way, and I will follow at my leisure. If I am not the leader you cannot expect me to lead."

Thank heaven that there were two sane men – Lord John Roxton and myself – to prevent the petulance and folly of our learned Professors from sending us back empty-handed to London. Such arguing and pleading and explaining before we could get them mollified! Then at last Summerlee, with his sneer and his pipe, would move forwards, and Challenger would come rolling and grumbling after. By some good fortune we discovered about this time that both our savants had the very poorest opinion of Dr. Illingworth of Edinburgh. Thenceforward that was our one safety, and every strained situation was relieved by our introducing the name of the Scotch zoologist, when both our Professors would form a temporary alliance and friendship in their detestation and abuse of this common rival.

Advancing in single file along the bank of the stream, we soon found that it narrowed down to a mere brook, and finally that it lost itself in a great green morass of sponge-like mosses, into which we sank up to our knees. The place was horribly haunted by clouds of mosquitoes and every form of flying pest, so we were glad to find solid ground again and to make a circuit among the trees, which enabled us to outflank this pestilent morass, which droned like an organ in the distance, so loud was it with insect life.

On the second day after leaving our canoes we found that the whole character of the country changed. Our road was persistently upwards, and as we ascended the woods became thinner and lost their tropical luxuriance. The huge trees of the alluvial Amazonian plain gave place to the Phoenix and coco palms, growing in scattered clumps, with thick brushwood between. In the damper hollows the Mauritia palms threw out their graceful drooping fronds. We traveled entirely by compass, and once or twice there were differences of opinion between Challenger and the two Indians, when, to quote the Professor's indignant words, the whole party agreed to "trust the fallacious instincts of undeveloped savages rather than the highest product of modern European culture." That we were justified in doing so was shown upon the third day, when Challenger admitted that he recognized several landmarks of his former journey, and in one spot we actually came upon four fire-blackened stones, which must have marked a camping-place.

The road still ascended, and we crossed a rock-studded slope which took two days to traverse. The vegetation had again changed, and only the vegetable ivory tree remained, with a great profusion of wonderful orchids, among which I learned to recognize the rare Nuttonia Vexillaria and the glorious pink and scarlet blossoms of Cattleya and odontoglossum. Occasional brooks with pebbly bottoms and fern-draped banks gurgled down the shallow gorges in the hill, and offered good camping-grounds every evening on the banks of some rock-studded pool, where swarms of little blue-backed fish, about the size and shape of English trout, gave us a delicious supper.

On the ninth day after leaving the canoes, having done, as I reckon, about a hundred and twenty miles, we began to emerge from the trees, which had grown smaller until they were mere shrubs. Their place was taken by an immense wilderness of bamboo, which grew so thickly that we could only penetrate it by cutting a pathway with the machetes and billhooks of the Indians. It took us a long day, traveling from seven in the morning till eight at night, with only two breaks of one hour each, to get through this obstacle. Anything more monotonous and wearying could not be imagined, for, even at the most open places, I could not see more than ten or twelve yards, while usually my vision was limited to the back of Lord John's cotton jacket in front of me, and to the yellow wall within a foot of me on either side. From above came one thin knife-edge of sunshine, and fifteen feet over our heads one saw the tops of the reeds swaying against the deep blue sky. I do not know what kind of creatures inhabit such a thicket, but several times we heard the plunging of large, heavy animals quite close to us. From their sounds Lord John judged them to be some form of wild cattle. Just as night fell we cleared the belt of bamboos, and at once formed our camp, exhausted by the interminable day.

Early next morning we were again afoot, and found that the character of the country had changed once again. Behind us was the wall of bamboo, as definite as if it marked the course of a river. In front was an open plain, sloping slightly upwards and dotted with clumps of tree-ferns, the whole curving before us until it ended in a long, whale-backed ridge. This we reached about midday, only to find a shallow valley beyond, rising once again into a gentle incline which led to a low, rounded sky-line. It was here, while we crossed the first of these hills, that an incident occurred which may or may not have been important.

Professor Challenger, who with the two local Indians was in the van of the party, stopped suddenly and pointed excitedly to the right. As he did so we saw, at the distance of a mile or so, something which appeared to be a huge gray bird flap slowly up from the ground and skim smoothly off, flying very low and straight, until it was lost among the tree-ferns.

"Did you see it?" cried Challenger, in exultation. "Summerlee, did you see it?"

His colleague was staring at the spot where the creature had disappeared.

"What do you claim that it was?" he asked.

"To the best of my belief, a pterodactyl."

Summerlee burst into derisive laughter "A pter-fiddlestick!" said he. "It was a stork, if ever I saw one."

Challenger was too furious to speak. He simply swung his pack upon his back and continued upon his march. Lord John came abreast of me, however, and his face was more grave than was his wont. He had his Zeiss glasses in his hand.

"I focused it before it got over the trees," said he. "I won't undertake to say what it was, but I'll risk my reputation as a sportsman that it wasn't any bird that ever I clapped eyes on in my life."

So there the matter stands. Are we really just at the edge of the unknown, encountering the outlying pickets of this lost world of which our leader speaks? I give you the incident as it occurred and you will know as much as I do. It stands alone, for we saw nothing more which could be called remarkable.

And now, my readers, if ever I have any, I have brought you up the broad river, and through the screen of rushes, and down the green tunnel, and up the long slope of palm trees, and through the bamboo brake, and across the plain of tree-ferns. At last our destination lay in full sight of us. When we had crossed the second ridge we saw before us an irregular, palm-studded plain, and then the line of high red cliffs which I have seen in the picture. There it lies, even as I write, and there can be no question that it is the same. At the nearest point it is about seven miles from our present camp, and it curves away, stretching as far as I can see. Challenger struts about like a prize peacock, and Summerlee is silent, but still sceptical. Another day should bring some of our doubts to an end. Meanwhile, as Jose, whose arm was pierced by a broken bamboo, insists upon returning, I send this letter back in his charge, and only hope that it may eventually come to hand. I will write again as the occasion serves. I have enclosed with this a rough chart of our journey, which may have the effect of making the account rather easier to understand.

Chapter IX
'Who Could Have Foreseen It?'

A DREADFUL THING has happened to us. Who could have foreseen it? I cannot foresee any end to our troubles. It may be that we are condemned to spend our whole lives in this strange, inaccessible place. I am still so confused that I can hardly think clearly of the facts of the present or of the chances of the future. To my astounded senses the one seems most terrible and the other as black as night.

No men have ever found themselves in a worse position; nor is there any use in disclosing to you our exact geographical situation and asking our friends for a relief party. Even if they could send one, our fate will in all human probability be decided long before it could arrive in South America.

We are, in truth, as far from any human aid as if we were in the moon. If we are to win through, it is only our own qualities which can save us. I have as companions three remarkable men, men of great brain-power and of unshaken courage. There lies our one and only hope. It is only when I look upon the untroubled faces of my comrades that I see some glimmer through the darkness. Outwardly I trust that I appear as unconcerned as they. Inwardly I am filled with apprehension.

Let me give you, with as much detail as I can, the sequence of events which have led us to this catastrophe.

When I finished my last letter I stated that we were within seven miles from an enormous line of ruddy cliffs, which encircled, beyond all doubt, the plateau of which Professor Challenger spoke. Their height, as we approached them, seemed to me in some places to be greater than he had stated – running up in parts to at least a thousand feet – and they were curiously striated, in a manner which is, I believe, characteristic of basaltic upheavals. Something of the sort is to be seen in Salisbury Crags at Edinburgh. The summit showed every sign of a luxuriant vegetation, with bushes near the edge, and farther back many high trees. There was no indication of any life that we could see.

That night we pitched our camp immediately under the cliff – a most wild and desolate spot. The crags above us were not merely perpendicular, but curved outwards at the top, so that ascent was out of the question. Close to us was the high thin pinnacle of rock which I believe I mentioned earlier in this narrative. It is like a broad red church spire, the top of it being level with the plateau, but a great chasm gaping between. On the summit of it there grew one high tree. Both pinnacle and cliff were comparatively low – some five or six hundred feet, I should think.

"It was on that," said Professor Challenger, pointing to this tree, "that the pterodactyl was perched. I climbed half-way up the rock before I shot him. I am inclined to think that a good mountaineer like myself could ascend the rock to the top, though he would, of course, be no nearer to the plateau when he had done so."

As Challenger spoke of his pterodactyl I glanced at Professor Summerlee, and for the first time I seemed to see some signs of a dawning credulity and repentance. There was no sneer upon his thin lips, but, on the contrary, a gray, drawn look of excitement and amazement. Challenger saw it, too, and reveled in the first taste of victory.

"Of course," said he, with his clumsy and ponderous sarcasm, "Professor Summerlee will understand that when I speak of a pterodactyl I mean a stork – only it is the kind of stork which has no feathers, a leathery skin, membranous wings, and teeth in its jaws." He grinned and blinked and bowed until his colleague turned and walked away.

In the morning, after a frugal breakfast of coffee and manioc – we had to be economical of our stores – we held a council of war as to the best method of ascending to the plateau above us.

Challenger presided with a solemnity as if he were the Lord Chief Justice on the Bench. Picture him seated upon a rock, his absurd boyish straw hat tilted on the back of his head, his supercilious eyes dominating us from under his drooping lids, his great black beard wagging as he slowly defined our present situation and our future movements.

Beneath him you might have seen the three of us – myself, sunburnt, young, and vigorous after our open-air tramp; Summerlee, solemn but still critical, behind his eternal pipe; Lord John, as keen as a razor-edge, with his supple, alert figure leaning upon his rifle, and his eager eyes fixed eagerly upon the speaker. Behind us were grouped the two swarthy half-breeds and the little knot of Indians, while in front and above us towered those huge, ruddy ribs of rocks which kept us from our goal.

"I need not say," said our leader, "that on the occasion of my last visit I exhausted every means of climbing the cliff, and where I failed I do not think that anyone else is likely to succeed, for I am something of a mountaineer. I had none of the appliances of a rock-climber with me, but I have taken the precaution to bring them now. With their aid I am positive I could climb that detached pinnacle to the summit; but so long as the main cliff overhangs, it is vain to attempt ascending that. I was hurried upon my last visit by the approach of the rainy season and by the exhaustion of my supplies. These considerations limited my time, and I can only claim that I have surveyed about six miles of the cliff to the east of us, finding no possible way up. What, then, shall we now do?"

"There seems to be only one reasonable course," said Professor Summerlee. "If you have explored the east, we should travel along the base of the cliff to the west, and seek for a practicable point for our ascent."

"That's it," said Lord John. "The odds are that this plateau is of no great size, and we shall travel round it until we either find an easy way up it, or come back to the point from which we started."

"I have already explained to our young friend here," said Challenger (he has a way of alluding to me as if I were a school child ten years old), "that it is quite impossible that there should be an easy way up anywhere, for the simple reason that if there were the summit would not be isolated, and those conditions would not obtain which have effected so singular an interference with the general laws of survival. Yet I admit that there may very well be places where an expert human climber may reach the summit, and yet a cumbrous and heavy animal be unable to descend. It is certain that there is a point where an ascent is possible."

"How do you know that, sir?" asked Summerlee, sharply.

"Because my predecessor, the American Maple White, actually made such an ascent. How otherwise could he have seen the monster which he sketched in his notebook?"

"There you reason somewhat ahead of the proved facts," said the stubborn Summerlee. "I admit your plateau, because I have seen it; but I have not as yet satisfied myself that it contains any form of life whatever."

"What you admit, sir, or what you do not admit, is really of inconceivably small importance. I am glad to perceive that the plateau itself has actually obtruded itself upon your intelligence." He glanced up at it, and then, to our amazement, he sprang from his rock, and, seizing Summerlee by the neck, he tilted his face into the air. "Now sir!" he shouted, hoarse with excitement. "Do I help you to realize that the plateau contains some animal life?"

I have said that a thick fringe of green overhung the edge of the cliff. Out of this there had emerged a black, glistening object. As it came slowly forth and overhung the chasm, we saw that it was a very large snake with a peculiar flat, spade-like head. It wavered and quivered above us for a minute, the morning sun gleaming upon its sleek, sinuous coils. Then it slowly drew inwards and disappeared.

Summerlee had been so interested that he had stood unresisting while Challenger tilted his head into the air. Now he shook his colleague off and came back to his dignity.

"I should be glad, Professor Challenger," said he, "if you could see your way to make any remarks which may occur to you without seizing me by the chin. Even the appearance of a very ordinary rock python does not appear to justify such a liberty."

"But there is life upon the plateau all the same," his colleague replied in triumph. "And now, having demonstrated this important conclusion so that it is clear to anyone, however prejudiced or obtuse, I am of opinion that we cannot do better than break up our camp and travel to westward until we find some means of ascent."

The ground at the foot of the cliff was rocky and broken so that the going was slow and difficult. Suddenly we came, however, upon something which cheered our hearts. It was the site of an old encampment, with several empty Chicago meat tins, a bottle labeled 'Brandy,' a broken tin-opener, and a quantity of other travelers' debris. A crumpled, disintegrated newspaper revealed itself as the Chicago Democrat, though the date had been obliterated.

"Not mine," said Challenger. "It must be Maple White's."

Lord John had been gazing curiously at a great tree-fern which overshadowed the encampment. "I say, look at this," said he. "I believe it is meant for a sign-post."

A slip of hard wood had been nailed to the tree in such a way as to point to the westward.

"Most certainly a sign-post," said Challenger. "What else? Finding himself upon a dangerous errand, our pioneer has left this sign so that any party which follows him may know the way he has taken. Perhaps we shall come upon some other indications as we proceed."

We did indeed, but they were of a terrible and most unexpected nature. Immediately beneath the cliff there grew a considerable patch of high bamboo, like that which we had traversed in our journey. Many of these stems were twenty feet high, with sharp, strong tops, so that even as they stood they made formidable spears. We were passing along the edge of this cover when my eye was caught by the gleam of something white within it. Thrusting in my head between the stems, I found myself gazing at a fleshless skull. The whole skeleton was there, but the skull had detached itself and lay some feet nearer to the open.

With a few blows from the machetes of our Indians we cleared the spot and were able to study the details of this old tragedy. Only a few shreds of clothes could still be distinguished, but there were the remains of boots upon the bony feet, and it was very clear that the dead man was a European. A gold watch by Hudson, of New York, and a chain which held a stylographic pen, lay among the bones. There was also a silver cigarette-case, with 'J.C., from A.E.S.,' upon the lid. The state of the metal seemed to show that the catastrophe had occurred no great time before.

"Who can he be?" asked Lord John. "Poor devil! Every bone in his body seems to be broken."

"And the bamboo grows through his smashed ribs," said Summerlee. "It is a fast-growing plant, but it is surely inconceivable that this body could have been here while the canes grew to be twenty feet in length."

"As to the man's identity," said Professor Challenger, "I have no doubt whatever upon that point. As I made my way up the river before I reached you at the fazenda I instituted very particular inquiries about Maple White. At Para they knew nothing. Fortunately, I had a definite clew, for there was a particular picture in his sketch-book which showed him taking lunch with a certain ecclesiastic at Rosario. This priest I was able to find, and though he proved a very argumentative fellow, who took it absurdly amiss that I should point out to him the corrosive effect which modern science must have upon his beliefs, he none the less gave me some positive information. Maple White passed Rosario four years ago, or two years before I saw his dead body. He was not alone at the time, but there was a friend, an American named James Colver, who remained in the boat and did not meet this ecclesiastic. I think, therefore, that there can be no doubt that we are now looking upon the remains of this James Colver."

"Nor," said Lord John, "is there much doubt as to how he met his death. He has fallen or been chucked from the top, and so been impaled. How else could he come by his broken bones, and how could he have been stuck through by these canes with their points so high above our heads?"

A hush came over us as we stood round these shattered remains and realized the truth of Lord John Roxton's words. The beetling head of the cliff projected over the cane-brake. Undoubtedly he had fallen from above. But had he fallen? Had it been an accident? Or – already ominous and terrible possibilities began to form round that unknown land.

We moved off in silence, and continued to coast round the line of cliffs, which were as even and unbroken as some of those monstrous Antarctic ice-fields which I have seen depicted as stretching from horizon to horizon and towering high above the mast-heads of the exploring vessel.

In five miles we saw no rift or break. And then suddenly we perceived something which filled us with new hope. In a hollow of the rock, protected from rain, there was drawn a rough arrow in chalk, pointing still to the westwards.

"Maple White again," said Professor Challenger. "He had some presentiment that worthy footsteps would follow close behind him."

"He had chalk, then?"

"A box of coloured chalks was among the effects I found in his knapsack. I remember that the white one was worn to a stump."

"That is certainly good evidence," said Summerlee. "We can only accept his guidance and follow on to the westward."

We had proceeded some five more miles when again we saw a white arrow upon the rocks. It was at a point where the face of the cliff was for the first time split into a narrow cleft. Inside the cleft was a second guidance mark, which pointed right up it with the tip somewhat elevated, as if the spot indicated were above the level of the ground.

It was a solemn place, for the walls were so gigantic and the slit of blue sky so narrow and so obscured by a double fringe of verdure, that only a dim and shadowy light penetrated to the bottom. We had had no food for many hours, and were very weary with the stony and irregular journey, but our nerves were too strung to allow us to halt. We ordered the camp to be pitched, however, and, leaving the Indians to arrange it, we four, with the two half-breeds, proceeded up the narrow gorge.

It was not more than forty feet across at the mouth, but it rapidly closed until it ended in an acute angle, too straight and smooth for an ascent. Certainly it was not this which our pioneer had attempted to indicate. We made our way back – the whole gorge was not more than a quarter of a mile deep – and then suddenly the quick eyes of Lord John fell upon what we were seeking. High up above our heads, amid the dark shadows, there was one circle of deeper gloom. Surely it could only be the opening of a cave.

The base of the cliff was heaped with loose stones at the spot, and it was not difficult to clamber up. When we reached it, all doubt was removed. Not only was it an opening into the rock, but on the side of it there was marked once again the sign of the arrow.

Here was the point, and this the means by which Maple White and his ill-fated comrade had made their ascent.

We were too excited to return to the camp, but must make our first exploration at once. Lord John had an electric torch in his knapsack, and this had to serve us as light. He advanced, throwing his little clear circlet of yellow radiance before him, while in single file we followed at his heels.

The cave had evidently been water-worn, the sides being smooth and the floor covered with rounded stones. It was of such a size that a single man could just fit through by stooping. For fifty yards it ran almost straight into the rock, and then it ascended at an angle of forty-five. Presently this incline became even steeper, and we found ourselves climbing upon hands and knees among loose rubble which slid from beneath us. Suddenly an exclamation broke from Lord Roxton.

"It's blocked!" said he.

Clustering behind him we saw in the yellow field of light a wall of broken basalt which extended to the ceiling.

"The roof has fallen in!"

In vain we dragged out some of the pieces. The only effect was that the larger ones became detached and threatened to roll down the gradient and crush us. It was evident that the obstacle was far beyond any efforts which we could make to remove it. The road by which Maple White had ascended was no longer available.

Too much cast down to speak, we stumbled down the dark tunnel and made our way back to the camp.

One incident occurred, however, before we left the gorge, which is of importance in view of what came afterwards.

We had gathered in a little group at the bottom of the chasm, some forty feet beneath the mouth of the cave, when a huge rock rolled suddenly downwards – and shot past us with tremendous force. It was the narrowest escape for one or all of us. We could not ourselves see whence the rock had come, but our half-breed servants, who were still at the opening of the cave, said that it had flown past them, and must therefore have fallen from the summit. Looking upwards, we could see no sign of movement above us amidst the green jungle which topped the cliff. There could be little doubt, however, that the stone was aimed at us, so the incident surely pointed to humanity – and malevolent humanity – upon the plateau.

We withdrew hurriedly from the chasm, our minds full of this new development and its bearing upon our plans. The situation was difficult enough before, but if the obstructions of Nature were increased by the deliberate opposition of man, then our case was indeed a hopeless one. And yet, as we looked up at that beautiful fringe of verdure only a few hundreds of feet above our heads, there was not one of us who could conceive the idea of returning to London until we had explored it to its depths.

On discussing the situation, we determined that our best course was to continue to coast round the plateau in the hope of finding some other means of reaching the top. The line of cliffs, which had decreased considerably in height, had already begun to trend from west to north, and if we could take this as representing the arc of a circle, the whole circumference could not be very great. At the worst, then, we should be back in a few days at our starting-point.

We made a march that day which totaled some two-and-twenty miles, without any change in our prospects. I may mention that our aneroid shows us that in the continual incline which we have ascended since we abandoned our canoes we have risen to no less than three thousand feet above sea-level. Hence there is a considerable change both in the temperature and in the vegetation. We have shaken off some of that horrible insect life which is the bane of tropical travel. A few palms still survive, and many tree-ferns, but the Amazonian trees have been all left behind. It was pleasant to see the convolvulus, the passion-flower, and the begonia, all reminding me of home, here among these inhospitable rocks. There was a red begonia just the same colour as one that is kept in a pot in the window of a certain villa in Streatham – but I am drifting into private reminiscence.

That night – I am still speaking of the first day of our circumnavigation of the plateau – a great experience awaited us, and one which for ever set at rest any doubt which we could have had as to the wonders so near us.

You will realize as you read it, my dear Mr. McArdle, and possibly for the first time that the paper has not sent me on a wild-goose chase, and that there is inconceivably fine copy waiting for the world whenever we have the Professor's leave to make use of it. I shall not dare to publish these articles unless I can bring back my proofs to England, or I shall be hailed as the journalistic Munchausen of all time. I have no doubt that you feel the same way yourself, and that you would not care to stake the whole credit of the Gazette upon this adventure until we can meet the chorus of criticism and scepticism which such articles must of necessity elicit. So this wonderful incident, which would make such a headline for the old paper, must still wait its turn in the editorial drawer.

And yet it was all over in a flash, and there was no sequel to it, save in our own convictions.

What occurred was this. Lord John had shot an ajouti – which is a small, pig-like animal – and, half of it having been given to the Indians, we were cooking the other half upon our fire. There is a chill in the air after dark, and we had all drawn close to the blaze. The night was moonless, but there were some stars, and one could see for a little distance across the plain. Well, suddenly out of the darkness, out of the night, there swooped something with a swish like an aeroplane. The whole group of us were covered for an instant by a canopy of leathery wings, and I had a momentary vision of a long, snake-like neck, a fierce, red, greedy eye, and a great snapping beak, filled, to my amazement, with little, gleaming teeth. The next instant it was gone – and so was our dinner. A huge black shadow, twenty feet across, skimmed up into the air; for an instant the monster wings blotted out the stars, and then it vanished over the brow of the cliff above us. We all sat in amazed silence round the fire, like the heroes of Virgil when the Harpies came down upon them. It was Summerlee who was the first to speak.

"Professor Challenger," said he, in a solemn voice, which quavered with emotion, "I owe you an apology. Sir, I am very much in the wrong, and I beg that you will forget what is past."

It was handsomely said, and the two men for the first time shook hands. So much we have gained by this clear vision of our first pterodactyl. It was worth a stolen supper to bring two such men together.

But if prehistoric life existed upon the plateau it was not superabundant, for we had no further glimpse of it during the next three days. During this time we traversed a barren and forbidding country, which alternated between stony desert and desolate marshes full of many wild-fowl, upon the north and east of the cliffs. From that direction the place is really inaccessible, and, were it not for a hardish ledge which runs at the very base of the precipice, we should have had to turn back. Many times we were up to our waists in the slime and blubber of an old, semi-tropical swamp. To make matters worse, the place seemed to be a favourite breeding-place of the Jaracaca snake, the most venomous and aggressive in South America. Again and again these horrible creatures came writhing and springing towards us across the surface of this putrid bog, and it was only by keeping our shot-guns for ever ready that we could feel safe from them. One funnel-shaped depression in the morass, of a livid green in colour from some lichen which festered in it, will always remain as a nightmare memory in my mind. It seems to have been a special nest of these vermin, and the slopes were alive with them, all writhing in our direction, for it is a peculiarity of the Jaracaca that he will always attack man at first sight. There were too many for us to shoot, so we fairly took to our heels and ran until we were exhausted. I shall always remember as we looked back how far behind we could see the heads and necks of our horrible pursuers rising and falling amid the reeds. Jaracaca Swamp we named it in the map which we are constructing.

The cliffs upon the farther side had lost their ruddy tint, being chocolate-brown in colour; the vegetation was more scattered along the top of them, and they had sunk to three or four hundred feet in height, but in no place did we find any point where they could be ascended. If anything, they were more impossible than at the first point where we had met them. Their absolute steepness is indicated in the photograph which I took over the stony desert.

"Surely," said I, as we discussed the situation, "the rain must find its way down somehow. There are bound to be water-channels in the rocks."

"Our young friend has glimpses of lucidity," said Professor Challenger, patting me upon the shoulder.

"The rain must go somewhere," I repeated.

"He keeps a firm grip upon actuality. The only drawback is that we have conclusively proved by ocular demonstration that there are no water channels down the rocks."

"Where, then, does it go?" I persisted.

"I think it may be fairly assumed that if it does not come outwards it must run inwards."

"Then there is a lake in the centre."

"So I should suppose."

"It is more than likely that the lake may be an old crater," said Summerlee. "The whole formation is, of course, highly volcanic. But, however that may be, I should expect to find the surface of the plateau slope inwards with a considerable sheet of water in the centre, which may drain off, by some subterranean channel, into the marshes of the Jaracaca Swamp."

"Or evaporation might preserve an equilibrium," remarked Challenger, and the two learned men wandered off into one of their usual scientific arguments, which were as comprehensible as Chinese to the layman.

On the sixth day we completed our first circuit of the cliffs, and found ourselves back at the first camp, beside the isolated pinnacle of rock. We were a disconsolate party, for nothing could have been more minute than our investigation, and it was absolutely certain that there was no single point where the most active human being could possibly hope to scale the cliff. The place which Maple White's chalk-marks had indicated as his own means of access was now entirely impassable.

What were we to do now? Our stores of provisions, supplemented by our guns, were holding out well, but the day must come when they would need replenishment. In a couple of months the rains might be expected, and we should be washed out of our camp. The rock was harder than marble, and any attempt at cutting a path for so great a height was more than our time or resources would admit. No wonder that we looked gloomily at each other that night, and sought our blankets with hardly a word exchanged. I remember that as I dropped off to sleep my last recollection was that Challenger was squatting, like a monstrous bull-frog, by the fire, his huge head in his hands, sunk apparently in the deepest thought, and entirely oblivious to the goodnight which I wished him.

But it was a very different Challenger who greeted us in the morning – a Challenger with contentment and self-congratulation shining from his whole person. He faced us as we assembled for breakfast with a deprecating false modesty in his eyes, as who should say, "I know that I deserve all that you can say, but I pray you to spare my blushes by not saying it." His beard bristled exultantly, his chest was thrown out, and his hand was thrust into the front of his jacket. So, in his fancy, may he see himself sometimes, gracing the vacant pedestal in Trafalgar Square, and adding one more to the horrors of the London streets.

"Eureka!" he cried, his teeth shining through his beard. "Gentlemen, you may congratulate me and we may congratulate each other. The problem is solved."

"You have found a way up?"

"I venture to think so."

"And where?"

For answer he pointed to the spire-like pinnacle upon our right.

Our faces – or mine, at least – fell as we surveyed it. That it could be climbed we had our companion's assurance. But a horrible abyss lay between it and the plateau.

"We can never get across," I gasped.

"We can at least all reach the summit," said he. "When we are up I may be able to show you that the resources of an inventive mind are not yet exhausted."

After breakfast we unpacked the bundle in which our leader had brought his climbing accessories. From it he took a coil of the strongest and lightest rope, a hundred and fifty feet in length, with climbing irons, clamps, and other devices. Lord John was an experienced mountaineer, and Summerlee had done some rough climbing at various times, so that I was really the novice at rock-work of the party; but my strength and activity may have made up for my want of experience.

It was not in reality a very stiff task, though there were moments which made my hair bristle upon my head. The first half was perfectly easy, but from there upwards it became continually steeper until, for the last fifty feet, we were literally clinging with our fingers and toes to tiny ledges and crevices in the rock. I could not have accomplished it, nor could Summerlee, if Challenger had not gained the summit (it was extraordinary to see such activity in so unwieldy a creature) and there fixed the rope round the trunk of the considerable tree which grew there. With this as our support, we were soon able to scramble up the jagged wall until we found ourselves upon the small grassy platform, some twenty-five feet each way, which formed the summit.

The first impression which I received when I had recovered my breath was of the extraordinary view over the country which we had traversed. The whole Brazilian plain seemed to lie beneath us, extending away and away until it ended in dim blue mists upon the farthest sky-line. In the foreground was the long slope, strewn with rocks and dotted with tree-ferns; farther off in the middle distance, looking over the saddle-back hill, I could just see the yellow and green mass of bamboos through which we had passed; and then, gradually, the vegetation increased until it formed the huge forest which extended as far as the eyes could reach, and for a good two thousand miles beyond.

I was still drinking in this wonderful panorama when the heavy hand of the Professor fell upon my shoulder.

"This way, my young friend," said he; "*vestigia nulla retrorsum*. Never look rearwards, but always to our glorious goal."

The level of the plateau, when I turned, was exactly that on which we stood, and the green bank of bushes, with occasional trees, was so near that it was difficult to realize how inaccessible it remained. At a rough guess the gulf was forty feet across, but, so far as I could see, it might as well have been forty miles. I placed one arm round the trunk of the tree and leaned over the abyss. Far down were the small dark figures of our servants, looking up at us. The wall was absolutely precipitous, as was that which faced me.

"This is indeed curious," said the creaking voice of Professor Summerlee.

I turned, and found that he was examining with great interest the tree to which I clung. That smooth bark and those small, ribbed leaves seemed familiar to my eyes. "Why," I cried, "it's a beech!"

"Exactly," said Summerlee. "A fellow-countryman in a far land."

"Not only a fellow-countryman, my good sir," said Challenger, "but also, if I may be allowed to enlarge your simile, an ally of the first value. This beech tree will be our saviour."

"By George!" cried Lord John, "A bridge!"

"Exactly, my friends, a bridge! It is not for nothing that I expended an hour last night in focusing my mind upon the situation. I have some recollection of once remarking to our young friend here that G.E.C. is at his best when his back is to the wall. Last night you will admit that all our backs were to the wall. But where will-power and intellect go together, there is always a way out. A drawbridge had to be found which could be dropped across the abyss. Behold it!"

It was certainly a brilliant idea. The tree was a good sixty feet in height, and if it only fell the right way it would easily cross the chasm. Challenger had slung the camp axe over his shoulder when he ascended. Now he handed it to me.

"Our young friend has the thews and sinews," said he. "I think he will be the most useful at this task. I must beg, however, that you will kindly refrain from thinking for yourself, and that you will do exactly what you are told."

Under his direction I cut such gashes in the sides of the trees as would ensure that it should fall as we desired. It had already a strong, natural tilt in the direction of the plateau, so that the matter was not difficult. Finally I set to work in earnest upon the trunk, taking turn and turn with Lord John. In a little over an hour there was a loud crack, the tree swayed forward, and then crashed over, burying its branches among the bushes on the farther side. The severed trunk rolled to the very edge of our platform, and for one terrible second we all thought it was over. It balanced itself, however, a few inches from the edge, and there was our bridge to the unknown.

All of us, without a word, shook hands with Professor Challenger, who raised his straw hat and bowed deeply to each in turn.

"I claim the honour," said he, "to be the first to cross to the unknown land – a fitting subject, no doubt, for some future historical painting."

He had approached the bridge when Lord John laid his hand upon his coat.

"My dear chap," said he, "I really cannot allow it."

"Cannot allow it, sir!" The head went back and the beard forward.

"When it is a matter of science, don't you know, I follow your lead because you are by way of bein' a man of science. But it's up to you to follow me when you come into my department."

"Your department, sir?"

"We all have our professions, and soldierin' is mine. We are, accordin' to my ideas, invadin' a new country, which may or may not be chock-full of enemies of sorts. To barge blindly into it for want of a little common sense and patience isn't my notion of management."

The remonstrance was too reasonable to be disregarded. Challenger tossed his head and shrugged his heavy shoulders.

"Well, sir, what do you propose?"

"For all I know there may be a tribe of cannibals waitin' for lunch-time among those very bushes," said Lord John, looking across the bridge. "It's better to learn wisdom before you get into a cookin'-pot; so we will content ourselves with hopin' that there is no trouble waitin' for us, and at the same time we will act as if there were. Malone and I will go down again, therefore, and we will fetch up the four rifles, together with Gomez and the other. One man can then go across and the rest will cover him with guns, until he sees that it is safe for the whole crowd to come along."

Challenger sat down upon the cut stump and groaned his impatience; but Summerlee and I were of one mind that Lord John was our leader when such practical details were in question. The climb was a more simple thing now that the rope dangled down the face of the worst part of the ascent. Within an hour we had brought up the rifles and a shot-gun. The half-breeds had ascended also, and under Lord John's orders they had carried up a bale of provisions in case our first exploration should be a long one. We had each bandoliers of cartridges.

"Now, Challenger, if you really insist upon being the first man in," said Lord John, when every preparation was complete.

"I am much indebted to you for your gracious permission," said the angry Professor; for never was a man so intolerant of every form of authority. "Since you are good enough to allow it, I shall most certainly take it upon myself to act as pioneer upon this occasion."

Seating himself with a leg overhanging the abyss on each side, and his hatchet slung upon his back, Challenger hopped his way across the trunk and was soon at the other side. He clambered up and waved his arms in the air.

"At last!" he cried; "at last!"

I gazed anxiously at him, with a vague expectation that some terrible fate would dart at him from the curtain of green behind him. But all was quiet, save that a strange, many-coloured bird flew up from under his feet and vanished among the trees.

Summerlee was the second. His wiry energy is wonderful in so frail a frame. He insisted upon having two rifles slung upon his back, so that both Professors were armed when he had made his transit. I came next, and tried hard not to look down into the horrible gulf over which I was passing. Summerlee held out the butt-end of his rifle, and an instant later I was able to grasp his hand. As to Lord John, he walked across – actually walked without support! He must have nerves of iron.

And there we were, the four of us, upon the dreamland, the lost world, of Maple White. To all of us it seemed the moment of our supreme triumph. Who could have guessed that it was the prelude to our supreme disaster? Let me say in a few words how the crushing blow fell upon us.

We had turned away from the edge, and had penetrated about fifty yards of close brushwood, when there came a frightful rending crash from behind us. With one impulse we rushed back the way that we had come. The bridge was gone!

Far down at the base of the cliff I saw, as I looked over, a tangled mass of branches and splintered trunk. It was our beech tree. Had the edge of the platform crumbled and let it through? For a moment this explanation was in all our minds. The next, from the farther side of the rocky pinnacle before us a swarthy face, the face of Gomez the half-breed, was slowly protruded. Yes, it was Gomez, but no longer the Gomez of the demure smile and the mask-like expression. Here was a face with flashing eyes and distorted features, a face convulsed with hatred and with the mad joy of gratified revenge.

"Lord Roxton!" he shouted. "Lord John Roxton!"

"Well," said our companion, "here I am."

A shriek of laughter came across the abyss.

"Yes, there you are, you English dog, and there you will remain! I have waited and waited, and now has come my chance. You found it hard to get up; you will find it harder to get down. You cursed fools, you are trapped, every one of you!"

We were too astounded to speak. We could only stand there staring in amazement. A great broken bough upon the grass showed whence he had gained his leverage to tilt over our bridge. The face had vanished, but presently it was up again, more frantic than before.

"We nearly killed you with a stone at the cave," he cried; "but this is better. It is slower and more terrible. Your bones will whiten up there, and none will know where you lie or come to cover them. As you lie dying, think of Lopez, whom you shot five years ago on the Putomayo River. I am his brother, and, come what will I will die happy now, for his memory has been avenged." A furious hand was shaken at us, and then all was quiet.

Had the half-breed simply wrought his vengeance and then escaped, all might have been well with him. It was that foolish, irresistible Latin impulse to be dramatic which brought his own downfall. Roxton, the man who had earned himself the name of the Flail of the Lord through three countries, was not one who could be safely taunted. The half-breed was descending on the farther side of the pinnacle; but before he could reach the ground Lord John had run along the edge of the plateau and gained a point from which he could see his man. There was a single crack of his rifle, and, though we saw nothing, we heard the scream and then the distant thud of the falling body. Roxton came back to us with a face of granite.

"I have been a blind simpleton," said he, bitterly, "It's my folly that has brought you all into this trouble. I should have remembered that these people have long memories for blood-feuds, and have been more upon my guard."

"What about the other one? It took two of them to lever that tree over the edge."

"I could have shot him, but I let him go. He may have had no part in it. Perhaps it would have been better if I had killed him, for he must, as you say, have lent a hand."

Now that we had the clue to his action, each of us could cast back and remember some sinister act upon the part of the half-breed – his constant desire to know our plans, his arrest outside our tent when he was over-hearing them, the furtive looks of hatred which from time to time one or other of us had surprised. We were still discussing it, endeavoring to adjust our minds to these new conditions, when a singular scene in the plain below arrested our attention.

A man in white clothes, who could only be the surviving half-breed, was running as one does run when Death is the pacemaker. Behind him, only a few yards in his rear, bounded the huge ebony figure of Zambo, our devoted negro. Even as we looked, he sprang upon the back of the fugitive and flung his arms round his neck. They rolled on the ground together. An instant afterwards Zambo rose, looked at the prostrate man, and then, waving his hand joyously to us, came running in our direction. The white figure lay motionless in the middle of the great plain.

Our two traitors had been destroyed, but the mischief that they had done lived after them. By no possible means could we get back to the pinnacle. We had been natives of the world; now we were natives of the plateau. The two things were separate and apart. There was the plain which led to the canoes. Yonder, beyond the violet, hazy horizon, was the stream which led back to civilization. But the link between was missing. No human ingenuity could suggest a means of bridging the chasm which yawned between ourselves and our past lives. One instant had altered the whole conditions of our existence.

It was at such a moment that I learned the stuff of which my three comrades were composed. They were grave, it is true, and thoughtful, but of an invincible serenity. For the moment we could only sit among the bushes in patience and wait the coming of Zambo. Presently his honest black face topped the rocks and his Herculean figure emerged upon the top of the pinnacle.

"What I do now?" he cried. "You tell me and I do it."

It was a question which it was easier to ask than to answer. One thing only was clear. He was our one trusty link with the outside world. On no account must he leave us.

"No no!" he cried. "I not leave you. Whatever come, you always find me here. But no able to keep Indians. Already they say too much Curupuri live on this place, and they go home. Now you leave them me no able to keep them."

It was a fact that our Indians had shown in many ways of late that they were weary of their journey and anxious to return. We realized that Zambo spoke the truth, and that it would be impossible for him to keep them.

"Make them wait till tomorrow, Zambo," I shouted; "then I can send letter back by them."

"Very good, sarr! I promise they wait till tomorrow," said the negro. "But what I do for you now?"

There was plenty for him to do, and admirably the faithful fellow did it. First of all, under our directions, he undid the rope from the tree-stump and threw one end of it across to us. It was not thicker than a clothes-line, but it was of great strength, and though we could not make a bridge of it, we might well find it invaluable if we had any climbing to do. He then fastened his end of the rope to the package of supplies which had been carried up, and we were able to drag it across. This gave us the means of life for at least a week, even if we found nothing else. Finally he descended and carried up two other packets of mixed goods – a box of ammunition and a number of other things, all of which we got across by throwing our rope to him and hauling it back. It was evening when he at last climbed down, with a final assurance that he would keep the Indians till next morning.

And so it is that I have spent nearly the whole of this our first night upon the plateau writing up our experiences by the light of a single candle-lantern.

We supped and camped at the very edge of the cliff, quenching our thirst with two bottles of Apollinaris which were in one of the cases. It is vital to us to find water, but I think even Lord John himself had had adventures enough for one day, and none of us felt inclined to make the first push into the unknown. We forbore to light a fire or to make any unnecessary sound.

Tomorrow (or today, rather, for it is already dawn as I write) we shall make our first venture into this strange land. When I shall be able to write again – or if I ever shall write again – I know not. Meanwhile, I can see that the Indians are still in their place, and I am sure that the faithful Zambo will be here presently to get my letter. I only trust that it will come to hand.

P.S. – The more I think the more desperate does our position seem. I see no possible hope of our return. If there were a high tree near the edge of the plateau we might drop a return bridge across, but there is none within fifty yards. Our united strength could not carry a trunk which would serve our purpose. The rope, of course, is far too short that we could descend by it. No, our position is hopeless – hopeless!

Chapter X
'The Most Wonderful Things Have Happened'

THE MOST wonderful things have happened and are continually happening to us. All the paper that I possess consists of five old note-books and a lot of scraps, and I have only the one stylographic pencil; but so long as I can move my hand I will continue to set down our experiences and impressions, for, since we are the only men of the whole human race to see such things, it is of enormous importance that I should record them whilst they are fresh in my memory and before that fate which seems to be constantly impending does actually overtake us. Whether Zambo can at last take these letters to the river, or whether I shall myself in some miraculous way carry them back with me, or, finally, whether some daring explorer, coming upon our tracks with the advantage, perhaps, of a perfected monoplane, should find this bundle of manuscript, in any case I can see that what I am writing is destined to immortality as a classic of true adventure.

On the morning after our being trapped upon the plateau by the villainous Gomez we began a new stage in our experiences. The first incident in it was not such as to give me a very favourable opinion of the place to which we had wandered. As I roused myself from a short nap after day had dawned, my eyes fell upon a most singular appearance upon my own leg. My trouser had slipped up, exposing a few inches of my skin above my sock. On this there rested a large, purplish grape. Astonished at the sight, I leaned forward to pick it off, when, to my horror, it burst between my finger and thumb, squirting blood in every direction. My cry of disgust had brought the two professors to my side.

"Most interesting," said Summerlee, bending over my shin. "An enormous blood-tick, as yet, I believe, unclassified."

"The first-fruits of our labors," said Challenger in his booming, pedantic fashion. "We cannot do less than call it *Ixodes Maloni*. The very small inconvenience of being bitten, my young friend, cannot, I am sure, weigh with you as against the glorious privilege of having your name inscribed in the deathless roll of zoology. Unhappily you have crushed this fine specimen at the moment of satiation."

"Filthy vermin!" I cried.

Professor Challenger raised his great eyebrows in protest, and placed a soothing paw upon my shoulder.

"You should cultivate the scientific eye and the detached scientific mind," said he. "To a man of philosophic temperament like myself the blood-tick, with its lancet-like proboscis and its distending stomach, is as beautiful a work of Nature as the peacock or, for that matter, the aurora borealis. It pains me to hear you speak of it in so unappreciative a fashion. No doubt, with due diligence, we can secure some other specimen."

"There can be no doubt of that," said Summerlee, grimly, "for one has just disappeared behind your shirt-collar."

Challenger sprang into the air bellowing like a bull, and tore frantically at his coat and shirt to get them off. Summerlee and I laughed so that we could hardly help him. At last we exposed that monstrous torso (fifty-four inches, by the tailor's tape). His body was all matted with black hair, out of which jungle we picked the wandering tick before it had bitten him. But the bushes round were full of the horrible pests, and it was clear that we must shift our camp.

But first of all it was necessary to make our arrangements with the faithful negro, who appeared presently on the pinnacle with a number of tins of cocoa and biscuits, which he tossed over to us. Of the stores which remained below he was ordered to retain as much as would keep him for two months. The Indians were to have the remainder as a reward for their services and as payment for taking our letters back to the Amazon. Some hours later we saw them in single file far out upon the plain, each with a bundle on his head, making their way back along the path we had come. Zambo occupied our little tent at the base of the pinnacle, and there he remained, our one link with the world below.

And now we had to decide upon our immediate movements. We shifted our position from among the tick-laden bushes until we came to a small clearing thickly surrounded by trees upon all sides. There were some flat slabs of rock in the centre, with an excellent well close by, and there we sat in cleanly comfort while we made our first plans for the invasion of this new country. Birds were calling among the foliage – especially one with a peculiar whooping cry which was new to us – but beyond these sounds there were no signs of life.

Our first care was to make some sort of list of our own stores, so that we might know what we had to rely upon. What with the things we had ourselves brought up and those which Zambo had sent across on the rope, we were fairly well supplied. Most important of all, in view of the dangers which might surround us, we had our four rifles and one thousand three hundred rounds, also a shot-gun, but not more than a hundred and fifty medium pellet cartridges. In the matter of provisions we had enough to last for several weeks, with a sufficiency of tobacco and a few scientific implements, including a large telescope and a good field-glass. All these things we collected together in the clearing, and as a first precaution, we cut down with our hatchet and knives a number of thorny bushes, which we piled round in a circle some fifteen yards in diameter. This was to be our headquarters for the time – our place of refuge against sudden danger and the guard-house for our stores. Fort Challenger, we called it.

It was midday before we had made ourselves secure, but the heat was not oppressive, and the general character of the plateau, both in its temperature and in its vegetation, was almost temperate. The beech, the oak, and even the birch were to be found among the tangle of trees which girt us in. One huge gingko tree, topping all the others, shot its great limbs and maidenhair foliage over the fort which we had constructed. In its shade we continued our discussion, while Lord John, who had quickly taken command in the hour of action, gave us his views.

"So long as neither man nor beast has seen or heard us, we are safe," said he. "From the time they know we are here our troubles begin. There are no signs that they have found us out as yet. So our game surely is to lie low for a time and spy out the land. We want to have a good look at our neighbours before we get on visitin' terms."

"But we must advance," I ventured to remark.

"By all means, sonny my boy! We will advance. But with common sense. We must never go so far that we can't get back to our base. Above all, we must never, unless it is life or death, fire off our guns."

"But *you* fired yesterday," said Summerlee.

"Well, it couldn't be helped. However, the wind was strong and blew outwards. It is not likely that the sound could have traveled far into the plateau. By the way, what shall we call this place? I suppose it is up to us to give it a name?"

There were several suggestions, more or less happy, but Challenger's was final.

"It can only have one name," said he. "It is called after the pioneer who discovered it. It is Maple White Land."

Maple White Land it became, and so it is named in that chart which has become my special task. So it will, I trust, appear in the atlas of the future.

The peaceful penetration of Maple White Land was the pressing subject before us. We had the evidence of our own eyes that the place was inhabited by some unknown creatures, and there was that of Maple White's sketch-book to show that more dreadful and more dangerous monsters might still appear. That there might also prove to be human occupants and that they were of a malevolent character was suggested by the skeleton impaled upon the bamboos, which could not have got there had it not been dropped from above. Our situation, stranded without possibility of escape in such a land, was clearly full of danger, and our reasons endorsed every measure of caution which Lord John's experience could suggest. Yet it was surely impossible that we should halt on the edge of this world of mystery when our very souls were tingling with impatience to push forward and to pluck the heart from it.

We therefore blocked the entrance to our zareba by filling it up with several thorny bushes, and left our camp with the stores entirely surrounded by this protecting hedge. We then slowly and cautiously set forth into the unknown, following the course of the little stream which flowed from our spring, as it should always serve us as a guide on our return.

Hardly had we started when we came across signs that there were indeed wonders awaiting us. After a few hundred yards of thick forest, containing many trees which were quite unknown to me, but which Summerlee, who was the botanist of the party, recognized as forms of conifera and of cycadaceous plants which have long passed away in the world below, we entered a region where the stream widened out and formed a considerable bog. High reeds of a peculiar type grew thickly before us, which were pronounced to be equisetacea, or mare's-tails, with tree-ferns scattered amongst them, all of them swaying in a brisk wind. Suddenly Lord John, who was walking first, halted with uplifted hand.

"Look at this!" said he. "By George, this must be the trail of the father of all birds!"

An enormous three-toed track was imprinted in the soft mud before us. The creature, whatever it was, had crossed the swamp and had passed on into the forest. We all stopped to examine that monstrous spoor. If it were indeed a bird – and what animal could leave such a mark? – its foot was so much larger than an ostrich's that its height upon the same scale must be enormous. Lord John looked eagerly round him and slipped two cartridges into his elephant-gun.

"I'll stake my good name as a shikarree," said he, "that the track is a fresh one. The creature has not passed ten minutes. Look how the water is still oozing into that deeper print! By Jove! See, here is the mark of a little one!"

Sure enough, smaller tracks of the same general form were running parallel to the large ones.

"But what do you make of this?" cried Professor Summerlee, triumphantly, pointing to what looked like the huge print of a five-fingered human hand appearing among the three-toed marks.

"Wealden!" cried Challenger, in an ecstasy. "I've seen them in the Wealden clay. It is a creature walking erect upon three-toed feet, and occasionally putting one of its five-fingered forepaws upon the ground. Not a bird, my dear Roxton – not a bird."

"A beast?"

"No; a reptile – a dinosaur. Nothing else could have left such a track. They puzzled a worthy Sussex doctor some ninety years ago; but who in the world could have hoped – hoped – to have seen a sight like that?"

His words died away into a whisper, and we all stood in motionless amazement. Following the tracks, we had left the morass and passed through a screen of brushwood and trees. Beyond was an open glade, and in this were five of the most extraordinary creatures that I have ever seen. Crouching down among the bushes, we observed them at our leisure.

There were, as I say, five of them, two being adults and three young ones. In size they were enormous. Even the babies were as big as elephants, while the two large ones were far beyond all creatures I have ever seen. They had slate-coloured skin, which was scaled like a lizard's and shimmered where the sun shone upon it. All five were sitting up, balancing themselves upon their broad, powerful tails and their huge three-toed hind-feet, while with their small five-fingered front-feet they pulled down the branches upon which they browsed. I do not know that I can bring their appearance home to you better than by saying that they looked like monstrous kangaroos, twenty feet in length, and with skins like black crocodiles.

I do not know how long we stayed motionless gazing at this marvelous spectacle. A strong wind blew towards us and we were well concealed, so there was no chance of discovery. From time to time the little ones played round their parents in unwieldy gambols, the great beasts bounding into the air and falling with dull thuds upon the earth. The strength of the parents seemed to be limitless, for one of them, having some difficulty in reaching a bunch of foliage which grew upon a considerable-sized tree, put his fore-legs round the trunk and tore it down as if it had been a sapling. The action seemed, as I thought, to show not only the great development of its muscles, but also the small one of its brain, for the whole weight came crashing down upon the top of it, and it uttered a series of shrill yelps to show that, big as it was, there was a limit to what it could endure. The incident made it think, apparently, that the neighbourhood was dangerous, for it slowly lurched off through the wood, followed by its mate and its three enormous infants. We saw the shimmering slaty gleam of their skins between the tree-trunks, and their heads undulating high above the brush-wood. Then they vanished from our sight.

I looked at my comrades. Lord John was standing at gaze with his finger on the trigger of his elephant-gun, his eager hunter's soul shining from his fierce eyes. What would he not give for one such head to place between the two crossed oars above the mantelpiece in his snuggery at the Albany! And yet his reason held him in, for all our exploration of the wonders of this unknown land depended upon our presence being concealed from its inhabitants. The two professors were in silent ecstasy. In their excitement they had unconsciously seized each other by the hand, and stood like two little children in the presence of a marvel, Challenger's cheeks bunched up into a seraphic smile, and Summerlee's sardonic face softening for the moment into wonder and reverence.

"*Nunc dimittis*!" he cried at last. "What will they say in England of this?"

"My dear Summerlee, I will tell you with great confidence exactly what they will say in England," said Challenger. "They will say that you are an infernal liar and a scientific charlatan, exactly as you and others said of me."

"In the face of photographs?"

"Faked, Summerlee! Clumsily faked!"

"In the face of specimens?"

"Ah, there we may have them! Malone and his filthy Fleet Street crew may be all yelping our praises yet. August the twenty-eighth – the day we saw five live iguanodons in a glade of Maple White Land. Put it down in your diary, my young friend, and send it to your rag."

"And be ready to get the toe-end of the editorial boot in return," said Lord John. "Things look a bit different from the latitude of London, young fellah my lad. There's many a man who never tells his adventures, for he can't hope to be believed. Who's to blame them? For this will seem a bit of a dream to ourselves in a month or two. *What* did you say they were?"

"Iguanodons," said Summerlee. "You'll find their footmarks all over the Hastings sands, in Kent, and in Sussex. The South of England was alive with them when there was plenty of good lush green-stuff to keep them going. Conditions have changed, and the beasts died. Here it seems that the conditions have not changed, and the beasts have lived."

"If ever we get out of this alive, I must have a head with me," said Lord John. "Lord, how some of that Somaliland-Uganda crowd would turn a beautiful pea-green if they saw it! I don't know what you chaps think, but it strikes me that we are on mighty thin ice all this time."

I had the same feeling of mystery and danger around us. In the gloom of the trees there seemed a constant menace and as we looked up into their shadowy foliage vague terrors crept into one's heart. It is true that these monstrous creatures which we had seen were lumbering, inoffensive brutes which were unlikely to hurt anyone, but in this world of wonders what other survivals might there not be – what fierce, active horrors ready to pounce upon us from their lair among the rocks or brushwood? I knew little of prehistoric life, but I had a clear remembrance of one book which I had read in which it spoke of creatures who would live upon our lions and tigers as a cat lives upon mice. What if these also were to be found in the woods of Maple White Land!

It was destined that on this very morning – our first in the new country – we were to find out what strange hazards lay around us. It was a loathsome adventure, and one of which I hate to think. If, as Lord John said, the glade of the iguanodons will remain with us as a dream, then surely the swamp of the pterodactyls will forever be our nightmare. Let me set down exactly what occurred.

We passed very slowly through the woods, partly because Lord Roxton acted as scout before he would let us advance, and partly because at every second step one or other of our professors would fall, with a cry of wonder, before some flower or insect which presented him with a new type. We may have traveled two or three miles in all, keeping to the right of the line of the stream, when we came upon a considerable opening in the trees. A belt of brushwood led up to a tangle of rocks – the whole plateau was strewn with boulders. We were walking slowly towards these rocks, among bushes which reached over our waists, when we became aware of a strange low gabbling and whistling sound, which filled the air with a constant clamour and appeared to come from some spot immediately before us. Lord John held up his hand as a signal for us to stop, and he made his way swiftly, stooping and running, to the line of rocks. We saw him peep over them and give a gesture of amazement. Then he stood staring as if forgetting us, so utterly entranced was he by what he saw. Finally he waved us to come on, holding up his hand as a signal for caution. His whole bearing made me feel that something wonderful but dangerous lay before us.

Creeping to his side, we looked over the rocks. The place into which we gazed was a pit, and may, in the early days, have been one of the smaller volcanic blow-holes of the plateau. It was bowl-shaped and at the bottom, some hundreds of yards from where we lay, were pools of green-scummed, stagnant water, fringed with bullrushes. It was a weird place in itself, but its occupants made it seem like a scene from the Seven Circles of Dante. The place was a rookery of pterodactyls. There were hundreds of them congregated within view. All the bottom area round the water-edge was alive with their young ones, and with hideous mothers brooding upon their leathery, yellowish eggs. From this crawling flapping mass of obscene reptilian life came the shocking clamour which filled the air and the mephitic, horrible, musty odour which turned us sick. But above, perched each upon its own stone, tall, gray, and withered, more like dead and dried specimens than actual living creatures, sat the horrible males, absolutely motionless save for the rolling of their red eyes or an occasional snap of their rat-trap beaks as a dragon-fly went past them. Their huge, membranous wings were closed by folding their fore-arms, so that they sat like gigantic old women, wrapped in hideous web-coloured shawls, and with their ferocious heads protruding above them. Large and small, not less than a thousand of these filthy creatures lay in the hollow before us.

Our professors would gladly have stayed there all day, so entranced were they by this opportunity of studying the life of a prehistoric age. They pointed out the fish and dead birds lying about among the rocks as proving the nature of the food of these creatures, and I heard them congratulating each other on having cleared up the point why the bones of this flying dragon are found in such great numbers in certain well-defined areas, as in the Cambridge Green-sand, since it was now seen that, like penguins, they lived in gregarious fashion.

Finally, however, Challenger, bent upon proving some point which Summerlee had contested, thrust his head over the rock and nearly brought destruction upon us all. In an instant the nearest male gave a shrill, whistling cry, and flapped its twenty-foot span of leathery wings as it soared up into the air. The females and young ones huddled together beside the water, while the whole circle of sentinels rose one after the other and sailed off into the sky. It was a wonderful sight to see at least a hundred creatures of such enormous size and hideous appearance all swooping like swallows with swift, shearing wing-strokes above us; but soon we realized that it was not one on which we could afford to linger. At first the great brutes flew round in a huge ring, as if to make sure what the exact extent of the danger might be. Then, the flight grew lower and the circle narrower, until they were whizzing round and round us, the dry, rustling flap of their huge slate-coloured wings filling the air with a volume of sound that made me think of Hendon aerodrome upon a race day.

"Make for the wood and keep together," cried Lord John, clubbing his rifle. "The brutes mean mischief."

The moment we attempted to retreat the circle closed in upon us, until the tips of the wings of those nearest to us nearly touched our faces. We beat at them with the stocks of our guns, but there was nothing solid or vulnerable to strike. Then suddenly out of the whizzing, slate-coloured circle a long neck shot out, and a fierce beak made a thrust at us. Another and another followed. Summerlee gave a cry and put his hand to his face, from which the blood was streaming. I felt a prod at the back of my neck, and turned dizzy with the shock. Challenger fell, and as I stooped to pick him up I was again struck from behind and dropped on the top of him. At the same instant I heard the crash of Lord John's elephant-gun, and, looking up, saw one of the creatures with a broken wing struggling upon the ground, spitting and gurgling at us with a wide-opened beak and blood-shot, goggled eyes, like some devil in a medieval picture. Its comrades had flown higher at the sudden sound, and were circling above our heads.

"Now," cried Lord John, "now for our lives!"

We staggered through the brushwood, and even as we reached the trees the harpies were on us again. Summerlee was knocked down, but we tore him up and rushed among the trunks. Once there we were safe, for those huge wings had no space for their sweep beneath the branches. As we limped homewards, sadly mauled and discomfited, we saw them for a long time flying at a great height against the deep blue sky above our heads, soaring round and round, no bigger than wood-pigeons, with their eyes no doubt still following our progress. At last, however, as we reached the thicker woods they gave up the chase, and we saw them no more.

"A most interesting and convincing experience," said Challenger, as we halted beside the brook and he bathed a swollen knee. "We are exceptionally well informed, Summerlee, as to the habits of the enraged pterodactyl."

Summerlee was wiping the blood from a cut in his forehead, while I was tying up a nasty stab in the muscle of the neck. Lord John had the shoulder of his coat torn away, but the creature's teeth had only grazed the flesh.

"It is worth noting," Challenger continued, "that our young friend has received an undoubted stab, while Lord John's coat could only have been torn by a bite. In my own case, I was beaten about the head by their wings, so we have had a remarkable exhibition of their various methods of offence."

"It has been touch and go for our lives," said Lord John, gravely, "and I could not think of a more rotten sort of death than to be outed by such filthy vermin. I was sorry to fire my rifle, but, by Jove! There was no great choice."

"We should not be here if you hadn't," said I, with conviction.

"It may do no harm," said he. "Among these woods there must be many loud cracks from splitting or falling trees which would be just like the sound of a gun. But now, if you are of my opinion, we have had thrills enough for one day, and had best get back to the surgical box at the camp for some carbolic. Who knows what venom these beasts may have in their hideous jaws?"

But surely no men ever had just such a day since the world began. Some fresh surprise was ever in store for us. When, following the course of our brook, we at last reached our glade and saw the thorny barricade of our camp, we thought that our adventures were at an end. But we had something more to think of before we could rest. The gate of Fort Challenger had been untouched, the walls were unbroken, and yet it had been visited by some strange and powerful creature in our absence. No foot-mark showed a trace of its nature, and only the overhanging branch of the enormous ginko tree suggested how it might have come and gone; but of its malevolent strength there was ample evidence in the condition of our stores. They were strewn at random all over the ground, and one tin of meat had been crushed into pieces so as to extract the contents. A case of cartridges had been shattered into matchwood, and one of the brass shells lay shredded into pieces beside it. Again the feeling of vague horror came upon our souls, and we gazed round with frightened eyes at the dark shadows which lay around us, in all of which some fearsome shape might be lurking. How good it was when we were hailed by the voice of Zambo, and, going to the edge of the plateau, saw him sitting grinning at us upon the top of the opposite pinnacle.

"All well, Massa Challenger, all well!" he cried. "Me stay here. No fear. You always find me when you want."

His honest black face, and the immense view before us, which carried us half-way back to the affluent of the Amazon, helped us to remember that we really were upon this earth in the twentieth century, and had not by some magic been conveyed to some raw planet in its earliest and wildest state. How difficult it was to realize that the violet line upon the far horizon was well advanced to that great river upon which huge steamers ran, and folk talked of the small affairs of life, while we, marooned among the creatures of a bygone age, could but gaze towards it and yearn for all that it meant!

One other memory remains with me of this wonderful day, and with it I will close this letter. The two professors, their tempers aggravated no doubt by their injuries, had fallen out as to whether our assailants were of the genus pterodactylus or dimorphodon, and high words had ensued. To avoid their wrangling I moved some little way apart, and was seated smoking upon the trunk of a fallen tree, when Lord John strolled over in my direction.

"I say, Malone," said he, "do you remember that place where those beasts were?"

"Very clearly."

"A sort of volcanic pit, was it not?"

"Exactly," said I.

"Did you notice the soil?"

"Rocks."

"But round the water – where the reeds were?"

"It was a bluish soil. It looked like clay."

"Exactly. A volcanic tube full of blue clay."

"What of that?" I asked.

"Oh, nothing, nothing," said he, and strolled back to where the voices of the contending men of science rose in a prolonged duet, the high, strident note of Summerlee rising and falling to the sonorous bass of Challenger. I should have thought no more of Lord John's remark were it not that once again that night I heard him mutter to himself: "Blue clay – clay in a volcanic tube!" They were the last words I heard before I dropped into an exhausted sleep.

The complete and unabridged text is available online, from *flametreepublishing.com/extras*

Wolf Brother's Song

Ronald D. Ferguson

"Love! Love like swirling lights in the winter sky. Love! Love like –"

Wolf Brother touched my mind. *Must you make that awful racket, Kopasz Kutya? Something follows.*

I glanced up to the snowy ridge. Wolf Brother glided along the uneven upper path with a free and easy four-legged lope, his hundi-moodi shape outlined by the setting sun. I sloshed human-legged across the flat, hard-packed pass and hoped not to trip over my own sneskos.

I laughed and teased, "You have no heart, no soul, to appreciate my song."

Of course, he ignored me. I knew he stood sentry for sounds I could never hear, for sounds my song would have drowned.

Music hater. I tempered the mental message with the vision of a playful smile across my face. Nevertheless, I ceased my noise and slogged along content to hum.

Soon, we would arrive at the outpost, and I would see Ann – if she and the other colonists still survived. Using dirigibles, we had fled our enemies and crossed the great ocean, only to have a storm crash our caravan in the rugged mountains that guarded the shore of this unknown land. Soon after, illness swept our colony until we were too ill to continue the mountain journey on foot. Jack, our healer, identified a toxin from a prevalent fungus as the source, but Ann and I were not as sick as most others.

When we first were stranded, I convinced Ann we should try local plants for food. After all, I was the colony's plant and animal specialist, who else better for the experiment. Soon I realized that the local plants, particularly Zivot, contained an anti-toxin against the fungus. We harvested and refined what we could through the rugged winter, but the high mountains never yielded enough for our needs. Ten died, the others weakened.

With the first thaw, Jack and I set forth to find a better source for Zivot. Now, after seven long months away, I carried the refined Zivot anti-toxin in my backpack. With it, we could push back the sickness and stave off death. The colony would survive the coming winter.

I was exuberant.

I did not hear the warning from Wolf Brother's mate, Silver Back – she barely tolerated me and seldom directed thoughts my way – but Wolf Brother relayed the message. *Ice-needle storm, seven minutes away.*

Shelter.

Ice-needles could slice through all but the heaviest body armor, and I had dressed for speed not protection. Even Wolf Brother's thick fur offered scant barrier against ice-needles.

Winter already rode the mountains closer than I anticipated, and we needed shelter now. I searched the passageway walls for any crevice, any overhang that might shield us.

Wolf Brother. He was the unexpected surprise in my journey, the welcomed help after Jack died. What would Ann make of Wolf Brother? What would all of the colonist make of Wolf Brother? What had I made of Wolf Brother when we first met five months ago?

I searched the darkening sky. Unlike Silver Back, I could not smell the coming storm. No shelter revealed itself in either direction.

What of the cave we passed two kilometers back? I thought.

Wolf Brother gave his unspoken answer to my unspoken question. *The storm is already upon Silver Back, and she has taken shelter in the cave. We must go forward.*

I tried to run, but the sneskos dragged my feet across the snow and forced me into a clumsy shuffle. Oh, for a clean slope where I could swap sneskos for the makeshift broad skis I carried on my back, and then I would schuss down the mountain.

From the ridge, Wolf Brother angled down the steep incline to intercept me. We met just where the passage walls narrowed, and his shoulder bumped hard against my elbow. The force staggered me to the passage wall. I grabbed his furry mane to steady myself. Together, we struggled through the constricted passage until the pathway widened again.

"How long?" I gasped, but already I heard the storm scream. Cold, hard blackness pursued us through the mountain pass.

Quickly, Little Brother, on my back. You are not very big, but you are incredibly slow.

I checked my pocket for the ancient device, the power stone, which Wolf Brother had shown me among the crumbling ruins of the lost city. Although I had no supporting evidence, I suspected that the city's powerful civilization, now long dead, had started with the ulven species and bred into them for intelligence and other abilities until they became the hundi-moodi species that produced Wolf Brother.

I tugged at the straps of my backpack to be sure the anti-toxin remained secure. Yanking the sneskos free of my boots, I swung onto Wolf Brother's back. While I fought to tangle my hands into the long fur of his neck, he exploded down the pathway.

I risked a backwards look. Like a living wall of death, ice-needles rained into the mountain pass behind us. Wolf Brother howled a challenge at the weather with a voice so strong that it compelled me to join him. A loud kerr-crack overhead answered our defiance. I glanced up. Already, large shelves of snow separated from the mountain walls and cascaded toward us.

A small ice-needle stung my arm, and Wolf Brother's right ear freely bled from another strike. But the ice-needles were as nothing compared to the on-rushing avalanche.

The passageway widened again, and the powerful hundi-moodi swerved towards a collection of massive boulders in the path of the avalanche. I gulped. Even if the imposing rocks managed to absorb the force of the avalanche, we would still be buried by the snow. Perhaps the ice-needles were more merciful.

Heat. Use the power stone, Little Brother.

I seized the stone in my pocket. Wolf brother slowed his pace and then wedged us into the narrow shadow of the boulders. An ice-needle grazed my cheek and broke my focus. Still, warmth welled up from the power stone and coated me with a dull blue glow. Wolf Brother joined my effort, and the glow spread to engulf him. I pushed harder and the glow deepened to orange, expanded, and enclosed us in a warming bubble.

A storm of ice-needles sizzled and exploded against the heated barrier. How long could we hold it? Not long, I feared, certainly not long enough to endure the storm. Again I pushed the boundary. The bubble expanded towards solidity just before the avalanche flooded the passage and consumed us.

Cushioned by the irregular bubble of heated force, we rolled and slid with the first frantic flush of snow. With one last effort, I directed the bubble's boundary to a red-hot glow. The heat melted the snow pressed against the bubble. Then while our tumble with the snow slowed, my strength waned, and the bubble faded to blue. With rapid efficiency, the melted snow refroze into ice.

Exhausted, I released my hold on the power stone, and the pale bubble collapsed. The dull blue light faded to black, but the crusty ice dome held back the snow. Unable to maintain my grasp on his mane, I slipped from Wolf Brother's back into the darkness. The snow could not have buried us too deeply because the steady rat-a-tat of ice-needles pounding against our icy shield became a lullaby. Wolf Brother nuzzled my face, just before I drifted off.

* * *

I dreamed. I had dreamed the same dream many times before.

Jack and I backed away from the pond, and the three ulven – so exotic in appearance, so wolf-like in size and behavior – lowered their heads in unison and stalked us. A massive tree with low slung limbs waited forty meters away, but I had no illusion about my speed. The ulven would catch us before we covered half the distance.

We had no other choice. "Run," I shouted to Jack, and I broke for the tree.

And run Jack did, straight at the ulven. Even back home across the sea, you could rarely confuse a ferocious predator by aggressive display. I had observed enough ulven to know that they were incredibly cunning. You might intimidate a single ulven, but ulven always ran with a pack, and you could never bluff the pack.

When Jack charged the three ulven, he shouted to me, "Tell Karen I lov..."

I stopped when I heard his voice and looked back. The ulven were already on him. One tore out his throat before he could scream. Two more ulven circled the pond, and ran to join the three that ripped Jack to pieces. With deep yellow eyes, one ulven looked up from the feast as if to measure whether I was worth immediate pursuit. I hesitated no longer and raced for the tree.

How I managed the precarious climb, I don't know. At that moment, I could not tear my eyes from the grisly scene. The five ulven growled and fought among themselves over what was left of Jack. Here was the perfect opportunity for me to study the feeding habits of a vicious predator. My mind told me that was my job in this new land, to observe and learn, but my stomach told me no. I turned away.

Perched among the tree limbs, the enormity of losing Jack whelmed me. Now, I realized that Jack had not run toward the ulven out of stupid bravado. He did it because I understood the Zivot plant better than he did. Sure, I was more competent for the fieldwork to harvest and refine Zivot, but in the final measure, Jack was simply a better friend than me. His sacrifice was the most precious gift that one human could offer another.

Now, the fate of the colony rested with me.

Finished with their feast, the ulven left two watchers at my tree base. Apparently, I was marked to become their next meal. The other three ulven plodded away – whether to join a larger pack or to hunt, I didn't know. In my backpack, I had water for a couple of days, and with rationing, food for a week, but I had no idea of how patient, how persistent ulven could be. By the next day, I realized that sleep would become a problem if I could not find some way to strap myself to the tree.

On waking the second day I climbed higher in the tree to survey my surroundings. One of the ulven watched me while the other slept. Beyond the morning mist, a flash of light and a glimmer of silver caught my eye beyond the next hill. A city?

Searching for help, I strained to see through the mist, but it did not clear until the noon sun burned it away. Then the gaps and breaks in a soaring tower became obvious among the scattered ruins. Yes, a city, but a city long dead by its appearance. No help would come from there.

Late the third day, two larger beasts, creatures who resembled ulven but at twice the size, drove away the ulven watchers and took up the guardianship of my tree. I named them hundi-moodi for their gray wolf behavior. That night, I first heard the voices in my mind.

" ...Go?"

" ...Different...intelligent. Hear its thoughts...."

Although without formal introduction, that's how I met Wolf Brother – me in the tree, him on the ground – and there, I learned to listen to Wolf Brother's mind. Not a sensible scene at all, but such is the confusion of a dream when it summarizes reality.

Neither did Silver Back's comment surprise me while she paced beneath the tree. "Intelligent? Can we eat it?"

* * *

Wolf Brother coaxed me awake. *We must hurry.*

I opened my eyes, but could not see. The air tasted stale.

"How long have we been here?"

Twenty minutes to a half-hour. The storm is past, but now ulven trail us.

Ulven. I shuddered. I thought we had escaped the plains-loving ulven once we reached the mountains. Apparently, the pack hated all hundi-moodi – and Wolf Brother and his mate in particular – or perhaps they just hungered for me.

"How –"

The ulven have trapped Silver Back in the cave. We must be free of the snow before they finish with her and track us here.

Silver Back? I tried to quell my questions, but the harsh wall that rose in Wolf Brother's mind suggested Silver Back's fate. I pulled the power stone from my pocket and clasped it with both hands. The stone responded, and the pale blue light pushed back the darkness once more. I extended my will through the stone into a narrow heat beam and angled it up about thirty degrees. Once the stone melted a path, we would need to climb out. I reconsidered our situation and slightly increased the angle for our escape hole. I dared not try too long a tunnel, not all at once. Not only would the extra effort weaken me, but without great care, the bubble could collapse and trap us beneath the snow.

A sudden gush of water suggested that the beam had broken through an ice plug. I paused, then redirected the beam overhead. After a few seconds, a satisfying pop sounded, and the heat from the beam provided a chimney to suck fresh air down the escape route hole and into the bubble. I refocused the beam to enlarge the escape hole into an escape tunnel.

As the beam did its slow work, a steady stream of icy water flowed into our hollow. The cold water seeped into my boots, and my feet numbed. I glanced at Wolf Brother. Waiting for me to free us, he patiently lay in the chilling pool of water. The rising water turned ominously dark near his rear leg. Blood. A lot of fresh blood.

A sudden slush of snow slid through the enlarged opening and almost knocked me down. Pale silver light reflected down the fresh exit. I hesitated and waited to see whether the tunnel would collapse. Wolf Brother slowly rose and then examined the passage. After a brief glance my way, he limped up the incline. Thoroughly soaked and freezing, I set the power stone with the selfish task of warming me, and then I followed Wolf Brother up the short passageway.

In the winter, night came quickly. When we emerged from the snow, twilight had already surrendered its fading light to the moons. Overhead, Vaike neared her apex while the larger companion moon, Suur, followed close behind. The two moon gibbous glow reflected from the silver snow. All lay eerily quiet.

Wolf Brother sniffed the air, his mind listening beyond what I could sense.

He turned his head and focused his yellow eyes on me. The luminescent irises shifted color to orange, then back to yellow.

The ulven are here, Kopasz Kutya. No time remains. I will lure away the pack. You must make your way down the mountain side alone.

I measured the sharp down slope of the mountain only a hundred meters away. Treacherous, but I had skied steeper. I looked to Wolf Brother. "But –"

We cannot stand against them. A large pack, at least a dozen ulven come. Perhaps, I could defeat three or four. You, Little Brother, would be lucky to prevail against one. Go now. You will make your way home, and you will save your people. I will lead them from you, and then I shall join Silver Back. With a mighty leap, he sought higher ground and worked his way upward, toward an overhanging bluff.

"Join Silver Back," I whispered, "but she's dead."

Wolf Brother's thoughts no longer answered mine.

The anti-toxin. I had responsibilities to the colony. I tugged at the shoulder straps to retrieve the short, broad skis hooked across my backpack.

I grimaced. One ski was badly cracked from the avalanche. The other had lost its binding.

With no alternative, I waded through the powdery snow toward the down slope. At the precipice, I sat in the snow to rework the skis. I removed the binding from the cracked ski, and threw the broken board away. All the while, I watched the shadows for sign of the ulven.

A hundred meters back, outlined by the moon Suur against the clearing sky, Wolf Brother climbed fifteen meters atop the projecting bluff. At the edge of the bluff, he stopped and shook himself as if to free his mind and body from all distraction. Below him, an amorphous black shadow moved, separated, and reformed as a dozen individual shapes, each with a glistening pair of glowing, yellow eyes.

I struggled to fit the loose binding to the good ski. A quick glance told me that the dozen pair of ulven eyes now tracked me. Even though I knew that I could never finish rigging the ski before the ulven reached me, I fumbled to secure the last knots.

The air filled with a mournful cry that grew in volume and echoed from the mountains. I had never heard another bay like it. The rabid challenge jerked all ulven eyes upward.

The sound ululated, its timbre cycled, and the voice carved the air with a story, an aria that I did not comprehend. Atop the bluff, Wolf Brother sang. I struggled to understand the song and failed. At last, his voice deepened into a rumbling growl that swelled to a defiance which chilled me beyond my wet clothes or the cold mountain pass.

While I finished wrapping the makeshift binding to my primitive ski, the ulven counter-pointed Wolf Brother's challenge with a chorus of yelps and barks. Nine ulven tested the incline and sought a path up the steep mountain wall. The remaining three turned their eyes on me and separated from the pack.

Cunning! Too cunning, but perhaps, too late. Wolf Brother's song had bought me the needed time.

I snapped my left boot against the ski binding and secured the straps. Now dispersed along the incline, the nine ulven scaled the mountain towards the bluff and Wolf Brother. The remaining three ulven lowered their heads and stalked me.

After one last check of the ski binding, I stood. I had always disdained the snowboard in favor of skis, but now I would have to manage. The ulven took my action as the cue to charge. I turned from them and plunged down the steep slope on my single ski.

Farewell, Kopasz Kutya. All that remains of me, Little Brother, I leave with you.

I tried to look back, but my weight shifted, the clumsy board dug into the snow, and I had to adjust to keep from tripping. I lightly dragged my right foot to serve as rudder and brake.

Goodbye, Wolf Brother. Sing well.

Because I did not trust my skill on the single ski, I swerved well in advance of the first tree. Behind me, the ulven plodded with steady gait, as if they knew I could never maintain this pace into the tree line.

At the next flurry of trees, my right foot dragged too heavily, but I managed to recover without spilling. I slowed my descent and looked back. The ulven had lost ground to my downhill flight. I stopped near a low-hanging tree limb. A quick handful of snow stolen from the branches refreshed my face and moistened my dry mouth.

From far away, the faint cry of battle echoed. I imagined ulven reaching the plateau one or two at a time to be dispatched by Wolf Brother's fury. But what if they attacked four or five at a time? What of his wound? What if his endurance faded? What if....

The bay of ulven on my trail drew me back. I shook my head free of speculation, and cast off down the slope. Now, the landscape looked more familiar, but the precarious twists and turns in the pathway impeded my flight. The trees thickened. The pathway narrowed. I slowed again. A spill could mean my death.

Five kilometers. Surely, the colony was no more than five kilometers away, but at this slower pace, the ulven would catch me long before I made even three kilometers. If only I could touch Ann's mind like Wolf Brother touched mine.

I recalled my trip up the path seven months ago. Only two kilometers from the colony, a large gulley, fully twenty meters deep, slashed diagonally across the slope. Where the gulley narrowed to ten meters wide, woody, flood debris collected at the bottom. When last I passed, the debris was stone dry and excellent for firewood. If I could start a bonfire to attract the colony's attention, they might send help.

If only someone were alert to a fire this time of night. If the wood were still dry. If....

The trees thinned. On the glide down the open slope, I removed the power stone from my pocket.

Focus like Wolf Brother had shown me. Imagine the gulley. Focus. Imagine the debris. Imagine a spark, a flicker of flame. Imagine –

The low branch swiped across my face and shoulder and knocked me aside. I plowed into a snow bank. Frantically, I recovered and pulled myself free of the snow. My ski binding had loosened. When I stooped to tighten the straps, I realized that somewhere in the snow, I had lost the power stone.

I turned to dig into the snow bank, but a triumphant howl halted my search. A hundred meters up the slope, the three ulven raced toward me. I pushed away from the snow bank and attacked the open slope. Crouching low, I shushed downhill, until the next clump of trees forced me to slalom.

The landscape, the trees, the moonlit snow, all blurred while I focused on flexing past the next rise, navigating the next bank, or avoiding the next obstacle. Then, I skied to a narrow, powdery stretch bordered by a thin line of trees. I glanced over my left shoulder when I made a wide turn to follow the deeper, snowy path to the far side of the tree line. On the other side of the trees, nearly abreast with me, the ulven raced along the dryer, parallel trail. Only brush and drifted snow among the sparse trees separated us. The ulven's hot breath puffed into the cold air, and their powerful strides kicked up small flurries of snow.

Dappled moonlight revealed that the trees dwindled ahead. My pathway curved left to track the gulley, and there my trail merged with the ulven's pursuit. If I followed the curve, the ulven would intercept me against the gulley. I had only one chance.

I pulled my right foot up tightly behind my left on the crude snowboard and leaned as low and as far forward as I dared to gather speed. The landscape hurtled past me. Ahead, a mysterious yellow glow outlined the gulley.

The ulven issued an elated cry because they closed on me. The tree line petered-out. From the corner of my eye, I saw the ulven slant to intercept me with the lead ulven scant meters away. But I did not follow the worn pathway. I did not curve into the waiting jaws. I plowed straight ahead to the gulley edge, and at the last moment, I uncoiled and sailed into the air.

I heard the lead ulven howl when its momentum carried it over the precipice and to the dimly lit rocks fifteen meters below. Light and heat rose from the gulley to warm my face. I watched the opposite edge of the gulley approach, and I wondered whether I would strike short of safety and join the first ulven in the debris below.

Strange. Just before I hit the ground, I noticed a fire brewing among the debris at the bottom of the gully. My ski caught the gulley edge and twisted from my foot. Pain exploded in my ankle, and the impact against the frozen ground knocked the air from my lungs.

I tumbled and rolled several meters, and then lay still for a long moment gasping for breath. Dazed, I looked across the gulley. Illuminated by moonlight and the flickering light from the fire in the gulley, the remaining two ulven paced the precipice. One quickly gave up the chase and trotted up the slope toward the sparse forest. The other waited. The creature's yellow eyes reflected the firelight while it watched me.

A light snow began. Finally, the last ulven yelped in frustration and slunk after its companion.

* * *

Late the next morning, I limped into the colony. The familiar storage structures of the camp, the individual huts, the common meeting dorm, all retained a soft coat of fresh snow. Beyond the central campfire, the winter sun gleamed off the thoroughly scavenged remnants of our dirigibles.

Ann saw me first. My guess was that she spent more time watching for me than the others did. I managed a smile and held up my backpack.

"Matt," she yelled. The name sounded peculiar. My name is Kopasz Kutya, the Hairless Puppy. With effort, I remembered that I was also Matt.

The anti-toxin was secure, and we could – we would – make it through the coming winter. With the spring thaw, I would lead the healthy colony down the perilous path from the mountains to the far river valley, where the anti-toxin producing Zivot flowers grew in abundance. There we would live. There we would teach the ulven respect. There we would rebuild the lost city.

I couldn't run, but Ann could, and she reached me with an embrace that drove away the cold and melted the icy heaviness in my heart.

* * *

Twilight shifted towards night. I forced the raucous community celebration from my mind and wandered toward the edge of the settlement. Fresh from comforting Karen, Ann put her hand on my shoulder when I passed Jack's hut, but then she read my face and answered my need for solitude with an understanding smile. She let me pass without comment.

Away from the noise of our village, outside the warm glow of the campfires, near the massive snow banks that bordered the surrounding forest, I found a dry log and sat…and watched…and waited.

Vaike lazily rose above the eastern horizon. Suur would soon follow. The breeze from the north picked up as a pale prelude of the coming winter storms. From deep within the woods, the moan of the errant wind sounded through the trees. Intrigued, I tilted my head to listen. The woodwind notes rose and fell like the ululating hundi-moodi song of life, like a warrior's last challenge against the inevitability of death.

I could no longer touch Wolf Brother's mind, but I felt him with me. Some part of him haunted me, and I treasured his spirit. Then, I understood the last song that Wolf Brother sang from that barren bluff.

My homecoming was a gift from Jack and Wolf Brother. Each of us survives some critical juncture of life because of another's sacrifice, the sacred gift that only one friend can offer another. The stars sparkled their agreement with my melancholy reflection.

I closed my eyes, smiled, and recalled the best and worst memories from my journey. Soon, the unremitting winter winds would come unabated to the mountains. Soon, gray would coat each day and bitter cold would stalk each night.

When the cold months lurk too long, when others complain of the insistent, constant gale, when our harsh new land demanded more sacrifice, I promised myself that I would stand against the howling wind and remember the comforting melody of Wolf Brother's love song.

Baryonyx Crossing

Kevin M. Folliard

JESSIE HARDING'S skimmer glided under the dense canopy of one of Dactyl Flowage's many murky passageways. The 12-foot vessel was perfect for day fishing, with cutting-edge solar cells and paneling. But it was ill-equipped for what stirred after sunset: the predators her seventeen-year-old son Chase had been hunting when he went missing twenty-four hours ago.

She reduced speed around a bend. These days, one could never tell what was waiting in the lake system.

Dactyl Flowage had been one of the safer places to settle in New Pangea when Jessie's parents were young. The fishing industry was booming, and the flowage became a popular vacation destination, a rare spot outside the walls of city compounds without large man-eating predators.

Jessie grew up loving the settlement. She married a local and did exactly what her parents had done. Fished. Life was good away from overregulated compounds. People around Dactyl Flowage took care of each other. And it stayed that way, until after Chase's sixth birthday, when the Baryonyx migration started.

Jessie examined both shores at the end of the passage. All clear. She sped into the six-hundred acre opening, Orion's Lake, then glided to a floating stop and lifted her binoculars.

She scoured the rippling blue expanse. It was unlikely that Chase and his three man crew would have been hunting for Onyx there, but she had to check it off the search list.

Across the water, a forty-foot Iguanodon drank from the sandy shore. An indigo stripe ran down her back; her tail coiled gracefully behind her. The Iguanodons were technically invasive too, no natural predators in the lake system. But they were harmless herbivores, and they hated the hum of solar generators, so they stayed away from town. Besides, tourists loved to spot them out on the water.

Silver-backed Istiodactyls roosted in the trees, downy tan wings wrapped around them like blankets. They hoisted toothy bills in the air and crooned at one another.

Jessie pined for the days when the dactyls were the biggest nuisance in the flowage. Now and then, a bold Istiodactlyus would swoop and steal a catch. Leave a haul unguarded, and they would swarm it. Worst case scenario, a dactyl could deliver a nasty bite that might get infected.

But even with a fourteen-foot wingspan, the dactyls were lightweights. A quick shock prod always scared them off. Back then, the locals never carried pulse rifles.

The skimmer drifted toward the center of the open water. Jessie did a full three-hundred-and-sixty degree surveillance, scoured every nook and inlet, but no sign of Chase. Her heart sank. Tears welled in her eyes.

She reached for her radio. "Checked all the western branches the *Challenger* could have accessed." She sighed. "No sign. No wreckage. Not a damn thing."

Static crackled. "Sorry to hear, Jessie," came Sheriff Grant Jensen. "We've been searching the upper and eastern branches. Nothing yet, but there's a lot more water to cover. We will find them."

Jessie checked her compass. "I'm heading to the Narrow Lake."

The radio crackled. "Gosh, Jess, that's far north. You and Chase never hunted up there did you?"

"I know it's a long shot, but Gunner could have talked him into trying."

"How long have you had Gunner, Russel, and Bobby under contract, Jess?"

"Six months. I know you don't like me paying under the table, but they're decent. They just owe the compounds and need to keep their heads down."

"Still," Jensen said, "this was Chase's first time on the water alone with them, right? Maybe they're stealing your boat."

"The *Challenger*'s too big to make it out of the Flowage. But they could have hit a shallow patch," Jessie suggested. "Hasn't been a lot of rain lately."

"Could be stuck, yeah. It's an idea." The Sheriff's voice drooped with doubt. "Might be a good idea to come back and recharge though."

"The skimmer has eight hours." Jessie steered toward the northeastern canal.

"Jess, listen," came Jensen. "You're worried. I get it. But head back in with the rest of us."

"I want a quick look up there. We've got another hour of daylight."

"We've got twenty minutes of light, and a whole lot of dusk." Static crackled. "Devils' suppertime. They'll be out soon."

The skimmer floated. Jessie glared at the sinking orange sun. Dactyls chittered in the treetops.

The radio sputtered. "Nobody knows these animals better than you, Jessie. Except maybe Chase. Would he want his mom out in that little surface skimmer after dark?"

Jessie clenched the wheel. Gritted her teeth.

"Even if you make it up there, you still gotta come *all* the way back down."

"You're right, Grant," she snapped. "Of course I know that."

"Come on back. We'll recharge everyone's equipment and resume at dawn."

"I won't ask anyone else to stay out," she said. "But this is my risk to take. If it was your kid…"

Static. "Check in on the hour if you're still out there. Got it?"

"Roger." She hit the button once more. "Thank you, Grant. Thank you to everyone who searched today."

"It's what we do. Be safe."

Jessie studied the surface in her path, no humps or ripple patterns. She accelerated toward the passage. She couldn't remember that last time she cut loose at top speed this far out in such a small boat, but she was racing the sun now.

The Sheriff was correct: Jessie was making a mistake. "Anything for you, Chase," she said.

Chase had always been a happy kid. He had his father's sandy brown hair and green eyes, and his mother's adventurous spirit. She'd been taking Chase onto the water since birth. He knew the lake system as well as she did. He knew the business almost as well too.

Lately, Jessie had taken on more of the daily operations, so once she had thoroughly vetted Gunner and the crew, she felt it was time to start transitioning Chase to an official captaincy of the big boat: the *Challenger*.

After the death of her husband Phil, Jessie harbored a fiery hatred for Baryonyx. They were invasive. Territorial. Difficult to detect without expensive sonar equipment that few could afford. And worst of all, the Onyx thrived where her family made their livelihood.

Urban sprawl from the compounds was always driving bigger, more dangerous predators into new territory. Dactyl Flowage had contingency plans for large therapod dinosaurs, but they never anticipated medium-sized carnivores like Onyx to settle in such large numbers.

The Baryonyx had taken the love of her life and robbed Chase of his father. That first year after she lost Phil, Jessie would sneak out at night on a small boat, not unlike the skimmer she was on now. She wanted them to come. She wanted revenge.

And she was good at it.

It was a technique she adopted from the Iguanodons, who took low defensive positions and jabbed at bigger dinosaurs' throats with their sharp thumb spikes. Jessie would deliver a shock to the Onyx's snout, a second shock to the side, and then skewer a hunter's knife in the soft tissue beneath the jaw.

She managed to kill three of them in one month without capsizing. But the fourth one wasn't as predictable. She went under. Floundering in the water, she barely managed to gouge its eye and get to shore.

She had come so close to making her son an orphan.

Sheriff Jenson had been the one who found her that following morning. On the way back to town, he gave her a piece of advice that stuck: "Behind every crisis is opportunity. You just have to know where to look."

That week, Jessie invested Phil's life insurance payout into the *Challenger*, an eighty-foot-long, twenty-five-ton, custom designed hunting ship. She equipped it with an industrial crane and capture mechanism. The cage was a steel trap which snapped together, breaking the spine of large, upright predators. Desert folk used the trap on Utahraptors, but when Jessie imported it, she had it reengineered for the water.

The first year was rough, but once they perfected the process, Jessie became the most efficient trapper of Baryonyx in the lake system. She had effectively monetized Dactyl Flowage's nightmare.

Once in steady supply, Onyx meat become a local delicacy and a novelty for visitors. The teeth, 12 inch front claws, and skulls could be sold as tourist keepsakes as well. On a good night, Jessie and Chase could catch five Onyx and trade them for twelve-hundred coppers each.

Now and then, Jessie would even get a request for a live specimen for zoos and private collectors. She had definitely turned crisis to opportunity, for her and Chase, as well as the town. But she never lost her hatred for the things.

She knew the animal that snapped up Phil and pulled him into a death roll didn't really do it with malice. It was a natural predator doing what came naturally. Still, the business gave Jessie a sense of vindication. When something hunts the Harding clan, they hunt back.

Jessie carefully navigated the northern passages. Jittery chicken-sized Scipionyx darted amid the leafy shore. They chirped and pecked for water beetles. As always, Jessie kept her eyes peeled for wake patterns and surface bumps. She fingered the shock prod strapped to her belt. It would have been better to have a pulse rifle of course, but all the Hardings' best weapons were on the *Challenger*.

Distant Iguanodon calls reverbed like cello strings. The skimmer sped into a new passageway as Jessie struggled to rationalize the *Challenger*'s disappearance.

A radio malfunction she could believe. Damaged or faulty equipment, perhaps, though the *Challenger*'s solar cells were brand new. Chase was too smart to get stuck in the muddy shallows. And the perfect storm of an accident *and* a radio failure was too much to swallow. Even the weather last night had been eerily calm.

The reality horrified her: Chase and the crew had to have been attacked. And to take out a ship like the *Challenger*, engineered to trap and carry several tons worth of Baryonyx, the culprit would have been enormous.

The sun slipped behind the evergreen horizon. Jessie picked up speed through a wide gap. A murder of Vectidraco fluttered into the air. They spread into a cloud of leathery wings against the pink sky. The tiny Pterosaurs were taking flight to hunt insects. And she knew they weren't the only things stirring at sundown.

The skimmer reached a shady stretch where the canopy hung low over muddy water. Jessie decelerated. The *Challenger* could never have made it through this way, but Chase and the crew could have reached the Narrow Lake via any of the other spidery canals. This was a shortcut, but was it safe?

Jessie grabbed a flashlight off its charger, shined it across dark surfaces and between trees. Soft hooting echoed: Hypsilophodons. The small lithe herbivores were plentiful this time of year. Hypsies were a favored treat of ambush predators like Baryonyx.

Daylight waned behind the low branches that blocked the passage. It wasn't far to the Narrow Lake. Jessie took her shock prod in hand and glided along, heart pounding. Shadows shifted across the water. She pushed overgrown fronds out of her face as the skimmer swept past them.

Some day, she thought. *We'll clear this passage, dig a channel wide enough for ships like the Challenger.* It comforted her to think of a future where the business, her family, her future was expanding rather than shrinking. She imagined Chase out on the water with his own kids. They could even work with the settlement to build a preserve, a place to farm predators instead of hunt them.

A curtain of willow branches obscured the water to the left. Jessie steered right, and the boat scraped against something large and hard. The skimmer jolted. Her muscles tensed. She stopped the engine.

She unhooked the shock prod from her belt and flicked it on with an electric hum. Jessie stood to examine the obstruction. A sunken tree trunk blocked the right path.

"Shoot," she whispered. She could back up and hug the left bank. Hope it wasn't too shallow. Hope nothing lurked under the willow. *Not worth it,* she decided.

Jessie grabbed an oar and prodded the tree trunk. Her eyes followed the trunk toward a split branch that blocked the skimmer. Maybe she could get enough leverage with the oar to spin and flip the obstructing side toward the right shore.

She made her way to the front of the boat, switched off the shock prod, and set it down. Then she dipped the oar under the sturdy protruding branch. She attempted to pry it up, but it wouldn't budge. Her back strained. She groaned and gave up. "Damn."

The sky was already tinting purple. Tears welled in Jessie's eyes.

A metallic blue dragonfly vibrated past her ear and landed on the tree trunk. Jessie remembered how Chase used to catch them near shore when he was little, and then let them go. She and Phil would sip moonshine on the porch and watch him race along the edge of the water.

Nobody let their kids play near shore at night anymore.

The hairs stood up on Jessie's neck. She took a closer look at the silvery-winged insect. Something was wrong.

The branch beneath the dragonfly was a different shade of muddy green than the rest of the tree trunk. She studied it closer. A long, flat snout took shape in her perception, about a yard long, with a discolored whitish bump that could almost pass for wet fungus.

A black eye glinted, half sunk below the water. Jessie followed the shape further up shore, past the smaller branches of the overturned tree, and she spotted the animal's mud-crusted hide, half submerged. Practically invisible against the shoreline.

It was one of them. A Baryonyx waiting patiently for an unsuspecting Hypsilophodon to take a drink.

Jessie trained her eyes on the animal's snout, not even six feet from the skimmer. Slowly, she lowered her arm toward the shock prod.

Water erupted. The Onyx launched over the fallen tree trunk. Huge front claws scraped the gunwale, and a long crocodilian snout snapped forward. Jessie dropped onto her back. The bow tipped forward under the weight of the animal. Water gushed inside.

Time seemed to slow down as Jessie focused on the exposed, vulnerable, pale throat above her head. If only her hunting knife had been in her hand, instead of still strapped to her ankle. If only the shock prod had been live and in hand. Instead, she clutched the wooden oar with both hands and cracked the Baryonyx in the skull as hard as she could.

The predator recoiled and snorted in frustration. The skimmer teetered. Jessie grabbed the shock prod and kicked her way toward the stern. She struggled to her feet.

The Baryonyx shook his head, dazed. He stood hip deep in the murky water. He was a big one for sure, 10 feet tall, almost 25 feet long, she guessed. Water dripped from his 12 inch front talons. A muddy green tail swayed behind him, flinging water left and right. He flexed his front claws, tilted his crocodilian smile and lurched forward again. His jaw chomped, talons scraped the hull, but he was coming up a few feet short of Jessie.

The tree trunk blocked his full assault, but Jessie knew he could easily climb over or swim around. And once he put his one ton body weight down on her vessel, she was sunk.

Jessie worked furiously to dry the wet tip of the shock prod. A throaty snarl escaped the back of the Baryonyx's throat, and he opened his jaws wide to reveal a broad pink tongue. The animal lurched closer to shore; his wake tilted the skimmer, and Jessie tumbled against the equipment chest, which popped open. She momentarily lost sight of the creature as the boat rocked, but then she saw the tip of his dark tail wiggling above her.

He's trying to get behind me, she realized. She searched for the shock prod, but couldn't find it. It would still take too long to unstrap her knife. In a panic, she reached into the equipment chest and grabbed a large fishing hook. As a dark shape swiveled above her, she spun and lodged the hook into the fleshy side of the Baryonyx.

The animal howled and swiped down. Jessie rolled to the side. A loud rip sounded as his front claw slashed her back. Jessie screamed. Her hands found the rubber handle of the shock prod and she jabbed it upward, flicking the switch.

The electric hum sounded. Dripping serrated jaws spread over her, and she squeezed the trigger. A huge spark flashed between them. The Baryonyx snarled and slammed against the stern. The stern dunked below water. Jessie watched the radio and half her equipment plunge into the murk.

She shouted as the skimmer flipped backward. She dunked underwater. Her head popped up into the darkness beneath the capsized vessel. Water rippled. The upside-down skimmer rocked.

Outside, the Onyx snarled. She heard the unmistakable sloshing sound of him shoving his enormous body underwater, getting into a swimming position, but was he heading toward shore? Out to deeper water? Or was he looping back around to finish the job?

Her hands felt among the floating equipment for anything useful. The skimmer's radio was an old model, not water-proof, but the shock prod, another hook, even a water-sealed flare might come in handy. All she found were sticks and debris.

Jessie's heart pounded. *I've been studying these animals for years,* she thought. *What's he most likely to do now? They don't eat boats. They don't hold grudges. He's just hungry, and he's not hidden anymore. He's going to find a new hiding spot.*

She listened closely. The water calmed. The upside-down skimmer steadied.

He's not coming back.

Jessie whispered a prayer and took a deep breath. She dunked under the edge of the capsized skimmer and surfaced on the other side. She glanced in every direction then swam for the opposite shore. Tangled willow branches stuck to her face, snagged at her arms, but once she was close to the edge, she was able to grab hold of the low-hanging vines to free her legs from the muck.

Jessie huffed and crawled up shore. She found stable ground, rested against a tree, and caught her breath. Her hunting knife was still secured at her ankle. The binoculars remained around her neck. Everything else was back in the water. No shock prod.

High above, a green and yellow spotted Hypsilophodon stared down at her with muddy, inquisitive eyes, hands wrapped around a leafy branch.

Jessie nodded up at the Hypsie. "That could have been you, you know." She gave a weak laugh. "I guess we're both lucky. So far."

The sky darkened beyond the trees. Insects chittered. Hypsies hooted and Iguanodons sang. Jessie forced herself back on her feet. Her back stung where the Baryonyx had cut her. She felt the wound. It didn't feel deep, but she had no way to examine it at the moment.

There's still some light. I'm close. She put one foot in front of the other and hiked through the foliage. She was determined to get one good look at the Narrow Lake. She had to know if Chase was there.

As she pushed through the brush, she felt something in her bones. A slight tremor that shook the ground. She paused. Held her breath. Waited.

There it was again, faint vibrations in the earth. Iguanodons were the biggest animals in Dactyl Flowage, and they were decently light on their feet. But Jessie had felt the impact tremors of larger dinosaurs when she traveled with her father years ago. Something was out there, and it was close. She quickened her pace.

Branches whipped her face. Thorny brush scraped her mud-crusted legs. Finally, she found an opening and stepped onto the shore.

Fifty yards out, the maroon and white hull of the *Challenger* tilted high into the air, half-sunk. The crane rested against starboard quarter, half-submerged, ripped from the deck. Wreckage and debris floated all around it.

Jessie's hands shook as she wiped the binoculars' lenses on her wet vest. She took a closer look. The solar panels on the upper deck were shattered. The damage was extensive enough to cause a total electrical failure. Thick metal scrapes carved through the paint on the hull, in rows of three, the claws of a three-fingered monster.

A red stain streaked the wooden deck.

Jessie fell to her knees. "Chase!" she screamed. To hell with whatever horrible new arrival to the Flowage might hear her. Whatever monster had demolished the *Challenger*.

All she wanted now was for Chase to be okay. She shouted and screamed his name until her throat hurt. Then she lay in the wet sand and cried. Water lapped at her fingers. One by one, the first stars punctured the darkening sky.

The earth trembled.

"Come and get me," she growled. She reached down and unfastened her mud-caked hunting knife. She cleaned it on her shirt and held the blade across her heart. "Just come and get me, but don't think I'm going to make it easy."

The ground vibrated again.

Then suddenly a light shined down on her. And a voice whispered: "Mom!"

Chase stood behind the ray of his flashlight, a tall, muscular shadow that reminded her of his father. He reached down and clutched her hands. "Mom!" He whispered with urgency. "Oh my God! You were attacked!"

"Chase," she gasped his name. He helped her to her feet. "Chase! Thank God!" She collapsed in his arms, squeezed him tight. "We've been searching all day. The Sheriff and everyone headed back in, and I was so close, but a damn Onyx capsized the skimmer. I'm just –"

"Shh." Chase whispered, "I'm okay. But something's out there. We have to keep it down." Chase felt the tear in her clothes. "You're injured."

"It's not bad," she insisted. "And in any event, not much to do about it. I'm just glad you're…" The lightness in her chest faded. "Gunner. The crew."

Tears glinted in the glow of Chase's flashlight. His voice cracked. "They didn't make it."

Chase's lips puckered. His face was still so young, smeared with mud, eyes puffy. Even though he was on the cusp of manhood, he looked as devastated, as terrified as he had when she'd broken the news about his father.

"It was a huge, two-legged, carnivore," Chase explained. "Biggest I've ever seen in person for sure. Hard to make out in the spotlights, brown coloring, at least a fifty-footer. Maybe longer. Had a sail or fin or something. It came fast. Snatched up Russel and Bobby. Pulled the crane down. Gunner fired off a couple of shots with his pulse rifle, but that only made it angrier. It circled back and hit us a second time, ruptured the hull.

"The stern started tanking, and we didn't risk going for the panic box below deck. We took the escape raft, but Gunner got pulled in on the way back. By the time I was ashore, the thing that started it all was gone. This morning, I glimpsed it through the trees." He lowered his voice further. "It's still on this side of shore. I've been trying to climb as high as I can but…"

Chase cried. "I'm sorry, Mom. We thought we'd get a good haul out here. We never expected anything that big."

"You're alive," she said. "That's what matters to me right now. That and staying safe. Sheriff Jenson and the others are heading out to search again tomorrow. When I don't check in, they'll be concerned, but for their own safety, they won't resume the search until daylight. How's the raft?"

Chase pointed with his flashlight. "Tied up shore. Still floating. I lost our radio and a rifle when Gunner went down. But I still have a shock prod." He patted the metal rod fastened to his belt.

"Good. Most of my equipment is sunk under the skimmer." Jessie pointed in the direction of her own attack. "Nothing worth going back for."

The ground shook again. Chase tensed up.

Jessie reached for Chase's flashlight. She shined across the water. "The *Challenger*'s not sinking any further. Russ and Bobby had guns when they got snatched up?"

"They did," Chase said solemnly.

"The panic box is probably floating at the base of the ladder below deck. We should go for it. Beats waiting around for whatever's shaking the ground." Jessie had her suspicions about the fifty-footer, but she didn't want to name the predator out loud. She hoped she was wrong.

She shined the light along the surface of the lake, between shore and the wreck. Scores of Baryonyx eyes reflected green.

"We'll get attacked if we cross," Chase said. "It's suicide."

The ground shook.

"Staying here is too." She took her son by the shoulders. "I'm not saying it won't be dangerous, but we *can* make that crossing. I've been out at night in Onyx territory in small boats before."

Chase's voice quaked. "Not a raft though, Mom."

"You'll be my extra eyes and ears. You row. I'll take point. Between my knife and your shock prod, I can defend us. But if the big one shows up," she pointed into the pitch black woods. "And we don't even have rifles." The ground shook again. "Then we're really sunk."

Chase shook his head.

"Out on the *Challenger*, we'll have guns, flares, spare solar cells, and a radio. We could wait topside until sun-up. It's that, or we climb a tree and hope for the best."

Chase sighed. "That's what I did last night. But the big one's tall. I got lucky." Chase unstrapped his shock prod and handed it to her. "I trust you, Mom." He nodded. "Get us through this."

A chorus of cicadas grew louder as night darkened. Chase led her up shore to where he had tied the eight by five foot aluminum framed raft. Although it was much better than an inflatable, Chase was right, the raft was pitiful in the face of even one Baryonyx, and there had to be at least a dozen of them gliding between them and the wreck of the *Challenger*.

The oars remained tucked under the seats. Chase took the back end, and Jessie crouched toward the front. She kept her shock prod in her right hand, and aimed the flashlight in her left. She kept the hunting knife loose in its ankle sheath, unstrapped for easy access.

Jessie illuminated the course to the *Challenger*. "We're clear for thirty feet or so, take us dead ahead to start." Chase rowed them across the water. Jessie caught a hump in her flashlight beam. "Veer left."

Chase steered, and they passed the tail-end of the animal, with a wide buffer. Jessie wanted to make sure that if they did come across an Onyx, they would come against it from behind. She had taken them out head on before, but how much of that had been luck?

"Keep left," Jessie instructed. "Let's loop around, too many eyes off the starboard quarter, kiddo."

The oars splashed as Chase widened the girth between the raft and the ship. The shock prod hummed. Jessie scoured the water, taking stock of every direction, occasionally chancing a glance over Chase's shoulders. So far nothing appeared to be following them.

"We've got Onyx eyes at nine o'clock, two sets, don't seem to be moving. Keep circling." Suddenly something rustled back on the shore. Jessie glanced up. A gaggle of dactyls took flight as the treetops shook. Snapping branches echoed, and a massive spine-tipped sail surfaced through the canopy, like a shark's dorsal fin.

Chase started to turn, but Jessie instructed: "Eyes forward, Chase. Big boy's still on shore." She turned her attention back to the water. "Keep rounding the ship. Come in a little tighter." Jessie spied the cargo net in the beam of her flashlight. It had been torn half loose, and draped from the port bow.

Onyx eyes reflected green near the submerged end of the *Challenger*, but the water was clear by the net. "Head for the cargo net. We'll climb up there. Let's keep our eyes on two o'clock over there."

They rounded the *Challenger* just as more branches cracked near shore. The big dinosaur had to be moving closer to water, but they didn't have a good vantage point anymore. An ear-splitting roar echoed from shore.

A loud splash sounded. Water sloshed as something enormous dove into the lake. The color drained from Chase's face.

"Stay on task, buddy," Jessie said with steely resolve. "No sense worrying about him until we're up on that deck. We're close."

She kept her eyes on the two Baryonyx to the right. Their snouts glided past, just ten feet away, but when the wake of the larger animal rippled past the *Challenger*, the Onyx picked up speed.

The raft bobbed. Chase stopped rowing, steadied himself.

Jessie whispered, "The big one's probably heading up shore. Its wake is parallel to us, means its swimming east or west." She gave Chase a confident wink, but her hands were trembling.

The raft steadied, and Chase continued to row. Jessie did a one-eighty sweep as they closed in on the net. Then suddenly, one attacked.

She heard it before she saw it, splashing from behind. She knew immediately it had been gliding under the raised hull of the *Challenger*, completely out of sight. But Jessie was already pulling the trigger of the shock prod as she whipped around.

Fortunately, it was going for her, not Chase. She sparked its snout. The disoriented Onyx twitched, but momentum drove it against the raft, pushing them away from the cargo net.

The raft spun and rocked. Jessie lost her sense of direction. She released the flashlight and unsheathed her knife.

The raft spiralled. Water erupted behind Chase.

Jessie screamed: "Get down!" She leapt toward her son as he ducked and covered. She thrust the shock prod at the Onyx's crocodile jaws.

Electric blue flashed. She stabbed upward with her left hand. The blade stuck deep under the lower jaw of the creature, jammed below his skull. Hot blood gushed over her hand as she pulled the blade free.

The Baryonyx's head bumped the raft as it went limp, momentarily pulling the aluminum frame under before the dead weight of its body drifted away. Water gushed around their ankles before the raft leveled out.

Jessie scrambled to snatch up the waterproof flashlight from red-tinted water. Chase frantically searched for his oars. Blood speckled his hair and face. "Hands in the boat!" she shouted.

Chase pulled his arms in. "Mom are you okay? Did you seriously just–" he stuttered. "That was incredible!"

Jessie scanned their surroundings. The cargo net dangled twenty feet away.

She handed Chase the flashlight. "We have to swim."

"What if –"

"We can't argue," Jessie snapped. "Just move and stay close to –"

Something hit them from behind, plowing them forward. Huge, foot long claws tipped the raft. Another Baryonyx was pushing them. They were heading toward the *Challenger*.

Jessie shocked the dinosaur's claws, and it released. The raft plopped back down. In desperation, Jessie sparked at the empty air in the attacker's direction, but it was back underwater. "Go!" she shouted. "I'm covering you. I'll be right there."

Chase leapt into the water. She heard him swimming away behind her. She prayed for his safety, gripping the shock prod and knife in both hands.

The Baryonyx hit the raft from underneath and knocked it into the air. Jessie flipped over. She lost the shock prod when she hit water, but she held onto the knife. She didn't waste any time. She clenched the knife between her teeth and swam as fast as she could, making a bee-line toward the dancing beam of Chase's flashlight.

Between splashes, she made out Chase's muscular arms and legs climbing the cargo net. She was close. Behind her, water sloshed.

Chase stopped halfway, and reached for her. "Mom! Hurry!"

She wanted to scream to him to keep climbing, but the knife kept her jaw clenched. Finally, she reached the net. Chase helped her up, and they climbed as fast as they could. The strands of the net pulled taught, almost throwing Jessie off balance. She glanced down, and spied two Baryonyx tugging at the bottom, but the cargo net held tight. The Onyx frayed the lower strands with their teeth and claws, but they were too heavy, too clumsy to climb.

Chase made it over the slanted surface of the deck and helped her up. They both collapsed. Jessie pulled the knife from her mouth and slowly caught her breath. Her heart rate steadied.

"That was too close, Mom," Chase panted. Then he laughed.

Jessie laughed too, until she took in the damage up close.

The deck was gouged, scraped, and torn up. Whole panels were missing. The crane's wiring had been pulled out and exposed, the metal snapped under stress. Shards of solar paneling were scattered everywhere. Jessie didn't want to think about the damage, about how much business they were going to lose before they could get the insurance settled. About what the next boat would look like, or if there would even be a next boat.

Instead she just leaned back and gazed at the thousands of stars twinkling down on them.

After a breather, Jessie took the flashlight from Chase and shined it down at the hatch that led below deck. "Stay up here, Chase. Something happens to me down there, the search party will come this way tomorrow. Be sure to warn them about what's out there."

"I don't want you going down there alone, Mom."

"There's no advantage to two of us going. We have one knife and one light. I have two hands. All I have to do is find the panic box and drag it above deck."

"Then give me the knife, and I'll be the one who –"

"Chase, some day, God-willing, you will be captain, and I will have to respect your chain of command." She squeezed his shoulder. "But not today, buddy." She kissed his cheek. "I love you. Stay right here."

Jessie inched down the diagonal deck, past the missing crane, around the dented holding cage, and over missing floorboards. If she slipped and tumbled, it wouldn't be pretty.

She reached the hatch and pulled it open. Dark steps led below deck. Water sloshed and echoed. Dactyl calls carried across the lake. She spotted the surface of the water in her flashlight beam, lapping at the bottom of the ladder. She had hoped the bright orange stripe of the panic box would be floating right there, but no such luck. The water must have pushed it toward the back corner.

She crept down the jagged, metal steps. The compartment was half underwater. Tools, a fire extinguisher, and kitchen utensils from the galley floated among the debris. Jessie spotted Gunner's khaki hat.

She closed her eyes for a moment and took a deep, controlled breath. *They knew the risks of being out here. We all do,* she thought. Still, she couldn't help but feel responsible. All this time, she had stayed focused on Chase. Now her son was safe for the moment, and they were gone.

Jessie exhaled and continued to search. A narrow rectangle with a neon orange stripe bobbed in the nook between the ceiling and the submerged hold: the panic box.

Jessie cautiously dipped her ankles and legs into the water, and waded down the slope. She held the flashlight upright, gripped the knife above water in her right hand. The floor dipped away, and she floated toward where the ceiling met the water. She reached for the handle of the panic box. Fortunately, it doubled as a flotation device, so it would be easy to pull to the ladder. Getting it topside would be harder, but one problem at a time.

She pulled the panic box toward her. A narrow snout, white bump and squinting black eye rested just behind it.

Jessie gasped and splashed away. She frantically kicked backwards, gripping the handle of the panic box tight.

The Baryonyx stirred. Water sprayed from its nostrils as it snorted at her. Long claws reached toward her.

Jessie dropped the flashlight and twisted around, yanking the floating box. She kicked frantically. Something scraped her leg, but she kept going.

She was close to the ladder. The Baryonyx hissed. Her soaked boots found the floor, and she pulled the panic box behind her. She grunted and struggled over the first few steps. Yanked the panic box over the next step, and then suddenly realized, the Onyx wasn't following.

He remained nestled on the far, deep edge of the compartment. His eyes squinted. Arms tucked defensively under his neck. In the faint light of the sunken flashlight, Jessie made out the shape of the hook she had lodged in his side. This was the same animal that had attacked her at sundown. He was injured. Hiding.

At first she smiled. But the cowering beast was so unlike the monster who snapped at her earlier. Vulnerable. Pathetic.

Part of Jessie wanted to go back. To put the beast out of his misery. But that wasn't nature. And she wasn't stupid.

"Sorry, pal," she whispered. "You're on your own."

Jessie started to lug the panic box up, step-by-step, when a massive force shook the *Challenger*. The entire vessel lurched to the starboard side. The water below deck sloshed. The injured Baryonyx dunked further below deck.

"Mom, stay down!" Chase was sliding down the deck, swiftly making his way around overturned objects.

The *Challenger* was hit a second time, from the front. Wood splintered. Beams cracked. Then the bow started tilting down. Chase crawled into the passageway. Huge clawed hands curled around the edges of the deck. A loud snarl vibrated the air.

The *Challenger* continued to lean forward. The big dinosaur was putting its full weight on the forward deck. It had to weigh as much as the *Challenger* itself.

Chase huddled with her at the base of the ladder, now practically horizontal. Finally, the forward deck snapped. A series of ear-splitting cracks thundered as the front of the *Challenger* broke off. A huge splash sounded. The predator climbed over the wrecked deck and loomed above them.

Chase hadn't been exaggerating. And Jessie's guess had been correct.

"Spinosaurus," she whispered. They had them on the Southern Islands, but she'd never heard of one this far north before. At a glance, she could almost mistake it for an incredibly oversized Baryonyx, but the towering back sail, supported by sharp, rigid spines was unmistakable.

Chase tensed up next to her. She handed him her knife. "Get behind me, buddy. Watch your back, there's a wounded Onyx under the water back there."

Jessie unbuckled and flipped open the panic box: two pulse rifles, two shock prods, a row of solar cells, flares, first aid kit, radio. Everything was intact. She handed Chase a shock prod. "Check the charge! Cover the water behind us!"

An electric hum sounded over her shoulder.

The Spinosaurus tore at what remained of the upper-deck with his three-clawed hands. He snarled and shredded the wood. His huge crocodile snout pushed forward and sniffed toward the hatch. The *Challenger* strained under his weight. Water sloshed below them. Hot, foul breath washed over them.

You found a snack here last night, Jessie thought. *Why not try again, right?* She began to assemble the rifle. The Spinosaurus climbed further over the ruined *Challenger*, his weight shifted, and the lower half started sinking forward. Water trickled down the ladder.

"We're going under!" Chase shouted.

"Sit tight." Jessie remained calm. She finished assembling the rifle, then inched up the steps.

"Mom!" Chase whispered. "You're too close!"

"I have one good shot, buddy!" She checked the battery. Full charge. A hint of ozone filled the air as she flicked off the safety. The pulse rifle hummed.

The Spinosaurus craned his neck down. Banana-sized teeth inched toward the passageway. His nostrils flared.

Gunner and the crew had been shooting at an unknown, hitting its side, the sail, she thought. *Well-insulated places, extremities. They riled him up.* But Jessie knew that on the highest setting, a well-placed hit could drive even the biggest ones away.

Just like with Onyx on the water, it wasn't about size. It was about accuracy.

"Come on," Jessie whispered. "Open wide."

The Spinosaurus reared back. His enormous hands dug at the bulkheads. Everything shook. Debris rained from overhead. Water gushed through the open hatch. Jessie dropped her rifle as the whole vessel lurched again. Water splashed up from below deck. Chase called to her.

Jessie's head throbbed, the wound on her back suddenly seared with pain, but she retrieved the rifle and got back into position.

The Spinosaurus stooped, snarled, and roared, rattling the bulkheads, stinging Jessie's eardrums. His fleshy pink mouth was fully exposed. Jessie charged a shot on the highest setting. An electric blue beam pulsed and split through the back of its throat like a bolt of lightning. For a moment, the air smelled like burning tires.

The Spinosaurus gave a loud, scratchy call. He reared away from the hatch. More of the demolished *Challenger* splintered and cracked as he retreated. A huge splash of water sounded, and the stern swiftly tilted to its original position. Water drained back down the ladder.

Jessie glimpsed the Spinosaur's shadowy sail and muscular tail slipping back into the lake. The animal roared in frustration a few more times, its noises fading into the distance.

She turned to check on Chase and found her son presenting the slack head of the wounded Onyx with one hand. His other hand was soaked in blood. He yanked the hunting knife free from the predator's throat. "I got your back, Mom."

Jessie smiled as she strapped the rifle around her chest. She pulled the radio out of the panic box then closed it back up. Chase helped her get the equipment up the ladder, and they huddled against what remained of the upper deck.

"Think it'll stay away the rest of the night?" Chase asked.

Jessie considered it. "I do," she said. In the distance, the shadowy sail glided toward the eastern half of the Narrow Lake. "That was more than just a headache I gave him. The problem is what do we do about him tomorrow? And the next day?"

Chase smiled. "Get a bigger boat."

She laughed and reached for the radio. But then she paused. Her bones ached. Her back stung. She handed the radio to her son. "I'm ready to go part time. You want to call this in, Captain Harding?"

Herland
Chapters I–II
Charlotte Perkins Gilman

Chapter I
A Not Unnatural Enterprise

THIS IS WRITTEN from memory, unfortunately. If I could have brought with me the material I so carefully prepared, this would be a very different story. Whole books full of notes, carefully copied records, firsthand descriptions, and the pictures – that's the worst loss. We had some bird's-eyes of the cities and parks; a lot of lovely views of streets, of buildings, outside and in, and some of those gorgeous gardens, and, most important of all, of the women themselves.

Nobody will ever believe how they looked. Descriptions aren't any good when it comes to women, and I never was good at descriptions anyhow. But it's got to be done somehow; the rest of the world needs to know about that country.

I haven't said where it was for fear some self-appointed missionaries, or traders, or land-greedy expansionists, will take it upon themselves to push in. They will not be wanted, I can tell them that, and will fare worse than we did if they do find it.

It began this way. There were three of us, classmates and friends – Terry O. Nicholson (we used to call him the Old Nick, with good reason), Jeff Margrave, and I, Vandyck Jennings.

We had known each other years and years, and in spite of our differences we had a good deal in common. All of us were interested in science.

Terry was rich enough to do as he pleased. His great aim was exploration. He used to make all kinds of a row because there was nothing left to explore now, only patchwork and filling in, he said. He filled in well enough – he had a lot of talents – great on mechanics and electricity. Had all kinds of boats and motorcars, and was one of the best of our airmen.

We never could have done the thing at all without Terry.

Jeff Margrave was born to be a poet, a botanist – or both – but his folks persuaded him to be a doctor instead. He was a good one, for his age, but his real interest was in what he loved to call "the wonders of science."

As for me, sociology's my major. You have to back that up with a lot of other sciences, of course. I'm interested in them all.

Terry was strong on facts – geography and meteorology and those; Jeff could beat him any time on biology, and I didn't care what it was they talked about, so long as it connected with human life, somehow. There are few things that don't.

We three had a chance to join a big scientific expedition. They needed a doctor, and that gave Jeff an excuse for dropping his just opening practice; they needed Terry's experience, his machine, and his money; and as for me, I got in through Terry's influence.

The expedition was up among the thousand tributaries and enormous hinterland of a great river, up where the maps had to be made, savage dialects studied, and all manner of strange flora and fauna expected.

But this story is not about that expedition. That was only the merest starter for ours.

My interest was first roused by talk among our guides. I'm quick at languages, know a good many, and pick them up readily. What with that and a really good interpreter we took with us, I made out quite a few legends and folk myths of these scattered tribes.

And as we got farther and farther upstream, in a dark tangle of rivers, lakes, morasses, and dense forests, with here and there an unexpected long spur running out from the big mountains beyond, I noticed that more and more of these savages had a story about a strange and terrible Woman Land in the high distance.

"Up yonder," "Over there," "Way up" – was all the direction they could offer, but their legends all agreed on the main point – that there was this strange country where no men lived – only women and girl children.

None of them had ever seen it. It was dangerous, deadly, they said, for any man to go there. But there were tales of long ago, when some brave investigator had seen it – a Big Country, Big Houses, Plenty People – All Women.

Had no one else gone? Yes – a good many – but they never came back. It was no place for men – of that they seemed sure.

I told the boys about these stories, and they laughed at them. Naturally I did myself. I knew the stuff that savage dreams are made of.

But when we had reached our farthest point, just the day before we all had to turn around and start for home again, as the best of expeditions must in time, we three made a discovery.

The main encampment was on a spit of land running out into the main stream, or what we thought was the main stream. It had the same muddy color we had been seeing for weeks past, the same taste.

I happened to speak of that river to our last guide, a rather superior fellow with quick, bright eyes.

He told me that there was another river – "over there, short river, sweet water, red and blue."

I was interested in this and anxious to see if I had understood, so I showed him a red and blue pencil I carried, and asked again.

Yes, he pointed to the river, and then to the southwestward. "River – good water – red and blue."

Terry was close by and interested in the fellow's pointing.

"What does he say, Van?"

I told him.

Terry blazed up at once.

"Ask him how far it is."

The man indicated a short journey; I judged about two hours, maybe three.

"Let's go," urged Terry. "Just us three. Maybe we can really find something. May be cinnabar in it."

"May be indigo," Jeff suggested, with his lazy smile.

It was early yet; we had just breakfasted; and leaving word that we'd be back before night, we got away quietly, not wishing to be thought too gullible if we failed, and secretly hoping to have some nice little discovery all to ourselves.

It was a long two hours, nearer three. I fancy the savage could have done it alone much quicker. There was a desperate tangle of wood and water and a swampy patch we never should have found our way across alone. But there was one, and I could see Terry, with compass and notebook, marking directions and trying to place landmarks.

We came after a while to a sort of marshy lake, very big, so that the circling forest looked quite low and dim across it. Our guide told us that boats could go from there to our camp – but "long way – all day."

This water was somewhat clearer than that we had left, but we could not judge well from the margin. We skirted it for another half hour or so, the ground growing firmer as we advanced, and presently we turned the corner of a wooded promontory and saw a quite different country – a sudden view of mountains, steep and bare.

"One of those long easterly spurs," Terry said appraisingly. "May be hundreds of miles from the range. They crop out like that."

Suddenly we left the lake and struck directly toward the cliffs. We heard running water before we reached it, and the guide pointed proudly to his river.

It was short. We could see where it poured down a narrow vertical cataract from an opening in the face of the cliff. It was sweet water. The guide drank eagerly and so did we.

"That's snow water," Terry announced. "Must come from way back in the hills."

But as to being red and blue – it was greenish in tint. The guide seemed not at all surprised. He hunted about a little and showed us a quiet marginal pool where there were smears of red along the border; yes, and of blue.

Terry got out his magnifying glass and squatted down to investigate.

"Chemicals of some sort – I can't tell on the spot. Look to me like dyestuffs. Let's get nearer," he urged, "up there by the fall."

We scrambled along the steep banks and got close to the pool that foamed and boiled beneath the falling water. Here we searched the border and found traces of color beyond dispute. More – Jeff suddenly held up an unlooked-for trophy.

It was only a rag, a long, raveled fragment of cloth. But it was a well-woven fabric, with a pattern, and of a clear scarlet that the water had not faded. No savage tribe that we had heard of made such fabrics.

The guide stood serenely on the bank, well pleased with our excitement.

"One day blue – one day red – one day green," he told us, and pulled from his pouch another strip of bright-hued cloth.

"Come down," he said, pointing to the cataract. "Woman Country – up there."

Then we were interested. We had our rest and lunch right there and pumped the man for further information. He could tell us only what the others had – a land of women – no men – babies, but all girls. No place for men – dangerous. Some had gone to see – none had come back.

I could see Terry's jaw set at that. No place for men? Dangerous? He looked as if he might shin up the waterfall on the spot. But the guide would not hear of going up, even if there had been any possible method of scaling that sheer cliff, and we had to get back to our party before night.

"They might stay if we told them," I suggested.

But Terry stopped in his tracks. "Look here, fellows," he said. "This is our find. Let's not tell those cocky old professors. Let's go on home with 'em, and then come back – just us – have a little expedition of our own."

We looked at him, much impressed. There was something attractive to a bunch of unattached young men in finding an undiscovered country of a strictly Amazonian nature.

Of course we didn't believe the story – but yet!

"There is no such cloth made by any of these local tribes," I announced, examining those rags with great care. "Somewhere up yonder they spin and weave and dye – as well as we do."

"That would mean a considerable civilization, Van. There couldn't be such a place – and not known about."

"Oh, well, I don't know. What's that old republic up in the Pyrenees somewhere – Andorra? Precious few people know anything about that, and it's been minding its own business for a thousand years. Then there's Montenegro – splendid little state – you could lose a dozen Montenegroes up and down these great ranges."

We discussed it hotly all the way back to camp. We discussed it with care and privacy on the voyage home. We discussed it after that, still only among ourselves, while Terry was making his arrangements.

He was hot about it. Lucky he had so much money – we might have had to beg and advertise for years to start the thing, and then it would have been a matter of public amusement – just sport for the papers.

But T.O. Nicholson could fix up his big steam yacht, load his specially-made big motorboat aboard, and tuck in a 'dissembled' biplane without any more notice than a snip in the society column.

We had provisions and preventives and all manner of supplies. His previous experience stood him in good stead there. It was a very complete little outfit.

We were to leave the yacht at the nearest safe port and go up that endless river in our motorboat, just the three of us and a pilot; then drop the pilot when we got to that last stopping place of the previous party, and hunt up that clear water stream ourselves.

The motorboat we were going to leave at anchor in that wide shallow lake. It had a special covering of fitted armor, thin but strong, shut up like a clamshell.

"Those natives can't get into it, or hurt it, or move it," Terry explained proudly. "We'll start our flier from the lake and leave the boat as a base to come back to."

"If we come back," I suggested cheerfully.

"'Fraid the ladies will eat you?" he scoffed.

"We're not so sure about those ladies, you know," drawled Jeff. "There may be a contingent of gentlemen with poisoned arrows or something."

"You don't need to go if you don't want to," Terry remarked drily.

"Go? You'll have to get an injunction to stop me!" Both Jeff and I were sure about that.

But we did have differences of opinion, all the long way.

An ocean voyage is an excellent time for discussion. Now we had no eavesdroppers, we could loll and loaf in our deck chairs and talk and talk – there was nothing else to do. Our absolute lack of facts only made the field of discussion wider.

"We'll leave papers with our consul where the yacht stays," Terry planned. "If we don't come back in – say a month – they can send a relief party after us."

"A punitive expedition," I urged. "If the ladies do eat us we must make reprisals."

"They can locate that last stopping place easy enough, and I've made a sort of chart of that lake and cliff and waterfall."

"Yes, but how will they get up?" asked Jeff.

"Same way we do, of course. If three valuable American citizens are lost up there, they will follow somehow – to say nothing of the glittering attractions of that fair land – let's call it 'Feminisia,'" he broke off.

"You're right, Terry. Once the story gets out, the river will crawl with expeditions and the airships rise like a swarm of mosquitoes." I laughed as I thought of it. "We've made a great mistake not to let Mr. Yellow Press in on this. Save us! What headlines!"

"Not much!" said Terry grimly. "This is our party. We're going to find that place alone."

"What are you going to do with it when you do find it – if you do?" Jeff asked mildly.

Jeff was a tender soul. I think he thought that country – if there was one – was just blossoming with roses and babies and canaries and tidies, and all that sort of thing.

And Terry, in his secret heart, had visions of a sort of sublimated summer resort – just Girls and Girls and Girls – and that he was going to be – well, Terry was popular among women even when there were other men around, and it's not to be wondered at that he had pleasant dreams of what might happen. I could see it in his eyes as he lay there, looking at the long blue rollers slipping by, and fingering that impressive mustache of his.

But I thought – then – that I could form a far clearer idea of what was before us than either of them.

"You're all off, boys," I insisted. "If there is such a place – and there does seem some foundation for believing it – you'll find it's built on a sort of matriarchal principle, that's all. The men have a separate cult of their own, less socially developed than the women, and make them an annual visit – a sort of wedding call. This is a condition known to have existed – here's just a survival. They've got some peculiarly isolated valley or tableland up there, and their primeval customs have survived. That's all there is to it."

"How about the boys?" Jeff asked.

"Oh, the men take them away as soon as they are five or six, you see."

"And how about this danger theory all our guides were so sure of?"

"Danger enough, Terry, and we'll have to be mighty careful. Women of that stage of culture are quite able to defend themselves and have no welcome for unseasonable visitors."

We talked and talked.

And with all my airs of sociological superiority I was no nearer than any of them.

It was funny though, in the light of what we did find, those extremely clear ideas of ours as to what a country of women would be like. It was no use to tell ourselves and one another that all this was idle speculation. We were idle and we did speculate, on the ocean voyage and the river voyage, too.

"Admitting the improbability," we'd begin solemnly, and then launch out again.

"They would fight among themselves," Terry insisted. "Women always do. We mustn't look to find any sort of order and organization."

"You're dead wrong," Jeff told him. "It will be like a nunnery under an abbess – a peaceful, harmonious sisterhood."

I snorted derision at this idea.

"Nuns, indeed! Your peaceful sisterhoods were all celibate, Jeff, and under vows of obedience. These are just women, and mothers, and where there's motherhood you don't find sisterhood – not much."

"No, sir – they'll scrap," agreed Terry. "Also we mustn't look for inventions and progress; it'll be awfully primitive."

"How about that cloth mill?" Jeff suggested.

"Oh, cloth! Women have always been spinsters. But there they stop – you'll see."

We joked Terry about his modest impression that he would be warmly received, but he held his ground.

"You'll see," he insisted. "I'll get solid with them all – and play one bunch against another. I'll get myself elected king in no time – whew! Solomon will have to take a back seat!"

"Where do we come in on that deal?" I demanded. "Aren't we Viziers or anything?"

"Couldn't risk it," he asserted solemnly. "You might start a revolution – probably would. No, you'll have to be beheaded, or bowstrung – or whatever the popular method of execution is."

"You'd have to do it yourself, remember," grinned Jeff. "No husky black slaves and mamelukes! And there'd be two of us and only one of you – eh, Van?"

Jeff's ideas and Terry's were so far apart that sometimes it was all I could do to keep the peace between them. Jeff idealized women in the best Southern style. He was full of chivalry and sentiment, and all that. And he was a good boy; he lived up to his ideals.

You might say Terry did, too, if you can call his views about women anything so polite as ideals. I always liked Terry. He was a man's man, very much so, generous and brave and clever; but I don't think any of us in college days was quite pleased to have him with our sisters. We weren't very stringent, heavens no! But Terry was 'the limit.' Later on – why, of course a man's life is his own, we held, and asked no questions.

But barring a possible exception in favor of a not impossible wife, or of his mother, or, of course, the fair relatives of his friends, Terry's idea seemed to be that pretty women were just so much game and homely ones not worth considering.

It was really unpleasant sometimes to see the notions he had.

But I got out of patience with Jeff, too. He had such rose-colored halos on his womenfolks. I held a middle ground, highly scientific, of course, and used to argue learnedly about the physiological limitations of the sex.

We were not in the least 'advanced' on the woman question, any of us, then.

So we joked and disputed and speculated, and after an interminable journey, we got to our old camping place at last.

It was not hard to find the river, just poking along that side till we came to it, and it was navigable as far as the lake.

When we reached that and slid out on its broad glistening bosom, with that high gray promontory running out toward us, and the straight white fall clearly visible, it began to be really exciting.

There was some talk, even then, of skirting the rock wall and seeking a possible footway up, but the marshy jungle made that method look not only difficult but dangerous.

Terry dismissed the plan sharply.

"Nonsense, fellows! We've decided that. It might take months – we haven't got the provisions. No, sir – we've got to take our chances. If we get back safe – all right. If we don't, why, we're not the first explorers to get lost in the shuffle. There are plenty to come after us."

So we got the big biplane together and loaded it with our scientifically compressed baggage: the camera, of course; the glasses; a supply of concentrated food. Our pockets were magazines of small necessities, and we had our guns, of course – there was no knowing what might happen.

Up and up and up we sailed, way up at first, to get "the lay of the land" and make note of it.

Out of that dark green sea of crowding forest this high-standing spur rose steeply. It ran back on either side, apparently, to the far-off white-crowned peaks in the distance, themselves probably inaccessible.

"Let's make the first trip geographical," I suggested. "Spy out the land, and drop back here for more gasoline. With your tremendous speed we can reach that range and back all right. Then we can leave a sort of map on board – for that relief expedition."

"There's sense in that," Terry agreed. "I'll put off being king of Ladyland for one more day."

So we made a long skirting voyage, turned the point of the cape which was close by, ran up one side of the triangle at our best speed, crossed over the base where it left the higher mountains, and so back to our lake by moonlight.

"That's not a bad little kingdom," we agreed when it was roughly drawn and measured. We could tell the size fairly by our speed. And from what we could see of the sides – and that icy ridge at the back end – "It's a pretty enterprising savage who would manage to get into it," Jeff said.

Of course we had looked at the land itself – eagerly, but we were too high and going too fast to see much. It appeared to be well forested about the edges, but in the interior there were wide plains, and everywhere parklike meadows and open places.

There were cities, too; that I insisted. It looked – well, it looked like any other country – a civilized one, I mean.

We had to sleep after that long sweep through the air, but we turned out early enough next day, and again we rose softly up the height till we could top the crowning trees and see the broad fair land at our pleasure.

"Semitropical. Looks like a first-rate climate. It's wonderful what a little height will do for temperature." Terry was studying the forest growth.

"Little height! Is that what you call little?" I asked. Our instruments measured it clearly. We had not realized the long gentle rise from the coast perhaps.

"Mighty lucky piece of land, I call it," Terry pursued. "Now for the folks – I've had enough scenery."

So we sailed low, crossing back and forth, quartering the country as we went, and studying it. We saw – I can't remember now how much of this we noted then and how much was supplemented by our later knowledge, but we could not help seeing this much, even on that excited day – a land in a state of perfect cultivation, where even the forests looked as if they were cared for; a land that looked like an enormous park, only it was even more evidently an enormous garden.

"I don't see any cattle," I suggested, but Terry was silent. We were approaching a village.

I confess that we paid small attention to the clean, well-built roads, to the attractive architecture, to the ordered beauty of the little town. We had our glasses out; even Terry, setting his machine for a spiral glide, clapped the binoculars to his eyes.

They heard our whirring screw. They ran out of the houses – they gathered in from the fields, swift-running light figures, crowds of them. We stared and stared until it was almost too late to catch the levers, sweep off and rise again; and then we held our peace for a long run upward.

"Gosh!" said Terry, after a while.

"Only women there – and children," Jeff urged excitedly.

"But they look – why, this is a *civilized* country!" I protested. "There must be men."

"Of course there are men," said Terry. "Come on, let's find 'em."

He refused to listen to Jeff's suggestion that we examine the country further before we risked leaving our machine.

"There's a fine landing place right there where we came over," he insisted, and it was an excellent one – a wide, flat-topped rock, overlooking the lake, and quite out of sight from the interior.

"They won't find this in a hurry," he asserted, as we scrambled with the utmost difficulty down to safer footing. "Come on, boys – there were some good lookers in that bunch."

Of course it was unwise of us.

It was quite easy to see afterward that our best plan was to have studied the country more fully before we left our swooping airship and trusted ourselves to mere foot service. But we were three young men. We had been talking about this country for over a year, hardly believing that there was such a place, and now – we were in it.

It looked safe and civilized enough, and among those upturned, crowding faces, though some were terrified enough, there was great beauty – on that we all agreed.

"Come on!" cried Terry, pushing forward. "Oh, come on! Here goes for Herland!"

Chapter II
Rash Advances

NOT MORE than ten or fifteen miles we judged it from our landing rock to that last village. For all our eagerness we thought it wise to keep to the woods and go carefully.

Even Terry's ardor was held in check by his firm conviction that there were men to be met, and we saw to it that each of us had a good stock of cartridges.

"They may be scarce, and they may be hidden away somewhere – some kind of a matriarchate, as Jeff tells us; for that matter, they may live up in the mountains yonder and keep the women in this part of the country – sort of a national harem! But there are men somewhere – didn't you see the babies?"

We had all seen babies, children big and little, everywhere that we had come near enough to distinguish the people. And though by dress we could not be sure of all the grown persons, still there had not been one man that we were certain of.

"I always liked that Arab saying, 'First tie your camel and then trust in the Lord,'" Jeff murmured; so we all had our weapons in hand, and stole cautiously through the forest. Terry studied it as we progressed.

"Talk of civilization," he cried softly in restrained enthusiasm. "I never saw a forest so petted, even in Germany. Look, there's not a dead bough – the vines are trained – actually! And see here" – he stopped and looked about him, calling Jeff's attention to the kinds of trees.

They left me for a landmark and made a limited excursion on either side.

"Food-bearing, practically all of them," they announced returning. "The rest, splendid hardwood. Call this a forest? It's a truck farm!"

"Good thing to have a botanist on hand," I agreed. "Sure there are no medicinal ones? Or any for pure ornament?"

As a matter of fact they were quite right. These towering trees were under as careful cultivation as so many cabbages. In other conditions we should have found those woods full of fair foresters and fruit gatherers; but an airship is a conspicuous object, and by no means quiet – and women are cautious.

All we found moving in those woods, as we started through them, were birds, some gorgeous, some musical, all so tame that it seemed almost to contradict our theory of cultivation – at least until we came upon occasional little glades, where carved stone seats and tables stood in the shade beside clear fountains, with shallow bird baths always added.

"They don't kill birds, and apparently they do kill cats," Terry declared. "*Must* be men here. Hark!"

We had heard something: something not in the least like a birdsong, and very much like a suppressed whisper of laughter – a little happy sound, instantly smothered. We stood like so many pointers, and then used our glasses, swiftly, carefully.

"It couldn't have been far off," said Terry excitedly. "How about this big tree?"

There was a very large and beautiful tree in the glade we had just entered, with thick wide-spreading branches that sloped out in lapping fans like a beech or pine. It was trimmed underneath some twenty feet up, and stood there like a huge umbrella, with circling seats beneath.

"Look," he pursued. "There are short stumps of branches left to climb on. There's someone up that tree, I believe."

We stole near, cautiously.

"Look out for a poisoned arrow in your eye," I suggested, but Terry pressed forward, sprang up on the seat-back, and grasped the trunk. "In my heart, more likely," he answered. "Gee! Look, boys!"

We rushed close in and looked up. There among the boughs overhead was something – more than one something – that clung motionless, close to the great trunk at first, and then, as one and all we started up the tree, separated into three swift-moving figures and fled upward. As we climbed we could catch glimpses of them scattering above us. By the time we had reached about as far as three men together dared push, they had left the main trunk and moved outward, each one balanced on a long branch that dipped and swayed beneath the weight.

We paused uncertain. If we pursued further, the boughs would break under the double burden. We might shake them off, perhaps, but none of us was so inclined. In the soft dappled light of these high regions, breathless with our rapid climb, we rested awhile, eagerly studying our objects of pursuit; while they in turn, with no more terror than a set of frolicsome children in a game of tag, sat as lightly as so many big bright birds on their precarious perches and frankly, curiously, stared at us.

"Girls!" whispered Jeff, under his breath, as if they might fly if he spoke aloud.

"Peaches!" added Terry, scarcely louder. "Peacherinos – apricot-nectarines! Whew!"

They were girls, of course, no boys could ever have shown that sparkling beauty, and yet none of us was certain at first.

We saw short hair, hatless, loose, and shining; a suit of some light firm stuff, the closest of tunics and kneebreeches, met by trim gaiters. As bright and smooth as parrots and as unaware of danger, they swung there before us, wholly at ease, staring as we stared, till first one, and then all of them burst into peals of delighted laughter.

Then there was a torrent of soft talk tossed back and forth; no savage sing-song, but clear musical fluent speech.

We met their laughter cordially, and doffed our hats to them, at which they laughed again, delightedly.

Then Terry, wholly in his element, made a polite speech, with explanatory gestures, and proceeded to introduce us, with pointing finger. "Mr. Jeff Margrave," he said clearly; Jeff bowed as gracefully as a man could in the fork of a great limb. "Mr. Vandyck Jennings" – I also tried to make an effective salute and nearly lost my balance.

Then Terry laid his hand upon his chest – a fine chest he had, too, and introduced himself; he was braced carefully for the occasion and achieved an excellent obeisance.

Again they laughed delightedly, and the one nearest me followed his tactics.

"Celis," she said distinctly, pointing to the one in blue; "Alima" – the one in rose; then, with a vivid imitation of Terry's impressive manner, she laid a firm delicate hand on her gold-green jerkin – "Ellador." This was pleasant, but we got no nearer.

"We can't sit here and learn the language," Terry protested. He beckoned to them to come nearer, most winningly – but they gaily shook their heads. He suggested, by signs, that we all go down together; but again they shook their heads, still merrily. Then Ellador clearly indicated that we should go down, pointing to each and all of us, with unmistakable firmness; and further seeming to imply by the sweep of a lithe arm that we not only go downward, but go away altogether – at which we shook our heads in turn.

"Have to use bait," grinned Terry. "I don't know about you fellows, but I came prepared." He produced from an inner pocket a little box of purple velvet, that opened with a snap – and out of it he drew a long sparkling thing, a necklace of big varicolored stones that would have been worth a million if real ones. He held it up, swung it, glittering in the sun, offered it first to one, then to another, holding it out as far as he could reach toward the girl nearest him. He stood braced in the fork, held firmly by one hand – the other, swinging his bright temptation, reached far out along the bough, but not quite to his full stretch.

She was visibly moved, I noted, hesitated, spoke to her companions. They chattered softly together, one evidently warning her, the other encouraging. Then, softly and slowly, she drew nearer. This was Alima, a tall long-limbed lass, well-knit and evidently both strong and agile. Her eyes were splendid, wide, fearless, as free from suspicion as a child's who has never been rebuked. Her interest was more that of an intent boy playing a fascinating game than of a girl lured by an ornament.

The others moved a bit farther out, holding firmly, watching. Terry's smile was irreproachable, but I did not like the look in his eyes – it was like a creature about to spring. I could already see it happen – the dropped necklace, the sudden clutching hand, the girl's sharp cry as he seized her and drew her in. But it didn't happen. She made a timid reach with her right hand for the gay swinging thing – he held it a little nearer – then, swift as light, she seized it from him with her left, and dropped on the instant to the bough below.

He made his snatch, quite vainly, almost losing his position as his hand clutched only air; and then, with inconceivable rapidity, the three bright creatures were gone. They dropped from the ends of the big boughs to those below, fairly pouring themselves off the tree, while we climbed downward as swiftly as we could. We heard their vanishing gay laughter, we saw them fleeting away in the wide open reaches of the forest, and gave chase, but we might as well have chased wild antelopes; so we stopped at length somewhat breathless.

"No use," gasped Terry. "They got away with it. My word! The men of this country must be good sprinters!"

"Inhabitants evidently arboreal," I grimly suggested. "Civilized and still arboreal – peculiar people."

"You shouldn't have tried that way," Jeff protested. "They were perfectly friendly; now we've scared them."

But it was no use grumbling, and Terry refused to admit any mistake. "Nonsense," he said. "They expected it. Women like to be run after. Come on, let's get to that town; maybe we'll find them there. Let's see, it was in this direction and not far from the woods, as I remember."

When we reached the edge of the open country we reconnoitered with our field glasses. There it was, about four miles off, the same town, we concluded, unless, as Jeff ventured, they all had pink houses. The broad green fields and closely cultivated gardens sloped away at our feet, a long easy slant, with good roads winding pleasantly here and there, and narrower paths besides.

"Look at that!" cried Jeff suddenly. "There they go!"

Sure enough, close to the town, across a wide meadow, three bright-hued figures were running swiftly.

"How could they have got that far in this time? It can't be the same ones," I urged. But through the glasses we could identify our pretty tree-climbers quite plainly, at least by costume.

Terry watched them, we all did for that matter, till they disappeared among the houses. Then he put down his glass and turned to us, drawing a long breath. "Mother of Mike, boys – what Gorgeous Girls! To climb like that! To run like that! And afraid of nothing. This country suits me all right. Let's get ahead."

"Nothing venture, nothing have," I suggested, but Terry preferred "Faint heart ne'er won fair lady."

We set forth in the open, walking briskly. "If there are any men, we'd better keep an eye out," I suggested, but Jeff seemed lost in heavenly dreams, and Terry in highly practical plans.

"What a perfect road! What a heavenly country! See the flowers, will you?"

This was Jeff, always an enthusiast; but we could agree with him fully.

The road was some sort of hard manufactured stuff, sloped slightly to shed rain, with every curve and grade and gutter as perfect as if it were Europe's best. "No men, eh?" sneered Terry. On either side a double row of trees shaded the footpaths; between the trees bushes or vines, all fruit-bearing, now and then seats and little wayside fountains; everywhere flowers.

"We'd better import some of these ladies and set 'em to parking the United States," I suggested. "Mighty nice place they've got here." We rested a few moments by one of the fountains, tested the fruit that looked ripe, and went on, impressed, for all our gay bravado by the sense of quiet potency which lay about us.

Here was evidently a people highly skilled, efficient, caring for their country as a florist cares for his costliest orchids. Under the soft brilliant blue of that clear sky, in the pleasant shade of those endless rows of trees, we walked unharmed, the placid silence broken only by the birds.

Presently there lay before us at the foot of a long hill the town or village we were aiming for. We stopped and studied it.

Jeff drew a long breath. "I wouldn't have believed a collection of houses could look so lovely," he said.

"They've got architects and landscape gardeners in plenty, that's sure," agreed Terry.

I was astonished myself. You see, I come from California, and there's no country lovelier, but when it comes to towns –! I have often groaned at home to see the offensive mess man made in the face of nature, even though I'm no art sharp, like Jeff. But this place! It was built mostly of a sort of dull rose-colored stone, with here and there some clear white houses; and it lay abroad among the green groves and gardens like a broken rosary of pink coral.

"Those big white ones are public buildings evidently," Terry declared. "This is no savage country, my friend. But no men? Boys, it behooves us to go forward most politely."

The place had an odd look, more impressive as we approached. "It's like an exposition." "It's too pretty to be true." "Plenty of palaces, but where are the homes?" "Oh there are little ones enough – but –." It certainly was different from any towns we had ever seen.

"There's no dirt," said Jeff suddenly. "There's no smoke," he added after a little.

"There's no noise," I offered; but Terry snubbed me – "That's because they are laying low for us; we'd better be careful how we go in there."

Nothing could induce him to stay out, however, so we walked on.

Everything was beauty, order, perfect cleanness, and the pleasantest sense of home over it all. As we neared the center of the town the houses stood thicker, ran together as it were, grew into rambling palaces grouped among parks and open squares, something as college buildings stand in their quiet greens.

And then, turning a corner, we came into a broad paved space and saw before us a band of women standing close together in even order, evidently waiting for us.

We stopped a moment and looked back. The street behind was closed by another band, marching steadily, shoulder to shoulder. We went on – there seemed no other way to go – and presently found ourselves quite surrounded by this close-massed multitude, women, all of them, but –

They were not young. They were not old. They were not, in the girl sense, beautiful. They were not in the least ferocious. And yet, as I looked from face to face, calm, grave, wise, wholly unafraid, evidently assured and determined, I had the funniest feeling – a very early feeling – a feeling that I traced back and back in memory until I caught up with it at last. It was that sense of being hopelessly in the wrong that I had so often felt in early youth when my short legs' utmost effort failed to overcome the fact that I was late to school.

Jeff felt it too; I could see he did. We felt like small boys, very small boys, caught doing mischief in some gracious lady's house. But Terry showed no such consciousness. I saw his quick eyes darting here and there, estimating numbers, measuring distances, judging chances of escape. He examined the close ranks about us, reaching back far on every side, and murmured softly to me, "Every one of 'em over forty as I'm a sinner."

Yet they were not old women. Each was in the full bloom of rosy health, erect, serene, standing sure-footed and light as any pugilist. They had no weapons, and we had, but we had no wish to shoot.

"I'd as soon shoot my aunts," muttered Terry again. "What do they want with us anyhow? They seem to mean business." But in spite of that businesslike aspect, he determined to try his favorite tactics. Terry had come armed with a theory.

He stepped forward, with his brilliant ingratiating smile, and made low obeisance to the women before him. Then he produced another tribute, a broad soft scarf of filmy texture, rich in color and pattern, a lovely thing, even to my eye, and offered it with a deep bow to the tall unsmiling woman who seemed to head the ranks before him. She took it with a gracious nod of acknowledgment, and passed it on to those behind her.

He tried again, this time bringing out a circlet of rhinestones, a glittering crown that should have pleased any woman on earth. He made a brief address, including Jeff and me as partners in his enterprise, and with another bow presented this. Again his gift was accepted and, as before, passed out of sight.

"If they were only younger," he muttered between his teeth. "What on earth is a fellow to say to a regiment of old Colonels like this?"

In all our discussions and speculations we had always unconsciously assumed that the women, whatever else they might be, would be young. Most men do think that way, I fancy.

'Woman' in the abstract is young, and, we assume, charming. As they get older they pass off the stage, somehow, into private ownership mostly, or out of it altogether. But these good ladies were very much on the stage, and yet any one of them might have been a grandmother.

We looked for nervousness – there was none.

For terror, perhaps – there was none.

For uneasiness, for curiosity, for excitement – and all we saw was what might have been a vigilance committee of women doctors, as cool as cucumbers, and evidently meaning to take us to task for being there.

Six of them stepped forward now, one on either side of each of us, and indicated that we were to go with them. We thought it best to accede, at first anyway, and marched along, one of these close at each elbow, and the others in close masses before, behind, on both sides.

A large building opened before us, a very heavy thick-walled impressive place, big, and old-looking; of gray stone, not like the rest of the town.

"This won't do!" said Terry to us, quickly. "We mustn't let them get us in this, boys. All together, now –"

We stopped in our tracks. We began to explain, to make signs pointing away toward the big forest – indicating that we would go back to it – at once.

It makes me laugh, knowing all I do now, to think of us three boys – nothing else; three audacious impertinent boys – butting into an unknown country without any sort of a guard or defense. We seemed to think that if there were men we could fight them, and if there were only women – why, they would be no obstacles at all.

Jeff, with his gentle romantic old-fashioned notions of women as clinging vines. Terry, with his clear decided practical theories that there were two kinds of women – those he wanted and those he didn't; Desirable and Undesirable was his demarcation. The latter as a large class, but negligible – he had never thought about them at all.

And now here they were, in great numbers, evidently indifferent to what he might think, evidently determined on some purpose of their own regarding him, and apparently well able to enforce their purpose.

We all thought hard just then. It had not seemed wise to object to going with them, even if we could have; our one chance was friendliness – a civilized attitude on both sides.

But once inside that building, there was no knowing what these determined ladies might do to us. Even a peaceful detention was not to our minds, and when we named it imprisonment it looked even worse.

So we made a stand, trying to make clear that we preferred the open country. One of them came forward with a sketch of our flier, asking by signs if we were the aerial visitors they had seen.

This we admitted.

They pointed to it again, and to the outlying country, in different directions – but we pretended we did not know where it was, and in truth we were not quite sure and gave a rather wild indication of its whereabouts.

Again they motioned us to advance, standing so packed about the door that there remained but the one straight path open. All around us and behind they were massed solidly – there was simply nothing to do but go forward – or fight.

We held a consultation.

"I never fought with women in my life," said Terry, greatly perturbed, "but I'm not going in there. I'm not going to be – herded in – as if we were in a cattle chute."

"We can't fight them, of course," Jeff urged. "They're all women, in spite of their nondescript clothes; nice women, too; good strong sensible faces. I guess we'll have to go in."

"We may never get out, if we do," I told them. "Strong and sensible, yes; but I'm not so sure about the good. Look at those faces!"

They had stood at ease, waiting while we conferred together, but never relaxing their close attention.

Their attitude was not the rigid discipline of soldiers; there was no sense of compulsion about them. Terry's term of a 'vigilance committee' was highly descriptive. They had just the aspect of sturdy burghers, gathered hastily to meet some common need or peril, all moved by precisely the same feelings, to the same end.

Never, anywhere before, had I seen women of precisely this quality. Fishwives and market women might show similar strength, but it was coarse and heavy. These were merely athletic – light and powerful. College professors, teachers, writers – many women showed similar intelligence but often wore a strained nervous look, while these were as calm as cows, for all their evident intellect.

We observed pretty closely just then, for all of us felt that it was a crucial moment.

The leader gave some word of command and beckoned us on, and the surrounding mass moved a step nearer.

"We've got to decide quick," said Terry.

"I vote to go in," Jeff urged. But we were two to one against him and he loyally stood by us. We made one more effort to be let go, urgent, but not imploring. In vain.

"Now for a rush, boys!" Terry said. "And if we can't break 'em, I'll shoot in the air."

Then we found ourselves much in the position of the suffragette trying to get to the Parliament buildings through a triple cordon of London police.

The solidity of those women was something amazing. Terry soon found that it was useless, tore himself loose for a moment, pulled his revolver, and fired upward. As they caught at it, he fired again – we heard a cry –

Instantly each of us was seized by five women, each holding arm or leg or head; we were lifted like children, straddling helpless children, and borne onward, wriggling indeed, but most ineffectually.

We were borne inside, struggling manfully, but held secure most womanfully, in spite of our best endeavors.

So carried and so held, we came into a high inner hall, gray and bare, and were brought before a majestic gray-haired woman who seemed to hold a judicial position.

There was some talk, not much, among them, and then suddenly there fell upon each of us at once a firm hand holding a wetted cloth before mouth and nose – an order of swimming sweetness – anesthesia.

The complete and unabridged text is available online, from *flametreepublishing.com/extras*

King Solomon's Mines

Chapters VIII–XIII

H. Rider Haggard

[Publisher's Note: At this point in the story Allan Quatermain and his friends Sir Henry Curtis and Captain Good have been travelling for a while, looking for Sir Henry's brother who was last seen in King Solomon's Mines. They enter Kukuanaland with Scragga, son of the great king Twala; and Infadoos, son of Kafa who was once king of the Kukuana people.]

Chapter VIII
We Enter Kukuanaland

ALL THAT AFTERNOON we travelled along the magnificent roadway, which trended steadily in a north-westerly direction. Infadoos and Scragga walked with us, but their followers marched about one hundred paces ahead.

"Infadoos," I said at length, "who made this road?"

"It was made, my lord, of old time, none know how or when, not even the wise woman Gagool, who has lived for generations. We are not old enough to remember its making. None can fashion such roads now, but the king suffers no grass to grow upon it."

"And whose are the writings on the wall of the caves through which we have passed on the road?" I asked, referring to the Egyptian-like sculptures that we had seen.

"My lord, the hands that made the road wrote the wonderful writings. We know not who wrote them."

"When did the Kukuana people come into this country?"

"My lord, the race came down here like the breath of a storm ten thousand thousand moons ago, from the great lands which lie there beyond," and he pointed to the north. "They could travel no further because of the high mountains which ring in the land, so say the old voices of our fathers that have descended to us the children, and so says Gagool, the wise woman, the smeller out of witches," and again he pointed to the snow-clad peaks. "The country, too, was good, so they settled here and grew strong and powerful, and now our numbers are like the sea sand, and when Twala the king calls up his regiments their plumes cover the plain so far as the eye of man can reach."

"And if the land is walled in with mountains, who is there for the regiments to fight with?"

"Nay, my lord, the country is open there towards the north, and now and again warriors sweep down upon us in clouds from a land we know not, and we slay them. It is the third part of the life of a man since there was a war. Many thousands died in it, but we destroyed those who came to eat us up. So since then there has been no war."

"Your warriors must grow weary of resting on their spears, Infadoos."

"My lord, there was one war, just after we destroyed the people that came down upon us, but it was a civil war; dog ate dog."

"How was that?"

"My lord the king, my half-brother, had a brother born at the same birth, and of the same woman. It is not our custom, my lord, to suffer twins to live; the weaker must always die. But the mother of the king hid away the feebler child, which was born the last, for her heart yearned over it, and that child is Twala the king. I am his younger brother, born of another wife."

"Well?"

"My lord, Kafa, our father, died when we came to manhood, and my brother Imotu was made king in his place, and for a space reigned and had a son by his favourite wife. When the babe was three years old, just after the great war, during which no man could sow or reap, a famine came upon the land, and the people murmured because of the famine, and looked round like a starved lion for something to rend. Then it was that Gagool, the wise and terrible woman, who does not die, made a proclamation to the people, saying, 'The king Imotu is no king.' And at the time Imotu was sick with a wound, and lay in his kraal not able to move.

"Then Gagool went into a hut and led out Twala, my half-brother, and twin brother to the king, whom she had hidden among the caves and rocks since he was born, and stripping the '*moocha*' (waist-cloth) off his loins, showed the people of the Kukuanas the mark of the sacred snake coiled round his middle, wherewith the eldest son of the king is marked at birth, and cried out loud, 'Behold your king whom I have saved for you even to this day!'

"Now the people being mad with hunger, and altogether bereft of reason and the knowledge of truth, cried out – '*The king! The king!*' but I knew that it was not so, for Imotu my brother was the elder of the twins, and our lawful king. Then just as the tumult was at its height Imotu the king, though he was very sick, crawled from his hut holding his wife by the hand, and followed by his little son Ignosi – that is, by interpretation, the Lightning.

"'What is this noise?' he asked. 'Why cry ye *The king! The king!*'

"Then Twala, his twin brother, born of the same woman, and in the same hour, ran to him, and taking him by the hair, stabbed him through the heart with his knife. And the people being fickle, and ever ready to worship the rising sun, clapped their hands and cried, '*Twala is king!* Now we know that Twala is king!'"

"And what became of Imotu's wife and her son Ignosi? Did Twala kill them too?"

"Nay, my lord. When she saw that her lord was dead the queen seized the child with a cry and ran away. Two days afterward she came to a kraal very hungry, and none would give her milk or food, now that her lord the king was dead, for all men hate the unfortunate. But at nightfall a little child, a girl, crept out and brought her corn to eat, and she blessed the child, and went on towards the mountains with her boy before the sun rose again, and there she must have perished, for none have seen her since, nor the child Ignosi."

"Then if this child Ignosi had lived he would be the true king of the Kukuana people?"

"That is so, my lord; the sacred snake is round his middle. If he lives he is king; but, alas! He is long dead."

"See, my lord," and Infadoos pointed to a vast collection of huts surrounded by a fence, which was in its turn encircled by a great ditch, that lay on the plain beneath us.

"That is the kraal where the wife of Imotu was last seen with the child Ignosi. It is there that we shall sleep tonight, if, indeed," he added doubtfully, "my lords sleep at all upon this earth."

"When we are among the Kukuanas, my good friend Infadoos, we do as the Kukuanas do," I said majestically, and turned round quickly to address Good, who was tramping along sullenly behind, his mind fully occupied with unsatisfactory attempts to prevent his flannel shirt from flapping in the evening breeze. To my astonishment I butted into Umbopa, who was walking along immediately behind me, and very evidently had been listening with the greatest interest to my conversation with Infadoos. The expression on his face was most curious, and gave me the idea of a man who was struggling with partial success to bring something long ago forgotten back into his mind.

All this while we had been pressing on at a good rate towards the undulating plain beneath us. The mountains we had crossed now loomed high above our heads, and Sheba's Breasts were veiled modestly in diaphanous wreaths of mist. As we went the country grew more and more lovely. The vegetation was luxuriant, without being tropical; the sun was bright and warm, but not burning; and a gracious breeze blew softly along the odorous slopes of the mountains. Indeed, this new land was little less than an earthly paradise; in beauty, in natural wealth, and in climate I have never seen its like. The Transvaal is a fine country, but it is nothing to Kukuanaland.

So soon as we started Infadoos had despatched a runner to warn the people of the kraal, which, by the way, was in his military command, of our arrival. This man had departed at an extraordinary speed, which Infadoos informed me he would keep up all the way, as running was an exercise much practised among his people.

The result of this message now became apparent. When we arrived within two miles of the kraal we could see that company after company of men were issuing from its gates and marching towards us.

Sir Henry laid his hand upon my arm, and remarked that it looked as though we were going to meet with a warm reception. Something in his tone attracted Infadoos' attention.

"Let not my lords be afraid," he said hastily, "for in my breast there dwells no guile. This regiment is one under my command, and comes out by my orders to greet you."

I nodded easily, though I was not quite easy in my mind.

About half a mile from the gates of this kraal is a long stretch of rising ground sloping gently upwards from the road, and here the companies formed. It was a splendid sight to see them, each company about three hundred strong, charging swiftly up the rise, with flashing spears and waving plumes, to take their appointed place. By the time we reached the slope twelve such companies, or in all three thousand six hundred men, had passed out and taken up their positions along the road.

Presently we came to the first company, and were able to gaze in astonishment on the most magnificent set of warriors that I have ever seen. They were all men of mature age, mostly veterans of about forty, and not one of them was under six feet in height, whilst many stood six feet three or four. They wore upon their heads heavy black plumes of Sakaboola feathers, like those which adorned our guides. About their waists and beneath the right knees were bound circlets of white ox tails, while in their left hands they carried round shields measuring about twenty inches across. These shields are very curious. The framework is made of an iron plate beaten out thin, over which is stretched milk-white ox-hide.

The weapons that each man bore were simple, but most effective, consisting of a short and very heavy two-edged spear with a wooden shaft, the blade being about six inches across at the widest part. These spears are not used for throwing but like the Zulu '*bangwan*,' or stabbing assegai, are for close quarters only, when the wound inflicted by them is terrible. In addition to his *bangwan* every man carried three large and heavy knives, each knife weighing about two pounds. One knife was fixed in the ox-tail girdle, and the other two at the back of the round shield. These knives, which are called '*tollas*' by the Kukuanas, take the place of the throwing assegai of the Zulus. The Kukuana warriors can cast them with great accuracy to a distance of fifty yards, and it is their custom on charging to hurl a volley of them at the enemy as they come to close quarters.

Each company remained still as a collection of bronze statues till we were opposite to it, when at a signal given by its commanding officer, who, distinguished by a leopard skin cloak, stood some paces in front, every spear was raised into the air, and from three hundred throats sprang forth with a sudden roar the royal salute of '*Koom*.' Then, so soon as we had passed, the company formed up behind us and followed us towards the kraal, till at last the whole regiment of the 'Greys' – so called from their white shields – the crack corps of the Kukuana people, was marching in our rear with a tread that shook the ground.

At length, branching off from Solomon's Great Road, we came to the wide fosse surrounding the kraal, which is at least a mile round, and fenced with a strong palisade of piles formed of the trunks of trees. At the gateway this fosse is spanned by a primitive drawbridge, which was let down by the guard to allow us to pass in. The kraal is exceedingly well laid out. Through the centre runs a wide pathway intersected at right angles by other pathways so arranged as to cut the huts into square blocks, each block being the quarters of a company. The huts are dome-shaped, and built, like those of the Zulus, of a framework of wattle, beautifully thatched with grass; but, unlike the Zulu huts, they have doorways through which men could walk. Also they are much larger, and surrounded by a verandah about six feet wide, beautifully paved with powdered lime trodden hard.

All along each side of this wide pathway that pierces the kraal were ranged hundreds of women, brought out by curiosity to look at us. These women, for a native race, are exceedingly handsome. They are tall and graceful, and their figures are wonderfully fine. The hair, though short, is rather curly than woolly, the features are frequently aquiline, and the lips are not unpleasantly thick, as is the case among most African races. But what struck us most was their exceedingly quiet and dignified air. They were as well-bred in their way as the *habituées* of a fashionable drawing-room, and in this respect they differ from Zulu women and their cousins the Masai who inhabit the district beyond Zanzibar. Their curiosity had brought them out to see us, but they allowed no rude expressions of astonishment or savage criticism to pass their lips as we trudged wearily in front of them. Not even when old Infadoos with a surreptitious motion of the hand pointed out the crowning wonder of poor Good's 'beautiful white legs,' did they suffer the feeling of intense admiration which evidently mastered their minds to find expression. They fixed their dark eyes upon this new and snowy loveliness, for, as I think I have said, Good's skin is exceedingly white, and that was all. But it was quite enough for Good, who is modest by nature.

When we reached the centre of the kraal, Infadoos halted at the door of a large hut, which was surrounded at a distance by a circle of smaller ones.

"Enter, Sons of the Stars," he said, in a magniloquent voice, "and deign to rest awhile in our humble habitations. A little food shall be brought to you, so that ye may have no need to draw your belts tight from hunger; some honey and some milk, and an ox or two, and a few sheep; not much, my lords, but still a little food."

"It is good," said I. "Infadoos; we are weary with travelling through realms of air; now let us rest."

Accordingly we entered the hut, which we found amply prepared for our comfort. Couches of tanned skins were spread for us to lie on, and water was placed for us to wash in.

Presently we heard a shouting outside, and stepping to the door, saw a line of damsels bearing milk and roasted mealies, and honey in a pot. Behind these were some youths driving a fat young ox. We received the gifts, and then one of the young men drew the knife from his girdle and dexterously cut the ox's throat. In ten minutes it was dead, skinned, and jointed. The best of the meat was then cut off for us, and the rest, in the name of our party, I presented to the warriors round us, who took it and distributed the 'white lords' gift.'

Umbopa set to work, with the assistance of an extremely prepossessing young woman, to boil our portion in a large earthenware pot over a fire which was built outside the hut, and when it was nearly ready we sent a message to Infadoos, and asked him and Scragga, the king's son, to join us.

Presently they came, and sitting down upon little stools, of which there were several about the hut, for the Kukuanas do not in general squat upon their haunches like the Zulus, they helped us to get through our dinner. The old gentleman was most affable and polite, but it struck me that the young one regarded us with doubt. Together with the rest of the party, he had been overawed by our white appearance and by our magic properties; but it seemed to me that, on discovering that we ate, drank, and slept like other mortals, his awe was beginning to wear off, and to be replaced by a sullen suspicion – which made me feel rather uncomfortable.

In the course of our meal Sir Henry suggested to me that it might be well to try to discover if our hosts knew anything of his brother's fate, or if they had ever seen or heard of him; but, on the whole, I thought that it would be wiser to say nothing of the matter at this time. It was difficult to explain a relative lost from 'the Stars.'

After supper we produced our pipes and lit them; a proceeding which filled Infadoos and Scragga with astonishment. The Kukuanas were evidently unacquainted with the divine delights of tobacco-smoke. The herb is grown among them extensively; but, like the Zulus, they use it for snuff only, and quite failed to identify it in its new form.

Presently I asked Infadoos when we were to proceed on our journey, and was delighted to learn that preparations had been made for us to leave on the following morning, messengers having already departed to inform Twala the king of our coming.

It appeared that Twala was at his principal place, known as Loo, making ready for the great annual feast which was to be held in the first week of June. At this gathering all the regiments, with the exception of certain detachments left behind for garrison purposes, are brought up and paraded before the king; and the great annual witch-hunt, of which more by-and-by, is held.

We were to start at dawn; and Infadoos, who was to accompany us, expected that we should reach Loo on the night of the second day, unless we were detained by accident or by swollen rivers.

When they had given us this information our visitors bade us goodnight; and, having arranged to watch turn and turn about, three of us flung ourselves down and slept the sweet sleep of the weary, whilst the fourth sat up on the look-out for possible treachery.

Chapter IX
Twala the King

IT WILL NOT be necessary for me to detail at length the incidents of our journey to Loo. It took two full days' travelling along Solomon's Great Road, which pursued its even course right into the heart of Kukuanaland. Suffice it to say that as we went the country seemed to grow richer and richer, and the kraals, with their wide surrounding belts of cultivation, more and more numerous. They were all built upon the same principles as the first camp which we had reached, and were guarded by ample garrisons of troops. Indeed, in Kukuanaland, as among the Germans, the Zulus, and the Masai, every able-bodied man is a soldier, so that the whole force of the nation is available for its wars, offensive or defensive. As we travelled we were overtaken by thousands of warriors hurrying up to Loo to be present at the great annual review and festival, and more splendid troops I never saw.

At sunset on the second day, we stopped to rest awhile upon the summit of some heights over which the road ran, and there on a beautiful and fertile plain before us lay Loo itself. For a native town it is an enormous place, quite five miles round, I should say, with outlying kraals projecting from it, that serve on grand occasions as cantonments for the regiments, and a curious horseshoe-shaped hill, with which we were destined to become better acquainted, about two miles to the north. It is beautifully situated, and through the centre of the kraal, dividing it into two portions, runs a river, which appeared to be bridged in several places, the same indeed that we had seen from the slopes of Sheba's Breasts. Sixty or seventy miles away three great snow-capped mountains, placed at the points of a triangle, started out of the level plain. The conformation of these mountains is unlike that of Sheba's Breasts, being sheer and precipitous, instead of smooth and rounded.

Infadoos saw us looking at them, and volunteered a remark.

"The road ends there," he said, pointing to the mountains known among the Kukuanas as the 'Three Witches.'

"Why does it end?" I asked.

"Who knows?" he answered with a shrug; "the mountains are full of caves, and there is a great pit between them. It is there that the wise men of old time used to go to get whatever it was they came for to this country, and it is there now that our kings are buried in the Place of Death."

"What was it they came for?" I asked eagerly.

"Nay, I know not. My lords who have dropped from the Stars should know," he answered with a quick look. Evidently he knew more than he chose to say.

"Yes," I went on, "you are right, in the Stars we learn many things. I have heard, for instance, that the wise men of old came to these mountains to find bright stones, pretty playthings, and yellow iron."

"My lord is wise," he answered coldly; "I am but a child and cannot talk with my lord on such matters. My lord must speak with Gagool the old, at the king's place, who is wise even as my lord," and he went away.

So soon as he was gone I turned to the others, and pointed out the mountains. "There are Solomon's diamond mines," I said.

Umbopa was standing with them, apparently plunged in one of the fits of abstraction which were common to him, and caught my words.

"Yes, Macumazahn," he put in, in Zulu, "the diamonds are surely there, and you shall have them, since you white men are so fond of toys and money."

"How dost thou know that, Umbopa?" I asked sharply, for I did not like his mysterious ways.

He laughed. "I dreamed it in the night, white men;" then he too turned on his heel and went.

"Now what," said Sir Henry, "is our black friend driving at? He knows more than he chooses to say, that is clear. By the way, Quatermain, has he heard anything of – of my brother?"

"Nothing; he has asked everyone he has become friendly with, but they all declare that no white man has ever been seen in the country before."

"Do you suppose that he got here at all?" suggested Good; "we have only reached the place by a miracle; is it likely he could have reached it without the map?"

"I don't know," said Sir Henry gloomily, "but somehow I think that I shall find him."

Slowly the sun sank, then suddenly darkness rushed down on the land like a tangible thing. There was no breathing-space between the day and night, no soft transformation scene, for in these latitudes twilight does not exist. The change from day to night is as quick and as absolute as the change from life to death. The sun sank and the world was wreathed in shadows. But not for long, for see in the west there is a glow, then come rays of silver light, and at last the full and glorious moon lights up the plain and shoots its gleaming arrows far and wide, filling the earth with a faint refulgence.

We stood and watched the lovely sight, whilst the stars grew pale before this chastened majesty, and felt our hearts lifted up in the presence of a beauty that I cannot describe. Mine has been a rough life, but there are a few things I am thankful to have lived for, and one of them is to have seen that moon shine over Kukuanaland.

Presently our meditations were broken in upon by our polite friend Infadoos.

"If my lords are rested we will journey on to Loo, where a hut is made ready for my lords tonight. The moon is now bright, so that we shall not fall by the way."

We assented, and in an hour's time were at the outskirts of the town, of which the extent, mapped out as it was by thousands of camp fires, appeared absolutely endless. Indeed, Good, who is always fond of a bad joke, christened it 'Unlimited Loo.' Soon we came to a moat with a drawbridge, where we were met by the rattling of arms and the hoarse challenge of a sentry. Infadoos gave some password that I could not catch, which was met with a salute, and we passed on through the central street of the great grass city. After nearly half an hour's tramp, past endless lines of huts, Infadoos halted at last by the gate of a little group of huts which surrounded a small courtyard of powdered limestone, and informed us that these were to be our 'poor' quarters.

We entered, and found that a hut had been assigned to each of us. These huts were superior to any that we had yet seen, and in each was a most comfortable bed made of tanned skins, spread upon mattresses of aromatic grass. Food too was ready for us, and so soon as we had washed ourselves with water, which stood ready in earthenware jars, some young women of handsome appearance brought us roasted meats, and mealie cobs daintily served on wooden platters, and presented them to us with deep obeisances.

We ate and drank, and then, the beds having been all moved into one hut by our request, a precaution at which the amiable young ladies smiled, we flung ourselves down to sleep, thoroughly wearied with our long journey.

When we woke it was to find the sun high in the heavens, and the female attendants, who did not seem to be troubled by any false shame, already standing inside the hut, having been ordered to attend and help us to "make ready."

"Make ready, indeed," growled Good; "when one has only a flannel shirt and a pair of boots, that does not take long. I wish you would ask them for my trousers, Quatermain."

I asked accordingly, but was informed that these sacred relics had already been taken to the king, who would see us in the forenoon.

Somewhat to their astonishment and disappointment, having requested the young ladies to step outside, we proceeded to make the best toilet of which the circumstances admitted. Good even went the length of again shaving the right side of his face; the left, on which now appeared a very fair crop of whiskers, we impressed upon him he must on no account touch. As for ourselves, we were contented with a good wash and combing our hair. Sir Henry's yellow locks were now almost upon his shoulders, and he looked more like an ancient Dane than ever, while my grizzled scrub was fully an inch long, instead of half an inch, which in a general way I considered my maximum length.

By the time that we had eaten our breakfast, and smoked a pipe, a message was brought to us by no less a personage than Infadoos himself that Twala the king was ready to see us, if we would be pleased to come.

We remarked in reply that we should prefer to wait till the sun was a little higher, we were yet weary with our journey, etc., etc. It is always well, when dealing with uncivilised people, not to be in too great a hurry. They are apt to mistake politeness for awe or servility. So, although we were quite as anxious to see Twala as Twala could be to see us, we sat down and waited for an hour, employing the interval in preparing such presents as our slender stock of goods permitted – namely, the Winchester rifle which had been used by poor Ventvögel, and some beads. The rifle and ammunition we determined to present to his royal highness, and the beads were for his wives and courtiers. We had already given a few to Infadoos and Scragga, and found that they were delighted with them, never having seen such things before. At length we declared that we were ready, and guided by Infadoos, started off to the audience, Umbopa carrying the rifle and beads.

After walking a few hundred yards we came to an enclosure, something like that surrounding the huts which had been allotted to us, only fifty times as big, for it could not have covered less than six or seven acres of ground. All round the outside fence stood a row of huts, which were the habitations of the king's wives. Exactly opposite the gateway, on the further side of the open space, was a very large hut, built by itself, in which his majesty resided. All the rest was open ground; that is to say, it would have been open had it not been filled by company after company of warriors, who were mustered there to the number of seven or eight thousand. These men stood still as statues as we advanced through them, and it would be impossible to give an adequate idea of the grandeur of the spectacle which they presented, with their waving plumes, their glancing spears, and iron-backed ox-hide shields.

The space in front of the large hut was empty, but before it were placed several stools. On three of these, at a sign from Infadoos, we seated ourselves, Umbopa standing behind us. As for Infadoos, he took up a position by the door of the hut. So we waited for ten minutes or more in the midst of a dead silence, but conscious that we were the object of the concentrated gaze of some eight thousand pairs of eyes. It was a somewhat trying ordeal, but we carried it off as best we could. At length the door of the hut opened, and a gigantic figure, with a splendid tiger-skin karross flung over its shoulders, stepped out, followed by the boy Scragga, and what appeared to us to be a withered-up monkey, wrapped in a fur cloak. The figure seated itself upon a stool, Scragga took his stand behind it, and the withered-up monkey crept on all fours into the shade of the hut and squatted down.

Still there was silence.

Then the gigantic figure slipped off the karross and stood up before us, a truly alarming spectacle. It was that of an enormous man with the most entirely repulsive countenance we had ever beheld. This man's lips were as thick as a Negro's, the nose was flat, he had but one gleaming black eye, for the other was represented by a hollow in the face, and his whole expression was cruel and sensual to a degree. From the large head rose a magnificent plume of white ostrich feathers, his body was clad in a shirt of shining chain armour, whilst round the waist and right knee were the usual garnishes of white ox-tail. In his right hand was a huge spear, about the neck a thick torque of gold, and bound on the forehead shone dully a single and enormous uncut diamond.

Still there was silence; but not for long. Presently the man, whom we rightly guessed to be the king, raised the great javelin in his hand. Instantly eight thousand spears were lifted in answer, and from eight thousand throats rang out the royal salute of '*Koom*.' Three times this was repeated, and each time the earth shook with the noise, that can only be compared to the deepest notes of thunder.

"Be humble, O people," piped out a thin voice which seemed to come from the monkey in the shade, "it is the king."

"*It is the king*," boomed out the eight thousand throats in answer. "*Be humble, O people, it is the king*."

Then there was silence again – dead silence. Presently, however, it was broken. A soldier on our left dropped his shield, which fell with a clatter on to the limestone flooring.

Twala turned his one cold eye in the direction of the noise.

"Come hither, thou," he said, in a cold voice.

A fine young man stepped out of the ranks, and stood before him.

"It was thy shield that fell, thou awkward dog. Wilt thou make me a reproach in the eyes of these strangers from the Stars? What hast thou to say for thyself?"

We saw the poor fellow turn pale under his dusky skin.

"It was by chance, O Calf of the Black Cow," he murmured.

"Then it is a chance for which thou must pay. Thou hast made me foolish; prepare for death."

"I am the king's ox," was the low answer.

"Scragga," roared the king, "let me see how thou canst use thy spear. Kill me this blundering fool."

Scragga stepped forward with an ill-favoured grin, and lifted his spear. The poor victim covered his eyes with his hand and stood still. As for us, we were petrified with horror.

"Once, twice," he waved the spear, and then struck, ah! Right home – the spear stood out a foot behind the soldier's back. He flung up his hands and dropped dead. From the multitude about us rose something like a murmur, it rolled round and round, and died away. The tragedy was finished; there lay the corpse, and we had not yet realised that it had been enacted. Sir Henry sprang up and swore a great oath, then, overpowered by the sense of silence, sat down again.

"The thrust was a good one," said the king; "take him away."

Four men stepped out of the ranks, and lifting the body of the murdered man, carried it thence.

"Cover up the blood-stains, cover them up," piped out the thin voice that proceeded from the monkey-like figure; "the king's word is spoken, the king's doom is done!"

Thereupon a girl came forward from behind the hut, bearing a jar filled with powdered lime, which she scattered over the red mark, blotting it from sight.

Sir Henry meanwhile was boiling with rage at what had happened; indeed, it was with difficulty that we could keep him still.

"Sit down, for heaven's sake," I whispered; "our lives depend on it."

He yielded and remained quiet.

Twala sat silent until the traces of the tragedy had been removed, then he addressed us.

"White people," he said, "who come hither, whence I know not, and why I know not, greeting."

"Greeting, Twala, King of the Kukuanas," I answered.

"White people, whence come ye, and what seek ye?"

"We come from the Stars, ask us not how. We come to see this land."

"Ye journey from far to see a little thing. And that man with you," pointing to Umbopa, "does he also come from the Stars?"

"Even so; there are people of thy colour in the heavens above; but ask not of matters too high for thee, Twala the king."

"Ye speak with a loud voice, people of the Stars," Twala answered in a tone which I scarcely liked. "Remember that the Stars are far off, and ye are here. How if I make you as him whom they bore away?"

I laughed out loud, though there was little laughter in my heart.

"O king," I said, "be careful, walk warily over hot stones, lest thou shouldst burn thy feet; hold the spear by the handle, lest thou should cut thy hands. Touch but one hair of our heads, and destruction shall come upon thee. What, have not these" – pointing to Infadoos and Scragga, who, young villain that he was, was employed in cleaning the blood of the soldier off his spear – "told thee what manner of men we are? Hast thou seen the like of us?" and I pointed to Good, feeling quite sure that he had never seen anybody before who looked in the least like *him* as he then appeared.

"It is true, I have not," said the king, surveying Good with interest.

"Have they not told thee how we strike with death from afar?" I went on.

"They have told me, but I believe them not. Let me see you kill. Kill me a man among those who stand yonder" – and he pointed to the opposite side of the kraal – "and I will believe."

"Nay," I answered; "we shed no blood of men except in just punishment; but if thou wilt see, bid thy servants drive in an ox through the kraal gates, and before he has run twenty paces I will strike him dead."

"Nay," laughed the king, "kill me a man and I will believe."

"Good, O king, so be it," I answered coolly; "do thou walk across the open space, and before thy feet reach the gate thou shalt be dead; or if thou wilt not, send thy son Scragga" (whom at that moment it would have given me much pleasure to shoot).

On hearing this suggestion Scragga uttered a sort of howl, and bolted into the hut.

Twala frowned majestically; the suggestion did not please him.

"Let a young ox be driven in," he said.

Two men at once departed, running swiftly.

"Now, Sir Henry," said I, "do you shoot. I want to show this ruffian that I am not the only magician of the party."

Sir Henry accordingly took his "express," and made ready.

"I hope I shall make a good shot," he groaned.

"You must," I answered. "If you miss with the first barrel, let him have the second. Sight for 150 yards, and wait till the beast turns broadside on."

Then came a pause, until presently we caught sight of an ox running straight for the kraal gate. It came on through the gate, then, catching sight of the vast concourse of people, stopped stupidly, turned round, and bellowed.

"Now's your time," I whispered.

Up went the rifle.

Bang! *Thud*! And the ox was kicking on his back, shot in the ribs. The semi-hollow bullet had done its work well, and a sigh of astonishment went up from the assembled thousands.

I turned round coolly –

"Have I lied, O king?"

"Nay, white man, it is the truth," was the somewhat awed answer.

"Listen, Twala," I went on. "Thou hast seen. Now know we come in peace, not in war. See," and I held up the Winchester repeater; "here is a hollow staff that shall enable thee to kill even as we kill, only I lay this charm upon it, thou shalt kill no man with it. If thou liftest it against a man, it shall kill thee. Stay, I will show thee. Bid a soldier step forty paces and place the shaft of a spear in the ground so that the flat blade looks towards us."

In a few seconds it was done.

"Now, see, I will break yonder spear."

Taking a careful sight I fired. The bullet struck the flat of the spear, and shattered the blade into fragments.

Again the sigh of astonishment went up.

"Now, Twala, we give this magic tube to thee, and by-and-by I will show thee how to use it; but beware how thou turnest the magic of the Stars against a man of earth," and I handed him the rifle.

The king took it very gingerly, and laid it down at his feet. As he did so I observed the wizened monkey-like figure creeping from the shadow of the hut. It crept on all fours, but when it reached the place where the king sat it rose upon its feet, and throwing the furry covering from its face, revealed a most extraordinary and weird countenance. Apparently it was that of a woman of great age so shrunken that in size it seemed no larger than the face of a year-old child, although made up of a number of deep and yellow wrinkles. Set in these wrinkles was a sunken slit, that represented the mouth, beneath which the chin curved outwards to a point. There was no nose to speak of; indeed, the visage might have been taken for that of a sun-dried corpse had it not been for a pair of large black eyes, still full of fire and intelligence, which gleamed and played under the snow-white eyebrows, and the projecting parchment-coloured skull, like jewels in a charnel-house. As for the head itself, it was perfectly bare, and yellow in hue, while its wrinkled scalp moved and contracted like the hood of a cobra.

The figure to which this fearful countenance belonged, a countenance so fearful indeed that it caused a shiver of fear to pass through us as we gazed on it, stood still for a moment. Then suddenly it projected a skinny claw armed with nails nearly an inch long, and laying it on the shoulder of Twala the king, began to speak in a thin and piercing voice –

"Listen, O king! Listen, O warriors! Listen, O mountains and plains and rivers, home of the Kukuana race! Listen, O skies and sun, O rain and storm and mist! Listen, O men and women, O youths and maidens, and O ye babes unborn! Listen, all things that live and must die! Listen, all dead things that shall live again – again to die! Listen, the spirit of life is in me and I prophesy. I prophesy! I prophesy!"

The words died away in a faint wail, and dread seemed to seize upon the hearts of all who heard them, including our own. This old woman was very terrible.

"*Blood! Blood! Blood!* Rivers of blood; blood everywhere. I see it, I smell it, I taste it – it is salt! it runs red upon the ground, it rains down from the skies.

"*Footsteps! Footsteps! Footsteps!* The tread of the white man coming from afar. It shakes the earth; the earth trembles before her master.

"Blood is good, the red blood is bright; there is no smell like the smell of new-shed blood. The lions shall lap it and roar, the vultures shall wash their wings in it and shriek with joy.

"I am old! I am old! I have seen much blood; *ha, ha!* But I shall see more ere I die, and be merry. How old am I, think ye? Your fathers knew me, and *their* fathers knew me, and *their* fathers' fathers' fathers. I have seen the white man and know his desires. I am old, but the mountains are older than I. Who made the great road, tell me? Who wrote the pictures on the rocks, tell me? Who reared up the three Silent Ones yonder, that gaze across the pit, tell me?" and she pointed towards the three precipitous mountains which we had noticed on the previous night.

"Ye know not, but I know. It was a white people who were before ye are, who shall be when ye are not, who shall eat you up and destroy you. *Yea! Yea! Yea!*

"And what came they for, the White Ones, the Terrible Ones, the skilled in magic and all learning, the strong, the unswerving? What is that bright stone upon thy forehead, O king? Whose hands made the iron garments upon thy breast, O king? Ye know not, but I know. I the Old One, I the Wise One, I the *Isanusi*, the witch doctress!"

Then she turned her bald vulture-head towards us.

"What seek ye, white men of the Stars – ah, yes, of the Stars? Do ye seek a lost one? Ye shall not find him here. He is not here. Never for ages upon ages has a white foot pressed this land; never except once, and I remember that he left it but to die. Ye come for bright stones; I know it – I know it; ye shall find them when the blood is dry; but shall ye return whence ye came, or shall ye stop with me? *Ha! Ha! Ha!*

"And thou, thou with the dark skin and the proud bearing," and she pointed her skinny finger at Umbopa, "who art *thou*, and what seekest *thou*? Not stones that shine, not yellow metal that gleams, these thou leavest to 'white men from the Stars.' Methinks I know thee; methinks I can smell the smell of the blood in thy heart. Strip off the girdle –"

Here the features of this extraordinary creature became convulsed, and she fell to the ground foaming in an epileptic fit, and was carried into the hut.

The king rose up trembling, and waved his hand. Instantly the regiments began to file off, and in ten minutes, save for ourselves, the king, and a few attendants, the great space was left empty.

"White people," he said, "it passes in my mind to kill you. Gagool has spoken strange words. What say ye?"

I laughed. "Be careful, O king, we are not easy to slay. Thou hast seen the fate of the ox; wouldst thou be as the ox is?"

The king frowned. "It is not well to threaten a king."

"We threaten not, we speak what is true. Try to kill us, O king, and learn."

The great savage put his hand to his forehead and thought.

"Go in peace," he said at length. "Tonight is the great dance. Ye shall see it. Fear not that I shall set a snare for you. Tomorrow I will think."

"It is well, O king," I answered unconcernedly, and then, accompanied by Infadoos, we rose and went back to our kraal.

Chapter X
The Witch Hunt

ON REACHING OUR HUT I motioned to Infadoos to enter with us.

"Now, Infadoos," I said, "we would speak with thee."

"Let my lords say on."

"It seems to us, Infadoos, that Twala the king is a cruel man."

"It is so, my lords. Alas! The land cries out because of his cruelties. Tonight ye shall see. It is the great witch-hunt, and many will be smelt out as wizards and slain. No man's life is safe. If the king covets a man's cattle, or a man's wife, or if he fears a man that he should excite a rebellion against him, then Gagool, whom ye saw, or some of the witch-finding women whom she has taught, will smell that man out as a wizard, and he will be killed. Many must die before the moon grows pale tonight. It is ever so. Perhaps I too shall be killed. As yet I have been spared because I am skilled in war, and am beloved by the soldiers; but I know not how long I have to live. The land groans at the cruelties of Twala the king; it is wearied of him and his red ways."

"Then why is it, Infadoos, that the people do not cast him down?"

"Nay, my lords, he is the king, and if he were killed Scragga would reign in his place, and the heart of Scragga is blacker than the heart of Twala his father. If Scragga were king his yoke upon our neck would be heavier than the yoke of Twala. If Imotu had never been slain, or if Ignosi his son had lived, it might have been otherwise; but they are both dead."

"How knowest thou that Ignosi is dead?" said a voice behind us. We looked round astonished to see who spoke. It was Umbopa.

"What meanest thou, boy?" asked Infadoos; "who told thee to speak?"

"Listen, Infadoos," was the answer, "and I will tell thee a story. Years ago the king Imotu was killed in this country and his wife fled with the boy Ignosi. Is it not so?"

"It is so."

"It was said that the woman and her son died upon the mountains. Is it not so?"

"It is even so."

"Well, it came to pass that the mother and the boy Ignosi did not die. They crossed the mountains and were led by a tribe of wandering desert men across the sands beyond, till at last they came to water and grass and trees again."

"How knowest thou this?"

"Listen. They travelled on and on, many months' journey, till they reached a land where a people called the Amazulu, who also are of the Kukuana stock, live by war, and with them they tarried many years, till at length the mother died. Then the son Ignosi became a wanderer again, and journeyed into a land of wonders, where white people live, and for many more years he learned the wisdom of the white people."

"It is a pretty story," said Infadoos incredulously.

"For years he lived there working as a servant and a soldier, but holding in his heart all that his mother had told him of his own place, and casting about in his mind to find how he might journey thither to see his people and his father's house before he died. For long years he lived and waited, and at last the time came, as it ever comes to him who can wait for it, and he met some white men who would seek this unknown land, and joined himself to them. The white men started and travelled on and on, seeking for one who is lost. They crossed the burning desert, they crossed the snow-clad mountains, and at last reached the land of the Kukuanas, and there they found *thee*, O Infadoos."

"Surely thou art mad to talk thus," said the astonished old soldier.

"Thou thinkest so; see, I will show thee, O my uncle.

"*I am Ignosi, rightful king of the Kukuanas!*"

Then with a single movement Umbopa slipped off his '*moocha*' or girdle, and stood naked before us.

"Look," he said; "what is this?" and he pointed to the picture of a great snake tattooed in blue round his middle, its tail disappearing into its open mouth just above where the thighs are set into the body.

Infadoos looked, his eyes starting nearly out of his head. Then he fell upon his knees.

"*Koom! Koom!*" he ejaculated; "it is my brother's son; it is the king."

"Did I not tell thee so, my uncle? Rise; I am not yet the king, but with thy help, and with the help of these brave white men, who are my friends, I shall be. Yet the old witch Gagool was right, the land shall run with blood first, and hers shall run with it, if she has any and can die, for she killed my father with her words, and drove my mother forth. And now, Infadoos, choose thou. Wilt thou put thy hands between my hands and be my man? Wilt thou share the dangers that lie before me, and help me to overthrow this tyrant and murderer, or wilt thou not? Choose thou."

The old man put his hand to his head and thought. Then he rose, and advancing to where Umbopa, or rather Ignosi, stood, he knelt before him, and took his hand.

"Ignosi, rightful king of the Kukuanas, I put my hand between thy hands, and am thy man till death. When thou wast a babe I dandled thee upon my knees, now shall my old arm strike for thee and freedom."

"It is well, Infadoos; if I conquer, thou shalt be the greatest man in the kingdom after its king. If I fail, thou canst only die, and death is not far off from thee. Rise, my uncle."

"And ye, white men, will ye help me? What have I to offer you! The white stones! If I conquer and can find them, ye shall have as many as ye can carry hence. Will that suffice you?"

I translated this remark.

"Tell him," answered Sir Henry, "that he mistakes an Englishman. Wealth is good, and if it comes in our way we will take it; but a gentleman does not sell himself for wealth. Still, speaking for myself, I say this. I have always liked Umbopa, and so far as lies in me I will stand by him in this business. It will be very pleasant to me to try to square matters with that cruel devil Twala. What do you say, Good, and you, Quatermain?"

"Well," said Good, "to adopt the language of hyperbole, in which all these people seem to indulge, you can tell him that a row is surely good, and warms the cockles of the heart, and that so far as I am concerned I'm his boy. My only stipulation is that he allows me to wear trousers."

I translated the substance of these answers.

"It is well, my friends," said Ignosi, late Umbopa; "and what sayest thou, Macumazahn, art thou also with me, old hunter, cleverer than a wounded buffalo?"

I thought awhile and scratched my head.

"Umbopa, or Ignosi," I said, "I don't like revolutions. I am a man of peace and a bit of a coward" – here Umbopa smiled – "but, on the other hand, I stick up for my friends, Ignosi. You have stuck to us and played the part of a man, and I will stick by you. But mind you, I am a trader, and have to make my living, so I accept your offer about those diamonds in case we should ever be in a position to avail ourselves of it. Another thing: we came, as you know, to look for Incubu's (Sir Henry's) lost brother. You must help us to find him."

"That I will do," answered Ignosi. "Stay, Infadoos, by the sign of the snake about my middle, tell me the truth. Has any white man to thy knowledge set his foot within the land?"

"None, O Ignosi."

"If any white man had been seen or heard of, wouldst thou have known?"

"I should certainly have known."

"Thou hearest, Incubu," said Ignosi to Sir Henry; "he has not been here."

"Well, well," said Sir Henry, with a sigh; "there it is; I suppose that he never got so far. Poor fellow, poor fellow! So it has all been for nothing. God's will be done."

"Now for business," I put in, anxious to escape from a painful subject. "It is very well to be a king by right divine, Ignosi, but how dost thou propose to become a king indeed?"

"Nay, I know not. Infadoos, hast thou a plan?"

"Ignosi, Son of the Lightning," answered his uncle, "tonight is the great dance and witch-hunt. Many shall be smelt out and perish, and in the hearts of many others there will be grief and anguish and fury against the king Twala. When the dance is over, then I will speak to some of the great chiefs, who in turn, if I can win them over, will speak to their regiments. I shall speak to the chiefs softly at first, and bring them to see that thou art indeed the king, and I think that by tomorrow's light thou shalt have twenty thousand spears at thy command. And now I must go and think, and hear, and make ready. After the dance is done, if I am yet alive, and we are all alive, I will meet thee here, and we can talk. At the best there must be war."

At this moment our conference was interrupted by the cry that messengers had come from the king. Advancing to the door of the hut we ordered that they should be admitted, and presently three men entered, each bearing a shining shirt of chain armour, and a magnificent battle-axe.

"The gifts of my lord the king to the white men from the Stars!" said a herald who came with them.

"We thank the king," I answered; "withdraw."

The men went, and we examined the armour with great interest. It was the most wonderful chain work that either of us had ever seen. A whole coat fell together so closely that it formed a mass of links scarcely too big to be covered with both hands.

"Do you make these things in this country, Infadoos?" I asked; "they are very beautiful."

"Nay, my lord, they came down to us from our forefathers. We know not who made them, and there are but few left. None but those of royal blood may be clad in them.

They are magic coats through which no spear can pass, and those who wear them are well-nigh safe in the battle. The king is well pleased or much afraid, or he would not have sent these garments of steel. Clothe yourselves in them tonight, my lords."

The remainder of that day we spent quietly, resting and talking over the situation, which was sufficiently exciting. At last the sun went down, the thousand watch fires glowed out, and through the darkness we heard the tramp of many feet and the clashing of hundreds of spears, as the regiments passed to their appointed places to be ready for the great dance. Then the full moon shone out in splendour, and as we stood watching her rays, Infadoos arrived, clad in his war dress, and accompanied by a guard of twenty men to escort us to the dance. As he recommended, we had already donned the shirts of chain armour which the king had sent us, putting them on under our ordinary clothing, and finding to our surprise that they were neither very heavy nor uncomfortable. These steel shirts, which evidently had been made for men of a very large stature, hung somewhat loosely upon Good and myself, but Sir Henry's fitted his magnificent frame like a glove. Then strapping our revolvers round our waists, and taking in our hands the battle-axes which the king had sent with the armour, we started.

On arriving at the great kraal, where we had that morning been received by the king, we found that it was closely packed with some twenty thousand men arranged round it in regiments. These regiments were in turn divided into companies, and between each company ran a little path to allow space for the witch-finders to pass up and down. Anything more imposing than the sight that was presented by this vast and orderly concourse of armed men it is impossible to conceive. There they stood perfectly silent, and the moon poured her light upon the forest of their raised spears, upon their majestic forms, waving plumes, and the harmonious shading of their various-coloured shields. Wherever we looked were line upon line of dim faces surmounted by range upon range of shimmering spears.

"Surely," I said to Infadoos, "the whole army is here?"

"Nay, Macumazahn," he answered, "but a third of it. One third is present at this dance each year, another third is mustered outside in case there should be trouble when the killing begins, ten thousand more garrison the outposts round Loo, and the rest watch at the kraals in the country. Thou seest it is a great people."

"They are very silent," said Good; and indeed the intense stillness among such a vast concourse of living men was almost overpowering.

"What says Bougwan?" asked Infadoos.

I translated.

"Those over whom the shadow of Death is hovering are silent," he answered grimly.

"Will many be killed?"

"Very many."

"It seems," I said to the others, "that we are going to assist at a gladiatorial show arranged regardless of expense."

Sir Henry shivered, and Good said he wished that we could get out of it.

"Tell me," I asked Infadoos, "are we in danger?"

"I know not, my lords, I trust not; but do not seem afraid. If ye live through the night all may go well with you. The soldiers murmur against the king."

All this while we had been advancing steadily towards the centre of the open space, in the midst of which were placed some stools. As we proceeded we perceived another small party coming from the direction of the royal hut.

"It is the king Twala, Scragga his son, and Gagool the old; and see, with them are those who slay," said Infadoos, pointing to a little group of about a dozen gigantic and savage-looking men, armed with spears in one hand and heavy kerries in the other.

The king seated himself upon the centre stool, Gagool crouched at his feet, and the others stood behind him.

"Greeting, white lords," Twala cried, as we came up; "be seated, waste not precious time – the night is all too short for the deeds that must be done. Ye come in a good hour, and shall see a glorious show. Look round, white lords; look round," and he rolled his one wicked eye from regiment to regiment. "Can the Stars show you such a sight as this? See how they shake in their wickedness, all those who have evil in their hearts and fear the judgment of 'Heaven above.'"

"*Begin! Begin!*" piped Gagool, in her thin piercing voice; "the hyenas are hungry, they howl for food. *Begin! Begin!*"

Then for a moment there was intense stillness, made horrible by a presage of what was to come.

The king lifted his spear, and suddenly twenty thousand feet were raised, as though they belonged to one man, and brought down with a stamp upon the earth. This was repeated three times, causing the solid ground to shake and tremble. Then from a far point of the circle a solitary voice began a wailing song, of which the refrain ran something as follows: –

"*What is the lot of man born of woman?*"

Back came the answer rolling out from every throat in that vast company –

"*Death!*"

Gradually, however, the song was taken up by company after company, till the whole armed multitude were singing it, and I could no longer follow the words, except in so far as they appeared to represent various phases of human passions, fears, and joys. Now it seemed to be a love song, now a majestic swelling war chant, and last of all a death dirge ending suddenly in one heart-breaking wail that went echoing and rolling away in a volume of blood-curdling sound.

Again silence fell upon the place, and again it was broken by the king lifting his hand. Instantly we heard a pattering of feet, and from out of the masses of warriors strange and awful figures appeared running towards us. As they drew near we saw that these were women, most of them aged, for their white hair, ornamented with small bladders taken from fish, streamed out behind them. Their faces were painted in stripes of white and yellow; down their backs hung snake-skins, and round their waists rattled circlets of human bones, while each held a small forked wand in her shrivelled hand. In all there were ten of them. When they arrived in front of us they halted, and one of them, pointing with her wand towards the crouching figure of Gagool, cried out –

"Mother, old mother, we are here."

"*Good! Good! Good!*" answered that aged Iniquity. "Are your eyes keen, *Isanusis* [witch doctresses], ye seers in dark places?"

"Mother, they are keen."

"*Good! Good! Good!* Are your ears open, *Isanusis*, ye who hear words that come not from the tongue?"

"Mother, they are open."

"*Good! Good! Good!* Are your senses awake, *Isanusis* – can ye smell blood, can ye purge the land of the wicked ones who compass evil against the king and against their neighbours?

Are ye ready to do the justice of 'Heaven above,' ye whom I have taught, who have eaten of the bread of my wisdom, and drunk of the water of my magic?"

"Mother, we can."

"Then go! Tarry not, ye vultures; see, the slayers" – pointing to the ominous group of executioners behind – "make sharp their spears; the white men from afar are hungry to see. *Go!*"

With a wild yell Gagool's horrid ministers broke away in every direction, like fragments from a shell, the dry bones round their waists rattling as they ran, and headed for various points of the dense human circle. We could not watch them all, so we fixed our eyes upon the *Isanusi* nearest to us. When she came to within a few paces of the warriors she halted and began to dance wildly, turning round and round with an almost incredible rapidity, and shrieking out sentences such as "I smell him, the evil-doer!" "He is near, he who poisoned his mother!" "I hear the thoughts of him who thought evil of the king!"

Quicker and quicker she danced, till she lashed herself into such a frenzy of excitement that the foam flew in specks from her gnashing jaws, till her eyes seemed to start from her head, and her flesh to quiver visibly. Suddenly she stopped dead and stiffened all over, like a pointer dog when he scents game, and then with outstretched wand she began to creep stealthily towards the soldiers before her. It seemed to us that as she came their stoicism gave way, and that they shrank from her. As for ourselves, we followed her movements with a horrible fascination. Presently, still creeping and crouching like a dog, the *Isanusi* was before them. Then she halted and pointed, and again crept on a pace or two.

Suddenly the end came. With a shriek she sprang in and touched a tall warrior with her forked wand. Instantly two of his comrades, those standing immediately next to him, seized the doomed man, each by one arm, and advanced with him towards the king.

He did not resist, but we saw that he dragged his limbs as though they were paralysed, and that his fingers, from which the spear had fallen, were limp like those of a man newly dead.

As he came, two of the villainous executioners stepped forward to meet him. Presently they met, and the executioners turned round, looking towards the king as though for orders.

"*Kill!*" said the king.

"*Kill!*" squeaked Gagool.

"*Kill!*" re-echoed Scragga, with a hollow chuckle.

Almost before the words were uttered the horrible deed was done. One man had driven his spear into the victim's heart, and to make assurance double sure, the other had dashed out his brains with a great club.

"*One*," counted Twala the king, just like a black Madame Defarge, as Good said, and the body was dragged a few paces away and stretched out.

Hardly was the thing done before another poor wretch was brought up, like an ox to the slaughter. This time we could see, from the leopard-skin cloak which he wore, that the man was a person of rank. Again the awful syllables were spoken, and the victim fell dead.

"*Two*," counted the king.

And so the deadly game went on, till about a hundred bodies were stretched in rows behind us. I have heard of the gladiatorial shows of the Caesars, and of the Spanish bull-fights, but I take the liberty of doubting if either of them could be half so horrible as this Kukuana witch-hunt. Gladiatorial shows and Spanish bull-fights at any rate contributed to the public amusement, which certainly was not the case here. The most confirmed sensation-monger would fight shy of sensation if he knew that it was well on the cards that he would, in his own proper person, be the subject of the next 'event.'

Once we rose and tried to remonstrate, but were sternly repressed by Twala.

"Let the law take its course, white men. These dogs are magicians and evil-doers; it is well that they should die," was the only answer vouchsafed to us.

About half-past ten there was a pause. The witch-finders gathered themselves together, apparently exhausted with their bloody work, and we thought that the performance was done with. But it was not so, for presently, to our surprise, the ancient woman, Gagool, rose from her crouching position, and supporting herself with a stick, staggered off into the open space. It was an extraordinary sight to see this frightful vulture-headed old creature, bent nearly double with extreme age, gather strength by degrees, until at last she rushed about almost as actively as her ill-omened pupils. To and fro she ran, chanting to herself, till suddenly she made a dash at a tall man standing in front of one of the regiments, and touched him. As she did this a sort of groan went up from the regiment which evidently he commanded. But two of its officers seized him all the same, and brought him up for execution. We learned afterwards that he was a man of great wealth and importance, being indeed a cousin of the king.

He was slain, and Twala counted one hundred and three. Then Gagool again sprang to and fro, gradually drawing nearer and nearer to ourselves.

"Hang me if I don't believe she is going to try her games on us," ejaculated Good in horror.

"Nonsense!" said Sir Henry.

As for myself, when I saw that old fiend dancing nearer and nearer, my heart positively sank into my boots. I glanced behind us at the long rows of corpses, and shivered.

Nearer and nearer waltzed Gagool, looking for all the world like an animated crooked stick or comma, her horrid eyes gleaming and glowing with a most unholy lustre.

Nearer she came, and yet nearer, every creature in that vast assemblage watching her movements with intense anxiety. At last she stood still and pointed.

"Which is it to be?" asked Sir Henry to himself.

In a moment all doubts were at rest, for the old hag had rushed in and touched Umbopa, alias Ignosi, on the shoulder.

"I smell him out," she shrieked. "Kill him, kill him, he is full of evil; kill him, the stranger, before blood flows from him. Slay him, O king."

There was a pause, of which I instantly took advantage.

"O king," I called out, rising from my seat, "this man is the servant of thy guests, he is their dog; whosoever sheds the blood of our dog sheds our blood. By the sacred law of hospitality I claim protection for him."

"Gagool, mother of the witch-finders, has smelt him out; he must die, white men," was the sullen answer.

"Nay, he shall not die," I replied; "he who tries to touch him shall die indeed."

"Seize him!" roared Twala to the executioners; who stood round red to the eyes with the blood of their victims.

They advanced towards us, and then hesitated. As for Ignosi, he clutched his spear, and raised it as though determined to sell his life dearly.

"Stand back, ye dogs!" I shouted, "if ye would see tomorrow's light. Touch one hair of his head and your king dies," and I covered Twala with my revolver. Sir Henry and Good also drew their pistols, Sir Henry pointing his at the leading executioner, who was advancing to carry out the sentence, and Good taking a deliberate aim at Gagool.

Twala winced perceptibly as my barrel came in a line with his broad chest.

"Well," I said, "what is it to be, Twala?"

Then he spoke.

"Put away your magic tubes," he said; "ye have adjured me in the name of hospitality, and for that reason, but not from fear of what ye can do, I spare him. Go in peace."

"It is well," I answered unconcernedly; "we are weary of slaughter, and would sleep. Is the dance ended?"

"It is ended," Twala answered sulkily. "Let these dead dogs," pointing to the long rows of corpses, "be flung out to the hyenas and the vultures," and he lifted his spear.

Instantly the regiments began to defile through the kraal gateway in perfect silence, a fatigue party only remaining behind to drag away the corpses of those who had been sacrificed.

Then we rose also, and making our salaam to his majesty, which he hardly deigned to acknowledge, we departed to our huts.

"Well," said Sir Henry, as we sat down, having first lit a lamp of the sort used by the Kukuanas, of which the wick is made from the fibre of a species of palm leaf, and the oil from clarified hippopotamus fat, "well, I feel uncommonly inclined to be sick."

"If I had any doubts about helping Umbopa to rebel against that infernal blackguard," put in Good, "they are gone now. It was as much as I could do to sit still while that slaughter was going on. I tried to keep my eyes shut, but they would open just at the wrong time. I wonder where Infadoos is. Umbopa, my friend, you ought to be grateful to us; your skin came near to having an air-hole made in it."

"I am grateful, Bougwan," was Umbopa's answer, when I had translated, "and I shall not forget. As for Infadoos, he will be here by-and-by. We must wait."

So we lit our pipes and waited.

Chapter XI
We Give a Sign

FOR A LONG WHILE – two hours, I should think – we sat there in silence, being too much overwhelmed by the recollection of the horrors we had seen to talk. At last, just as we were thinking of turning in – for the night drew nigh to dawn – we heard a sound of steps. Then came the challenge of a sentry posted at the kraal gate, which apparently was answered, though not in an audible tone, for the steps still advanced; and in another second Infadoos had entered the hut, followed by some half-dozen stately-looking chiefs.

"My lords," he said, "I have come according to my word. My lords and Ignosi, rightful king of the Kukuanas, I have brought with me these men," pointing to the row of chiefs, "who are great men among us, having each one of them the command of three thousand soldiers, that live but to do their bidding, under the king's. I have told them of what I have seen, and what my ears have heard. Now let them also behold the sacred snake around thee, and hear thy story, Ignosi, that they may say whether or no they will make cause with thee against Twala the king."

By way of answer Ignosi again stripped off his girdle, and exhibited the snake tattooed about him. Each chief in turn drew near and examined the sign by the dim light of the lamp, and without saying a word passed on to the other side.

Then Ignosi resumed his *moocha*, and addressing them, repeated the history he had detailed in the morning.

"Now ye have heard, chiefs," said Infadoos, when he had done, "what say ye: will ye stand by this man and help him to his father's throne, or will ye not? The land cries out against Twala, and the blood of the people flows like the waters in spring. Ye have seen tonight. Two other chiefs there were with whom I had it in my mind to speak, and where are they now? The hyenas howl over their corpses. Soon shall ye be as they are if ye strike not. Choose then, my brothers."

The eldest of the six men, a short, thick-set warrior, with white hair, stepped forward a pace and answered –

"Thy words are true, Infadoos; the land cries out. My own brother is among those who died tonight; but this is a great matter, and the thing is hard to believe. How know we that if we lift our spears it may not be for a thief and a liar? It is a great matter, I say, of which none can see the end. For of this be sure, blood will flow in rivers before the deed is done; many will still cleave to the king, for men worship the sun that still shines bright in the heavens, rather than that which has not risen. These white men from the Stars, their magic is great, and Ignosi is under the cover of their wing. If he be indeed the rightful king, let them give us a sign, and let the people have a sign, that all may see. So shall men cleave to us, knowing of a truth that the white man's magic is with them."

"Ye have the sign of the snake," I answered.

"My lord, it is not enough. The snake may have been placed there since the man's childhood. Show us a sign, and it will suffice. But we will not move without a sign."

The others gave a decided assent, and I turned in perplexity to Sir Henry and Good, and explained the situation.

"I think that I have it," said Good exultingly; "ask them to give us a moment to think."

I did so, and the chiefs withdrew. So soon as they had gone Good went to the little box where he kept his medicines, unlocked it, and took out a note-book, in the fly-leaves of which was an almanack. "Now look here, you fellows, isn't tomorrow the 4th of June?" he said.

We had kept a careful note of the days, so were able to answer that it was.

"Very good; then here we have it – '4 June, total eclipse of the moon commences at 8.15 Greenwich time, visible in Teneriffe – *South Africa*, etc.' There's a sign for you. Tell them we will darken the moon tomorrow night."

The idea was a splendid one; indeed, the only weak spot about it was a fear lest Good's almanack might be incorrect. If we made a false prophecy on such a subject, our prestige would be gone for ever, and so would Ignosi's chance of the throne of the Kukuanas.

"Suppose that the almanack is wrong," suggested Sir Henry to Good, who was busily employed in working out something on a blank page of the book.

"I see no reason to suppose anything of the sort," was his answer. "Eclipses always come up to time; at least that is my experience of them, and it especially states that this one will be visible in South Africa. I have worked out the reckonings as well as I can, without knowing our exact position; and I make out that the eclipse should begin here about ten o'clock tomorrow night, and last till half-past twelve. For an hour and a half or so there should be almost total darkness."

"Well," said Sir Henry, "I suppose we had better risk it."

I acquiesced, though doubtfully, for eclipses are queer cattle to deal with – it might be a cloudy night, for instance, or our dates might be wrong – and sent Umbopa to summon the chiefs back. Presently they came, and I addressed them thus –

"Great men of the Kukuanas, and thou, Infadoos, listen. We love not to show our powers, for to do so is to interfere with the course of nature, and to plunge the world into fear and confusion. But since this matter is a great one, and as we are angered against the king because of the slaughter we have seen, and because of the act of the *Isanusi* Gagool, who would have put our friend Ignosi to death, we have determined to break a rule, and to give such a sign as all men may see. Come hither"; and I led them to the door of the hut and pointed to the red ball of the moon. "What see ye there?"

"We see the sinking moon," answered the spokesman of the party.

"It is so. Now tell me, can any mortal man put out that moon before her hour of setting, and bring the curtain of black night down upon the land?"

The chief laughed a little at the question. "No, my lord, that no man can do. The moon is stronger than man who looks on her, nor can she vary in her courses."

"Ye say so. Yet I tell you that tomorrow night, about two hours before midnight, we will cause the moon to be eaten up for a space of an hour and half an hour. Yes, deep darkness shall cover the earth, and it shall be for a sign that Ignosi is indeed king of the Kukuanas. If we do this thing, will ye be satisfied?"

"Yea, my lords," answered the old chief with a smile, which was reflected on the faces of his companions; "*if* ye do this thing, we will be satisfied indeed."

"It shall be done; we three, Incubu, Bougwan, and Macumazahn, have said it, and it shall be done. Dost thou hear, Infadoos?"

"I hear, my lord, but it is a wonderful thing that ye promise, to put out the moon, the mother of the world, when she is at her full."

"Yet shall we do it, Infadoos."

"It is well, my lords. Today, two hours after sunset, Twala will send for my lords to witness the girls dance, and one hour after the dance begins the girl whom Twala thinks the fairest shall be killed by Scragga, the king's son, as a sacrifice to the Silent Ones, who sit and keep watch by the mountains yonder," and he pointed towards the three strange-looking peaks where Solomon's road was supposed to end. "Then let my lords darken the moon, and save the maiden's life, and the people will believe indeed."

"Ay," said the old chief, still smiling a little, "the people will believe indeed."

"Two miles from Loo," went on Infadoos, "there is a hill curved like a new moon, a stronghold, where my regiment, and three other regiments which these chiefs command, are stationed. This morning we will make a plan whereby two or three other regiments may be moved there also. Then, if in truth my lords can darken the moon, in the darkness I will take my lords by the hand and lead them out of Loo to this place, where they shall be safe, and thence we can make war upon Twala the king."

"It is good," said I. "Let leave us to sleep awhile and to make ready our magic."

Infadoos rose, and, having saluted us, departed with the chiefs.

"My friends," said Ignosi, so soon as they were gone, "can ye do this wonderful thing, or were ye speaking empty words to the captains?"

"We believe that we can do it, Umbopa – Ignosi, I mean."

"It is strange," he answered, "and had ye not been Englishmen I would not have believed it; but I have learned that English 'gentlemen' tell no lies. If we live through the matter, be sure that I will repay you."

"Ignosi," said Sir Henry, "promise me one thing."

"I will promise, Incubu, my friend, even before I hear it," answered the big man with a smile. "What is it?"

"This: that if ever you come to be king of this people you will do away with the smelling out of wizards such as we saw last night; and that the killing of men without trial shall no longer take place in the land."

Ignosi thought for a moment after I had translated this request, and then answered –

"The ways of black people are not as the ways of white men, Incubu, nor do we value life so highly. Yet I will promise. If it be in my power to hold them back, the witch-finders shall hunt no more, nor shall any man die the death without trial or judgment."

"That's a bargain, then," said Sir Henry; "and now let us get a little rest."

Thoroughly wearied out, we were soon sound asleep, and slept till Ignosi woke us about eleven o'clock. Then we rose, washed, and ate a hearty breakfast. After that we went outside the hut and walked about, amusing ourselves with examining the structure of the Kukuana huts and observing the customs of the women.

"I hope that eclipse will come off," said Sir Henry presently.

"If it does not it will soon be all up with us," I answered mournfully; "for so sure as we are living men some of those chiefs will tell the whole story to the king, and then there will be another sort of eclipse, and one that we shall certainly not like."

Returning to the hut we ate some dinner, and passed the rest of the day in receiving visits of ceremony and curiosity. At length the sun set, and we enjoyed a couple of hours of such quiet as our melancholy forebodings would allow to us. Finally, about half-past eight, a messenger came from Twala to bid us to the great annual 'dance of girls' which was about to be celebrated.

Hastily we put on the chain shirts that the king had sent us, and taking our rifles and ammunition with us, so as to have them handy in case we had to fly, as suggested by Infadoos, we started boldly enough, though with inward fear and trembling. The great space in front of the king's kraal bore a very different appearance from that which it had presented on the previous evening. In place of the grim ranks of serried warriors were company after company of Kukuana girls, not over-dressed, so far as clothing went, but each crowned with a wreath of flowers, and holding a palm leaf in one hand and a white arum lily in the other. In the centre of the open moonlit space sat Twala the king, with old Gagool at his feet, attended by Infadoos, the boy Scragga, and twelve guards. There were also present about a score of chiefs, amongst whom I recognised most of our friends of the night before.

Twala greeted us with much apparent cordiality, though I saw him fix his one eye viciously on Umbopa.

"Welcome, white men from the Stars," he said; "this is another sight from that which your eyes gazed on by the light of last night's moon, but it is not so good a sight. Girls are pleasant, and were it not for such as these," and he pointed round him, "we should none of us be here this day; but men are better. Kisses and the tender words of women are sweet, but the sound of the clashing of the spears of warriors, and the smell of men's blood, are sweeter far! Would ye have wives from among our people, white men?

If so, choose the fairest here, and ye shall have them, as many as ye will," and he paused for an answer.

As the prospect did not seem to be without attractions for Good, who, like most sailors, is of a susceptible nature, – being elderly and wise, foreseeing the endless complications that anything of the sort would involve, for women bring trouble so surely as the night follows the day, I put in a hasty answer –

"Thanks to thee, O king, but we white men wed only with white women like ourselves. Your maidens are fair, but they are not for us!"

The king laughed. "It is well. In our land there is a proverb which runs, 'Women's eyes are always bright, whatever the colour,' and another that says, 'Love her who is present, for be sure she who is absent is false to thee;' but perhaps these things are not so in the Stars. In a land where men are white all things are possible. So be it, white men; the girls will not go begging! Welcome again; and welcome, too, thou black one; if Gagool here had won her way, thou wouldst have been stiff and cold by now. It is lucky for thee that thou too camest from the Stars; ha! Ha!"

"I can kill thee before thou killest me, O king," was Ignosi's calm answer, "and thou shalt be stiff before my limbs cease to bend."

Twala started. "Thou speakest boldly, boy," he replied angrily; "presume not too far."

"He may well be bold in whose lips are truth. The truth is a sharp spear which flies home and misses not. It is a message from 'the Stars,' O king."

Twala scowled, and his one eye gleamed fiercely, but he said nothing more.

"Let the dance begin," he cried, and then the flower-crowned girls sprang forward in companies, singing a sweet song and waving the delicate palms and white lilies. On they danced, looking faint and spiritual in the soft, sad light of the risen moon; now whirling round and round, now meeting in mimic warfare, swaying, eddying here and there, coming forward, falling back in an ordered confusion delightful to witness. At last they paused, and a beautiful young woman sprang out of the ranks and began to pirouette in front of us with a grace and vigour which would have put most ballet girls to shame. At length she retired exhausted, and another took her place, then another and another, but none of them, either in grace, skill, or personal attractions, came up to the first.

When the chosen girls had all danced, the king lifted his hand.

"Which deem ye the fairest, white men?" he asked.

"The first," said I unthinkingly. Next second I regretted it, for I remembered that Infadoos had told us that the fairest woman must be offered up as a sacrifice.

"Then is my mind as your minds, and my eyes as your eyes. She is the fairest! And a sorry thing it is for her, for she must die!"

"*Ay, must die!*" piped out Gagool, casting a glance of her quick eyes in the direction of the poor girl, who, as yet ignorant of the awful fate in store for her, was standing some ten yards off in front of a company of maidens, engaged in nervously picking a flower from her wreath to pieces, petal by petal.

"Why, O king?" said I, restraining my indignation with difficulty; "the girl has danced well, and pleased us; she is fair too; it would be hard to reward her with death."

Twala laughed as he answered –

"It is our custom, and the figures who sit in stone yonder," and he pointed towards the three distant peaks, "must have their due. Did I fail to put the fairest girl to death today, misfortune would fall upon me and my house. Thus runs the prophecy of my people: 'If the king offer not a sacrifice of a fair girl, on the day of the dance of maidens, to the Old Ones who sit and watch on the mountains, then shall he fall, and his house.' Look ye, white men, my brother who reigned before me offered not the sacrifice, because of the tears of the woman, and he fell, and his house, and I reign in his stead. It is finished; she must die!" Then turning to the guards – "Bring her hither; Scragga, make sharp thy spear."

Two of the men stepped forward, and as they advanced, the girl, for the first time realising her impending fate, screamed aloud and turned to fly. But the strong hands caught her fast, and brought her, struggling and weeping, before us.

"What is thy name, girl?" piped Gagool. "What! Wilt thou not answer? Shall the king's son do his work at once?"

At this hint, Scragga, looking more evil than ever, advanced a step and lifted his great spear, and at that moment I saw Good's hand creep to his revolver. The poor girl caught the faint glint of steel through her tears, and it sobered her anguish. She ceased struggling, and clasping her hands convulsively, stood shuddering from head to foot.

"See," cried Scragga in high glee, "she shrinks from the sight of my little plaything even before she has tasted it," and he tapped the broad blade of his spear.

"If ever I get the chance you shall pay for that, you young hound!" I heard Good mutter beneath his breath.

"Now that thou art quiet, give us thy name, my dear. Come, speak out, and fear not," said Gagool in mockery.

"Oh, mother," answered the girl, in trembling accents, "my name is Foulata, of the house of Suko. Oh, mother, why must I die? I have done no wrong!"

"Be comforted," went on the old woman in her hateful tone of mockery. "Thou must die, indeed, as a sacrifice to the Old Ones who sit yonder," and she pointed to the peaks; "but it is better to sleep in the night than to toil in the daytime; it is better to die than to live, and thou shalt die by the royal hand of the king's own son."

The girl Foulata wrung her hands in anguish, and cried out aloud, "Oh, cruel! And I so young! What have I done that I should never again see the sun rise out of the night, or the stars come following on his track in the evening, that I may no more gather the flowers when the dew is heavy, or listen to the laughing of the waters? Woe is me, that I shall never see my father's hut again, nor feel my mother's kiss, nor tend the lamb that is sick! Woe is me, that no lover shall put his arm around me and look into my eyes, nor shall men children be born of me! Oh, cruel, cruel!"

And again she wrung her hands and turned her tear-stained flower-crowned face to Heaven, looking so lovely in her despair – for she was indeed a beautiful woman – that assuredly the sight of her would have melted the hearts of any less cruel than were the three fiends before us. Prince Arthur's appeal to the ruffians who came to blind him was not more touching than that of this savage girl.

But it did not move Gagool or Gagool's master, though I saw signs of pity among the guards behind, and on the faces of the chiefs; and as for Good, he gave a fierce snort of indignation, and made a motion as though to go to her assistance. With all a woman's quickness, the doomed girl interpreted what was passing in his mind, and by a sudden movement flung herself before him, and clasped his 'beautiful white legs' with her hands.

"Oh, white father from the Stars!" she cried, "throw over me the mantle of thy protection; let me creep into the shadow of thy strength, that I may be saved. Oh, keep me from these cruel men and from the mercies of Gagool!"

"All right, my hearty, I'll look after you," sang out Good in nervous Saxon. "Come, get up, there's a good girl," and he stooped and caught her hand.

Twala turned and motioned to his son, who advanced with his spear lifted.

"Now's your time," whispered Sir Henry to me; "what are you waiting for?"

"I am waiting for that eclipse," I answered; "I have had my eye on the moon for the last half-hour, and I never saw it look healthier."

"Well, you must risk it now, or the girl will be killed. Twala is losing patience."

Recognising the force of the argument, and having cast one more despairing look at the bright face of the moon, for never did the most ardent astronomer with a theory to prove await a celestial event with such anxiety, I stepped with all the dignity that I could command between the prostrate girl and the advancing spear of Scragga.

"King," I said, "it shall not be; we will not endure this thing; let the girl go in safety."

Twala rose from his seat in wrath and astonishment, and from the chiefs and serried ranks of maidens who had closed in slowly upon us in anticipation of the tragedy came a murmur of amazement.

"*Shall not be!* Thou white dog, that yappest at the lion in his cave; *shall not be!* Art thou mad? Be careful, lest this chicken's fate overtake thee, and those with thee. How canst thou save her or thyself? Who art thou that thou settest thyself between me and my will? Back, I say. Scragga, kill her! Ho, guards! Seize these men."

At his cry armed men ran swiftly from behind the hut, where they had evidently been placed beforehand.

Sir Henry, Good, and Umbopa ranged themselves alongside of me, and lifted their rifles.

"Stop!" I shouted boldly, though at the moment my heart was in my boots. "Stop! We, the white men from the Stars, say that it shall not be. Come but one pace nearer, and we will put out the moon like a wind-blown lamp, as we who dwell in her House can do, and plunge the land in darkness. Dare to disobey, and ye shall taste of our magic."

My threat produced an effect; the men halted, and Scragga stood still before us, his spear lifted.

"Hear him! Hear him!" piped Gagool; "hear the liar who says that he will put out the moon like a lamp. Let him do it, and the girl shall be spared. Yes, let him do it, or die by the girl, he and those with him."

I glanced up at the moon despairingly, and now to my intense joy and relief saw that we – or rather the almanack – had made no mistake. On the edge of the great orb lay a faint rim of shadow, while a smoky hue grew and gathered upon its bright surface. Never shall I forget that supreme, that superb moment of relief.

Then I lifted my hand solemnly towards the sky, an example which Sir Henry and Good followed, and quoted a line or two from the *Ingoldsby Legends* at it in the most impressive tones that I could command. Sir Henry followed suit with a verse out of the Old Testament, and something about Balbus building a wall, in Latin, whilst Good addressed the Queen of Night in a volume of the most classical bad language which he could think of.

Slowly the penumbra, the shadow of a shadow, crept on over the bright surface, and as it crept I heard deep gasps of fear rising from the multitude around.

"Look, O king!" I cried; "Look, Gagool! Look, chiefs and people and women, and see if the white men from the Stars keep their word, or if they be but empty liars!

"The moon grows black before your eyes; soon there will be darkness – ay, darkness in the hour of the full moon. Ye have asked for a sign; it is given to you. Grow dark, O Moon! Withdraw thy light, thou pure and holy One; bring the proud heart of usurping murderers to the dust, and eat up the world with shadows."

A groan of terror burst from the onlookers. Some stood petrified with dread, others threw themselves upon their knees and cried aloud. As for the king, he sat still and turned pale beneath his dusky skin. Only Gagool kept her courage.

"It will pass," she cried; "I have often seen the like before; no man can put out the moon; lose not heart; sit still – the shadow will pass."

"Wait, and ye shall see," I replied, hopping with excitement. "O Moon! Moon! Moon! Wherefore art thou so cold and fickle?" This appropriate quotation was from the pages of a popular romance that I chanced to have read recently, though now I come to think of it, it was ungrateful of me to abuse the Lady of the Heavens, who was showing herself to be the truest of friends to us, however she may have behaved to the impassioned lover in the novel. Then I added: "Keep it up, Good, I can't remember any more poetry. Curse away, there's a good fellow."

Good responded nobly to this tax upon his inventive faculties. Never before had I the faintest conception of the breadth and depth and height of a naval officer's objurgatory powers. For ten minutes he went on in several languages without stopping, and he scarcely ever repeated himself.

Meanwhile the dark ring crept on, while all that great assembly fixed their eyes upon the sky and stared and stared in fascinated silence. Strange and unholy shadows encroached upon the moonlight, an ominous quiet filled the place. Everything grew still as death. Slowly and in the midst of this most solemn silence the minutes sped away, and while they sped the full moon passed deeper and deeper into the shadow of the earth, as the inky segment of its circle slid in awful majesty across the lunar craters. The great pale orb seemed to draw near and to grow in size. She turned a coppery hue, then that portion of her surface which was unobscured as yet grew grey and ashen, and at length, as totality approached, her mountains and her plains were to be seen glowing luridly through a crimson gloom.

On, yet on, crept the ring of darkness; it was now more than half across the blood-red orb. The air grew thick, and still more deeply tinged with dusky crimson. On, yet on, till we could scarcely see the fierce faces of the group before us. No sound rose now from the spectators, and at last Good stopped swearing.

"The moon is dying – the white wizards have killed the moon," yelled the prince Scragga at last. "We shall all perish in the dark," and animated by fear or fury, or by both, he lifted his spear and drove it with all his force at Sir Henry's breast. But he forgot the mail shirts that the king had given us, and which we wore beneath our clothing. The steel rebounded harmless, and before he could repeat the blow Curtis had snatched the spear from his hand and sent it straight through him.

Scragga dropped dead.

At the sight, and driven mad with fear of the gathering darkness, and of the unholy shadow which, as they believed, was swallowing the moon, the companies of girls broke up in wild confusion, and ran screeching for the gateways. Nor did the panic stop there. The king himself, followed by his guards, some of the chiefs, and Gagool, who hobbled away after them with marvellous alacrity, fled for the huts, so that in another minute we ourselves, the would-be victim Foulata, Infadoos, and most of the chiefs who had interviewed us on the previous night, were left alone upon the scene, together with the dead body of Scragga, Twala's son.

"Chiefs," I said, "we have given you the sign. If ye are satisfied, let us fly swiftly to the place of which ye spoke. The charm cannot now be stopped. It will work for an hour and the half of an hour. Let us cover ourselves in the darkness."

"Come," said Infadoos, turning to go, an example which was followed by the awed captains, ourselves, and the girl Foulata, whom Good took by the arm.

Before we reached the gate of the kraal the moon went out utterly, and from every quarter of the firmament the stars rushed forth into the inky sky.

Holding each other by the hand we stumbled on through the darkness.

Chapter XII
Before the Battle

LUCKILY FOR US, Infadoos and the chiefs knew all the paths of the great town perfectly, so that we passed by side-ways unmolested, and notwithstanding the gloom we made fair progress.

For an hour or more we journeyed on, till at length the eclipse began to pass, and that edge of the moon which had disappeared the first became again visible. Suddenly, as we watched, there burst from it a silver streak of light, accompanied by a wondrous ruddy glow, which hung upon the blackness of the sky like a celestial lamp, and a wild and lovely sight it was. In another five minutes the stars began to fade, and there was sufficient light to see our whereabouts. We then discovered that we were clear of the town of Loo, and approaching a large flat-topped hill, measuring some two miles in circumference. This hill, which is of a formation common in South Africa, is not very high; indeed, its greatest elevation is scarcely more than 200 feet, but it is shaped like a horseshoe, and its sides are rather precipitous and strewn with boulders. On the grass table-land at its summit is ample camping-ground, which had been utilised as a military cantonment of no mean strength. Its ordinary garrison was one regiment of three thousand men, but as we toiled up the steep side of the mountain in the returning moonlight we perceived that there were several of such regiments encamped there.

Reaching the table-land at last, we found crowds of men roused from their sleep, shivering with fear and huddled up together in the utmost consternation at the natural phenomenon which they were witnessing. Passing through these without a word, we gained a hut in the centre of the ground, where we were astonished to find two men waiting, laden with our few goods and chattels, which of course we had been obliged to leave behind in our hasty flight.

"I sent for them," explained Infadoos; "and also for these," and he lifted up Good's long-lost trousers.

With an exclamation of rapturous delight Good sprang at them, and instantly proceeded to put them on.

"Surely my lord will not hide his beautiful white legs!" exclaimed Infadoos regretfully.

But Good persisted, and once only did the Kukuana people get the chance of seeing his beautiful legs again. Good is a very modest man. Henceforward they had to satisfy their aesthetic longings with his one whisker, his transparent eye, and his movable teeth.

Still gazing with fond remembrance at Good's trousers, Infadoos next informed us that he had commanded the regiments to muster so soon as the day broke, in order to explain to them fully the origin and circumstances of the rebellion which was decided on by the chiefs, and to introduce to them the rightful heir to the throne, Ignosi.

Accordingly, when the sun was up, the troops – in all some twenty thousand men, and the flower of the Kukuana army – were mustered on a large open space, to which we went. The men were drawn up in three sides of a dense square, and presented a magnificent spectacle. We took our station on the open side of the square, and were speedily surrounded by all the principal chiefs and officers.

These, after silence had been proclaimed, Infadoos proceeded to address. He narrated to them in vigorous and graceful language – for, like most Kukuanas of high rank, he was a born orator – the history of Ignosi's father, and of how he had been basely murdered by Twala the king, and his wife and child driven out to starve. Then he pointed out that the people suffered and groaned under Twala's cruel rule, instancing the proceedings of the previous night, when, under pretence of their being evil-doers, many of the noblest in the land had been dragged forth and wickedly done to death. Next he went on to say that the white lords from the Stars, looking down upon their country, had perceived its trouble, and determined, at great personal inconvenience, to alleviate its lot: That they had accordingly taken the real king of the Kukuanas, Ignosi, who was languishing in exile, by the hand, and led him over the mountains: That they had seen the wickedness of Twala's doings, and for a sign to the wavering, and to save the life of the girl Foulata, actually, by the exercise of their high magic, had put out the moon and slain the young fiend Scragga; and that they were prepared to stand by them, and assist them to overthrow Twala, and set up the rightful king, Ignosi, in his place.

He finished his discourse amidst a murmur of approbation. Then Ignosi stepped forward and began to speak. Having reiterated all that Infadoos his uncle had said, he concluded a powerful speech in these words: –

"O chiefs, captains, soldiers, and people, ye have heard my words. Now must ye make choice between me and him who sits upon my throne, the uncle who killed his brother, and hunted his brother's child forth to die in the cold and the night. That I am indeed the king these" – pointing to the chiefs – "can tell you, for they have seen the snake about my middle. If I were not the king, would these white men be on my side with all their magic? Tremble, chiefs, captains, soldiers, and people! Is not the darkness they have brought upon the land to confound Twala and cover our flight, darkness even in the hour of the full moon, yet before your eyes?"

"It is," answered the soldiers.

"I am the king; I say to you, I am the king," went on Ignosi, drawing up his great stature to its full, and lifting his broad-bladed battle-axe above his head. "If there be any man among you who says that it is not so, let him stand forth and I will fight him now, and his blood shall be a red token that I tell you true. Let him stand forth, I say;" and he shook the great axe till it flashed in the sunlight.

As nobody seemed inclined to respond to this heroic version of "Dilly, Dilly, come and be killed," our late henchman proceeded with his address.

"I am indeed the king, and should ye stand by my side in the battle, if I win the day ye shall go with me to victory and honour. I will give you oxen and wives, and ye shall take place of all the regiments; and if ye fall, I will fall with you.

"And behold, I give you this promise, that when I sit upon the seat of my fathers, bloodshed shall cease in the land. No longer shall ye cry for justice to find slaughter, no longer shall the witch-finder hunt you out so that ye may be slain without a cause. No man shall die save he who offends against the laws. The 'eating up' of your kraals shall cease; each one of you shall sleep secure in his own hut and fear naught, and justice shall walk blindfold throughout the land. Have ye chosen, chiefs, captains, soldiers, and people?"

"We have chosen, O king," came back the answer.

"It is well. Turn your heads and see how Twala's messengers go forth from the great town, east and west, and north and south, to gather a mighty army to slay me and you, and these my friends and protectors. Tomorrow, or perchance the next day, he will come against us with all who are faithful to him. Then I shall see the man who is indeed my man, the man who fears not to die for his cause; and I tell you that he shall not be forgotten in the time of spoil. I have spoken, O chiefs, captains, soldiers, and people. Now go to your huts and make you ready for war."

There was a pause, till presently one of the chiefs lifted his hand, and out rolled the royal salute, '*Koom.*' It was a sign that the soldiers accepted Ignosi as their king. Then they marched off in battalions.

Half an hour afterwards we held a council of war, at which all the commanders of regiments were present. It was evident to us that before very long we should be attacked in overwhelming force. Indeed, from our point of vantage on the hill we could see troops mustering, and runners going forth from Loo in every direction, doubtless to summon soldiers to the king's assistance. We had on our side about twenty thousand men, composed of seven of the best regiments in the country. Twala, so Infadoos and the chiefs calculated, had at least thirty to thirty-five thousand on whom he could rely at present assembled in Loo, and they thought that by midday on the morrow he would be able to gather another five thousand or more to his aid. It was, of course, possible that some of his troops would desert and come over to us, but it was not a contingency which could be reckoned on. Meanwhile, it was clear that active preparations were being made by Twala to subdue us. Already strong bodies of armed men were patrolling round and round the foot of the hill, and there were other signs also of coming assault.

Infadoos and the chiefs, however, were of opinion that no attack would take place that day, which would be devoted to preparation and to the removal of every available means of the moral effect produced upon the minds of the soldiery by the supposed magical darkening of the moon. The onslaught would be on the morrow, they said, and they proved to be right.

Meanwhile, we set to work to strengthen the position in all ways possible. Almost every man was turned out, and in the course of the day, which seemed far too short, much was done. The paths up the hill – that was rather a sanatorium than a fortress, being used generally as the camping place of regiments suffering from recent service in unhealthy portions of the country – were carefully blocked with masses of stones, and every other approach was made as impregnable as time would allow. Piles of boulders were collected at various spots to be rolled down upon an advancing enemy, stations were appointed to the different regiments, and all preparation was made which our joint ingenuity could suggest.

Just before sundown, as we rested after our toil, we perceived a small company of men advancing towards us from the direction of Loo, one of whom bore a palm leaf in his hand for a sign that he came as a herald.

As he drew near, Ignosi, Infadoos, one or two chiefs and ourselves, went down to the foot of the mountain to meet him. He was a gallant-looking fellow, wearing the regulation leopard-skin cloak.

"Greeting!" he cried, as he came; "the king's greeting to those who make unholy war against the king; the lion's greeting to the jackals that snarl around his heels."

"Speak," I said.

"These are the king's words. Surrender to the king's mercy ere a worse thing befall you. Already the shoulder has been torn from the black bull, and the king drives him bleeding about the camp **(footnote 1)**."

"What are Twala's terms?" I asked from curiosity.

"His terms are merciful, worthy of a great king. These are the words of Twala, the one-eyed, the mighty, the husband of a thousand wives, lord of the Kukuanas, keeper of the Great Road (Solomon's Road), beloved of the Strange Ones who sit in silence at the mountains yonder (the Three Witches), Calf of the Black Cow, Elephant whose tread shakes the earth, Terror of the evil-doer, Ostrich whose feet devour the desert, huge One, black One, wise One, king from generation to generation! These are the words of Twala: 'I will have mercy and be satisfied with a little blood. One in every ten shall die, the rest shall go free; but the white man Incubu, who slew Scragga my son, and the black man his servant, who pretends to my throne, and Infadoos my brother, who brews rebellion against me, these shall die by torture as an offering to the Silent Ones.' Such are the merciful words of Twala."

After consulting with the others a little, I answered him in a loud voice, so that the soldiers might hear, thus –

"Go back, thou dog, to Twala, who sent thee, and say that we, Ignosi, veritable king of the Kukuanas, Incubu, Bougwan, and Macumazahn, the wise ones from the Stars, who make dark the moon, Infadoos, of the royal house, and the chiefs, captains, and people here gathered, make answer and say, 'That we will not surrender; that before the sun has gone down twice, Twala's corpse shall stiffen at Twala's gate, and Ignosi, whose father Twala slew, shall reign in his stead.' Now go, ere we whip thee away, and beware how thou dost lift a hand against such as we are."

The herald laughed loudly. "Ye frighten not men with such swelling words," he cried out. "Show yourselves as bold tomorrow, O ye who darken the moon. Be bold, fight, and be merry, before the crows pick your bones till they are whiter than your faces. Farewell; perhaps we may meet in the fight; fly not to the Stars, but wait for me, I pray, white men." With this shaft of sarcasm he retired, and almost immediately the sun sank.

That night was a busy one, for weary as we were, so far as was possible by the moonlight all preparations for the morrow's fight were continued, and messengers were constantly coming and going from the place where we sat in council. At last, about an hour after midnight, everything that could be done was done, and the camp, save for the occasional challenge of a sentry, sank into silence. Sir Henry and I, accompanied by Ignosi and one of the chiefs, descended the hill and made a round of the pickets. As we went, suddenly, from all sorts of unexpected places, spears gleamed out in the moonlight, only to vanish again when we uttered the password. It was clear to us that none were sleeping at their posts. Then we returned, picking our way warily through thousands of sleeping warriors, many of whom were taking their last earthly rest.

The moonlight flickering along their spears, played upon their features and made them ghastly; the chilly night wind tossed their tall and hearse-like plumes. There they lay in wild confusion, with arms outstretched and twisted limbs; their stern, stalwart forms looking weird and unhuman in the moonlight.

"How many of these do you suppose will be alive at this time tomorrow?" asked Sir Henry.

I shook my head and looked again at the sleeping men, and to my tired and yet excited imagination it seemed as though Death had already touched them. My mind's eye singled out those who were sealed to slaughter, and there rushed in upon my heart a great sense of the mystery of human life, and an overwhelming sorrow at its futility and sadness. Tonight these thousands slept their healthy sleep, tomorrow they, and many others with them, ourselves perhaps among them, would be stiffening in the cold; their wives would be widows, their children fatherless, and their place know them no more for ever. Only the old moon would shine on serenely, the night wind would stir the grasses, and the wide earth would take its rest, even as it did eons before we were, and will do eons after we have been forgotten.

Yet man dies not whilst the world, at once his mother and his monument, remains. His name is lost, indeed, but the breath he breathed still stirs the pine-tops on the mountains, the sound of the words he spoke yet echoes on through space; the thoughts his brain gave birth to we have inherited today; his passions are our cause of life; the joys and sorrows that he knew are our familiar friends – the end from which he fled aghast will surely overtake us also!

Truly the universe is full of ghosts, not sheeted churchyard spectres, but the inextinguishable elements of individual life, which having once been, can never *die*, though they blend and change, and change again for ever.

All sorts of reflections of this nature passed through my mind – for as I grow older I regret to say that a detestable habit of thinking seems to be getting a hold of me – while I stood and stared at those grim yet fantastic lines of warriors, sleeping, as their saying goes, 'upon their spears.'

"Curtis," I said, "I am in a condition of pitiable fear."

Sir Henry stroked his yellow beard and laughed, as he answered –

"I have heard you make that sort of remark before, Quatermain."

"Well, I mean it now. Do you know, I very much doubt if one of us will be alive tomorrow night. We shall be attacked in overwhelming force, and it is quite a chance if we can hold this place."

"We'll give a good account of some of them, at any rate. Look here, Quatermain, this business is nasty, and one with which, properly speaking, we ought not to be mixed up, but we are in for it, so we must make the best of our job. Speaking personally, I had rather be killed fighting than any other way, and now that there seems little chance of our finding my poor brother, it makes the idea easier to me. But fortune favours the brave, and we may succeed. Anyway, the battle will be awful, and having a reputation to keep up, we shall need to be in the thick of the thing."

He made this last remark in a mournful voice, but there was a gleam in his eye which belied its melancholy. I have an idea Sir Henry Curtis actually likes fighting.

After this we went to sleep for a couple of hours or so.

Just about dawn we were awakened by Infadoos, who came to say that great activity was to be observed in Loo, and that parties of the king's skirmishers were driving in our outposts.

We rose and dressed ourselves for the fray, each putting on his chain armour shirt, for which garments at the present juncture we felt exceedingly thankful. Sir Henry went the whole length about the matter, and dressed himself like a native warrior. "When you are in Kukuanaland, do as the Kukuanas do," he remarked, as he drew the shining steel over his broad breast, which it fitted like a glove. Nor did he stop there. At his request Infadoos had provided him with a complete set of native war uniform. Round his throat he fastened the leopard-skin cloak of a commanding officer, on his brows he bound the plume of black ostrich feathers worn only by generals of high rank, and about his middle a magnificent *moocha* of white ox-tails. A pair of sandals, a leglet of goat's hair, a heavy battle-axe with a rhinoceros-horn handle, a round iron shield covered with white ox-hide, and the regulation number of *tollas*, or throwing-knives, made up his equipment, to which, however, he added his revolver. The dress was, no doubt, a savage one, but I am bound to say that I seldom saw a finer sight than Sir Henry Curtis presented in this guise. It showed off his magnificent physique to the greatest advantage, and when Ignosi arrived presently, arrayed in a similar costume, I thought to myself that I had never before seen two such splendid men.

As for Good and myself, the armour did not suit us nearly so well. To begin with, Good insisted upon keeping on his new-found trousers, and a stout, short gentleman with an eye-glass, and one half of his face shaved, arrayed in a mail shirt, carefully tucked into a very seedy pair of corduroys, looks more remarkable than imposing. In my case, the chain shirt being too big for me, I put it on over all my clothes, which caused it to bulge in a somewhat ungainly fashion. I discarded my trousers, however, retaining only my veldtschoons, having determined to go into battle with bare legs, in order to be the lighter for running, in case it became necessary to retire quickly. The mail coat, a spear, a shield, that I did not know how to use, a couple of *tollas*, a revolver, and a huge plume, which I pinned into the top of my shooting hat, in order to give a bloodthirsty finish to my appearance, completed my modest equipment. In addition to all these articles, of course we had our rifles, but as ammunition was scarce, and as they would be useless in case of a charge, we arranged that they should be carried behind us by bearers.

When at length we had equipped ourselves, we swallowed some food hastily, and then started out to see how things were going on. At one point in the table-land of the mountain, there was a little koppie of brown stone, which served the double purpose of head-quarters and of a conning tower. Here we found Infadoos surrounded by his own regiment, the Greys, which was undoubtedly the finest in the Kukuana army, and the same that we had first seen at the outlying kraal. This regiment, now three thousand five hundred strong, was being held in reserve, and the men were lying down on the grass in companies, and watching the king's forces creep out of Loo in long ant-like columns. There seemed to be no end to the length of these columns – three in all, and each of them numbering, as we judged, at least eleven or twelve thousand men.

As soon as they were clear of the town the regiments formed up. Then one body marched off to the right, one to the left, and the third came on slowly towards us.

"Ah," said Infadoos, "they are going to attack us on three sides at once."

This seemed rather serious news, for our position on the top of the mountain, which measured a mile and a half in circumference, being an extended one, it was important to us to concentrate our comparatively small defending force as much as possible. But since it was impossible for us to dictate in what way we should be assailed, we had to make the best of it, and accordingly sent orders to the various regiments to prepare to receive the separate onslaughts.

Footnote 1. This cruel custom is not confined to the Kukuanas, but is by no means uncommon amongst African tribes on the occasion of the outbreak of war or any other important public event. – A.Q.

Chapter XIII
The Attack

SLOWLY, AND WITHOUT the slightest appearance of haste or excitement, the three columns crept on. When within about five hundred yards of us, the main or centre column halted at the root of a tongue of open plain which ran up into the hill, to give time to the other divisions to circumvent our position, which was shaped more or less in the form of a horse-shoe, with its two points facing towards the town of Loo. The object of this manoeuvre was that the threefold assault should be delivered simultaneously.

"Oh, for a gatling!" groaned Good, as he contemplated the serried phalanxes beneath us. "I would clear that plain in twenty minutes."

"We have not got one, so it is no use yearning for it; but suppose you try a shot, Quatermain," said Sir Henry. "See how near you can go to that tall fellow who appears to be in command. Two to one you miss him, and an even sovereign, to be honestly paid if ever we get out of this, that you don't drop the bullet within five yards."

This piqued me, so, loading the express with solid ball, I waited till my friend walked some ten yards out from his force, in order to get a better view of our position, accompanied only by an orderly; then, lying down and resting the express on a rock, I covered him. The rifle, like all expresses, was only sighted to three hundred and fifty yards, so to allow for the drop in trajectory I took him half-way down the neck, which ought, I calculated, to find him in the chest. He stood quite still and gave me every opportunity, but whether it was the excitement or the wind, or the fact of the man being a long shot, I don't know, but this was what happened. Getting dead on, as I thought, a fine sight, I pressed, and when the puff of smoke had cleared away, to my disgust, I saw my man standing there unharmed, whilst his orderly, who was at least three paces to the left, was stretched upon the ground apparently dead. Turning swiftly, the officer I had aimed at began to run towards his men in evident alarm.

"Bravo, Quatermain!" sang out Good; "You've frightened him."

This made me very angry, for, if possible to avoid it, I hate to miss in public. When a man is master of only one art he likes to keep up his reputation in that art. Moved quite out of myself at my failure, I did a rash thing. Rapidly covering the general as he ran, I let drive with the second barrel. Instantly the poor man threw up his arms, and fell forward on to his face. This time I had made no mistake; and – I say it as a proof of how little we think of others when our own safety, pride, or reputation is in question – I was brute enough to feel delighted at the sight.

The regiments who had seen the feat cheered wildly at this exhibition of the white man's magic, which they took as an omen of success, while the force the general had belonged to – which, indeed, as we ascertained afterwards, he had commanded – fell back in confusion. Sir Henry and Good now took up their rifles and began to fire, the latter industriously 'browning' the dense mass before him with another Winchester repeater, and I also had another shot or two, with the result, so far as we could judge, that we put some six or eight men *hors de combat* before they were out of range.

Just as we stopped firing there came an ominous roar from our far right, then a similar roar rose on our left. The two other divisions were engaging us.

At the sound, the mass of men before us opened out a little, and advanced towards the hill and up the spit of bare grass land at a slow trot, singing a deep-throated song as they ran. We kept up a steady fire from our rifles as they came, Ignosi joining in occasionally, and accounted for several men, but of course we produced no more effect upon that mighty rush of armed humanity than he who throws pebbles does on the breaking wave.

On they came, with a shout and the clashing of spears; now they were driving in the pickets we had placed among the rocks at the foot of the hill. After that the advance was a little slower, for though as yet we had offered no serious opposition, the attacking forces must climb up hill, and they came slowly to save their breath. Our first line of defence was about half-way down the side of the slope, our second fifty yards further back, while our third occupied the edge of the plateau.

On they stormed, shouting their war-cry, "*Twala! Twala! Chiele! Chiele!*" (Twala! Twala! Smite! Smite!) "*Ignosi! Ignosi! Chiele! Chiele!*" answered our people. They were quite close now, and the *tollas*, or throwing-knives, began to flash backwards and forwards, and now with an awful yell the battle closed in.

To and fro swayed the mass of struggling warriors, men falling fast as leaves in an autumn wind; but before long the superior weight of the attacking force began to tell, and our first line of defence was slowly pressed back till it merged into the second. Here the struggle was very fierce, but again our people were driven back and up, till at length, within twenty minutes of the commencement of the fight, our third line came into action.

But by this time the assailants were much exhausted, and besides had lost many men killed and wounded, and to break through that third impenetrable hedge of spears proved beyond their powers. For a while the seething lines of savages swung backwards and forwards, in the fierce ebb and flow of battle, and the issue was doubtful. Sir Henry watched the desperate struggle with a kindling eye, and then without a word he rushed off, followed by Good, and flung himself into the hottest of the fray. As for myself, I stopped where I was.

The soldiers caught sight of his tall form as he plunged into battle, and there rose a cry of –

"*Nanzia Incubu! Nanzia Unkungunklovo!*" (Here is the Elephant!) "*Chiele! Chiele!*"

From that moment the end was no longer in doubt. Inch by inch, fighting with splendid gallantry, the attacking force was pressed back down the hillside, till at last it retreated upon its reserves in something like confusion. At that instant, too, a messenger arrived to say that the left attack had been repulsed; and I was just beginning to congratulate myself, believing that the affair was over for the present, when, to our horror, we perceived our men who had been engaged in the right defence being driven towards us across the plain, followed by swarms of the enemy, who had evidently succeeded at this point.

Ignosi, who was standing by me, took in the situation at a glance, and issued a rapid order. Instantly the reserve regiment around us, the Greys, extended itself.

Again Ignosi gave a word of command, which was taken up and repeated by the captains, and in another second, to my intense disgust, I found myself involved in a furious onslaught upon the advancing foe. Getting as much as I could behind Ignosi's huge frame, I made the best of a bad job, and toddled along to be killed as though I liked it. In a minute or two – we were plunging through the flying groups of our men, who at once began to re-form behind us, and then I am sure I do not know what happened. All I can remember is a dreadful rolling noise of the meeting of shields, and the sudden apparition of a huge ruffian, whose eyes seemed literally to be starting out of his head, making straight at me with a bloody spear. But – I say it with pride – I rose – or rather sank – to the occasion. It was one before which most people would have collapsed once and for all. Seeing that if I stood where I was I must be killed, as the horrid apparition came I flung myself down in front of him so cleverly that, being unable to stop himself, he took a header right over my prostrate form. Before he could rise again, *I* had risen and settled the matter from behind with my revolver.

Shortly after this somebody knocked me down, and I remember no more of that charge.

When I came to I found myself back at the koppie, with Good bending over me holding some water in a gourd.

"How do you feel, old fellow?" he asked anxiously.

I got up and shook myself before replying.

"Pretty well, thank you," I answered.

"Thank Heaven! When I saw them carry you in, I felt quite sick; I thought you were done for."

"Not this time, my boy. I fancy I only got a rap on the head, which knocked me stupid. How has it ended?"

"They are repulsed at every point for a while. The loss is dreadfully heavy; we have quite two thousand killed and wounded, and they must have lost three. Look, there's a sight!" and he pointed to long lines of men advancing by fours.

In the centre of every group of four, and being borne by it, was a kind of hide tray, of which a Kukuana force always carries a quantity, with a loop for a handle at each corner. On these trays – and their number seemed endless – lay wounded men, who as they arrived were hastily examined by the medicine men, of whom ten were attached to a regiment. If the wound was not of a fatal character the sufferer was taken away and attended to as carefully as circumstances would allow. But if, on the other hand, the injured man's condition proved hopeless, what followed was very dreadful, though doubtless it may have been the truest mercy. One of the doctors, under pretence of carrying out an examination, swiftly opened an artery with a sharp knife, and in a minute or two the sufferer expired painlessly. There were many cases that day in which this was done. In fact, it was done in the majority of cases when the wound was in the body, for the gash made by the entry of the enormously broad spears used by the Kukuanas generally rendered recovery impossible. In most instances the poor sufferers were already unconscious, and in others the fatal 'nick' of the artery was inflicted so swiftly and painlessly that they did not seem to notice it. Still it was a ghastly sight, and one from which we were glad to escape; indeed, I never remember anything of the kind that affected me more than seeing those gallant soldiers thus put out of pain by the red-handed medicine men, except, indeed, on one occasion when, after an attack, I saw a force of Swazis burying their hopelessly wounded *alive*.

Hurrying from this dreadful scene to the further side of the koppie, we found Sir Henry, who still held a battle-axe in his hand, Ignosi, Infadoos, and one or two of the chiefs in deep consultation.

"Thank Heaven, here you are, Quatermain! I can't quite make out what Ignosi wants to do. It seems that though we have beaten off the attack, Twala is now receiving large reinforcements, and is showing a disposition to invest us, with the view of starving us out."

"That's awkward."

"Yes; especially as Infadoos says that the water supply has given out."

"My lord, that is so," said Infadoos; "the spring cannot supply the wants of so great a multitude, and it is failing rapidly. Before night we shall all be thirsty. Listen, Macumazahn. Thou art wise, and hast doubtless seen many wars in the lands from whence thou camest – that is if indeed they make wars in the Stars. Now tell us, what shall we do? Twala has brought up many fresh men to take the place of those who have fallen. Yet Twala has learnt his lesson; the hawk did not think to find the heron ready; but our beak has pierced his breast; he fears to strike at us again. We too are wounded, and he will wait for us to die; he will wind himself round us like a snake round a buck, and fight the fight of 'sit down.'"

"I hear thee," I said.

"So, Macumazahn, thou seest we have no water here, and but a little food, and we must choose between these three things – to languish like a starving lion in his den, or to strive to break away towards the north, or" – and here he rose and pointed towards the dense mass of our foes – "to launch ourselves straight at Twala's throat. Incubu, the great warrior – for today he fought like a buffalo in a net, and Twala's soldiers went down before his axe like young corn before the hail; with these eyes I saw it – Incubu says 'Charge'; but the Elephant is ever prone to charge. Now what says Macumazahn, the wily old fox, who has seen much, and loves to bite his enemy from behind? The last word is in Ignosi the king, for it is a king's right to speak of war; but let us hear thy voice, O Macumazahn, who watchest by night, and the voice too of him of the transparent eye."

"What sayest thou, Ignosi," I asked.

"Nay, my father," answered our quondam servant, who now, clad as he was in the full panoply of savage war, looked every inch a warrior king, "do thou speak, and let me, who am but a child in wisdom beside thee, hearken to thy words."

Thus adjured, after taking hasty counsel with Good and Sir Henry, I delivered my opinion briefly to the effect that, being trapped, our best chance, especially in view of the failure of our water supply, was to initiate an attack upon Twala's forces. Then I recommended that the attack should be delivered at once, 'before our wounds grew stiff,' and also before the sight of Twala's overpowering force caused the hearts of our soldiers 'to wax small like fat before a fire.' Otherwise, I pointed out, some of the captains might change their minds, and, making peace with Twala, desert to him, or even betray us into his hands.

This expression of opinion seemed, on the whole, to be favourably received; indeed, among the Kukuanas my utterances met with a respect which has never been accorded to them before or since. But the real decision as to our plans lay with Ignosi, who, since he had been recognised as rightful king, could exercise the almost unbounded rights of sovereignty, including, of course, the final decision on matters of generalship, and it was to him that all eyes were now turned.

At length, after a pause, during which he appeared to be thinking deeply, he spoke.

"Incubu, Macumazahn, and Bougwan, brave white men, and my friends; Infadoos, my uncle, and chiefs; my heart is fixed. I will strike at Twala this day, and set my fortunes on the blow, ay, and my life – my life and your lives also. Listen; thus will I strike. Ye see how the hill curves round like the half-moon, and how the plain runs like a green tongue towards us within the curve?"

"We see," I answered.

"Good; it is now mid-day, and the men eat and rest after the toil of battle. When the sun has turned and travelled a little way towards the darkness, let thy regiment, my uncle, advance with one other down to the green tongue, and it shall be that when Twala sees it he will hurl his force at it to crush it. But the spot is narrow, and the regiments can come against thee one at a time only; so may they be destroyed one by one, and the eyes of all Twala's army shall be fixed upon a struggle the like of which has not been seen by living man. And with thee, my uncle, shall go Incubu my friend, that when Twala sees his battle-axe flashing in the first rank of the Greys his heart may grow faint. And I will come with the second regiment, that which follows thee, so that if ye are destroyed, as it might happen, there may yet be a king left to fight for; and with me shall come Macumazahn the wise."

"It is well, O king," said Infadoos, apparently contemplating the certainty of the complete annihilation of his regiment with perfect calmness. Truly, these Kukuanas are a wonderful people. Death has no terrors for them when it is incurred in the course of duty.

"And whilst the eyes of the multitude of Twala's soldiers are thus fixed upon the fight," went on Ignosi, "behold, one-third of the men who are left alive to us (i.e. about 6,000) shall creep along the right horn of the hill and fall upon the left flank of Twala's force, and one-third shall creep along the left horn and fall upon Twala's right flank. And when I see that the horns are ready to toss Twala, then will I, with the men who remain to me, charge home in Twala's face, and if fortune goes with us the day will be ours, and before Night drives her black oxen from the mountains to the mountains we shall sit in peace at Loo. And now let us eat and make ready; and, Infadoos, do thou prepare, that the plan be carried out without fail; and stay, let my white father Bougwan go with the right horn, that his shining eye may give courage to the captains."

The arrangements for attack thus briefly indicated were set in motion with a rapidity that spoke well for the perfection of the Kukuana military system. Within little more than an hour rations had been served out and devoured, the divisions were formed, the scheme of onslaught was explained to the leaders, and the whole force, numbering about 18,000 men, was ready to move, with the exception of a guard left in charge of the wounded.

Presently Good came up to Sir Henry and myself.

"Goodbye, you fellows," he said; "I am off with the right wing according to orders; and so I have come to shake hands, in case we should not meet again, you know," he added significantly.

We shook hands in silence, and not without the exhibition of as much emotion as Anglo-Saxons are wont to show.

"It is a queer business," said Sir Henry, his deep voice shaking a little, "and I confess I never expect to see tomorrow's sun. So far as I can make out, the Greys, with whom I am to go, are to fight until they are wiped out in order to enable the wings to slip round unawares and outflank Twala. Well, so be it; at any rate, it will be a man's death. Goodbye, old fellow. God bless you! I hope you will pull through and live to collar the diamonds; but if you do, take my advice and don't have anything more to do with Pretenders!"

In another second Good had wrung us both by the hand and gone; and then Infadoos came up and led off Sir Henry to his place in the forefront of the Greys, whilst, with many misgivings, I departed with Ignosi to my station in the second attacking regiment.

The complete and unabridged text is available online, from *flametreepublishing.com/extras*

The Shell-Spire

Sara M. Harvey

I THINK it was perhaps because I was a child that they passed me by. I cannot think of another reason I had been marked as different from the others. Why I was the only one who survived.

My parents carefully selected their team for each and every excursion. This one was no different. My father had received a letter, describing this place and hinting at the treasures we would find. Not riches, not necessarily, but information, art, and artifacts. It was a long trip, meticulously planned with barely contained excitement that I did not feel.

We had five in our group: Jean-Marc Arnold, the Haitian pilot and ancient language specialist, Howard Keith, the British cartographer, my parents, Ruby and Arthur Phillips, professors of anthropology and ancient religions with a special interest in the occult, and me. My parents took me everywhere with them. Giza, Machu Picchu, Newgrange, Uluru, Teotihuacan, Stonehenge, anywhere where there had once been spiritual practice done in the far-distant past, my parents were there with me in tow. I sat crammed between them in the tiny helicopter that took us to the island.

I say 'island' and you're likely imaging a landmass made up of soil and trees with a beach and all of that. But this place was unlike that in every way imaginable.

It rose up from the blue-grey Pacific, an incredibly small projection, the same pinkish-ivory color and undulating shape as a conch shell but crafted with platforms and steps like the turret of a castle. We circled it at least a dozen times with my mother and Howard taking pictures and video leaning so far out of the helicopter I feared they'd tumble into the sea.

It was as remote and thrilling as the letter had promised, my father marveled.

Jean-Marc brought us down into the largest of the outcroppings that projected from the spire in a weirdly organic shape, like a flat mushroom growing from the side of a tree, about three-quarters of the way to the top.

Howard was out of his seat first, scrambling up the steps to the very top with his tablet in hand, taking a panoramic shot of the view from there while waiting for a sync with a satellite to confirm our location.

I watched the adults step out onto the platform and felt a sense of dreadful foreboding so strong that I thought I would vomit.

"Come along, now," my mother reached in and took my hand. They were always so steady and sure, my mother's hands, but that day they trembled.

The surface was just as strangely shell-like as the shape and color. My father, who favored studying architecture, immediately began to take notes. He dropped to his knees scratching and knocking and rubbing the floor, then scuttling over to the wall to do the same.

"Remarkable…there is no sign of the type of erosion I was expecting in this environment… can't even see the joins in the masonry…amazing…" he said into his pocket recorder and crawled around the corner, out of sight.

Jean-Marc and my mother were already stepping inside, heads together murmuring about interior inscriptions and murals and Egyptians and Minoans who sought to protect their sacred work from the harsh elements by keeping it inside.

I stood alone in the small space between the helicopter and the wall of the tower. I heard the wind through the structure: it whispered and it moaned and I could swear that it laughed.

What I didn't hear were their voices.

I followed my mother and Jean-Marc through the curved opening. The walls were smooth to the touch, smooth as satin, smooth as the inside of a seashell. I thought perhaps that it had been eroded that way, but as I felt the stinging ocean spray against my face, I remembered that even sea glass was pitted and cloudy.

Crossing the threshold, the silence within enveloped me. No more wind and still, no voices.

Stairs had been cut into the interior wall, spiraling down from the topmost platform to the roundish bottom floor where all of the adults now gathered. Their devices held loosely in their hands, momentarily forgotten, as they beheld the full magnitude of what surrounded them.

Absolutely nothing.

There were no paintings, no carvings, no inscriptions, no artifacts, no signs of habitation or activity except for the steps. The platforms and doorways even seemed too organic, almost accidental, my parents would certainly not have counted them as part of a master build plan. No, they would certainly decide that the builders of this place had simply incorporated these existing elements into their design. But without any other evidence, what could the purpose of such a remote location be?

Coming down the steps towards them, I saw something else missing: dust. The edges and corners of each step were completely free of dust. Also missing were the signs of animal habitation we usually came across: birds' nests and excrement, bones, fur, eggshells, and the various detritus of living things. Even this far out into the ocean, I knew that seabirds should have flocked to this lonely outpost, free from predators and offering shelter for their nests, gliding miles and miles on the same gusts that moved tradeships of old. But there were no signs of them, not a twig, not a feather.

The chatter started up again, slowly, with hypotheses flying between them, bordering on bickering. Howard threw up his hands and tucked his tablet into his backpack.

"I'm going to take a peek outside," he said to no one in particular.

I followed him, lagging behind as much as the small space would allow. Unlike the platform above, a sweeping set of stairs led down from the only outlet on the ground floor. They went straight into the sea, reminding me quite a bit of Santorini Island in Greece.

He sat down and gazed across the gently rolling waves. We were far beyond the sight of land. I hovered at the opening, looking at those steps. No algae, no barnacles, no mussels. Just gleaming ivory vanishing into blue.

"Would you look at that?" He'd taken off his shoes, setting them on the step behind him and was soaking his feet. He tilted his head one direction and another, leaning forward. "Does that look like...*rooftops* to you?"

He pointed a few yards out and, perhaps, yes, if I squinted, I thought I could see an entire intact city of rooftops and steps and paths and bridges all looking like they were carved of the same silky shell-like material.

"The sonar reads here were just bonkers, why we had J-M fly us in, you know. I didn't trust those readings to bring in a boat, looked too shallow. Figured it was coral reefs, maybe ruins if we were lucky....But this..." He scooted down another step and the water lapped at his pale ankles. "This is something entirely different." He twisted back to look up at me. "Go get your folks, they'll want to see this."

As he turned around, but before I did, I spotted it. The only artifact we'd encountered here in this strange place. It looked like the knight piece from a chess set, vaguely shaped like a horse's head and made of the same material as everything else. It stood maybe a foot and a half in height had been placed on one of the steps just below the waterline, the step where Howard rested his feet. He rose into an awkward half-squat, trying to peer deeper into the sea without falling in. The horse head statue fell over, landing across his left ankle and effectively pinning it to the step. Howard fell back and immediately tried to jerk his leg free to no avail.

"Bloody hell! Don't just stand there, go get the rest to help me move this thing. It's damned heavy for its size!"

His struggle sent a flurry of ripples out from those steps.

The ripples met the waves.

And from the waves they rose.

For a long, stunned moment I could only stare at the sea as it seemed to come to life. The wave crests formed into spheres, those spheres were perched on necks that were balanced on shoulders, looking just like people if people were made entirely out of water. They rose out of the waves, three and four quickly turned into a dozen of them, faceless except for two hollowed-out places where eyes should have been.

Howard froze, eyes stretched wide as his mouth in silent fright as these beings advanced up the steps, coming straight for him. It was only as the first one made contact that he screamed. It was not the simple shout of a man surprised, or even one that'd been hurt, but a rending, primal scream of pure agony and terror.

I bolted back into the spire, crashing hard into my parents in the doorway. Unable to put into words what I had seen I could only push them backwards, sobbing hysterically. Howard's voice turned hoarse, cracking into several octaves at once like the adolescent boys we often hired to carry our luggage.

I squeezed past, between my parents, knocking Jean-Marc to the floor in my manic scramble for the stairs. I saw my mother decide to follow me and my father take one step outside the spire but quickly return as Howard's cries abruptly stopped. He came up the steps behind us, looking wildly around for Jean-Marc.

The water-beings were fast, faster than I could have reckoned, and not all that human-like once I saw them fully out of the sea. Their torsos merged into a column of swirling water that seemed to float across the floor and their arms were impossibly long and thin with no indication of hands at the end until they reached to grab and the appendage split into slender strips like the tentacles of a squid. That is how they snared my father. Poor Jean-Marc was simply enveloped by one of them lying completely atop his body. He never got the chance to scream.

"Run," my father shouted at us because we were rooted to the spot, too horrified to unlock our muscles and make an attempt to save ourselves.

My mother snapped back to herself first and stepped around me, her arm coming around my waist as she passed. I'm certain she meant to sling me over her shoulder and run for the helicopter. She wasn't certified, but I knew she could fly it. I relaxed into her sure grip as my father went down, caught and held fast by two of the creatures.

She never climbed the next step. Two more beings sloshed up the steps, their lower halves splitting apart like legs, more than two legs, I couldn't count how many but they seemed to have a leg for every step between us and them.

They passed right by me and took my mother.

One peeled her arm away from my body as if it had no bones and the other tackled her to the stairs. They spilled one into the other as they did whatever it was they were doing, half rape, half devouring.

She turned her head, an effort that ruffled the bodies of her attackers. What she meant to say to me was lost in the gush of blood that poured forth when she opened her mouth.

I ran.

I didn't want to touch these things, but I could not help but put a foot through the shoulder of one. Through my shoe, my sock, the leg of my pants I could feel its surging heartbeat like the eternal movement of the waves. I could sense in that fleeting moment, that these beings were interconnected and that there were hundreds, if not thousands more in the city below, and those were connected to something larger and greater that lay deeper still.

Your kind calls us many things...fallen angels...demons...gods, but we have been here longer than all of those words.

There was more, a message that I sensed bubbling through them from someplace else, but I plucked my foot from that creature's body and ran for the helicopter. Once free, the screaming intruded once more, the desperate bleating of the dying, a howling chorus that echoes through my dreams still.

Once inside the helicopter, I locked the doors and turned on the distress beacon. I cried into the radio, calling for anyone, anywhere to help me.

No one answered and the sun went down.

Fitful sleep finally overtook me, but I awoke with a terrible start at each creak and every subtle motion of the copter. The water beings never came for me.

With the rising of the sun came the familiar chopping beat of another helicopter. It was large, military-grade. Whoever they were, they must have flown all night to get to me. We had launched from a ship several miles away, and the ride before that had taken more than a day.

I don't know why they never answered the radio call, but I didn't care. They unrolled a rescue ladder and I stepped out of the helicopter to take it.

My shoe, sock, and entire pants leg were still wet. In a panic I'm sure they didn't understand, I undressed from the waist down before scrambling up that ladder into safety.

They didn't ask about my parents or any of the others, they simply turned their craft around and headed away. I watched that spire, looking heavenly pink in the morning light, grow smaller and smaller until it vanished over the horizon. Then I closed my eyes.

When I opened them, it was some days later. I was in a small hospital on Tahiti. I never learned the identities of my rescuers. The hospital staff had found me on the doorstep to the emergency room and had no idea who had brought me in. They gave me fluids, treated me for shock, and hoped I would wake up.

The rental outfit went back for the boat we'd taken out. And although they had the coordinates of the helicopter's location, they never found it. Nor did they ever find a strange tower that looked like it was carved from a giant conch shell, nor any evidence of a great underwater city.

My last living relative, a maiden great-aunt on my father's side, came to collect me a few weeks later. There was some hubbub about it since all of my papers had been aboard the missing helicopter, but she finally took me home with her to a pleasant ranch in New Mexico, where there wasn't much water. She took it upon herself to decline all inquiries from the press and never asked me what had happened.

I sometimes wish she did, though, keeping all this inside of me is maddening.

A few months ago, I started waking up with my foot wet. The same one that stepped through the creature. In my dreams, I can see straight through it, as if it has turned to water, just like one of them.

When this happens, I go outside, even if it is the dead of night, and rub my foot into the sandy soil until it is dry. This is the only way I can do it, towels and hairdryers do nothing.

Whispers of colleagues over the years had hinted at that place in the middle of the Pacific, so ancient and so rare, undocumented by scholars. A career-making find. My father received a letter one day, that letter held the plausible coordinates of this speculated wonder of the world. Basically, Atlantis. My parents could not resist.

When a letter from one of my father's colleagues arrived for me, I was surprised. My great-aunt was now long passed and so should this man have been, twice my father's age twenty years ago.

The letter, carefully typed with an old-fashioned manual machine, asked if I wanted to continue my father's research. The time had come once again, the letter stated. It gave me the purported coordinates of the mythical lost city beneath the waves where the ancients dwelled. The rest frightened me to the bone to read.

People call them fallen angels or demons or gods, but they have been here longer than all of those words.

I put down this letter and went to the box in the hall closet that held the last of my parents' things, accumulated over the years from this university and that, sent to me as tokens of respect and admiration for their work. I searched until I found the letter that started this entire affair. Bringing the two together, I saw that they were typed in the same manner, upon the same paper, and contained nearly the same wording. This professor in Prague wished my father to carry on the research of his father. That the time had come once again. The coordinates. The same sentence.

People call them fallen angels or demons or gods, but they have been here longer than all of those words.

I sat down at my desk, shaking too hard to remain standing.

When I looked down, I saw that my foot was wet.

The Lost Race

Robert E. Howard

CORORUC glanced about him and hastened his pace. He was no coward, but he did not like the place. Tall trees rose all about, their sullen branches shutting out the sunlight. The dim trail led in and out among them, sometimes skirting the edge of a ravine, where Cororuc could gaze down at the treetops beneath. Occasionally, through a rift in the forest, he could see away to the forbidding hills that hinted of the ranges much farther to the west, that were the mountains of Cornwall.

In those mountains the bandit chief, Buruc the Cruel, was supposed to lurk, to descend upon such victims as might pass that way. Cororuc shifted his grip on his spear and quickened his step. His haste was due not only to the menace of the outlaws, but also to the fact that he wished once more to be in his native land. He had been on a secret mission to the wild Cornish tribesmen; and though he had been more or less successful, he was impatient to be out of their inhospitable country. It had been a long, wearisome trip, and he still had nearly the whole of Britain to traverse. He threw a glance of aversion about him. He longed for the pleasant woodlands, with scampering deer, and chirping birds, to which he was used. He longed for the tall white cliff, where the blue sea lapped merrily. The forest through which he was passing seemed uninhabited. There were no birds, no animals; nor had he seen a sign of human habitation.

His comrades still lingered at the savage court of the Cornish king, enjoying his crude hospitality, in no hurry to be away. But Cororuc was not content. So he had left them to follow at their leisure and had set out alone.

Rather a fine figure of a man was Cororuc. Some six feet in height, strongly though leanly built, he was, with gray eyes, a pure Briton but not a pure Celt, his long yellow hair revealing, in him as in all his race, a trace of Belgae.

He was clad in skillfully dressed deerskin, for the Celts had not yet perfected the coarse cloth which they made, and most of the race preferred the hides of deer.

He was armed with a long bow of yew wood, made with no especial skill but an efficient weapon; a long bronze broadsword, with a buckskin sheath; a long bronze dagger and a small, round shield, rimmed with a band of bronze and covered with tough buffalo hide. A crude bronze helmet was on his head. Faint devices were painted in woad on his arms and cheeks.

His beardless face was of the highest type of Briton, clear, straightforward, the shrewd, practical determination of the Nordic mingling with the reckless courage and dreamy artistry of the Celt.

So Cororuc trod the forest path, warily, ready to flee or fight, but preferring to do neither just then.

The trail led away from the ravine, disappearing around a great tree. And from the other side of the tree, Cororuc heard sounds of conflict. Gliding warily forward, and wondering whether he should see some of the elves and dwarfs that were reputed to haunt those woodlands, he peered around the great tree.

A few feet from him he saw a strange tableau. Backed against another tree stood a large wolf, at bay, blood trickling from gashes about his shoulder; while before him, crouching for a spring, the warrior saw a great panther. Cororuc wondered at the cause of the battle. Not often the lords of the forest met in warfare. And he was puzzled by the snarls of the great cat. Savage, blood-lusting, yet they held a strange note of fear; and the beast seemed hesitant to spring in.

Just why Cororuc chose to take the part of the wolf, he himself could not have said. Doubtless it was just the reckless chivalry of the Celt in him, an admiration for the dauntless attitude of the wolf against his far more powerful foe. Be that as it may, Cororuc, characteristically forgetting his bow and taking the more reckless course, drew his sword and leaped in front of the panther. But he had no chance to use it. The panther, whose nerve appeared to be already somewhat shaken, uttered a startled screech and disappeared among the trees so quickly that Cororuc wondered if he had really seen a panther. He turned to the wolf, wondering if it would leap upon him. It was watching him, half crouching; slowly it stepped away from the tree, and still watching him, backed away a few yards, then turned and made off with a strange shambling gait. As the warrior watched it vanish into the forest, an uncanny feeling came over him; he had seen many wolves, he had hunted them and had been hunted by them, but he had never seen such a wolf before.

He hesitated and then walked warily after the wolf, following the tracks that were plainly defined in the soft loam. He did not hasten, being merely content to follow the tracks. After a short distance, he stopped short, the hairs on his neck seeming to bristle. *Only the tracks of the hind feet showed: the wolf was walking erect.*

He glanced about him. There was no sound; the forest was silent. He felt an impulse to turn and put as much territory between him and the mystery as possible, but his Celtic curiosity would not allow it. He followed the trail. And then it ceased altogether. Beneath a great tree the tracks vanished. Cororuc felt the cold sweat on his forehead. What kind of place was that forest? Was he being led astray and eluded by some inhuman, supernatural monster of the woodlands, who sought to ensnare him? And Cororuc backed away, his sword lifted, his courage not allowing him to run, but greatly desiring to do so. And so he came again to the tree where he had first seen the wolf. The trail he had followed led away from it in another direction and Cororuc took it up, almost running in his haste to get out of the vicinity of a wolf who walked on two legs and then vanished in the air.

The trail wound about more tediously than ever, appearing and disappearing within a dozen feet, but it was well for Cororuc that it did, for thus he heard the voices of the men coming up the path before they saw him. He took to a tall tree that branched over the trail, lying close to the great bole, along a wide-flung branch.

Three men were coming down the forest path.

One was a big, burly fellow, vastly over six feet in height, with a long red beard and a great mop of red hair. In contrast, his eyes were a beady black. He was dressed in deerskins, and armed with a great sword.

Of the two others, one was a lanky, villainous-looking scoundrel, with only one eye, and the other was a small, wizened man, who squinted hideously with both beady eyes.

Cororuc knew them, by descriptions the Cornishmen had made between curses, and it was in his excitement to get a better view of the most villainous murderer in Britain that he slipped from the tree branch and plunged to the ground directly between them.

He was up on the instant, his sword out. He could expect no mercy; for he knew that the red-haired man was Buruc the Cruel, the scourge of Cornwall.

The bandit chief bellowed a foul curse and whipped out his great sword. He avoided the Briton's furious thrust by a swift backward leap and then the battle was on. Buruc rushed the warrior from the front, striving to beat him down by sheer weight; while the lanky, one-eyed villain slipped around, trying to get behind him. The smaller man had retreated to the edge of the forest. The fine art of the fence was unknown to those early swordsmen. It was hack, slash, stab, the full weight of the arm behind each blow. The terrific blows crashing on his shield beat Cororuc to the ground, and the lanky, one-eyed villain rushed in to finish him. Cororuc spun about without rising, cut the bandit's legs from under him and stabbed him as he fell, then threw himself to one side and to his feet, in time to avoid Buruc's sword. Again, driving his shield up to catch the bandit's sword in midair, he deflected it and whirled his own with all his power. Buruc's head flew from his shoulders.

Then Cororuc, turning, saw the wizened bandit scurry into the forest. He raced after him, but the fellow had disappeared among the trees. Knowing the uselessness of attempting to pursue him, Cororuc turned and raced down the trail. He did not know if there were more bandits in that direction, but he did know that if he expected to get out of the forest at all, he would have to do it swiftly. Without doubt the villain who had escaped would have all the other bandits out, and soon they would be beating the woodlands for him.

After running for some distance down the path and seeing no sign of any enemy, he stopped and climbed into the topmost branches of a tall tree that towered above its fellows.

On all sides he seemed surrounded by a leafy ocean. To the west he could see the hills he had avoided. To the north, far in the distance, other hills rose; to the south the forest ran, an unbroken sea. But to the east, far away, he could barely see the line that marked the thinning out of the forest into the fertile plains. Miles and miles away, he knew not how many, but it meant more pleasant travel, villages of men, people of his own race. He was surprized that he was able to see that far, but the tree in which he stood was a giant of its kind.

Before he started to descend, he glanced about nearer at hand. He could trace the faintly marked line of the trail he had been following, running away into the east; and could make out other trails leading into it, or away from it. Then a glint caught his eye. He fixed his gaze on a glade some distance down the trail and saw, presently, a party of men enter and vanish. Here and there, on every trail, he caught glances of the glint of accouterments, the waving of foliage. So the squinting villain had already roused the bandits. They were all around him; he was virtually surrounded.

A faintly heard burst of savage yells, from back up the trail, startled him. So, they had already thrown a cordon about the place of the fight and had found him gone. Had he not fled swiftly, he would have been caught. He was outside the cordon, but the bandits were all about him. Swiftly he slipped from the tree and glided into the forest.

Then began the most exciting hunt Cororuc had ever engaged in; for he was the hunted and men were the hunters. Gliding, slipping from bush to bush and from tree to tree, now running swiftly, now crouching in a covert, Cororuc fled, ever eastward, not daring to turn back lest he be driven farther back into the forest. At times he was forced to turn his course; in fact, he very seldom fled in a straight course, yet always he managed to work farther eastward.

Sometimes he crouched in bushes or lay along some leafy branch, and saw bandits pass so close to him that he could have touched them. Once or twice they sighted him and he fled, bounding over logs and bushes, darting in and out among the trees; and always he eluded them.

It was in one of those headlong flights that he noticed he had entered a defile of small hills, of which he had been unaware, and looking back over his shoulder, saw that his pursuers had halted, within full sight. Without pausing to ruminate on so strange a thing, he darted around a great boulder, felt a vine or something catch his foot, and was thrown headlong. Simultaneously, something struck the youth's head, knocking him senseless.

When Cororuc recovered his senses, he found that he was bound, hand and foot. He was being borne along, over rough ground. He looked about him. Men carried him on their shoulders, but such men as he had never seen before. Scarce above four feet stood the tallest, and they were small of build and very dark of complexion. Their eyes were black; and most of them went stooped forward, as if from a lifetime spent in crouching and hiding; peering furtively on all sides. They were armed with small bows, arrows, spears and daggers, all pointed, not with crudely worked bronze but with flint and obsidian, of the finest workmanship. They were dressed in finely dressed hides of rabbits and other small animals, and a kind of coarse cloth; and many were tattooed from head to foot in ocher and woad. There were perhaps twenty in all. What sort of men were they? Cororuc had never seen the like.

They were going down a ravine, on both sides of which steep cliffs rose. Presently they seemed to come to a blank wall, where the ravine appeared to come to an abrupt stop. Here, at a word from one who seemed to be in command, they set the Briton down, and seizing hold of a large boulder, drew it to one side. A small cavern was exposed, seeming to vanish away into the earth; then the strange men picked up the Briton and moved forward.

Cororuc's hair bristled at the thought of being borne into that forbidding-looking cave. What manner of men were they? In all Britain and Alba, in Cornwall or Ireland, Cororuc had never seen such men. Small dwarfish men, who dwelt in the earth. Cold sweat broke out on the youth's forehead. Surely they were the malevolent dwarfs of whom the Cornish people had spoken, who dwelt in their caverns by day, and by night sallied forth to steal and burn dwellings, even slaying if the opportunity arose! You will hear of them, even today, if you journey in Cornwall.

The men, or elves, if such they were, bore him into the cavern, others entering and drawing the boulder back into place. For a moment all was darkness, and then torches began to glow, away off. And at a shout they moved on. Other men of the caves came forward, with the torches.

Cororuc looked about him. The torches shed a vague glow over the scene. Sometimes one, sometimes another wall of the cave showed for an instant, and the Briton was vaguely aware that they were covered with paintings, crudely done, yet with a certain skill his own race could not equal. But always the roof remained unseen. Cororuc knew that the seemingly small cavern had merged into a cave of surprizing size. Through the vague light of the torches the strange people moved, came and went, silently, like shadows of the dim past.

He felt the cords of thongs that bound his feet loosened. He was lifted upright.

"Walk straight ahead," said a voice, speaking the language of his own race, and he felt a spear point touch the back of his neck.

And straight ahead he walked, feeling his sandals scrape on the stone floor of the cave, until they came to a place where the floor tilted upward. The pitch was steep and the stone was so slippery that Cororuc could not have climbed it alone. But his captors pushed him, and pulled him, and he saw that long, strong vines were strung from somewhere at the top.

Those the strange men seized, and bracing their feet against the slippery ascent, went up swiftly. When their feet found level surface again, the cave made a turn, and Cororuc blundered out into a fire-lit scene that made him gasp.

The cave debouched into a cavern so vast as to be almost incredible. The mighty walls swept up into a great arched roof that vanished in the darkness. A level floor lay between, and through it flowed a river; an underground river. From under one wall it flowed to vanish silently under the other. An arched stone bridge, seemingly of natural make, spanned the current.

All around the walls of the great cavern, which was roughly circular, were smaller caves, and before each glowed a fire. Higher up were other caves, regularly arranged, tier on tier. Surely human men could not have built such a city.

In and out among the caves, on the level floor of the main cavern, people were going about what seemed daily tasks. Men were talking together and mending weapons, some were fishing from the river; women were replenishing fires, preparing garments; and altogether it might have been any other village in Britain, to judge from their occupations. But it all struck Cororuc as extremely unreal; the strange place, the small, silent people, going about their tasks, the river flowing silently through it all.

Then they became aware of the prisoner and flocked about him. There was none of the shouting, abuse and indignities, such as savages usually heap on their captives, as the small men drew about Cororuc, silently eying him with malevolent, wolfish stares. The warrior shuddered, in spite of himself.

But his captors pushed through the throng, driving the Briton before them. Close to the bank of the river, they stopped and drew away from around him.

Two great fires leaped and flickered in front of him and there was something between them. He focused his gaze and presently made out the object. A high stone seat, like a throne; and in it seated an aged man, with a long white beard, silent, motionless, but with black eyes that gleamed like a wolf's.

The ancient was clothed in some kind of a single, flowing garment. One claw-like hand rested on the seat near him, skinny, crooked fingers, with talons like a hawk's. The other hand was hidden among his garments.

The firelight danced and flickered; now the old man stood out clearly, his hooked, beak-like nose and long beard thrown into bold relief; now he seemed to recede until he was invisible to the gaze of the Briton, except for his glittering eyes.

"Speak, Briton!" The words came suddenly, strong, clear, without a hint of age. "Speak, what would ye say?"

Cororuc, taken aback, stammered and said, "Why, why – what manner people are you? Why have you taken me prisoner? Are you elves?"

"We are Picts," was the stern reply.

"Picts!" Cororuc had heard tales of those ancient people from the Gaelic Britons; some said that they still lurked in the hills of Siluria, but –

"I have fought Picts in Caledonia," the Briton protested; "they are short but massive and misshapen; not at all like you!"

"They are not true Picts," came the stern retort. "Look about you, Briton," with a wave of an arm, "you see the remnants of a vanishing race; a race that once ruled Britain from sea to sea."

The Briton stared, bewildered.

"Harken, Briton," the voice continued; "harken, barbarian, while I tell to you the tale of the lost race."

The firelight flickered and danced, throwing vague reflections on the towering walls and on the rushing, silent current.

The ancient's voice echoed through the mighty cavern.

"Our people came from the south. Over the islands, over the Inland Sea. Over the snow-topped mountains, where some remained, to slay any enemies who might follow. Down into the fertile plains we came. Over all the land we spread. We became wealthy and prosperous. Then two kings arose in the land, and he who conquered, drove out the conquered. So many of us made boats and set sail for the far-off cliffs that gleamed white in the sunlight. We found a fair land with fertile plains. We found a race of red-haired barbarians, who dwelt in caves. Mighty giants, of great bodies and small minds.

"We built our huts of wattle. We tilled the soil. We cleared the forest. We drove the red-haired giants back into the forest. Farther we drove them back until at last they fled to the mountains of the west and the mountains of the north. We were rich. We were prosperous.

"Then," and his voice thrilled with rage and hate, until it seemed to reverberate through the cavern, "then the Celts came. From the isles of the west, in their rude coracles they came. In the west they landed, but they were not satisfied with the west. They marched eastward and seized the fertile plains. We fought. They were stronger. They were fierce fighters and they were armed with weapons of bronze, whereas we had only weapons of flint.

"We were driven out. They enslaved us. They drove us into the forest. Some of us fled into the mountains of the west. Many fled into the mountains of the north. There they mingled with the red-haired giants we drove out so long ago, and became a race of monstrous dwarfs, losing all the arts of peace and gaining only the ability to fight.

"But some of us swore that we would never leave the land we had fought for. But the Celts pressed us. There were many, and more came. So we took to caverns, to ravines, to caves. We, who had always dwelt in huts that let in much light, who had always tilled the soil, we learned to dwell like beasts, in caves where no sunlight ever entered. Caves we found, of which this is the greatest; caves we made.

"You, Briton," the voice became a shriek and a long arm was outstretched in accusation, "you and your race! You have made a free, prosperous nation into a race of earth-rats! We who never fled, who dwelt in the air and the sunlight close by the sea where traders came, we must flee like hunted beasts and burrow like moles! But at night! Ah, then for our vengeance! Then we slip from our hiding places, ravines and caves, with torch and dagger! Look, Briton!"

And following the gesture, Cororuc saw a rounded post of some kind of very hard wood, set in a niche in the stone floor, close to the bank. The floor about the niche was charred as if by old fires.

Cororuc stared, uncomprehending. Indeed, he understood little of what had passed. That these people were even human, he was not at all certain. He had heard so much of them as 'little people.' Tales of their doings, their hatred of the race of man, and their maliciousness flocked back to him. Little he knew that he was gazing on one of the mysteries of the ages. That the tales which the ancient Gaels told of the Picts, already warped, would become even more warped from age to age, to result in tales of elves, dwarfs, trolls and fairies, at first accepted and then rejected, entire, by the race of men, just as the Neanderthal monsters resulted in tales of goblins and ogres. But of that Cororuc neither knew nor cared, and the ancient was speaking again.

"There, there, Briton," exulted he, pointing to the post, "there you shall pay! A scant payment for the debt your race owes mine, but to the fullest of your extent."

The old man's exultation would have been fiendish, except for a certain high purpose in his face. He was sincere. He believed that he was only taking just vengeance; and he seemed like some great patriot for a mighty, lost cause.

"But I am a Briton!" stammered Cororuc. "It was not my people who drove your race into exile! They were Gaels, from Ireland. I am a Briton and my race came from Gallia only a hundred years ago. We conquered the Gaels and drove them into Erin, Wales and Caledonia, even as they drove your race."

"No matter!" The ancient chief was on his feet. "A Celt is a Celt. Briton, or Gael, it makes no difference. Had it not been Gael, it would have been Briton. Every Celt who falls into our hands must pay, be it warrior or woman, babe or king. Seize him and bind him to the post."

In an instant Cororuc was bound to the post, and he saw, with horror, the Picts piling firewood about his feet.

"And when you are sufficiently burned, Briton," said the ancient, "this dagger that has drunk the blood of a hundred Britons, shall quench its thirst in yours."

"But never have I harmed a Pict!" Cororuc gasped, struggling with his bonds.

"You pay, not for what you did, but for what your race has done," answered the ancient sternly. "Well do I remember the deeds of the Celts when first they landed on Britain – the shrieks of the slaughtered, the screams of ravished girls, the smokes of burning villages, the plundering."

Cororuc felt his short neck-hairs bristle. When first the Celts landed on Britain! That was over five hundred years ago!

And his Celtic curiosity would not let him keep still, even at the stake with the Picts preparing to light firewood piled about him.

"You could not remember that. That was ages ago."

The ancient looked at him somberly. "And I am age-old. In my youth I was a witch-finder, and an old woman witch cursed me as she writhed at the stake. She said I should live until the last child of the Pictish race had passed. That I should see the once mighty nation go down into oblivion and then – and only then – should I follow it. For she put upon me the curse of life everlasting."

Then his voice rose until it filled the cavern. "But the curse was nothing. Words can do no harm, can do nothing, to a man. I live. A hundred generations have I seen come and go, and yet another hundred. What is time? The sun rises and sets, and another day has passed into oblivion. Men watch the sun and set their lives by it. They league themselves on every hand with time. They count the minutes that race them into eternity. Man outlived the centuries ere he began to reckon time. Time is man-made. Eternity is the work of the gods. In this cavern there is no such thing as time. There are no stars, no sun. Without is time; within is eternity. We count not time. Nothing marks the speeding of the hours. The youths go forth. They see the sun, the stars. They reckon time. And they pass. I was a young man when I entered this cavern. I have never left it. As you reckon time, I may have dwelt here a thousand years; or an hour. When not banded by time, the soul, the mind, call it what you will, can conquer the body. And the wise men of the race, in my youth, knew more than the outer world will ever learn. When I feel that my body begins to weaken, I take the magic draft, that is known only to me, of all the world. It does not give immortality; that is the work of the mind alone; but it rebuilds the body. The race of Picts vanish; they fade like the snow on the mountain. And when the last is gone, this dagger shall free me from the world." Then in a swift change of tone, "Light the fagots!"

Cororuc's mind was fairly reeling. He did not in the least understand what he had just heard. He was positive that he was going mad; and what he saw the next minute assured him of it.

Through the throng came a wolf; and he knew that it was the wolf whom he had rescued from the panther close by the ravine in the forest!

Strange, how long ago and far away that seemed! Yes, it was the same wolf. That same strange, shambling gait. Then the thing stood erect and raised its front feet to its head. What nameless horror was that?

Then the wolf's head fell back, disclosing a man's face. The face of a Pict; one of the first 'werewolves.' The man stepped out of the wolfskin and strode forward, calling something. A Pict just starting to light the wood about the Briton's feet drew back the torch and hesitated.

The wolf-Pict stepped forward and began to speak to the chief, using Celtic, evidently for the prisoner's benefit. Cororuc was surprized to hear so many speak his language, not reflecting upon its comparative simplicity, and the ability of the Picts.

"What is this?" asked the Pict who had played wolf. "A man is to be burned who should not be!"

"How?" exclaimed the old man fiercely, clutching his long beard. "Who are you to go against a custom of age-old antiquity?"

"I met a panther," answered the other, "and this Briton risked his life to save mine. Shall a Pict show ingratitude?"

And as the ancient hesitated, evidently pulled one way by his fanatical lust for revenge, and the other by his equally fierce racial pride, the Pict burst into a wild flight of oration, carried on in his own language. At last the ancient chief nodded.

"A Pict ever paid his debts," said he with impressive grandeur. "Never a Pict forgets. Unbind him. No Celt shall ever say that a Pict showed ingratitude."

Cororuc was released, and as, like a man in a daze, he tried to stammer his thanks, the chief waved them aside.

"A Pict never forgets a foe, ever remembers a friendly deed," he replied.

"Come," murmured his Pictish friend, tugging at the Celt's arm.

He led the way into a cave leading away from the main cavern. As they went, Cororuc looked back, to see the ancient chief seated upon his stone throne, his eyes gleaming as he seemed to gaze back through the lost glories of the ages; on each hand the fires leaped and flickered. A figure of grandeur, the king of a lost race.

On and on Cororuc's guide led him. And at last they emerged and the Briton saw the starlit sky above him.

"In that way is a village of your tribesmen," said the Pict, pointing, "where you will find a welcome until you wish to take up your journey anew."

And he pressed gifts on the Celt; gifts of garments of cloth and finely worked deerskin, beaded belts, a fine horn bow with arrows skillfully tipped with obsidian. Gifts of food. His own weapons were returned to him.

"But an instant," said the Briton, as the Pict turned to go. "I followed your tracks in the forest. They vanished." There was a question in his voice.

The Pict laughed softly. "I leaped into the branches of the tree. Had you looked up, you would have seen me. If ever you wish a friend, you will ever find one in Berula, chief among the Alban Picts."

He turned and vanished. And Cororuc strode through the moonlight toward the Celtic village.

The Man Who Would Be King

Rudyard Kipling

'Brother to a Prince and fellow to a beggar if he be found worthy.'

THE LAW, as quoted, lays down a fair conduct of life, and one not easy to follow. I have been fellow to a beggar again and again under circumstances which prevented either of us finding out whether the other was worthy. I have still to be brother to a Prince, though I once came near to kinship with what might have been a veritable King, and was promised the reversion of a Kingdom – army, law-courts, revenue, and policy all complete. But, today, I greatly fear that my King is dead, and if I want a crown I must go hunt it for myself.

The beginning of everything was in a railway-train upon the road to Mhow from Ajmir. There had been a Deficit in the Budget, which necessitated travelling, not Second-class, which is only half as dear as First-Class, but by Intermediate, which is very awful indeed. There are no cushions in the Intermediate class, and the population are either Intermediate, which is Eurasian, or native, which for a long night journey is nasty, or Loafer, which is amusing though intoxicated. Intermediates do not buy from refreshment-rooms. They carry their food in bundles and pots, and buy sweets from the native sweetmeat-sellers, and drink the roadside water. This is why in hot weather Intermediates are taken out of the carriages dead, and in all weathers are most properly looked down upon.

My particular Intermediate happened to be empty till I reached Nasirabad, when the big black-browed gentleman in shirt-sleeves entered, and, following the custom of Intermediates, passed the time of day. He was a wanderer and a vagabond like myself, but with an educated taste for whisky. He told tales of things he had seen and done, of out-of-the-way corners of the Empire into which he had penetrated, and of adventures in which he risked his life for a few days' food.

"If India was filled with men like you and me, not knowing more than the crows where they'd get their next day's rations, it isn't seventy millions of revenue the land would be paying – it's seven hundred millions," said he; and as I looked at his mouth and chin I was disposed to agree with him.

We talked politics – the politics of Loaferdom that sees things from the under side where the lath and plaster is not smoothed off – and we talked postal arrangements because my friend wanted to send a telegram back from the next station to Ajmir, the turning-off place from the Bombay to the Mhow line as you travel westward. My friend had no money beyond eight annas which he wanted for dinner, and I had no money at all, owing to the hitch in the Budget before mentioned. Further, I was going into a wilderness where, though I should resume touch with the Treasury, there were no telegraph offices. I was, therefore, unable to help him in any way.

"We might threaten a Station-master, and make him send a wire on tick," said my friend, "but that'd mean inquiries for you and for me, and I've got my hands full these days. Did you say you were travelling back along this line within any days?"

"Within ten," I said.

"Can't you make it eight?" said he. "Mine is rather urgent business."

"I can send your telegrams within ten days if that will serve you," I said.

"I couldn't trust the wire to fetch him, now I think of it. It's this way. He leaves Delhi on the 23rd for Bombay. That means he'll be running through Ajmir about the night of the 23rd."

"But I'm going into the Indian Desert," I explained.

"Well and good," said he. "You'll be changing at Marwar Junction to get into Jodhpore territory – you must do that – and he'll be coming through Marwar Junction in the early morning of the 24th by the Bombay Mail. Can you be at Marwar Junction on that time? 'T won't be inconveniencing you, because I know that there's precious few pickings to be got out of these Central India States – even though you pretend to be correspondent of the 'Backwoodsman.'"

"Have you ever tried that trick?" I asked.

"Again and again, but the Residents find you out, and then you get escorted to the Border before you've time to get your knife into them. But about my friend here. I must give him a word o' mouth to tell him what's come to me, or else he won't know where to go. I would take it more than kind of you if you was to come out of Central India in time to catch him at Marwar Junction, and say to him, 'He has gone South for the week.' He'll know what that means. He's a big man with a red beard, and a great swell he is. You'll find him sleeping like a gentleman with all his luggage round him in a Second-class apartment. But don't you be afraid. Slip down the window and say, 'He has gone South for the week,' and he'll tumble. It's only cutting your time of stay in those parts by two days. I ask you as a stranger – going to the West," he said, with emphasis.

"Where have you come from?" said I.

"From the East," said he, "and I am hoping that you will give him the message on the Square – for the sake of my Mother as well as your own."

Englishmen are not usually softened by appeals to the memory of their mothers; but for certain reasons, which will be fully apparent, I saw fit to agree.

"It's more than a little matter," said he, "and that's why I asked you to do it – and now I know that I can depend on you doing it. A Second-class carriage at Marwar Junction, and a red-haired man asleep in it. You'll be sure to remember. I get out at the next station, and I must hold on there till he comes or sends me what I want."

"I'll give the message if I catch him," I said, "and for the sake of your Mother as well as mine I'll give you a word of advice. Don't try to run the Central India States just now as the correspondent of the 'Backwoodsman.' There's a real one knocking about here, and it might lead to trouble."

"Thank you," said he, simply; "and when will the swine be gone? I can't starve because he's ruining my work. I wanted to get hold of the Degumber Rajah down here about his father's widow, and give him a jump."

"What did he do to his father's widow, then?"

"Filled her up with red pepper and slippered her to death as she hung from a beam. I found that out myself, and I'm the only man that would dare going into the State to get hush-money for it. They'll try to poison me, same as they did in Chortumna when I went on the loot there. But you'll give the man at Marwar Junction my message?"

He got out at a little roadside station, and I reflected. I had heard, more than once, of men personating correspondents of newspapers and bleeding small Native States with threats of exposure, but I had never met any of the caste before. They lead a hard life, and generally die with great suddenness. The Native States have a wholesome horror of English newspapers, which may throw light on their peculiar methods of government, and do their best to choke correspondents with champagne, or drive them out of their mind with four-inhand barouches. They do not understand that nobody cares a straw for the internal administration of Native States so long as oppression and crime are kept within decent limits, and the ruler is not drugged, drunk, or diseased from one end of the year to the other. They are the dark places of the earth, full of unimaginable cruelty, touching the Railway and the Telegraph on one side, and, on the other, the days of Harun-al-Raschid. When I left the train I did business with divers Kings, and in eight days passed through many changes of life. Sometimes I wore dress-clothes and consorted with Princes and Politicals, drinking from crystal and eating from silver. Sometimes I lay out upon the ground and devoured what I could get, from a plate made of leaves, and drank the running water, and slept under the same rug as my servant. It was all in the day's work.

Then I headed for the Great Indian Desert upon the proper date, as I had promised, and the night Mail set me down at Marwar Junction, where a funny little, happy-go-lucky, native-managed railway runs to Jodhpore. The Bombay Mail from Delhi makes a short halt at Marwar. She arrived just as I got in, and I had just time to hurry to her platform and go down the carriages. There was only one Second-class on the train. I slipped the window and looked down upon a flaming-red beard, half covered by a railway-rug. That was my man, fast asleep, and I dug him gently in the ribs. He woke with a grunt, and I saw his face in the light of the lamps. It was a great and shining face.

"Tickets again?" said he.

"No," said I. "I am to tell you that he is gone South for the week. He has gone South for the week!"

The train had begun to move out. The red man rubbed his eyes. "He has gone South for the week," he repeated. "Now that's just like his impidence. Did he say that I was to give you anything? 'Cause I won't."

"He didn't," I said, and dropped away, and watched the red lights die out in the dark. It was horribly cold because the wind was blowing off the sands. I climbed into my own train – not an Intermediate carriage this time – and went to sleep.

If the man with the beard had given me a rupee I should have kept it as a memento of a rather curious affair. But the consciousness of having done my duty was my only reward.

Later on I reflected that two gentlemen like my friends could not do any good if they foregathered and personated correspondents of newspapers, and might, if they blackmailed one of the little rat-trap States of Central India or Southern Rajputana, get themselves into serious difficulties. I therefore took some trouble to describe them as accurately as I could remember to people who would be interested in deporting them; and succeeded, so I was later informed, in having them headed back from the Degumber borders.

Then I became respectable, and returned to an office where there were no Kings and no incidents outside the daily manufacture of a newspaper. A newspaper office seems to attract every conceivable sort of person, to the prejudice of discipline. Zenana-mission ladies arrive, and beg that the Editor will instantly abandon all his duties to describe a Christian prize-giving in a back slum of a perfectly inaccessible village; Colonels who have been overpassed for command sit down and sketch the outline of a series of ten, twelve, or twenty-four leading articles on Seniority versus Selection; missionaries wish to know why they have not been permitted to escape from their regular vehicles of abuse, and swear at a brother missionary under special patronage of the editorial We; stranded theatrical companies troop up to explain that they cannot pay for their advertisements, but on their return from New Zealand or Tahiti will do so with interest; inventors of patent punka-pulling machines, carriage couplings, and unbreakable swords and axletrees call with specifications in their pockets and hours at their disposal; tea companies enter and elaborate their prospectuses with the office pens; secretaries of ball committees clamour to have the glories of their last dance more fully described; strange ladies rustle in and say, "I want a hundred lady's cards printed at once, please," which is manifestly part of an Editor's duty; and every dissolute ruffian that ever tramped the Grand Trunk Road makes it his business to ask for employment as a proof-reader. And, all the time, the telephone-bell is ringing madly, and Kings are being killed on the Continent, and Empires are saying, "You're another," and Mister Gladstone is calling down brimstone upon the British Dominions, and the little black copyboys are whining, "kaa-pi chay-ha-yeh" ('Copy wanted'), like tired bees, and most of the paper is as blank as Modred's shield.

But that is the amusing part of the year. There are six other months when none ever come to call, and the thermometer walks inch by inch up to the top of the glass, and the office is darkened to just above reading-light, and the press-machines are red-hot to touch, and nobody writes anything but accounts of amusements in the Hill-stations or obituary notices. Then the telephone becomes a tinkling terror, because it tells you of the sudden deaths of men and women that you knew intimately, and the prickly heat covers you with a garment, and you sit down and write: 'A slight increase of sickness is reported from the Khuda Janta Khan District. The outbreak is purely sporadic in its nature, and, thanks to the energetic efforts of the District authorities, is now almost at an end. It is, however, with deep regret we record the death,' etc.

Then the sickness really breaks out, and the less recording and reporting the better for the peace of the subscribers. But the Empires and the Kings continue to divert themselves as selfishly as before, and the Foreman thinks that a daily paper really ought to come out once in twenty-four hours, and all the people at the Hill-stations in the middle of their amusements say, "Good gracious! why can't the paper be sparkling? I'm sure there's plenty going on up here."

That is the dark half of the moon, and, as the advertisements say, "must be experienced to be appreciated."

It was in that season, and a remarkably evil season, that the paper began running the last issue of the week on Saturday night, which is to say Sunday morning, after the custom of a London paper. This was a great convenience, for immediately after the paper was put to bed the dawn would lower the thermometer from 96 degrees to almost 84 degrees for half an hour, and in that chill – you have no idea how cold is 84 degrees on the grass until you begin to pray for it – a very tired man could get off to sleep ere the heat roused him.

One Saturday night it was my pleasant duty to put the paper to bed alone. A King or courtier or a courtesan or a Community was going to die or get a new Constitution, or do something that was important on the other side of the world, and the paper was to be held open till the latest possible minute in order to catch the telegram.

It was a pitchy-black night, as stifling as a June night can be, and the loo, the red-hot wind from the westward, was booming among the tinder-dry trees and pretending that the rain was on its heels. Now and again a spot of almost boiling water would fall on the dust with the flop of a frog, but all our weary world knew that was only pretence. It was a shade cooler in the press-room than the office, so I sat there, while the type ticked and clicked, and the night-jars hooted at the windows, and the all but naked compositors wiped the sweat from their foreheads and called for water. The thing that was keeping us back, whatever it was, would not come off, though the loo dropped and the last type was set, and the whole round earth stood still in the choking heat, with its finger on its lip, to wait the event. I drowsed, and wondered whether the telegraph was a blessing, and whether this dying man, or struggling people, might be aware of the inconvenience the delay was causing. There was no special reason beyond the heat and worry to make tension, but, as the clock-hands crept up to three o-clock and the machines spun their fly-wheels two and three times to see that all was in order, before I said the word that would set them off, I could have shrieked aloud.

Then the roar and rattle of the wheels shivered the quiet into little bits. I rose to go away, but two men in white clothes stood in front of me. The first one said, "It's him!" The second said, "So it is!" And they both laughed almost as loudly as the machinery roared, and mopped their foreheads. "We seed there was a light burning across the road, and we were sleeping in that ditch there for coolness, and I said to my friend here, 'The office is open. Let's come along and speak to him as turned us back from Degumber State,'" said the smaller of the two. He was the man I had met in the Mhow train, and his fellow was the red-bearded man of Marwar Junction. There was no mistaking the eyebrows of the one or the beard of the other.

I was not pleased, because I wished to go to sleep, not to squabble with loafers. "What do you want?" I asked.

"Half an hour's talk with you, cool and comfortable, in the office," said the red-bearded man. "We'd like some drink – the Contrack doesn't begin yet, Peachey, so you needn't look – but what we really want is advice. We don't want money. We ask you as a favour, because we found out you did us a bad turn about Degumber State."

I led from the press-room to the stifling office with the maps on the walls, and the red-haired man rubbed his hands. "That's something like," said he. "This was the proper shop to come to. Now, Sir, let me introduce you to Brother Peachey Carnehan, that's him, and Brother Daniel Dravot, that is me, and the less said about our professions the better, for we have been most things in our time – soldier, sailor, compositor, photographer, proof-reader, street-preacher, and correspondents of the 'Backwoodsman' when we thought the paper wanted one. Carnehan is sober, and so am I. Look at us first, and see that's sure. It will save you cutting into my talk. We'll take one of your cigars apiece, and you shall see us light up."

I watched the test. The men were absolutely sober, so I gave them each a tepid whisky-and-soda.

"Well and good," said Carnehan of the eyebrows, wiping the froth from his moustache. "Let me talk now, Dan. We have been all over India, mostly on foot. We have been boiler-fitters, engine-drivers, petty contractors, and all that, and we have decided that India isn't big enough for such as us."

They certainly were too big for the office. Dravot's beard seemed to fill half the room and Carnehan's shoulders the other half, as they sat on the big table. Carnehan continued: "The country isn't half worked out because they that governs it won't let you touch it. They spend all their blessed time in governing it, and you can't lift a spade, nor chip a rock, nor look for oil, nor anything like that, without all the Government saying, 'Leave it alone, and let us govern.' Therefore, such as it is, we will let it alone, and go away to some other place where a man isn't crowded and can come to his own. We are not little men, and there is nothing that we are afraid of except Drink, and we have signed a Contrack on that. Therefore we are going away to be Kings."

"Kings in our own right," muttered Dravot.

"Yes, of course," I said. "You've been tramping in the sun, and it's a very warm night, and hadn't you better sleep over the notion? Come tomorrow."

"Neither drunk nor sunstruck," said Dravot. "We have slept over the notion half a year, and require to see Books and Atlases, and we have decided that there is only one place now in the world that two strong men can Sar-a-whack. They call it Kafiristan. By my reckoning it's the top right-hand corner of Afghanistan, not more than three hundred miles from Peshawar. They have two and thirty heathen idols there, and we'll be the thirty-third and fourth. It's a mountainous country, the women of those parts are very beautiful."

"But that is provided against in the Contrack," said Carnehan. "Neither Women nor Liquor, Daniel."

"And that's all we know, except that no one has gone there, and they fight, and in any place where they fight a man who knows how to drill men can always be a King. We shall go to those parts and say to any King we find, 'D' you want to vanquish your foes?' and we will show him how to drill men; for that we know better than anything else. Then we will subvert that King and seize his Throne and establish a Dynasty."

"You'll be cut to pieces before you're fifty miles across the Border," I said. "You have to travel through Afghanistan to get to that country. It's one mass of mountains and peaks and glaciers, and no Englishman has been through it. The people are utter brutes, and even if you reached them you couldn't do anything."

"That's more like," said Carnehan. "If you could think us a little more mad we would be more pleased. We have come to you to know about this country, to read a book about it, and to be shown maps. We want you to tell us that we are fools and to show us your books." He turned to the bookcases.

"Are you at all in earnest?" I said.

"A little," said Dravot, sweetly. "As big a map as you have got, even if it's all blank where Kafiristan is, and any books you've got. We can read, though we aren't very educated."

I uncased the big thirty-two-miles-to-the-inch map of India and two smaller Frontier maps, hauled down volume INF-KAN of the *Encyclopaedia Britannica*, and the men consulted them.

"See here!" said Dravot, his thumb on the map. "Up to Jagdallak, Peachey and me know the road. We was there with Robert's Army. We'll have to turn off to the right at Jagdallak through Laghmann territory. Then we get among the hills – fourteen thousand feet – fifteen thousand – it will be cold work there, but it don't look very far on the map."

I handed him Wood on the 'Sources of the Oxus.' Carnehan was deep in the *Encyclopaedia*.

"They're a mixed lot," said Dravot, reflectively; "and it won't help us to know the names of their tribes. The more tribes the more they'll fight, and the better for us. From Jagdallak to Ashang. H'mm!"

"But all the information about the country is as sketchy and inaccurate as can be," I protested. "No one knows anything about it really. Here's the file of the 'United Services' Institute.' Read what Bellew says."

"Blow Bellew!" said Carnehan. "Dan, they're a stinkin' lot of heathens, but this book here says they think they're related to us English."

I smoked while the men poured over Raverty, Wood, the maps, and the *Encyclopaedia*.

"There is no use your waiting," said Dravot, politely. "It's about four o'clock now. We'll go before six o'clock if you want to sleep, and we won't steal any of the papers. Don't you sit up. We're two harmless lunatics, and if you come tomorrow evening down to the Serai we'll say good-bye to you."

"You are two fools," I answered. "You'll be turned back at the Frontier or cut up the minute you set foot in Afghanistan. Do you want any money or a recommendation down-country? I can help you to the chance of work next week."

"Next week we shall be hard at work ourselves, thank you," said Dravot. "It isn't so easy being a King as it looks. When we've got our Kingdom in going order we'll let you know, and you can come up and help us govern it."

"Would two lunatics make a Contrack like that?" said Carnehan, with subdued pride, showing me a greasy half-sheet of notepaper on which was written the following. I copied it, then and there, as a curiosity.

This Contract between me and you persuing witnesseth in the name of God – Amen and so forth.
(One) *That me and you will settle this matter together; i.e., to be Kings of Kafiristan.*
(Two) *That you and me will not, while this matter is being settled, look at any Liquor, nor any Woman, black, white, or brown, so as to get mixed up with one or the other harmful.*
(Three) *That we conduct ourselves with Dignity and Discretion, and if one of us gets into trouble the other will stay by him.*
Signed by you and me this day.
Peachey Taliaferro Carnehan.
Daniel Dravot.
Both Gentlemen at Large.

"There was no need for the last article," said Carnehan, blushing modestly; "but it looks regular. Now you know the sort of men that loafers are – we *are* loafers, Dan, until we get out of India – and *do* you think that we would sign a Contrack like that unless we was in earnest? We have kept away from the two things that make life worth having."

"You won't enjoy your lives much longer if you are going to try this idiotic adventure. Don't set the office on fire," I said, "and go away before nine o'clock."

I left them still poring over the maps and making notes on the back of the 'Contrack.' "Be sure to come down to the Serai tomorrow," were their parting words.

The Kumharsen Serai is the great foursquare sink of humanity where the strings of camels and horses from the North load and unload. All the nationalities of Central Asia may be found there, and most of the folk of India proper. Balkh and

Bokhara there meet Bengal and Bombay, and try to draw eye-teeth. You can buy ponies, turquoises, Persian pussy-cats, saddle-bags, fat-tailed sheep, and musk in the Kumharsen Serai, and get many strange things for nothing. In the afternoon I went down to see whether my friends intended to keep their word or were lying there drunk.

A priest attired in fragments of ribbons and rags stalked up to me, gravely twisting a child's paper whirligig. Behind him was his servant bending under the load of a crate of mud toys. The two were loading up two camels, and the inhabitants of the Serai watched them with shrieks of laughter.

"The priest is mad," said a horse-dealer to me. "He is going up to Kabul to sell toys to the Amir. He will either be raised to honour or have his head cut off. He came in here this morning and has been behaving madly ever since."

"The witless are under the protection of God," stammered a flat-cheeked Usbeg in broken Hindi. "They foretell future events."

"Would they could have foretold that my caravan would have been cut up by the Shinwaris almost within shadow of the Pass!" grunted the Eusufzai agent of a Rajputana trading-house whose goods had been diverted into the hands of other robbers just across the Border, and whose misfortunes were the laughing-stock of the bazaar. "Ohé, priest, whence come you and whither do you go?"

"From Roum have I come," shouted the priest, waving his whirligig; "from Roum, blown by the breath of a hundred devils across the sea! O thieves, robbers, liars, the blessing of Pir Khan on pigs, dogs, and perjurers! Who will take the Protected of God to the North to sell charms that are never still to the Amir? The camels shall not gall, the sons shall not fall sick, and the wives shall remain faithful while they are away, of the men who give me place in their caravan. Who will assist me to slipper the King of the Roos with a golden slipper with a silver heel? The protection of Pir Khan be upon his labours!" He spread out the skirts of his gabardine and pirouetted between the lines of tethered horses.

"There starts a caravan from Peshawar to Kabul in twenty days, *Huzrut*," said the Eusufzai trader. "My camels go therewith. Do thou also go and bring us good luck."

"I will go even now!" shouted the priest. "I will depart upon my winged camels, and be at Peshawar in a day! Ho! Hazar Mir Khan," he yelled to his servant, "drive out the camels, but let me first mount my own."

He leaped on the back of his beast as it knelt, and, turning round to me, cried, "Come thou also, Sahib, a little along the road, and I will sell thee a charm – an amulet that shall make thee King of Kafiristan."

Then the light broke upon me, and I followed the two camels out of the Serai till we reached open road and the priest halted.

"What d' you think o' that?" said he in English. "Carnehan can't talk their patter, so I've made him my servant. He makes a handsome servant. 'T isn't for nothing that I've been knocking about the country for fourteen years. Didn't I do that talk neat? We'll hitch on to a caravan at Peshawar till we get to Jagdallak, and then we'll see if we can get donkeys for our camels, and strike into Kafiristan. Whirligigs for the Amir, O Lor'! Put your hand under the camelbags and tell me what you feel."

I felt the butt of a Martini, and another and another.

"Twenty of 'em," said Dravot, placidly. "Twenty of 'em and ammunition to correspond, under the whirligigs and the mud dolls."

"Heaven help you if you are caught with those things!" I said. "A Martini is worth her weight in silver among the Pathans."

"Fifteen hundred rupees of capital – every rupee we could beg, borrow, or steal – are invested on these two camels," said Dravot. "We won't get caught. We're going through the Khaiber with a regular caravan. Who'd touch a poor mad priest?"

"Have you got everything you want?" I asked, overcome with astonishment.

"Not yet, but we shall soon. Give us a memento of your kindness, *Brother*. You did me a service yesterday, and that time in Marwar. Half my Kingdom shall you have, as the saying is." I slipped a small charm compass from my watch-chain and handed it up to the priest.

"Good-bye," said Dravot, giving me hand cautiously. "It's the last time we'll shake hands with an Englishman these many days. Shake hands with him, Carnehan," he cried, as the second camel passed me.

Carnehan leaned down and shook hands. Then the camels passed away along the dusty road, and I was left alone to wonder. My eye could detect no failure in the disguises. The scene in the Serai proved that they were complete to the native mind. There was just the chance, therefore, that Carnehan and Dravot would be able to wander through Afghanistan without detection. But, beyond, they would find death – certain and awful death.

Ten days later a native correspondent, giving me the news of the day from Peshawar, wound up his letter with: "There has been much laughter here on account of a certain mad priest who is going in his estimation to sell petty gauds and insignificant trinkets which he ascribes as great charms to H.H. the Amir of Bokhara. He passed through Peshawar and associated himself to the Second Summer caravan that goes to Kabul. The merchants are pleased because through superstition they imagine that such mad fellows bring good fortune."

The two, then, were beyond the Border. I would have prayed for them, but that night a real King died in Europe, and demanded an obituary notice.

The wheel of the world swings through the same phases again and again. Summer passed and winter thereafter, and came and passed again. The daily paper continued and I with it, and upon the third summer there fell a hot night, a night issue, and a strained waiting for something to be telegraphed from the other side of the world, exactly as had happened before. A few great men had died in the past two years, the machines worked with more clatter, and some of the trees in the office garden were a few feet taller. But that was all the difference.

I passed over to the press-room, and went through just such a scene as I have already described. The nervous tension was stronger than it had been two years before, and I felt the heat more acutely. At three o'clock I cried, "Print off," and turned to go, when there crept to my chair what was left of a man. He was bent into a circle, his head was sunk between his shoulders, and he moved his feet one over the other like a bear. I could hardly see whether he walked or crawled – this rag-wrapped, whining cripple who addressed me by name, crying that he was come back. "Can you give me a drink?" he whimpered. "For the Lord's sake, give me a drink!"

I went back to the office, the man following with groans of pain, and I turned up the lamp.

"Don't you know me?" he gasped, dropping into a chair, and he turned his drawn face, surmounted by a shock of grey hair, to the light.

I looked at him intently. Once before had I seen eyebrows that met over the nose in an inch-broad black band, but for the life of me I could not tell where.

"I don't know you," I said, handing him the whisky. "What can I do for you?"

He took a gulp of the spirit raw, and shivered in spite of the suffocating heat.

"I've come back," he repeated; "and I was the King of Kafiristan – me and Dravot – crowned Kings we was! In this office we settled it – you setting there and giving us the books. I am Peachey – Peachey Taliaferro Carnehan – and you've been setting here ever since – O Lord!"

I was more than a little astonished, and expressed my feelings accordingly.

"It's true," said Carnehan, with a dry cackle, nursing his feet, which were wrapped in rags –"true as gospel. Kings we were, with crowns upon our heads – me and Dravot – poor Dan – oh, poor, poor Dan, that would never take advice, not though I begged of him!"

"Take the whisky," I said, "and take your own time. Tell me all you can recollect of everything from beginning to end. You got across the Border on your camels, Dravot dressed as a mad priest and you his servant. Do you remember that?"

"I ain't mad – yet, but I shall be that way soon. Of course I remember. Keep looking at me, or maybe my words will go all to pieces. Keep looking at me in my eyes and don't say anything."

I leaned forward and looked into his face as steadily as I could. He dropped one hand upon the table and I grasped it by the wrist. It was twisted like a bird's claw, and upon the back was a ragged, red, diamond-shaped scar.

"No, don't look there. Look at *me*," said Carnehan. "That comes afterward, but for the Lord's sake don't distrack me. We left with that caravan, me and Dravot playing all sorts of antics to amuse the people we were with. Dravot used to make us laugh in the evenings when all the people was cooking their dinners – cooking their dinners, and...what did they do then? They lit little fires with sparks that went into Dravot's beard, and we all laughed – fit to die. Little red fires they was, going into Dravot's big red beard – so funny." His eyes left mine and he smiled foolishly.

"You went as far as Jagdallak with that caravan," I said, at a venture, "after you had lit those fires. To Jagdallak, where you turned off to try to get into Kafiristan."

"No, we didn't, neither. What are you talking about? We turned off before Jagdallak, because we heard the roads was good. But they wasn't good enough for our two camels – mine and Dravot's. When we left the caravan, Dravot took off all his clothes and mine too, and said we would be heathen, because the Kafirs didn't allow Mohammedans to talk to them. So we dressed betwixt and between, and such a sight as Daniel Dravot I never saw yet nor expect to see again. He burned half his beard, and slung a sheepskin over his shoulder, and shaved his head into patterns. He shaved mine too, and made me wear outrageous things to look like a heathen. That was in a most mountainous country, and our camels couldn't go along any more because of the mountains. They were tall and black, and coming home I saw them fight like wild goats – there are lots of goats in Kafiristan. And these mountains, they never keep still, no more than the goats. Always fighting they are, and don't let you sleep at night."

"Take some more whisky," I said, very slowly. "What did you and Daniel Dravot do when the camels could go no farther because of the rough roads that led into Kafiristan?"

"What did which do? There was a party called Peachey Taliaferro Carnehan that was with Dravot. Shall I tell you about him? He died out there in the cold. Slap from the bridge fell old Peachey, turning and twisting in the air like a penny whirligig that you can sell to the Amir. No; they was two for three ha'pence, those whirligigs, or I am much mistaken and woeful sore....And then these camels were no use, and Peachey said to Dravot, 'For the Lord's sake let's get out of this before our heads are chopped off,' and with that they killed the camels all among the mountains, not having anything in particular to eat, but first they took off the boxes with the guns and the ammunition, till two men came along driving four mules. Dravot up and dances in front of them, singing, 'Sell me four mules.' Says the first man, 'If you are rich enough to buy, you are rich enough to rob;' but before ever he could put his hand to his knife, Dravot breaks his neck over his knee, and the other party runs away. So Carnehan loaded the mules with the rifles that was taken off the camels, and together we starts forward into those bitter-cold mountainous parts, and never a road broader than the back of your hand."

He paused for a moment, while I asked him if he could remember the nature of the country through which he had journeyed.

"I am telling you as straight as I can, but my head isn't as good as it might be. They drove nails through it to make me hear better how Dravot died. The country was mountainous and the mules were most contrary, and the inhabitants was dispersed and solitary. They went up and up, and down and down, and that other party, Carnehan, was imploring of Dravot not to sing and whistle so loud, for fear of bringing down the tremenjus avalanches. But Dravot says that if a King couldn't sing it wasn't worth being King, and whacked the mules over the rump, and never took no heed for ten cold days. We came to a big level valley all among the mountains, and the mules were near dead, so we killed them, not having anything in special for them or us to eat. We sat upon the boxes, and played odd and even with the cartridges that was jolted out.

"Then ten men with bows and arrows ran down that valley, chasing twenty men with bows and arrows, and the row was tremenjus. They was fair men – fairer than you or me – with yellow hair and remarkable well built. Says Dravot, unpacking the guns, 'This is the beginning of the business. We'll fight for the ten men,' and with that he fires two rifles at the twenty men, and drops one of them at two hundred yards from the rock where he was sitting. The other men began to run, but Carnehan and Dravot sits on the boxes picking them off at all ranges, up and down the valley. Then we goes up to the ten men that had run across the snow too, and they fires a footy little arrow at us. Dravot he shoots above their heads, and they all falls down flat. Then he walks over them and kicks them, and then he lifts them up and shakes hands all round to make them friendly like. He calls them and gives them the boxes to carry, and waves his hand for all the world as though he was King already. They takes the boxes and him across the valley and up the hill into a pine wood on the top, where there was half a dozen big stone idols. Dravot he goes to the biggest – a fellow they call Imbra – and lays a rifle and a cartridge at his feet, rubbing his nose respectfully with his own nose, patting him on the head, and nods his head, and says, 'That's all right. I'm in the know too, and these old jimjams are my friends.' Then he opens his mouth and points down it, and when the first man brings him food, he says, 'No;' and when the second man brings him food, he says 'no;' but when one of the old priests and the boss of the village brings him food, he says, 'Yes;' very haughty, and eats it slow. That was how we came to our first village without any trouble, just as though we had tumbled from the skies. But we tumbled from one of those damned rope-bridges, you see, and – you couldn't expect a man to laugh much after that?"

"Take some more whisky and go on," I said. "That was the first village you came into. How did you get to be King?"

"I wasn't King," said Carnehan. "Dravot, he was the King, and a handsome man he looked with the gold crown on his head and all. Him and the other party stayed in that village, and every morning Dravot sat by the side of old Imbra, and the people came and worshipped. That was Dravot's order. Then a lot of men came into the valley, and Carnehan and Dravot picks them off with the rifles before they knew where they was, and runs down into the valley and up again the other side, and finds another village, same as the first one, and the people all falls down flat on their faces, and Dravot says, 'Now what is the trouble between you two villages?' and the people points to a woman, as fair as you or me, that was carried off, and Dravot takes her back to the first village and counts up the dead – eight there was. For each dead man Dravot pours a little milk on the ground and waves his arms like a whirligig, and 'That's all right,' says he. Then he and Carnehan takes the big boss of each village by the arm, and walks them down the valley, and shows them how to scratch a line with a spear right down the valley, and gives each a sod of turf from both sides of the line. Then all the people comes down and shouts like the devil and all, and Dravot says, 'Go and dig the land, and be fruitful and multiply,' which they did, though they didn't understand. Then we asks the names of things in their lingo – bread and water and fire and idols and such; and Dravot leads the priest of each village up to the idol, and says he must sit there and judge the people, and if anything goes wrong he is to be shot.

"Next week they was all turning up the land in the valley as quiet as bees and much prettier, and the priests heard all the complaints and told Dravot in dumb-show what it was about. 'That's just the beginning,' says Dravot. 'They think we're Gods.' He and Carnehan picks out twenty good men and shows them how to click off a rifle and form fours and advance in line; and they was very pleased to do so, and clever to see the hang of it. Then he takes out his pipe and his baccy-pouch, and leaves one at one village and one at the other, and off we two goes to see what was to be done in the next valley. That was all rock, and there was a little village there, and Carnehan says, 'Send 'em to the old valley to plant,' and takes 'em there and gives 'em some land that wasn't took before. They were a poor lot, and we blooded 'em with a kid before letting 'em into the new Kingdom. That was to impress the people, and then they settled down quiet, and Carnehan went back to Dravot, who had got into another valley, all snow and ice and most mountaineous. There was no people there, and the Army got afraid; so Dravot shoots one of them, and goes on till he finds some people in a village, and the Army explains that unless the people wants to be killed they had better not shoot their little matchlocks, for they had matchlocks. We makes friends with the priest, and I stays there alone with two of the Army, teaching the men how to drill; and a thundering big Chief comes across the snow with kettledrums and horns twanging, because he heard there was a new God kicking about. Carnehan sights for the brown of the men half a mile across the snow and wings one of them. Then he sends a message to the Chief that, unless he wished to be killed, he must come and shake hands with me and leave his arms behind. The Chief comes alone first, and Carnehan shakes hands with him and whirls his arms about, same as Dravot used, and very much surprised that Chief was, and strokes my eyebrows. Then Carnehan goes alone to the Chief, and asks him in dumb-show if he had an enemy he hated. 'I have,' says the chief. So Carnehan weeds out the pick of his men, and sets the two of the Army to show them drill, and at the end of two weeks the men can manoeuvre about as well as Volunteers. So he marches with the Chief to a great big plain on the top of a mountain, and the Chief's men rushes into a village and takes it; we three Martinis firing into the brown of the enemy. So we took that village too, and I gives the Chief a rag from my coat, and says, 'Occupy till I come;' which was scriptural. By way of a reminder, when me and the Army was eighteen hundred yards away, I drops a bullet near him standing on the snow, and all the people falls flat on their faces. Then I sends a letter to Dravot wherever he be by land or by sea."

At the risk of throwing the creature out of train I interrupted: "How could you write a letter up yonder?"

"The letter? – Oh! – The letter! Keep looking at me between the eyes, please. It was a string-talk letter, that we'd learned the way of it from a blind beggar in the Punjab."

I remember that there had once come to the office a blind man with a knotted twig, and a piece of string which he wound round the twig according to some cipher of his own. He could, after the lapse of days or hours, repeat the sentence which he had reeled up. He had reduced the alphabet to eleven primitive sounds, and tried to teach me his method, but I could not understand.

"I sent that letter to Dravot," said Carnehan, "and told him to come back because this Kingdom was growing too big for me to handle; and then I struck for the first valley, to see how the priests were working. They called the village we took along with the Chief, Bashkai, and the first village we took, Er-Heb. The priests at Er-Heb was doing all right, but they had a lot of pending cases about land to show me, and some men from another village had been firing arrows at night. I went out and looked for that village, and fired four rounds at it from a thousand yards. That used all the cartridges I cared to spend, and I waited for Dravot, who had been away two or three months, and I kept my people quiet.

"One morning I heard the devil's own noise of drums and horns, and Dan Dravot marches down the hill with his Army and a tail of hundreds of men, and, which was the most amazing, a great gold crown on his head. 'My Gord, Carnehan,' says Daniel, 'this is a tremenjus business, and we've got the whole country as far as it's worth having. I am the son of Alexander by Queen Semiramis, and you're my younger brother and a God too! It's the biggest thing we've ever seen. I've been marching and fighting for six weeks with the Army, and every footy little village for fifty miles has come in rejoiceful; and more than that, I've got the key of the whole show, as you'll see, and I've got a crown for you! I told 'em to make two of 'em at a place called Shu, where the gold lies in the rock like suet in mutton. Gold I've seen, and turquoise I've kicked out of the cliffs, and there's garnets in the sands of the river, and here's a chunk of amber that a man brought me. Call up all the priests and, here, take your crown.'

"One of the men opens a black hair bag, and I slips the crown on. It was too small and too heavy, but I wore it for the glory. Hammered gold it was – five pounds weight, like a hoop of a barrel.

"'Peachey,' says Dravot, 'we don't want to fight no more. The Craft's the trick, so help me!' and he brings forward that same Chief that I left at Bashkai – Billy Fish we called him afterward, because he was so like Billy Fish that drove the big tank-engine at Mach on the Bolan in the old days. 'Shake hands with him,' says Dravot; and I shook hands and nearly dropped, for Billy Fish gave me the Grip. I said nothing, but tried him with the Fellow-craft Grip. He answers all right, and I tried the Master's Grip, but that was a slip. 'A Fellow-craft he is!' I says to Dan. 'Does he know the word?' 'He does,' says Dan, 'and all the priests know. It's a miracle! The Chiefs and the priests can work a Fellow-craft Lodge in a way that's very like ours, and they've cut the marks on the rocks, but they don't know the Third Degree, and they've come to find out. It's Gord's Truth. I've known these long years that the Afghans knew up to the Fellow-craft Degree, but this is a miracle. A God and a Grand Master of the Craft am I, and a Lodge in the Third Degree I will open, and we'll raise the head priests and the Chiefs of the villages.'

"'It's against all the law,' I says, 'holding a Lodge without warrant from any one; and you know we never held office in any Lodge.'

"'It's a master stroke o' policy,' says Dravot. 'It means running the country as easy as a four-wheeled bogie on a down grade. We can't stop to inquire now, or they'll turn against us. I've forty Chiefs at my heel, and passed and raised according to their merit they shall be. Billet these men on the villages, and see that we run up a Lodge of some kind. The temple of Imbra will do for a Lodge-room. The women must make aprons as you show them. I'll hold a levee of Chiefs tonight and Lodge tomorrow.'

"I was fair run off my legs, but I wasn't such a fool as not to see what a pull this Craft business gave us. I showed the priests' families how to make aprons of the degrees, but for Dravot's apron the blue border and marks was made of turquoise lumps on white hide, not cloth. We took a great square stone in the temple for the Master's chair, and little stones for the officer's chairs, and painted the black pavement with white squares, and did what we could to make things regular.

"At the levee which was held that night on the hillside with big bonfires, Dravot gives out that him and me were Gods and sons of Alexander, and Passed Grand Masters in the Craft, and was come to make Kafiristan a country where every man should eat in peace and drink in quiet, and specially obey us. Then the Chiefs come round to shake hands, and they were so hairy and white and fair it was just shaking hands with old friends. We gave them names according as they was like men we had known in India – Billy Fish, Holly Dilworth, Pikky Kergan, that was Bazaar-master when I was at Mhow, and so on, and so on.

"*The* most amazing miracles was at Lodge next night. One of the old priests was watching us continuous, and I felt uneasy, for I knew we'd have to fudge the Ritual, and I didn't know what the men knew. The old priest was a stranger come in from beyond the village of Bashkai. The minute Dravot puts on the Master's apron that the girls had made for him, the priest fetches a whoop and a howl, and tries to overturn the stone that Dravot was sitting on. 'It's all up now,' I says. 'That comes of meddling with the Craft without warrant!' Dravot never winked an eye, not when ten priests took and tilted over the Grand Master's chair – which was to say, the stone of Imbra. The priest begins rubbing the bottom end of it to clear away the black dirt, and presently he shows all the other priests the Master's Mark, same as was on Dravot's apron, cut into the stone. Not even the priests of the temple of Imbra knew it was there. The old chap falls flat on his face at Dravot's feet and kisses 'em. 'Luck again,' says Dravot, across the Lodge, to me; 'they say it's the missing Mark that no one could understand the why of. We're more than safe now.' Then he bangs the butt of his gun for a gavel and says, 'By virtue of the authority vested in me by my own right hand and the help of Peachey, I declare myself Grand Master of all Freemasonry in Kafiristan in this the Mother Lodge o' the country, and King of Kafiristan equally with Peachey!' At that he puts on his crown and I puts on mine – I was doing Senior Warden – and we opens the Lodge in most ample form. It was an amazing miracle! The priests moved in Lodge through the first two degrees almost without telling, as if the memory was coming back to them. After that Peachey and Dravot raised such as was worthy – high priests and Chiefs of far-off villages. Billy Fish was the first, and I can tell you we scared the soul out of him. It was not in any way according to Ritual, but it served our turn. We didn't raise more than ten of the biggest men, because we didn't want to make the Degree common. And they was clamouring to be raised.

"'In another six months,' says Dravot, 'we'll hold another Communication and see how you are working.' Then he asks them about their villages, and learns that they was fighting one against the other, and were sick and tired of it. And when they wasn't doing that they was fighting with the Mohammedans. 'You can fight those when they come into our country,' says Dravot. 'Tell off every tenth man of your tribes for a Frontier guard, and send two hundred at a time to this valley to be drilled. Nobody is going to be shot or speared any more so long as he does well, and I know that you won't cheat me, because you're white people – sons of Alexander – and not like common black Mohammedans. You are *my* people, and, by God,' says he, running off into English at the end, 'I'll make a damned fine Nation of you, or I'll die in the making!'

"I can't tell all we did for the next six months, because Dravot did a lot I couldn't see the hang of, and he learned their lingo in a way I never could. My work was to help the people plough, and now and again go out with some of the Army and see what the other villages were doing, and make 'em throw rope bridges across the ravines which cut up the country horrid. Dravot was very kind to me, but when he walked up and down in the pine wood pulling that bloody red beard of his with both fists I knew he was thinking plans I could not advise about, and I just waited for orders.

"But Dravot never showed me disrespect before the people. They were afraid of me and the Army, but they loved Dan. He was the best of friends with the priests and the Chiefs; but any one could come across the hills with a complaint, and Dravot would hear him out fair, and call four priests together and say what was to be done. He used to call in Billy Fish from Bashkai, and Pikky Kergan from Shu, and an old Chief we called Kafuzelum – it was like enough to his real name – and hold councils with 'em when there was any fighting to be done in small villages. That was his Council of War, and the four priests of Bashkai, Shu, Khawak, and Madora was his Privy Council. Between the lot of 'em they sent me, with forty men and twenty rifles, and sixty men carrying turquoises, into the Ghorband country to buy those hand-made Martini rifles, that come out of the Amir's workshops at Kabul, from one of the Amir's Herati regiments that would have sold the very teeth out of their mouths for turquoises.

"I stayed in Ghorband a month, and gave the Governor there the pick of my baskets for hush-money, and bribed the Colonel of the regiment some more, and, between the two and the tribes-people, we got more than a hundred hand-made Martinis, a hundred good Kohat Jezails that'll throw to six hundred yards, and forty man-loads of very bad ammunition for the rifles. I came back with what I had, and distributed 'em among the men that the Chiefs sent in to me to drill. Dravot was too busy to attend to those things, but the old Army that we first made helped me, and we turned out five hundred men that could drill, and two hundred that knew how to hold arms pretty straight. Even those cork-screwed, hand-made guns was a miracle to them. Dravot talked big about powder-shops and factories, walking up and down in the pine wood when the winter was coming on.

"'I won't make a Nation,' says he. 'I'll make an Empire! These men aren't niggers; they're English! Look at their eyes – look at their mouths. Look at the way they stand up. They sit on chairs in their own houses. They're the Lost Tribes, or something like it, and they've grown to be English. I'll take a census in the spring if the priests don't get frightened. There must be a fair two million of 'em in these hills. The villages are full o' little children. Two million people – two hundred and fifty thousand fighting men – and all English! They only want the rifles and a little drilling. Two hundred and fifty thousand men, ready to cut in on Russia's right flank when she tries for India! Peachey, man,' he says, chewing his beard in great hunks, 'we shall be Emperors – Emperors of the Earth! Rajah Brooke will be a suckling to us. I'll treat with the Viceroy on equal terms. I'll ask him to send me twelve picked English – twelve that I know of – to help us govern a bit. There's Mackray, Serjeant Pensioner at Segowli – many's the good dinner he's given me, and his wife a pair of trousers. There's Donkin, the Warder of Tounghoo Jail; there's hundreds that I could lay my hand on if I was in India. The Viceroy shall do it for me; I'll send a man through in the spring for those men, and I'll write for a dispensation from the Grand Lodge for what I've done as Grand Master. That – and all the Sniders that'll be thrown out when the native troops in India take up the Martini. They'll be worn smooth, but they'll do for fighting in these hills. Twelve English, a hundred thousand Sniders run through the Amir's country in driblets – I'd be content with twenty thousand in one year – and we'd be an Empire. When everything was shipshape I'd hand over the crown – this crown I'm wearing now – to Queen Victoria on my knees, and she'd say, "Rise up, Sir Daniel Dravot." Oh, it's big! It's big, I tell you! But there's so much to be done in every place – Bashkai, Khawak, Shu, and everywhere else.'

"'What is it?' I says. 'There are no more men coming in to be drilled this autumn. Look at those fat black clouds. They're bringing the snow.'

"'It isn't that,' says Daniel, putting his hand very hard on my shoulder; 'and I don't wish to say anything that's against you, for no other living man would have followed me and made me what I am as you have done. You're a first-class Commander-in-Chief, and the people know you; but – it's a big country, and somehow you can't help me, Peachey, in the way I want to be helped.'

"'Go to your blasted priests, then!' I said, and I was sorry when I made that remark, but it did hurt me sore to find Daniel talking so superior, when I'd drilled all the men and done all he told me.

"'Don't let's quarrel, Peachey,' says Daniel, without cursing. 'You're a King too, and the half of this Kingdom is yours; but can't you see, Peachey, we want cleverer men than us now – three or four of 'em, that we can scatter about for our Deputies. It's a hugeous great State, and I can't always tell the right thing to do, and I haven't time for all I want to do, and here's the winter coming on and all.' He put half his beard into his mouth, all red like the gold of his crown.

"'I'm sorry, Daniel,' says I. 'I've done all I could. I've drilled the men and shown the people how to stack their oats better; and I've brought in those tinware rifles from Ghorband – but I know what you're driving at. I take it Kings always feel oppressed that way.'

"'There's another thing too,' says Dravot, walking up and down. 'The winter's coming, and these people won't be giving much trouble, and if they do we can't move about. I want a wife.'

"'For Gord's sake leave the women alone!' I says. 'We've both got all the work we can, though I *am* a fool. Remember the Contrack, and keep clear o' women.'"

"'The Contrack only lasted till such time as we was Kings; and Kings we have been these months past,' says Dravot, weighing his crown in his hand. 'You go get a wife too, Peachey – a nice, strappin', plump girl that'll keep you warm in the winter. They're prettier than English girls, and we can take the pick of 'em. Boil 'em once or twice in hot water, and they'll come out like chicken and ham.'

"'Don't tempt me!' I says. 'I will not have any dealings with a woman, not till we are a dam' side more settled than we are now. I've been doing the work o' two men, and you've been doing the work of three. Let's lie off a bit, and see if we can get some better tobacco from Afghan country and run in some good liquor; and no women.'"

"'Who's talking o' *women*?' says Dravot. 'I said *wife* – a Queen to breed a King's son for the King. A Queen out of the strongest tribe, that'll make them your blood-brothers, and that'll lie by your side and tell you all the people thinks about you and their own affairs. That's what I want.'

"'Do you remember that Bengali woman I kept at Mogul Serai when I was a plate-layer?' says I. 'A fat lot o' good she was to me. She taught me the lingo and one or two other things; but what happened? She ran away with the Station-master's servant and half my month's pay. Then she turned up at Dadur Junction in tow of a half-caste, and had the impudence to say I was her husband – all among the drivers in the running-shed too!'

"'We've done with that,' says Dravot; 'these women are whiter than you or me, and a Queen I will have for the winter months.'

"'For the last time o' asking, Dan, do *not*,' I says. 'It'll only bring us harm. The Bible says that Kings ain't to waste their strength on women, 'specially when they've got a new raw Kingdom to work over.'

"'For the last time of answering, I will,' said Dravot, and he went away through the pine-trees looking like a big red devil, the sun being on his crown and beard and all.

"But getting a wife was not as easy as Dan thought. He put it before the Council, and there was no answer till Billy Fish said that he'd better ask the girls. Dravot damned them all round. 'What's wrong with me?' he shouts, standing by the idol Imbra. 'Am I a dog, or am I not enough of a man for your wenches? Haven't I put the shadow of my hand over this country? Who stopped the last Afghan raid?' It was me really, but Dravot was too angry to remember. 'Who bought your guns? Who repaired the bridges? Who's the Grand Master of the sign cut in the stone?' says he, and he thumped his hand on the block that he used to sit on in Lodge, and at Council, which opened like Lodge always. Billy Fish said nothing, and no more did the others. 'Keep your hair on, Dan,' said I, 'and ask the girls. That's how it's done at Home, and these people are quite English.'

"'The marriage of the King is a matter of State,' says Dan, in a white-hot rage, for he could feel, I hope, that he was going against his better mind. He walked out of the Council-room, and the others sat still, looking at the ground.

"'Billy Fish,' says I to the Chief of Bashkai, 'what's the difficulty here? A straight answer to a true friend.'

"'You know,' says Billy Fish. 'How should a man tell you who knows everything? How can daughters of men marry Gods or Devils? It's not proper.'

"I remembered something like that in the Bible; but, if after seeing us as long as they had, they still believed we were Gods, it wasn't for me to undeceive them.

"'A God can do anything,' says I. 'If the King is fond of a girl he'll not let her die.' 'She'll have to,' said Billy Fish. 'There are all sorts of Gods and Devils in these mountains, and now and again a girl marries one of them and isn't seen any more. Besides, you two know the Mark cut in the stone. Only the Gods know that. We thought you were men till you showed the sign of the Master.'

"I wished then that we had explained about the loss of the genuine secrets of a Master Mason at the first go-off; but I said nothing. All that night there was a blowing of horns in a little dark temple half-way down the hill, and I heard the girl crying fit to die. One of the priests told us that she was being prepared to marry the King.

"'I'll have no nonsense of that kind,' says Dan. 'I don't want to interfere with your customs, but I'll take my own wife.' 'The girl's a little bit afraid,' says the priest. 'She thinks she's going to die, and they are a-heartening of her up down in the temple.'

"'Hearten her very tender, then,' says Dravot, 'or I'll hearten you with the butt of a gun so you'll never want to be heartened again.' He licked his lips, did Dan, and stayed up walking about more than half the night, thinking of the wife that he was going to get in the morning. I wasn't any means comfortable, for I knew that dealings with a woman in foreign parts, though you was a crowned King twenty times over, could not but be risky. I got up very early in the morning while Dravot was asleep, and I saw the priests talking together in whispers, and the Chiefs talking together too, and they looked at me out of the corners of their eyes.

"'What is up, Fish?' I say to the Bashkai man, who was wrapped up in his furs and looking splendid to behold.

"'I can't rightly say,' says he; 'but if you can make the King drop all this nonsense about marriage, you'll be doing him and me and yourself a great service.'

"'That I do believe,' says I. 'But sure, you know, Billy, as well as me, having fought against and for us, that the King and me are nothing more than two of the finest men that God Almighty ever made. Nothing more, I do assure you.'

"'That may be,' says Billy Fish, 'and yet I should be sorry if it was.' He sinks his head upon his great fur cloak for a minute and thinks. 'King,' says he, 'be you man or God or Devil, I'll stick by you today. I have twenty of my men with me, and they will follow me. We'll go to Bashkai until the storm blows over.'

"A little snow had fallen in the night, and everything was white except the greasy fat clouds that blew down and down from the north. Dravot came out with his crown on his head, swinging his arms and stamping his feet, and looking more pleased than Punch.

"'For the last time, drop it, Dan,' says I, in a whisper; 'Billy Fish here says that there will be a row.'

"'A row among my people!' says Dravot. 'Not much. Peachey, you're a fool not to get a wife too. Where's the girl?' says he, with a voice as loud as the braying of a jackass. 'Call up all the Chiefs and priests, and let the Emperor see if his wife suits him.'

"There was no need to call any one. They were all there leaning on their guns and spears round the clearing in the centre of the pine wood. A lot of priests went down to the little temple to bring up the girl, and the horns blew fit to wake the dead. Billy Fish saunters round and gets as close to Daniel as he could, and behind him stood his twenty men with matchlocks – not a man of them under six feet. I was next to Dravot, and behind me was twenty men of the regular Army. Up comes the girl, and a strapping wench she was, covered with silver and turquoises, but white as death, and looking back every minute at the priests.

"'She'll do,' said Dan, looking her over. 'What's to be afraid of, lass? Come and kiss me.' He puts his arm round her. She shuts her eyes, gives a bit of a squeak, and down goes her face in the side of Dan's flaming-red beard.

"'The slut's bitten me!' says he, clapping his hand to his neck, and, sure enough, his hand was red with blood. Billy Fish and two of his matchlock men catches hold of Dan by the shoulders and drags him into the Bashkai lot, while the priests howls in their lingo, 'Neither God nor Devil, but a man!' I was all taken aback, for a priest cut at me in front, and the Army behind began firing into the Bashkai men.

"'God A'mighty!' says Dan, 'what is the meaning o' this?'

"'Come back! Come away!' says Billy Fish. 'Ruin and Mutiny is the matter. We'll break for Bashkai if we can.'

"I tried to give some sort of orders to my men – the men o' the regular Army – but it was no use, so I fired into the brown of 'em with an English Martini and drilled three beggars in a line. The valley was full of shouting, howling creatures, and every soul was shrieking, 'Not a God nor a Devil, but only a man!' The Bashkai troops stuck to Billy Fish all they were worth, but their matchlocks wasn't half as good as the Kabul breech-loaders, and four of them dropped. Dan was bellowing like a bull, for he was very wrathy; and Billy Fish had a hard job to prevent him running out at the crowd.

"'We can't stand,' says Billy Fish. 'Make a run for it down the valley! The whole place is against us.' The matchlock-men ran, and we went down the valley in spite of Dravot. He was swearing horrible and crying out that he was a King. The priests rolled great stones on us, and the regular Army fired hard, and there wasn't more than six men, not counting Dan, Billy Fish, and Me, that came down to the bottom of the valley alive.

"Then they stopped firing, and the horns in the temple blew again. 'Come away – for Gord's sake come away!' says Billy Fish. 'They'll send runners out to all the villages before ever we get to Bashkai. I can protect you there, but I can't do anything now."

"My own notion is that Dan began to go mad in his head from that hour. He stared up and down like a stuck pig. Then he was all for walking back alone and killing the priests with his bare hands; which he could have done. 'An Emperor am I,' says Daniel, 'and next year I shall be a Knight of the Queen.'

"'All right, Dan,' says I; 'but come along now while there's time.'

"'It's your fault,' says he, 'for not looking after your Army better. There was mutiny in the midst, and you didn't know – you damned engine-driving, plate-laying, missionary's-pass-hunting hound!' He sat upon a rock and called me every foul name he could lay tongue to. I was too heart-sick to care, though it was all his foolishness that brought the smash.

"'I'm sorry, Dan,' says I, 'but there's no accounting for natives. This business is our Fifty-seven. Maybe we'll make something out of it yet, when we've got to Bashkai.'

"'Let's get to Bashkai, then,' says Dan, 'and, by God, when I come back here again I'll sweep the valley so there isn't a bug in a blanket left!'

"We walked all that day, and all that night Dan was stumping up and down on the snow, chewing his beard and muttering to himself.

"'There's no hope o' getting clear,' said Billy Fish. 'The priests have sent runners to the villages to say that you are only men. Why didn't you stick on as Gods till things was more settled? I'm a dead man,' says Billy Fish, and he throws himself down on the snow and begins to pray to his Gods.

"Next morning we was in a cruel bad country – all up and down, no level ground at all, and no food, either. The six Bashkai men looked at Billy Fish hungry-way as if they wanted to ask something, but they never said a word. At noon we came to the top of a flat mountain all covered with snow, and when we climbed up into it, behold, there was an Army in position waiting in the middle!

"'The runners have been very quick,' says Billy Fish, with a little bit of a laugh. 'They are waiting for us.'

"Three or four men began to fire from the enemy's side, and a chance shot took Daniel in the calf of the leg. That brought him to his senses. He looks across the snow at the Army, and sees the rifles that we had brought into the country.

"'We're done for,' says he. 'They are Englishmen, these people – and it's my blasted nonsense that has brought you to this. Get back, Billy Fish, and take your men away; you've done what you could, and now cut for it. Carnehan,' says he, 'shake hands with me and go along with Billy. Maybe they won't kill you. I'll go and meet 'em alone. It's me that did it! Me, the King!'

"'Go!' says I. 'Go to Hell, Dan! I'm with you here. Billy Fish, you clear out, and we two will meet those folk.'

"'I'm a Chief,' says Billy Fish, quite quiet. 'I stay with you. My men can go.'

"The Bashkai fellows didn't wait for a second word, but ran off, and Dan and Me and Billy Fish walked across to where the drums were drumming and the horns were horning. It was cold – awful cold. I've got that cold in the back of my head now. There's a lump of it there."

The punka-coolies had gone to sleep. Two kerosene lamps were blazing in the office, and the perspiration poured down my face and splashed on the blotter as I leaned forward. Carnehan was shivering, and I feared that his mind might go. I wiped my face, took a fresh grip of the piteously mangled hands, and said, "What happened after that?"

The momentary shift of my eyes had broken the clear current.

"What was you pleased to say?" whined Carnehan. "They took them without any sound. Not a little whisper all along the snow, not though the King knocked down the first man that set hand on him – not though old Peachey fired his last cartridge into the brown of 'em. Not a single solitary sound did those swines make. They just closed up tight, and I tell you their furs stunk. There was a man called Billy Fish, a good friend of us all, and they cut his throat, Sir, then and there, like a pig; and the King kicks up the bloody snow and says, 'We've had a dashed fine run for our money. What's coming next?' But Peachey, Peachey Taliaferro, I tell you, Sir, in confidence as betwixt two friends, he lost his head, Sir. No, he didn't, neither. The King lost his head, so he did, all along o' one of those cunning rope bridges. Kindly let me have the paper-cutter, Sir. It tilted this way. They marched him a mile across that snow to a rope bridge over a ravine with a river at the bottom. You may have seen such. They prodded him behind like an ox. 'Damn your eyes!' says the King. 'D' you suppose I can't die like a gentleman?' He turns to Peachey – Peachey that was crying like a child. 'I've brought you to this, Peachey,' says he. 'Brought you out of your happy life to be killed in Kafiristan, where you was late Commander-inChief of the Emperor's forces. Say you forgive me, Peachey.' 'I do,' says Peachey. 'Fully and freely do I forgive you, Dan.' 'Shake hands, Peachey,' says he. 'I'm going now.' Out he goes, looking neither right nor left, and when he was plumb in the middle of those dizzy dancing ropes, 'Cut you beggars,' he shouts; and they cut, and old Dan fell, turning round and round and round, twenty thousand miles, for he took half an hour to fall till he struck the water, and I could see his body caught on a rock with the gold crown close beside.

"But do you know what they did to Peachey between two pine-trees? They crucified him, Sir, as Peachey's hand will show. They used wooden pegs for his hands and feet; but he didn't die. He hung there and screamed, and they took him down next day, and said it was a miracle that he wasn't dead. They took him down – poor old Peachey that hadn't done them any harm – that hadn't done them any –"

He rocked to and fro and wept bitterly, wiping his eyes with the back of his scarred hands and moaning like a child for some ten minutes.

"They was cruel enough to feed him up in the temple, because they said he was more of a God than old Daniel that was a man. Then they turned him out on the snow, and told him to go home, and Peachey came home in about a year, begging along the roads quite safe; for Daniel Dravot he walked before and said, 'Come along, Peachey. It's a big thing we're doing.' The mountains they danced at night, and the mountains they tried to fall on Peachey's head, but Dan he held up his hand, and Peachey came along bent double. He never let go of Dan's hand, and he never let go of Dan's head. They gave it to him as a present in the temple, to remind him not to come again; and though the crown was pure gold and Peachey was starving, never would Peachey sell the same. You know Dravot, Sir! You knew Right Worshipful Brother Dravot! Look at him now!"

He fumbled in the mass of rags round his bent waist; brought out a black horsehair bag embroidered with silver thread; and shook therefrom on to my table – the dried, withered head of Daniel Dravot! The morning sun, that had long been paling the lamps, struck the red beard and blind sunken eyes; struck, too, a heavy circlet of gold studded with raw turquoises, that Carnehan placed tenderly on the battered temples.

"You be'old now," said Carnehan, "the Emperor in his 'abit as he lived – the King of Kafiristan with his crown upon his head. Poor old Daniel that was a monarch once!"

I shuddered, for, in spite of defacements manifold, I recognised the head of the man of Marwar Junction. Carnehan rose to go. I attempted to stop him. He was not fit to walk abroad. "Let me take away the whisky, and give me a little money," he gasped. "I was a King once. I'll go to the Deputy Commissioner and ask to set in the Poorhouse till I get my health. No, thank you, I can't wait till you get a carriage for me. I've urgent private affairs – in the south – at Marwar."

He shambled out of the office and departed in the direction of the Deputy Commissioner's house. That day at noon I had occasion to go down the blinding-hot Mall, and I saw a crooked man crawling along the white dust of the roadside, his hat in his hand, quavering dolorously after the fashion of street-singers at Home. There was not a soul in sight, and he was out of all possible earshot of the houses. And he sang through his nose, turning his head from right to left:

"The Son of Man goes forth to war,
A golden crown to gain;
His blood-red banner streams afar –
Who follows in His train?"

I waited to hear no more, but put the poor wretch into my carriage and drove him off to the nearest missionary for eventual transfer to the Asylum. He repeated the hymn twice while he was with me, whom he did not in the least recognise, and I left him singing it to the missionary.

Two days later I inquired after his welfare of the Superintendent of the Asylum.

"He was admitted suffering from sunstroke. He died early yesterday morning," said the Superintendent. "Is it true that he was half an hour bareheaded in the sun at midday?"

"Yes," said I; "but do you happen to know if he had anything upon him by any chance when he died?"

"Not to my knowledge," said the Superintendent.

And there the matter rests.

At the Mountains of Madness

H.P. Lovecraft

Chapter I

I AM FORCED into speech because men of science have refused to follow my advice without knowing why. It is altogether against my will that I tell my reasons for opposing this contemplated invasion of the antarctic – with its vast fossil hunt and its wholesale boring and melting of the ancient ice caps. And I am the more reluctant because my warning may be in vain.

Doubt of the real facts, as I must reveal them, is inevitable; yet, if I suppressed what will seem extravagant and incredible, there would be nothing left. The hitherto withheld photographs, both ordinary and aerial, will count in my favor, for they are damnably vivid and graphic. Still, they will be doubted because of the great lengths to which clever fakery can be carried. The ink drawings, of course, will be jeered at as obvious impostures, notwithstanding a strangeness of technique which art experts ought to remark and puzzle over.

In the end I must rely on the judgment and standing of the few scientific leaders who have, on the one hand, sufficient independence of thought to weigh my data on its own hideously convincing merits or in the light of certain primordial and highly baffling myth cycles; and on the other hand, sufficient influence to deter the exploring world in general from any rash and over-ambitious program in the region of those mountains of madness. It is an unfortunate fact that relatively obscure men like myself and my associates, connected only with a small university, have little chance of making an impression where matters of a wildly bizarre or highly controversial nature are concerned.

It is further against us that we are not, in the strictest sense, specialists in the fields which came primarily to be concerned. As a geologist, my object in leading the Miskatonic University Expedition was wholly that of securing deep-level specimens of rock and soil from various parts of the antarctic continent, aided by the remarkable drill devised by Professor Frank H. Pabodie of our engineering department. I had no wish to be a pioneer in any other field than this, but I did hope that the use of this new mechanical appliance at different points along previously explored paths would bring to light materials of a sort hitherto unreached by the ordinary methods of collection.

Pabodie's drilling apparatus, as the public already knows from our reports, was unique and radical in its lightness, portability, and capacity to combine the ordinary artesian drill principle with the principle of the small circular rock drill in such a way as to cope quickly with strata of varying hardness. Steel head, jointed rods, gasoline motor, collapsible wooden derrick, dynamiting paraphernalia, cording, rubbish-removal auger, and sectional piping for bores five inches wide and up to one thousand feet deep all formed, with needed accessories, no greater load than three seven-dog sledges could carry. This was made possible by the clever aluminum alloy of which most of the metal objects were fashioned. Four large Dornier aeroplanes, designed especially for the tremendous altitude flying necessary on the antarctic plateau and with added fuel-warming and quick-starting devices worked out by Pabodie, could transport our entire expedition from a base at the edge of the great ice barrier to various suitable inland points, and from these points a sufficient quota of dogs would serve us.

We planned to cover as great an area as one antarctic season – or longer, if absolutely necessary – would permit, operating mostly in the mountain ranges and on the plateau south of Ross Sea; regions explored in varying degree by Shackleton, Amundsen, Scott, and Byrd. With frequent changes of camp, made by aeroplane and involving distances great enough to be of geological significance, we expected to unearth a quite unprecedented amount of material – especially in the pre-Cambrian strata of which so narrow a range of antarctic specimens had previously been secured. We wished also to obtain as great as possible a variety of the upper fossiliferous rocks, since the primal life history of this bleak realm of ice and death is of the highest importance to our knowledge of the earth's past. That the antarctic continent was once temperate and even tropical, with a teeming vegetable and animal life of which the lichens, marine fauna, arachnida, and penguins of the northern edge are the only survivals, is a matter of common information; and we hoped to expand that information in variety, accuracy, and detail. When a simple boring revealed fossiliferous signs, we would enlarge the aperture by blasting, in order to get specimens of suitable size and condition.

Our borings, of varying depth according to the promise held out by the upper soil or rock, were to be confined to exposed, or nearly exposed, land surfaces – these inevitably being slopes and ridges because of the mile or two-mile thickness of solid ice overlying the lower levels. We could not afford to waste drilling the depth of any considerable amount of mere glaciation, though Pabodie had worked out a plan for sinking copper electrodes in thick clusters of borings and melting off limited areas of ice with current from a gasoline-driven dynamo. It is this plan – which we could not put into effect except experimentally on an expedition such as ours – that the coming Starkweather-Moore Expedition proposes to follow, despite the warnings I have issued since our return from the antarctic.

The public knows of the Miskatonic Expedition through our frequent wireless reports to the Arkham Advertiser and Associated Press, and through the later articles of Pabodie and myself. We consisted of four men from the University – Pabodie, Lake of the biology department, Atwood of the physics department – also a meteorologist – and myself, representing geology and having nominal command – besides sixteen assistants: seven graduate students from Miskatonic and nine skilled mechanics. Of these sixteen, twelve were qualified aeroplane pilots, all but two of whom were competent wireless operators. Eight of them understood navigation with compass and sextant, as did Pabodie, Atwood, and I. In addition, of course, our two ships – wooden ex-whalers, reinforced for ice conditions and having auxiliary steam – were fully manned.

The Nathaniel Derby Pickman Foundation, aided by a few special contributions, financed the expedition; hence our preparations were extremely thorough, despite the absence of great publicity. The dogs, sledges, machines, camp materials, and unassembled parts of our five planes were delivered in Boston, and there our ships were loaded.

We were marvelously well-equipped for our specific purposes, and in all matters pertaining to supplies, regimen, transportation, and camp construction we profited by the excellent example of our many recent and exceptionally brilliant predecessors. It was the unusual number and fame of these predecessors which made our own expedition – ample though it was – so little noticed by the world at large.

As the newspapers told, we sailed from Boston Harbor on September 2nd, 1930, taking a leisurely course down the coast and through the Panama Canal, and stopping at Samoa and Hobart, Tasmania, at which latter place we took on final supplies. None of our exploring party had ever been in the polar regions before, hence we all relied greatly on our ship captains – J.B. Douglas, commanding the brig Arkham, and serving as commander of the sea party, and Georg Thorfinnssen, commanding the barque Miskatonic – both veteran whalers in antarctic waters.

As we left the inhabited world behind, the sun sank lower and lower in the north, and stayed longer and longer above the horizon each day. At about 62° South Latitude we sighted our first icebergs – table-like objects with vertical sides – and just before reaching the antarctic circle, which we crossed on October 20th with appropriately quaint ceremonies, we were considerably troubled with field ice. The falling temperature bothered me considerably after our long voyage through the tropics, but I tried to brace up for the worse rigors to come. On many occasions the curious atmospheric effects enchanted me vastly; these including a strikingly vivid mirage – the first I had ever seen – in which distant bergs became the battlements of unimaginable cosmic castles.

Pushing through the ice, which was fortunately neither extensive nor thickly packed, we regained open water at South Latitude 67°, East Longitude 175° On the morning of October 26th a strong land blink appeared on the south, and before noon we all felt a thrill of excitement at beholding a vast, lofty, and snow-clad mountain chain which opened out and covered the whole vista ahead. At last we had encountered an outpost of the great unknown continent and its cryptic world of frozen death. These peaks were obviously the Admiralty Range discovered by Ross, and it would now be our task to round Cape Adare and sail down the east coast of Victoria Land to our contemplated base on the shore of McMurdo Sound, at the foot of the volcano Erebus in South Latitude 77° 9'.

The last lap of the voyage was vivid and fancy-stirring. Great barren peaks of mystery loomed up constantly against the west as the low northern sun of noon or the still lower horizon-grazing southern sun of midnight poured its hazy reddish rays over the white snow, bluish ice and water lanes, and black bits of exposed granite slope. Through the desolate summits swept ranging, intermittent gusts of the terrible antarctic wind; whose cadences sometimes held vague suggestions of a wild and half-sentient musical piping, with notes extending over a wide range, and which for some subconscious mnemonic reason seemed to me disquieting and even dimly terrible. Something about the scene reminded me of the strange and disturbing Asian paintings of Nicholas Roerich, and of the still stranger and more disturbing descriptions of the evilly fabled plateau of Leng which occur in the dreaded *Necronomicon* of the mad Arab Abdul Alhazred. I was rather sorry, later on, that I had ever looked into that monstrous book at the college library.

On the 7th of November, sight of the westward range having been temporarily lost, we passed Franklin Island; and the next day descried the cones of Mts. Erebus and Terror on Ross Island ahead, with the long line of the Parry Mountains beyond. There now stretched off to the east the low, white line of the great ice barrier, rising perpendicularly to a height of two hundred feet like the rocky cliffs of Quebec, and marking the end of southward navigation. In the afternoon we entered McMurdo Sound and stood off the coast in the lee of smoking Mt. Erebus. The scoriac peak towered up some twelve thousand, seven hundred feet against the eastern sky, like a Japanese print of the sacred Fujiyama, while beyond it rose the white, ghostlike height of Mt. Terror, ten thousand, nine hundred feet in altitude, and now extinct as a volcano.

Puffs of smoke from Erebus came intermittently, and one of the graduate assistants – a brilliant young fellow named Danforth – pointed out what looked like lava on the snowy slope, remarking that this mountain, discovered in 1840, had undoubtedly been the source of Poe's image when he wrote seven years later:

– the lavas that restlessly roll
Their sulphurous currents down Yaanek
In the ultimate climes of the pole –
That groan as they roll down Mount Yaanek
In the realms of the boreal pole.

Danforth was a great reader of bizarre material, and had talked a good deal of Poe. I was interested myself because of the antarctic scene of Poe's only long story – the disturbing and enigmatical Arthur Gordon Pym. On the barren shore, and on the lofty ice barrier in the background, myriads of grotesque penguins squawked and flapped their fins, while many fat seals were visible on the water, swimming or sprawling across large cakes of slowly drifting ice.

Using small boats, we effected a difficult landing on Ross Island shortly after midnight on the morning of the 9th, carrying a line of cable from each of the ships and preparing to unload supplies by means of a breeches-buoy arrangement. Our sensations on first treading Antarctic soil were poignant and complex, even though at this particular point the Scott and Shackleton expeditions had preceded us. Our camp on the frozen shore below the volcano's slope was only a provisional one, headquarters being kept aboard the Arkham. We landed all our drilling apparatus, dogs, sledges, tents, provisions, gasoline tanks, experimental ice-melting outfit, cameras, both ordinary and aerial, aeroplane parts, and other accessories, including three small portable wireless outfits – besides those in the planes – capable of communicating with the Arkham's large outfit from any part of the antarctic continent that we would be likely to visit. The ship's outfit, communicating with the outside world, was to convey press reports to the Arkham Advertiser's powerful wireless station on Kingsport Head, Massachusetts. We hoped to complete our work during a single antarctic summer; but if this proved impossible, we would winter on the Arkham, sending the Miskatonic north before the freezing of the ice for another summer's supplies.

I need not repeat what the newspapers have already published about our early work: of our ascent of Mt. Erebus; our successful mineral borings at several points on Ross Island and the singular speed with which Pabodie's apparatus accomplished them, even through solid rock layers; our provisional test of the small ice-melting equipment; our perilous ascent of the great barrier with sledges and supplies; and our final assembling of five huge aeroplanes at the camp atop the barrier. The health of our land party – twenty men and fifty-five Alaskan sledge dogs – was remarkable, though of course we had so far encountered no really destructive temperatures or windstorms. For the most part, the thermometer varied between zero and 20° or 25° above, and our experience with

New England winters had accustomed us to rigors of this sort. The barrier camp was semi-permanent, and destined to be a storage cache for gasoline, provisions, dynamite, and other supplies.

Only four of our planes were needed to carry the actual exploring material, the fifth being left with a pilot and two men from the ships at the storage cache to form a means of reaching us from the Arkham in case all our exploring planes were lost. Later, when not using all the other planes for moving apparatus, we would employ one or two in a shuttle transportation service between this cache and another permanent base on the great plateau from six hundred to seven hundred miles southward, beyond Beardmore Glacier. Despite the almost unanimous accounts of appalling winds and tempests that pour down from the plateau, we determined to dispense with intermediate bases, taking our chances in the interest of economy and probable efficiency.

Wireless reports have spoken of the breathtaking, four-hour, nonstop flight of our squadron on November 21st over the lofty shelf ice, with vast peaks rising on the west, and the unfathomed silences echoing to the sound of our engines. Wind troubled us only moderately, and our radio compasses helped us through the one opaque fog we encountered. When the vast rise loomed ahead, between Latitudes 83° and 84°, we knew we had reached Beardmore Glacier, the largest valley glacier in the world, and that the frozen sea was now giving place to a frowning and mountainous coast line. At last we were truly entering the white, aeon-dead world of the ultimate south. Even as we realized it we saw the peak of Mt. Nansen in the eastern distance, towering up to its height of almost fifteen thousand feet.

The successful establishment of the southern base above the glacier in Latitude 86° 7', East Longitude 174° 23', and the phenomenally rapid and effective borings and blastings made at various points reached by our sledge trips and short aeroplane flights, are matters of history; as is the arduous and triumphant ascent of Mt. Nansen by Pabodie and two of the graduate students – Gedney and Carroll – on December 13–15. We were some eight thousand, five hundred feet above sea-level, and when experimental drillings revealed solid ground only twelve feet down through the snow and ice at certain points, we made considerable use of the small melting apparatus and sunk bores and performed dynamiting at many places where no previous explorer had ever thought of securing mineral specimens. The pre-Cambrian granites and beacon sandstones thus obtained confirmed our belief that this plateau was homogeneous, with the great bulk of the continent to the west, but somewhat different from the parts lying eastward below South America – which we then thought to form a separate and smaller continent divided from the larger one by a frozen junction of Ross and Weddell Seas, though Byrd has since disproved the hypothesis.

In certain of the sandstones, dynamited and chiseled after boring revealed their nature, we found some highly interesting fossil markings and fragments; notably ferns, seaweeds, trilobites, crinoids, and such mollusks as linguellae and gastropods – all of which seemed of real significance in connection with the region's primordial history. There was also a queer triangular, striated marking, about a foot in greatest diameter, which Lake pieced together from three fragments of slate brought up from a deep-blasted aperture. These fragments came from a point to the westward, near the Queen Alexandra Range; and Lake, as a biologist, seemed to find their curious marking unusually puzzling and provocative, though to my geological eye it looked not unlike some of the ripple effects reasonably common in the sedimentary rocks. Since slate is no more than a metamorphic formation into which a sedimentary stratum is pressed, and since the pressure itself produces odd distorting effects on any markings which may exist, I saw no reason for extreme wonder over the striated depression.

On January 6th, 1931, Lake, Pabodie, Danforth, the other six students, and myself flew directly over the south pole in two of the great planes, being forced down once by a sudden high wind, which, fortunately, did not develop into a typical storm. This was, as the papers have stated, one of several observation flights, during others of which we tried to discern new topographical features in areas unreached by previous explorers. Our early flights were disappointing in this latter respect, though they afforded us some magnificent examples of the richly fantastic and deceptive mirages of the polar regions, of which our sea voyage had given us some brief foretastes. Distant mountains floated in the sky as enchanted cities, and often the whole white world would dissolve into a gold, silver, and scarlet land of Dunsanian dreams and adventurous expectancy under the magic of the low midnight sun. On cloudy days we had considerable trouble in flying owing to the tendency of snowy earth and sky to merge into one mystical opalescent void with no visible horizon to mark the junction of the two.

At length we resolved to carry out our original plan of flying five hundred miles eastward with all four exploring planes and establishing a fresh sub-base at a point which would probably be on the smaller continental division, as we mistakenly conceived it. Geological specimens obtained there would be desirable for purposes of comparison. Our health so far had remained excellent – lime juice well offsetting the steady diet of tinned and salted food, and temperatures generally above zero enabling us to do without our thickest furs. It was now midsummer, and with haste and care we might be able to conclude work by March and avoid a tedious wintering through the long antarctic night. Several savage windstorms had burst upon us from the west, but we had escaped damage through the skill of Atwood in devising rudimentary aeroplane shelters and windbreaks of heavy snow blocks, and reinforcing the principal camp buildings with snow. Our good luck and efficiency had indeed been almost uncanny.

The outside world knew, of course, of our program, and was told also of Lake's strange and dogged insistence on a westward – or rather, northwestward – prospecting trip before our radical shift to the new base. It seems that he had pondered a great deal, and with alarmingly radical daring, over that triangular striated marking in the slate; reading into it certain contradictions in nature and geological period which whetted his curiosity to the utmost, and made him avid to sink more borings and blastings in the west-stretching formation to which the exhumed fragments evidently belonged. He was strangely convinced that the marking was the print of some bulky, unknown, and radically unclassifiable organism of considerably advanced evolution, notwithstanding that the rock which bore it was of so vastly ancient a date – Cambrian if not actually pre-Cambrian – as to preclude the probable existence not only of all highly evolved life, but of any life at all above the unicellular or at most the trilobite stage. These fragments, with their odd marking, must have been five hundred million to a thousand million years old.

Chapter II

POPULAR IMAGINATION, I judge, responded actively to our wireless bulletins of Lake's start northwestward into regions never trodden by human foot or penetrated by human imagination, though we did not mention his wild hopes of revolutionizing the entire sciences of biology and geology. His preliminary sledging and boring journey of

January 11th to 18th with Pabodie and five others – marred by the loss of two dogs in an upset when crossing one of the great pressure ridges in the ice – had brought up more and more of the Archaean slate; and even I was interested by the singular profusion of evident fossil markings in that unbelievably ancient stratum. These markings, however, were of very primitive life forms involving no great paradox except that any life forms should occur in rock as definitely pre-Cambrian as this seemed to be; hence I still failed to see the good sense of Lake's demand for an interlude in our time-saving program – an interlude requiring the use of all four planes, many men, and the whole of the expedition's mechanical apparatus. I did not, in the end, veto the plan, though I decided not to accompany the northwestward party despite Lake's plea for my geological advice. While they were gone, I would remain at the base with Pabodie and five men and work out final plans for the eastward shift. In preparation for this transfer, one of the planes had begun to move up a good gasoline supply from McMurdo Sound; but this could wait temporarily. I kept with me one sledge and nine dogs, since it is unwise to be at any time without possible transportation in an utterly tenantless world of aeon-long death.

Lake's sub-expedition into the unknown, as everyone will recall, sent out its own reports from the shortwave transmitters on the planes; these being simultaneously picked up by our apparatus at the southern base and by the Arkham at McMurdo Sound, whence they were relayed to the outside world on wave lengths up to fifty meters. The start was made January 22nd at 4 a.m., and the first wireless message we received came only two hours later, when Lake spoke of descending and starting a small-scale ice-melting and bore at a point some three hundred miles away from us. Six hours after that a second and very excited message told of the frantic, beaver-like work whereby a shallow shaft had been sunk and blasted, culminating in the discovery of slate fragments with several markings approximately like the one which had caused the original puzzlement.

Three hours later a brief bulletin announced the resumption of the flight in the teeth of a raw and piercing gale; and when I dispatched a message of protest against further hazards, Lake replied curtly that his new specimens made any hazard worth taking. I saw that his excitement had reached the point of mutiny, and that I could do nothing to check this headlong risk of the whole expedition's success; but it was appalling to think of his plunging deeper and deeper into that treacherous and sinister white immensity of tempests and unfathomed mysteries which stretched off for some fifteen hundred miles to the half-known, half-suspected coast line of Queen Mary and Knox Lands.

Then, in about an hour and a half more, came that doubly excited message from Lake's moving plane, which almost reversed my sentiments and made me wish I had accompanied the party:

"**10:05 p.m**. On the wing. After snowstorm, have spied mountain range ahead higher than any hitherto seen. May equal Himalayas, allowing for height of plateau. Probable Latitude 76° 15', Longitude 113° 10' E. Reaches far as can see to right and left. Suspicion of two smoking cones. All peaks black and bare of snow. Gale blowing off them impedes navigation."

After that Pabodie, the men and I hung breathlessly over the receiver. Thought of this titanic mountain rampart seven hundred miles away inflamed our deepest sense of adventure; and we rejoiced that our expedition, if not ourselves personally, had been its discoverers. In half an hour Lake called us again:

"Moulton's plane forced down on plateau in foothills, but nobody hurt and perhaps can repair. Shall transfer essentials to other three for return or further moves if necessary, but no more heavy plane travel needed just now. Mountains surpass anything in imagination. Am going up scouting in Carroll's plane, with all weight out.

"You can't imagine anything like this. Highest peaks must go over thirty-five thousand feet. Everest out of the running. Atwood to work out height with theodolite while Carroll and I go up. Probably wrong about cones, for formations look stratified. Possibly pre-Cambrian slate with other strata mixed in. Queer skyline effects – regular sections of cubes clinging to highest peaks. Whole thing marvelous in red-gold light of low sun. Like land of mystery in a dream or gateway to forbidden world of untrodden wonder. Wish you were here to study."

Though it was technically sleeping time, not one of us listeners thought for a moment of retiring. It must have been a good deal the same at McMurdo Sound, where the supply cache and the Arkham were also getting the messages; for Captain Douglas gave out a call congratulating everybody on the important find, and Sherman, the cache operator, seconded his sentiments. We were sorry, of course, about the damaged aeroplane, but hoped it could be easily mended. Then, at 11 p.m., came another call from Lake:

"Up with Carroll over highest foothills. Don't dare try really tall peaks in present weather, but shall later. Frightful work climbing, and hard going at this altitude, but worth it. Great range fairly solid, hence can't get any glimpses beyond. Main summits exceed Himalayas, and very queer. Range looks like pre-Cambrian slate, with plain signs of many other upheaved strata. Was wrong about volcanism. Goes farther in either direction than we can see. Swept clear of snow above about twenty-one thousand feet.

"Odd formations on slopes of highest mountains. Great low square blocks with exactly vertical sides, and rectangular lines of low, vertical ramparts, like the old Asian castles clinging to steep mountains in Roerich's paintings. Impressive from distance. Flew close to some, and Carroll thought they were formed of smaller separate pieces, but that is probably weathering. Most edges crumbled and rounded off as if exposed to storms and climate changes for millions of years.

"Parts, especially upper parts, seem to be of lighter-colored rock than any visible strata on slopes proper, hence of evidently crystalline origin. Close flying shows many cave mouths, some unusually regular in outline, square or semicircular. You must come and investigate. Think I saw rampart squarely on top of one peak. Height seems about thirty thousand to thirty-five thousand feet. Am up twenty-one thousand, five hundred myself, in devilish, gnawing cold. Wind whistles and pipes through passes and in and out of caves, but no flying danger so far."

From then on for another half hour Lake kept up a running fire of comment, and expressed his intention of climbing some of the peaks on foot. I replied that I would join him as soon as he could send a plane, and that Pabodie and I would work out the best gasoline plan – just where and how to concentrate our supply in view of the expedition's altered character. Obviously, Lake's boring operations, as well as his aeroplane activities, would require a great deal for the new base which he planned to establish at the foot of the mountains; and it was possible that the eastward flight might not be made, after all, this season. In connection with this business I called Captain Douglas and asked him to get as much as possible out of the ships and up the barrier with the single dog team we had left there. A direct route across the unknown region between Lake and McMurdo Sound was what we really ought to establish.

Lake called me later to say that he had decided to let the camp stay where Moulton's plane had been forced down, and where repairs had already progressed somewhat.

The ice sheet was very thin, with dark ground here and there visible, and he would sink some borings and blasts at that very point before making any sledge trips or climbing expeditions. He spoke of the ineffable majesty of the whole scene, and the queer state of his sensations at being in the lee of vast, silent pinnacles whose ranks shot up like a wall reaching the sky at the world's rim. Atwood's theodolite observations had placed the height of the five tallest peaks at from thirty thousand to thirty-four thousand feet. The windswept nature of the terrain clearly disturbed Lake, for it argued the occasional existence of prodigious gales, violent beyond anything we had so far encountered. His camp lay a little more than five miles from where the higher foothills rose abruptly. I could almost trace a note of subconscious alarm in his words – flashed across a glacial void of seven hundred miles – as he urged that we all hasten with the matter and get the strange, new region disposed of as soon as possible. He was about to rest now, after a continuous day's work of almost unparalleled speed, strenuousness, and results.

In the morning I had a three-cornered wireless talk with Lake and Captain Douglas at their widely separated bases. It was agreed that one of Lake's planes would come to my base for Pabodie, the five men, and myself, as well as for all the fuel it could carry. The rest of the fuel question, depending on our decision about an easterly trip, could wait for a few days, since Lake had enough for immediate camp heat and borings. Eventually the old southern base ought to be restocked, but if we postponed the easterly trip we would not use it till the next summer, and, meanwhile, Lake must send a plane to explore a direct route between his new mountains and McMurdo Sound.

Pabodie and I prepared to close our base for a short or long period, as the case might be. If we wintered in the antarctic we would probably fly straight from Lake's base to the Arkham without returning to this spot. Some of our conical tents had already been reinforced by blocks of hard snow, and now we decided to complete the job of making a permanent village. Owing to a very liberal tent supply, Lake had with him all that his base would need, even after our arrival. I wirelessed that Pabodie and I would be ready for the northwestward move after one day's work and one night's rest.

Our labors, however, were not very steady after 4 p.m., for about that time Lake began sending in the most extraordinary and excited messages. His working day had started unpropitiously, since an aeroplane survey of the nearly-exposed rock surfaces showed an entire absence of those Archaean and primordial strata for which he was looking, and which formed so great a part of the colossal peaks that loomed up at a tantalizing distance from the camp. Most of the rocks glimpsed were apparently Jurassic and Comanchian sandstones and Permian and Triassic schists, with now and then a glossy black outcropping suggesting a hard and slaty coal. This rather discouraged Lake, whose plans all hinged on unearthing specimens more than five hundred million years older. It was clear to him that in order to recover the Archaean slate vein in which he had found the odd markings, he would have to make a long sledge trip from these foothills to the steep slopes of the gigantic mountains themselves.

He had resolved, nevertheless, to do some local boring as part of the expedition's general program; hence he set up the drill and put five men to work with it while the rest finished settling the camp and repairing the damaged aeroplane. The softest visible rock – a sandstone about a quarter of a mile from the camp – had been chosen for the first sampling; and the drill made excellent progress without much supplementary blasting. It was about three hours afterward, following the first really heavy blast of the operation, that the shouting of the drill crew was heard; and that young Gedney – the acting foreman – rushed into the camp with the startling news.

They had struck a cave. Early in the boring the sandstone had given place to a vein of Comanchian limestone, full of minute fossil cephalopods, corals, echini, and spirifera, and with occasional suggestions of siliceous sponges and marine vertebrate bones – the latter probably of teleosts, sharks, and ganoids. This, in itself, was important enough, as affording the first vertebrate fossils the expedition had yet secured; but when shortly afterward the drill head dropped through the stratum into apparent vacancy, a wholly new and doubly intense wave of excitement spread among the excavators. A good-sized blast had laid open the subterrene secret; and now, through a jagged aperture perhaps five feet across and three feet thick, there yawned before the avid searchers a section of shallow limestone hollowing worn more than fifty million years ago by the trickling ground waters of a bygone tropic world.

The hollowed layer was not more than seven or eight feet deep but extended off indefinitely in all directions and had a fresh, slightly moving air which suggested its membership in an extensive subterranean system. Its roof and floor were abundantly equipped with large stalactites and stalagmites, some of which met in columnar form: but important above all else was the vast deposit of shells and bones, which in places nearly choked the passage. Washed down from unknown jungles of Mesozoic tree ferns and fungi, and forests of Tertiary cycads, fan palms, and primitive angiosperms, this osseous medley contained representatives of more Cretaceous, Eocene, and other animal species than the greatest paleontologist could have counted or classified in a year. Mollusks, crustacean armor, fishes, amphibians, reptiles, birds, and early mammals – great and small, known and unknown. No wonder Gedney ran back to the camp shouting, and no wonder everyone else dropped work and rushed headlong through the biting cold to where the tall derrick marked a new-found gateway to secrets of inner earth and vanished aeons.

When Lake had satisfied the first keen edge of his curiosity, he scribbled a message in his notebook and had young Moulton run back to the camp to dispatch it by wireless. This was my first word of the discovery, and it told of the identification of early shells, bones of ganoids and placoderms, remnants of labyrinthodonts and thecodonts, great mosasaur skull fragments, dinosaur vertebrae and armor plates, pterodactyl teeth and wing bones, Archaeopteryx debris, Miocene sharks' teeth, primitive bird skulls, and other bones of archaic mammals such as palaeotheres, Xiphodons, Eohippi, Oreodons, and titanotheres. There was nothing as recent as a mastodon, elephant, true camel, deer, or bovine animal; hence Lake concluded that the last deposits had occurred during the Oligocene Age, and that the hollowed stratum had lain in its present dried, dead, and inaccessible state for at least thirty million years.

On the other hand, the prevalence of very early life forms was singular in the highest degree. Though the limestone formation was, on the evidence of such typical imbedded fossils as ventriculites, positively and unmistakably Comanchian and not a particle earlier, the free fragments in the hollow space included a surprising proportion from organisms hitherto considered as peculiar to far older periods – even rudimentary fishes, mollusks, and corals as remote as the Silurian or Ordovician. The inevitable inference was that in this part of the world there had been a remarkable and unique degree of continuity between the life of over three hundred million years ago and that of only thirty million years ago. How far this continuity had extended beyond the Oligocene Age when the cavern was closed was of course past all speculation. In any event, the coming of the frightful ice in the Pleistocene some five hundred thousand years ago – a mere yesterday as compared with the age of this cavity – must have put an end to any of the primal forms which had locally managed to outlive their common terms.

Lake was not content to let his first message stand, but had another bulletin written and dispatched across the snow to the camp before Moulton could get back. After that Moulton stayed at the wireless in one of the planes, transmitting to me – and to the Arkham for relaying to the outside world – the frequent postscripts which Lake sent him by a succession of messengers. Those who followed the newspapers will remember the excitement created among men of science by that afternoon's reports – reports which have finally led, after all these years, to the organization of that very Starkweather-Moore Expedition which I am so anxious to dissuade from its purposes. I had better give the messages literally as Lake sent them, and as our base operator McTighe translated them from the pencil shorthand:

"Fowler makes discovery of highest importance in sandstone and limestone fragments from blasts. Several distinct triangular striated prints like those in Archaean slate, proving that source survived from over six hundred million years ago to Comanchian times without more than moderate morphological changes and decrease in average size. Comanchian prints apparently more primitive or decadent, if anything, than older ones. Emphasize importance of discovery in press. Will mean to biology what Einstein has meant to mathematics and physics. Joins up with my previous work and amplifies conclusions.

"Appears to indicate, as I suspected, that earth has seen whole cycle or cycles of organic life before known one that begins with Archaeozoic cells. Was evolved and specialized not later than a thousand million years ago, when planet was young and recently uninhabitable for any life forms or normal protoplasmic structure. Question arises when, where, and how development took place."

"Later. Examining certain skeletal fragments of large land and marine saurians and primitive mammals, find singular local wounds or injuries to bony structure not attributable to any known predatory or carnivorous animal of any period, of two sorts – straight, penetrant bores, and apparently hacking incisions. One or two cases of cleanly severed bones. Not many specimens affected. Am sending to camp for electric torches. Will extend search area underground by hacking away stalactites."

"Still later. Have found peculiar soapstone fragment about six inches across and an inch and a half thick, wholly unlike any visible local formation – greenish, but no evidences to place its period. Has curious smoothness and regularity. Shaped like five-pointed star with tips broken off, and signs of other cleavage at inward angles and in center of surface. Small, smooth depression in center of unbroken surface. Arouses much curiosity as to source and weathering. Probably some freak of water action. Carroll, with magnifier, thinks he can make out additional markings of geologic significance. Groups of tiny dots in regular patterns. Dogs growing uneasy as we work, and seem to hate this soapstone. Must see if it has any peculiar odor. Will report again when Mills gets back with light and we start on underground area."

"**10:15 p.m.** Important discovery. Orrendorf and Watkins, working underground at 9:45 with light, found monstrous barrel-shaped fossil of wholly unknown nature; probably vegetable unless overgrown specimen of unknown marine radiata. Tissue evidently preserved by mineral salts. Tough as leather, but astonishing flexibility retained in places.

Marks of broken-off parts at ends and around sides. Six feet end to end, three and five-tenths feet central diameter, tapering to one foot at each end. Like a barrel with five bulging ridges in place of staves. Lateral breakages, as of thinnish stalks, are at equator in middle of these ridges. In furrows between ridges are curious growths – combs or wings that fold up and spread out like fans. All greatly damaged but one, which gives almost seven-foot wing spread. Arrangement reminds one of certain monsters of primal myth, especially fabled Elder Things in the *Necronomicon*.

"Their wings seem to be membranous, stretched on frame work of glandular tubing. Apparent minute orifices in frame tubing at wing tips. Ends of body shriveled, giving no clue to interior or to what has been broken off there. Must dissect when we get back to camp. Can't decide whether vegetable or animal. Many features obviously of almost incredible primitiveness. Have set all hands cutting stalactites and looking for further specimens. Additional scarred bones found, but these must wait. Having trouble with dogs. They can't endure the new specimen, and would probably tear it to pieces if we didn't keep it at a distance from them."

"**11:30 p.m.** Attention, Dyer, Pabodie, Douglas. Matter of highest – I might say transcendent – importance. Arkham must relay to Kingsport Head Station at once. Strange barrel growth is the Archaean thing that left prints in rocks. Mills, Boudreau, and Fowler discover cluster of thirteen more at underground point forty feet from aperture. Mixed with curiously rounded and configured soapstone fragments smaller than one previously found – star-shaped, but no marks of breakage except at some of the points.

"Of organic specimens, eight apparently perfect, with all appendages. Have brought all to surface, leading off dogs to distance. They cannot stand the things. Give close attention to description and repeat back for accuracy Papers must get this right.

"Objects are eight feet long all over. Six-foot, five-ridged barrel torso three and five-tenths feet central diameter, one foot end diameters. Dark gray, flexible, and infinitely tough. Seven-foot membranous wings of same color, found folded, spread out of furrows between ridges. Wing framework tubular or glandular, of lighter gray, with orifices at wing tips. Spread wings have serrated edge. Around equator, one at central apex of each of the five vertical, stave-like ridges are five systems of light gray flexible arms or tentacles found tightly folded to torso but expansible to maximum length of over three feet. Like arms of primitive crinoid. Single stalks three inches diameter branch after six inches into five substalks, each of which branches after eight inches into small, tapering tentacles or tendrils, giving each stalk a total of twenty-five tentacles.

"At top of torso blunt, bulbous neck of lighter gray, with gill-like suggestions, holds yellowish five-pointed starfish-shaped apparent head covered with three-inch wiry cilia of various prismatic colors.

"Head thick and puffy, about two feet point to point, with three-inch flexible yellowish tubes projecting from each point. Slit in exact center of top probably breathing aperture. At end of each tube is spherical expansion where yellowish membrane rolls back on handling to reveal glassy, red-irised globe, evidently an eye.

"Five slightly longer reddish tubes start from inner angles of starfish-shaped head and end in saclike swellings of same color which, upon pressure, open to bell-shaped orifices two inches maximum diameter and lined with sharp, white tooth like projections – probably mouths. All these tubes, cilia, and points of starfish head, found folded tightly down; tubes and points clinging to bulbous neck and torso. Flexibility surprising despite vast toughness.

"At bottom of torso, rough but dissimilarly functioning counterparts of head arrangements exist. Bulbous light-gray pseudo-neck, without gill suggestions, holds greenish five-pointed starfish arrangement.

"Tough, muscular arms four feet long and tapering from seven inches diameter at base to about two and five-tenths at point. To each point is attached small end of a greenish five-veined membranous triangle eight inches long and six wide at farther end. This is the paddle, fin, or pseudofoot which has made prints in rocks from a thousand million to fifty or sixty million years old.

"From inner angles of starfish arrangement project two-foot reddish tubes tapering from three inches diameter at base to one at tip. Orifices at tips.

All these parts infinitely tough and leathery, but extremely flexible. Four-foot arms with paddles undoubtedly used for locomotion of some sort, marine or otherwise. When moved, display suggestions of exaggerated muscularity. As found, all these projections tightly folded over pseudoneck and end of torso, corresponding to projections at other end.

"Cannot yet assign positively to animal or vegetable kingdom, but odds now favor animal. Probably represents incredibly advanced evolution of radiata without loss of certain primitive features. Echinoderm resemblances unmistakable despite local contradictory evidences.

"Wing structure puzzles in view of probable marine habitat, but may have use in water navigation. Symmetry is curiously vegetablelike, suggesting vegetable's essential up-and-down structure rather than animal's fore-and-aft structure. Fabulously early date of evolution, preceding even simplest Archaean protozoa hitherto known, baffles all conjecture as to origin.

"Complete specimens have such uncanny resemblance to certain creatures of primal myth that suggestion of ancient existence outside antarctic becomes inevitable. Dyer and Pabodie have read Necronomicon and seen Clark Ashton Smith's nightmare paintings based on text, and will understand when I speak of Elder Things supposed to have created all earth life as jest or mistake. Students have always thought conception formed from morbid imaginative treatment of very ancient tropical radiata. Also like prehistoric folklore things Wilmarth has spoken of – Cthulhu cult appendages, etc.

"Vast field of study opened. Deposits probably of late Cretaceous or early Eocene period, judging from associated specimens. Massive stalagmites deposited above them. Hard work hewing out, but toughness prevented damage. State of preservation miraculous, evidently owing to limestone action. No more found so far, but will resume search later. Job now to get fourteen huge specimens to camp without dogs, which bark furiously and can't be trusted near them.

"With nine men – three left to guard the dogs – we ought to manage the three sledges fairly well, though wind is bad. Must establish plane communication with McMurdo Sound and begin shipping material. But I've got to dissect one of these things before we take any rest. Wish I had a real laboratory here. Dyer better kick himself for having tried to stop my westward trip. First the world's greatest mountains, and then this. If this last isn't the high spot of the expedition, I don't know what is. We're made scientifically. Congrats, Pabodie, on the drill that opened up the cave. Now will Arkham please repeat description?"

The sensations of Pabodie and myself at receipt of this report were almost beyond description, nor were our companions much behind us in enthusiasm. McTighe, who had hastily translated a few high spots as they came from the droning receiving set, wrote out the entire message from his shorthand version as soon as Lake's operator signed off. All appreciated the epoch-making significance of the discovery, and I sent Lake congratulations as soon as the Arkham's operator had repeated back the descriptive parts as requested; and my example was followed by Sherman from his station at the McMurdo Sound supply cache, as well as by Captain Douglas of the Arkham. Later, as head of the expedition, I added some remarks to be relayed through the Arkham to the outside world. Of course, rest was an absurd thought amidst this excitement; and my only wish was to get to Lake's camp as quickly as I could. It disappointed me when he sent word that a rising mountain gale made early aerial travel impossible.

But within an hour and a half interest again rose to banish disappointment. Lake, sending more messages, told of the completely successful transportation of the fourteen great specimens to the camp. It had been a hard pull, for the things were surprisingly heavy; but nine men had accomplished it very neatly. Now some of the party were hurriedly building a snow corral at a safe distance from the camp, to which the dogs could be brought for greater convenience in feeding. The specimens were laid out on the hard snow near the camp, save for one on which Lake was making crude attempts at dissection.

This dissection seemed to be a greater task than had been expected, for, despite the heat of a gasoline stove in the newly raised laboratory tent, the deceptively flexible tissues of the chosen specimen – a powerful and intact one – lost nothing of their more than leathery toughness. Lake was puzzled as to how he might make the requisite incisions without violence destructive enough to upset all the structural niceties he was looking for. He had, it is true, seven more perfect specimens; but these were too few to use up recklessly unless the cave might later yield an unlimited supply. Accordingly he removed the specimen and dragged in one which, though having remnants of the starfish arrangements at both ends, was badly crushed and partly disrupted along one of the great torso furrows.

Results, quickly reported over the wireless, were baffling and provocative indeed. Nothing like delicacy or accuracy was possible with instruments hardly able to cut the anomalous tissue, but the little that was achieved left us all awed and bewildered. Existing biology would have to be wholly revised, for this thing was no product of any cell growth science knows about. There had been scarcely any mineral replacement, and despite an age of perhaps forty million years, the internal organs were wholly intact. The leathery, undeteriorative, and almost indestructible quality was an inherent attribute of the thing's form of organization, and pertained to some paleogean cycle of invertebrate evolution utterly beyond our powers of speculation. At first all that Lake found was dry, but as the heated tent produced its thawing effect, organic moisture of pungent and offensive odor was encountered toward the thing's uninjured side. It was not blood, but a thick, dark-green fluid apparently answering the same purpose. By the time Lake reached this stage, all thirty-seven dogs had been brought to the still uncompleted corral near the camp, and even at that distance set up a savage barking and show of restlessness at the acrid, diffusive smell.

Far from helping to place the strange entity, this provisional dissection merely deepened its mystery. All guesses about its external members had been correct, and on the evidence of these one could hardly hesitate to call the thing animal; but internal inspection brought up so many vegetable evidences that Lake was left hopelessly at sea.

It had digestion and circulation, and eliminated waste matter through the reddish tubes of its starfish-shaped base. Cursorily, one would say that its respiration apparatus handled oxygen rather than carbon dioxide, and there were odd evidences of air-storage chambers and methods of shifting respiration from the external orifice to at least two other fully developed breathing systems – gills and pores. Clearly, it was amphibian, and probably adapted to long airless hibernation periods as well. Vocal organs seemed present in connection with the main respiratory system, but they presented anomalies beyond immediate solution. Articulate speech, in the sense of syllable utterance, seemed barely conceivable, but musical piping notes covering a wide range were highly probable. The muscular system was almost prematurely developed.

The nervous system was so complex and highly developed as to leave Lake aghast. Though excessively primitive and archaic in some respects, the thing had a set of ganglial centers and connectives arguing the very extremes of specialized development. Its five-lobed brain was surprisingly advanced, and there were signs of a sensory equipment, served in part through the wiry cilia of the head, involving factors alien to any other terrestrial organism. Probably it has more than five senses, so that its habits could not be predicted from any existing analogy. It must, Lake thought, have been a creature of keen sensitiveness and delicately differentiated functions in its primal world – much like the ants and bees of today. It reproduced like the vegetable cryptogams, especially the Pteridophyta, having spore cases at the tips of the wings and evidently developing from a thallus or prothallus.

But to give it a name at this stage was mere folly. It looked like a radiate, but was clearly something more. It was partly vegetable, but had three-fourths of the essentials of animal structure. That it was marine in origin, its symmetrical contour and certain other attributes clearly indicated; yet one could not be exact as to the limit of its later adaptations. The wings, after all, held a persistent suggestion of the aerial. How it could have undergone its tremendously complex evolution on a new-born earth in time to leave prints in Archaean rocks was so far beyond conception as to make Lake whimsically recall the primal myths about Great Old Ones who filtered down from the stars and concocted earth life as a joke or mistake; and the wild tales of cosmic hill things from outside told by a folklorist colleague in Miskatonic's English department.

Naturally, he considered the possibility of the pre-Cambrian prints having been made by a less evolved ancestor of the present specimens, but quickly rejected this too-facile theory upon considering the advanced structural qualities of the older fossils. If anything, the later contours showed decadence rather than higher evolution. The size of the pseudofeet had decreased, and the whole morphology seemed coarsened and simplified. Moreover, the nerves and organs just examined held singular suggestions of retrogression from forms still more complex. Atrophied and vestigial parts were surprisingly prevalent. Altogether, little could be said to have been solved; and Lake fell back on mythology for a provisional name – jocosely dubbing his finds 'The Elder Ones.'

At about 2:30 a.m., having decided to postpone further work and get a little rest, he covered the dissected organism with a tarpaulin, emerged from the laboratory tent, and studied the intact specimens with renewed interest. The ceaseless antarctic sun had begun to limber up their tissues a trifle, so that the head points and tubes of two or three showed signs of unfolding; but Lake did not believe there was any danger of immediate decomposition in the almost subzero air. He did, however, move all the undissected specimens close together and throw a spare tent over them in order to keep off the direct solar rays. That would also help to keep their possible scent away from the dogs, whose hostile unrest was really becoming a problem, even at their substantial distance and behind the higher and higher snow walls which an increased quota of the men were hastening to raise around their quarters. He had to weight down the corners of the tent cloth with heavy blocks of snow to hold it in place amidst the rising gale, for the titan mountains seemed about to deliver some gravely severe blasts. Early apprehensions about sudden antarctic winds were revived, and under Atwood's supervision precautions were taken to bank the tents, new dog corral, and crude aeroplane shelters with snow on the mountainward side. These latter shelters, begun with hard snow blocks during odd moments, were by no means as high as they should have been; and Lake finally detached all hands from other tasks to work on them.

It was after four when Lake at last prepared to sign off and advised us all to share the rest period his outfit would take when the shelter walls were a little higher. He held some friendly chat with Pabodie over the ether, and repeated his praise of the really marvelous drills that had helped him make his discovery. Atwood also sent greetings and praises. I gave Lake a warm word of congratulations, owning up that he was right about the western trip, and we all agreed to get in touch by wireless at ten in the morning. If the gale was then over, Lake would send a plane for the party at my base. Just before retiring I dispatched a final message to the Arkham with instructions about toning down the day's news for the outside world, since the full details seemed radical enough to rouse a wave of incredulity until further substantiated.

Chapter III

NONE OF US, I imagine, slept very heavily or continuously that morning. Both the excitement of Lake's discovery and the mounting fury of the wind were against such a thing. So savage was the blast, even where we were, that we could not help wondering how much worse it was at Lake's camp, directly under the vast unknown peaks that bred and delivered it. McTighe was awake at ten o'clock and tried to get Lake on the wireless, as agreed, but some electrical condition in the disturbed air to the westward seemed to prevent communication. We did, however, get the Arkham, and Douglas told me that he had likewise been vainly trying to reach Lake. He had not known about the wind, for very little was blowing at McMurdo Sound, despite its persistent rage where we were.

Throughout the day we all listened anxiously and tried to get Lake at intervals, but invariably without results. About noon a positive frenzy of wind stampeded out of the west, causing us to fear for the safety of our camp; but it eventually died down, with only a moderate relapse at 2 p.m. After three o'clock it was very quiet, and we redoubled our efforts to get Lake. Reflecting that he had four planes, each provided with an excellent short-wave outfit, we could not imagine any ordinary accident capable of crippling all his wireless equipment at once. Nevertheless the stony silence continued, and when we thought of the delirious force the wind must have had in his locality we could not help making the more direful conjectures.

By six o'clock our fears had become intense and definite, and after a wireless consultation with Douglas and Thorfinnssen I resolved to take steps toward investigation. The fifth aeroplane, which we had left at the McMurdo Sound supply cache with Sherman and two sailors, was in good shape and ready for instant use, and it seemed that the very emergency for which it had been saved was now upon us. I got Sherman by wireless and ordered him to join me with the plane and the two sailors at the southern base as quickly as possible, the air conditions being apparently highly favorable. We then talked over the personnel of the coming investigation party, and decided that we would include all hands, together with the sledge and dogs which I had kept with me. Even so great a load would not be too much for one of the huge planes built to our special orders for heavy machinery transportation. At intervals I still tried to reach Lake with the wireless, but all to no purpose.

Sherman, with the sailors Gunnarsson and Larsen, took off at 7:30, and reported a quiet flight from several points on the wing. They arrived at our base at midnight, and all hands at once discussed the next move. It was risky business sailing over the antarctic in a single aeroplane without any line of bases, but no one drew back from what seemed like the plainest necessity. We turned in at two o'clock for a brief rest after some preliminary loading of the plane, but were up again in four hours to finish the loading and packing.

At 7:15 a.m., January 25th, we started flying northwestward under McTighe's pilotage with ten men, seven dogs, a sledge, a fuel and food supply, and other items including the plane's wireless outfit. The atmosphere was clear, fairly quiet, and relatively mild in temperature, and we anticipated very little trouble in reaching the latitude and longitude designated by Lake as the site of his camp. Our apprehensions were over what we might find, or fail to find, at the end of our journey, for silence continued to answer all calls dispatched to the camp.

Every incident of that four-and-a-half-hour flight is burned into my recollection because of its crucial position in my life. It marked my loss, at the age of fifty-four, of all that peace and balance which the normal mind possesses through its accustomed conception of external nature and nature's laws. Thenceforward the ten of us – but the student Danforth and myself above all others – were to face a hideously amplified world of lurking horrors which nothing can erase from our emotions, and which we would refrain from sharing with mankind in general if we could. The newspapers have printed the bulletins we sent from the moving plane, telling of our nonstop course, our two battles with treacherous upper-air gales, our glimpse of the broken surface where Lake had sunk his mid-journey shaft three days before, and our sight of a group of those strange fluffy snow cylinders noted by Amundsen and Byrd as rolling in the wind across the endless leagues of frozen plateau. There came a point, though, when our sensations could not be conveyed in any words the press would understand, and a latter point when we had to adopt an actual rule of strict censorship.

The sailor Larsen was first to spy the jagged line of witchlike cones and pinnacles ahead, and his shouts sent everyone to the windows of the great cabined plane. Despite our speed, they were very slow in gaining prominence; hence we knew that they must be infinitely far off, and visible only because of their abnormal height. Little by little, however, they rose grimly into the western sky; allowing us to distinguish various bare, bleak, blackish summits, and to catch the curious sense of fantasy which they inspired as seen in the reddish antarctic light against the provocative background of iridescent ice-dust clouds. In the whole spectacle there was a persistent, pervasive hint of stupendous secrecy and potential revelation. It was as if these stark, nightmare spires marked the pylons of a frightful gateway into forbidden spheres of dream, and complex gulfs of remote time, space, and ultra-dimensionality. I could not help feeling that they were evil things – mountains of madness whose farther slopes looked out over some accursed ultimate abyss. That seething, half-luminous cloud background held ineffable suggestions of a vague, ethereal beyondness far more than terrestrially spatial, and gave appalling reminders of the utter remoteness, separateness, desolation, and aeon-long death of this untrodden and unfathomed austral world.

It was young Danforth who drew our notice to the curious regularities of the higher mountain skyline – regularities like clinging fragments of perfect cubes, which Lake had mentioned in his messages, and which indeed justified his comparison with the dreamlike suggestions of primordial temple ruins, on cloudy Asian mountaintops so subtly and strangely painted by Roerich. There was indeed something hauntingly Roerich-like about this whole unearthly continent of mountainous mystery. I had felt it in October when we first caught sight of Victoria Land, and I felt it afresh now. I felt, too, another wave of uneasy consciousness of Archaean mythical resemblances; of how disturbingly this lethal realm corresponded to the evilly famed plateau of Leng in the primal writings. Mythologists have placed Leng in Central Asia; but the racial memory of man – or of his predecessors – is long, and it may well be that certain tales have come down from lands and mountains and temples of horror earlier than Asia and earlier than any human world we know. A few daring mystics have hinted at a pre-Pleistocene origin for the fragmentary Pnakotic Manuscripts, and have suggested that the devotees of Tsathoggua were as alien to mankind as Tsathoggua itself. Leng, wherever in space or time it might brood, was not a region I would care to be in or near, nor did I relish the proximity of a world that had ever bred such ambiguous and Archaean monstrosities as those Lake had just mentioned. At the moment I felt sorry that I had ever read the abhorred *Necronomicon*, or talked so much with that unpleasantly erudite folklorist Wilmarth at the university.

This mood undoubtedly served to aggravate my reaction to the bizarre mirage which burst upon us from the increasingly opalescent zenith as we drew near the mountains and began to make out the cumulative undulations of the foothills. I had seen dozens of polar mirages during the preceding weeks, some of them quite as uncanny and fantastically vivid as the present example; but this one had a wholly novel and obscure quality of menacing symbolism, and I shuddered as the seething labyrinth of fabulous walls and towers and minarets loomed out of the troubled ice vapors above our heads.

The effect was that of a Cyclopean city of no architecture known to man or to human imagination, with vast aggregations of night-black masonry embodying monstrous perversions of geometrical laws. There were truncated cones, sometimes terraced or fluted, surmounted by tall cylindrical shafts here and there bulbously enlarged and often capped with tiers of thinnish scalloped disks; and strange beetling, table-like constructions suggesting piles of multitudinous rectangular slabs or circular plates or five-pointed stars with each one overlapping the one beneath. There were composite cones and pyramids either alone or surmounting cylinders or cubes or flatter truncated cones and pyramids, and occasional needle-like spires in curious clusters of five. All of these febrile structures seemed knit together by tubular bridges crossing from one to the other at various dizzy heights, and the implied scale of the whole was terrifying and oppressive in its sheer gigantism. The general type of mirage was not unlike some of the wilder forms observed and drawn by the arctic whaler Scoresby in 1820, but at this time and place, with those dark, unknown mountain peaks soaring stupendously ahead, that anomalous elder-world discovery in our minds, and the pall of probable disaster enveloping the greater part of our expedition, we all seemed to find in it a taint of latent malignity and infinitely evil portent.

I was glad when the mirage began to break up, though in the process the various nightmare turrets and cones assumed distorted, temporary forms of even vaster hideousness. As the whole illusion dissolved to churning opalescence we began to look earthward again, and saw that our journey's end was not far off. The unknown mountains ahead rose dizzily up like a fearsome rampart of giants, their curious regularities showing with startling clearness even without a field glass. We were over the lowest foothills now, and could see amidst the snow, ice, and bare patches of their main plateau a couple of darkish spots which we took to be Lake's camp and boring. The higher foothills shot up between five and six miles away, forming a range almost distinct from the terrifying line of more than Himalayan peaks beyond them. At length Ropes – the student who had relieved McTighe at the controls – began to head downward toward the left-hand dark spot whose size marked it as the camp. As he did so, McTighe sent out the last uncensored wireless message the world was to receive from our expedition.

Everyone, of course, has read the brief and unsatisfying bulletins of the rest of our antarctic sojourn. Some hours after our landing we sent a guarded report of the tragedy we found, and reluctantly announced the wiping out of the whole Lake party by the frightful wind of the preceding day, or of the night before that. Eleven known dead, young Gedney missing. People pardoned our hazy lack of details through realization of the shock the sad event must have caused us, and believed us when we explained that the mangling action of the wind had rendered all eleven bodies unsuitable for transportation outside. Indeed, I flatter myself that even in the midst of our distress, utter bewilderment, and soul-clutching horror, we scarcely went beyond the truth in any specific instance. The tremendous significance lies in what we dared not tell; what I would not tell now but for the need of warning others off from nameless terrors.

It is a fact that the wind had brought dreadful havoc. Whether all could have lived through it, even without the other thing, is gravely open to doubt. The storm, with its fury of madly driven ice particles, must have been beyond anything our expedition had encountered before. One aeroplane shelter-wall, it seems, had been left in a far too flimsy and inadequate state – was nearly pulverized – and the derrick at the distant boring was entirely shaken to pieces. The exposed metal of the grounded planes and drilling machinery was bruised into a high polish, and two of the small tents were flattened despite their snow banking. Wooden surfaces left out in the blaster were pitted and denuded of paint, and all signs of tracks in the snow were completely obliterated. It is also true that we found none of the Archaean biological objects in a condition to take outside as a whole. We did gather some minerals from a vast, tumbled pile, including several of the greenish soapstone fragments whose odd five-pointed rounding and faint patterns of grouped dots caused so many doubtful comparisons; and some fossil bones, among which were the most typical of the curiously injured specimens.

None of the dogs survived, their hurriedly built snow inclosure near the camp being almost wholly destroyed. The wind may have done that, though the greater breakage on the side next the camp, which was not the windward one, suggests an outward leap or break of the frantic beasts themselves. All three sledges were gone, and we have tried to explain that the wind may have blown them off into the unknown. The drill and ice-melting machinery at the boring were too badly damaged to warrant salvage, so we used them to choke up that subtly disturbing gateway to the past which Lake had blasted. We likewise left at the camp the two most shaken up of the planes; since our surviving party had only four real pilots – Sherman, Danforth, McTighe, and Ropes – in all, with Danforth in a poor nervous shape to navigate. We brought back all the books, scientific equipment, and other incidentals we could find, though much was rather unaccountably blown away. Spare tents and furs were either missing or badly out of condition.

It was approximately 4 p.m., after wide plane cruising had forced us to give Gedney up for lost, that we sent our guarded message to the Arkham for relaying; and I think we did well to keep it as calm and noncommittal as we succeeded in doing. The most we said about agitation concerned our dogs, whose frantic uneasiness near the biological specimens was to be expected from poor Lake's accounts. We did not mention, I think, their display of the same uneasiness when sniffing around the queer greenish soapstones and certain other objects in the disordered region-objects including scientific instruments, aeroplanes, and machinery, both at the camp and at the boring, whose parts had been loosened, moved, or otherwise tampered with by winds that must have harbored singular curiosity and investigativeness.

About the fourteen biological specimens, we were pardonably indefinite. We said that the only ones we discovered were damaged, but that enough was left of them to prove Lake's description wholly and impressively accurate. It was hard work keeping our personal emotions out of this matter – and we did not mention numbers or say exactly how we had found those which we did find. We had by that time agreed not to transmit anything suggesting madness on the part of Lake's men, and it surely looked like madness to find six imperfect monstrosities carefully buried upright in nine-foot snow graves under five-pointed mounds punched over with groups of dots in patterns exactly those on the queer greenish soapstones dug up from Mesozoic or Tertiary times. The eight perfect specimens mentioned by Lake seemed to have been completely blown away.

We were careful, too, about the public's general peace of mind; hence Danforth and I said little about that frightful trip over the mountains the next day. It was the fact that only a radically lightened plane could possibly cross a range of such height, which mercifully limited that scouting tour to the two of us. On our return at one a.m., Danforth was close to hysterics, but kept an admirably stiff upper lip. It took no persuasion to make him promise not to show our sketches and the other things we brought away in our pockets, not to say anything more to the others than what we had agreed to relay outside, and to hide our camera films for private development later on; so that part of my present story will be as new to Pabodie, McTighe, Ropes, Sherman, and the rest as it will be to the world in general. Indeed, Danforth is closer mouthed than I: for he saw, or thinks he saw, one thing he will not tell even me.

As all know, our report included a tale of a hard ascent – a confirmation of Lake's opinion that the great peaks are of Archaean slate and other very primal crumpled strata unchanged since at least middle Comanchian times; a conventional comment on the regularity of the clinging cube and rampart formations; a decision that the cave mouths indicate dissolved calcaerous veins; a conjecture that certain slopes and passes would permit of the scaling and crossing of the entire range by seasoned mountaineers; and a remark that the mysterious other side holds a lofty and immense superplateau as ancient and unchanging as the mountains themselves – twenty thousand feet in elevation, with grotesque rock formations protruding through a thin glacial layer and with low gradual foothills between the general plateau surface and the sheer precipices of the highest peaks.

This body of data is in every respect true so far as it goes, and it completely satisfied the men at the camp. We laid our absence of sixteen hours – a longer time than our announced flying, landing, reconnoitering, and rock-collecting program called for – to a long mythical spell of adverse wind conditions, and told truly of our landing on the farther foothills. Fortunately our tale sounded realistic and prosaic enough not to tempt any of the others into emulating our flight. Had any tried to do that, I would have used every ounce of my persuasion to stop them – and I do not know what Danforth would have done. While we were gone, Pabodie, Sherman, Ropes, McTighe, and Williamson had worked like beavers over Lake's two best planes, fitting them again for use despite the altogether unaccountable juggling of their operative mechanism.

We decided to load all the planes the next morning and start back for our old base as soon as possible. Even though indirect, that was the safest way to work toward McMurdo Sound; for a straightline flight across the most utterly unknown stretches of the aeon-dead continent would involve many additional hazards. Further exploration was hardly feasible in view of our tragic decimation and the ruin of our drilling machinery. The doubts and horrors around us – which we did not reveal – made us wish only to escape from this austral world of desolation and brooding madness as swiftly as we could.

As the public knows, our return to the world was accomplished without further disasters. All planes reached the old base on the evening of the next day – January 27th – after a swift nonstop flight; and on the 28th we made McMurdo Sound in two laps, the one pause being very brief, and occasioned by a faulty rudder in the furious wind over the ice shelf after we had cleared the great plateau. In five days more, the Arkham and Miskatonic, with all hands and equipment on board, were shaking clear of the thickening field ice and working up Ross Sea with the mocking mountains of Victoria Land looming westward against a troubled antarctic sky and twisting the wind's wails into a wide-ranged musical piping which chilled my soul to the quick. Less than a fortnight later we left the last hint of polar land behind us and thanked heaven that we were clear of a haunted, accursed realm where life and death, space and time, have made black and blasphemous alliances, in the unknown epochs since matter first writhed and swam on the planet's scarce-cooled crust.

Since our return we have all constantly worked to discourage antarctic exploration, and have kept certain doubts and guesses to ourselves with splendid unity and faithfulness. Even young Danforth, with his nervous breakdown, has not flinched or babbled to his doctors – indeed, as I have said, there is one thing he thinks he alone saw which he will not tell even me, though I think it would help his psychological state if he would consent to do so. It might explain and relieve much, though perhaps the thing was no more than the delusive aftermath of an earlier shock. That is the impression I gather after those rare, irresponsible moments when he whispers disjointed things to me – things which he repudiates vehemently as soon as he gets a grip on himself again.

It will be hard work deterring others from the great white south, and some of our efforts may directly harm our cause by drawing inquiring notice. We might have known from the first that human curiosity is undying, and that the results we announced would be enough to spur others ahead on the same age-long pursuit of the unknown. Lake's reports of those biological monstrosities had aroused naturalists and paleontologists to the highest pitch, though we were sensible enough not to show the detached parts we had taken from the actual buried specimens, or our photographs of those specimens as they were found. We also refrained from showing the more puzzling of the scarred bones and greenish soapstones; while Danforth and I have closely guarded the pictures we took or drew on the superplateau across the range, and the crumpled things we smoothed, studied in terror, and brought away in our pockets.

But now that Starkweather-Moore party is organizing, and with a thoroughness far beyond anything our outfit attempted. If not dissuaded, they will get to the innermost nucleus of the antarctic and melt and bore till they bring up that which we know may end the world. So I must break through all reticences at last – even about that ultimate, nameless thing beyond the mountains of madness.

Chapter IV

IT IS ONLY with vast hesitancy and repugnance that I let my mind go back to Lake's camp and what we really found there – and to that other thing beyond the mountains of madness. I am constantly tempted to shirk the details, and to let hints stand for actual facts and ineluctable deductions. I hope I have said enough already to let me glide briefly over the rest; the rest, that is, of the horror at the camp. I have told of the wind-ravaged terrain, the damaged shelters, the disarranged machinery, the varied uneasiness of our dogs, the missing sledges and other items, the deaths of men and dogs, the absence of Gedney, and the six insanely buried biological specimens, strangely sound in texture for all their structural injuries, from a world forty million years dead. I do not recall whether I mentioned that upon checking up the canine bodies we found one dog missing. We did not think much about that till later – indeed, only Danforth and I have thought of it at all.

The principal things I have been keeping back relate to the bodies, and to certain subtle points which may or may not lend a hideous and incredible kind of rationale to the apparent chaos. At the time, I tried to keep the men's minds off those points; for it was so much simpler – so much more normal – to lay everything to an outbreak of madness on the part of some of Lake's party. From the look of things, that demon mountain wind must have been enough to drive any man mad in the midst of this center of all earthly mystery and desolation.

The crowning abnormality, of course, was the condition of the bodies – men and dogs alike. They had all been in some terrible kind of conflict, and were torn and mangled in fiendish and altogether inexplicable ways. Death, so far as we could judge, had in each case come from strangulation or laceration. The dogs had evidently started the trouble, for the state of their ill-built corral bore witness to its forcible breakage from within. It had been set some distance from the camp because of the hatred of the animals for those hellish Archaean organisms, but the precaution seemed to have been taken in vain. When left alone in that monstrous wind, behind flimsy walls of insufficient height, they must have stampeded – whether from the wind itself, or from some subtle, increasing odor emitted by the nightmare specimens, one could not say.

But whatever had happened, it was hideous and revolting enough. Perhaps I had better put squeamishness aside and tell the worst at last – though with a categorical statement of opinion, based on the first-hand observations and most rigid deductions of both Danforth and myself, that the then missing Gedney was in no way responsible for the loathsome horrors we found. I have said that the bodies were frightfully mangled.

Now I must add that some were incised and subtracted from in the most curious, cold-blooded, and inhuman fashion. It was the same with dogs and men. All the healthier, fatter bodies, quadrupedal or bipedal, had had their most solid masses of tissue cut out and removed, as by a careful butcher; and around them was a strange sprinkling of salt – taken from the ravaged provision chests on the planes – which conjured up the most horrible associations. The thing had occurred in one of the crude aeroplane shelters from which the plane had been dragged out, and subsequent winds had effaced all tracks which could have supplied any plausible theory. Scattered bits of clothing, roughly slashed from the human incision subjects, hinted no clues. It is useless to bring up the half impression of certain faint snow prints in one shielded corner of the ruined inclosure – because that impression did not concern human prints at all, but was clearly mixed up with all the talk of fossil prints which poor Lake had been giving throughout the preceding weeks. One had to be careful of one's imagination in the lee of those overshadowing mountains of madness.

As I have indicated, Gedney and one dog turned out to be missing in the end. When we came on that terrible shelter we had missed two dogs and two men; but the fairly unharmed dissecting tent, which we entered after investigating the monstrous graves, had something to reveal. It was not as Lake had left it, for the covered parts of the primal monstrosity had been removed from the improvised table. Indeed, we had already realized that one of the six imperfect and insanely buried things we had found – the one with the trace of a peculiarly hateful odor – must represent the collected sections of the entity which Lake had tried to analyze. On and around that laboratory table were strewn other things, and it did not take long for us to guess that those things were the carefully though oddly and inexpertly dissected parts of one man and one dog. I shall spare the feelings of survivors by omitting mention of the man's identity. Lake's anatomical instruments were missing, but there were evidences of their careful cleansing. The gasoline stove was also gone, though around it we found a curious litter of matches. We buried the human parts beside the other ten men; and the canine parts with the other thirty-five dogs. Concerning the bizarre smudges on the laboratory table, and on the jumble of roughly handled illustrated books scattered near it, we were much too bewildered to speculate.

This formed the worst of the camp horror, but other things were equally perplexing. The disappearance of Gedney, the one dog, the eight uninjured biological specimens, the three sledges, and certain instruments, illustrated technical and scientific books, writing materials, electric torches and batteries, food and fuel, heating apparatus, spare tents, fur suits, and the like, was utterly beyond sane conjecture; as were likewise the spatter-fringed ink blots on certain pieces of paper, and the evidences of curious alien fumbling and experimentation around the planes and all other mechanical devices both at the camp and at the boring. The dogs seemed to abhor this oddly disordered machinery. Then, too, there was the upsetting of the larder, the disappearance of certain staples, and the jarringly comical heap of tin cans pried open in the most unlikely ways and at the most unlikely places. The profusion of scattered matches, intact, broken, or spent, formed another minor enigma – as did the two or three tent cloths and fur suits which we found lying about with peculiar and unorthodox slashings conceivably due to clumsy efforts at unimaginable adaptations. The maltreatment of the human and canine bodies, and the crazy burial of the damaged Archaean specimens, were all of a piece with this apparent disintegrative madness. In view of just such an eventuality as the present one, we carefully photographed all the main evidences of insane disorder at the camp; and shall use the prints to buttress our pleas against the departure of the proposed Starkweather-Moore Expedition.

Our first act after finding the bodies in the shelter was to photograph and open the row of insane graves with the five-pointed snow mounds. We could not help noticing the resemblance of these monstrous mounds, with their clusters of grouped dots, to poor Lake's descriptions of the strange greenish soapstones; and when we came on some of the soapstones themselves in the great mineral pile, we found the likeness very close indeed. The whole general formation, it must be made clear, seemed abominably suggestive of the starfish head of the Archaean entities; and we agreed that the suggestion must have worked potently upon the sensitized minds of Lake's overwrought party.

For madness – centering in Gedney as the only possible surviving agent – was the explanation spontaneously adopted by everybody so far as spoken utterance was concerned; though I will not be so naive as to deny that each of us may have harbored wild guesses which sanity forbade him to formulate completely. Sherman, Pabodie, and McTighe made an exhaustive aeroplane cruise over all the surrounding territory in the afternoon, sweeping the horizon with field glasses in quest of Gedney and of the various missing things; but nothing came to light. The party reported that the titan barrier range extended endlessly to right and left alike, without any diminution in height or essential structure. On some of the peaks, though, the regular cube and rampart formations were bolder and plainer, having doubly fantastic similitudes to Roerich-painted Asian hill ruins. The distribution of cryptical cave mouths on the black snow-denuded summits seemed roughly even as far as the range could be traced.

In spite of all the prevailing horrors, we were left with enough sheer scientific zeal and adventurousness to wonder about the unknown realm beyond those mysterious mountains. As our guarded messages stated, we rested at midnight after our day of terror and bafflement – but not without a tentative plan for one or more range-crossing altitude flights in a lightened plane with aerial camera and geologist's outfit, beginning the following morning. It was decided that Danforth and I try it first, and we awaked at 7 a.m. intending an early flight; however, heavy winds – mentioned in our brief bulletin to the outside world – delayed our start till nearly nine o'clock.

I have already repeated the noncommittal story we told the men at camp – and relayed outside – after our return sixteen hours later. It is now my terrible duty to amplify this account by filling in the merciful blanks with hints of what we really saw in the hidden transmontane world – hints of the revelations which have finally driven Danforth to a nervous collapse. I wish he would add a really frank word about the thing which he thinks he alone saw – even though it was probably a nervous delusion – and which was perhaps the last straw that put him where he is; but he is firm against that. All I can do is to repeat his later disjointed whispers about what set him shrieking as the plane soared back through the wind-tortured mountain pass after that real and tangible shock which I shared. This will form my last word. If the plain signs of surviving elder horrors in what I disclose be not enough to keep others from meddling with the inner antarctic – or at least from prying too deeply beneath the surface of that ultimate waste of forbidden secrets and inhuman, aeon-cursed desolation – the responsibility for unnamable and perhaps immeasurable evils will not be mine.

Danforth and I, studying the notes made by Pabodie in his afternoon flight and checking up with a sextant, had calculated that the lowest available pass in the range lay somewhat to the right of us, within sight of camp, and about twenty-three thousand or twenty-four thousand feet above sea level. For this point, then, we first headed in the lightened plane as we embarked on our flight of discovery. The camp itself, on foothills which sprang from a high continental plateau, was some twelve thousand feet in altitude; hence the actual height increase necessary was not so vast as it might seem. Nevertheless we were acutely conscious of the rarefied air and intense cold as we rose; for, on account of visibility conditions, we had to leave the cabin windows open. We were dressed, of course, in our heaviest furs.

As we drew near the forbidding peaks, dark and sinister above the line of crevasse-riven snow and interstitial glaciers, we noticed more and more the curiously regular formations clinging to the slopes; and thought again of the strange Asian paintings of Nicholas Roerich. The ancient and wind-weathered rock strata fully verified all of Lake's bulletins, and proved that these pinnacles had been towering up in exactly the same way since a surprisingly early time in earth's history – perhaps over fifty million years. How much higher they had once been, it was futile to guess; but everything about this strange region pointed to obscure atmospheric influences unfavorable to change, and calculated to retard the usual climatic processes of rock disintegration.

But it was the mountainside tangle of regular cubes, ramparts, and cave mouths which fascinated and disturbed us most. I studied them with a field glass and took aerial photographs while Danforth drove; and at times I relieved him at the controls – though my aviation knowledge was purely an amateur's – in order to let him use the binoculars. We could easily see that much of the material of the things was a lightish Archaean quartzite, unlike any formation visible over broad areas of the general surface; and that their regularity was extreme and uncanny to an extent which poor Lake had scarcely hinted.

As he had said, their edges were crumbled and rounded from untold aeons of savage weathering; but their preternatural solidity and tough material had saved them from obliteration. Many parts, especially those closest to the slopes, seemed identical in substance with the surrounding rock surface. The whole arrangement looked like the ruins of Macchu Picchu in the Andes, or the primal foundation walls of Kish as dug up by the Oxford Field Museum Expedition in 1929; and both Danforth and I obtained that occasional impression of separate Cyclopean blocks which Lake had attributed to his flight-companion Carroll. How to account for such things in this place was frankly beyond me, and I felt queerly humbled as a geologist. Igneous formations often have strange regularities – like the famous Giants' Causeway in Ireland – but this stupendous range, despite Lake's original suspicion of smoking cones, was above all else nonvolcanic in evident structure.

The curious cave mouths, near which the odd formations seemed most abundant, presented another albeit a lesser puzzle because of their regularity of outline. They were, as Lake's bulletin had said, often approximately square or semicircular; as if the natural orifices had been shaped to greater symmetry by some magic hand. Their numerousness and wide distribution were remarkable, and suggested that the whole region was honeycombed with tunnels dissolved out of limestone strata. Such glimpses as we secured did not extend far within the caverns, but we saw that they were apparently clear of stalactites and stalagmites. Outside, those parts of the mountain slopes adjoining the apertures seemed invariably smooth and regular; and Danforth thought that the slight cracks and pittings of the weathering tended toward unusual patterns. Filled as he was with the horrors and strangenesses discovered at the camp, he hinted that the pittings vaguely resembled those baffling groups of dots sprinkled over the primeval greenish soapstones, so hideously duplicated on the madly conceived snow mounds above those six buried monstrosities.

We had risen gradually in flying over the higher foothills and along toward the relatively low pass we had selected. As we advanced we occasionally looked down at the snow and ice of the land route, wondering whether we could have attempted the trip with the simpler equipment of earlier days. Somewhat to our surprise we saw that the terrain was far from difficult as such things go; and that despite the crevasses and other bad spots it would not have been likely to deter the sledges of a Scott, a Shackleton, or an Amundsen. Some of the glaciers appeared to lead up to wind-bared passes with unusual continuity, and upon reaching our chosen pass we found that its case formed no exception.

Our sensations of tense expectancy as we prepared to round the crest and peer out over an untrodden world can hardly be described on paper; even though we had no cause to think the regions beyond the range essentially different from those already seen and traversed. The touch of evil mystery in these barrier mountains, and in the beckoning sea of opalescent sky glimpsed betwixt their summits, was a highly subtle and attenuated matter not to be explained in literal words. Rather was it an affair of vague psychological symbolism and aesthetic association – a thing mixed up with exotic poetry and paintings, and with archaic myths lurking in shunned and forbidden volumes. Even the wind's burden held a peculiar strain of conscious malignity; and for a second it seemed that the composite sound included a bizarre musical whistling or piping over a wide range as the blast swept in and out of the omnipresent and resonant cave mouths. There was a cloudy note of reminiscent repulsion in this sound, as complex and unplaceable as any of the other dark impressions.

We were now, after a slow ascent, at a height of twenty-three thousand, five hundred and seventy feet according to the aneroid; and had left the region of clinging snow definitely below us. Up here were only dark, bare rock slopes and the start of rough-ribbed glaciers – but with those provocative cubes, ramparts, and echoing cave mouths to add a portent of the unnatural, the fantastic, and the dreamlike. Looking along the line of high peaks, I thought I could see the one mentioned by poor Lake, with a rampart exactly on top. It seemed to be half lost in a queer antarctic haze – such a haze, perhaps, as had been responsible for Lake's early notion of volcanism. The pass loomed directly before us, smooth and windswept between its jagged and malignly frowning pylons. Beyond it was a sky fretted with swirling vapors and lighted by the low polar sun – the sky of that mysterious farther realm upon which we felt no human eye had ever gazed.

A few more feet of altitude and we would behold that realm. Danforth and I, unable to speak except in shouts amidst the howling, piping wind that raced through the pass and added to the noise of the unmuffled engines, exchanged eloquent glances. And then, having gained those last few feet, we did indeed stare across the momentous divide and over the unsampled secrets of an elder and utterly alien earth.

Chapter V

I THINK THAT both of us simultaneously cried out in mixed awe, wonder, terror, and disbelief in our own senses as we finally cleared the pass and saw what lay beyond. Of course, we must have had some natural theory in the back of our heads to steady our faculties for the moment. Probably we thought of such things as the grotesquely weathered stones of the Garden of the Gods in Colorado, or the fantastically symmetrical wind-carved rocks of the Arizona desert. Perhaps we even half thought the sight a mirage like that we had seen the morning before on first approaching those mountains of madness. We must have had some such normal notions to fall back upon as our eyes swept that limitless, tempest-scarred plateau and grasped the almost endless labyrinth of colossal, regular, and geometrically eurythmic stone masses which reared their crumbled and pitted crests above a glacial sheet not more than forty or fifty feet deep at its thickest, and in places obviously thinner.

The effect of the monstrous sight was indescribable, for some fiendish violation of known natural law seemed certain at the outset. Here, on a hellishly ancient table-land fully twenty thousand feet high, and in a climate deadly to habitation since a prehuman age not less than five hundred thousand years ago, there stretched nearly to the vision's limit a tangle of orderly stone which only the desperation of mental self-defense could possibly attribute to any but conscious and artificial cause. We had previously dismissed, so far as serious thought was concerned, any theory that the cubes and ramparts of the mountainsides were other than natural in origin. How could they be otherwise, when man himself could scarcely have been differentiated from the great apes at the time when this region succumbed to the present unbroken reign of glacial death?

Yet now the sway of reason seemed irrefutably shaken, for this Cyclopean maze of squared, curved, and angled blocks had features which cut off all comfortable refuge. It was, very clearly, the blasphemous city of the mirage in stark, objective, and ineluctable reality. That damnable portent had had a material basis after all – there had been some horizontal stratum of ice dust in the upper air, and this shocking stone survival had projected its image across the mountains according to the simple laws of reflection, Of course, the phantom had been twisted and exaggerated, and had contained things which the real source did not contain; yet now, as we saw that real source, we thought it even more hideous and menacing than its distant image.

Only the incredible, unhuman massiveness of these vast stone towers and ramparts had saved the frightful things from utter annihilation in the hundreds of thousands – perhaps millions – of years it had brooded there amidst the blasts of a bleak upland. 'Corona Mundi – Roof of the World –' All sorts of fantastic phrases sprang to our lips as we looked dizzily down at the unbelievable spectacle. I thought again of the eldritch primal myths that had so persistently haunted me since my first sight of this dead antarctic world – of the demoniac plateau of Leng, of the Mi-Go, or abominable Snow Men of the Himalayas, of the Pnakotic Manuscripts with their prehuman implications, of the Cthulhu cult, of the *Necronomicon*, and of the Hyperborean legends of formless Tsathoggua and the worse than formless star spawn associated with that semientity.

For boundless miles in every direction the thing stretched off with very little thinning; indeed, as our eyes followed it to the right and left along the base of the low, gradual foothills which separated it from the actual mountain rim, we decided that we could see no thinning at all except for an interruption at the left of the pass through which we had come. We had merely struck, at random, a limited part of something of incalculable extent. The foothills were more sparsely sprinkled with grotesque stone structures, linking the terrible city to the already familiar cubes and ramparts which evidently formed its mountain outposts. These latter, as well as the queer cave mouths, were as thick on the inner as on the outer sides of the mountains.

The nameless stone labyrinth consisted, for the most part, of walls from ten to one hundred and fifty feet in ice-clear height, and of a thickness varying from five to ten feet. It was composed mostly of prodigious blocks of dark primordial slate, schist, and sandstone – blocks in many cases as large as 4 x 6 x 8 feet – though in several places it seemed to be carved out of a solid, uneven bed rock of pre-Cambrian slate. The buildings were far from equal in size, there being innumerable honeycomb arrangements of enormous extent as well as smaller separate structures. The general shape of these things tended to be conical, pyramidal, or terraced; though there were many perfect cylinders, perfect cubes, clusters of cubes, and other rectangular forms, and a peculiar sprinkling of angled edifices whose five-pointed ground plan roughly suggested modern fortifications. The builders had made constant and expert use of the principle of the arch, and domes had probably existed in the city's heyday.

The whole tangle was monstrously weathered, and the glacial surface from which the towers projected was strewn with fallen blocks and immemorial debris. Where the glaciation was transparent we could see the lower parts of the gigantic piles, and we noticed the ice-preserved stone bridges which connected the different towers at varying distances above the ground. On the exposed walls we could detect the scarred places where other and higher bridges of the same sort had existed. Closer inspection revealed countless largish windows; some of which were closed with shutters of a petrified material originally wood, though most gaped open in a sinister and menacing fashion. Many of the ruins, of course, were roofless, and with uneven though wind-rounded upper edges; whilst others, of a more sharply conical or pyramidal model or else protected by higher surrounding structures, preserved intact outlines despite the omnipresent crumbling and pitting. With the field glass we could barely make out what seemed to be sculptural decorations in horizontal bands – decorations including those curious groups of dots whose presence on the ancient soapstones now assumed a vastly larger significance.

In many places the buildings were totally ruined and the ice sheet deeply riven from various geologic causes. In other places the stonework was worn down to the very level of the glaciation. One broad swath, extending from the plateau's interior, to a cleft in the foothills about a mile to the left of the pass we had traversed, was wholly free from buildings. It probably represented, we concluded, the course of some great river which in Tertiary times – millions of years ago – had poured through the city and into some prodigious subterranean abyss of the great barrier range. Certainly, this was above all a region of caves, gulfs, and underground secrets beyond human penetration.

Looking back to our sensations, and recalling our dazedness at viewing this monstrous survival from aeons we had thought prehuman, I can only wonder that we preserved the semblance of equilibrium, which we did. Of course, we knew that something – chronology, scientific theory, or our own consciousness – was woefully awry; yet we kept enough poise to guide the plane, observe many things quite minutely, and take a careful series of photographs which may yet serve both us and the world in good stead. In my case, ingrained scientific habit may have helped; for above all my bewilderment and sense of menace, there burned a dominant curiosity to fathom more of this age-old secret – to know what sort of beings had built and lived in this incalculably gigantic place, and what relation to the general world of its time or of other times so unique a concentration of life could have had.

For this place could be no ordinary city. It must have formed the primary nucleus and center of some archaic and unbelievable chapter of earth's history whose outward ramifications, recalled only dimly in the most obscure and distorted myths, had vanished utterly amidst the chaos of terrene convulsions long before any human race we know had shambled out of apedom. Here sprawled a Palaeogaean megalopolis compared with which the fabled Atlantis and Lemuria, Commoriom and Uzuldaroum, and Olathoc in the land of Lomar, are recent things of today – not even of yesterday; a megalopolis ranking with such whispered prehuman blasphemies as Valusia, R'lyeh, Ib in the land of Mnar, and the Nameless city of Arabia Deserta. As we flew above that tangle of stark titan towers my imagination sometimes escaped all bounds and roved aimlessly in realms of fantastic associations – even weaving links betwixt this lost world and some of my own wildest dreams concerning the mad horror at the camp.

The plane's fuel tank, in the interest of greater lightness, had been only partly filled; hence we now had to exert caution in our explorations. Even so, however, we covered an enormous extent of ground – or, rather, air – after swooping down to a level where the wind became virtually negligible. There seemed to be no limit to the mountain range, or to the length of the frightful stone city which bordered its inner foothills. Fifty miles of flight in each direction showed no major change in the labyrinth of rock and masonry that clawed up corpselike through the eternal ice. There were, though, some highly absorbing diversifications; such as the carvings on the canyon where that broad river had once pierced the foothills and approached its sinking place in the great range. The headlands at the stream's entrance had been boldly carved into Cyclopean pylons; and something about the ridgy, barrel-shaped designs stirred up oddly vague, hateful, and confusing semi-remembrances in both Danforth and me.

We also came upon several star-shaped open spaces, evidently public squares, and noted various undulations in the terrain. Where a sharp hill rose, it was generally hollowed out into some sort of rambling-stone edifice; but there were at least two exceptions. Of these latter, one was too badly weathered to disclose what had been on the jutting eminence, while the other still bore a fantastic conical monument carved out of the solid rock and roughly resembling such things as the well-known Snake Tomb in the ancient valley of Petra.

Flying inland from the mountains, we discovered that the city was not of infinite width, even though its length along the foothills seemed endless. After about thirty miles the grotesque stone buildings began to thin out, and in ten more miles we came to an unbroken waste virtually without signs of sentient artifice. The course of the river beyond the city seemed marked by a broad, depressed line, while the land assumed a somewhat greater ruggedness, seeming to slope slightly upward as it receded in the mist-hazed west.

So far we had made no landing, yet to leave the plateau without an attempt at entering some of the monstrous structures would have been inconceivable. Accordingly, we decided to find a smooth place on the foothills near our navigable pass, there grounding the plane and preparing to do some exploration on foot. Though these gradual slopes were partly covered with a scattering of ruins, low flying soon disclosed an ampler number of possible landing places. Selecting that nearest to the pass, since our flight would be across the great range and back to camp, we succeeded about 12:30 p.m. in effecting a landing on a smooth, hard snow field wholly devoid of obstacles and well adapted to a swift and favorable take-off later on.

It did not seem necessary to protect the plane with a snow banking for so brief a time and in so comfortable an absence of high winds at this level; hence we merely saw that the landing skis were safely lodged, and that the vital parts of the mechanism were guarded against the cold. For our foot journey we discarded the heaviest of our flying furs, and took with us a small outfit consisting of pocket compass, hand camera, light provisions, voluminous notebooks and paper, geologist's hammer and chisel, specimen bags, coil of climbing rope, and powerful electric torches with extra batteries; this equipment having been carried in the plane on the chance that we might be able to effect a landing, take ground pictures, make drawings and topographical sketches, and obtain rock specimens from some bare slope, outcropping, or mountain cave. Fortunately we had a supply of extra paper to tear up, place in a spare specimen bag, and use on the ancient principle of hare and hounds for marking our course in any interior mazes we might be able to penetrate. This had been brought in case we found some cave system with air quiet enough to allow such a rapid and easy method in place of the usual rock-chipping method of trail blazing.

Walking cautiously downhill over the crusted snow toward the stupendous stone labyrinth that loomed against the opalescent west, we felt almost as keen a sense of imminent marvels as we had felt on approaching the unfathomed mountain pass four hours previously. True, we had become visually familiar with the incredible secret concealed by the barrier peaks; yet the prospect of actually entering primordial walls reared by conscious beings perhaps millions of years ago – before any known race of men could have existed – was none the less awesome and potentially terrible in its implications of cosmic abnormality. Though the thinness of the air at this prodigious altitude made exertion somewhat more difficult than usual, both Danforth and I found ourselves bearing up very well, and felt equal to almost any task which might fall to our lot. It took only a few steps to bring us to a shapeless ruin worn level with the snow, while ten or fifteen rods farther on there was a huge, roofless rampart still complete in its gigantic five-pointed outline and rising to an irregular height of ten or eleven feet. For this latter we headed; and when at last we were actually able to touch its weathered Cyclopean blocks, we felt that we had established an unprecedented and almost blasphemous link with forgotten aeons normally closed to our species.

This rampart, shaped like a star and perhaps three hundred feet from point to point, was built of Jurassic sandstone blocks of irregular size, averaging 6 x 8 feet in surface. There was a row of arched loopholes or windows about four feet wide and five feet high, spaced quite symmetrically along the points of the star and at its inner angles, and with the bottoms about four feet from the glaciated surface. Looking through these, we could see that the masonry was fully five feet thick, that there were no partitions remaining within, and that there were traces of banded carvings or bas-reliefs on the interior walls – facts we had indeed guessed before, when flying low over this rampart and others like it. Though lower parts must have originally existed, all traces of such things were now wholly obscured by the deep layer of ice and snow at this point.

We crawled through one of the windows and vainly tried to decipher the nearly effaced mural designs, but did not attempt to disturb the glaciated floor. Our orientation flights had indicated that many buildings in the city proper were less ice-choked, and that we might perhaps find wholly clear interiors leading down to the true ground level if we entered those structures still roofed at the top. Before we left the rampart we photographed it carefully, and studied its mortar-less Cyclopean masonry with complete bewilderment.

We wished that Pabodie were present, for his engineering knowledge might have helped us guess how such titanic blocks could have been handled in that unbelievably remote age when the city and its outskirts were built up.

The half-mile walk downhill to the actual city, with the upper wind shrieking vainly and savagely through the skyward peaks in the background, was something of which the smallest details will always remain engraved on my mind. Only in fantastic nightmares could any human beings but Danforth and me conceive such optical effects. Between us and the churning vapors of the west lay that monstrous tangle of dark stone towers, its outre and incredible forms impressing us afresh at every new angle of vision. It was a mirage in solid stone, and were it not for the photographs, I would still doubt that such a thing could be. The general type of masonry was identical with that of the rampart we had examined; but the extravagant shapes which this masonry took in its urban manifestations were past all description.

Even the pictures illustrate only one or two phases of its endless variety, preternatural massiveness, and utterly alien exoticism. There were geometrical forms for which an Euclid would scarcely find a name – cones of all degrees of irregularity and truncation, terraces of every sort of provocative disproportion, shafts with odd bulbous enlargements, broken columns in curious groups, and five-pointed or five-ridged arrangements of mad grotesqueness. As we drew nearer we could see beneath certain transparent parts of the ice sheet, and detect some of the tubular stone bridges that connected the crazily sprinkled structures at various heights. Of orderly streets there seemed to be none, the only broad open swath being a mile to the left, where the ancient river had doubtless flowed through the town into the mountains.

Our field glasses showed the external, horizontal bands of nearly effaced sculptures and dot groups to be very prevalent, and we could half imagine what the city must once have looked like – even though most of the roofs and tower tops had necessarily perished. As a whole, it had been a complex tangle of twisted lanes and alleys, all of them deep canyons, and some little better than tunnels because of the overhanging masonry or overarching bridges. Now, outspread below us, it loomed like a dream fantasy against a westward mist through whose northern end the low, reddish antarctic sun of early afternoon was struggling to shine; and when, for a moment, that sun encountered a denser obstruction and plunged the scene into temporary shadow, the effect was subtly menacing in a way I can never hope to depict. Even the faint howling and piping of the unfelt wind in the great mountain passes behind us took on a wilder note of purposeful malignity. The last stage of our descent to the town was unusually steep and abrupt, and a rock outcropping at the edge where the grade changed led us to think that an artificial terrace had once existed there. Under the glaciation, we believed, there must be a flight of steps or its equivalent.

When at last we plunged into the town itself, clambering over fallen masonry and shrinking from the oppressive nearness and dwarfing height of omnipresent crumbling and pitted walls, our sensations again became such that I marvel at the amount of self-control we retained. Danforth was frankly jumpy, and began making some offensively irrelevant speculations about the horror at the camp – which I resented all the more because I could not help sharing certain conclusions forced upon us by many features of this morbid survival from nightmare antiquity. The speculations worked on his imagination, too; for in one place – where a debris-littered alley turned a sharp corner – he insisted that he saw faint traces of ground markings which he did not like;

whilst elsewhere he stopped to listen to a subtle, imaginary sound from some undefined point – a muffled musical piping, he said, not unlike that of the wind in the mountain caves, yet somehow disturbingly different. The ceaseless five-pointedness of the surrounding architecture and of the few distinguishable mural arabesques had a dimly sinister suggestiveness we could not escape, and gave us a touch of terrible subconscious certainty concerning the primal entities which had reared and dwelt in this unhallowed place.

Nevertheless, our scientific and adventurous souls were not wholly dead, and we mechanically carried out our program of chipping specimens from all the different rock types represented in the masonry. We wished a rather full set in order to draw better conclusions regarding the age of the place. Nothing in the great outer walls seemed to date from later than the Jurassic and Comanchian periods, nor was any piece of stone in the entire place of a greater recency than the Pliocene Age. In stark certainty, we were wandering amidst a death which had reigned at least five hundred thousand years, and in all probability even longer.

As we proceeded through this maze of stone-shadowed twilight we stopped at all available apertures to study interiors and investigate entrance possibilities. Some were above our reach, whilst others led only into ice-choked ruins as unroofed and barren as the rampart on the hill. One, though spacious and inviting, opened on a seemingly bottomless abyss without visible means of descent. Now and then we had a chance to study the petrified wood of a surviving shutter, and were impressed by the fabulous antiquity implied in the still discernible grain. These things had come from Mesozoic gymnosperms and conifers – especially Cretaceous cycads – and from fan palms and early angiosperms of plainly Tertiary date. Nothing definitely later than the Pliocene could be discovered. In the placing of these shutters – whose edges showed the former presence of queer and long-vanished hinges – usage seemed to be varied – some being on the outer and some on the inner side of the deep embrasures. They seemed to have become wedged in place, thus surviving the rusting of their former and probably metallic fixtures and fastenings.

After a time we came across a row of windows – in the bulges of a colossal five-edged cone of undamaged apex – which led into a vast, well-preserved room with stone flooring; but these were too high in the room to permit descent without a rope. We had a rope with us, but did not wish to bother with this twenty-foot drop unless obliged to – especially in this thin plateau air where great demands were made upon the heart action. This enormous room was probably a hall or concourse of some sort, and our electric torches showed bold, distinct, and potentially startling sculptures arranged round the walls in broad, horizontal bands separated by equally broad strips of conventional arabesques. We took careful note of this spot, planning to enter here unless a more easily gained interior were encountered.

Finally, though, we did encounter exactly the opening we wished; an archway about six feet wide and ten feet high, marking the former end of an aerial bridge which had spanned an alley about five feet above the present level of glaciation. These archways, of course, were flush with upper-story floors, and in this case one of the floors still existed. The building thus accessible was a series of rectangular terraces on our left facing westward. That across the alley, where the other archway yawned, was a decrepit cylinder with no windows and with a curious bulge about ten feet above the aperture. It was totally dark inside, and the archway seemed to open on a well of illimitable emptiness.

Heaped debris made the entrance to the vast left-hand building doubly easy, yet for a moment we hesitated before taking advantage of the long-wished chance. For though we had penetrated into this tangle of archaic mystery, it required fresh resolution to carry us actually inside a complete and surviving building of a fabulous elder world whose nature was becoming more and more hideously plain to us. In the end, however, we made the plunge, and scrambled up over the rubble into the gaping embrasure. The floor beyond was of great slate slabs, and seemed to form the outlet of a long, high corridor with sculptured walls.

Observing the many inner archways which led off from it, and realizing the probable complexity of the nest of apartments within, we decided that we must begin our system of hare-and-hound trail blazing. Hitherto our compasses, together with frequent glimpses of the vast mountain range between the towers in our rear, had been enough to prevent our losing our way; but from now on, the artificial substitute would be necessary. Accordingly we reduced our extra paper to shreds of suitable size, placed these in a bag to be carried by Danforth, and prepared to use them as economically as safety would allow. This method would probably gain us immunity from straying, since there did not appear to be any strong air currents inside the primordial masonry. If such should develop, or if our paper supply should give out, we could of course fall back on the more secure though more tedious and retarding method of rock chipping.

Just how extensive a territory we had opened up, it was impossible to guess without a trial. The close and frequent connection of the different buildings made it likely that we might cross from one to another on bridges underneath the ice, except where impeded by local collapses and geologic rifts, for very little glaciation seemed to have entered the massive constructions. Almost all the areas of transparent ice had revealed the submerged windows as tightly shuttered, as if the town had been left in that uniform state until the glacial sheet came to crystallize the lower part for all succeeding time. Indeed, one gained a curious impression that this place had been deliberately closed and deserted in some dim, bygone aeon, rather than overwhelmed by any sudden calamity or even gradual decay. Had the coming of the ice been foreseen, and had a nameless population left en masse to seek a less doomed abode? The precise physiographic conditions attending the formation of the ice sheet at this point would have to wait for later solution. It had not, very plainly, been a grinding drive. Perhaps the pressure of accumulated snows had been responsible, and perhaps some flood from the river, or from the bursting of some ancient glacial dam in the great range, had helped to create the special state now observable. Imagination could conceive almost anything in connection with this place.

Chapter VI

IT WOULD BE CUMBROUS to give a detailed, consecutive account of our wanderings inside that cavernous, aeon-dead honeycomb of primal masonry – that monstrous lair of elder secrets which now echoed for the first time, after uncounted epochs, to the tread of human feet. This is especially true because so much of the horrible drama and revelation came from a mere study of the omnipresent mural carvings. Our flashlight photographs of those carvings will do much toward proving the truth of what we are now disclosing, and it is lamentable that we had not a larger film supply with us. As it was, we made crude notebook sketches of certain salient features after all our films were used up.

The building which we had entered was one of great size and elaborateness, and gave us an impressive notion of the architecture of that nameless geologic past. The inner partitions were less massive than the outer walls, but on the lower levels were excellently preserved. Labyrinthine complexity, involving curiously irregular difference in floor levels, characterized the entire arrangement; and we should certainly have been lost at the very outset but for the trail of torn paper left behind us. We decided to explore the more decrepit upper parts first of all, hence climbed aloft in the maze for a distance of some one hundred feet, to where the topmost tier of chambers yawned snowily and ruinously open to the polar sky. Ascent was effected over the steep, transversely ribbed stone ramps or inclined planes which everywhere served in lieu of stairs. The rooms we encountered were of all imaginable shapes and proportions, ranging from five-pointed stars to triangles and perfect cubes. It might be safe to say that their general average was about 30 x 30 feet in floor area, and 20 feet in height, though many larger apartments existed. After thoroughly examining the upper regions and the glacial level, we descended, story by story, into the submerged part, where indeed we soon saw we were in a continuous maze of connected chambers and passages probably leading over unlimited areas outside this particular building. The Cyclopean massiveness and gigantism of everything about us became curiously oppressive; and there was something vaguely but deeply unhuman in all the contours, dimensions, proportions, decorations, and constructional nuances of the blasphemously archaic stonework. We soon realized, from what the carvings revealed, that this monstrous city was many million years old.

We cannot yet explain the engineering principles used in the anomalous balancing and adjustment of the vast rock masses, though the function of the arch was clearly much relied on. The rooms we visited were wholly bare of all portable contents, a circumstance which sustained our belief in the city's deliberate desertion. The prime decorative feature was the almost universal system of mural sculpture, which tended to run in continuous horizontal bands three feet wide and arranged from floor to ceiling in alternation with bands of equal width given over to geometrical arabesques. There were exceptions to this rule of arrangement, but its preponderance was overwhelming. Often, however, a series of smooth cartouches containing oddly patterned groups of dots would be sunk along one of the arabesque bands.

The technique, we soon saw, was mature, accomplished, and aesthetically evolved to the highest degree of civilized mastery, though utterly alien in every detail to any known art tradition of the human race. In delicacy of execution no sculpture I have ever seen could approach it. The minutest details of elaborate vegetation, or of animal life, were rendered with astonishing vividness despite the bold scale of the carvings; whilst the conventional designs were marvels of skillful intricacy. The arabesques displayed a profound use of mathematical principles, and were made up of obscurely symmetrical curves and angles based on the quantity of five. The pictorial bands followed a highly formalized tradition, and involved a peculiar treatment of perspective, but had an artistic force that moved us profoundly, notwithstanding the intervening gulf of vast geologic periods. Their method of design hinged on a singular juxtaposition of the cross section with the two-dimensional silhouette, and embodied an analytical psychology beyond that of any known race of antiquity. It is useless to try to compare this art with any represented in our museums. Those who see our photographs will probably find its closest analogue in certain grotesque conceptions of the most daring futurists.

The arabesque tracery consisted altogether of depressed lines, whose depth on unweathered walls varied from one to two inches. When cartouches with dot groups appeared – evidently as inscriptions in some unknown and primordial language and alphabet – the depression of the smooth surface was perhaps an inch and a half, and of the dots perhaps a half inch more. The pictorial bands were in countersunk low relief, their background being depressed about two inches from the original wall surface. In some specimens marks of a former coloration could be detected, though for the most part the untold aeons had disintegrated and banished any pigments which may have been applied. The more one studied the marvelous technique, the more one admired the things. Beneath their strict conventionalization one could grasp the minute and accurate observation and graphic skill of the artists; and indeed, the very conventions themselves served to symbolize and accentuate the real essence or vital differentiation of every object delineated. We felt, too, that besides these recognizable excellences there were others lurking beyond the reach of our perceptions. Certain touches here and there gave vague hints of latent symbols and stimuli which another mental and emotional background, and a fuller or different sensory equipment, might have made of profound and poignant significance to us.

The subject matter of the sculptures obviously came from the life of the vanished epoch of their creation, and contained a large proportion of evident history. It is this abnormal historic-mindedness of the primal race – a chance circumstance operating, through coincidence, miraculously in our favor – which made the carvings so awesomely informative to us, and which caused us to place their photography and transcription above all other considerations. In certain rooms the dominant arrangement was varied by the presence of maps, astronomical charts, and other scientific designs of an enlarged scale – these things giving a naive and terrible corroboration to what we gathered from the pictorial friezes and dadoes. In hinting at what the whole revealed, I can only hope that my account will not arouse a curiosity greater than sane caution on the part of those who believe me at all. It would be tragic if any were to be allured to that realm of death and horror by the very warning meant to discourage them.

Interrupting these sculptured walls were high windows and massive twelve-foot doorways; both now and then retaining the petrified wooden planks – elaborately carved and polished – of the actual shutters and doors. All metal fixtures had long ago vanished, but some of the doors remained in place and had to be forced aside as we progressed from room to room. Window frames with odd transparent panes – mostly elliptical – survived here and there, though in no considerable quantity. There were also frequent niches of great magnitude, generally empty, but once in a while containing some bizarre object carved from green soapstone which was either broken or perhaps held too inferior to warrant removal. Other apertures were undoubtedly connected with bygone mechanical facilities – heating, lighting, and the like – of a sort suggested in many of the carvings. Ceilings tended to be plain, but had sometimes been inlaid with green soapstone or other tiles, mostly fallen now. Floors were also paved with such tiles, though plain stonework predominated.

As I have said, all furniture and other movables were absent; but the sculptures gave a clear idea of the strange devices which had once filled these tomblike, echoing rooms. Above the glacial sheet the floors were generally thick with detritus, litter, and debris, but farther down this condition decreased. In some of the lower chambers and corridors there was little more than gritty dust or ancient incrustations, while occasional areas had an uncanny air of newly swept immaculateness. Of course, where rifts or collapses had occurred, the lower levels were as littered as the upper ones. A central court – as in other structures we had seen from the air – saved the inner regions from total darkness; so that we seldom had to use our electric torches in the upper rooms except when studying sculptured details. Below the ice cap, however, the twilight deepened; and in many parts of the tangled ground level there was an approach to absolute blackness.

To form even a rudimentary idea of our thoughts and feelings as we penetrated this aeon-silent maze of unhuman masonry, one must correlate a hopelessly bewildering chaos of fugitive moods, memories, and impressions. The sheer appalling antiquity and lethal desolation of the place were enough to overwhelm almost any sensitive person, but added to these elements were the recent unexplained horror at the camp, and the revelations all too soon effected by the terrible mural sculptures around us. The moment we came upon a perfect section of carving, where no ambiguity of interpretation could exist, it took only a brief study to give us the hideous truth – a truth which it would be naive to claim Danforth and I had not independently suspected before, though we had carefully refrained from even hinting it to each other. There could now be no further merciful doubt about the nature of the beings which had built and inhabited this monstrous dead city millions of years ago, when man's ancestors were primitive archaic mammals, and vast dinosaurs roamed the tropical steppes of Europe and Asia.

We had previously clung to a desperate alternative and insisted – each to himself – that the omnipresence of the five-pointed motifs meant only some cultural or religious exaltation of the Archaean natural object which had so patently embodied the quality of five-pointedness; as the decorative motifs of Minoan Crete exalted the sacred bull, those of Egypt the scarabaeus, those of Rome the wolf and the eagle, and those of various savage tribes some chosen totem animal. But this lone refuge was now stripped from us, and we were forced to face definitely the reason-shaking realization which the reader of these pages has doubtless long ago anticipated. I can scarcely bear to write it down in black and white even now, but perhaps that will not be necessary.

The things once rearing and dwelling in this frightful masonry in the age of dinosaurs were not indeed dinosaurs, but far worse. Mere dinosaurs were new and almost brainless objects – but the builders of the city were wise and old, and had left certain traces in rocks even then laid down well nigh a thousand million years – rocks laid down before the true life of earth had advanced beyond plastic groups of cells – rocks laid down before the true life of earth had existed at all. They were the makers and enslavers of that life, and above all doubt the originals of the fiendish elder myths which things like the *Pnakotic Manuscripts* and the *Necronomicon* affrightedly hint about. They were the great 'Old Ones' that had filtered down from the stars when earth was young – the beings whose substance an alien evolution had shaped, and whose powers were such as this planet had never bred. And to think that only the day before, Danforth and I had actually looked upon fragments of their millennially fossilized substance, and that poor Lake and his party had seen their complete outlines. It is of course impossible for me to relate in proper order the stages by which we picked up what we know of that monstrous chapter of prehuman life. After the first shock of the certain revelation, we had to pause a while to recuperate, and it was fully three o'clock before we got started on our actual tour of systematic research. The sculptures in the building we entered were of relatively late date – perhaps two million years ago – as checked up by geological, biological, and astronomical features – and embodied an art which would be called decadent in comparison with that of specimens we found in older buildings after crossing bridges under the glacial sheet. One edifice hewn from the solid rock seemed to go back forty or possibly even fifty million years – to the lower Eocene or upper Cretaceous – and contained bas-reliefs of an artistry surpassing anything else, with one tremendous exception, that we encountered. That was, we have since agreed, the oldest domestic structure we traversed.

Were it not for the support of those flashlights soon to be made public, I would refrain from telling what I found and inferred, lest I be confined as a madman. Of course, the infinitely early parts of the patchwork tale – representing the preterrestrial life of the star-headed beings on other planets, in other galaxies, and in other universes – can readily be interpreted as the fantastic mythology of those beings themselves; yet such parts sometimes involved designs and diagrams so uncannily close to the latest findings of mathematics and astrophysics that I scarcely know what to think. Let others judge when they see the photographs I shall publish.

Naturally, no one set of carvings which we encountered told more than a fraction of any connected story, nor did we even begin to come upon the various stages of that story in their proper order. Some of the vast rooms were independent units so far as their designs were concerned, whilst in other cases a continuous chronicle would be carried through a series of rooms and corridors. The best of the maps and diagrams were on the walls of a frightful abyss below even the ancient ground level – a cavern perhaps two hundred feet square and sixty feet high, which had almost undoubtedly been an educational center of some sort. There were many provoking repetitions of the same material in different rooms and buildings, since certain chapters of experience, and certain summaries or phases of racial history, had evidently been favorites with different decorators or dwellers. Sometimes, though, variant versions of the same theme proved useful in settling debatable points and filling up gaps.

I still wonder that we deduced so much in the short time at our disposal. Of course, we even now have only the barest outline – and much of that was obtained later on from a study of the photographs and sketches we made. It may be the effect of this later study – the revived memories and vague impressions acting in conjunction with his general sensitiveness and with that final supposed horror-glimpse whose essence he will not reveal even to me – which has been the immediate source of Danforth's present breakdown. But it had to be; for we could not issue our warning intelligently without the fullest possible information, and the issuance of that warning is a prime necessity. Certain lingering influences in that unknown antarctic world of disordered time and alien natural law make it imperative that further exploration be discouraged.

Chapter VII

THE FULL STORY, so far as deciphered, will eventually appear in an official bulletin of Miskatonic University. Here I shall sketch only the salient highlights in a formless, rambling way. Myth or otherwise, the sculptures told of the coming of those star-headed things to the nascent, lifeless earth out of cosmic space – their coming, and the coming of many other alien entities such as at certain times embark upon spatial pioneering. They seemed able to traverse the interstellar ether on their vast membranous wings – thus oddly confirming some curious hill folklore long ago told me by an antiquarian colleague. They had lived under the sea a good deal, building fantastic cities and fighting terrific battles with nameless adversaries by means of intricate devices employing unknown principles of energy. Evidently their scientific and mechanical knowledge far surpassed man's today, though they made use of its more widespread and elaborate forms only when obliged to. Some of the sculptures suggested that they had passed through a stage of mechanized life on other planets, but had receded upon finding its effects emotionally unsatisfying. Their preternatural toughness of organization and simplicity of natural wants made them peculiarly able to live on a high plane without the more specialized fruits of artificial manufacture, and even without garments, except for occasional protection against the elements.

It was under the sea, at first for food and later for other purposes, that they first created earth life – using available substances according to long-known methods. The more elaborate experiments came after the annihilation of various cosmic enemies. They had done the same thing on other planets, having manufactured not only necessary foods, but certain multicellular protoplasmic masses capable of molding their tissues into all sorts of temporary organs under hypnotic influence and thereby forming ideal slaves to perform the heavy work of the community. These viscous masses were without doubt what Abdul Alhazred whispered about as the 'Shoggoths' in his frightful *Necronomicon*, though even that mad Arab had not hinted that any existed on earth except in the dreams of those who had chewed a certain alkaloidal herb. When the star-headed Old Ones on this planet had synthesized their simple food forms and bred a good supply of Shoggoths, they allowed other cell groups to develop into other forms of animal and vegetable life for sundry purposes, extirpating any whose presence became troublesome.

With the aid of the Shoggoths, whose expansions could be made to lift prodigious weights, the small, low cities under the sea grew to vast and imposing labyrinths of stone not unlike those which later rose on land. Indeed, the highly adaptable Old Ones had lived much on land in other parts of the universe, and probably retained many traditions of land construction. As we studied the architecture of all these sculptured palaeogean cities, including that whose aeon-dead corridors we were even then traversing, we were impressed by a curious coincidence which we have not yet tried to explain, even to ourselves. The tops of the buildings, which in the actual city around us had, of course, been weathered into shapeless ruins ages ago, were clearly displayed in the bas-reliefs, and showed vast clusters of needle-like spires, delicate finials on certain cone and pyramid apexes, and tiers of thin, horizontal scalloped disks capping cylindrical shafts. This was exactly what we had seen in that monstrous and portentous mirage, cast by a dead city whence such skyline features had been absent for thousands and tens of thousands of years, which loomed on our ignorant eyes across the unfathomed mountains of madness as we first approached poor Lake's ill-fated camp.

Of the life of the Old Ones, both under the sea and after part of them migrated to land, volumes could be written. Those in shallow water had continued the fullest use of the eyes at the ends of their five main head tentacles, and had practiced the arts of sculpture and of writing in quite the usual way – the writing accomplished with a stylus on waterproof waxen surfaces. Those lower down in the ocean depths, though they used a curious phosphorescent organism to furnish light, pieced out their vision with obscure special senses operating through the prismatic cilia on their heads – senses which rendered all the Old Ones partly independent of light in emergencies. Their forms of sculpture and writing had changed curiously during the descent, embodying certain apparently chemical coating processes – probably to secure phosphorescence – which the bas-reliefs could not make clear to us. The beings moved in the sea partly by swimming – using the lateral crinoid arms – and partly by wriggling with the lower tier of tentacles containing the pseudofeet. Occasionally they accomplished long swoops with the auxiliary use of two or more sets of their fanlike folding wings. On land they locally used the pseudofeet, but now and then flew to great heights or over long distances with their wings. The many slender tentacles into which the crinoid arms branched were infinitely delicate, flexible, strong, and accurate in muscular-nervous coordination – ensuring the utmost skill and dexterity in all artistic and other manual operations.

The toughness of the things was almost incredible. Even the terrific pressure of the deepest sea bottoms appeared powerless to harm them. Very few seemed to die at all except by violence, and their burial places were very limited. The fact that they covered their vertically inhumed dead with five-pointed inscribed mounds set up thoughts in Danforth and me which made a fresh pause and recuperation necessary after the sculptures revealed it. The beings multiplied by means of spores – like vegetable pteridophytes, as Lake had suspected – but, owing to their prodigious toughness and longevity, and consequent lack of replacement needs, they did not encourage the large-scale development of new prothallia except when they had new regions to colonize. The young matured swiftly, and received an education evidently beyond any standard we can imagine. The prevailing intellectual and aesthetic life was highly evolved, and produced a tenaciously enduring set of customs and institutions which I shall describe more fully in my coming monograph. These varied slightly according to sea or land residence, but had the same foundations and essentials.

Though able, like vegetables, to derive nourishment from inorganic substances, they vastly preferred organic and especially animal food. They ate uncooked marine life under the sea, but cooked their viands on land. They hunted game and raised meat herds – slaughtering with sharp weapons whose odd marks on certain fossil bones our expedition had noted. They resisted all ordinary temperatures marvelously, and in their natural state could live in water down to freezing. When the great chill of the Pleistocene drew on, however – nearly a million years ago – the land dwellers had to resort to special measures, including artificial heating – until at last the deadly cold appears to have driven them back into the sea. For their prehistoric flights through cosmic space, legend said, they absorbed certain chemicals and became almost independent of eating, breathing, or heat conditions – but by the time of the great cold they had lost track of the method. In any case they could not have prolonged the artificial state indefinitely without harm.

Being nonpairing and semivegetable in structure, the Old Ones had no biological basis for the family phase of mammal life, but seemed to organize large households on the principles of comfortable space-utility and – as we deduced from the pictured occupations and diversions of co-dwellers – congenial mental association. In furnishing their homes they kept everything in the center of the huge rooms, leaving all the wall spaces free for decorative treatment. Lighting, in the case of the land inhabitants, was accomplished by a device probably electro-chemical in nature. Both on land and under water they used curious tables, chairs and couches like cylindrical frames – for they rested and slept upright with folded-down tentacles – and racks for hinged sets of dotted surfaces forming their books.

Government was evidently complex and probably socialistic, though no certainties in this regard could be deduced from the sculptures we saw. There was extensive commerce, both local and between different cities – certain small, flat counters, five-pointed and inscribed, serving as money. Probably the smaller of the various greenish soapstones found by our expedition were pieces of such currency. Though the culture was mainly urban, some agriculture and much stock raising existed. Mining and a limited amount of manufacturing were also practiced. Travel was very frequent, but permanent migration seemed relatively rare except for the vast colonizing movements by which the race expanded. For personal locomotion no external aid was used, since in land, air, and water movement alike the Old Ones seemed to possess excessively vast capacities for speed. Loads, however, were drawn by beasts of burden – Shoggoths under the sea, and a curious variety of primitive vertebrates in the later years of land existence.

These vertebrates, as well as an infinity of other life forms – animal and vegetable, marine, terrestrial, and aerial – were the products of unguided evolution acting on life cells made by the Old Ones, but escaping beyond their radius of attention. They had been suffered to develop unchecked because they had not come in conflict with the dominant beings. Bothersome forms, of course, were mechanically exterminated. It interested us to see in some of the very last and most decadent sculptures a shambling, primitive mammal, used sometimes for food and sometimes as an amusing buffoon by the land dwellers, whose vaguely simian and human foreshadowings were unmistakable. In the building of land cities the huge stone blocks of the high towers were generally lifted by vast-winged pterodactyls of a species heretofore unknown to paleontology.

The persistence with which the Old Ones survived various geologic changes and convulsions of the earth's crust was little short of miraculous. Though few or none of their first cities seem to have remained beyond the Archaean Age, there was no interruption in their civilization or in the transmission of their records. Their original place of advent to the planet was the Antarctic Ocean, and it is likely that they came not long after the matter forming the moon was wrenched from the neighboring South Pacific. According to one of the sculptured maps the whole globe was then under water, with stone cities scattered farther and farther from the antarctic as aeons passed. Another map shows a vast bulk of dry land around the south pole, where it is evident that some of the beings made experimental settlements, though their main centers were transferred to the nearest sea bottom. Later maps, which display the land mass as cracking and drifting, and sending certain detached parts northward, uphold in a striking way the theories of continental drift lately advanced by Taylor, Wegener, and Joly.

With the upheaval of new land in the South Pacific tremendous events began. Some of the marine cities were hopelessly shattered, yet that was not the worst misfortune. Another race – a land race of beings shaped like octopi and probably corresponding to fabulous prehuman spawn of Cthulhu – soon began filtering down from cosmic infinity and precipitated a – monstrous war which for a time drove the Old Ones wholly back to the sea – a colossal blow in view of the increasing land settlements. Later peace was made, and the new lands were given to the Cthulhu spawn whilst the Old Ones held the sea and the older lands. New land cities were founded – the greatest of them in the antarctic, for this region of first arrival was sacred. From then on, as before, the antarctic remained the center of the Old Ones' civilization, and all the cities built there by the Cthulhu spawn were blotted out. Then suddenly the lands of the Pacific sank again, taking with them the frightful stone city of R'lyeh and all the cosmic octopi, so that the Old Ones were again supreme on the planet except for one shadowy fear about which they did not like to speak. At a rather later age their cities dotted all the land and water areas of the globe – hence the recommendation in my coming monograph that some archaeologist make systematic borings with Pabodie's type of apparatus in certain widely separated regions.

The steady trend down the ages was from water to land – a movement encouraged by the rise of new land masses, though the ocean was never wholly deserted. Another cause of the landward movement was the new difficulty in breeding and managing the Shoggoths upon which successful sea life depended. With the march of time, as the sculptures sadly confessed, the art of creating new life from inorganic matter had been lost, so that the Old Ones had to depend on the molding of forms already in existence. On land the great reptiles proved highly tractable; but the Shoggoths of the sea, reproducing by fission and acquiring a dangerous degree of accidental intelligence, presented for a time a formidable problem.

They had always been controlled through the hypnotic suggestions of the Old Ones, and had modeled their tough plasticity into various useful temporary limbs and organs; but now their self-modeling powers were sometimes exercised independently, and in various imitative forms implanted by past suggestion. They had, it seems, developed a semistable brain whose separate and occasionally stubborn volition echoed the will of the Old Ones without always obeying it. Sculptured images of these Shoggoths filled Danforth and me with horror and loathing. They were normally shapeless entities composed of a viscous jelly which looked like an agglutination of bubbles, and each averaged about fifteen feet in diameter when a sphere. They had, however, a constantly shifting shape and volume – throwing out temporary developments or forming apparent organs of sight, hearing, and speech in imitation of their masters, either spontaneously or according to suggestion.

They seem to have become peculiarly intractable toward the middle of the Permian Age, perhaps one hundred and fifty million years ago, when a veritable war of resubjugation was waged upon them by the marine Old Ones. Pictures of this war, and of the headless, slime-coated fashion in which the Shoggoths typically left their slain victims, held a marvelously fearsome quality despite the intervening abyss of untold ages. The Old Ones had used curious weapons of molecular and atomic disturbances against the rebel entities, and in the end had achieved a complete victory. Thereafter the sculptures showed a period in which Shoggoths were tamed and broken by armed Old Ones as the wild horses of the American west were tamed by cowboys. Though during the rebellion the Shoggoths had shown an ability to live out of water, this transition was not encouraged – since their usefulness on land would hardly have been commensurate with the trouble of their management.

During the Jurassic Age the Old Ones met fresh adversity in the form of a new invasion from outer space – this time by half-fungous, half-crustacean creatures – creatures undoubtedly the same as those figuring in certain whispered hill legends of the north, and remembered in the Himalayas as the Mi-Go, or Abominable Snow Men. To fight these beings the Old Ones attempted, for the first time since their terrene advent, to sally forth again into the planetary ether; but, despite all traditional preparations, found it no longer possible to leave the earth's atmosphere. Whatever the old secret of interstellar travel had been, it was now definitely lost to the race. In the end the Mi-Go drove the Old Ones out of all the northern lands, though they were powerless to disturb those in the sea. Little by little the slow retreat of the elder race to their original antarctic habitat was beginning.

It was curious to note from the pictured battles that both the Cthulhu spawn and the Mi-Go seem to have been composed of matter more widely different from that which we know than was the substance of the Old Ones. They were able to undergo transformations and reintegrations impossible for their adversaries, and seem therefore to have originally come from even remoter gulfs of the cosmic space. The Old Ones, but for their abnormal toughness and peculiar vital properties, were strictly material, and must have had their absolute origin within the known space-time continuum – whereas the first sources of the other beings can only be guessed at with bated breath. All this, of course, assuming that the non-terrestrial linkages and the anomalies ascribed to the invading foes are not pure mythology. Conceivably, the Old Ones might have invented a cosmic framework to account for their occasional defeats, since historical interest and pride obviously formed their chief psychological element. It is significant that their annals failed to mention many advanced and potent races of beings whose mighty cultures and towering cities figure persistently in certain obscure legends.

The changing state of the world through long geologic ages appeared with startling vividness in many of the sculptured maps and scenes. In certain cases existing science will require revision, while in other cases its bold deductions are magnificently confirmed. As I have said, the hypothesis of Taylor, Wegener, and Joly that all the continents are fragments of an original antarctic land mass which cracked from centrifugal force and drifted apart over a technically viscous lower surface – an hypothesis suggested by such things as the complementary outlines of Africa and South America, and the way the great mountain chains are rolled and shoved up – receives striking support from this uncanny source.

Maps evidently showing the Carboniferous world of an hundred million or more years ago displayed significant rifts and chasms destined later to separate Africa from the once continuous realms of Europe (then the Valusia of primal legend), Asia, the Americas, and the antarctic continent. Other charts – and most significantly one in connection with the founding fifty million years ago of the vast dead city around us – showed all the present continents well differentiated. And in the latest discoverable specimen – dating perhaps from the Pliocene Age – the approximate world of today appeared quite clearly despite the linkage of Alaska with Siberia, of North America with Europe through Greenland, and of South America with the antarctic continent through Graham Land. In the Carboniferous map the whole globe-ocean floor and rifted land mass alike – bore symbols of the Old Ones' vast stone cities, but in the later charts the gradual recession toward the antarctic became very plain. The final Pliocene specimen showed no land cities except on the antarctic continent and the tip of South America, nor any ocean cities north of the fiftieth parallel of South Latitude. Knowledge and interest in the northern world, save for a study of coast lines probably made during long exploration flights on those fanlike membranous wings, had evidently declined to zero among the Old Ones.

Destruction of cities through the upthrust of mountains, the centrifugal rending of continents, the seismic convulsions of land or sea bottom, and other natural causes, was a matter of common record; and it was curious to observe how fewer and fewer replacements were made as the ages wore on. The vast dead megalopolis that yawned around us seemed to be the last general center of the race – built early in the Cretaceous

Age after a titanic earth buckling had obliterated a still vaster predecessor not far distant. It appeared that this general region was the most sacred spot of all, where reputedly the first Old Ones had settled on a primal sea bottom. In the new city – many of whose features we could recognize in the sculptures, but which stretched fully a hundred miles along the mountain range in each direction beyond the farthest limits of our aerial survey – there were reputed to be preserved certain sacred stones forming part of the first sea-bottom city, which thrust up to light after long epochs in the course of the general crumbling of strata.

Chapter VIII

NATURALLY, Danforth and I studied with especial interest and a peculiarly personal sense of awe everything pertaining to the immediate district in which we were. Of this local material there was naturally a vast abundance; and on the tangled ground level of the city we were lucky enough to find a house of very late date whose walls, though somewhat damaged by a neighboring rift, contained sculptures of decadent workmanship carrying the story of the region much beyond the period of the Pliocene map whence we derived our last general glimpse of the prehuman world. This was the last place we examined in detail, since what we found there gave us a fresh immediate objective.

Certainly, we were in one of the strangest, weirdest, and most terrible of all the corners of earth's globe. Of all existing lands, it was infinitely the most ancient. The conviction grew upon us that this hideous upland must indeed be the fabled nightmare plateau of Leng which even the mad author of the *Necronomicon* was reluctant to discuss. The great mountain chain was tremendously long – starting as a low range at Luitpold Land on the east coast of Weddell Sea and virtually crossing the entire continent. That really high part stretched in a mighty arc from about Latitude 82°, E. Longitude 60° to Latitude 70°, E. Longitude 115°, with its concave side toward our camp and its seaward end in the region of that long, ice-locked coast whose hills were glimpsed by Wilkes and Mawson at the antarctic circle.

Yet even more monstrous exaggerations of nature seemed disturbingly close at hand. I have said that these peaks are higher than the Himalayas, but the sculptures forbid me to say that they are earth's highest. That grim honor is beyond doubt reserved for something which half the sculptures hesitated to record at all, whilst others approached it with obvious repugnance and trepidation. It seems that there was one part of the ancient land – the first part that ever rose from the waters after the earth had flung off the moon and the Old Ones had seeped down, from the stars – which had come to be shunned as vaguely and namelessly evil. Cities built there had crumbled before their time, and had been found suddenly deserted. Then when the first great earth buckling had convulsed the region in the Comanchian Age, a frightful line of peaks had shot suddenly up amidst the most appalling din and chaos – and earth had received her loftiest and most terrible mountains.

If the scale of the carvings was correct, these abhorred things must have been much over forty thousand feet high – radically vaster than even the shocking mountains of madness we had crossed. They extended, it appeared, from about Latitude 77°, E. Longitude 70° to Latitude 70°, E. Longitude 100° – less than three hundred miles away from the dead city, so that we would have spied their dreaded summits in the dim western distance had it not been for that vague, opalescent haze. Their northern end must likewise be visible from the long antarctic circle coast line at Queen Mary Land.

Some of the Old Ones, in the decadent days, had made strange prayers to those mountains – but none ever went near them or dared to guess what lay beyond. No human eye had ever seen them, and as I studied the emotions conveyed in the carvings, I prayed that none ever might. There are protecting hills along the coast beyond them – Queen Mary and Kaiser Wilhelm Lands – and I thank Heaven no one has been able to land and climb those hills. I am not as sceptical about old tales and fears as I used to be, and I do not laugh now at the prehuman sculptor's notion that lightning paused meaningfully now and then at each of the brooding crests, and that an unexplained glow shone from one of those terrible pinnacles all through the long polar night. There may be a very real and very monstrous meaning in the old Pnakotic whispers about Kadath in the Cold Waste.

But the terrain close at hand was hardly less strange, even if less namelessly accursed. Soon after the founding of the city the great mountain range became the seat of the principal temples, and many carvings showed what grotesque and fantastic towers had pierced the sky where now we saw only the curiously clinging cubes and ramparts. In the course of ages the caves had appeared, and had been shaped into adjuncts of the temples. With the advance of still later epochs, all the limestone veins of the region were hollowed out by ground waters, so that the mountains, the foothills, and the plains below them were a veritable network of connected caverns and galleries. Many graphic sculptures told of explorations deep underground, and of the final discovery of the Stygian sunless sea that lurked at earth's bowels.

This vast nighted gulf had undoubtedly been worn by the great river which flowed down from the nameless and horrible westward mountains, and which had formerly turned at the base of the Old Ones' range and flowed beside that chain into the Indian Ocean between Budd and Totten Lands on Wilkes's coast line. Little by little it had eaten away the limestone hill base at its turning, till at last its sapping currents reached the caverns of the ground waters and joined with them in digging a deeper abyss. Finally its whole bulk emptied into the hollow hills and left the old bed toward the ocean dry. Much of the later city as we now found it had been built over that former bed. The Old Ones, understanding what had happened, and exercising their always keen artistic sense, had carved into ornate pylons those headlands of the foothills where the great stream began its descent into eternal darkness.

This river, once crossed by scores of noble stone bridges, was plainly the one whose extinct course we had seen in our aeroplane survey. Its position in different carvings of the city helped us to orient ourselves to the scene as it had been at various stages of the region's age-long, aeon-dead history, so that we were able to sketch a hasty but careful map of the salient features – squares, important buildings, and the like – for guidance in further explorations. We could soon reconstruct in fancy the whole stupendous thing as it was a million or ten million or fifty million years ago, for the sculptures told us exactly what the buildings and mountains and squares and suburbs and landscape setting and luxuriant Tertiary vegetation had looked like. It must have had a marvelous and mystic beauty, and as I thought of it, I almost forgot the clammy sense of sinister oppression with which the city's inhuman age and massiveness and deadness and remoteness and glacial twilight had choked and weighed on my spirit. Yet according to certain carvings, the denizens of that city had themselves known the clutch of oppressive terror; for there was a somber and recurrent type of scene in which the Old Ones were shown in the act of recoiling affrightedly from some object – never allowed to appear in the design – found in the great river and indicated as having been washed down through waving, vine-draped cycad forests from those horrible westward mountains.

It was only in the one late-built house with the decadent carvings that we obtained any foreshadowing of the final calamity leading to the city's desertion. Undoubtedly there must have been many sculptures of the same age elsewhere, even allowing for the slackened energies and aspirations of a stressful and uncertain period; indeed, very certain evidence of the existence of others came to us shortly afterward. But this was the first and only set we directly encountered. We meant to look farther later on; but as I have said, immediate conditions dictated another present objective. There would, though, have been a limit – for after all hope of a long future occupancy of the place had perished among the Old Ones, there could not but have been a complete cessation of mural decoration. The ultimate blow, of course, was the coming of the great cold which once held most of the earth in thrall, and which has never departed from the ill-fated poles – the great cold that, at the world's other extremity, put an end to the fabled lands of Lomar and Hyperborea.

Just when this tendency began in the antarctic, it would be hard to say in terms of exact years. Nowadays we set the beginning of the general glacial periods at a distance of about five hundred thousand years from the present, but at the poles the terrible scourge must have commenced much earlier. All quantitative estimates are partly guesswork, but it is quite likely that the decadent sculptures were made considerably less than a million years ago, and that the actual desertion of the city was complete long before the conventional opening of the Pleistocene – five hundred thousand years ago – as reckoned in terms of the earth's whole surface.

In the decadent sculptures there were signs of thinner vegetation everywhere, and of a decreased country life on the part of the Old Ones. Heating devices were shown in the houses, and winter travelers were represented as muffled in protective fabrics. Then we saw a series of cartouches – the continuous band arrangement being frequently interrupted in these late carvings – depicting a constantly growing migration to the nearest refuges of greater warmth – some fleeing to cities under the sea off the far-away coast, and some clambering down through networks of limestone caverns in the hollow hills to the neighboring black abyss of subterrene waters.

In the end it seems to have been the neighboring abyss which received the greatest colonization. This was partly due, no doubt, to the traditional sacredness of this special region, but may have been more conclusively determined by the opportunities it gave for continuing the use of the great temples on the honeycombed mountains, and for retaining the vast land city as a place of summer residence and base of communication with various mines. The linkage of old and new abodes was made more effective by means of several gradings and improvements along the connecting routes, including the chiseling of numerous direct tunnels from the ancient metropolis to the black abyss – sharply down-pointing tunnels whose mouths we carefully drew, according to our most thoughtful estimates, on the guide map we were compiling. It was obvious that at least two of these tunnels lay within a reasonable exploring distance of where we were – both being on the mountainward edge of the city, one less than a quarter of a mile toward the ancient river course, and the other perhaps twice that distance in the opposite direction.

The abyss, it seems, had shelving shores of dry land at certain places, but the Old Ones built their new city under water – no doubt because of its greater certainty of uniform warmth. The depth of the hidden sea appears to have been very great, so that the earth's internal heat could ensure its habitability for an indefinite period. The beings seemed to have had no trouble in adapting themselves to part-time – and eventually, of course, whole-time – residence under water, since they had never allowed their gill systems to atrophy. There were many sculptures which showed how they had always frequently visited their submarine kinsfolk elsewhere, and how they had habitually bathed on the deep bottom of their great river. The darkness of inner earth could likewise have been no deterrent to a race accustomed to long antarctic nights.

Decadent though their style undoubtedly was, these latest carvings had a truly epic quality where they told of the building of the new city in the cavern sea. The Old Ones had gone about it scientifically – quarrying insoluble rocks from the heart of the honeycombed mountains, and employing expert workers from the nearest submarine city to perform the construction according to the best methods. These workers brought with them all that was necessary to establish the new venture – Shoggoth tissue from which to breed stone lifters and subsequent beasts of burden for the cavern city, and other protoplasmic matter to mold into phosphorescent organisms for lighting purposes.

At last a mighty metropolis rose on the bottom of that Stygian sea, its architecture much like that of the city above, and its workmanship displaying relatively little decadence because of the precise mathematical element inherent in building operations. The newly bred Shoggoths grew to enormous size and singular intelligence, and were represented as taking and executing orders with marvelous quickness. They seemed to converse with the Old Ones by mimicking their voices – a sort of musical piping over a wide range, if poor Lake's dissection had indicated aright – and to work more from spoken commands than from hypnotic suggestions as in earlier times. They were, however, kept in admirable control. The phosphorescent organisms supplied light with vast effectiveness, and doubtless atoned for the loss of the familiar polar auroras of the outer-world night.

Art and decoration were pursued, though of course with a certain decadence. The Old Ones seemed to realize this falling off themselves, and in many cases anticipated the policy of Constantine the Great by transplanting especially fine blocks of ancient carving from their land city, just as the emperor, in a similar age of decline, stripped Greece and Asia of their finest art to give his new Byzantine capital greater splendors than its own people could create. That the transfer of sculptured blocks had not been more extensive was doubtless owing to the fact that the land city was not at first wholly abandoned. By the time total abandonment did occur – and it surely must have occurred before the polar Pleistocene was far advanced – the Old Ones had perhaps become satisfied with their decadent art – or had ceased to recognize the superior merit of the older carvings. At any rate, the aeon-silent ruins around us had certainly undergone no wholesale sculptural denudation, though all the best separate statues, like other movables, had been taken away.

The decadent cartouches and dadoes telling this story were, as I have said, the latest we could find in our limited search. They left us with a picture of the Old Ones shuttling back and forth betwixt the land city in summer and the sea-cavern city in winter, and sometimes trading with the sea-bottom cities off the antarctic coast. By this time the ultimate doom of the land city must have been recognized, for the sculptures showed many signs of the cold's malign encroachments. Vegetation was declining, and the terrible snows of the winter no longer melted completely even in midsummer. The saurian livestock were nearly all dead, and the mammals were standing it none too well. To keep on with the work of the upper world it had become necessary to adapt some of the amorphous and curiously cold-resistant Shoggoths to land life – a thing the Old Ones had formerly been reluctant to do. The great river was now lifeless, and the upper sea had lost most of its denizens except the seals and whales. All the birds had flown away, save only the great, grotesque penguins.

What had happened afterward we could only guess. How long had the new sea-cavern city survived? Was it still down there, a stony corpse in eternal blackness? Had the subterranean waters frozen at last? To what fate had the ocean-bottom cities of the outer world been delivered? Had any of the Old Ones shifted north ahead of the creeping ice cap? Existing geology shows no trace of their presence. Had the frightful Mi-Go been still a menace in the outer land world of the north? Could one be sure of what might or might not linger, even to this day, in the lightless and unplumbed abysses of earth's deepest waters? Those things had seemingly been able to withstand any amount of pressure – and men of the sea have fished up curious objects at times. And has the killer-whale theory really explained the savage and mysterious scars on antarctic seals noticed a generation ago by Borchgrevingk?

The specimens found by poor Lake did not enter into these guesses, for their geologic setting proved them to have lived at what must have been a very early date in the land city's history. They were, according to their location, certainly not less than thirty million years old, and we reflected that in their day the sea-cavern city, and indeed the cavern itself, had had no existence. They would have remembered an older scene, with lush Tertiary vegetation everywhere, a younger land city of flourishing arts around them, and a great river sweeping northward along the base of the mighty mountains toward a far-away tropic ocean.

And yet we could not help thinking about these specimens – especially about the eight perfect ones that were missing from Lake's hideously ravaged camp. There was something abnormal about that whole business – the strange things we had tried so hard to lay to somebody's madness – those frightful graves – the amount and nature of the missing material – Gedney – the unearthly toughness of those archaic monstrosities, and the queer vital freaks the sculptures now showed the race to have – Danforth and I had seen a good deal in the last few hours, and were prepared to believe and keep silent about many appalling and incredible secrets of primal nature.

Chapter IX

I HAVE SAID that our study of the decadent sculptures brought about a change in our immediate objective. This, of course, had to do with the chiseled avenues to the black inner world, of whose existence we had not known before, but which we were now eager to find and traverse. From the evident scale of the carvings we deduced that a steeply descending walk of about a mile through either of the neighboring tunnels would bring us to the brink of the dizzy, sunless cliffs about the great abyss; down whose sides paths, improved by the Old Ones, led to the rocky shore of the hidden and nighted ocean. To behold this fabulous gulf in stark reality was a lure which seemed impossible of resistance once we knew of the thing – yet we realized we must begin the quest at once if we expected to include it in our present trip.

It was now 8 p.m., and we did not have enough battery replacements to let our torches burn on forever. We had done so much studying and copying below the glacial level that our battery supply had had at least five hours of nearly continuous use, and despite the special dry cell formula, would obviously be good for only about four more – though by keeping one torch unused, except for especially interesting or difficult places, we might manage to eke out a safe margin beyond that. It would not do to be without a light in these Cyclopean catacombs, hence in order to make the abyss trip we must give up all further mural deciphering. Of course we intended to revisit the place for days and perhaps weeks of intensive study and photography – curiosity having long ago got the better of horror – but just now we must hasten.

Our supply of trail-blazing paper was far from unlimited, and we were reluctant to sacrifice spare notebooks or sketching paper to augment it, but we did let one large notebook go. If worse came to worst we could resort to rock chipping – and of course it would be possible, even in case of really lost direction, to work up to full daylight by one channel or another if granted sufficient time for plentiful trial and error. So at last we set off eagerly in the indicated direction of the nearest tunnel.

According to the carvings from which we had made our map, the desired tunnel mouth could not be much more than a quarter of a mile from where we stood; the intervening space showing solid-looking buildings quite likely to be penetrable still at a sub-glacial level. The opening itself would be in the basement – on the angle nearest the foothills – of a vast five-pointed structure of evidently public and perhaps ceremonial nature, which we tried to identify from our aerial survey of the ruins.

No such structure came to our minds as we recalled our flight, hence we concluded that its upper parts had been greatly damaged, or that it had been totally shattered in an ice rift we had noticed. In the latter case the tunnel would probably turn out to be choked, so that we would have to try the next nearest one – the one less than a mile to the north. The intervening river course prevented our trying any of the more southern tunnels on this trip; and indeed, if both of the neighboring ones were choked it was doubtful whether our batteries would warrant an attempt on the next northerly one – about a mile beyond our second choice.

As we threaded our dim way through the labyrinth with the aid of map and compass – traversing rooms and corridors in every stage of ruin or preservation, clambering up ramps, crossing upper floors and bridges and clambering down again, encountering choked doorways and piles of debris, hastening now and then along finely preserved and uncannily immaculate stretches, taking false leads and retracing our way (in such cases removing the blind paper trail we had left), and once in a while striking the bottom of an open shaft through which daylight poured or trickled down – we were repeatedly tantalized by the sculptured walls along our route. Many must have told tales of immense historical importance, and only the prospect of later visits reconciled us to the need of passing them by. As it was, we slowed down once in a while and turned on our second torch. If we had had more films, we would certainly have paused briefly to photograph certain bas-reliefs, but time-consuming hand-copying was clearly out of the question.

I come now once more to a place where the temptation to hesitate, or to hint rather than state, is very strong. It is necessary, however, to reveal the rest in order to justify my course in discouraging further exploration. We had wormed our way very close to the computed site of the tunnel's mouth – having crossed a second-story bridge to what seemed plainly the tip of a pointed wall, and descended to a ruinous corridor especially rich in decadently elaborate and apparently ritualistic sculptures of late workmanship – when, shortly before 8:30 p.m., Danforth's keen young nostrils gave us the first hint of something unusual. If we had had a dog with us, I suppose we would have been warned before. At first we could not precisely say what was wrong with the formerly crystal-pure air, but after a few seconds our memories reacted only too definitely. Let me try to state the thing without flinching. There was an odor – and that odor was vaguely, subtly, and unmistakably akin to what had nauseated us upon opening the insane grave of the horror poor Lake had dissected.

Of course the revelation was not as clearly cut at the time as it sounds now. There were several conceivable explanations, and we did a good deal of indecisive whispering. Most important of all, we did not retreat without further investigation; for having come this far, we were loath to be balked by anything short of certain disaster. Anyway, what we must have suspected was altogether too wild to believe. Such things did not happen in any normal world. It was probably sheer irrational instinct which made us dim our single torch – tempted no longer by the decadent and sinister sculptures that leered menacingly from the oppressive walls – and which softened our progress to a cautious tiptoeing and crawling over the increasingly littered floor and heaps of debris.

Danforth's eyes as well as nose proved better than mine, for it was likewise he who first noticed the queer aspect of the debris after we had passed many half-choked arches leading to chambers and corridors on the ground level. It did not look quite as it ought after countless thousands of years of desertion, and when we cautiously turned on more light we saw that a kind of swath seemed to have been lately tracked through it. The irregular nature of the litter precluded any definite marks, but in the smoother places there were suggestions of the dragging of heavy objects. Once we thought there was a hint of parallel tracks as if of runners. This was what made us pause again.

It was during that pause that we caught – simultaneously this time – the other odor ahead. Paradoxically, it was both a less frightful and more frightful odor – less frightful intrinsically, but infinitely appalling in this place under the known circumstances – unless, of course, Gedney – for the odor was the plain and familiar one of common petrol – every-day gasoline.

Our motivation after that is something I will leave to psychologists. We knew now that some terrible extension of the camp horrors must have crawled into this nighted burial place of the aeons, hence could not doubt any longer the existence of nameless conditions – present or at least recent just ahead. Yet in the end we did let sheer burning curiosity – or anxiety – or autohypnotism – or vague thoughts of responsibility toward Gedney – or what not – drive us on. Danforth whispered again of the print he thought he had seen at the alley turning in the ruins above; and of the faint musical piping – potentially of tremendous significance in the light of Lake's dissection report, despite its close resemblance to the cave-mouth echoes of the windy peaks – which he thought he had shortly afterward half heard from unknown depths below. I, in my turn, whispered of how the camp was left – of what had disappeared, and of how the madness of a lone survivor might have conceived the inconceivable – a wild trip across the monstrous mountains and a descent into the unknown, primal masonry.

But we could not convince each other, or even ourselves, of anything definite. We had turned off all light as we stood still, and vaguely noticed that a trace of deeply filtered upper day kept the blackness from being absolute. Having automatically begun to move ahead, we guided ourselves by occasional flashes from our torch. The disturbed debris formed an impression we could not shake off, and the smell of gasoline grew stronger. More and more ruin met our eyes and hampered our feet, until very soon we saw that the forward way was about to cease. We had been all too correct in our pessimistic guess about that rift glimpsed from the air. Our tunnel quest was a blind one, and we were not even going to be able to reach the basement out of which the abyssward aperture opened.

The torch, flashing over the grotesquely carved walls of the blocked corridor in which we stood, showed several doorways in various states of obstruction; and from one of them the gasoline odor – quite submerging that other hint of odor – came with especial distinctness. As we looked more steadily, we saw that beyond a doubt there had been a slight and recent clearing away of debris from that particular opening. Whatever the lurking horror might be, we believed the direct avenue toward it was now plainly manifest. I do not think anyone will wonder that we waited an appreciable time before making any further motion.

And yet, when we did venture inside that black arch, our first impression was one of anticlimax. For amidst the littered expanse of that sculptured crypt – a perfect cube with sides of about twenty feet – there remained no recent object of instantly discernible size; so that we looked instinctively, though in vain, for a farther doorway. In another moment, however, Danforth's sharp vision had descried a place where the floor debris had been disturbed; and we turned on both torches full strength. Though what we saw in that light was actually simple and trifling, I am none the less reluctant to tell of it because of what it implied. It was a rough leveling of the debris, upon which several small objects lay carelessly scattered, and at one corner of which a considerable amount of gasoline must have been spilled lately enough to leave a strong odor even at this extreme superplateau altitude. In other words, it could not be other than a sort of camp – a camp made by questing beings who, like us, had been turned back by the unexpectedly choked way to the abyss.

Let me be plain. The scattered objects were, so far as substance was concerned, all from Lake's camp; and consisted of tin cans as queerly opened as those we had seen at that ravaged place, many spent matches, three illustrated books more or less curiously smudged, an empty ink bottle with its pictorial and instructional carton, a broken fountain pen, some oddly snipped fragments of fur and tent cloth, a used electric battery with circular of directions, a folder that came with our type of tent heater, and a sprinkling of crumpled papers. It was all bad enough but when we smoothed out the papers and looked at what was on them, we felt we had come to the worst. We had found certain inexplicably blotted papers at the camp which might have prepared us, yet the effect of the sight down there in the prehuman vaults of a nightmare city was almost too much to bear.

A mad Gedney might have made the groups of dots in imitation of those found on the greenish soapstones, just as the dots on those insane five-pointed grave mounds might have been made; and he might conceivably have prepared rough, hasty sketches – varying in their accuracy or lack of it – which outlined the neighboring parts of the city and traced the way from a circularly represented place outside our previous route – a place we identified as a great cylindrical tower in the carvings and as a vast circular gulf glimpsed in our aerial survey – to the present five-pointed structure and the tunnel mouth therein.

He might, I repeat, have prepared such sketches; for those before us were quite obviously compiled, as our own had been, from late sculptures somewhere in the glacial labyrinth, though not from the ones which we had seen and used. But what the art-blind bungler could never have done was to execute those sketches in a strange and assured technique perhaps superior, despite haste and carelessness, to any of the decadent carvings from which they were taken – the characteristic and unmistakable technique of the Old Ones themselves in the dead city's heyday.

There are those who will say Danforth and I were utterly mad not to flee for our lives after that; since our conclusions were now – notwithstanding their wildness – completely fixed, and of a nature I need not even mention to those who have read my account as far as this. Perhaps we were mad – for have I not said those horrible peaks were mountains of madness? But I think I can detect something of the same spirit – albeit in a less extreme form – in the men who stalk deadly beasts through African jungles to photograph them or study their habits. Half paralyzed with terror though we were, there was nevertheless fanned within us a blazing flame of awe and curiosity which triumphed in the end.

Of course we did not mean to face that – or those – which we knew had been there, but we felt that they must be gone by now. They would by this time have found the other neighboring entrance to the abyss, and have passed within, to whatever night-black fragments of the past might await them in the ultimate gulf – the ultimate gulf they had never seen. Or if that entrance, too, was blocked, they would have gone on to the north seeking another. They were, we remembered, partly independent of light.

Looking back to that moment, I can scarcely recall just what precise form our new emotions took – just what change of immediate objective it was that so sharpened our sense of expectancy. We certainly did not mean to face what we feared – yet I will not deny that we may have had a lurking, unconscious wish to spy certain things from some hidden vantage point. Probably we had not given up our zeal to glimpse the abyss itself, though there was interposed a new goal in the form of that great circular place shown on the crumpled sketches we had found. We had at once recognized it as a monstrous cylindrical tower figuring in the very earliest carvings, but appearing only as a prodigious round aperture from above. Something about the impressiveness of its rendering, even in these hasty diagrams, made us think that its subglacial levels must still form a feature of peculiar importance. Perhaps it embodied architectural marvels as yet unencountered by us. It was certainly of incredible age according to the sculptures in which it figured – being indeed among the first things built in the city. Its carvings, if preserved, could not but be highly significant. Moreover, it might form a good present link with the upper world – a shorter route than the one we were so carefully blazing, and probably that by which those others had descended.

At any rate, the thing we did was to study the terrible sketches – which quite perfectly confirmed our own – and start back over the indicated course to the circular place; the course which our nameless predecessors must have traversed twice before us. The other neighboring gate to the abyss would lie beyond that. I need not speak of our journey – during which we continued to leave an economical trail of paper – for it was precisely the same in kind as that by which we had reached the cul-de-sac; except that it tended to adhere more closely to the ground level and even descend to basement corridors. Every now and then we could trace certain disturbing marks in the debris or litter underfoot; and after we had passed outside the radius of the gasoline scent, we were again faintly conscious – spasmodically – of that more hideous and more persistent scent. After the way had branched from our former course, we sometimes gave the rays of our single torch a furtive sweep along the walls; noting in almost every case the well-nigh omnipresent sculptures, which indeed seem to have formed a main aesthetic outlet for the Old Ones.

About 9:30 p.m., while traversing a long, vaulted corridor whose increasingly glaciated floor seemed somewhat below the ground level and whose roof grew lower as we advanced, we began to see strong daylight ahead and were able to turn off our torch. It appeared that we were coming to the vast circular place, and that our distance from the upper air could not be very great. The corridor ended in an arch surprisingly low for these megalithic ruins, but we could see much through it even before we emerged. Beyond there stretched a prodigious round space – fully two hundred feet in diameter – strewn with debris and containing many choked archways corresponding to the one we were about to cross. The walls were – in available spaces – boldly sculptured into a spiral band of heroic proportions; and displayed, despite the destructive weathering caused by the openness of the spot, an artistic splendor far beyond anything we had encountered before. The littered floor was quite heavily glaciated, and we fancied that the true bottom lay at a considerably lower depth.

But the salient object of the place was the titanic stone ramp which, eluding the archways by a sharp turn outward into the open floor, wound spirally up the stupendous cylindrical wall like an inside counterpart of those once climbing outside the monstrous towers or ziggurats of antique Babylon. Only the rapidity of our flight, and the perspective which confounded the descent with the tower's inner wall, had prevented our noticing this feature from the air, and thus caused us to seek another avenue to the subglacial level. Pabodie might have been able to tell what sort of engineering held it in place, but Danforth and I could merely admire and marvel. We could see mighty stone corbels and pillars here and there, but what we saw seemed inadequate to the function performed. The thing was excellently preserved up to the present top of the tower – a highly remarkable circumstance in view of its exposure – and its shelter had done much to protect the bizarre and disturbing cosmic sculptures on the walls.

As we stepped out into the awesome half daylight of this monstrous cylinder bottom – fifty million years old, and without doubt the most primally ancient structure ever to meet our eyes – we saw that the ramp-traversed sides stretched dizzily up to a height of fully sixty feet. This, we recalled from our aerial survey, meant an outside glaciation of some forty feet; since the yawning gulf we had seen from the plane had been at the top of an approximately twenty-foot mound of crumbled masonry, somewhat sheltered for three-fourths of its circumference by the massive curving walls of a line of higher ruins. According to the sculptures, the original tower had stood in the center of an immense circular plaza, and had been perhaps five hundred or six hundred feet high, with tiers of horizontal disks near the top, and a row of needlelike spires along the upper rim. Most of the masonry had obviously toppled outward rather than inward – a fortunate happening, since otherwise the ramp might have been shattered and the whole interior choked. As it was, the ramp showed sad battering; whilst the choking was such that all the archways at the bottom seemed to have been recently cleared.

It took us only a moment to conclude that this was indeed the route by which those others had descended, and that this would be the logical route for our own ascent despite the long trail of paper we had left elsewhere. The tower's mouth was no farther from the foothills and our waiting plane than was the great terraced building we had entered, and any further subglacial exploration we might make on this trip would lie in this general region. Oddly, we were still thinking about possible later trips – even after all we had seen and guessed. Then, as we picked our way cautiously over the debris of the great floor, there came a sight which for the time excluded all other matters.

It was the neatly huddled array of three sledges in that farther angle of the ramp's lower and outward-projecting course which had hitherto been screened from our view. There they were – the three sledges missing from Lake's camp – shaken by a hard usage which must have included forcible dragging along great reaches of snowless masonry and debris, as well as much hand portage over utterly unnavigable places. They were carefully and intelligently packed and strapped, and contained things memorably familiar enough: the gasoline stove, fuel cans, instrument cases, provision tins, tarpaulins obviously bulging with books, and some bulging with less obvious contents – everything derived from Lake's equipment.

After what we had found in that other room, we were in a measure prepared for this encounter. The really great shock came when we stepped over and undid one tarpaulin whose outlines had peculiarly disquieted us. It seems that others as well as Lake had been interested in collecting typical specimens; for there were two here, both stiffly frozen, perfectly preserved, patched with adhesive plaster where some wounds around the neck had occurred, and wrapped with care to prevent further damage. They were the bodies of young Gedney and the missing dog.

Chapter X

MANY PEOPLE will probably judge us callous as well as mad for thinking about the northward tunnel and the abyss so soon after our somber discovery, and I am not prepared to say that we would have immediately revived such thoughts but for a specific circumstance which broke in upon us and set up a whole new train of speculations. We had replaced the tarpaulin over poor Gedney and were standing in a kind of mute bewilderment when the sounds finally reached our consciousness – the first sounds we had heard since descending out of the open where the mountain wind whined faintly from its unearthly heights. Well-known and mundane though they were, their presence in this remote world of death was more unexpected and unnerving than any grotesque or fabulous tones could possibly have been – since they gave a fresh upsetting to all our notions of cosmic harmony.

Had it been some trace of that bizarre musical piping over a wide range which Lake's dissection report had led us to expect in those others – and which, indeed, our overwrought fancies had been reading into every wind howl we had heard since coming on the camp horror – it would have had a kind of hellish congruity with the aeon-dead region around us. A voice from other epochs belongs in a graveyard of other epochs. As it was, however, the noise shattered all our profoundly seated adjustments – all our tacit acceptance of the inner antarctic as a waste utterly and irrevocably void of every vestige of normal life. What we heard was not the fabulous note of any buried blasphemy of elder earth from whose supernal toughness an age-denied polar sun had evoked a monstrous response. Instead, it was a thing so mockingly normal and so unerringly familiarized by our sea days off Victoria Land and our camp days at McMurdo Sound that we shuddered to think of it here, where such things ought not to be. To be brief – it was simply the raucous squawking of a penguin.

The muffled sound floated from subglacial recesses nearly opposite to the corridor whence we had come – regions manifestly in the direction of that other tunnel to the vast abyss. The presence of a living water bird in such a direction – in a world whose surface was one of age-long and uniform lifelessness – could lead to only one conclusion; hence our first thought was to verify the objective reality of the sound. It was, indeed, repeated, and seemed at times to come from more than one throat. Seeking its source, we entered an archway from which much debris had been cleared; resuming our trail blazing – with an added paper supply taken with curious repugnance from one of the tarpaulin bundles on the sledges – when we left daylight behind.

As the glaciated floor gave place to a litter of detritus, we plainly discerned some curious, dragging tracks; and once Danforth found a distinct print of a sort whose description would be only too superfluous. The course indicated by the penguin cries was precisely what our map and compass prescribed as an approach to the more northerly tunnel mouth, and we were glad to find that a bridgeless thoroughfare on the ground and basement levels seemed open. The tunnel, according to the chart, ought to start from the basement of a large pyramidal structure which we seemed vaguely to recall from our aerial survey as remarkably well-preserved. Along our path the single torch showed a customary profusion of carvings, but we did not pause to examine any of these.

Suddenly a bulky white shape loomed up ahead of us, and we flashed on the second torch. It is odd how wholly this new quest had turned our minds from earlier fears of what might lurk near. Those other ones, having left their supplies in the great circular place, must have planned to return after their scouting trip toward or into the abyss; yet we had now discarded all caution concerning them as completely as if they had never existed. This white, waddling thing was fully six feet high, yet we seemed to realize at once that it was not one of those others. They were larger and dark, and, according to the sculptures, their motion over land surfaces was a swift, assured matter despite the queerness of their sea-born tentacle equipment. But to say that the white thing did not profoundly frighten us would be vain. We were indeed clutched for an instant by primitive dread almost sharper than the worst of our reasoned fears regarding those others. Then came a flash of anticlimax as the white shape sidled into a lateral archway to our left to join two others of its kind which had summoned it in raucous tones. For it was only a penguin – albeit of a huge, unknown species larger than the greatest of the known king penguins, and monstrous in its combined albinism and virtual eyelessness.

When we had followed the thing into the archway and turned both our torches on the indifferent and unheeding group of three, we saw that they were all eyeless albinos of the same unknown and gigantic species. Their size reminded us of some of the archaic penguins depicted in the Old Ones' sculptures, and it did not take us long to conclude that they were descended from the same stock – undoubtedly surviving through a retreat to some warmer inner region whose perpetual blackness had destroyed their pigmentation and atrophied their eyes to mere useless slits. That their present habitat was the vast abyss we sought, was not for a moment to be doubted; and this evidence of the gulf's continued warmth and habitability filled us with the most curious and subtly perturbing fancies.

We wondered, too, what had caused these three birds to venture out of their usual domain. The state and silence of the great dead city made it clear that it had at no time been an habitual seasonal rookery, whilst the manifest indifference of the trio to our presence made it seem odd that any passing party of those others should have startled them. Was it possible that those others had taken some aggressive action or tried to increase their meat supply? We doubted whether that pungent odor which the dogs had hated could cause an equal antipathy in these penguins, since their ancestors had obviously lived on excellent terms with the Old Ones – an amicable relationship which must have survived in the abyss below as long as any of the Old Ones remained. Regretting – in a flare-up of the old spirit of pure science – that we could not photograph these anomalous creatures, we shortly left them to their squawking and pushed on toward the abyss whose openness was now so positively proved to us, and whose exact direction occasional penguin tracks made clear.

Not long afterward a steep descent in a long, low, doorless, and peculiarly sculptureless corridor led us to believe that we were approaching the tunnel mouth at last. We had passed two more penguins, and heard others immediately ahead. Then the corridor ended in a prodigious open space which made us gasp involuntarily – a perfect inverted hemisphere, obviously deep underground; fully a hundred feet in diameter and fifty feet high, with low archways opening around all parts of the circumference but one, and that one yawning cavernously with a black, arched aperture which broke the symmetry of the vault to a height of nearly fifteen feet. It was the entrance to the great abyss.

In this vast hemisphere, whose concave roof was impressively though decadently carved to a likeness of the primordial celestial dome, a few albino penguins waddled – aliens there, but indifferent and unseeing. The black tunnel yawned indefinitely off at a steep, descending grade, its aperture adorned with grotesquely chiseled jambs and lintel. From that cryptical mouth we fancied a current of slightly warmer air, and perhaps even a suspicion of vapor proceeded; and we wondered what living entities other than penguins the limitless void below, and the contiguous honeycombings of the land and the titan mountains, might conceal. We wondered, too, whether the trace of mountaintop smoke at first suspected by poor Lake, as well as the odd haze we had ourselves perceived around the rampart-crowned peak, might not be caused by the tortuous-channeled rising of some such vapor from the unfathomed regions of earth's core.

Entering the tunnel, we saw that its outline was – at least at the start – about fifteen feet each way – sides, floor, and arched roof composed of the usual megalithic masonry. The sides were sparsely decorated with cartouches of conventional designs in a late, decadent style; and all the construction and carving were marvelously well-preserved. The floor was quite clear, except for a slight detritus bearing outgoing penguin tracks and the inward tracks of these others. The farther one advanced, the warmer it became; so that we were soon unbuttoning our heavy garments. We wondered whether there were any actually igneous manifestations below, and whether the waters of that sunless sea were hot. After a short distance the masonry gave place to solid rock, though the tunnel kept the same proportions and presented the same aspect of carved regularity. Occasionally its varying grade became so steep that grooves were cut in the floor. Several times we noted the mouths of small lateral galleries not recorded in our diagrams; none of them such as to complicate the problem of our return, and all of them welcome as possible refuges in case we met unwelcome entities on their way back from the abyss.

The nameless scent of such things was very distinct. Doubtless it was suicidally foolish to venture into that tunnel under the known conditions, but the lure of the unplumbed is stronger in certain persons than most suspect – indeed, it was just such a lure which had brought us to this unearthly polar waste in the first place. We saw several penguins as we passed along, and speculated on the distance we would have to traverse. The carvings had led us to expect a steep downhill walk of about a mile to the abyss, but our previous wanderings had shown us that matters of scale were not wholly to be depended on.

After about a quarter of a mile that nameless scent became greatly accentuated, and we kept very careful track of the various lateral openings we passed. There was no visible vapor as at the mouth, but this was doubtless due to the lack of contrasting cooler air. The temperature was rapidly ascending, and we were not surprised to come upon a careless heap of material shudderingly familiar to us. It was composed of furs and tent cloth taken from Lake's camp, and we did not pause to study the bizarre forms into which the fabrics had been slashed. Slightly beyond this point we noticed a decided increase in the size and number of the side galleries, and concluded that the densely honeycombed region beneath the higher foothills must now have been reached. The nameless scent was now curiously mixed with another and scarcely less offensive odor – of what nature we could not guess, though we thought of decaying organisms and perhaps unknown subterranean fungi. Then came a startling expansion of the tunnel for which the carvings had not prepared us – a broadening and rising into a lofty, natural-looking elliptical cavern with a level floor, some seventy-five feet long and fifty broad, and with many immense side passages leading away into cryptical darkness.

Though this cavern was natural in appearance, an inspection with both torches suggested that it had been formed by the artificial destruction of several walls between adjacent honeycombings. The walls were rough, and the high, vaulted roof was thick with stalactites; but the solid rock floor had been smoothed off, and was free from all debris, detritus, or even dust to a positively abnormal extent. Except for the avenue through which we had come, this was true of the floors of all the great galleries opening off from it; and the singularity of the condition was such as to set us vainly puzzling. The curious new fetor which had supplemented the nameless scent was excessively pungent here; so much so that it destroyed all trace of the other. Something about this whole place, with its polished and almost glistening floor, struck us as more vaguely baffling and horrible than any of the monstrous things we had previously encountered.

The regularity of the passage immediately ahead, as well as the larger proportion of penguin-droppings there, prevented all confusion as to the right course amidst this plethora of equally great cave mouths. Nevertheless we resolved to resume our paper trailblazing if any further complexity should develop; for dust tracks, of course, could no longer be expected. Upon resuming our direct progress we cast a beam of torchlight over the tunnel walls – and stopped short in amazement at the supremely radical change which had come over the carvings in this part of the passage. We realized, of course, the great decadence of the Old Ones' sculpture at the time of the tunneling, and had indeed noticed the inferior workmanship of the arabesques in the stretches behind us. But now, in this deeper section beyond the cavern, there was a sudden difference wholly transcending explanation – a difference in basic nature as well as in mere quality, and involving so profound and calamitous a degradation of skill that nothing in the hitherto observed rate of decline could have led one to expect it.

This new and degenerate work was coarse, bold, and wholly lacking in delicacy of detail. It was countersunk with exaggerated depth in bands following the same general line as the sparse cartouches of the earlier sections, but the height of the reliefs did not reach the level of the general surface. Danforth had the idea that it was a second carving – a sort of palimpsest formed after the obliteration of a previous design. In nature it was wholly decorative and conventional, and consisted of crude spirals and angles roughly following the quintile mathematical tradition of the Old Ones, yet seemingly more like a parody than a perpetuation of that tradition. We could not get it out of our minds that some subtly but profoundly alien element had been added to the aesthetic feeling behind the technique – an alien element, Danforth guessed, that was responsible for the laborious substitution. It was like, yet disturbingly unlike, what we had come to recognize as the Old Ones' art; and I was persistently reminded of such hybrid things as the ungainly Palmyrene sculptures fashioned in the Roman manner. That others had recently noticed this belt of carving was hinted by the presence of a used flashlight battery on the floor in front of one of the most characteristic cartouches.

Since we could not afford to spend any considerable time in study, we resumed our advance after a cursory look; though frequently casting beams over the walls to see if any further decorative changes developed. Nothing of the sort was perceived, though the carvings were in places rather sparse because of the numerous mouths of smooth-floored lateral tunnels. We saw and heard fewer penguins, but thought we caught a vague suspicion of an infinitely distant chorus of them somewhere deep within the earth. The new and inexplicable odor was abominably strong, and we could detect scarcely a sign of that other nameless scent. Puffs of visible vapor ahead bespoke increasing contrasts in temperature, and the relative nearness of the sunless sea cliffs of the great abyss. Then, quite unexpectedly, we saw certain obstructions on the polished floor ahead – obstructions which were quite definitely not penguins – and turned on our second torch after making sure that the objects were quite stationary.

Chapter XI

STILL ANOTHER TIME have I come to a place where it is very difficult to proceed. I ought to be hardened by this stage; but there are some experiences and intimations which scar too deeply to permit of healing, and leave only such an added sensitiveness that memory reinspires all the original horror. We saw, as I have said, certain obstructions on the polished floor ahead; and I may add that our nostrils were assailed almost simultaneously by a very curious intensification of the strange prevailing fetor, now quite plainly mixed with the nameless stench of those others which had gone before. The light of the second torch left no doubt of what the obstructions were, and we dared approach them only because we could see, even from a distance, that they were quite as past all harming power as had been the six similar specimens unearthed from the monstrous star-mounded graves at poor Lake's camp.

They were, indeed, as lacking in completeness as most of those we had unearthed – though it grew plain from the thick, dark green pool gathering around them that their incompleteness was of infinitely greater recency. There seemed to be only four of them, whereas Lake's bulletins would have suggested no less than eight as forming the group which had preceded us. To find them in this state was wholly unexpected, and we wondered what sort of monstrous struggle had occurred down here in the dark.

Penguins, attacked in a body, retaliate savagely with their beaks, and our ears now made certain the existence of a rookery far beyond. Had those others disturbed such a place and aroused murderous pursuit? The obstructions did not suggest it, for penguins' beaks against the tough tissues Lake had dissected could hardly account for the terrible damage our approaching glance was beginning to make out. Besides, the huge blind birds we had seen appeared to be singularly peaceful.

Had there, then, been a struggle among those others, and were the absent four responsible? If so, where were they? Were they close at hand and likely to form an immediate menace to us? We glanced anxiously at some of the smooth-floored lateral passages as we continued our slow and frankly reluctant approach. Whatever the conflict was, it had clearly been that which had frightened the penguins into their unaccustomed wandering. It must, then, have arisen near that faintly heard rookery in the incalculable gulf beyond, since there were no signs that any birds had normally dwelt here. Perhaps, we reflected, there had been a hideous running fight, with the weaker party seeking to get back to the cached sledges when their pursuers finished them. One could picture the demoniac fray between namelessly monstrous entities as it surged out of the black abyss with great clouds of frantic penguins squawking and scurrying ahead.

I say that we approached those sprawling and incomplete obstructions slowly and reluctantly. Would to Heaven we had never approached them at all, but had run back at top speed out of that blasphemous tunnel with the greasily smooth floors and the degenerate murals aping and mocking the things they had superseded – run back, before we had seen what we did see, and before our minds were burned with something which will never let us breathe easily again!

Both of our torches were turned on the prostrate objects, so that we soon realized the dominant factor in their incompleteness. Mauled, compressed, twisted, and ruptured as they were, their chief common injury was total decapitation. From each one the tentacled starfish head had been removed; and as we drew near we saw that the manner of removal looked more like some hellish tearing or suction than like any ordinary form of cleavage. Their noisome dark-green ichor formed a large, spreading pool; but its stench was half overshadowed by the newer and stranger stench, here more pungent than at any other point along our route. Only when we had come very close to the sprawling obstructions could we trace that second, unexplainable fetor to any immediate source – and the instant we did so Danforth, remembering certain very vivid sculptures of the Old Ones' history in the Permian Age one hundred and fifty million years ago, gave vent to a nerve-tortured cry which echoed hysterically through that vaulted and archaic passage with the evil, palimpsest carvings.

I came only just short of echoing his cry myself; for I had seen those primal sculptures, too, and had shudderingly admired the way the nameless artist had suggested that hideous slime coating found on certain incomplete and prostrate Old Ones – those whom the frightful Shoggoths had characteristically slain and sucked to a ghastly headlessness in the great war of resubjugation. They were infamous, nightmare sculptures even when telling of age-old, bygone things; for Shoggoths and their work ought not to be seen by human beings or portrayed by any beings. The mad author of the *Necronomicon* had nervously tried to swear that none had been bred on this planet, and that only drugged dreamers had even conceived them. Formless protoplasm able to mock and reflect all forms and organs and processes – viscous agglutinations of bubbling cells – rubbery fifteen-foot spheroids infinitely plastic and ductile – slaves of suggestion, builders of cities – more and more sullen, more and more intelligent, more and more amphibious, more and more imitative! Great God! What madness made even those blasphemous Old Ones willing to use and carve such things?

And now, when Danforth and I saw the freshly glistening and reflectively iridescent black slime which clung thickly to those headless bodies and stank obscenely with that new, unknown odor whose cause only a diseased fancy could envisage – clung to those bodies and sparkled less voluminously on a smooth part of the accursedly resculptured wall in a series of grouped dots – we understood the quality of cosmic fear to its uttermost depths. It was not fear of those four missing others – for all too well did we suspect they would do no harm again. Poor devils! After all, they were not evil things of their kind. They were the men of another age and another order of being. Nature had played a hellish jest on them – as it will on any others that human madness, callousness, or cruelty may hereafter dig up in that hideously dead or sleeping polar waste – and this was their tragic homecoming. They had not been even savages – for what indeed had they done? That awful awakening in the cold of an unknown epoch – perhaps an attack by the furry, frantically barking quadrupeds, and a dazed defense against them and the equally frantic white simians with the queer wrappings and paraphernalia...poor Lake, poor Gedney...and poor Old Ones! Scientists to the last – what had they done that we would not have done in their place? God, what intelligence and persistence! What a facing of the incredible, just as those carven kinsmen and forbears had faced things only a little less incredible! Radiates, vegetables, monstrosities, star spawn – whatever they had been, they were men!

They had crossed the icy peaks on whose templed slopes they had once worshipped and roamed among the tree ferns. They had found their dead city brooding under its curse, and had read its carven latter days as we had done. They had tried to reach their living fellows in fabled depths of blackness they had never seen – and what had they found? All this flashed in unison through the thoughts of Danforth and me as we looked from those headless, slime-coated shapes to the loathsome palimpsest sculptures and the diabolical dot groups of fresh slime on the wall beside them – looked and understood what must have triumphed and survived down there in the Cyclopean water city of that nighted, penguin-fringed abyss, whence even now a sinister curling mist had begun to belch pallidly as if in answer to Danforth's hysterical scream.

The shock of recognizing that monstrous slime and headlessness had frozen us into mute, motionless statues, and it is only through later conversations that we have learned of the complete identity of our thoughts at that moment. It seemed aeons that we stood there, but actually it could not have been more than ten or fifteen seconds. That hateful, pallid mist curled forward as if veritably driven by some remoter advancing bulk – and then came a sound which upset much of what we had just decided, and in so doing broke the spell and enabled us to run like mad past squawking, confused penguins over our former trail back to the city, along ice-sunken megalithic corridors to the great open circle, and up that archaic spiral ramp in a frenzied, automatic plunge for the sane outer air and light of day.

The new sound, as I have intimated, upset much that we had decided; because it was what poor Lake's dissection had led us to attribute to those we had judged dead. It was, Danforth later told me, precisely what he had caught in infinitely muffled form when at that spot beyond the alley corner above the glacial level; and it certainly had a shocking resemblance to the wind pipings we had both heard around the lofty mountain caves. At the risk of seeming puerile I will add another thing, too, if only because of the surprising way Danforth's impressions chimed with mine. Of course common reading is what prepared us both to make the interpretation, though Danforth has hinted at queer notions about unsuspected and forbidden sources to which Poe may have had access when writing his Arthur Gordon Pym a century ago. It will be remembered that in that fantastic tale there is a word of unknown but terrible and prodigious significance connected with the antarctic and screamed eternally by the gigantic spectrally snowy birds of that malign region's core. "Tekeli-li! Tekeli-li!" That, I may admit, is exactly what we thought we heard conveyed by that sudden sound behind the advancing white mist – that insidious musical piping over a singularly wide range.

We were in full flight before three notes or syllables had been uttered, though we knew that the swiftness of the Old Ones would enable any scream-roused and pursuing survivor of the slaughter to overtake us in a moment if it really wished to do so. We had a vague hope, however, that nonaggressive conduct and a display of kindred reason might cause such a being to spare us in case of capture, if only from scientific curiosity. After all, if such an one had nothing to fear for itself, it would have no motive in harming us. Concealment being futile at this juncture, we used our torch for a running glance behind, and perceived that the mist was thinning. Would we see, at last, a complete and living specimen of those others? Again came that insidious musical piping – "Tekeli-li! Tekeli-li!" Then, noting that we were actually gaining on our pursuer, it occurred to us that the entity might be wounded. We could take no chances, however, since it was very obviously approaching in answer to Danforth's scream, rather than in flight from any other entity. The timing was too close to admit of doubt. Of the whereabouts of that less conceivable and less mentionable nightmare – that fetid, unglimpsed mountain of slime-spewing protoplasm whose race had conquered the abyss and sent land pioneers to recarve and squirm through the burrows of the hills – we could form no guess; and it cost us a genuine pang to leave this probably crippled Old One – perhaps a lone survivor – to the peril of recapture and a nameless fate.

Thank Heaven we did not slacken our run. The curling mist had thickened again, and was driving ahead with increased speed; whilst the straying penguins in our rear were squawking and screaming and displaying signs of a panic really surprising in view of their relatively minor confusion when we had passed them. Once more came that sinister, wide-ranged piping – "Tekeli-li! Tekeli-li!" We had been wrong. The thing was not wounded, but had merely paused on encountering the bodies of its fallen kindred and the hellish slime inscription above them. We could never know what that demon message was – but those burials at Lake's camp had shown how much importance the beings attached to their dead. Our recklessly used torch now revealed ahead of us the large open cavern where various ways converged, and we were glad to be leaving those morbid palimpsest sculptures – almost felt even when scarcely seen – behind. Another thought which the advent of the cave inspired was the possibility of losing our pursuer at this bewildering focus of large galleries. There were several of the blind albino penguins in the open space, and it seemed clear that their fear of the oncoming entity was extreme to the point of unaccountability. If at that point we dimmed our torch to the very lowest limit of traveling need, keeping it strictly in front of us, the frightened squawking motions of the huge birds in the mist might muffle our footfalls, screen our true course, and somehow set up a false lead. Amidst the churning, spiraling fog, the littered and unglistening floor of the main tunnel beyond this point, as differing from the other morbidly polished burrows, could hardly form a highly distinguishing feature; even, so far as we could conjecture, for those indicated special senses which made the Old Ones partly, though imperfectly, independent of light in emergencies. In fact, we were somewhat apprehensive lest we go astray ourselves in our haste. For we had, of course, decided to keep straight on toward the dead city; since the consequences of loss in those unknown foothill honeycombings would be unthinkable.

The fact that we survived and emerged is sufficient proof that the thing did take a wrong gallery whilst we providentially hit on the right one. The penguins alone could not have saved us, but in conjunction with the mist they seem to have done so. Only a benign fate kept the curling vapors thick enough at the right moment, for they were constantly shifting and threatening to vanish. Indeed, they did lift for a second just before we emerged from the nauseously resculptured tunnel into the cave; so that we actually caught one first and only half glimpse of the oncoming entity as we cast a final, desperately fearful glance backward before dimming the torch and mixing with the penguins in the hope of dodging pursuit. If the fate which screened us was benign, that which gave us the half glimpse was infinitely the opposite; for to that flash of semivision can be traced a full half of the horror which has ever since haunted us.

Our exact motive in looking back again was perhaps no more than the immemorial instinct of the pursued to gauge the nature and course of its pursuer; or perhaps it was an automatic attempt to answer a subconscious question raised by one of our senses. In the midst of our flight, with all our faculties centered on the problem of escape, we were in no condition to observe and analyze details; yet even so, our latent brain cells must have wondered at the message brought them by our nostrils. Afterward we realized what it was that our retreat from the fetid slime coating on those headless obstructions, and the coincident approach of the pursuing entity, had not brought us the exchange of stenches which logic called for. In the neighborhood of the prostrate things that new and lately unexplainable fetor had been wholly dominant; but by this time it ought to have largely given place to the nameless stench associated with those others. This it had not done – for instead, the newer and less bearable smell was now virtually undiluted, and growing more and more poisonously insistent each second.

So we glanced back simultaneously, it would appear; though no doubt the incipient motion of one prompted the imitation of the other. As we did so we flashed both torches full strength at the momentarily thinned mist; either from sheer primitive anxiety to see all we could, or in a less primitive but equally unconscious effort to dazzle the entity before we dimmed our light and dodged among the penguins of the labyrinth center ahead. Unhappy act! Not Orpheus himself, or Lot's wife, paid much more dearly for a backward glance. And again came that shocking, wide-ranged piping – "Tekeli-li! Tekeli-li!"

I might as well be frank – even if I cannot bear to be quite direct – in stating what we saw; though at the time we felt that it was not to be admitted even to each other. The words reaching the reader can never even suggest the awfulness of the sight itself. It crippled our consciousness so completely that I wonder we had the residual sense to dim our torches as planned, and to strike the right tunnel toward the dead city. Instinct alone must have carried us through – perhaps better than reason could have done; though if that was what saved us, we paid a high price. Of reason we certainly had little enough left.

Danforth was totally unstrung, and the first thing I remember of the rest of the journey was hearing him lightheadedly chant an hysterical formula in which I alone of mankind could have found anything but insane irrelevance. It reverberated in falsetto echoes among the squawks of the penguins; reverberated through the vaultings ahead, and – thank God – through the now empty vaultings behind. He could not have begun it at once – else we would not have been alive and blindly racing. I shudder to think of what a shade of difference in his nervous reactions might have brought.

"South Station Under – Washington Under – Park Street Under – Kendall – Central – Harvard –" The poor fellow was chanting the familiar stations of the Boston-Cambridge tunnel that burrowed through our peaceful native soil thousands of miles away in New England, yet to me the ritual had neither irrelevance nor home feeling. It had only horror, because I knew unerringly the monstrous, nefandous analogy that had suggested it. We had expected, upon looking back, to see a terrible and incredible moving entity if the mists were thin enough; but of that entity we had formed a clear idea. What we did see – for the mists were indeed all too malignly thinned – was something altogether different, and immeasurably more hideous and detestable. It was the utter, objective embodiment of the fantastic novelist's 'thing that should not be'; and its nearest comprehensible analogue is a vast, onrushing subway train as one sees it from a station platform – the great black front looming colossally out of infinite subterranean distance, constellated with strangely colored lights and filling the prodigious burrow as a piston fills a cylinder.

But we were not on a station platform. We were on the track ahead as the nightmare, plastic column of fetid black iridescence oozed tightly onward through its fifteen-foot sinus, gathering unholy speed and driving before it a spiral, rethickening cloud of the pallid abyss-vapor. It was a terrible, indescribable thing vaster than any subway train – a shapeless congeries of protoplasmic bubbles, faintly self-luminous, and with myriads of temporary eyes forming and un-forming as pustules of greenish light all over the tunnel-filling front that bore down upon us, crushing the frantic penguins and slithering over the glistening floor that it and its kind had swept so evilly free of all litter. Still came that eldritch, mocking cry – "Tekeli-li! Tekeli-li!" and at last we remembered that the demoniac Shoggoths – given life, thought, and plastic organ patterns solely by the Old Ones, and having no language save that which the dot groups expressed – had likewise no voice save the imitated accents of their bygone masters.

Chapter XII

DANFORTH AND I have recollections of emerging into the great sculptured hemisphere and of threading our back trail through the Cyclopean rooms and corridors of the dead city; yet these are purely dream fragments involving no memory of volition, details, or physical exertion. It was as if we floated in a nebulous world or dimension without time, causation, or orientation. The gray half-daylight of the vast circular space sobered us somewhat; but we did not go near those cached sledges or look again at poor Gedney and the dog. They have a strange and titanic mausoleum, and I hope the end of this planet will find them still undisturbed.

It was while struggling up the colossal spiral incline that we first felt the terrible fatigue and short breath which our race through the thin plateau air had produced; but not even fear of collapse could make us pause before reaching the normal outer realm of sun and sky. There was something vaguely appropriate about our departure from those buried epochs; for as we wound our panting way up the sixty-foot cylinder of primal masonry, we glimpsed beside us a continuous procession of heroic sculptures in the dead race's early and undecayed technique – a farewell from the Old Ones, written fifty million years ago.

Finally scrambling out at the top, we found ourselves on a great mound of tumbled blocks, with the curved walls of higher stonework rising westward, and the brooding peaks of the great mountains showing beyond the more crumbled structures toward the east. The low antarctic sun of midnight peered redly from the southern horizon through rifts in the jagged ruins, and the terrible age and deadness of the nightmare city seemed all the starker by contrast with such relatively known and accustomed things as the features of the polar landscape. The sky above was a churning and opalescent mass of tenuous ice-vapors, and the cold clutched at our vitals. Wearily resting the outfit-bags to which we had instinctively clung throughout our desperate flight, we rebuttoned our heavy garments for the stumbling climb down the mound and the walk through the aeon-old stone maze to the foothills where our aeroplane waited. Of what had set us fleeing from that darkness of earth's secret and archaic gulfs we said nothing at all.

In less than a quarter of an hour we had found the steep grade to the foothills – the probable ancient terrace – by which we had descended, and could see the dark bulk of our great plane amidst the sparse ruins on the rising slope ahead. Halfway uphill toward our goal we paused for a momentary breathing spell, and turned to look again at the fantastic tangle of incredible stone shapes below us – once more outlined mystically against an unknown west. As we did so we saw that the sky beyond had lost its morning haziness; the restless ice-vapors having moved up to the zenith, where their mocking outlines seemed on the point of settling into some bizarre pattern which they feared to make quite definite or conclusive.

There now lay revealed on the ultimate white horizon behind the grotesque city a dim, elfin line of pinnacled violet whose needle-pointed heights loomed dreamlike against the beckoning rose color of the western sky. Up toward this shimmering rim sloped the ancient table-land, the depressed course of the bygone river traversing it as an irregular ribbon of shadow. For a second we gasped in admiration of the scene's unearthly cosmic beauty, and then vague horror began to creep into our souls. For this far violet line could be nothing else than the terrible mountains of the forbidden land – highest of earth's peaks and focus of earth's evil; harborers of nameless horrors and Archaean secrets; shunned and prayed to by those who feared to carve their meaning; untrodden by any living thing on earth, but visited by the sinister lightnings and sending strange beams across the plains in the polar night – beyond doubt the unknown archetype of that dreaded Kadath in the Cold Waste beyond abhorrent Leng, whereof primal legends hint evasively.

If the sculptured maps and pictures in that prehuman city had told truly, these cryptic violet mountains could not be much less than three hundred miles away; yet none the less sharply did their dim elfin essence appear above that remote and snowy rim, like the serrated edge of a monstrous alien planet about to rise into unaccustomed heavens. Their height, then, must have been tremendous beyond all comparison – carrying them up into tenuous atmospheric strata peopled only by such gaseous wraiths as rash flyers have barely lived to whisper of after unexplainable falls. Looking at them, I thought nervously of certain sculptured hints of what the great bygone river had washed down into the city from their accursed slopes – and wondered how much sense and how much folly had lain in the fears of those Old Ones who carved them so reticently. I recalled how their northerly end must come near the coast at Queen Mary Land, where even at that moment Sir Douglas Mawson's expedition was doubtless working less than a thousand miles away; and hoped that no evil fate would give Sir Douglas and his men a glimpse of what might lie beyond the protecting coastal range. Such thoughts formed a measure of my overwrought condition at the time – and Danforth seemed to be even worse.

Yet long before we had passed the great star-shaped ruin and reached our plane, our fears had become transferred to the lesser but vast-enough range whose recrossing lay ahead of us. From these foothills the black, ruin-crusted slopes reared up starkly and hideously against the east, again reminding us of those strange Asian paintings of Nicholas Roerich; and when we thought of the frightful amorphous entities that might have pushed their fetidly squirming way even to the topmost hollow pinnacles, we could not face without panic the prospect of again sailing by those suggestive skyward cave mouths where the wind made sounds like an evil musical piping over a wide range. To make matters worse, we saw distinct traces of local mist around several of the summits – as poor Lake must have done when he made that early mistake about volcanism – and thought shiveringly of that kindred mist from which we had just escaped; of that, and of the blasphemous, horror-fostering abyss whence all such vapors came.

All was well with the plane, and we clumsily hauled on our heavy flying furs. Danforth got the engine started without trouble, and we made a very smooth take-off over the nightmare city. Below us the primal Cyclopean masonry spread out as it had done when first we saw it, and we began rising and turning to test the wind for our crossing through the pass. At a very high level there must have been great disturbance, since the ice-dust clouds of the zenith were doing all sorts of fantastic things; but at twenty-four thousand feet, the height we needed for the pass, we found navigation quite practicable. As we drew close to the jutting peaks the wind's strange piping again became manifest, and I could see Danforth's hands trembling at the controls. Rank amateur that I was, I thought at that moment that I might be a better navigator than he in effecting the dangerous crossing between pinnacles; and when I made motions to change seats and take over his duties he did not protest. I tried to keep all my skill and self-possession about me, and stared at the sector of reddish farther sky betwixt the walls of the pass – resolutely refusing to pay attention to the puffs of mountain-top vapor, and wishing that I had wax-stopped ears like Ulysses' men off the Siren's coast to keep that disturbing windpiping from my consciousness.

But Danforth, released from his piloting and keyed up to a dangerous nervous pitch, could not keep quiet. I felt him turning and wriggling about as he looked back at the terrible receding city, ahead at the cave-riddled, cube-barnacled peaks, sidewise at the bleak sea of snowy, rampart-strewn foothills, and upward at the seething, grotesquely clouded sky. It was then, just as I was trying to steer safely through the pass, that his mad shrieking brought us so close to disaster by shattering my tight hold on myself and causing me to fumble helplessly with the controls for a moment. A second afterward my resolution triumphed and we made the crossing safely – yet I am afraid that Danforth will never be the same again.

I have said that Danforth refused to tell me what final horror made him scream out so insanely – a horror which, I feel sadly sure, is mainly responsible for his present breakdown. We had snatches of shouted conversation above the wind's piping and the engine's buzzing as we reached the safe side of the range and swooped slowly down toward the camp, but that had mostly to do with the pledges of secrecy we had made as we prepared to leave the nightmare city. Certain things, we had agreed, were not for people to know and discuss lightly – and I would not speak of them now but for the need of heading off that Starkweather-Moore Expedition, and others, at any cost. It is absolutely necessary, for the peace and safety of mankind, that some of earth's dark, dead corners and unplumbed depths be let alone; lest sleeping abnormalities wake to resurgent life, and blasphemously surviving nightmares squirm and splash out of their black lairs to newer and wider conquests.

All that Danforth has ever hinted is that the final horror was a mirage. It was not, he declares, anything connected with the cubes and caves of those echoing, vaporous, wormily-honeycombed mountains of madness which we crossed; but a single fantastic, demoniac glimpse, among the churning zenith clouds, of what lay back of those other violet westward mountains which the Old Ones had shunned and feared. It is very probable that the thing was a sheer delusion born of the previous stresses we had passed through, and of the actual though unrecognized mirage of the dead transmontane city experienced near Lake's camp the day before; but it was so real to Danforth that he suffers from it still.

He has on rare occasions whispered disjointed and irresponsible things about "The black pit," "the carven rim," "the protoShoggoths," "the windowless solids with five dimensions," "the nameless cylinder," "the elder Pharos," "Yog-Sothoth," "the primal white jelly," "the color out of space," "the wings," "the eyes in darkness," "the moon-ladder," "the original, the eternal, the undying," and other bizarre conceptions; but when he is fully himself he repudiates all this and attributes it to his curious and macabre reading of earlier years. Danforth, indeed, is known to be among the few who have ever dared go completely through that worm-riddled copy of the *Necronomicon* kept under lock and key in the college library.

The higher sky, as we crossed the range, was surely vaporous and disturbed enough; and although I did not see the zenith, I can well imagine that its swirls of ice dust may have taken strange forms. Imagination, knowing how vividly distant scenes can sometimes be reflected, refracted, and magnified by such layers of restless cloud, might easily have supplied the rest – and, of course, Danforth did not hint any of these specific horrors till after his memory had had a chance to draw on his bygone reading. He could never have seen so much in one instantaneous glance.

At the time, his shrieks were confined to the repetition of a single, mad word of all too obvious source: "Tekeli-li! Tekeli-li!"

In Ice Entombed

K.G. McAbee

"WHAT THE HELL is that?" I pointed at the whirling maelstrom ahead of us, peculiar colors chasing each other through the massed ice.

Kirsch shrugged. He wiped condensate off the poly-glass window of our borer and hissed as the cold penetrated his thick glove.

Damn, it was cold. You'd think, with the globe warming and the icecaps melting, cold would no longer be an issue. You'd be right, mostly, but so wrong in Antarctica.

"Backwash?" Kirsch flipped switches and regarded dials. "Nope, everything within parameters. Maybe some sort of visual anomaly?"

I leaned closer to the window and examined the mass of ice before us. It didn't look like a snow mirage, like none I've seen, anyway. And I've seen a lot of them since we started mining here at the bottom of the world.

But this job, now. This job had been different from the get-go.

"It's a lake under nearly a mile of ice," my boss had told me back at our base on Heard Island. "And somebody with a lot of money wants a big hole in the ice sheath to get to the water." He handed me the work order and I whistled when I read it.

"Yeah," Johnson agreed. "He wants it bad. Seems that water beneath the ice hasn't been exposed since one of those prehistoric times, Jurassic or Triassic or some other -ic. So go bore us a hole and let's see why the water under it is so valuable."

"Any non-contamination procedures I need to be aware of?" I looked out the window in his office so I wouldn't have to see the smirk on his face. I knew his attitude towards rules and procedures: things to bypass when possible or buy out of when necessary.

"Just go and do your job," he said. "Take whatever crew you like."

"Triple time?"

This time he didn't limit it to a smirk but threw his bearded head back. A deep laugh erupted from his belly. "Hell, that's just to start. Remember, though. Your job is to get close then call me. A rep from the corporation wants to be there when the water is exposed."

"This corporation have a name?" I asked.

"I'm sure it does. Don't they all?"

Okay, then, as suspected. We were on our own. So we'd trekked all our equipment in, some by heli-transport, some by snow cats, and set up on the shores of Lake Vostok, deep in the Antarctic interior.

Now, three months later, Kirsch, Meehan and I were in a borer, which is basically a big-ass drill with seats inside. And we were damn close to the end of the ice sheath over the lake and the beginning of that ancient fresh water. That mysteriously valuable ancient water.

"How long ago is the Triassic?" Meehan asked as he looked out his own window. The maelstrom or whirlpool or, hell, visual anomaly, was getting closer.

"Sixty-five or seventy million years, give or take," I said. Yes, I'd read up on it.

"Long damn time," he said and went back to making notes on his pad. That's Meehan. It takes a lot to get his attention, unlike Kirsch, who's the excitable one.

The borer shuddered and moaned as it cut through the ice. Behind us, way behind, a long trail of chunks and slivers of glacier slush spewed out the top of the hole we were cutting. Not that we could see any of the debris; visibility was limited to the front and two side viewports. The borer jerked and hummed and gave an occasional irritated cough as it cut steadily downward at a 45 degree angle. I ran the calculations over in my head one more time – okay, I tell a lie. I'd been running the calculations over and over for days, in my head, on napkins, on the wall of my cubicle. It's what I do. I want my crew safe and myself safer. Sure, we were all in it for the money, but you can't spend your paycheck if you're dead, and it's no fun if you're shut up in the hospital with bits falling off you from frostbite.

I tapped the comm button behind my right ear. "Yamato, what do things look like from your end?" I don't like comm systems that use bone conduction; what's wrong with the old ways? But they don't work well when you're close to a mile down in solid ice.

Yamato's voice came back, setting my teeth on edge. Not Yamo's fault; she's got a great voice, calm and soothing. It's just the vibration.

"We've pumped out most of the detritus. Not much coming through now. You guys are too deep."

"Is our exit clear?" I asked. After all, I didn't want the hole we were cutting to freeze up behind us. I knew of at least three crews that had been lost that way, but never on my watch.

"Looks good. How close are you?"

I glanced at the readings. "About another twenty minutes to break-through."

"You know you're not supposed to break-through," Yamo reminded me.

Not that I needed the reminder. But ice miners like us are driven by, one, money, and two, curiosity, and not always in that order. Why did this nameless corporation want the old, old water below? I figured we could 'accidentally' miscalculate our rate of descent, snag a sample of water, then head up at right angles to our descent vector, as usual. Not that I'd mentioned this to Kirsch and Meehan, or Yamato either. It's called plausible deniability. I'm in charge, so all the fault would be mine.

"Later, Yamo," I said as I tapped the comm behind my ear. "Kirsch, how much further to approximate break-through?"

Kirsch did his gauge-tapping thing, but before he could speak, a new kind of shudder went through the borer, one I'd never felt before in all my drills.

Then it got weird.

Way weird.

The borer surged forward like it had broken through too soon, way too soon, and into, not water, but air. And we fell. For a long, long time.

Well, maybe not that long. But it sure as hell seemed like a long time before the borer stopped. Hit, really. We were lucky. I'm a stickler for seatbelts in the borer. That saved us.

"What the purple hell was that?" Kirsch coughed, slapped switches to turn off the borer, then bent over and puked up last night's beer and this morning's breakfast. And since Kirsch is a full-English-breakfast man, it wasn't pretty. Behind me, I could hear

Meehan breathing, but it sounded odd, a strangled kind of gasp. I struggled out of my belt and tried to reach him, but he was above me – the borer had landed butt upward. Then, with a swoop that threatened to empty my stomach, something slammed into the outside and the borer toppled in the other direction. I vaulted over Meehan's head to land in the back amongst the supplies. They'd all been strapped in too; thankfully, pretty much everything held.

Then another slam outside and we rolled. I grabbed a strap and held on. After what seemed like years but was probably seconds, the borer stopped, rocked a little, then was still.

"You okay, chief?" I heard Kirsch call. I took a deep breath, shoved a box of rations off my chest and grabbed another strap to lift myself up.

Meehan still hadn't said anything. I struggled – we were still at an angle, but not as acute as before – back to his seat. Unconscious, but his color looked okay and, when I lifted an eyelid, his pupil reacted. So no concussion. I hoped.

"Where are we?" I asked "Underwater? Were those waves knocking us around?"

"Nope," Kirsch was wiping the inside of his viewport.

"But we have to be," I insisted. "We're through the ice, and there's nothing but water below the ice."

"Guess we were misinformed."

Well, we could argue about it, but an ounce of fact is worth a ton of discussion. I leaned over my seat to my own port. It was impossible to see out so I reached to wipe the condensate away. I drew back my hand with a hiss of surprise.

"Hot? Mine too." Kirsch was wiping his port with his sleeve.

"It can't be hot."

But it was. Warm, anyway, very warm. I used my own sleeve to wipe away the moisture and peered out.

Then I shook my head and wiped my eyes.

Nope. Still there.

"Either I'm crazy, I'm dreaming, or we're not in Kansas anymore," I whispered.

"I'm voting for all of the above," Kirsch said in a matching whisper.

Outside the viewport was an impossibility. Instead of water, that clean pure prehistoric water we were after, I saw land. And not the rocky bare landscape of Antarctica that surrounded us in all directions a mile above our heads, but land with green, lush trees and greener, lusher ferns and plants with huge yellow and white blooms breaking up the incessant, constant green...

"Yes, I'm crazy. Or I hit my head," I said as I turned away from the port and blinked, hard.

"Are you seeing lots of green?" Kirsch asked.

"Yep."

"Then we both hit our head and we're both sharing the same illusion. Which, I'm guessing, is a scientific impossibility."

A groan from Meehan punctuated his remark. Good, my other crewmember was awake. I went to help him out of his belts; he looked as groggy as I felt.

"Wha...who...where...?" he mumbled.

"Where. That is the question of the hour...or the century." I turned back to the viewport, shook my head again, then said, "Report, Kirsch. Systems, exterior, everything."

Kirsch checked his dials and gauges and readouts. "The borer seems okay, far as I can tell. Outside...well, outside ought to be colder'n ice at this depth, water under pressure, but the temp readings," he tapped a dial and shook his head, "say it's nearly thirty-five °C out there. And we're not underwater."

"Almost body temp? In the Antarctic? That can't be right…" I shut up when I recalled how hot the viewport was.

Meehan was leaning against his viewport. He mumbled, "What's that big green thing?"

"Tree," I said, not bothering to look. Not wanting to look.

"Tree…with legs?"

I dived for his seat and, I admit, sat right in his lap while I looked outside. My aim may have been wonky, considering his gasp of protest.

"Guys, I still think we might all be crazy or dreaming, but…does that look like a dinosaur to you?"

Damn it, it did look like a dinosaur. I'm not an expert, mind you, but we do run across a lot of fossils in our line of work, so I had read up on them. Not a very big one, maybe the size of a cow, but covered in scales and spiky in places you wouldn't expect. So, dinosaur. I couldn't put a name to it – why do archaeologists love Latin polysyllabics? – but it sure ticked all the boxes.

And it was staring at us. And it had friends. Or possibly family. And they were all pawing at the lush green ground, and one started a lumbering charge at us. It disappeared from the viewport and, a second later, a shudder went through the borer.

"Chief, what the hell?" Kirsch had scrambled back to Meehan's seat.

"I think the local boys don't much like us being here. We need to be gone," I said. "And quick."

Kirsch climbed back into his seat. I followed and buckled in as I flipped switches and he hit buttons. A whine, an irritated-sounding growl.

No, not the dinosaur; the borer.

"Something's wrong," Kirsch said.

I looked at him. "Ya think?"

"Sure," he spread his hands, "shoot the messenger. But I think we've got some sort of exterior issue."

"Exterior issue?" I shook my head. "Of course we do." I unbuckled my seatbelt.

"What? You can't go out there! There's a, well, pissed bunch of lizards out there and we don't know what else."

"Guess I'm going to find out." I shrugged out of my thermal jacket, only just then realizing how hot it was inside the borer. "You're the pilot, Meehan is injured, and I'm chief of this expedition. Open the hatch, but be ready to close it fast behind me. And open it even faster when I need back in, okay?"

Kirsch opened his mouth to protest, but closed it at once. I mean, what other choice did we have? I stumbled back to the supplies, grabbed a crowbar we keep strapped to the wall, and stood in front of the hatch. I nodded at Kirsch and he hit a switch.

The hatch hesitated just long enough for an 'oh shit' to start from my brain to my mouth, but not long enough to complete the journey. It cracked open and the richest, purest air swooshed in, slamming into my face.

"Whoa," I heard Kirsch say, and Meehan took a deep breath behind me. If we could bottle that stuff, we'd all be able to retire.

Then the hatch opened, the steps ratcheted out and I stood at the top, surveying. And breathing. Sucking in this air, rich in oxygen and who knew what else; it was almost stupefying. I shook my head and tried to concentrate. The dinosaur herd were cropping undergrowth and keeping wary eyes on us except for one, who was shaking his head and looking pissed. I stifled thoughts of T-Rex and stepped onto the springy ground. Trying to keep one eye on my surroundings and one looking for damage – yep, it's as hard as it sounds – I walked around the borer and almost fell into a lake. Okay, here was the water we were looking for; I took a minute to scoop us a sample in the vial I had in my pocket, then continued around the borer. I saw the problem when I reached the tail. A cluster of rocks was jamming the blades. I cleared them away and tapped my comm.

"Kirsch? Do you read?"

"Got you, chief. Find anything?"

I backed away from the borer and said, "Try her again." The blades seemed free now so I headed for the hatch and climbed the steps. Now that I wasn't so worried about being eaten, I looked up to see what we'd come through.

If I'd thought the landscape was amazing, the sky overhead was even more so. I say sky for want of a better word. It appeared to be a swirling silver dome with fragments of color that melded and blended and swirled incessantly. And yes, I hear you thinking, is this the first time you wondered where the light was coming from? Yes, it was, but in my defense, I had had a few other things on my mind. The dome radiated a warm, constant light – no wonder the growth was so lush – and I noticed that I didn't cast a shadow. Weird.

Directly above us, there was a disturbance in the dome, a darkish spot threaded through with tendrils of silver and blue, almost like the dome was repairing itself. I looked back down and around, trying to imprint everything in my mind's eye. I wanted to explore. I wanted to examine. I wanted to know this place so much I ached with it.

But Kirsch and Meehan were depending on me. I had to get them back home.

Question was, how?

"Chief, where to?" Kirsch said behind me.

"Have you looked above us?"

He nodded. "I've been standing here staring while I waited for you. That spot up there is probably where we broke through. But how the hell can we get back?"

I patted the borer. "Well, this baby can't fly, but it can swim. I guess our only option is to dive into that lake and see where it takes us. With any luck, we can strike the edge of the dome where it hits ice and find a way out."

Meehan was standing behind him. "You don't believe that, do you?"

"Nope. But what else can we do?"

He scratched his head. "Looks kind of…nice here. Clean. Not like the rest of the world. It'd be a shame to have something bad happen to it. Some developer putting up condos."

I shrugged. "Yes, it would. But that's what we do, right?"

The big dinosaurs had decided we weren't worth bothering with and were wandering off. I watched them until they disappeared into the undergrowth.

Kirsch cranked up the engines and the borer trundled like a fat duck across the thick turf. Finally, after a few heart-in-mouth moments where it looked as if we might get stuck, we slid into water.

A collective sigh of relief echoed through the cabin.

Kirsch looked at me.

"Direction, chief?"

"Hell, I don't know. Ideas?"

"I've got one," Meehan said.

"Got for it."

He tapped his viewport, where dark water caressed the plastic. "Down."

I looked at the goofy grin on a face I'd never seen even crack a smile. "Down?"

"Sure. You know the rules as well as I do. We don't come back, the contract's cancelled. We don't come back, support packs up and leaves. We don't come back, no one drills in this area again for the foreseeable future."

"We don't come back, we die," Kirsch murmured.

"Well, yeah, there is that," Meehan admitted. He took a deep breath. The borer was still full of that amazing, oxygen-rich air.

Of course. "You're, I don't know, air-drunk or whatever," I said. "Something was in that place's atmosphere. It's got us all addled or hallucinating. That's it; maybe we all just thought we saw what we saw back there."

I was babbling, trying to change his mind – trying to change my mind, maybe, since I was starting to think he was right. And he was, about one thing at least: every contract had a death-clause. If the borer team died, the contract was null and no one could jump-start it for decades. Decades doesn't seem long when I'd been thinking in millions of years, but decades might be long enough for humans to get off this poor old planet and give it a chance to revive. The Mars missions were going strong. Moon Base Heinlein was growing bigger and becoming more self-supporting every day. The Europa Mission. The three generation ships heading to different exoplanets, gone for nearly twenty years.

Why open up this final, maybe this last pocket of beauty on damaged old Terra to the depredations of humankind? Especially when we've sent out our seed to other planets?

Kirsch said, "It's a tough call, chief."

I looked at him. I looked at Meehan. I shrugged.

"Tough calls are our specialty."

The borer slid through the warm waters of Lake Vostok like some kind of ancient, extinct beast, its thrumming engines sending out ripples behind us...ripples in time...

Aren't we all just ripples in time?

The Face in the Abyss

Chapters I–V

A. Merritt

Chapter I
Suarra

NICHOLAS GRAYDON ran into Starrett in Quito. Rather, Starrett sought him out there. Graydon had often heard of the big West Coast adventurer, but their trails had never crossed. It was with lively curiosity that he opened his door to his visitor.

Starrett came to the point at once. Graydon had heard the legend of the treasure train bringing to Pizarro the ransom of the Inca Atahualpa? And that its leaders, learning of the murder of their monarch by the butcher-boy Conquistador, had turned aside and hidden the treasure somewhere in the Andean wilderness?

Graydon had heard it, hundreds of times; had even considered hunting for it. He said so. Starrett nodded.

"I know where it is," he said.

Graydon laughed.

In the end Starrett convinced him; convinced him, at least, that he had something worth looking into.

Graydon rather liked the big man. There was a bluff directness that made him overlook the hint of cruelty in eyes and jaw. There were two others with him, Starrett said, both old companions. Graydon asked why they had picked him out. Starrett bluntly told him – because they knew he could afford to pay the expenses of the expedition. They would all share equally in the treasure. If they didn't find it, Graydon was a first-class mining engineer, and the region they were going into was rich in minerals. He was practically sure of making some valuable discovery on which they could cash in.

Graydon considered. There were no calls upon him. He had just passed his thirty-fourth birthday, and since he had been graduated from the Harvard School of Mines eleven years ago he had never had a real holiday. He could well afford the cost. There would be some excitement, if nothing else.

After he had looked over Starrett's two comrades – Soames, a lanky, saturnine, hard-bitten Yankee, and Dancret, a cynical, amusing little Frenchman – they had drawn up an agreement and he had signed it.

They went down by rail to Cerro de Pasco for their outfit, that being the town of any size closest to where their trek into the wilderness would begin. A week later with eight burros and six arrieros, or packmen, they were within the welter of peaks through which, Starrett's map indicated, lay their road.

It had been the map which had persuaded Graydon. It was no parchment, but a sheet of thin gold quite as flexible. Starrett drew it out of a small golden tube of ancient workmanship, and unrolled it. Graydon examined it and was unable to see any map upon it – or anything else. Starrett held it at a peculiar angle – and the markings upon it became plain.

It was a beautiful piece of cartography. It was, in fact, less a map than a picture. Here and there were curious symbols which Starrett said were signs cut upon the rocks along the way; guiding marks for those of the old race who would set forth to recover the treasure when the Spaniards had been swept from the land.

Whether it was clue to Atahualpa's ransom hoard or to something else – Graydon did not know. Starrett said it was. But Graydon did not believe his story of how the golden sheet had come into his possession. Nevertheless, there had been purpose in the making of the map, and stranger purpose in the cunning with which the markings had been concealed. Something interesting lay at the end of that trail.

They found the signs cut in the rocks exactly as the sheet of gold had indicated. Gay, spirits high with anticipation, three of them spending in advance their share of the booty, they followed the symbols. Steadily they were led into the uncharted wilderness.

At last the arrieros began to murmur. They were approaching, they said, a region that was accursed, the Cordillera de Carabaya, where only demons dwelt Promises of more money, threats, pleadings, took them along a little further. One morning the four awakened to find the arrieros gone, and with them half the burros and the major portion of their supplies.

They pressed on. Then the signs failed them. Either they had lost the trail, or the map which had led them truthfully so far had lied at the last.

The country into which they had penetrated was a curiously lonely one. There had been no sign of Indians since more than a fortnight before, when they had stopped at a Quicha village and Starrett had gotten mad drunk on the fiery spirit the Quichas distill. Food was hard to find. There were few animals and fewer birds.

Worst of all was the change which had come over Graydon's companions. As high as they had been lifted by their certitude of success, just so deep were they in depression. Starrett kept himself at a steady level of drunkenness, alternately quarrelsome and noisy, or brooding in sullen rage.

Dancret was silent and irritable. Soames seemed to have come to the conclusion that Starrett, Graydon and Dancret had combined against him; that they had either deliberately missed the trail or had erased the signs. Only when the pair of them joined Starrett and drank with him the Quicha brew with which they had laden one of the burros did the three relax. At such times Graydon had the uneasy feeling that all were holding the failure against him, and that his life might be hanging on a thin thread.

The day that Graydon's great adventure really began, he was on his way back to the camp. He had been hunting since morning. Dancret and Soames had gone off together on another desperate search for the missing marks.

Cut off in mid-flight, the girl's cry came to him as the answer to all his apprehensions; materialization of the menace toward which his vague fears had been groping since he had left Starrett alone at the camp, hours ago. He had sensed some culminating misfortune close – and here it was! He broke into a run, stumbling up the slope to the group of gray-green algarrobas, where the tent was pitched.

He crashed through the thick undergrowth to the clearing.

Why didn't the girl cry out again, he wondered. A chuckle reached him, thick, satyr-toned.

Half crouching, Starrett was holding the girl bow fashion over one knee. A thick arm was clenched about her neck, the fingers clutching her mouth brutally, silencing her; his right hand fettered her wrists; her knees were caught in the vise of his bent right leg.

Graydon caught him by the hair, and locked his arm under his chin. He drew his head sharply back.

"Drop her!" he ordered.

Half paralyzed, Starrett relaxed – he writhed, then twisted to his feet.

"What the hell are you butting in for?"

His hand struck down toward his pistol. Graydon's fist caught him on the point of the jaw. The half-drawn gun slipped to the ground and Starrett toppled over.

The girl leaped up, and away.

Graydon did not look after her. She had gone, no doubt, to bring down upon them her people, some tribe of the fierce Aymara whom even the Incas of old had never quite conquered. And who would avenge her in ways that Graydon did not like to visualize.

He bent over Starrett. Between the blow and the drink he would probably be out for some time. Graydon picked up the pistol. He wished that Dancret and Soames would get back soon to camp. The three of them could put up a good fight at any rate...might even have a chance to escape...but they would have to get back quickly...the girl would soon return with her avengers...was probably at that moment telling them of her wrongs. He turned –

She stood there, looking at him.

Drinking in her loveliness, Graydon forgot the man at his feet – forgot all else.

Her skin was palest ivory. It gleamed through the rents of the soft amber fabric, like thickest silk, which swathed her. Her eyes were oval, a little tilted, Egyptian in the wide midnight of her pupils. Her nose was small and straight; her brows level and black, almost meeting. Her hair was cloudy, jet, misty and shadowed. A narrow fillet of gold bound her low broad forehead. In it was entwined a sable and silver feather of the caraquenque – that bird whose plumage in lost centuries was sacred to the princesses of the Incas alone.

Above her elbows were golden bracelets, reaching almost to the slender shoulders. Her little high-arched feet were shod with high buskins of deerskin. She was lithe and slender as the Willow Maid who waits on Kwannon when she passes through the World of Trees pouring into them new fire of green life.

She was no Indian...nor daughter of ancient Incas...nor was she Spanish...she was of no race that he knew. There were bruises on her cheeks – the marks of Starrett's fingers. Her long, slim hands touched them. She spoke – in the Aymara tongue.

"Is he dead?"

"No," Graydon answered.

In the depths of her eyes a small, hot flame flared; he could have sworn it was of gladness.

"That is well! I would not have him die –" her voice became meditative – "at least – not this way."

Starrett groaned. The girl again touched the bruises on her cheek.

"He is very strong," she murmured.

Graydon thought there was admiration in her whisper; wondered whether all her beaut was, after all, only a mask for primitive woman worshiping brute strength. "Who are you? he asked.

She looked at him for a long, long moment.

"I am – Suarra," she answered, at last.

"But where do you come from? What are you?" he asked again. She did not choose to answer these questions.

"Is he your enemy?"

"No," he said. "We travel together."

"Then why –" she pointed again to the outstretched figure – "why did you do this to him? Why did you not let him have his way with me?"

Graydon flushed. The question, with all its subtle implications, cut.

"What do you think I am?" he answered, hotly. "No man lets a thing like that go on!"

She looked at him, curiously. Her face softened. She took a step closer to him. She touched once more the bruises on her cheek.

"Do you not wonder," she said, "now do you not wonder why I do not call my people to deal him the punishment he has earned?"

"I do wonder," Graydon's perplexity was frank. "I wonder indeed. Why do you not call them – if they are close enough to hear?"

"And what would you do were they to come?"

"I would not let them have him – alive," he answered. "Nor me."

"Perhaps," she said, slowly – "perhaps that is why I do not call."

Suddenly she smiled upon him. He took a swift step toward her. She thrust out a warning hand. "I am – Suarra," she said. "And I am – Death!" A chill passed through Graydon. Again he realized the alien beauty of her. Could there be truth in these legends of the haunted Cordillera? He had never doubted that there was something real behind the terror of the Indians, the desertion of the arrieros. Was she one of its spirits, one of its – demons? For an instant the fantasy seemed no fantasy. Then reason returned. This girl a demon! He laughed.

"Do not laugh," she said. "The death I mean is not such as you who live beyond the high rim of our hidden land know. Your body may live on – yet it is death and more than death, since it is changed in – dreadful – ways. And that which tenants your body, that which speaks through your lips, is changed – in ways more dreadful still!...I would not have that death come to you."

Strange as were her words, Graydon hardly heard them: certainly did not then realize their meaning, lost as he was in wonder at her beauty.

"How you came by the Messengers, I do not know. How you could have passed unseen by them, I cannot understand. Nor how you came so far into this forbidden land. Tell me – why came you here at all?"

"We came from afar," he told her, "on the track of a great treasure of gold and gems; the treasure of Atahualpa, the Inca. There were certain signs that led us. We lost them. We found that we, too, were lost. And we wandered here."

"Of Atahualpa or of Incas," the girl said, "I know nothing. Whoever they were, they could not have come to this place. And their treasure, no matter how great, would have meant nothing to us – to us of Yu-Atlanchi, where treasures are as rocks in the bed of a stream. A grain of sand it would have been, among many –" she paused, then went on, perplexedly, as though voicing her thoughts to herself – "But it is why the Messengers did not see them that I cannot understand ...the Mother must know of this...I must go quickly to the Mother..."

"The Mother?" asked Graydon.

"The Snake Mother!" her gaze returned to him; she touched a bracelet on her right wrist. Graydon, drawing close, saw that this bracelet held a disk on which was carved in bas-relief a serpent with a woman's head and woman's breast and arms. It lay coiled upon what appeared to be a great bowl held high on the paws of four beasts. The shapes of these creatures did not at once register upon his consciousness, so absorbed was he in his study of that coiled figure. He stared close – and closer. And now he realized that the head reared upon the coils was not really that of a woman. No! It was reptilian.

Snake-like – yet so strongly had the artist feminized it, so great was the suggestion of womanhood modeled into every line of it, that constantly one saw it as woman, forgetting all that was of the serpent.

The eyes were of some intensely glittering purple stone. Graydon felt that those eyes were alive – that far, far away some living thing was looking at him through them. That they were, in fact, prolongations of some one's – some thing's – vision.

The girl touched one of the beasts that held up the bowl. "The Xinli," she said. Graydon's bewilderment increased. He knew what those animals were. Knowing, he also knew that he looked upon the incredible.

They were dinosaurs! The monstrous saurians that ruled earth millions upon millions of years ago, and, but for whose extinction, so he had been taught, man could never have developed.

Who in this Andean wilderness could know or could have known the dinosaurs? Who here could have carved the monsters with such life-like detail as these possessed? Why, it was only yesterday that science had learned what really were their huge bones, buried so long that the rocks had molded themselves around them in adamantine matrix. And laboriously, with every modern resource, haltingly and laboriously, science had set those bones together as a perplexed child would a picture puzzle, and put forth what it believed to be reconstructions of these long-vanished chimera of earth's nightmare youth.

Yet here, far from all science it must surely be, some; one had modeled those same monsters for a woman's; bracelet. Why then – it followed that whoever had done this must have had before him the living forms from which; to work. Or, if not, had copies of those forms set down by ancient men who had seen them. And either or both these things were incredible, Who were the people to whom she belonged? There had been a name – Yu-Atlanchi.

"Suarra," he said, "where is Yu-Atlanchi? Is it this place?"

"This?" She laughed. "No! Yu-Atlanchi is the Ancient Land. The Hidden Land where the six Lords and the Lords of Lords once ruled. And where now rules only the Snake Mother and – another. This place Yu-Atlanchi!" Again she laughed. "Now and then I hunt here with – the –" she hesitated, looking at him oddly – "So it was that he who lies there caught me. I was hunting. I had slipped away from my followers, for sometimes it pleases me to hunt alone. I came through these trees and saw your tetuane, your lodge. I came face to face with – him. And I was amazed – too amazed to strike with one of these." She pointed to a low knoll a few feet away. "Before I could conquer that amaze he had caught me. Then you came."

Graydon looked where she had pointed. Upon the ground lay three slender, shining spears. Their slim shafts were of gold; the arrow-shaped heads of two of them were of fine opal. The third – the third was a single emerald, translucent and flawless, all of six inches long and three at its widest, ground to keenest point and cutting edge.

There it lay, a priceless jewel tipping a spear of gold – and a swift panic shook Graydon. He had forgotten Soames and Dancret. Suppose they should return while this girl was there. This girl with her ornaments of gold, her gem-tipped spears – and her beauty!

"Suarra," he said, "you must go, and go quickly. This man and I are not all. There are two more, and even now they may be close. Take your spears, and go quickly. Else I may not be able to save you."

"You think I am –"

"I tell you to go," he interrupted. "Whoever you are, whatever you are, go now and keep away from this place. Tomorrow I will try to lead them away. If you have people to fight for you – well, let them come and fight if you so desire. But take your spears and go."

She crossed to the little knoll and picked up the spears. She held one out to him, the one that bore the emerald point.

"This," she said, "to remember – Suarra."

"No," he thrust it back. "Go!"

If the others saw that jewel, never, he knew, would he be able to start them on the back trail – if they could find it. Starrett had seen it, of course, but he might be able to convince them that Starrett's story was only a drunken dream.

The girl studied him – a quickened interest in her eyes.

She slipped the bracelets from her arms, held them out to him with the three spears.

"Will you take these – and leave your comrades?" she asked. "Here are gold and gems. They are treasure. They are what you have been seeking. Take them. Take them and go, leaving that man here. Consent – and I will show you a way out of this forbidden land."

Graydon hesitated. The emerald alone was worth a fortune. What loyalty did he owe the three, after all? And Starrett had brought this thing upon himself. Nevertheless – they were his comrades. Open-eyed he had gone into this venture with them. He had a vision of himself skulking away with the glittering booty, creeping off to safety while he left the three unwarned, unprepared, to meet – what?

He did not like that picture.

"No," he said. "These men are of my race, my comrades. Whatever is to come – I will meet it with them and help them fight it."

"Yet you would have fought them for my sake – indeed, did fight," she said. "Why then do you cling to them when you can save yourself, and go free, with treasure? And why, if you will not do this, do you let me go, knowing that if you kept me prisoner, or – killed me, I could not bring my people down upon you?"

Graydon laughed.

"I couldn't let them hurt you, of course," he said. "And I'm afraid to make you prisoner, because I might not be able to keep you free from hurt. And I won't run away. So talk no more, but go – go!"

She thrust the gleaming spears into the ground, slipped the golden bracelets back on her arms, held white hands out to him.

"Now," she whispered, "now, by the Wisdom of the Mother, I will save you – if I can."

There was the sound of a horn, far away and high in air it seemed. It was answered by others closer by; mellow, questing notes – with weirdly alien beat in them.

"They come," the girl said. "My followers. Light your fire tonight. Sleep without fear. But do not wander beyond these trees."

"Suarra –" he began.

"Quiet now," she warned. "Quiet – until I am gone."

The mellow horns sounded closer. She sprang from his side and darted away through the trees. From the ridge above the camp he heard her voice raised in one clear shout There was a tumult of the horns about her – elfin and troubling. Then silence.

Graydon stood listening. The sun touched the high snowfields of the majestic peaks toward which he faced, touched them and turned them into robes of molten gold. The amethyst shadows that draped their sides thickened, wavered and marched swiftly forward.

Still he listened, hardly breathing.

Far, far away the horns sounded again; faint echoings of the tumult that had swept about the girl – faint, faint and fairy sweet.

The sun dropped behind the peaks; the edges of their frozen mantels glittered as though sewn with diamonds; darkened into a fringe of gleaming rubies. The golden fields dulled, grew amber and then blushed forth a glowing rose. They changed to pearl and faded into a ghostly silver, shining like cloud wraiths in the highest heavens. Down upon the algarroba clump the quick Andean dusk fell.

Not till then did Graydon, shivering with sudden, inexplicable dread, realize that beyond the calling horns and the girl's clear shouting he had heard no other sound – no noise either of man or beast, no sweeping through of brush or grass, no fall of running feet.

Nothing but that mellow chorus of the horns.

Chapter II
The Unseen Watchers

STARRETT had drifted out of the paralysis of the blow into a drunken stupor. Graydon dragged him over to the tent, thrust a knapsack under his head, and threw a blanket over him. Then he went out and built up the fire. There was a trampling through the underbrush. Soames and Dancret came up through the trees.

"Find any signs?" he asked.

"Signs? Hell – no!" snarled the New Englander. "Say, Graydon, did you hear somethin' like a lot of horns? Damned queer horns, too. They seemed to be over here."

Graydon nodded, he realized that he must tell these men what had happened so that they could prepare some defense. But how much could he tell?

Tell them of Suarra's beauty, of her golden ornaments and her gem-tipped spears of gold? Tell them what she had said of Atahualpa's treasure?

If he did, there would be no further reasoning with them. They would go berserk with greed. Yet something of it he must tell them if they were to be ready for the attack which he was certain would come with the dawn.

And of the girl they would learn soon enough from Starrett.

He heard an exclamation from Dancret who had passed on into the tent; heard him come out; stood up and faced the wiry little Frenchman.

"What's the matter wit' Starrett, eh?" Dancret snapped. "First I t'ought he's drunk. Then I see he's scratched like wildcat and wit' a lump on his jaw as big as one orange. What you do to Starrett, eh?"

Graydon had made up his mind, and was ready to answer.

"Dancret," he said, "Soames – we're in a bad box. I came in from hunting less than an hour ago, and found Starrett wrestling with a girl. That's bad medicine down here – the worst, and you two know it. I had to knock Starrett out before I could get the girl away from him. Her people will probably be after us in the morning. There's no use trying to get away. We don't know a thing about this wilderness. Here is as good as any other place to meet them. We'd better spend the night getting it ready so we can put up a good scrap, if we have to."

"A girl, eh?" said Dancret. "What she look like? Where she come from? How she get away?"

Graydon chose the last question to answer.

"I let her go," he said.

"You let her go!" snarled Soames. "What the hell did you do that for? Why didn't you tie her up? We could have held her as a hostage, Graydon – had somethin' to do some tradin' with when her damned bunch of Indians came."

"She wasn't an Indian, Soames," said Graydon, then hesitated.

"You mean she was white – Spanish?" broke in Dancret, incredulously.

"No, not Spanish either. She was white. Yes, white as any of us. I don't know what she was."

The pair stared at him, then at each other.

"There's somethin' damned funny about this," growled Soames, at last "But what I want to know is why you let her go – whatever the hell she was?"

"Because I thought we'd have a better chance if I did than if I didn't." Graydon's own wrath was rising. "I tell you that we're up against something none of us knows anything about. And we've got just one chance of getting out of the mess. If I'd kept her there, we wouldn't have even that chance."

Dancret stooped, and picked up something from the ground, something that gleamed yellow in the firelight.

"Somet'ing funny is right, Soames," he said. "Look at this!"

He handed the gleaming object over. It was a golden bracelet, and as Soames turned it over in his hand there was the green glitter of emeralds. It had been torn from Suarra's arm, undoubtedly, in her struggle with Starrett.

"What that girl give you to let her go, Graydon, eh?" Dancret spat. "What she tell you, eh?"

Soames's hand dropped to his automatic.

"She gave me nothing. I took nothing," answered Graydon.

"I t'ink you damned liar," said Dancret, viciously. "We get Starrett awake," he turned to Soames. "We get him awake quick. I t'ink he tell us more about this, oui. A girl who wears stuff like this – and he lets her go! Lets her go when he knows there must be more where this come from – eh, Soames! Damned funny is right, eh? Come now, we see what Starrett tell us."

Graydon watched them go into the tent. Soon Soames came out, went to a spring that bubbled up from among the trees; returned, with water.

Well, let them waken Starrett; let him tell them whatever he would. They would not kill him that night, of that he was sure. They believed that he knew too much. And in the morning –

What was hidden in the morning for them all?

That even now they were prisoners, Graydon was sure. Suarra's warning not to leave the camp had been explicit Since that tumult of the elfin horns, her swift vanishing and the silence that had followed, he no longer doubted that they had strayed, as she had said, within the grasp of some power as formidable as it was mysterious.

The silence? Suddenly it came to him that the night had become strangely still. There was no sound either of insect or bird, nor any stirring of the familiar after-twilight life of the wilderness.

The camp was besieged by silence!

He walked away through the algarrobas. There was a scant score of the trees. They stood like a little leafy island peak within the brush-covered savanna. They were great trees, every one of them, and set with a curious regularity; as though they had not sprung up by chance; as though indeed they had been carefully planted.

Graydon reached the last of them, rested a hand against a bole that was like myriads of tiny grubs turned to soft brown wood. He peered out. The slope that lay before him was flooded with moonlight; the yellow blooms of the chiica shrubs that pressed to the very feet of the trees shone wanly in the silver flood. The faintly aromatic fragrance of the quenuar stole around him. Movement or sign of life there was none.

And yet –

The spaces seemed filled with watchers. He felt their gaze upon him. He knew that some hidden host girdled the camp. He scanned every bush and shadow – and saw nothing. The certainty of a hidden, unseen multitude persisted. A wave of nervous irritation passed through him. He would force them, whatever they were, to show themselves.

He stepped out boldly into the full moonlight.

On the instant the silence intensified. It seemed to draw taut, to lift itself up whole octaves of stillnesses. It became alert, expectant – as though poised to spring upon him should he take one step further.

A coldness wrapped him, and he shuddered. He drew swiftly back to the shadow of the trees; stood there, his heart beating furiously. The silence lost its poignancy, drooped back upon its haunches – watchful.

What had frightened him? What was there in that tightening of the stillness that had touched him with the finger of nightmare terror? He groped back, foot by foot, afraid to turn his face from the silence. Behind him the fire flared. His fear dropped from him.

His reaction from his panic was a heady recklessness. He threw a log upon the fire and laughed as the sparks shot up among the leaves. Soames, coming out of the tent for more water, stopped as he heard that laughter and scowled at him malevolently.

"Laugh," he said. "Laugh while you can. Maybe you'll laugh on the other side of your mouth when we get Starrett up and he tells us what he knows."

"That was a sound sleep I gave him, anyway," jeered Graydon.

"There are sounder sleeps. Don't forget it," Dancret's voice, cold and menacing came from the tent.

Graydon turned his back to the tent, and deliberately faced that silence from which he had just fled. He seated himself, and after a while he dozed.

He awakened with a jump. Halfway between him and the tent Starrett was charging on him like a madman, bellowing.

Graydon leaped to his feet, but before he could defend himself the giant was upon him. The next moment he was down, overborne by sheer weight. The big adventurer crunched a knee into his arm and gripped his throat.

"Let her go, did you!" he roared. "Knocked me out and then let her go! Here's where you go, too, damn you!"

Graydon tried to break the grip on his throat. His lungs labored; there was a deafening roaring in his ears, and flecks of crimson began to dance across his vision. Starrett was strangling him. Through fast dimming sight he saw two black shadows leap through the firelight and clutch the strangling hands.

The fingers relaxed. Graydon staggered up. A dozen paces away stood Starrett. Dancret, arms around his knees, was hanging to him like a little terrier. Beside him was Soames, the barrel of his automatic pressed against his stomach.

"Why don't you let me kill him!" raved Starrett. "Didn't I tell you the girl had enough green ice on her to set us up the rest of our lives? There's more where it came from! And he let her go! Let her go, the –"

Again his curses flowed.

"Now look here, Starrett," Soames's voice was deliberate. "You be quiet, or I'll do for you. We ain't goin' to let this thing get by us, me and Dancret. We ain't goin' to let this double-crossin' louse do us, and we ain't goin' to let you spill the beans by killin' him. We've struck somethin' big. All right, we're goin' to cash in on it. We're goin' to sit down peaceable, and Mister Graydon is goin' to tell us what happened after he put you out, what dicker he made with the girl and all of that. If he won't do it peaceable, then Mister Graydon is goin' to have things done to him that'll make him give up. That's all. Danc', let go his legs. Starrett, if you kick up any more trouble until I give the word I'm goin' to shoot you. From now on I boss this crowd – me and Danc'. You get me, Starrett?"

Graydon, head once more clear, slid a cautious hand down toward the pistol holster. It was empty. Soames grinned, sardonically.

"We got it, Graydon," he said. "Yours, too, Starrett. Fair enough. Sit down everybody."

He squatted by the fire, still keeping Starrett covered. And after a moment the latter, grumbling, followed suit. Dancret dropped beside him.

"Come over here, Graydon," said Soames. "Come over here and cough up. What're you holdin' out on us? Did you make a date with her to meet you after you got rid of us? If so, where is it – because we'll all go together."

"Where'd you hide those gold spears?" growled Starrett "You never let her get away with them, that's sure."

"Shut up, Starrett," ordered Soames. "I'm holdin' this inquest. Still – there's something in that. Was that it, Graydon? Did she give you the spears and her jewelry to let her go?"

"I've told you," answered Graydon. "I asked for nothing, and took nothing. Starrett's drunken folly had put us all in jeopardy. Letting the girl go free was the first vital step toward our own safety. I thought it was the best thing to do. I still think so."

"Yeah?" sneered the lank New Englander, "Is that so? Well, I'll tell you, Graydon, if she'd been an Indian maybe I'd agree with you. But not when she was the kind of lady Starrett says she was. No, sir, it ain't natural. You know damned well that if you'd been straight you'd have kept her here till Danc' and me got back. Then we could all have got together and figured what was the best thing to do. Hold her until her folks came along and paid up to get her back undamaged. Or give her the third degree until she gave up where all that gold and stuff she was carrying came from. That's what you would have done, Graydon – if you weren't a dirty, lyin', double-crossin' hound."

Graydon's anger flared up.

"All right, Soames," he said. "I'll tell you. What I've said about freeing her for our own safety is true. But outside of that I would as soon have thought of trusting a child to a bunch of hyenas as I would of trusting that girl to you three. I let her go a damned sight more for her sake than I did for our own. Does that satisfy you?"

"Aha!" jeered Dancret. "Now I see! Here is this strange lady of so much wealth and beauty. She is too pure and good for us to behold. He tell her so and bid her fly. 'My hero!' she say, 'take all I have and give up this bad company.' 'No, no,' he tell her, t'inking all the time if he play his cards right he get much more, and us out of the way so he need not divide, 'no, no,' he tell her. 'But long as these bad men stay here you will not be safe.' 'My hero,' she say. 'I will go and bring back my family and they shall dispose of your bad company. But you they shall reward, my hero, oui!' Aha, so that is what it was!"

Graydon flushed; the little Frenchman's malicious travesty had shot uncomfortably close. After all, Suarra's unasked promise to save him could be construed as Dancret had suggested. Suppose he told them he had warned her that whatever the fate in store for them he was determined to share it, and would stand by them to the last? They would not believe him.

Soames had been watching him, closely.

"By God, Danc'," he said, "I guess you hit it. He changed color. He's sold us out."

He raised his automatic, held it on Graydon – then lowered it.

"No," he said, deliberately. "This is too big a thing to let slip by bein' too quick on the trigger. If your dope is right, Danc', and I guess it is, the lady was mighty grateful. All right – we ain't got her, but we have got him. As I figure it, bein' grateful, she won't want him to get killed. She'll be back. Well, we'll trade him for what they got that we want. Tie him up."

He pointed the pistol at Graydon. Unresisting, Graydon let Starrett and Dancret bind his wrists. They pushed him over to one of the trees and sat him on the ground with his back against its bole. They passed a rope under his arms and hitched it securely around the trunk; they tied his feet.

"Now," said Soames, "if her gang show up in the morning, well let 'em see you, and find out how much you're worth. They won't rush us. There's bound to be a palaver. And if they don't come to terms – well, Graydon, the first bullet out of this gun goes through your guts. That'll give you time to see what we do to her before you die."

Graydon did not answer him. He knew that nothing he might say would change them from their purpose. He made himself as comfortable as possible, and closed his eyes. Once or twice he opened them, and looked at the others. They sat beside the fire, heads dose together, talking in whispers, their faces tense, and eyes feverish with the treasure lust. After a while Graydon's head dropped forward. He slept.

Chapter III
The White Llama

IT WAS DAWN when Graydon awakened.

Some one had thrown a blanket over him during the night, but he was, nevertheless, cold and stiff. He drew his legs up and down painfully, trying to start the sluggish blood. He heard the others stirring in the tent. He wondered which of them had thought of the blanket, and why he had been moved to that kindness.

Starrett lifted the tent flap, passed by him without a word and went on to the spring. He returned and busied himself, furtively, about the fire. Now and then he looked at the prisoner, but seemingly with neither anger nor resentment. He slipped at last to the tent listened, then trod softly over to Graydon.

"Sorry about this," he muttered. "But I can't do anything with Soames and Dancret. Had a hard time persuading 'em even to let you have that blanket. Take a drink of this."

He pressed a flask to Graydon's lips. He took a liberal swallow; it warmed him.

"Sh-h," warned Starrett. "Don't bear any grudge. Drunk last night. I'll help you, if –." He broke off, abruptly; busied himself with the burning logs. Out of the tent came Soames.

"I'm goin' to give you one last chance, Graydon," he began, without preliminary. "Come through clean with us on your dicker with the girl, and we'll take you back with us, and all work together and all share together. You had the edge on us yesterday, and I don't know that I blame you. But it's three to one now and the plain truth is you can't get away with it. So why not be reasonable?"

"What's the use of going over all that again, Soames?" Graydon asked, wearily. "I've told you everything. If you're wise, you'll let me loose, give me my guns and I'll fight for you when the trouble comes. For trouble is coming, man, sure – big trouble."

"Yeah!" snarled the New Englander. "Tryin' to scare us, are you? All right – there's a nice little trick of drivin' a wedge under each of your finger nails and a-keepin' drivin' 'em in. It makes 'most anybody talk after awhile. And if it don't, there's the good old fire dodge. Rollin' your feet up to it, closer and closer and closer. Yeah, anybody'll talk when their toes begin to crisp up and toast."

Suddenly he bent over and sniffed at Graydon's lips.

"So that's it!" he faced Starrett, tense, gun leveled from his hip pocket. "Been feedin' him liquor, have you? Been talkin' to him, have you? After we'd settled it last night that I was to do all the talkin'. All right, that settles you, Starrett. Dancret! Danc'! Come here, quick!" he roared.

The Frenchman came running out of the tent.

"Tie him up," Soames nodded toward Starrett. "Another damned double- crosser in the camp. Gave him liquor. Got their heads together while we were inside. Tie him."

"But, Soames," the Frenchman hesitated, "if we have to fight, it is not well to have half of us helpless, non. Perhaps Starrett he did nothing –"

"If we have to fight, two men will do as well as three," said Soames. "I ain't goin' to let this thing slip through my fingers, Danc'. I don't think we'll have to do any fightin'. If they come, I think it's goin' to be a tradin' job. Starrett's turnin' traitor, too. Tie him, I say."

"Well, I don't like it –" began Dancret; Soames made an impatient motion with his automatic; the little Frenchman went to the tent, returned with a coil of rope, and sidled up to Starrett.

"Put up your hands," ordered Soames. Starrett swung them up. But in mid- swing they closed on Dancret, lifted him like a doll and held him between himself and the gaunt New Englander.

"Now shoot, damn you!" he cried, and bore down on Soames, meeting every move of his pistol arm with Dancret's wriggling body. His own right hand swept down to the Frenchman's belt, drew from the holster his automatic, leveled it over the twisting shoulder at Soames.

"Drop your gun. Yank," grinned Starrett, triumphantly. "Or shoot if you want. But before your bullet's half through Dancret here, by Christ, I'll have you drilled clean."

There was a momentary, sinister silence – it was broken by a sudden pealing of tiny golden bells.

Their chiming cleft through the murk of murder that had fallen on the camp; lightened it; dissolved it as the sunshine does a cloud. Soames' pistol dropped; Starrett's iron grip upon Dancret relaxed.

Through the trees, not a hundred yards away, came Suarra.

A cloak of green covered the girl from neck almost to slender feet. In her hair gleamed a twisted string of emeralds. Bandlets of gold studded with the same gems circled her wrists and ankles. Behind her a snow-white llama paced, sedately. There was a broad golden collar around its neck from which dropped strands of little golden bells. At each of its silvery sides a pannier hung, woven it seemed from shining yellow rushes.

And there was no warrior host around her. She had brought neither avengers nor executioners. At the llama's side was a single attendant. Swathed in a voluminous robe of red and yellow, the hood of which covered his face. His only weapon was a long staff, vermilion. He was bent, and he fluttered and danced as he came on, taking little steps backward and forward – movements that carried the suggestion that his robes clothed less a human being than some huge bird. They drew closer, and Graydon saw that the hand that clutched the staff was thin and white with the transparent pallor of old, old age.

He strained at his bonds, a sick horror at his heart. Why had she come back – like this? Without strong men to guard her? With none but this one ancient? And decked in jewels and gold? He had warned her; she could not be ignorant of what threatened her. It was as though she had come thus deliberately – to fan the lusts from which she had most to fear.

"Diable!" whispered Dancret – "the emeralds!"

"God – what a girl!" muttered Starrett, thick nostrils distended, a red flicker in his eyes.

Soames said nothing, perplexity and suspicion replacing the astonishment with which he had watched the approach. Nor did he speak as the girl and her attendants halted close beside him. But the doubt in his eyes grew, and he scanned the path along which they had come, searching every tree, every bush. There was no sign of movement, no sound.

"Suarra!" cried Graydon, despairingly, "Suarra, why did you return?"

She stepped over to him, and drew a dagger from beneath her cloak. She cut the thongs binding him to the tree. She slipped the blade beneath the cords that fettered his wrists and ankles; freed him. He staggered to his feet.

"Was it not well for you that I did come?" she asked, sweetly.

Before he could answer, Soames strode forward. And Graydon saw that he had come to some decision, had resolved upon some course of action. He made a low, awkward, mocking bow to the girl; then spoke to Graydon.

"All right," he said, "you can stay loose – as long as you do what I want you to. The girl's back and that's the main thing. She seems to favor you a lot, Graydon. I reckon that gives us a way to persuade her to answer our questions. Yes, sir, and you favor her. That's useful, too. I reckon you won't want to be tied up an' watch certain things happen to her, eh –" he leered at Graydon. "But there's just one thing you've got to do if you want things to go along peaceable. Don't do any talkin' to her when I ain't close by. Remember, I know the Aymara as well as you do. And I want to be right alongside listenin' in all the time, do you see? That's all."

He turned to Suarra.

"Your visit has brought great happiness, maiden," he spoke in the Aymara. "It will not be a short one, if we have our way – and I think we will have our way –." There was covert menace in the phrase, yet if she noted it she gave no heed. "You are strange to us, as we must be to you. There is much for us each to learn, one of the other."

"That is true," she answered, tranquilly. "I think though that your desire to learn of me is much greater than mine to learn of you – since, as you surely know, I have had one not too pleasant lesson." She glanced at Starrett.

"The lessons," he said, "shall be pleasant – or not pleasant, as you choose."

This time there was no mistaking the menace in the words, nor did Suarra again let it pass. Her eyes blazed sudden wrath.

"Better not to threaten!" she warned. "I, Suarra, am not used to threats – and if you will take my counsel you will keep them to yourself hereafter!"

"Yeah, is that so?" Soames took a step toward her, face grown grim and ugly. There came a dry chuckling from the hooded figure in red and yellow. Suarra started; her wrath vanished, she became friendly once more.

"I was hasty," she said to Soames. "Nevertheless, it is never wise to threaten unless you know the strength of what it is you menace. And remember – of me you know nothing. Yet I know all that you wish to learn. You wish to know how I came by this – and this – and this –" she touched her coronal, her bracelet, her anklets. "You wish to know where they came from, and if there are more of them there, and if so, how you may possess yourself of as much as you can carry away. Well, you shall know all that. I have come to tell you."

At this announcement, so frank and open, all the doubt and suspicion returned to Soames. Again his eyes narrowed and he searched the trail up which Suarra had come.

"Soames," Dancret gripped his arm, and his voice and hand were both shaking, "the baskets on the llama. They're not rushes – they're gold, pure gold, pure soft gold, woven like straw! Diable! Soames, what have we struck!"

Soames's eyes glittered.

"Better go over and watch where they came up, Danc'," he answered. "I don't quite get this. It looks too cursed easy to be right. Take your rifle and squint out from the edge of the trees while I try to get down to what's what."

"There is nothing to fear," said the girl, as though she had understood the words, "no harm will come to you from me. If there is any evil in store for you, you yourselves will summon it – not we. I have come to show you the way to treasure. Only that. Come with me and you shall see where jewels like these" – she touched the gems meshed in her hair – "grow like flowers in a garden. You shall see the gold come streaming forth, living, from –" she hesitated; then went on as though reciting some lesson – "come streaming forth like water. You may bathe in that stream, drink from it if you will, carry away all that you can bear. Or if it causes you too much sorrow to leave it, why – you may stay with it forever; nay, become a part of it, even. Men of gold."

She turned from them, and walked toward the llama.

They stared at her and at each other; on the faces of three, greed and suspicion; bewilderment on Graydon's.

"It is a long journey," she faced them, one hand on the llama's head. "You are my guests – in a sense. Therefore, I have brought something for your entertainment before we start."

She began to unbuckle the panniers. Graydon was aware that this attendant of hers was a strange servant – if servant he was. He made no move to help her. Silent he stood, and motionless, face covered.

Graydon stepped forward to help the girl. She smiled up at him, half shyly. In the depths of her eyes was a glow warmer than friendliness; his hands leaped to touch hers.

Instantly Soames stepped between them.

"Better remember what I told you," he snapped.

"Help me," said Suarra. Graydon lifted the basket and set it down beside her. She slipped a hasp, bent back the soft metal withes, and drew out a shimmering packet. She shook it and it floated out on the dawn wind, a cloth of silver. It lay upon the ground like a web of gossamer spun by silver spiders.

Then from the hamper she brought forth cups of gold, and deep, boat- shaped golden dishes, two tall ewers whose handles were winged serpents, their scales made, it seemed, from molten rubies. After them small golden-withed baskets. She set the silver cloth with the dishes and the cups. She opened the little baskets. In them were unfamiliar, fragrant fruits and loaves and oddly colored cakes. All these Suarra placed upon the plates. She dropped to her knees at the head of the cloth, took up one of the ewers, snapped open its lid and from it poured into the cups clear amber wine.

She raised her eyes to them; waved a white hand, graciously.

"Sit," she said. "Eat and drink."

She beckoned to Graydon; pointed to the place beside her. Silently, gaze fixed upon the glittering hoard, Starrett and Dancret and Soames squatted before the other plates. Soames thrust out a hand, took up one and weighed it, scattering what it held upon the cloth.

"Gold!" he breathed.

Starrett laughed, crazily, and raised his wine-filled goblet to his lips.

"Wait!" Dancret caught his wrist 'Eat and drink,' she said, eh? "Eat, drink and be merry – for tomorrow we die, eh – is that it?"

Soames started, his face once more dark with suspicion.

"You think it's poisoned?" he snarled.

"Maybe no – maybe so," the little Frenchman shrugged. "Anyway I t'ink it better we say 'After you' to her."

The girl looked at them, then at Graydon, inquiringly. "They are afraid. They think it is – that you have –" Graydon stumbled. "That I have put sleep – or death in it? And you?" she asked.

For answer, Graydon raised his cup and drank.

"Yet it is natural," she turned to Soames. "Yes, it is natural that you three should fear this, since – is it not so – it is what you would do if you were we, and we were you? But you are wrong. I tell you again that what there may be to fear is only that which is in yourselves."

She poured wine into her own cup and drank it; broke off a bit of Starrett's bread and ate it; took a cake from Dancret's plate and ate that; set white teeth in one of the fruits.

"Are you satisfied?" she asked them. "Oh, be very sure that if it is in my wish to bring death to you, it is in no such shape as this."

For a moment Soames glared at her. He jumped to his feet strode over to the hooded figure and snatched aside the cowl. The uncovered face was like old ivory. It was seamed with scores of fine lines. It was a face stamped with an incredible ancientness – but the eyes were as bright and as youthful as their setting was ancient.

It stared at Soames, inscrutably. For a dozen heartbeats the gaunt New Englander stared back. Then, slowly, he let the hood drop. He returned to the silver cloth. As he passed, Graydon saw that all color had drained from his cheeks. He threw himself down at his place, and drank deep of the wine, the hand that raised the goblet shaking.

He drank, and drank again from the flagon. And soon, whatever the terror he had felt, the wine drowned it The first ewer and a second, drawn by Suarra from the llama's panniers, were emptied by the three before Soames lurched to his feet.

"You're all right, sister," he said, half-drunkenly. "Just keep on treatin' us like this, and we'll end by all bein' little pals together."

"What does he say?" asked Suarra of Graydon.

"He approves of your – entertainment," answered Graydon, dryly.

"Good," Suarra, too, arose. "Then let us be going."

"We're going, sister, never fear," grinned Soames. "Danc', you stay right here and watch things. Come on, Bill –" he slapped Starrett on the back. "Everything's just fine. Come on, Graydon – bygones is bygones."

Starrett scrambled up. He linked his arm in the New Englander's. They staggered over to the tent. Dancret, upon whom the wine seemed to have had little effect, settled down on a boulder just beyond the fire and began his watch, rifle at readiness.

Graydon lingered. Soames had forgotten him, for a time at least. He meant to make the best of that time with this strange maid whose beauty and sweetness had touched him as no other woman's ever had. He drew so close that the fragrance of her cloudy hair rocked him; so close that her touching shoulder sent a flame through him.

"Suarra –" he began. She turned, and silenced him with slender fingers on his lips.

"Not now –" she whispered. "Not now – tell me nothing now of what is in your heart – not now – nor, it may be, ever! I promised that I would save you – if I could. Of that promise was born another –" her glance turned to the silent figure, meaningly. "So speak to me not again," she went on hurriedly, "or if you must speak – let it be of – commonplace things."

She began packing the golden cups and dishes. He set about helping her. He thought, ruefully, that this was a commonplace thing enough to satisfy her. She accepted his aid without comment, looked at him no more.

When the last shining cup was in the pannier, he turned and went toward the tent to get together his duffle, pack his burro. The voices of Starrett and Soames came to him.

"But she's not Indian, Soames," Starrett was speaking. "She's whiter than you and me. What are they? And the girl – Christ!"

"What they are we'll find out, never fear," and Soames.

"To hell with the girl – take her if you want her. But I'd go through a dozen hells to get to the place where that stuff they're carryin' samples of comes from. Man – with what we could carry out on the burros and the llama and come back for – man, we could buy the world."

"Yes – unless there's a trap somewhere," said Starrett, dubiously.

"We've got the cards in our hands," the wine was wearing off Soames. "What's against us? An old dummy and a girl. Now, I'll tell you what I think. I don't know who or what they are, but whoever or whatever, you can bet there ain't many of 'em. If there was, they'd be landing on us hard. No – they're damned anxious to get us away and they're willin' to let us get out with what we can to get us away. They want to get rid of us, quick and cheap as possible. Yeah – that's what they want. Why – because they damn well know the three of us could wipe 'em all out."

"Three of us?" echoed Starrett. "Four, you mean. There's Graydon."

"Graydon don't count – the louse! Thought he'd sold us out, didn't he? All right – we'll fix Mister Graydon when the time comes. Just now he's useful to us on account of the girl. She's stuck on him. But when the time comes to divide – there'll be only three of us. And there'll only be two of us – if you do anything like you did this morning."

"Cut it out, Soames," growled Starrett. "I told you it was the hooch. I'm through with that, now that we've seen this stuff. I'm with you to the limit Do what you want with Graydon. But – I want the girl. I'd be willing to make a bargain with you – give up a part of my share."

"Oh, hell," drawled Soames. "We've been together a good many years. Bill. There's enough and plenty for the three of us. You can have the girl for nothing."

Little flecks of red danced before Graydon's eyes. Hand stretched to tear open the tent flap, he checked himself.

That was no way to help Suarra. Unarmed, what could he do? In some way, he must get his guns. And the danger was not imminent – they would do nothing before they reached that place of treasure to which Suarra had promised to lead them.

He stole back a dozen paces, waited for a moment or two; then went noisily to the tent. He thrust aside the flap and entered.

"Been a long time comin'," snarled Soames. "Been talkin' – after what I told you?"

"Not a word," lied Graydon, cheerfully – he busied himself with his belongings. "By the way, Soames, don't you think it's time to stop this nonsense and give me back my guns?"

Soames made no answer.

"Oh, all right then," said Graydon. "I only thought that they would come in handy when the pinch comes. But if you only want me to look on while you do the scrapping – well, I don't mind."

"You'd better mind," said Soames. "You'd better mind, Graydon! If the pinch comes – we're takin' no chances of a bullet in our backs. That's why you've got no guns. And if the pinch does come – well, we'll take no chances on you, anyway. Do you get me?"

Graydon shrugged. In silence the packing was completed; the tent struck; the burros loaded.

Suarra stood awaiting them at the side of the white llama. Soames walked up to her, drew from its holster his automatic, balanced it in outstretched hand.

"You know what this is?" he asked her.

"Why, yes," she answered. "It is the death weapon of your kind."

"Right," said Soames. "And it deals death quickly, quicker than spears or arrows –." He raised his voice so there could be no doubt that her silent attendant must also hear – "Now, I and these two men here carry these and others still more deadly. This man's we have taken from him. Your words may be clearest truth. I hope they are – for your sake and this man's and his who came with you. You understand me?" he asked, and grinned like a hungry wolf.

"I understand." Suarra's eyes and face were calm. "You need fear nothing from us."

"We don't," said Soames. "But you have much to fear – from us." Another moment he regarded her, menacingly; then shoved his pistol back into his holster.

"You go first," he ordered. "Your man behind you. And then him –" he pointed to Graydon. "We three march in the rear – death-weapons ready."

In that order they passed through the giant algarrobas, and out into the oddly park-like spaces beyond.

Chapter IV
The Thing that Fled

THEY HAD TRAVELED over the savanna for perhaps an hour when Suarra turned to the left, entering the forest that covered the flanks of a great mountain. The trees closed on them. Graydon could see no trail, yet she went on without pause. Another hour went by and the way began to climb, the shade to deepen. Deeper it became and deeper, until the girl was but a flitting shadow.

Once or twice Graydon had glanced at the three men behind him. The darkness was making them more and more uneasy. They walked close together, eyes and ears strained to catch the first faint stirrings of ambush. And now, as the green gloom grew denser still, Soames ordered him to join Dancret and Starrett. He hesitated, read murder in the New Englander's eyes, realized the futility of resistance and dropped back. Soames pressed forward until he was close behind the cowled figure. Dancret drew Graydon between himself and Starrett, grinning.

"Soames has changed his plan," he whispered. "If there is trouble, he shoot the old devil – quick. He keep the girl to make trade wit' her people. He keep you to make trade wit' the girl. How you like – eh?"

Graydon did not answer. When the Frenchman had pressed close to him, he had felt an automatic in his side pocket If an attack did come, he could leap upon Dancret, snatch the pistol and gain for himself a fighting chance. He would shoot Soames down as remorselessly as he knew Soames would shoot him.

Darker grew the woods until the figures in front were only a moving blur. Then the gloom began to lighten. They had been passing through some ravine, some gorge whose unseen walls had been pressing in upon them, and had now begun to retreat.

A few minutes longer, and ahead of them loomed a prodigious doorway, a cleft whose sides reached up for thousands of feet. Beyond was a flood of sunshine. Suarra stopped at the rocky threshold with a gesture of warning, peered through, and beckoned them on.

Blinking, Graydon walked through the portal. He looked out over a grass- covered plain strewn with huge, isolated rocks rising from the green like menhirs of the Druids. There were no trees. The plain was dish-shaped; an enormous oval as symmetrical as though it had been molded by the thumb of some Cyclopean potter. Straight across it, three miles or more away, the forests began again. They clothed the base of another gigantic mountain whose walls arose, perpendicularly, a mile at least in air. The smooth scarps described an arc of a tremendous circle – round as Fujiyama's sacred cone, but many times its girth.

They were on a wide ledge that bordered this vast bowl This shelf was a full hundred feet higher than the bottom of the valley whose side sloped up to it like the side of a saucer. And, again carrying out that suggestion of a huge dish, the ledge jutted out like a rim. Graydon guessed that there was a concavity under his feet, and that if one should fall over the side it would be well-nigh impossible to climb back because of the overhang. The surface was about twelve feet wide, and more like a road carefully leveled by human hands than work of nature. On one side was the curving bowl of the valley with its weird monoliths and the circular scarp of the mysterious mountain; on the other the wooded cliffs, unscalable.

They set forth along the rim-like way. Noon came, and in another ravine that opened upon the strange road they had snatched from saddle bags a hasty lunch. They did not waste time in unpacking the burros. There was a little brook singing in the pass, and from it they refilled their canteens, then watered the animals. This time Suarra did not join them.

By mid-afternoon they were nearing the northern end of the bowl. All through the day the circular mountain across the plain had unrolled its vast arc of cliff. A wind had arisen, sweeping from the distant forest and bending the tall heads of the grass far below them.

Suddenly, deep within the wind, Graydon heard a faint, far-off clamor, a shrill hissing, as of some on-rushing army of serpents. The girl halted, face turned toward the sound. It came again – and louder. Her face whitened, but when she spoke her voice was steady.

"There is danger," she said. "Deadly danger for you. It may pass and – it may not. Until we know what to expect you must hide. Take your animals and tether them in the underbrush there –" she pointed to the mountainside which here was broken enough for cover – "the four of you take trees and hide behind them. Tie the mouths of your animals so that they can make no noise."

"So!" snarled Soames. "So here's the trap, is it! All right, sister, you know what I told you. We'll go into the trees, but – you go with us where we can keep our hands on you."

"I will go with you," she answered, gravely.

Soames glared at her, then turned abruptly.

"Danc'," he ordered, "Starrett – get the burros in. And Graydon – you'll stay with the burros and see they make no noise. We'll be right close – with the guns. And we'll have the girl – don't forget that."

Again the hissing shrilled down the wind.

"Be quick," the girl commanded.

When the trees and underbrush had closed in upon them it flashed on Graydon, crouching behind the burros, that he had not seen the cloaked famulus of Suarra join the retreat and seek the shelter of the woods. He parted the bushes, and peered cautiously through them. There was no one upon the path.

A sudden gust of wind tore at the trees. It brought with it a burst of the hissing, closer and more strident, and in it an undertone that thrilled him with unfamiliar terror.

A thing of vivid scarlet streaked out from the trees which here were not more than a half a mile away. It scuttled over the plain until it reached the base of one of the monoliths. It swarmed up its side to the top. There it paused, apparently scanning the forest from which it had come. He caught the impression of some immense insect, but touched with a monstrous, an incredible suggestion of humanness.

The scarlet thing slipped down the monolith, and raced through the grasses toward him. Out of the forest burst what at first glance he took for a pack of huge hunting dogs – then realized that whatever they might be, dogs they certainly were not. They came forward leaping like kangaroos, and as they leaped they glittered green and blue in the sunlight, as though armored in mail of emeralds and sapphires. Nor did ever dogs give tongue as they did. From them came the hellish hissing.

The scarlet thing darted to right, to left, frantically; then crouched at the base of another monolith, motionless.

From the trees emerged another monstrous shape. Like the questing creatures, it glittered – but as though its body were cased in polished jet. Its bulk was that of a giant draft-horse. Its neck was long and reptilian. At the base of its neck, astride it, was a man.

Graydon cautiously raised his field glasses and focused them on the pack. Directly in his line of vision was one of the creatures which had come to gaze. It stood rigid, its side toward him, pointing like a hunting dog.

It was a dinosaur!

Dwarfed to the size of a Great Dane, still there was no mistaking it. He could see its blunt and spade-shaped tail which with its powerful, pillar-like hind legs made a tripod upon which it squatted. Its body was nearly erect Its short forelegs were muscled as powerfully as it's others. It held these forelegs half curved at its breast, as though ready to clutch. They ended in four long talons, chisel shaped. One of which thrust outward like a huge thumb.

And what he had taken for mail of sapphire and emerald were scales. They overlapped like those of the armadillo. From their burnished surfaces and edges the sun struck out the jewel glints.

The creature turned its head upon its short, bull neck. It seemed to stare straight at Graydon. He saw fiery red eyes set in a sloping, bony arch of broad forehead. Its muzzle was that of a crocodile, but smaller and blunted. The jaws were studded with yellow, pointed fangs.

The rider drew up beside it. Like the others, the creature he rode was a true dinosaur. It was black scaled and longer tailed, with serpentine neck thicker than the central coil of the giant python.

The rider was a man of Suarra's own race. There was the same ivory whiteness of skin, the more than classic regularity of feature. But his face was stamped with arrogance, indifferent cruelty. He wore a close-fitting suit of green that clung to him like a glove, and his hair was a shining golden. He sat upon a light saddle fastened at the base of the long neck of his steed. Heavy reins ran up to the jaws of the jetty dinosaur's small, snake-like head.

Graydon's glasses dropped from his shaking hand. What manner of man was this who hunted with dinosaurs for dogs and a dinosaur for steed!

He looked toward the base of the monolith where the scarlet thing had crouched. It was no longer there. He caught a gleam of scarlet in the high grass not a thousand feet away. The thing was scuttering toward the rim –

There was a shrieking clamor like a thousand hissing fumaroles. The pack had found the scent, were leaping forward like a glittering green and blue comber.

The scarlet thing jumped up out of the grasses. It swayed upon four long and stilt-like legs, its head a full twelve feet above the ground. High on these stilts of legs was its body, almost round and no bigger than a half-grown boy's. From the sides of the body stretched two sinewy arms – like human arms pulled out to twice their normal length. Body, arms and legs were covered with fine scarlet hair. Its face, turned toward its pursuers, Graydon could not see.

The pack rushed upon it. The thing hurled itself like a thunderbolt straight toward the rim.

Graydon heard beneath him a frantic scrambling and scratching. Gray hands came over the edge of the road, gripping the rock with foot-long fingers like blunt needles of bone. They clutched and drew forward. Behind them appeared spindling, scarlet-haired arms.

Over the edge peered a face, gray as the hands. Within it were two great unwinking round and golden eyes.

A man's face – and not a man's!

A face such as he had never seen upon any living creature…yet there could be no mistaking the humanness of it – the humanness which lay over the incredible visage like a veil.

He thought he saw a red rod dart out of air and touch the face – the red rod of Suarra's motley-garbed attendant Whether he saw it or not, the clutching claws opened and slid away. The gray face vanished.

Up from the hidden slope arose a wailing, agonized shriek, and a triumphant hissing. Then out into the range of his vision bounded the black dinosaur, its golden-haired rider shouting. Behind it leaped the pack. They crossed the plain like a thunder cloud pursued by emerald and sapphire lightnings. They passed into the forest, and were gone.

Suarra stepped out of the tree shadows, the three adventurers close behind her, white-faced and shaking. She stood looking where the dinosaurs had disappeared, and her face was set, and her eyes filled with loathing.

"Suarra!" gasped Graydon. "That thing – the thing that ran – what was it? God – it had the face of a man!"

"It was no man," she shook her head. "It was a – Weaver. Perhaps he had tried to escape. Or perhaps Lantlu opened a way for him that he might be tempted to escape. For Lantlu delights in hunting with the Xinli –" her voice shook with hatred – "and a Weaver will do when there is nothing better!"

"A Weaver? It had a man's face!" It was Soames, echoing Graydon.

"No," she repeated. "It was no – man. At least no man as you are. Long, long ago his ancestors were men like you – that is true. But now – he is – only a Weaver."

She turned to Graydon.

"Yu-Atlanchi by its arts fashioned him and his kind. Remember him, Graydon – when you come to our journey's end!"

She stepped out upon the path. There stood the cowled figure, waiting as tranquilly as though it had never stirred. She called to the white llama, and again took her place at the head of the little caravan. Soames touched Graydon, arousing him from the troubled thought into which her enigmatic warning had thrown him.

"Take your place, Graydon," he muttered. "We'll follow. Later I want to talk to you. Maybe you can get your guns back – if you're reasonable."

"Hurry," said Suarra, "the sun sinks, and we must go quickly. Before tomorrow's noon you shall see your garden of jewels, and the living gold streaming for you to do with it as you will – or the gold to do as it wills with you."

She looked the three over, swiftly, a shadow of mockery in her eyes. Soames' lips tightened.

"Get right along, sister," he said, sardonically. "All you have to do is show us. Then your work is done. We'll take care of the rest."

She shrugged, carelessly. They set forth once more along the rimmed path.

The plain was silent, deserted. From the far forests came no sound. Graydon strove for sane comprehension of what he had just beheld. A Weaver, Suarra had named the scarlet thing – and had said that once its ancestors had been men like themselves. He remembered what, at their first meeting, she had told him of the powers of this mysterious Yu-Atlanchi. Did she mean that her people had mastered the secrets of evolution so thoroughly that they had learned how to reverse its processes as well? Could control – devolution!

Well, why not? In man's long ascent from the primeval jelly on the shallow shores of the warm first seas, he had worn myriad shapes. And as he moved higher from one form to another, changing to vertebrate, discarding cold blood for warm, still was he kin to the fish he caught today, to the furred creatures whose pelts clothed his women, to the apes he brought from the jungles to study or to amuse him. Even the spiders that spun in his gardens, the scorpion that scuttled from the tread of his feet, were abysmally distant blood-brothers.

When St. Francis of Assisi had spoken of Brother Fly, Brother Wolf, Brother Snake, he had voiced scientific truth.

All life on earth had a common origin. Divergent now and Protean-shaped, still man and beast, fish and serpent, lizard and bird, ant and bee and spider, all had come from those once similar specks of jelly, adrift millions upon millions of years ago in the shallow littorals of the first seas. Protobion, Gregory of Edinburgh had named it – the first stuff of life from which all life was to develop.

Were the germs of all those shapes man had worn in his slow upward climb still dormant in him?

Roux, the great French scientist, had taken the eggs of frogs and, by manipulating them, had produced giant frogs and dwarfs, frogs with two heads and one body, frogs with one head and eight legs, three-headed frogs with legs numerous as centipedes'. And he had produced from these eggs, also, creatures which in no way resembled frogs at all.

Vornikoff, the Russian, and Schwartz, the German, had experimented with still higher forms of life, producing chimera, nightmare things they had been forced to slay – and quickly.

If Roux and the others had done all this – and they had done it, Graydon knew – then was it not possible for greater scientists to awaken those dormant germs in man, and similarly create – such creatures as the scarlet thing? A spider-man!

Nature, herself, had given them the hint. Nature from time to time produced such abnormalities – human monsters marked outwardly if not inwardly with the stigmata of the beast, the fish, even the crustacean. Babies with gill slits in their throats babies with tails; babies furred. The human embryo passed through all these stages, from the protoplasmic unicell up – compressing the age-long drama of evolution into less than a year.

Might it not well be, then, that in Yu-Atlanchi dwelt those to whom the crucible of birth held no secrets; who could dip within it and mold from its contents what they would?

A loom is a dead machine upon which fingers work more or less clumsily. The spider is both machine and artisan, spinning and weaving more surely, more exquisitely than can any lifeless mechanism worked by man. What man-made machine had ever approached the delicacy, the beauty of the spider's web?

Suddenly Graydon seemed to behold a whole new world of appalling grotesquerie – spider-men and spider-women spread upon huge webs and weaving with needled fingers wondrous fabrics, mole-men and mole-women burrowing, opening mazes of subterranean passages, cloacae, for those who had wrought them into being; amphibian folk busy about the waters – a phantasmagoria of humanity, monstrously twinned with Nature's perfect machine, while still plastic in the womb!

Shuddering, he thrust away that nightmare vision.

Chapter V
The Elfin Horns

THE SUN was halfway down the west when they came to the end of the oval plain. Here the mountain thrust out a bastion which almost touched the cliff at the right. Into the narrow cleft between the two they filed, and through the semi-gloom of this ravine they marched over a smooth rock floor, their way running always up, although at an easy grade. The sun was behind the westward peaks and dusk was falling when they emerged.

They stood at the edge of a little moor. Upon the left, the arc of the circular mountain resumed its march. The place was, indeed, less a moor than a barren. Its floor was clean white sand. It was dotted with hillocks, mounds flat-topped as though constantly swept by brooms of wind. Upon the slopes of these mounds a fall grass grew sparsely. The hillocks arose about a hundred feet apart, with a singular regularity, like tumuli, graves in a cemetery of giants. The little barren covered about five acres. Around it clustered the forest. He heard the gurgling of a brook.

Suarra led them across the sands until she reached a mound close to the center of the place.

"You will camp here," she said. "Water is close by. You may light a fire, and you can sleep without fear. By dawn we must be away."

She left them, and walked with red-and-yellow robe toward one of the neighboring knolls. The white llama followed her. Graydon had expected Soames to halt her, but he did not. Instead, his eyes flashed some message to Dancret and Starrett. It seemed to Graydon they were pleased that the girl was not to share their camp, that they welcomed the distance she had put between them.

And their manner toward him had changed. They were comradely once more.

"Mind takin' the burros over to water?" asked Soames. "Well get the fire goin', and chow ready."

Graydon nodded and led the animals over to the brook. Taking them back after they had drunk their fill, he looked over at the mound to which Suarra had gone. At its base stood a small square tent, glimmering in the twilight like silk. Tethered close to it was the white llama, placidly munching grass and grain. Its hampers of woven golden withes were still at its sides. Neither Suarra nor the hooded man was visible. They were, he supposed, within the tent.

At his own hillock a fire was crackling and supper being prepared. As he came up, Starrett jerked a thumb at the little tent.

"Took it out of the saddle-bags," he said. "Looked like a folded umbrella and went up like one. Who'd ever think to find anything like that in this wilderness!"

"Lots of things I t'ink in those saddle-bags we have not yet seen maybe," whispered Dancret.

"You bet," said Soames. "An' the loot we've already seen's enough to set us all up for life. Eh, Graydon?"

"She has promised you much more," answered Graydon, troubled by the undercurrent in the New Englander's voice.

"Yeah," said Soames, "yeah – I guess so. But – well, let's eat."

The four sat around the burning sticks, as they had for so many nights before his fight with Starrett. And, to Graydon's astonishment, they ignored the weird tragedy of the plain; avoided it, swiftly changed the subject when twice, to test them, he brought it up. Their talk was all of the treasure so close to them, and of what could be done with it when back in their own world. Piece by piece they went over the golden hoard in the white llama's packs; discussed Suarra's jewels and their worth. It was as though they were bent upon infecting him with their own avarice.

"Hell! Why, with only her emeralds none of us'd have to worry!" Starrett repeated, with variations, over and over.

Graydon listened with increasing disquiet There was something behind this studied avoidance of the destruction of the scarlet thing by the dinosaurs, this constant reference to the rich loot at hand, the reiterated emphasis upon what ease and luxuries it would bring them all.

Suddenly he realized that they were afraid, that terror of the unknown struggled with treasure-lust and that therefore they were doubly dangerous. Something was hidden in the minds of the three to whose uncovering all this talk was only the preamble.

At last Soames looked at his watch.

"Nearly eight," he said, abruptly. "Dawn breaks about five. Time to talk turkey. Graydon, come up close."

The four drew into a huddle in the shelter of the knoll. From where they crouched, Suarra's tent was hidden – as they were hidden to any watchers in that little silken pavilion looking now like a great silver moth at rest under the moonlight.

"Graydon," began the New Englander, "we've made up our minds on this thing. We're goin' to do it a little different. We're glad and willin' to let bygones be bygones. Here we are, four white men among a bunch of God knows what. White men ought to stick together. Ain't that so?"

Graydon nodded, waiting.

"All right, then," said Soames. "Now here's the situation. I don't deny that what we seen today gave us all a hell of a jolt. We ain't equipped to go up against anything like that pack of hissin' devils. But, an' here's the point, we can beat it out an' come back equipped. You get me?"

Again Graydon nodded, alert to meet what he sensed was coming.

"There's enough stuff on that llama and the girl to make all comfortable," went on Soames. "But also it's enough to finance the greatest little expedition that ever hit the trail for treasure. An' that's just what we plan doin', Graydon. Get the hampers an' all that's in 'em. Get the stuff on the girl. Beat it, an' come back. We'll get together a little crowd of hard- boiled guys. The four of us'll take half we find an' the others'll divide the other half. We'll pack along a couple of planes, an' damn soon find out where the girl comes from. I bet those hissin' devils wouldn't stand up long under machine guns an' some bombs dropped from the flyin' crates. An' when the smoke clears away we'll lift the loot an' go back an' sit on the top of the world. What you say to that?"

Graydon fenced for time.

"How will you get the stuff now?" he asked. "And if you get it, how will you get away with it?"

"Easy," Soames bent his head closer. "We got it all planned: There's only the girl an' that old devil in that tent. They ain't watchin', they're too sure of us. All right, if you're with us, we'll just slip over there. Starrett and Danc', they'll take care of the dummy. No shootin'. Just slip a knife' between his ribs. Me an' you'll attend to the girl. We won't hurt her. Just tie her up an' gag her. Then we'll stow the stuff on a couple of burros, an' beat it."

"Beat it where?" asked Graydon. He edged a bit closer to Dancret, ready to jerk the automatic from his pocket.

"Beat it out, damn it!" growled Soames. "Me an' Starrett seen a peak to the west both of us recognized when we come in here. Once we hit it I know where we are. An' travelin' light an' all night we can be well on our way to it by this time tomorrow. These woods ain't so thick an' it's full moon."

Graydon moved his hand cautiously and touched Dancret's pocket. The automatic was still there. Before he made that desperate move he would try one last appeal – to fear.

"But you've forgotten one thing, Soames," he said. "There would be pursuit. What could we do with those hell-beasts on our track? Why, man, they'd be after us in no time. You couldn't get away with anything like that."

Instantly he realized the weakness in the argument.

"Not a bit of it," Soames grinned evilly. "That's just the point Nobody's worryin' about that girl. Nobody knows where she is an' she don't want 'em to. She was damned anxious not to be seen this afternoon. No, Graydon – I figure she slipped away from her folks to help you out. I take my hat off to you – you're a quick worker an' you sure got her hooked. The only one that might raise trouble is the old devil. He'll get the knife before he knows it. Then there's only the girl. She'll be damned glad to show us the way out, happen we get lost again. But me an' Starrett know that peak, I tell you. We'll carry her along so she can't start anybody after us, an' when we get where we know the country we'll turn her loose for a walk back home. An' none the worse off either – eh, boys?"

Starrett and Dancret nodded.

Graydon feigned to consider. He knew exactly what was in Soames' mind – to use him in the cold-blooded murder the three had planned and, once beyond the reach of pursuit, to murder him, too. Nor would they ever allow Suarra to return to tell what they had done. She would be slain – after they had thrown her to Starrett.

"Come on, Graydon," whispered Soames, impatiently. "It's a good scheme, an' we can work it. Are you with us? If you ain't –"

His knife glittered in his hand. Simultaneously Starrett and Dancret pressed close. Their movement gave him the one advantage he needed. He thrust his hand into the Frenchman's pocket, plucked out the gun and as he did so landed a side kick that caught Starrett in the groin. The big man rolled over, groaning. Graydon leaped to his feet. But before he could cover Soames, Dancret's hands were around his ankles, his legs jerked from under him.

"Suarra!" shouted Graydon as he fell. At least, his cry might awaken and warn her. A second shout was choked in mid-utterance. Soames' bony hands were around his neck.

He reached up, and tried to break the strangling clutch. It gave a little, enough to let him grasp one breath. Instantly he dropped his hold on Soames' wrists, hooked the fingers of one hand in the corner of the New Englander's mouth, pulling with all his strength. There was a sputtering curse from Soames, and his hands let go. Graydon tried to spring up, but an arm of the gaunt man slipped over the back of his head and held his neck in the vise of bent elbow against shoulder.

"Knife him, Danc'," snarled Soames.

Graydon suddenly twisted, bringing the New Englander on top of him. He was barely in time for, as he did so, Dancret struck, his blade just missing Soames. Soames locked his legs around his, trying to jerk him over in range of the little Frenchman. Graydon sank his teeth in the shoulder pressing him. Soames roared with pain and rage; threshed and rolled trying to shake off the grip of Graydon's jaws. Around them danced Dancret, awaiting a chance to thrust.

There came a bellow from Starrett.

"The llama! It's running away! The llama!"

Involuntarily, Graydon loosed his teeth. Soames leaped – up. Graydon followed on the instant, shoulder lifted to meet the blow he expected from Dancret.

"Look, Soames, look!" the little Frenchman was pointing. "He's loose! Christ! There he goes – wit' the gold – wit' the jewels –"

The moon had gathered strength, and under its flood the white sands were a silver lake in which the hillocks stood like tiny islands. Golden hampers gleaming on its sides, the white llama was flitting across that lake of silver, a hundred paces away and headed for the cleft through which they had come.

"Stop it!" shouted Soames, forgetting all else. "After it, Starrett! That way, Danc'! I'll head it off!"

They ran out over the shining barren. The llama changed its pace, trotted leisurely to one of the mounds, and bounded to its top.

"Close in! We've got it," cried Soames. The three ran to the hillock, on which the white beast stood looking calmly around. They swarmed up the mound from three sides.

As their feet touched the sparse grass a mellow note rang out, one of those elfin horns Graydon had heard chorusing so gaily about Suarra that first day. It was answered by others, close and all about. Again the single note. And then the answering chorus swirled toward the hillock of the llama, hovered over it, and dropped like a shower of winged sounds upon it.

Graydon saw Starrett stagger as though under some blow, then whirl knotted arms as though warding off invisible attack. A moment the big man stood thus, flailing with frantic arms. He cast himself to the ground and rolled down to the sands. The notes of the elfin horns swarmed away from him, to concentrate upon Soames. He had thrown himself face downward on the slope of the mound and was doggedly crawling to the top. He held one arm stiffly, shielding his face.

Shielding his face against what?

All that Graydon could see was the hillock and on it the llama bathed in the moonlight, Starrett at the foot of the mound and Soames now nearly at its crest. Dancret, upon the opposite side, he could not see at all.

The horn notes were ringing in greater volume, scores of them, like the bugles of a fairy hunt. What it was that made those sounds was not visible to him, nor did they cast any shadow in the brilliant moonlight. But he heard a whirring as of hundreds of wings.

Soames had reached the edge of the mound's flat summit. The llama bent its head, contemplating him. As he scrambled over that edge and thrust out a hand to grasp its bridle, it flicked about, sprang to the opposite side and leaped to the sands.

The clamor of the elfin horns about Soames had never stilled. Graydon watched him wince, strike out, bend his head and guard his eyes as though from a shower of blows. And whatever was that attack of the invisible, it did not daunt him. He leaped across the mound and slid down its side, close behind the llama. As he reached the base, Starrett arose, swaying drunkenly.

The horn notes ceased abruptly, like candles blown out by a sudden blast. Dancret came running around the slope. The three stood arguing, gesticulating. Their clothes were ripped to rags, and as Soames shifted and the moonlight fell full upon him, his face showed streaked with blood.

The llama was walking across the sands, as slowly as though it were tempting them to further pursuit. It was strange how its shape now stood out sharply, and now faded almost to a ghostly tenuity. When it reappeared, it was as if the moonbeams thickened, swirled, wove swiftly, and spun it from themselves. The llama faded – and then grew again upon the warp and woof of the rays like a pattern on an enchanted loom.

Starrett's hand swept down to his belt. Before he could cover the white beast with his automatic, Soames caught his wrist. He spoke wrathfully, peremptorily. Graydon knew he was warning Starrett of the danger of the pistol crack, urging silence.

The three scattered, Dancret and Starrett to the left and right to flank the llama, Soames approaching it cautiously to keep from frightening it into a run. But as he neared it, the animal broke into a gentle lope and headed for another hillock.

For an instant Graydon thought he saw upon the crest of that mound the figure in motley, red staff raised and pointing at the llama. He looked more intently and decided his eyes had played a trick upon him, for the crest was empty. The llama leaped lightly up to it. As before, Soames and the two others closed in. They swarmed up the mound.

Instantly the elfin horns rang out – menacingly. The three hesitated, stopped their climbing. Then Starrett slid down, ran back a few paces, raised his pistol and fired. The white llama fell.

"The fool! The damned fool!" groaned Graydon.

The silence that followed the shot was broken by a tempest of the elfin horns. It swept down up the three. Dancret shrieked, and ran toward the camp, beating the air as he came. Halfway, he dropped and lay still. And Soames and Starrett they, too, were buffeting the air with great blows, ducking and dodging. The elfin horns were now a raging tumult – death creeping into their notes.

Starrett fell to his knees, arose and lurched away. He fell again, not far from Dancret and lay as still as he. And now Soames went down, fighting to the last. The three lay upon the sands, motionless.

Graydon shook himself into action, and leaped forward. He felt a touch upon his shoulder. A tingling numbness ran through his body. With difficulty he turned his head. Behind him was the figure in motley. His red staff it was that had taken from him all power to move, even as it had paralyzed the spider-man and sent him into the jaws of the dinosaurs.

The red staff pointed to the three bodies. Instantly, as at some command, the clamor of the horns lifted from around them, swirled high in air – and stilled. At the top of the hillock the white llama was struggling to its feet. A band of crimson ran across one silvery flank, the mark of Starrett's bullet. The llama limped down the mound.

As it passed Soames it nosed him. The New Englander's head lifted. He tried to arise, and fell back. The llama nosed him again. Soames squirmed up on hands and knees; eyes fixed upon the golden panniers, he began to crawl after the beast.

The white llama walked slowly, stiffly. It came to Starrett's body and touched him as it had Soames. And Starrett's massive head lifted and he tried to rise, and failing even as had Soames, began like him to crawl behind the animal.

The white llama paused beside Dancret. He stirred, and lurched, and followed it on knees and hands.

Over the moon-soaked sands, back to the camp they trailed – the limping beast with the blood dripping from its wounded side. Behind it the three crawling men, their eyes fixed upon the golden-withed panniers, their mouths gasping, like fish being drawn up to shore.

The llama reached the camp fire and passed on. The crawling men reached the fire and were passing in the llama's wake. The figure in motley lowered his rod.

The three men ceased their crawling. They collapsed beside the embers as though all life had abruptly been withdrawn.

The strange paralysis lifted from Graydon as swiftly as it had come upon him; his muscles relaxed, and power of movement returned, Suarra ran by him to the llama's side, caressed it, strove to stanch its blood.

He bent over the three. They were breathing stertorously, eyes half closed and turned upward so that only the whites were visible. Their shirts had been ripped to ribbons. And on their faces, their breasts and their backs were dozens of small punctures, the edges clean cut as though by sharp steel punches. Some were bleeding, but on most of them the blood had already dried.

He studied them, puzzled. The wounds were bad enough, of course, yet it did not seem to him that they accounted for the condition of the three. Certainly they had not lost enough blood to cause unconsciousness; no arteries had been touched, nor any of the large veins.

He took a bucket and drew water from the brook. Returning, he saw that Suarra had gotten the llama upon its feet again, and over to her tent. He stopped, loosed the golden panniers, and probed the wound. The bullet had plowed almost through the upper left flank, but without touching the bone. He extracted the lead and bathed and dressed the injury with strips of silken stuff the girl handed him. He did it all silently, nor did she speak.

He drew more water from the brook, and went back to his own camp. He saw that the hooded figure had joined the girl. He felt its hidden eyes upon him as he passed. He spread blankets, and pulled Soames, Dancret and Starrett up on them. They had passed out of the stupor, and seemed to be sleeping naturally. He washed the blood from their faces and bodies, and dabbed iodine into the deepest of the peck-like punctures. They showed no sign of awakening under his handling.

Graydon covered them with blankets, walked away from the fire, and threw himself down on the white sands. Foreboding rested heavily on him, a sense of doom. And as he sat there, fighting against the depression sapping his courage, he heard light footsteps, and Suarra sank beside him. His hand dropped upon hers, covering it. She leaned toward him, her shoulder touched him, her cloudy hair caressed his cheek.

"It is the last night, Graydon," she whispered, tremulously. "The last night! And so – I may talk with you for awhile."

He answered nothing to that, only looked at her and smiled. Correctly she interpreted that smile.

"Ah, but it is, Graydon," she said. "I have promised. I told you that I would save you if I could. I went to the Mother, and asked her to help you. She laughed – at first."

"But when she saw how serious it was with me, she was gentle. And at last she promised me, as woman to woman – for after all the Mother is woman – she promised me if there was that within you which would respond to her, she would help you when you stood before the Face and –"

"The Face, Suarra?" he interrupted her.

"The Face in the Abyss!" she said, and shivered. "I can tell you nothing more of it. You – must stand before it. You – and those three. And, oh Graydon – you must not let it conquer you…you must not…"

Her hand drew from beneath his, clenched it tight. He drew her close to him. For a moment she rested against his breast.

"The Mother promised," she said, "and then I knew hope. But she made this condition, Graydon – if by her help you escape the Face, then you must straightway go from this Forbidden Land, nor speak of it to any beyond its borders – to no one, no matter how near or dear. I made that promise for you, Graydon. And so" – she faltered – "and so – it is the last night."

In his heart was stubborn denial of that. But he did not speak, and after a little silence she said, wistfully –

"Is there any maid who loves you – or whom you love – in your own land, Graydon?"

"There is none, Suarra," he answered.

"I believe you," she said, simply, "and I would go away with you – if I could. But I cannot. The Mother loves and trusts me. And I love her – greatly. I could not leave her even for –"

Suddenly she wrenched her hand from his, clenched it and struck it against her breast.

"I am weary of Yu-Atlanchi! Yes, weary of its ancient wisdom and its deathless people! I would go into the new world where there are babes, and many of them, and the laughter of children, and life streams swiftly, passionately – even though it is through the opened Door of Death that it flows at last. For in Yu-Atlanchi not only the Door of Death but the Door of Life is closed. And there are few babes, and of the laughter of children – none."

He caught the beating hand and soothed her.

"Suarra," he said, "I walk in darkness, and your words give me little light. Tell me – who are your people?"

"The ancient people," she told him. "The most ancient. Ages upon ages ago they came here from the south where they had dwelt for other ages still. One day the earth rocked and swung. It was then that the great cold fell, and the darkness and the icy tempests. And many of my people died. Then those who remained journeyed north in their ships, bearing with them the remnant of the serpent-people who had taught them the most of their wisdom. And the Mother is the last of that people.

"They came to rest here. At that time the sea was close and the mountains had not yet been born. They found hordes of the Xinli occupying this land. They were larger, far larger, than now. My people destroyed most of them, and bred down and tamed those they spared, to their own uses. And here for another age they dwelt as they had in the south, where their cities were now beneath mountains of ice.

"Then there were earth-shakings, and the mountains began to lift. Their wisdom was not strong enough to keep the mountains from being born, but they could control their growth around their city. Slowly, steadily, through another age the mountains uprose. Until at last they girdled Yu-Atlanchi like a vast wall – a wall which could not be scaled. Nor did my people care; indeed, it gladdened them. Because by then the Lords and the Mother had closed the Gate of Death. And my people cared no more to go into the outer world. And so they have dwelt – for other ages more."

Again she was silent, musing. Graydon looked at her, struggling to hide his incredulity. A people who had conquered death! A people so old that their ancient cities were covered by the Antarctic ice! The latter – well, that was possible. Certainly, the South Polar continent had once basked beneath a warm sun. Its fossils of palms and other vegetation that could only have lived at tropical temperatures were proof of that. And quite as certainly what are now the poles at one time were not. Whether the change had come about from a sudden tipping of the earth's axis, or a gradual readjustment, science was not agreed. But whatever it was that had happened, it must have taken place at least a million years ago. If Suarra's story were true, if she were not merely reciting myth, it placed the origin of man back into an inconceivable antiquity.

And yet…it might be…there were many mysteries…legends of lost lands and lost civilizations that must have some basis in fact…the Mother Land of Mu, Atlantis, the unknown race that ruled Asia from the Gobi when that dread desert was a green Paradise…yes, it might be. But that they had conquered Death? No! That he did not believe.

He spoke with an irritation born of his doubts.

"If your people were so wise why did they not come forth and rule this world?"

"Why should they have?" she asked in turn. "If they had come forth what could they have done but build the rest of earth into likeness of this Yu- Atlanchi – as it was built in likeness of that older Yu-Atlanchi? There were none too many of them. Did I not say that when the Door of Death was closed so also was the Door of Life? It is true that always there have been some who elect to throw open these doors – my father and my mother were of these, Graydon. But they are few – so few! No, there was no reason why they should go beyond the barrier. All that they needed, all that they wanted, was here.

"And there was another reason. They had conquered dream. Through dream they create their own worlds; do therein as they will; live life upon life as they will it. In their dreams they shape world upon world – and each of these worlds is as real to them as this is to you. And so – many let the years stream by while they live in dream. Why should they have gone or why should they go out into this one world when they can create myriads of their own at will?"

"Suarra," he said, abruptly. "Just why do you want to save me?"

"Because," she murmured, slowly, "because you make me feel as I have never felt before. Because you make me happy – because you make me sorrowful! I want to be close to you. When you go – the world will be darkened –"

"Suarra!" he cried, and drew her, unresisting now, to him. His lips sought hers and her lips clung.

"I will come back," he whispered. "I will come back, Suarra."

"Come back!" her soft arms tightened round his neck, "Come back to me – Graydon!" She thrust him from her, leaped to her feet.

"No! No!" she sobbed. "No – Graydon! I am wicked. No – it would be death for you."

"As God lives," he told her, "I will come back to you."

She trembled; leaned forward, pressed her lips again to his, slipped from his arms and ran to the silken tent. For a moment she paused there – stretched wistful hands toward him; and was hidden in its folds. There seemed to come to him, faintly, heard only by his heart, her voice –

"Come back! Come back – to me!"

The complete and unabridged text is available online, from *flametreepublishing.com/extras*

If you enjoyed this, you might also like A. Merritt's *The Metal Monster*, also available online, from *flametreepublishing.com/extras*

A Strange Manuscript Found in a Copper Cylinder

Chapters I–VI

James De Mille

Chapter I
The Finding of the Copper Cylinder

IT OCCURRED as far back as February 15, 1850. It happened on that day that the yacht *Falcon* lay becalmed upon the ocean between the Canaries and the Madeira Islands. This yacht *Falcon* was the property of Lord Featherstone, who, being weary of life in England, had taken a few congenial friends for a winter's cruise in these southern latitudes. They had visited the Azores, the Canaries, and the Madeira Islands, and were now on their way to the Mediterranean.

The wind had failed, a deep calm had succeeded, and everywhere, as far as the eye could reach, the water was smooth and glassy. The yacht rose and fell at the impulse of the long ocean undulations, and the creaking of the spars sounded out a lazy accompaniment to the motion of the vessel. All around was a watery horizon, except in the one place only, toward the south, where far in the distance the Peak of Teneriffe rose into the air.

The profound calm, the warm atmosphere, the slow pitching of the yacht, and the dull creaking of the spars all combined to lull into a state of indolent repose the people on board. Forward were the crew; some asleep, others smoking, others playing cards. At the stern were Oxenden, the intimate friend of Featherstone, and Dr. Congreve, who had come in the double capacity of friend and medical attendant. These two, like the crew, were in a state of dull and languid repose. Suspended between the two masts, in an Indian hammock, lay Featherstone, with a cigar in his mouth and a novel in his hand, which he was pretending to read. The fourth member of the party, Melick, was seated near the mainmast, folding some papers in a peculiar way. His occupation at length attracted the roving eyes of Featherstone, who poked forth his head from his hammock, and said in a sleepy voice:

"I say, Melick, you're the most energetic fellah I ever saw. By Jove! You're the only one aboard that's busy. What are you doing?"

"Paper boats," said Melick, in a business-like tone.

"Paper boats! By Jove!" said Featherstone. "What for?"

"I'm going to have a regatta," said Melick. "Anything to kill time, you know."

"By Jove!" exclaimed Featherstone again, raising himself higher in his hammock, "that's not a bad idea. A wegatta! By Jove! Glowious! Glowious! I say, Oxenden, did you hear that?"

"What do you mean by a regatta?" asked Oxenden, lazily.

"Oh, I mean a race with these paper boats. We can bet on them, you know."

At this Featherstone sat upright, with his legs dangling out of the hammock.

"By Jove!" he exclaimed again. "Betting! So we can. Do you know, Melick, old chap, I think that's a wegular piece of inspiration. A wegatta! And we can bet on the best boat."

"But there isn't any wind," said Oxenden.

"Well, you know, that's the fun of it," said Melick, who went solemnly on as he spoke, folding his paper boats; "that's the fun of it. For you see if there was a wind we should be going on ourselves, and the regatta couldn't come off; but, as it is, the water is just right. You pick out your boat, and lay your bet on her to race to some given point."

"A given point? But how can we find any?"

"Oh, easily enough; something or anything – a bubble'll do, or we can pitch out a bit of wood."

Upon this Featherstone descended from his perch, and came near to examine the proceedings, while the other two, eager to take advantage of the new excitement, soon joined him. By this time Melick had finished his paper boats. There were four of them, and they were made of different colors, namely, red, green, yellow, and white.

"I'll put these in the water," said Melick, "and then we can lay our bets on them as we choose. But first let us see if there is anything that can be taken as a point of arrival. If there isn't anything, I can pitch out a bit of wood, in any direction which may seem best."

Saying this, he went to the side, followed by the others, and all looked out carefully over the water.

"There's a black speck out there," said Oxenden.

"So there is," said Featherstone. "That'll do. I wonder what it is?"

"Oh, a bit of timber," said Melick. "Probably the spar of some ship."

"It don't look like a spar," said the doctor; "it's only a round spot, like the float of some net."

"Oh, it's a spar," said Melick. "It's one end of it, the rest is under water."

The spot thus chosen was a dark, circular object, about a hundred yards away, and certainly did look very much like the extremity of some spar, the rest of which was under water. Whatever it was, however, it served well enough for their present purpose, and no one took any further interest in it, except as the point toward which the paper boats should run in their eventful race.

Melick now let himself down over the side, and placed the paper boats on the water as carefully as possible. After this the four stood watching the little fleet in silence. The water was perfectly still, and there was no perceptible wind, but there were draughts of air caused by the rise and fall of the yacht, and these affected the tiny boats. Gradually they drew apart, the green one drifting astern, the yellow one remaining under the vessel, while the red and the white were carried out in the direction where they were expected to go, with about a foot of space between them.

"Two to one on the red!" cried Featherstone, betting on the one which had gained the lead.

"Done," said Melick, promptly taking his offer.

Oxenden made the same bet, which was taken by Melick and the doctor.

Other bets were now made as to the direction which they would take, as to the distance by which the red would beat the white, as to the time which would be occupied by the race, and as to fifty other things which need not be mentioned. All took part in this; the excitement rose high and the betting went on merrily. At length it was noticed that the white was overhauling the red. The excitement grew intense; the betting changed its form, but was still kept up, until at last the two paper boats seemed blended together in one dim spot which gradually faded out of sight.

It was now necessary to determine the state of the race, so Featherstone ordered out the boat. The four were soon embarked, and the men rowed out toward the point which had been chosen as the end of the race. On coming near they found the paper boats stuck together, saturated with water, and floating limp on the surface. An animated discussion arose about this. Some of the bets were off, but others remained an open question, and each side insisted upon a different view of the case. In the midst of this, Featherstone's attention was drawn to the dark spot already mentioned as the goal of the race.

"That's a queer-looking thing," said he, suddenly. "Pull up, lads, a little; let's see what it is. It doesn't look to me like a spar."

The others, always on the lookout for some new object of interest, were attracted by these words, and looked closely at the thing in question. The men pulled. The boat drew nearer.

"It's some sort of floating vessel," said Oxenden.

"It's not a spar," said Melick, who was at the bow.

And as he said this he reached out and grasped at it. He failed to get it, and did no more than touch it. It moved easily and sank, but soon came up again. A second time he grasped at it, and with both hands. This time he caught it, and then lifted it out of the water into the boat. These proceedings had been watched with the deepest interest; and now, as this curious floating thing made its appearance among them, they all crowded around it in eager excitement.

"It looks like a can of preserved meat," said the doctor.

"It certainly is a can," said Melick, "for it's made of metal; but as to preserved meat, I have my doubts."

The article in question was made of metal and was cylindrical in shape. It was soldered tight and evidently contained something. It was about eighteen inches long and eight wide. The nature of the metal was not easily perceptible, for it was coated with slime, and covered over about half its surface with barnacles and seaweed. It was not heavy, and would have floated higher out of the water had it not been for these encumbrances.

"It's some kind of preserved meat," said the doctor. "Perhaps something good – game, I dare say – yes, Yorkshire game-pie. They pot all sorts of things now."

"If it's game," said Oxenden, "it'll be rather high by this time. Man alive! Look at those weeds and shells. It must have been floating for ages."

"It's my belief," said Featherstone, "that it's part of the provisions laid in by Noah for his long voyage in the ark. So come, let's open it, and see what sort of diet the antediluvians had."

"It may be liquor," said Oxenden.

Melick shook his head.

"No," said he; "there's something inside, but whatever it is, it isn't liquor. It's odd, too. The thing is of foreign make, evidently. I never saw anything like it before. It may be Chinese."

"By Jove!" cried Featherstone, "this is getting exciting. Let's go back to the yacht and open it."

The men rowed back to the yacht.

"It's meat of some sort," continued the doctor. "I'm certain of that. It has come in good time. We can have it for dinner."

"You may have my share, then," said Oxenden. "I hereby give and bequeath to you all my right, title, and interest in and to anything in the shape of meat that may be inside."

"Meat cans," said Melick, "are never so large as that."

"Oh, I don't know about that," said the doctor, "they make up pretty large packages of pemmican for the arctic expeditions."

"But they never pack up pemmican in copper cylinders," said Melick, who had been using his knife to scrape off the crust from the vessel.

"Copper!" exclaimed Oxenden. "Is it copper?"

"Look for yourselves," said Melick, quietly.

They all looked, and could see, where the knife had cut into the vessel, that it was as he said. It was copper.

"It's foreign work," said Melick. "In England we make tin cans for everything. It may be something that's drifted out from Mogadore or some port in Morocco."

"In that case," said Oxenden, "it may contain the mangled remains of one of the wives of some Moorish pasha."

By this time they had reached the yacht and hurried aboard. All were eager to satisfy their curiosity. Search was made for a cold-chisel, but to no purpose. Then Featherstone produced a knife which was used to open sardine boxes, but after a faithful trial this proved useless. At length Melick, who had gone off in search of something more effective, made his appearance armed with an axe. With this he attacked the copper cylinder, and by means of a few dexterous blows succeeded in cutting it open. Then he looked in.

"What do you see?" asked Featherstone.

"Something," said Melick, "but I can't quite make it out."

"If you can't make it out, then shake it out," said Oxenden.

Upon this Melick took the cylinder, turned it upside down, shook it smartly, and then lifted it and pounded it against the deck. This served to loosen the contents, which seemed tightly packed, but came gradually down until at length they could be seen and drawn forth. Melick drew them forth, and the contents of the mysterious copper cylinder resolved themselves into two packages.

The sight of these packages only served to intensify their curiosity. If it had been some species of food it would at once have revealed itself, but these packages suggested something more important. What could they be? Were there treasures inside – jewels, or golden ornaments from some Moorish seraglio, or strange coin from far Cathay?

One of the packages was very much larger than the other. It was enclosed in wrappers made of some coarse kind of felt, bound tight with strong cords. The other was much smaller, and, was folded in the same material without being bound. This Melick seized and began to open.

"Wait a minute," said Featherstone. "Let's make a bet on it. Five guineas that it's some sort of jewels!"

"Done," said Oxenden.

Melick opened the package, and it was seen that Featherstone had lost. There were no jewels, but one or two sheets of something that looked like paper. It was not paper however, but some vegetable product which was used for the same purpose. The surface was smooth, but the color was dingy, and the lines of the vegetable fibres were plainly discernible. These sheets were covered with writing.

"Halloa!" cried Melick. "Why, this is English!"

At this the others crowded around to look on, and Featherstone in his excitement forgot that he had lost his bet. There were three sheets, all covered with writing – one in English, another in French, and a third in German. It was the same message, written in these three different languages. But at that moment they scarcely noticed this. All that they saw was the message itself, with its mysterious meaning.

It was as follows:

To the finder of this:

Sir, – I am an Englishman, and have been carried by a series of incredible events to a land from which escape is as impossible as from the grave. I have written this and committed it to the sea, in the hope that the ocean currents may bear it within the reach of civilized man. Oh, unknown friend! whoever you are. I entreat you to let this message be made known in some way to my father, Henry More, Keswick, Cumberland, England, so that he may learn the fate of his son. The MS. accompanying this contains an account of my adventures, which I should like to have forwarded to him. Do this for the sake of that mercy which you may one day wish to have shown to yourself.

ADAM MORE.

"By Jove!" cried Featherstone, as he read the above, "this is really getting to be something tremendous."

"This other package must be the manuscript," said Oxenden, "and it'll tell all about it."

"Such a manuscript'll be better than meat," said the doctor, sententiously.

Melick said nothing, but, opening his knife, he cut the cords and unfolded the wrapper. He saw a great collection of leaves, just like those of the letter, of some vegetable substance, smooth as paper, and covered with writing.

"It looks like Egyptian papyrus," said the doctor. "That was the common paper of antiquity."

"Never mind the Egyptian papyrus," said Featherstone, in feverish curiosity. "Let's have the contents of the manuscript. You, Melick, read; you're the most energetic of the lot, and when you're tired the rest of us will take turns."

"Read? Why, it'll take a month to read all this," said Melick.

"All the better," said Featherstone; "this calm will probably last a month, and we shall have nothing to interest us."

Melick made no further objection. He was as excited as the rest, and so he began the reading of the manuscript.

Chapter II
Adrift in the Antarctic Ocean

MY NAME IS Adam More. I am the son of Henry More, apothecary, Keswick, Cumberland. I was mate of the ship *Trevelyan* (Bennet, master), which was chartered by the British Government to convey convicts to Van Dieman's Land. This was in 1843. We made our voyage without any casualty, landed our convicts in Hobart Town, and then set forth on our return home. It was the 17th of December when we left. From the first adverse winds prevailed, and in order to make any progress we were obliged to keep well to the south. At length, on the 6th of January, we sighted Desolation Island. We found it, indeed, a desolate spot. In its vicinity we saw a multitude of smaller islands, perhaps a thousand in number, which made navigation difficult, and forced us to hurry away as fast as possible. But the aspect of this dreary spot was of itself enough to repel us. There were no trees, and the multitude of islands seemed like moss-covered rocks; while the temperature, though in the middle of the antarctic summer, was from 38° to 58° Fahr.

In order to get rid of these dangerous islands we stood south and west, and at length found ourselves in south latitude 65°, longitude 60° east. We were fortunate enough not to find any ice, although we were within fifteen hundred miles of the South Pole, and far within that impenetrable icy barrier which, in 1773, had arrested the progress of Captain Cook. Here the wind failed us, and we lay becalmed and drifting. The sea was open all around us, except to the southeast, where there was a low line along the horizon terminating in a lofty promontory; but though it looked like land we took it for ice. All around us whales and grampuses were gambolling and spouting in vast numbers. The weather was remarkably fine and clear.

For two or three days the calm continued, and we drifted along helplessly, until at length we found ourselves within a few miles of the promontory above mentioned. It looked like land, and seemed to be a rocky island rising from the depths of the sea. It was, however, all covered with ice and snow, and from this there extended eastward as far as the eye could reach an interminable line of ice, but toward the southwest the sea seemed open to navigation. The promontory was very singular in shape, rising up to a peak which was at least a thousand feet in height, and forming a striking object, easily discovered and readily identified by any future explorer. We named it, after our ship, Trevelyan Peak, and then felt anxious to lose sight of it forever. But the calm continued, and at length we drifted in close enough to see immense flocks of seals dotting the ice at the foot of the peak.

Upon this I proposed to Agnew, the second mate, that we should go ashore, shoot some seals, and bring them back. This was partly for the excitement of the hunt, and partly for the honor of landing in a place never before trodden by the foot of man. Captain Bennet made some objections, but he was old and cautious, and we were young and venturesome, so we laughed away his scruples and set forth. We did not take any of the crew, owing to the captain's objections. He said that if we chose to throw away our own lives he could not help it, but that he would positively refuse to allow a single man to go with us. We thought this refusal an excess of caution amounting to positive cowardice, but were unable to change his mind. The distance was not great, the adventure was attractive, and so the captain's gig was lowered, and in this Agnew and I rowed ashore. We took with us a double-barrelled rifle apiece, and also a pistol. Agnew took a glass.

We rowed for about three miles, and reached the edge of the ice, which extended far out from the promontory. Here we landed, and secured the boat by means of a small grappling-iron, which we thrust into the ice. We then walked toward the promontory for about a mile, and here we found a multitude of seals. These animals were so fearless that they made not the slightest movement as we came up, but stared at us in an indifferent way. We killed two or three, and then debated whether to go to the promontory or not.

Agnew was eager to go, so as to touch the actual rock; but I was satisfied with what we had done, and was now desirous of returning. In the midst of this I felt a flake of snow on my cheek. I started and looked up. To my great surprise I saw that the sky had changed since I had last noticed it. When we left the ship it was clear and blue, but now it was overspread with dark, leaden-colored clouds, and the snowflakes that had fallen were ominous of evil. A snowstorm here, in the vicinity of the ice, was too serious a thing to be disregarded. But one course now remained, and that was an immediate return to the ship.

Each of us seized a seal and dragged it after us to the boat. We reached it and flung them in. Just at that moment a gun sounded over the water. It was from the ship – the signal of alarm – the summons from the captain for our return. We saw now that she had been drifting since we left her, and had moved southwest several miles. The row back promised to be far harder than the pull ashore, and, what was worse, the wind was coming up, the sea was rising, and the snow was thickening. Neither of us said a word. We saw that our situation was very serious, and that we had been very foolhardy; but the words were useless now. The only thing to be done was to pull for the ship with all our strength, and that was what we did.

So we pushed off, and rowed as we had never rowed before. Our progress was difficult. The sea grew steadily rougher; the wind increased; the snow thickened; and, worst of all, the day was drawing to a close. We had miscalculated both as to distance and time. Even if it had continued calm we should have had to row back in the dark; but now the sun was setting, and with the darkness we had to encounter the gathering storm and the blinding snow. We rowed in silence. At every stroke our situation grew more serious. The wind was from the south, and therefore favored us to some extent, and also made less of a sea than would have been produced by a wind from any other quarter; but then this south wind brought dangers of its own, which we were soon to feel – new dangers and worse ones. For this south wind drove the ship farther from us, and at the same time broke up the vast fields of ice and impelled the fractured masses northward. But this was a danger which we did not know just then. At that time we were rowing for the ship, and amid the darkness and the blinding snow and the dashing waves we heard from time to time the report of signal guns fired from the ship to guide us back. These were our only guide, for thc darkness and the snow had drawn the ship from our sight, and we had to be guided by our hearing only.

We were rowing for our lives, and we knew it; but every moment our situation grew more desperate. Each new report of the gun seemed to sound farther away. We seemed always to be rowing in the wrong direction. At each report we had to shift the boat's course somewhat, and pull toward the last point from which the gun seemed to sound. With all this the wind was increasing rapidly to a gale, the sea was rising and breaking over the boat, the snow was blinding us with its ever-thickening sleet. The darkness deepened and at length had grown so intense that nothing whatever could be seen – neither sea nor sky, not even the boat itself – yet we dared not stop; we had to row. Our lives depended on our efforts. We had to row, guided by the sound of the ship's gun, which the ever-varying wind incessantly changed, till our minds grew all confused, and we rowed blindly and mechanically.

So we labored for hours at the oars, and the storm continually increased, and the sea continually rose, while the snow fell thicker and the darkness grew intenser. The reports of the gun now grew fainter; what was worse, they were heard at longer intervals, and his showed us that Captain Bennet was losing heart; that he was giving us up; that he despaired of finding us, and was now firing only an occasional gun out of a mournful sense of duty. This thought reduced us to despair. It seemed as if all our efforts had only served to take us farther away from the ship, and deprived us of all motive for rowing any harder than was barely necessary to keep the boat steady. After a time Agnew dropped his oar and began to bail out the boat – a work which was needed; for, in spite of our care, she had shipped many seas, and was one third full of water. He worked away at this while I managed the boat, and then we took turns at bailing. In this way we passed the dreary night.

Morning came at last. The wind was not so violent, but the snow was so thick that we could only see for a little distance around us. The ship was nowhere visible, nor were there any signs of her. The last gun had been fired during the night. All that we could see was the outline of a gaunt iceberg – an ominous spectacle. Not knowing what else to do we rowed on as before, keeping in what seemed our best course, though this was mere conjecture, and we knew all the time that we might be going wrong. There was no compass in the boat, nor could we tell the sun's position through the thick snow. We rowed with the wind, thinking that it was blowing toward the north, and would carry us in that direction. We still hoped to come within sound of the ship's gun, and kept straining our ears incessantly to hear the wished-for report. But no such sound ever came again, and we heard nothing except the plash of the waves and the crash of breaking ice. Thus all that day we rowed along, resting at intervals when exhausted, and then resuming our labors, until at length night came; and again to the snow and ice and waves was added the horror of great darkness. We passed that night in deep misery. We had eaten nothing since we left the ship, but though exhausted by long fasting and severe labor, the despair of our hearts took away all desire for food. We were worn out with hard work, yet the cold was too great to allow us to take rest, and we were compelled to row so as to keep ourselves from perishing. But fatigue and drowsiness overcame us, and we often sank into sleep even while rowing; and then after a brief slumber we would awake with benumbed limbs to wrestle again with the oars. In this way we passed that night.

Another morning came, and we found to our great joy that the snow had ceased. We looked eagerly around to see if there were any signs of the ship. Nothing could be seen of her. Far away on one side rose a peak, which looked like the place where we had landed. Judging from the wind, which we still supposed to be southerly, the peak lay toward the northeast; in which case we had been carried steadily, in spite of all our efforts, toward the south. About a mile on one side of us the ice began, and extended far away; while on the other side, at the distance of some ten miles, there was another line of ice. We seemed to have been carried in a southwesterly direction along a broad strait that ran into the vast ice fields. This discovery showed how utterly useless our labors had been; for in spite of all, even with the wind in our favor, we had been drawn steadily in an opposite direction. It was evident that there was some current here, stronger than all our strength, which had brought us to this place.

We now determined to land on the ice, and try to cook a portion of our seals. On approaching it we noticed that there was a current which tended to draw us past the ice in what I supposed to be a southwesterly direction. This confirmed my worst fears. But now the labor of landing and building a fire on the ice served to interest us for a time and divert our thoughts. We brushed away the snow, and then broke up a box which was in the boat, and also the stern seats. This we used very sparingly, reservin the rest for another occasion. Then we cut portions from one of the seals, and laid ther in thin strips on the flames. The cooking was but slight, for the meat was merely singec but we were ravenous, and the contact of the fire was enough to give it an attractiv flavor. With this food we were greatly refreshed; and as for drink, we had all around u an endless extent of ice and snow. Then, taking our precious fragments of cooked meat we returned to the boat and put off. We could scarcely tell what to do next, and whil debating on this point we fell asleep. We slept far into the night, then awoke benumbec with cold; then took to the oars till we were weary; then fell asleep again, to be agair awakened by the cold and again to pull at the oars. So the night passed, and anothe day came.

The snow still held off, but the sky was overcast with dark, leaden-colored clouds, anc looked threatening. Ice was all around us as before; and the open water had diminishec now from ten miles to five miles of width. The ice on one side was low, but on the opposite side it arose to the height of one hundred feet. We saw here, as we watchec the shore, that the current which had already borne us thus far was now stronger than ever, and was carrying us along at a rate which made all efforts of ours against it utterly useless. And now a debate arose between us as to the direction of this current. Agnew suddenly declared his belief that it was running north, while I was firm in the conviction that it ran south.

"There's no use rowing any more," said Agnew. "If it runs south we can't resist it. It's too strong. But I always like to look on the bright side, and so I believe it runs north. In that case there is no use rowing, for it will carry us along fast enough."

Then I proposed that we should go ashore on the ice. To this Agnew objected, but afterward consented, at my earnest request. So we tried to get ashore, but this time found it impossible; for the ice consisted of a vast sheet of floating lumps, which looked like the ruin of bergs that had been broken up in some storm. After this I had nothing to say, nor was there anything left for us but to drift wherever the current might carry us.

So we drifted for some days, Agnew all the time maintaining that we were going north, while I was sure that we were going south. The sky remained as cloudy as ever, the wind varied incessantly, and there was nothing by which we could conjecture the points of the compass. We lived on our seal, and for drink we chewed ice and snow. One thing was certain – the climate was no colder. Agnew laid great stress on this.

"You see," said he, "we must be going north. If we were going south we should be frozen stiff by this time."

"Yes; but if we were going north," said I, "we ought to find it growing warmer."

"No," said he, "not with all this ice around us. It's the ice that keeps the temperature in this cold state."

Argument could do no good, and so we each remained true to our belief – his leading him to hope, and mine dragging me down to despair. At length we finished the last fragment of the seal that we had cooked, and, finding ourselves near some firm ice, we went ashore and cooked all that was left, using the remainder of our wood for fuel, and all that we dared to remove from the boat. Re-embarking with this, we drifted on as before.

Several more days passed. At last one night I was roused by Agnew. He pointed far away to the distant horizon, where I saw a deep red glow as of fire. We were both filled with wonder at the sight, and were utterly unable to account for it. We knew that it could not be caused by the sun or the moon, for it was midnight, and the cause lay on the earth and not in the skies. It was a deep, lurid glow, extending along the horizon, and seemed to be caused by some vast conflagration.

Chapter III
A World of Fire and Desolation

AT THE SIGHT of that deep red glow various feelings arose within us: in me there was new dejection; in Agnew there was stronger hope. I could not think but that it was our ship that was on fire, and was burning before our eyes. Agnew thought that it was some burning forest, and that it showed our approach to some habitable and inhabited land. For hour after hour we watched, and all the time the current drew us nearer, and the glow grew brighter and more intense. At last we were too weak to watch any longer, and we fell asleep.

On waking our first thoughts were about the fire, and we looked eagerly around. It was day, but the sky was as gloomy as ever, and the fire was there before our eyes, bright and terrible. We could now see it plainly, and discern the cause also. The fire came from two points, at some distance apart – two peaks rising above the horizon, from which there burst forth flames and smoke with incessant explosions. All was now manifest. It was no burning ship, no blazing forest, no land inhabited by man: those blazing peaks were two volcanoes in a state of active eruption, and at that sight I knew the worst.

"I know where we are now," I said, despairingly.

"Where?" asked Agnew.

"That," said I, "is the antarctic continent."

"The antarctic fiddlestick," said he, contemptuously. "It is far more likely to be some volcanic island in the South Sea. There's a tremendous volcano in the Sandwich Islands, and these are something like it."

"I believe," said I, "that these are the very volcanoes that Sir James Ross discovered last year."

"Do you happen to know where he found them?" Agnew asked.

"I do not," I answered.

"Well, I do," said he, "and they're thousands of miles away from this. They are south latitude 77°, east longitude 167°; while we, as I guess, are about south latitude 40°, east longitude 60°."

"At any rate," said I, "we're drifting straight toward them."

"So I see," said Agnew, dryly. "At any rate, the current will take us somewhere. We shall find ourselves carried past these volcanic islands, or through them, and then west to the Cape of Good Hope. Besides, even here we may find land with animals and vegetation; who knows?"

"What! amid all this ice?" I cried. "Are you mad?"

"Mad?" said he; "I should certainly go mad if I hadn't hope."

"Hope!" I repeated; "I have long since given up hope."

"Oh, well," said he, "enjoy your despair, and don't try to deprive me of my consolation. My hope sustains me, and helps me to cheer you up. It would never do, old fellow, for both of us to knock under."

I said nothing more, nor did Agnew. We drifted on, and all our thoughts were taken up with the two volcanoes, toward which we were every moment drawing nearer.

As we approached they grew larger and larger, towering up to a tremendous height I had seen Vesuvius and Stromboli and Etna and Cotopaxi; but these appeared far larger than any of them, not excepting the last. They rose, like the Peak of Teneriffe, abruptly from the sea, with no intervening hills to dwarf or diminish their proportions. They were ten or twelve miles apart, and the channel of water in which we were drifting flowed between them.

Here the ice and snow ended. We thus came at last to land; but it was a land that seemed more terrible than even the bleak expanse of ice and snow that lay behind, for nothing could be seen except a vast and drear accumulation of lava-blocks of every imaginable shape, without a trace of vegetation – uninhabited, uninhabitable, and unpassable to man. But just where the ice ended and the rocks began there was a long, low reef, which projected for more than a quarter of a mile into the water, affording the only possible landing place within sight. Here we decided to land, so as to rest and consider what was best to be done.

Here we landed, and walked up to where rugged lava-blocks prevented any further progress. But at this spot our attention was suddenly arrested by a sight of horror. It was a human figure lying prostrate, face downward.

At this sight there came over us a terrible sensation. Even Agnew's buoyant soul shrank back, and we stared at each other with quivering lips. It was some time before we could recover ourselves; then we went to the figure, and stooped down to examine it.

The clothes were those of a European and a sailor; the frame was emaciated and dried up, till it looked like a skeleton; the face was blackened and all withered, and the bony hands were clinched tight. It was evidently some sailor who had suffered shipwreck in these frightful solitudes, and had drifted here to starve to death in this appalling wilderness. It was a sight which seemed ominous of our own fate, and Agnew's boasted hope, which had so long upheld him, now sank down into a despair as deep as my own. What room was there now for hope, or how could we expect any other fate than this?

At length I began to search the pockets of the deceased.

"What are you doing?" asked Agnew, in a hoarse voice.

"I'm trying to find out who he is," I said. "Perhaps there may be papers."

As I said this I felt something in the breast pocket of his jacket, and drew it forth. It was a leather pocketbook, mouldy and rotten like the clothing. On opening it, it fell to pieces. There was nothing in it but a piece of paper, also mouldy and rotten. This I unfolded with great care, and saw writing there, which, though faded, was still legible. It was a letter, and there were still signs of long and frequent perusals, and marks, too, which looked as though made by tears – tears, perhaps of the writer, perhaps of the reader: who can tell? I have preserved this letter ever since, and I now fasten it here upon this sheet of my manuscript.

THE LETTER.

Bristol April 20. 1820.

my darling tom

*i writ you these few lines in hast i don like youar gon a walen an in the south sea dont go darlin tom or mebbe ill never se you agin for ave bad drems of you darlin tom an im afraid so don go my darlin tom but come back an take anoth ship for America baby i as wel as ever but mises is pa an as got a new tooth an i think yo otnt go a walen o darlin tom * * * sea as the wages was i in New York an better go thar an id*

like to go ther for good for they gives good wages in America. O come back my Darlin tom and take me to America an the baby an weel all live an love an di together
Your loving wife Polley Reed.

I began to read this, but there came a lump in my throat, and I had to stop. Agnew leaned on my shoulder, and we both read it in silence. He rubbed the back of his hand over his eyes and drew a long breath. Then he walked away for a little distance, and I put the letter carefully away in my own pocketbook. After a little while Agnew came back.

"More," said he, "do you remember any of the burial service?"

I understood his meaning at once.

"Yes," I said, "some of it – a good deal of it, I think."

"That's good," said he. "Let's put the poor fellow under ground."

"It would be hard to do that," I said; "we'll have to bury him in the snow."

At this Agnew went off for a little distance and clambered over the rocks. He was not gone long. When he returned he said, "I've found some crumbled pumice stone; we can scoop a grave for him there."

We then raised the body and carried it to the place which Agnew had found. So emaciated was the poor dead sailor that his remains were no heavier than a small boy. On reaching the spot, we found the crumbled pumice stone. We placed the body in a crevice among the lava rocks, and then I said what I could remember of the burial service. After this we carried in our hands the crumbled pumice stone until we had covered the body, and thus gave the poor fellow a Christian burial.

We then returned to the shore.

"More, old fellow," said Agnew, "I feel the better for this; the service has done me good."

"And me too," said I. "It has reminded me of what I had forgotten. This world is only a part of life. We may lose it and yet live on. There is another world; and if we can only keep that in our minds we sha'n't be so ready to sink into despair – that is, I sha'n't. Despair is my weakness; you are more hopeful."

"Yes," said Agnew, solemnly; "but my hope thus far has referred only to the safety of my skin. After this I shall try to think of my soul, and cultivate, not the hope of escape, but the hope full of immortality. Yes, More, after all we shall live, if not in England, then, let us hope, in heaven."

There was a long silence after this – that kind of silence which one may preserve who is at the point of death.

"I wonder how he got here?" said Agnew, at last. "The letter mentions a whaler. No doubt the ship has been driven too far south; it has foundered; he has escaped in a boat, either alone or with others; he has been carried along this channel, and has landed here, afraid to go any farther."

"But his boat, what has become of that?"

"His boat! That must have gone long ago. The letter was written in 1820. At any rate, let's look around."

We did so. After some search we found fragments of a rotted rope attached to a piece of rock.

"That," said Agnew, "must have been fastened to the boat; and as for the boat herself, she has long ago been swept away from this."

"What shall we do now?" I said, after a long silence.

"There's only one thing," said Agnew. "We must go on."

"Go on?" I asked, in wonder.

"Certainly," said he, confidently. "Will you stay here? No. Will you go back? You can We must, therefore, go on. That is our only hope."

"Hope!" I cried. "Do you still talk of hope?"

"Hope?" said Agnew; "of course. Why not? There are no limits to hope, are there One can hope anything anywhere. It is better to die while struggling like a man, full of hop and energy than to perish in inaction and despair. It is better to die in the storm and furiou waters than to waste away in this awful place. So come along. Let's drift as before. Let's se where this channel will take us. It will certainly take us somewhere. Such a stream as thi must have some outlet."

"This stream," said I, "will take us to death, and death only. The current grows swifte every hour. I've heard some old yarn of a vast opening at each of the poles, or one of them into which the waters of the ocean pour. They fall into one, and some say they go throug and come out at the other."

Agnew laughed.

"That," said he, "is a madman's dream. In the first place, I don't believe that we are approaching the south, but the north. The warmth of the climate here shows that. Yes, we are drawing north. We shall soon emerge into warm waters and bright skies. So come along and let us lose no more time."

I made no further objection. There was nothing else to be done, and at the very worst we could not be in greater danger while drifting on than in remaining behind. Soon, therefore, we were again in the boat, and the current swept us on as before.

The channel now was about four miles wide. On either side arose the lofty volcanoes vomiting forth flames and smoke with furious explosions; vast stones were hurled up into the air from the craters; streams of molten lava rolled down, and at intervals there fell great showers of ashes. The shores on either side were precipitous and rugged beyond all description, looking like fiery lava streams which had been arrested by the flood, and cooled into gloomy, overhanging cliffs. The lava rock was of a deep, dull slate color, which at a distance looked black; and the blackness which thus succeeded to the whiteness of the snow behind us seemed like the funeral pall of nature. Through scenes like these we drifted on, and the volcanoes on either side of the channel towered on high with their fiery floods of lava, their incessant explosions, their fierce outbursts of flames, and overhead there rolled a dense black canopy of smoke – altogether forming a terrific approach to that unknown and awful pathway upon which we were going. So we passed this dread portal, and then there lay before us – what? Was it a land of life or a land of death? Who could say?

It was evening when we passed through. Night came on, and the darkness was illuminated by the fiery glow of the volcanic flames. Worn out with fatigue, we fell asleep. So the night passed, and the current bore us on until, at length, the morning came. We awoke, and now, for the first time in many days, we saw the face of the sun. The clouds had at last broken, the sky was clear, and behind us the sun was shining. That sight told us all. It showed us where we were going.

I pointed to the sun.

"Look there," said I. "There is the sun in the northern sky – behind us. We have been drifting steadily toward the south."

At this Agnew was silent, and sat looking back for a long time. There we could still see the glow of the volcanic fires, though they were now many miles away; while the sun, but lately risen, was lying on a course closer to the horizon than we had ever seen it before.

"We are going south," said I – "to the South Pole. This swift current can have but one ending – there may be an opening at the South Pole, or a whirlpool like the Maelstrom."

Agnew looked around with a smile.

"All these notions," said he, "are dreams, or theories, or guesses. There is no evidence to prove them. Why trouble yourself about a guess? You and I can guess, and with better reason; for we have now, it seems, come farther south than any human being who has ever lived. Do not imagine that the surface of the earth is different at the poles from what it is anywhere else. If we get to the South Pole we shall see there what we have always seen – the open view of land or water, and the boundary of the horizon. As for this current, it seems to me like the Gulf Stream, and it evidently does an important work in the movement of the ocean waters. It pours on through vast fields of ice on its way to other oceans, where it will probably become united with new currents. Theories about openings at the poles, or whirlpools, must be given up. Since the Maelstrom has been found to be a fiction, no one need believe in any other whirlpool. For my own part, I now believe that this current will bear us on, due south, over the pole, and then still onward, until at last we shall find ourselves in the South Pacific Ocean. So cheer up – don't be downhearted; there's still hope. We have left the ice and snow behind, and already the air is warmer. Cheer up; we may find our luck turn at any moment."

To this I had no reply to make. Agnew's confidence seemed to me to be assumed, and certainly did not alleviate my own deep gloom, nor was the scene around calculated to rouse me in the slightest degree out of my despair. The channel had now lessened to a width of not more than two miles; the shores on either side were precipitous cliffs, broken by occasional declivities, but all of solid rock, so dark as to be almost black, and evidently of volcanic origin. At times there arose rugged eminences, scarred and riven, indescribably dismal and appalling. There was not only an utter absence of life here in these abhorrent regions, but an actual impossibility of life which was enough to make the stoutest heart quail. The rocks looked like iron. It seemed a land of iron penetrated by this ocean stream which had made for itself a channel, and now bore us onward to a destination which was beyond all conjecture.

Through such scenes we drifted all that day. Night came, and in the skies overhead there arose a brilliant display of the aurora australis, while toward the north the volcanic fires glowed with intense lustre. That night we slept. On awakening we noticed a change in the scene. The shores, though still black and forbidding, were no longer precipitous, but sloped down gradually to the water; the climate was sensibly milder, and far away before us there arose a line of giant mountains, whose summits were covered with ice and snow that gleamed white and purple in the rays of the sun.

Suddenly Agnew gave a cry, and pointed to the opposite shore.

"Look!" he cried – "do you see? They are men!"

I looked, and there I saw plainly some moving figures that were, beyond a doubt, human beings.

Chapter IV
The Sight of Human Beings

THE SIGHT of human beings, thus unexpectedly found, filled us with strange feelings – feelings which I cannot explain. The country was still iron-bound and dark and forbidding, and the stream ran on in a strong current, deep, black as ink, and resistless as fate; the sky behind was lighted up by the volcanic glare which still shone from afar;

and in front the view was bounded by the icy heights of a mountain chain. Here was, indeed, a strange country for a human habitation; and strange, indeed, were the human beings whom we saw.

"Shall we land?" said Agnew.

"Oh no," said I. "Don't be hasty. The elements are sometimes kinder than men, and I feel safer here, even in this river of death, than ashore with such creatures as those."

Agnew made no reply. We watched the figures on the shore. We saw them coming down staring and gesticulating. We drew on nearer to them till we were able to see them better. A nearer view did not improve them. They were human beings, certainly, but of such an appalling aspect that they could only be likened to animated mummies. They were small, thin, shrivelled, black, with long matted hair and hideous faces. They all had long spears, and wore about the waist short skirts that seemed to be made of the skin of some seafowl.

We could not imagine how these creatures lived, or where. There were no signs of vegetation of any kind – not a tree or a shrub. There were no animals; but there were great flocks of birds, some of which seemed different from anything that we had ever seen before. The long spears which the natives carried might possibly be used for catching these, or for fishing purposes. This thought made them seem less formidable, since they would thus be instruments of food rather than weapons of war. Meanwhile we drifted on as before, and the natives watched us, running along the shore abreast of us, so as to keep up with the boat. There seemed over a hundred of them. We could see no signs of any habitations – no huts, however humble; but we concluded that their abodes were farther inland. As for the natives themselves, the longer we looked at them the more abhorrent they grew. Even the wretched aborigines of Van Dieman's Land, who have been classed lowest in the scale of humanity, were pleasing and congenial when compared with these, and the land looked worse than Tierra del Fuego. It looked like a land of iron, and its inhabitants like fiends.

Agnew again proposed to land, but I refused.

"No," I said; "I'd rather starve for a week, and live on hope. Let us drift on. If we go on we may have hope if we choose, but if we land here we shall lose even that. Can we hope for anything from such things as these? Even if they prove friendly, can we live among them? To stay here is worse than death; our only hope is to go on."

Agnew made no reply, and we drifted on for two hours, still followed by the natives. They made no hostile demonstrations. They merely watched us, apparently from motives of curiosity. All this time we were drawing steadily nearer to the line of lofty mountains, which with their icy crests rose before us like an inaccessible and impassable barrier, apparently closing up all farther progress; nor was there any indication of any pass or any opening, however narrow, through which the great stream might run. Nothing was there but one unbroken wall of iron cliffs and icy summits. At last we saw that the sloping shores grew steeper, until, about a mile or two before us, they changed to towering cliffs that rose up on each side for about a thousand feet above the water; here the stream ran, and became lost to view as completely as though swallowed up by the earth.

"We can go no farther," said Agnew. "See – this stream seems to make a plunge there into the mountains. There must be some deep canyon there with cataracts. To go on is certain death. We must stop here, if only to deliberate. Say, shall we risk it among these natives? After all, there is not, perhaps, any danger among them. They are little creatures and seem harmless. They are certainly not very good-looking; but then, you know, appearances often deceive, and the devil's not so black as he's painted. What do you say?"

"I suppose we can do nothing else," said I.

In fact, I could see that we had reached a crisis in our fate. To go on seemed certain death. To stop was our only alternative; and as we were armed we should not be altogether at the mercy of these creatures. Having made this decision we acted upon it at once, for in such a current there was no time for delay; and so, seizing the oars, we soon brought the boat ashore.

As we approached, the crowd of natives stood awaiting us, and looked more repulsive than ever. We could see the emaciation of their bony frames; their toes and fingers were like birds' claws; their eyes were small and dull and weak, and sunken in cavernous hollows, from which they looked at us like corpses – a horrible sight. They stood quietly, however, and without any hostile demonstration, holding their spears carelessly resting upon the ground.

"I don't like the looks of them," said I. "I think I had better fire a gun."

"Why?" cried Agnew. "For Heaven's sake, man, don't hurt any of them!"

"Oh no," said I; "I only mean to inspire a little wholesome respect."

Saying this I fired in the air. The report rang out with long echoes, and as the smoke swept away it showed us all the natives on the ground. They had seated themselves with their hands crossed on their laps, and there they sat looking at us as before, but with no manifestation of fear or even surprise. I had expected to see them run, but there was nothing of the kind. This puzzled us. Still, there was no time now for any further hesitation. The current was sweeping us toward the chasm between the cliffs, and we had to land without delay. This we did, and as I had another barrel still loaded and a pistol, I felt that with these arms and those of Agnew we should be able to defend ourselves. It was in this state of mind that we landed, and secured the boat by means of the grappling iron.

The natives now all crowded around us, making many strange gestures, which we did not understand. Some of them bowed low, others prostrated themselves; on the whole these seemed like marks of respect, and it occurred to me that they regarded us as superior beings of some sort. It was evident that there was nothing like hostility in their minds. At the same time, the closer survey which I now made of them filled me with renewed horror; their meagre frames, small, watery, lack-lustre eyes, hollow, cavernous sockets, sunken cheeks, protruding teeth, claw-like fingers, and withered skins, all made them look more than ever like animated mummies, and I shrank from them involuntarily, as one shrinks from contact with a corpse.

Agnew, however, was very different, and it was evident that he felt no repugnance whatever. He bowed and smiled at them, and shook hands with half a dozen of them in succession. The hand-shaking was a new thing to them, but they accepted it in a proper spirit, and renewed their bows and prostrations. After this they all offered us their lances. This certainly seemed like an act of peace and goodwill. I shook my head and declined to touch them; but Agnew accepted one of them, and offered his rifle in return. The one to whom he offered it refused to take it. He seemed immensely gratified because Agnew had taken his lance, and the others seemed disappointed at his refusal to take theirs. But I felt my heart quake as I saw him offer his rifle, and still more when he offered it to one or two others, and only regained my composure as I perceived that his offer was refused by all.

They now made motions to us to follow, and we all set forth together.

"My dear More," said Agnew, cheerily, "they're not a bad lot. They mean well. They can't help their looks. You're too suspicious and reserved. Let's make friends with them, and get them to help us. Do as I do."

I tried to, but found it impossible, for my repugnance was immovable. It was like the horror which one feels toward rats, cockroaches, earwigs, or serpents. It was something that defied reason. These creatures seemed like human vermin.

We marched inland for about half a mile, crossed a ridge, and came to a valley, or rather a kind of hollow, at the other side of which we found a cave with a smouldering fire in front. The fire was made of coal, which must exist here somewhere. It was highly bituminous, and burned with a great blaze.

The day was now drawing to a close; far away I could see the lurid glow of the volcanoes, which grew brighter as the day declined: above, the skies twinkled with innumerable stars, and the air was filled with the moan of rushing waters.

We entered the cave. As we did so the natives heaped coal upon the fire, and the flames arose, lighting up the interior. We found here a number of women and children, who looked at us without either fear or curiosity. The children looked like little dwarfs; the women were hags, hideous beyond description. One old woman in particular, who seemed to be in authority, was actually terrible in her awful and repulsive ugliness. A nightmare dream never furnished forth a more frightful object. This nightmare hag prostrated herself before each of us with such an air of self-immolation that she looked as though she wished us to kill her at once. The rough cave, the red light of the fire, all made the scene more awful; and a wild thought came to me that we had actually reached, while yet living, the infernal world, and that this was the abode of devils. Yet their actions, it must be confessed, were far from devilish. Everyone seemed eager to serve us. Some spread out couches formed of the skins of birds for us to sit on; others attended to the fire; others offered us gifts of large and beautiful feathers, together with numerous trinkets of rare and curious workmanship. This kind attention on their part was a great puzzle to me, and I could not help suspecting that beneath all this there must be some sinister design. Resolving to be prepared for the worst, I quietly reloaded the empty barrel of my rifle and watched with the utmost vigilance. As for Agnew, he took it all in the most unsuspicious manner. He made signs to them, shook hands with them, accepted their gifts, and even tried to do the agreeable to the formidable hags and the child-fiends around him. He soon attracted the chief attention, and while all looked admiringly upon him, I was left to languish in comparative neglect.

At length a savory odor came through the cave, and a repast was spread before us. It consisted of some large fowl that looked like a goose, but was twice as large as the largest turkey that I had ever seen. The taste was like that of a wild goose, but rather fishy. Still to us it seemed delicious, for our prolonged diet of raw seal had made us ready to welcome any other food whatever; and this fowl, whatever it was, would not have been unwelcome to any hungry man. It was evident that these people lived on the flesh of birds of various sorts. All around us we saw the skins of birds dried with the feathers on, and used for clothing, for mats, and for ornaments.

The repast being finished, we both felt greatly strengthened and refreshed. Agnew continued to cultivate his new acquaintances, and seeing me holding back, he said,

"More, old fellow, these good people give me to understand that there is another place better than this, and want me to go with them. Will you go?"

At this a great fear seized me.

"Don't go!" I cried – "don't go! We are close by the boat here, and if anything happens we can easily get to it."

Agnew laughed in my face.

"Why, you don't mean to tell me," said he, "that you are still suspicious, and after that dinner? Why, man, if they wanted to harm us, would they feast us in this style? Nonsense, man! Drop your suspicions and come along."

I shook my head obstinately.

"Well," said he, "if I thought there was anything in your suspicions I would stay by you; but I'm confident they mean nothing but kindness, so I'm going off to see the place."

"You'll be back again?" said I.

"Oh yes," said he, "of course I'll come back, and sleep here."

With these words he left, and nearly all the people accompanied him. I was left behind with the women and children and about a dozen men. These men busied themselves with some work over bird skins; the women were occupied with some other work over feathers. No one took any notice of me. There did not seem to be any restraint upon me, nor was I watched in any way. Once the nightmare hag came and offered me a small roasted fowl, about the size of a woodcock. I declined it, but at the same time this delicate attention certainly surprised me.

I was now beginning to struggle with some success against my feelings of abhorrence, when suddenly I caught sight of something which chased away every other thought, and made my blood turn cold in my veins. It was something outside. At the mouth of the cave – by the fire which was still blazing bright, and lighting up the scene – I saw four men who had just come to the cave: they were carrying something which I at first supposed to be a sick or wounded companion. On reaching the fire they put it down, and I saw, with a thrill of dismay, that their burden was neither sick nor wounded, but dead, for the corpse lay rigid as they had placed it. Then I saw the nightmare hag approach it with a knife. An awful thought came to me – the crowning horror! The thought soon proved to be but too well founded. The nightmare hag began to cut, and in an instant had detached the arm of the corpse, which she thrust among the coals in the very place where lately she had cooked the fowl. Then she went back for more.

For a moment my brain reeled, and I gasped for breath. Then I rose and staggered out, I know not how. No one tried to stop me, nor did anyone follow me; and, for my part, I was ready to blow out the brains of the first who dared to approach me. In this way I reached the open air, and passed by the hag and the four men as they were busy at their awful work. But at this point I was observed and followed. A number of men and women came after me, jabbering their uncouth language and gesticulating. I warned them off, angrily. They persisted, and though none of them were armed, yet I saw that they were unwilling to have me leave the cave, and I supposed that they would try to prevent me by force.

The absence of Agnew made my position a difficult one. Had it not been for this I would have burst through them and fled to the boat; but as long as he was away I felt bound to wait; and though I longed to fly, I could not for his sake. The boat seemed to be a haven of rest. I longed to be in her once more, and drift away, even if it should be to my death. Nature was here less terrible than man; and it seemed better to drown in the waters, to perish amid rocks and whirlpools, than to linger here amid such horrors as these. These people were not like human beings. The vilest and lowest savages that

I had ever seen were not so odious as these. A herd of monkeys would be far more congenial, a flock of wolves less abhorrent. They had the caricature of the human form; they were the lowest of humanity; their speech was a mockery of language; their faces devilish, their kindness a cunning pretence; and most hideous of all was the nightmare hag that prepared the cannibal repast.

I could not begin hostilities, for I had to wait for Agnew; so I stood and looked, and then walked away for a little distance. They followed me closely, with eager words and gesticulations, though as yet no one touched me or threatened me. Their tone seemed rather one of persuasion. After a few paces I stood still, with all of them around me. The horrible repast showed plainly all that was in store for us. They received us kindly and fed us well only to devote us to the most abhorrent of deaths. Agnew, in his mad confidence, was only insuring his own doom. He was putting himself completely in the power of devils, who were incapable of pity and strangers to humanity. To make friends with such fiends was impossible, and I felt sure that our only plan was to rule by terror – to seize, to slay, to conquer. But still I had to wait for him, and did not dare to resort to violence while he was absent; so I waited, while the savages gathered round me, contenting themselves with guarding me, and neither touching me nor threatening me. And all this time the hag went on, intent on her preparation of the horrible repast.

While standing there looking, listening, waiting for Agnew, I noticed many things. Far away the volcanoes blazed, and the northern sky was red with a lurid light. There, too, higher up, the moon was shining overhead, the sky was gleaming with stars; and all over the heavens there shone the lustre of the aurora australis, brighter than any I had ever seen – surpassing the moon and illuminating all. It lighted up the haggard faces of the devils around me, and it again seemed to me as though I had died and gone to the land of woe – an iron land, a land of despair, with lurid fires all aglow and faces of fear.

Suddenly, there burst upon my ears the report of a gun, which sounded like a thunder-peal, and echoed in long reverberations. At once I understood it. My fears had proved true. These savages had enticed Agnew away to destroy him. In an instant I burst through the crowd around me, and ran wildly in the direction of that sound, calling his name, as I ran, at the top of my voice.

I heard a loud cry; then another report. I hurried on, shouting his name in a kind of frenzy. The strange courage of these savages had already impressed me deeply. They did not fear our guns. They were all attacking him, and he was alone, fighting for his life.

Then there was another report; it was his pistol. I still ran on, and still shouted to him.

At last I received an answer. He had perhaps heard me, and was answering, or, at any rate, he was warning me.

"More," he cried, "fly, fly, fly to the boat! Save yourself!"

"Where are you?" I cried, as I still rushed on.

"Fly, More, fly! Save yourself! You can't save me. I'm lost. Fly for your life!"

Judging from his cries, he did not seem far away. I hurried on. I could see nothing of him. All the time the savages followed me. None were armed; but it seemed to me that they were preparing to fling themselves upon me and overpower me with their numbers. They would capture me alive, I thought, bind me, and carry me back, reserving me for a future time!

I turned and waved them back. They took no notice of my gesture. Then I ran on once more. They followed. They could not run so fast as I did, and so I gained on them rapidly, still shouting to Agnew. But there was no response. I ran backward and forward, crossing and recrossing, doubling and turning, pursued all the time by the savages. At last, in rage and despair, I fired upon them, and one of them fell. But, to my dismay, the others did not seem to care one whit; they did not stop for one moment, but pursued as before.

My situation was now plain in all its truth. They had enticed Agnew away; they had attacked him. He had fought, and had been overpowered. He had tried to give me warning. His last words had been for me to fly – to fly: yes, for he well knew that it was better far for me to go to death through the raging torrent than to meet the fate which had fallen upon himself. For him there was now no more hope. That he was lost was plain. If he were still alive he would call to me; but his voice had been silenced for some time. All was over, and that noble heart that had withstood so bravely and cheerily the rigors of the storm, and the horrors of our desperate voyage, had been stilled in death by the vilest of miscreants.

I paused for a moment. Even though Agnew was dead, I could not bear to leave him, but felt as though I ought to share his fate. The savages came nearer. At their approach I hesitated no longer. That fate was too terrible: I must fly.

But before I fled I turned in fury to wreak vengeance upon them for their crimes. Full of rage and despair, I discharged my remaining rifle-barrel into the midst of the crowd. Then I fled toward the boat. On the way I had a frightful thought that she might have been sent adrift; but, on approaching the place, I found her there just as I had left her. The savages, with their usual fearlessness, still pursued. For a moment I stood on the shore, with the grapple in my hand and the boat close by, and as they came near I discharged my pistol into the midst of them. Then I sprang into the boat; the swift current bore me away, and in a few minutes the crowd of pursuing demons disappeared from view.

Chapter V
The Torrent Sweeping Under the Mountains

THE BOAT DRIFTED ON. The light given by the aurora and the low moon seemed to grow fainter; and as I looked behind I saw that the distant glow from the volcanic fires had become more brilliant in the increasing darkness. The sides of the channel grew steeper, until at last they became rocky precipices, rising to an unknown height. The channel itself grew narrower, till from a width of two miles it had contracted to a tenth of those dimensions; but with this lessening width the waters seemed to rush far more swiftly. Here I drifted helplessly, and saw the gloomy, rocky cliffs sweep past me as I was hurled onward on the breast of the tremendous flood. I was in despair. The fate of Agnew had prepared me for my own, and I was only thankful that my fate, since it was inevitable, would be less appalling. Death seemed certain, and my chief thought now was as to the moment when it would come. I was prepared. I felt that I could meet it calmly, sternly, even thankfully; far better was a death here amid the roar of waters than at the hands of those abhorrent beings by whose treachery my friend had fallen.

As I went on, the precipices rose higher and seemed to overhang, the channel grew narrower, the light grew fainter, until at last all around me grew dark. I was floating at the bottom of a vast chasm, where the sides seemed to rise precipitously for thousands of feet, where neither watery flood nor rocky wall was visible, and where, far above, I could see the line of sky between the summits of the cliffs, and watch the glowing stars. And as I watched them there came to me the thought that this was my last sight on earth, and I could only hope that the life which was so swiftly approaching its end might live again somewhere among those glittering orbs. So I thought; and with these thoughts I drifted on, I cannot tell how long, until at length there appeared a vast black mass, where the open sky above me terminated, and where the lustre of the stars and the light of the heavens were all swallowed up in utter darkness.

This, then, I thought, is the end. Here, amid this darkness, I must make the awful plunge and find my death I fell upon my knees in the bottom of the boat and prayed. As I knelt there the boat drew nearer, the black mass grew blacker. The current swept me on. There were no breakers; there was no phosphorescent sparkle of seething waters, and no whiteness of foam. I thought that I was on the brink of some tremendous cataract a thousand times deeper than Niagara; some fall where the waters plunged into the depths of the earth; and where, gathering for the terrific descent, all other movements – all dashings and writhings and twistings – were obliterated and lost in the one overwhelming onward rush. Suddenly all grew dark – dark beyond all expression; the sky above was in a moment snatched from view; I had been flung into some tremendous cavern; and there, on my knees, with terror in my heart, I waited for death.

The moments passed, and death delayed to come. The awful plunge was still put off; and though I remained on my knees and waited long, still the end came not. The waters seemed still, the boat motionless. It was borne upon the surface of a vast stream as smooth as glass; but who could tell how deep that stream was, or how wide? At length I rose from my knees and sank down upon the seat of the boat, and tried to peer through the gloom. In vain. Nothing was visible. It was the very blackness of darkness. I listened, but heard nothing save a deep, dull, droning sound, which seemed to fill all the air and make it all tremulous with its vibrations. I tried to collect my thoughts. I recalled that old theory which had been in my mind before this, and which I had mentioned to Agnew. This was the notion that at each pole there is a vast opening; that into one of them all the waters of the ocean pour themselves, and, after passing through the earth, come out at the other pole, to pass about its surface in innumerable streams. It was a wild fancy, which I had laughed at under other circumstances, but which now occurred to me once more, when I was overwhelmed with despair, and my mind was weakened by the horrors which I had experienced; and I had a vague fear that I had been drawn into the very channel through which the ocean waters flowed in their course to that terrific, that unparalleled abyss. Still, there was as yet no sign whatever of anything like a descent, for the boat was on even keel, and perfectly level as before, and it was impossible for me to tell whether I was moving swiftly or slowly, or standing perfectly still; for in that darkness there were no visible objects by which I could find out the rate of my progress; and as those who go up in balloons are utterly insensible of motion, so was I on those calm but swift waters.

At length there came into view something which arrested my attention and engrossed all my thoughts. It was faint glow that at first caught my gaze; and, on turning to see it better, I saw a round red spot glowing like fire. I had not seen this before. It looked like the moon when it rises from behind clouds, and glows red and lurid from the horizon; and so this glowed, but not with the steady light of the moon, for the light was fitful, and sometimes flashed into a baleful brightness, which soon subsided into a dimmer lustre. New alarm arose within me, for this new sight suggested something more terrible than anything that I had thus far thought of. This, then, I thought, was to be the end of my voyage; this was my goal – a pit of fire, into which I should be hurled! Would it be well, I thought, to wait for such a fate, and experience such a death-agony? Would it not be better for me to take my own life before I should know the worst? I took my pistol and loaded it, so as to be prepared, but hesitated to use it until my fate should be more apparent. So I sat, holding my pistol, prepared to use it, watching the light, and awaiting the time when the glowing fires should make all further hope impossible. But time passed, and the light grew no brighter; on the contrary, it seemed to grow fainter. There was also another change. Instead of shining before me, it appeared more on my left. From this it went on changing its position until at length it was astern. All the time it continued to grow fainter, and it seemed certain that I was moving away from it rather than toward it. In the midst of this there occurred a new thought, which seemed to account for this light – this was, that it arose from these same volcanoes which had illuminated the northern sky when I was ashore, and followed me still with their glare. I had been carried into this darkness, through some vast opening which now lay behind me, disclosing the red volcano glow, and this it was that caused that roundness and resemblance to the moon. I saw that I was still moving on away from that light as before, and that its changing position was due to the turning of the boat as the water drifted it along, now stern foremost, now sidewise, and again bow foremost. From this it seemed plainly evident that the waters had borne me into some vast cavern of unknown extent, which went under the mountains – a subterranean channel, whose issue I could not conjecture. Was this the beginning of that course which should ultimately become a plunge deep down into some unutterable abyss? or might I ever hope to emerge again into the light of day – perhaps in some other ocean – some land of ice and frost and eternal night? But the old theory of the flow of water through the earth had taken hold of me and could not be shaken off. I knew some scientific men held the opinion that the earth's interior is a mass of molten rock and pent-up fire, and that the earth itself had once been a burning orb, which had cooled down at the surface; yet, after all, this was only a theory, and there were other theories which were totally different. As a boy I had read wild works of fiction about lands in the interior of the earth, with a sun at the centre, which gave them the light of a perpetual day. These, I knew, were only the creations of fiction; yet, after all, it seemed possible that the earth might contain vast hollow spaces in its interior – realms of eternal darkness, caverns in comparison with which the hugest caves on the surface were but the tiniest cells. I was now being borne on to these. In that case there might be no sudden plunge, after all. The stream might run on for many thousand miles through this terrific cavern gloom, in accordance with natural laws; and I might thus live, and drift on in this darkness, until I should die a lingering death of horror and despair.

There was no possible way of forming any estimate as to speed. All was dark, and even the glow behind was fading away; nor could I make any conjecture whatever as to the size of the channel. At the opening it had been contracted and narrow; but here it might have expanded itself to miles, and its vaulted top might reach almost to the summit of the lofty mountains. While sight thus failed me, sound was equally unavailing, for it was always the same – a sustained and unintermittent roar, a low, droning sound, deep and terrible, with no variations of dashing breakers or rushing rapids or falling cataracts.

Vague thoughts of final escape came and went; but in such a situation hope could not be sustained. The thick darkness oppressed the soul; and at length even the glow of the distant volcanoes, which had been gradually diminishing, grew dimmer and fainter, and finally faded out altogether. That seemed to me to be my last sight of earthly things. After this nothing was left. There was no longer for me such a thing as sight; there was nothing but darkness – perpetual and eternal night. I was buried in a cavern of rushing waters, to which there would be no end, where I should be borne onward helplessly by the resistless tide to a mysterious and an appalling doom.

The darkness grew so intolerable that I longed for something to dispel it, if only for a moment. I struck a match. The air was still, and the flame flashed out, lighting up the boat and showing the black water around me. This made me eager to see more. I loaded both barrels of the rifle, keeping my pistol for another purpose, and then fired one of them. There was a tremendous report, that rang in my ears like a hundred thunder-volleys, and rolled and reverberated far along, and died away in endless echoes. The flash lighted up the scene for an instant, and for an instant only; like the sudden lightning, it revealed all around. I saw a wide expanse of water, black as ink – a Stygian pool; but no rocks were visible, and it seemed as though I had been carried into a subterranean sea.

I loaded the empty barrel and waited. The flash of light had revealed nothing, yet it had distracted my thoughts, and the work of reloading was an additional distraction. Anything was better than inaction. I did not wish to waste my ammunition, yet I thought that an occasional shot might serve some good purpose, if it was only to afford me some relief from despair.

And now, as I sat with the rifle in my hands, I was aware of a sound – new, exciting, different altogether from the murmur of innumerable waters that filled my ears, and in sharp contrast with the droning echoes of the rushing flood. It was a sound that spoke of life. I heard quick, heavy pantings, as of some great living thing; and with this there came the noise of regular movements in the water, and the foaming and gurgling of waves. It was as though some living, breathing creature were here, not far away, moving through these midnight waters; and with this discovery there came a new fear – the fear of pursuit. I thought that some sea monster had scented me in my boat, and had started to attack me. This new fear aroused me to action. It was a danger quite unlike any other which I had ever known; yet the fear which it inspired was a feeling that roused me to action, and prompted me, even though the coming danger might be as sure as death, to rise against it and resist to the last. So I stood up with my rifle and listened, with all my soul in my sense of hearing. The sounds arose more plainly. They had come nearer. They were immediately in front. I raised my rifle and took aim. Then in quick succession two reports thundered out with tremendous uproar and interminable echoes, but the long reverberations were unheeded in the blaze of sudden light and the vision that was revealed. For there full before me I saw, though but for an instant, a tremendous sight. It was a vast monster, moving in the waters against the stream and toward the boat. Its head was raised high, its eyes were inflamed with a baleful light, its jaws, opened wide, bristled with sharp teeth, and it had a long neck joined to a body of enormous bulk, with a tail that lashed all the water into foam. It was but for an instant that I saw it, and then with a sudden plunge the monster dived, while at the same moment all was as dark as before.

Full of terror and excitement, I loaded my rifle again and waited, listening for a renewal of the noise. I felt sure that the monster, balked of his prey, would return with redoubled fury, and that I should have to renew the conflict. I felt that the dangers of the subterranean passage and of the rushing waters had passed away, and that a new peril had arisen from the assault of this monster of the deep. Nor was it this one alone that was to be dreaded. Where one was, others were sure to be; and if this one should pass me by it would only leave me to be assailed by monsters of the same kind, and these would probably increase in number as I advanced farther into this realm of darkness. And yet, in spite of these grisly thoughts, I felt less of horror than before, for the fear which I had was now associated with action; and as I stood waiting for the onset and listening for the approach of the enemy, the excitement that ensued was a positive relief from the dull despair into which I had sunk but a moment before.

Yet, though I waited for a new attack, I waited in vain. The monster did not come back. Either the flash and the noise had terrified him, or the bullets had hit him, or else in his vastness he had been indifferent to so feeble a creature as myself; but whatever may have been the cause, he did not emerge again out of the darkness and silence into which he had sunk. For a long time I stood waiting; then I sat down, still watchful, still listening, but without any result, until at length I began to think that there was no chance of any new attack. Indeed, it seemed now as though there had been no attack at all, but that the monster had been swimming at random without any thought of me, in which case my rifle-flashes had terrified him more than his fearful form had terrified me. On the whole this incident had greatly benefited me. It had roused me from my despair. I grew reckless, and felt a disposition to acquiesce in whatever fate might have in store for me.

And now, worn out with fatigue and exhausted from long watchfulness and anxiety, I sank down in the bottom of the boat and fell into a deep sleep.

Chapter VI
The New World

HOW LONG I SLEPT I do not know. My sleep was profound, yet disturbed by troubled dreams, in which I lived over again all the eventful scenes of the past; and these were all intermingled in the wildest confusion. The cannibals beckoned to us from the peak, and we landed between the two volcanoes. There the body of the dead sailor received us, and afterward chased us to the boat. Then came snow and volcanic eruptions, and we drifted amid icebergs and molten lava until we entered an iron portal and plunged into darkness. Here there were vast swimming monsters and burning orbs of fire and thunderous cataracts falling from inconceivable heights, and the sweep of immeasurable tides and the circling of infinite whirlpools; while in my ears there rang the never-ending roar of remorseless waters that came after us, with all their waves and billows rolling upon us. It was a dream in which all the material terrors of the past were renewed; but these were all as nothing when compared with a certain deep underlying feeling that possessed my soul – a sense of loss irretrievable, an expectation of impending doom, a drear and immitigable despair.

In the midst of this I awoke. It was with a sudden start, and I looked all around in speechless bewilderment. The first thing of which I was conscious was a great blaze of light – light so lately lost, and supposed to be lost forever, but now filling all the universe – bright, brilliant, glowing bringing hope and joy and gladness, with all the splendor of deep blue skies and the multitudinous laughter of ocean waves that danced and sparkled in the sun. I flung up my arms and laughed aloud. Then I burst into tears, and falling on my knees, I thanked the Almighty Ruler of the skies for this marvellous deliverance.

Rising from my knees I looked around, and once more amazement overwhelmed me. I saw a long line of mountains towering up to immeasurable heights, their summits covered with eternal ice and snow. There the sun blazed low in the sky, elevated but a few degrees above the mountain crests, which gleamed in gold and purple under its fiery rays. The sun seemed enlarged to unusual dimensions, and the mountains ran away on every side like the segment of some infinite circle. At the base of the mountains lay a land all green with vegetation, where cultivated fields were visible, and vineyards and orchards and groves, together with forests of palm and all manner of trees of every variety of hue, which ran up the sides of the mountains till they reached the limits of vegetation and the regions of snow and ice.

Here in all directions there were unmistakable signs of human life – the outlines of populous cities and busy towns and hamlets; roads winding far away along the plain or up the mountainsides, and mighty works of industry in the shape of massive structures, terraced slopes, long rows of arches, ponderous pyramids, and battlemented walls.

From the land I turned to the sea. I saw before me an expanse of water intensely blue – an extent so vast that never before in all my ocean voyages had anything appeared at all comparable with it. Out at sea, wherever I had been, the water had always limited the view; the horizon had never seemed far away; ships soon sank below it, and the visible surface of the earth was thus always contracted; but here, to my bewilderment, the horizon appeared to be removed to an immeasurable distance and raised high in the air, while the waters were prolonged endlessly. Starting from where I was, they went away to inconceivable distances, and the view before me seemed like a watery declivity reaching for a thousand miles, till it approached the horizon far up in the sky. Nor was it any delusion of the senses that caused this unparalleled spectacle. I was familiar with the phenomena of the mirage, and knew well that there was nothing of that kind here; for the mirage always shows great surfaces of stillness, or a regular vibration – glassy tides and indistinct distances; but here everything was sharply defined in the clear atmosphere: the sky overhung a deep blue vault; the waves danced and sparkled in the sun; the waters rolled and foamed on every side; and the fresh breeze, as it blew over the ocean, brought with it such exhilarating influences that it acted upon me like some reviving cordial.

From the works of nature I turned to those of man. These were visible everywhere: on the land, in cities and cultivated fields and mighty constructions; on the sea, in floating craft, which appeared wherever I turned my eyes – boats like those of fishermen, ships long and low, some like galleys, propelled by a hundred oars, others provided with one huge square-sail, which enabled them to run before the wind. They were unlike any ships which I had ever seen; for neither in the Mediterranean nor in Chinese waters were there any craft like these, and they reminded me rather of those ancient galleys which I had seen in pictures.

I was lost in wonder as to where I was, and what land this could be to which I had been brought. I had not plunged into the interior of the earth, but I had been carried under the mountains, and had emerged again into the glad light of the sun. Could it be possible, I thought, that Agnew's hope had been realized, and that I had been carried into the warm regions of the South Pacific Ocean? Yet in the South Pacific there could be no place like this – no immeasurable expanse of waters, no horizon raised mountain high. It seemed like a vast basin-shaped world, for all around me the surface appeared to rise, and I was in what looked like a depression; yet I knew that the basin and the depression were an illusion, and that this appearance was due to the immense extent of level surface with the environment of lofty mountains. I had crossed the antarctic circle; I had been borne onward for an immense distance. Over all the known surface of the earth no one had ever seen anything like this; there were but two places where such an immeasurable plain was possible, and those were at the flattened poles. Where I was I now knew well. I had reached the antarctic pole. Here the earth was flat – an immense level with no roundness to lessen the reach of the horizon but an almost even surface that gave an unimpeded view for hundreds of miles.

The subterranean channel had rushed through the mountains and had carried me here. Here came all the waters of the Northern ocean pouring into this vast polar sea, perhaps to issue forth from it by some similar passage. Here, then, was the South Pole – a world by itself: and how different from that terrible, that iron land on the other side of the mountains! – not a world of ice and frost, but one of beauty and light, with a climate that was almost tropical in its warmth, and lands that were covered with the rank luxuriance of a teeming vegetable life. I had passed from that outer world to this inner one, and the passage was from death unto life, from agony and despair to sunlight and splendor and joy. Above all, in all around me that which most impressed me now was the rich and superabundant life, and a warmth of air which made me think of India. It was an amazing and an unaccountable thing, and I could only attribute it to the flattening of the poles, which brought the surface nearer to the supposed central fires of the earth, and therefore created a heat as great as that of the equatorial regions. Here I found a tropical climate – a land warmed not by the sun, but from the earth itself. Or another cause might be found in the warm ocean currents. Whatever the true one might be, I was utterly unable to form a conjecture.

But I had no time for such speculations as these. After the first emotions of wonder and admiration had somewhat subsided, I began to experience other sensations. I began to remember that I had eaten nothing for a length of time that I had no means of calculating, and to look around to see if there was any way of satisfying my hunger. The question arose now, What was to be done? After my recent terrible experience I naturally shrank from again committing myself to the tender mercies of strange tribes; yet further thought and examination showed me that the people of this strange land must be very different from those frightful savages on the other side of the mountains. Everywhere I beheld the manifest signs of cultivation and civilization. Still, I knew that even civilized people would not necessarily be any kinder than savages, and that I might be seized and flung into hopeless imprisonment or slavery.

So I hesitated, yet what could I do? My hunger was beginning to be insupportable. I had reached a place where I had to choose between starvation on the one hand, or a venture among these people on the other. To go back was impossible. Who could breast those waters in the tremendous subterranean channel, or force his way back through such appalling dangers? Or, if that were possible, who could ever hope to breast those mighty currents beyond, or work his way amid everlasting ice and immeasurable seas? No; return was impossible. I had been flung into this world of wonders, and here would be my home for the remainder of my days; though I could not now imagine whether those days would be passed in peace or in bitter slavery and sorrow. Yet the decision must be made and the risk must be run. It must be so. I must land here, venture among these people, and trust in that Providence which had hitherto sustained me.

Having thus resolved at all hazards to try my fate, I rowed in toward the shore. Thus far I had seen galleys passing and small boats, but they had taken no notice of me, for the reason that they were too far away to perceive anything about me that differed from any other boat; but now, as I rowed, I noticed a galley coming down toward me. She seemed to be going in toward the shore at the very point at which I was aiming, and her course and mine must soon meet if I continued to row. After some hesitation I concluded to make signals to her, so as to attract attention; for, now that I had resolved to venture among the people here, I was anxious to end my suspense as soon as possible. So I continued rowing, and gradually drew nearer. The galley was propelled by oars, of which there were fifty on either side. The stem was raised, and covered in like a cabin. At length I ceased rowing, and sat watching her. I soon saw that I was noticed, but this did not occur till the galley was close by me – so close, indeed, that I thought they would pass without perceiving me. I raised my hands, waved them, and gave a cry. The galley at once stopped, a boat was lowered, and some men descended and rowed toward me.

They were men of strange appearance – very small in stature and slender in frame. Their hair was black and straight, their features were quite regular, and their general expression was one of great gentleness. I was surprised to notice that they kept their eyes almost closed, as though they were weak and troubled by the glare of the sun. With their half-closed eyes they blinked at me, and then one who appeared to be their chief spoke to me. I understood not a word; and then I answered him in English, which, of course, was equally unintelligible to him. I then made signs, pointing to the mountains and endeavoring to make known to him that I had come from beyond them – that I had suffered shipwreck, that I had drifted here, and that I needed assistance. Of all this it was quite evident that they understood nothing except the fact that I needed help. The moment that they comprehended this they took me in tow and rowed back to the galley.

I found the galley to be about one hundred and fifty feet in length. For about two thirds of this length forward it was open and filled with seats, where there were about a hundred rowers, who all looked like those that I had first seen, all being of small stature, slender frames, and, moreover, all being apparently distressed by the sunlight. There was in all of them the same mild and gentle expression. In complexion and general outline of features they were not unlike Arabs, but they were entirely destitute of that hardness and austerity which the latter have. They all had beards, which were dressed in a peculiar way in plaits. Their costume varied. The rowers wore a coarse tunic, with a girdle of rope. The officers wore tunics of fine cloth and very elegant mantles, richly embroidered, and with borders of down. They all wore broad-brimmed hats, and the one who seemed to be chief had on his some golden ornaments.

Here once more I tried to explain to them who I was. They looked at me, examining me all over, inspecting my gun, pistol, coat, trousers, boots, and hat, and talking all the time among themselves. They did not touch me, but merely showed the natural curiosity which is felt at the sight of a foreigner who has appeared unexpectedly. There was a scrupulous delicacy and a careful and even ceremonious politeness in their attitude toward me which was at once amazing and delightful. All fear and anxiety had now left me; in the gentle manners and amiable faces of these people I saw enough to assure me of kind treatment; and in my deep joy and gratitude for this even my hunger was for a time forgotten.

At length the chief motioned to me to follow him. He led the way to the cabin, where, opening the door, he entered, and I followed, after which the others came in also and then the door was shut. At first I could see nothing. There were no windows whatever, and only one or two slight crevices through which the light came. After a time my eyes grew more accustomed to the darkness, and I could see that the cabin was a spacious compartment, adorned with rich hangings of some unknown material. There was a large table and seats. Taking me by the hand, the chief led me to this, where I seated myself, while the others remained standing. Then some of them went away, and soon returned with food and drink. The food was of different kinds – some tasting like goose, others like turkey, others like partridge. It was all the flesh of fowls, though, judging from the slices before me, they must have been of great size. I wondered much at the behavior of the officers of the ship, who all, and the chief himself more than all, stood and waited upon me; but it was a new world, and I supposed that this must be the fashion; so I made no objections, but accepted the situation and ate with a thankful heart.

As the first keenness of my appetite was satisfied I had more leisure to make observations. I noticed that the eyes of my new friends no longer blinked; they were wide open; and, so far as I could make them out, their faces were much improved. Weakness of eyes seemed common among these people, and therefore the officers had their cabin darkened, while the unfortunate rowers had to labor in the blazing sun. Such was my conclusion, and the fact reminded me of the miserable fellahin of Egypt, who have ophthalmia from the blazing sun and burning sand.

After the repast they brought me water in a basin, and all stood around me. One held the basin, another a towel, another a flask, another took a sponge and proceeded to wash my face and hands. This was all strange to me, yet there was nothing left for me but submission. Then the chief, who had stood looking on with a smile on his face took off his rich furred mantle and handed it to me. I was half inclined to refuse it, but was afraid of giving offence, so I accepted it, and he himself fastened it around my shoulders. The others seemed actually to envy the chief, as though he had gained some uncommon good-fortune. Then they offered me various drinks, of which I tasted several kinds. Some were sweet waters of different flavors, others tasted like mild wine, one was a fermented drink, light, sweet, and very agreeable to the palate. I now wished to show my generous entertainers that I was grateful; so I raised my cup, bowed to all of them, particularly the chief, and drank their health. They all watched this ceremony with very sober faces, and I could not quite make out whether they took my meaning or not. They certainly did not look pleased, and it seemed to me as though they felt hurt at any expression of gratitude, so I concluded for the future to abstain from all such demonstrations.

Yet with every moment the manners of these people grew more bewildering. It was strange, indeed, for me to find myself so suddenly the centre of interest and of generous intentions. For a moment the thought occurred to me that they regarded me as some wonderful being with superior powers, and were trying to propitiate me by these services; yet I soon saw that these services were not at all acts of propitiation; they looked rather like those loving and profuse attentions which a family showers down upon some dear one long absent and at last returned, and with this my wonder grew greater than ever.

The galley had long since resumed her progress. I heard the steady beat of the oars as they all moved in time, and at length the motion ceased. The chief then signed to me and went out. I followed, and the rest came after. And now as I emerged from the gloom of the cabin, I found myself once more in the glorious light of day, and saw that we had reached the land. The galley was hauled up alongside a stone quay, and on the shore there were buildings and walls and trees and people. The chief went ashore at once and I accompanied him. We walked for some distance along a road with stone walls on either side, from behind which there arose trees that from a distance had looked like palms. I now found them to be giant ferns, arching overhead with their broad fanlike leaves and branches in dense masses, making the roadway quite dark in the shadow. Astonished as I was at the sight of these trees, I soon forgot them in a still more astonishing sight, for after going onward about a hundred paces I stopped, and found myself in a wide space where four crossroads met. Here there were three birds of gigantic stature. They had vast bodies, short legs, short necks, and seemed as large as an ordinary-sized ox. Their wings were short, and evidently could not be used for flight; their beaks were like that of a seagull; each one had a man on his back, and was harnessed to a car. The chief motioned to me to enter one of these cars. I did so. He followed, and thereupon the driver started the bird, which set forth with long, rapid strides, at a pace fast as that of a trotting horse. So astonished was I that for some time I did not notice anything else; but at length, when my first feeling had subsided, I began to regard other objects. All the way the dense fern foliage arched overhead, throwing down deep shadows. They grew on either side in dense rows, but between their stalks I could see the country beyond, which lay all bright in the sunlight.

Here were broad fields, all green with verdure; farther away arose clumps of tree-ferns; at every step of the way new vistas opened; amid the verdure and the foliage were the roofs of structures that looked like pavilions, and more massive edifices with pyramidal roofs. Our road constantly ascended, and at length we came to a crossing. This was a wide terrace at the slope of the mountain; on the lower side was a row of massive stone edifices with pyramidal roofs, while on the upper there were portals which seemed to open into excavated caverns. Here, too, on either side arose the giant ferns, overarching and darkening the terrace with their deep shadow. From this point I looked back, and through the trunks of the tree-ferns I could see fields and pavilions and the pyramidal roofs of massive edifices, and broad, verdant slopes, while in the distance there were peeps of the boundless sea. We continued on our way without stopping, and passed several successive terraces like the first, with the same caverns on the upper side and massive edifices on the lower, until at last the ascent ended at the fifth terrace, and here we turned to the left. Now the view became more varied. The tree-ferns arose on either side, arching overhead; on my right were the portals that opened into caverns, on my left solid and massive houses, built of great blocks of stone, with pyramidal roofs. As far as I could judge, I was in a city built on the slope of a mountain, with its streets formed thus of successive terraces and their connecting crossways, one half its habitations consisting of caverns, while the other half were pavilions and massive stone structures. Few people, however, were to be seen. Occasionally I saw one or two groping along with their eyes half shut, seeking the darkest shadows; and it seemed to me that this extraordinary race of men had some natural and universal peculiarity of eyesight which made them shun the sunlight, and seek the darkness of caves and of dense, overshadowing foliage.

At length we came to a place where the terrace ran back till it formed a semicircle against the mountain slope, when several vast portals appeared. Here there was a large space, where the tree-ferns grew in long lines crossing each other, and making a denser shade than usual. On the lower side were several stone edifices of immense size; and in the middle of the place there arose a singular structure, shaped like a half pyramid, with three sides sloping, and the fourth perpendicular, flat on the top, which was approached by a flight of steps. We now went on until we reached the central portal of the range of caverns, and here we stopped. The chief got out and beckoned to me. I followed. He then led the way into the cavern, while I, full of wonder, walked behind him.

The complete and unabridged text is available online, from *flametreepublishing.com/extras*

The Diamond Lens

Fitz-James O'Brien

I

FROM a very early period of my life the entire bent of my inclinations had been toward microscopic investigations. When I was not more than ten years old, a distant relative of our family, hoping to astonish my inexperience, constructed a simple microscope for me by drilling in a disk of copper a small hole in which a drop of pure water was sustained by capillary attraction. This very primitive apparatus, magnifying some fifty diameters, presented, it is true, only indistinct and imperfect forms, but still sufficiently wonderful to work up my imagination to a preternatural state of excitement.

Seeing me so interested in this rude instrument, my cousin explained to me all that he knew about the principles of the microscope, related to me a few of the wonders which had been accomplished through its agency, and ended by promising to send me one regularly constructed, immediately on his return to the city. I counted the days, the hours, the minutes that intervened between that promise and his departure.

Meantime, I was not idle. Every transparent substance that bore the remotest resemblance to a lens I eagerly seized upon, and employed in vain attempts to realize that instrument the theory of whose construction I as yet only vaguely comprehended. All panes of glass containing those oblate spheroidal knots familiarly known as 'bull's-eyes' were ruthlessly destroyed in the hope of obtaining lenses of marvelous power. I even went so far as to extract the crystalline humor from the eyes of fishes and animals, and endeavored to press it into the microscopic service. I plead guilty to having stolen the glasses from my Aunt Agatha's spectacles, with a dim idea of grinding them into lenses of wondrous magnifying properties – in which attempt it is scarcely necessary to say that I totally failed.

At last the promised instrument came. It was of that order known as Field's simple microscope, and had cost perhaps about fifteen dollars. As far as educational purposes went, a better apparatus could not have been selected. Accompanying it was a small treatise on the microscope – its history, uses, and discoveries. I comprehended then for the first time the 'Arabian Nights' Entertainments'. The dull veil of ordinary existence that hung across the world seemed suddenly to roll away, and to lay bare a land of enchantments. I felt toward my companions as the seer might feel toward the ordinary masses of men. I held conversations with nature in a tongue which they could not understand. I was in daily communication with living wonders such as they never imagined in their wildest visions, I penetrated beyond the external portal of things, and roamed through the sanctuaries. Where they beheld only a drop of rain slowly rolling down the window-glass, I saw a universe of beings animated with all the passions common to physical life, and convulsing their minute sphere with struggles as fierce and protracted as those of men. In the common spots of mould, which my mother, good housekeeper that she was, fiercely scooped away from her jam-pots, there abode for me, under the name of mildew, enchanted gardens, filled with dells and avenues of the densest foliage and most astonishing verdure, while from the fantastic boughs of these microscopic forests hung strange fruits glittering with green and silver and gold.

It was no scientific thirst that at this time filled my mind. It was the pure enjoyment of a poet to whom a world of wonders has been disclosed. I talked of my solitary pleasures to none. Alone with my microscope, I dimmed my sight, day after day and night after night, poring over the marvels which it unfolded to me. I was like one who, having discovered the ancient Eden still existing in all its primitive glory, should resolve to enjoy it in solitude, and never betray to mortal the secret of its locality. The rod of my life was bent at this moment. I destined myself to be a microscopist.

Of course, like every novice, I fancied myself a discoverer. I was ignorant at the time of the thousands of acute intellects engaged in the same pursuit as myself, and with the advantage of instruments a thousand times more powerful than mine. The names of Leeuwenhoek, Williamson, Spencer, Ehrenberg, Schultz, Dujardin, Schact, and Schleiden were then entirely unknown to me, or, if known, I was ignorant of their patient and wonderful researches. In every fresh specimen of cryptogamia which I placed beneath my instrument I believed that I discovered wonders of which the world was as yet ignorant. I remember well the thrill of delight and admiration that shot through me the first time that I discovered the common wheel animalcule (*Rotifera vulgaris*) expanding and contracting its flexible spokes and seemingly rotating through the water. Alas! As I grew older, and obtained some works treating of my favorite study, I found that I was only on the threshold of a science to the investigation of which some of the greatest men of the age were devoting their lives and intellects.

As I grew up, my parents, who saw but little likelihood of anything practical resulting from the examination of bits of moss and drops of water through a brass tube and a piece of glass, were anxious that I should choose a profession.

It was their desire that I should enter the counting-house of my uncle, Ethan Blake, a prosperous merchant, who carried on business in New York. This suggestion I decisively combated. I had no taste for trade; I should only make a failure; in short, I refused to become a merchant.

But it was necessary for me to select some pursuit. My parents were staid New England people, who insisted on the necessity of labor, and therefore, although, thanks to the bequest of my poor Aunt Agatha, I should, on coming of age, inherit a small fortune sufficient to place me above want, it was decided that, instead of waiting for this, I should act the nobler part, and employ the intervening years in rendering myself independent.

After much cogitation, I complied with the wishes of my family, and selected a profession. I determined to study medicine at the New York Academy. This disposition of my future suited me. A removal from my relatives would enable me to dispose of my time as I pleased without fear of detection. As long as I paid my Academy fees, I might shirk attending the lectures if I chose; and, as I never had the remotest intention of standing an examination, there was no danger of my being 'plucked'. Besides, a metropolis was the place for me. There I could obtain excellent instruments, the newest publications, intimacy with men of pursuits kindred with my own – in short, all things necessary to ensure a profitable devotion of my life to my beloved science. I had an abundance of money, few desires that were not bounded by my illuminating mirror on one side and my object-glass on the other; what, therefore, was to prevent my becoming an illustrious investigator of the veiled worlds? It was with the most buoyant hope that I left my New England home and established myself in New York.

II

MY FIRST STEP, of course, was to find suitable apartments. These I obtained, after a couple of days' search, in Fourth Avenue; a very pretty second floor, unfurnished, containing sitting-room, bedroom, and a smaller apartment which I intended to fit up as a laboratory. I furnished my lodgings simply, but rather elegantly, and then devoted all my energies to the adornment of the temple of my worship. I visited Pike, the celebrated optician, and passed in review his splendid collection of microscopes – Field's Compound, Hingham's, Spencer's, Nachet's Binocular (that founded on the principles of the stereoscope), and at length fixed upon that form known as Spencer's Trunnion Microscope, as combining the greatest number of improvements with an almost perfect freedom from tremor. Along with this I purchased every possible accessory – draw-tubes, micrometers, a *camera lucida*, lever-stage, achromatic condensers, white cloud illuminators, prisms, parabolic condensers, polarizing apparatus, forceps, aquatic boxes, fishing-tubes, with a host of other articles, all of which would have been useful in the hands of an experienced microscopist, but, as I afterward discovered, were not of the slightest present value to me. It takes years of practice to know how to use a complicated microscope. The optician looked suspiciously at me as I made these valuable purchases. He evidently was uncertain whether to set me down as some scientific celebrity or a madman. I think he was inclined to the latter belief. I suppose I was mad. Every great genius is mad upon the subject in which he is greatest. The unsuccessful madman is disgraced and called a lunatic.

Mad or not, I set myself to work with a zeal which few scientific students have ever equaled. I had everything to learn relative to the delicate study upon which I had embarked – a study involving the most earnest patience, the most rigid analytic powers, the steadiest hand, the most untiring eye, the most refined and subtle manipulation.

For a long time half my apparatus lay inactively on the shelves of my laboratory, which was now most amply furnished with every possible contrivance for facilitating my investigations. The fact was that I did not know how to use some of my scientific implements – never having been taught microscopies – and those whose use I understood theoretically were of little avail until by practice I could attain the necessary delicacy of handling. Still, such was the fury of my ambition, such the untiring perseverance of my experiments, that, difficult of credit as it may be, in the course of one year I became theoretically and practically an accomplished microscopist.

During this period of my labors, in which I submitted specimens of every substance that came under my observation to the action of my lenses, I became a discoverer – in a small way, it is true, for I was very young, but still a discoverer. It was I who destroyed Ehrenberg's theory that the *Volvox globator* was an animal, and proved that his 'monads' with stomachs and eyes were merely phases of the formation of a vegetable cell, and were, when they reached their mature state, incapable of the act of conjugation, or any true generative act, without which no organism rising to any stage of life higher than vegetable can be said to be complete. It was I who resolved the singular problem of rotation in the cells and hairs of plants into ciliary attraction, in spite of the assertions of Wenham and others that my explanation was the result of an optical illusion.

But notwithstanding these discoveries, laboriously and painfully made as they were, I felt horribly dissatisfied. At every step I found myself stopped by the imperfections of my instruments. Like all active microscopists, I gave my imagination full play. Indeed, it is a common complaint against many such that they supply the defects of their instruments with the creations of their brains. I imagined depths beyond depths in nature which the limited power of my lenses prohibited me from exploring. I lay awake at night constructing imaginary microscopes of immeasurable power, with which I seemed to pierce through all the envelopes of matter down to its original atom. How I cursed those imperfect mediums which necessity through ignorance compelled me to use! How I longed to discover the secret of some perfect lens, whose magnifying power should be limited only by the resolvability of the object, and which at the same time should be free from spherical and chromatic aberrations – in short, from all the obstacles over which the poor microscopist finds himself continually stumbling! I felt convinced that the simple microscope, composed of a single lens of such vast yet perfect power, was possible of construction. To attempt to bring the compound microscope up to such a pitch would have been commencing at the wrong end; this latter being simply a partially successful endeavor to remedy those very defects of the simplest instrument which, if conquered, would leave nothing to be desired.

It was in this mood of mind that I became a constructive microscopist. After another year passed in this new pursuit, experimenting on every imaginable substance – glass, gems, flints, crystals, artificial crystals formed of the alloy of various vitreous materials – in short, having constructed as many varieties of lenses as Argus had eyes – I found myself precisely where I started, with nothing gained save an extensive knowledge of glass-making. I was almost dead with despair. My parents were surprised at my apparent want of progress in my medical studies (I had not attended one lecture since my arrival in the city), and the expenses of my mad pursuit had been so great as to embarrass me very seriously.

I was in this frame of mind one day, experimenting in my laboratory on a small diamond – that stone, from its great refracting power, having always occupied my attention more than any other – when a young Frenchman who lived on the floor above me, and who was in the habit of occasionally visiting me, entered the room.

I think that Jules Simon was a Jew. He had many traits of the Hebrew character: a love of jewelry, of dress, and of good living. There was something mysterious about him. He always had something to sell, and yet went into excellent society. When I say sell, I should perhaps have said peddle; for his operations were generally confined to the disposal of single articles – a picture, for instance, or a rare carving in ivory, or a pair of duelling-pistols, or the dress of a Mexican *caballero*. When I was first furnishing my rooms, he paid me a visit, which ended in my purchasing an antique silver lamp, which he assured me was a Cellini – it was handsome enough even for that – and some other knick-knacks for my sitting-room. Why Simon should pursue this petty trade I never could imagine. He apparently had plenty of money, and had the *entrée* of the best houses in the city – taking care, however, I suppose, to drive no bargains within the enchanted circle of the Upper Ten. I came at length to the conclusion that this peddling was but a mask to cover some greater object, and even went so far as to believe my young acquaintance to be implicated in the slave-trade. That, however, was none of my affair.

On the present occasion, Simon entered my room in a state of considerable excitement.

"*Ah! Mon ami!*" he cried, before I could even offer him the ordinary salutation, "it has occurred to me to be the witness of the most astonishing things in the world. I promenade myself to the house of Madame –. How does the little animal – *le renard* – name himself in the Latin?"

"*Vulpes*," I answered.

"Ah! Yes – *Vulpes*. I promenade myself to the house of Madame Vulpes."

"The spirit medium?"

"Yes, the great medium. Great heavens! What a woman! I write on a slip of paper many of questions concerning affairs of the most secret – affairs that conceal themselves in the abysses of my heart the most profound; and behold, by example, what occurs? This devil of a woman makes me replies the most truthful to all of them. She talks to me of things that I do not love to talk of to myself. What am I to think? I am fixed to the earth!"

"Am I to understand you, M. Simon, that this Mrs. Vulpes replied to questions secretly written by you, which questions related to events known only to yourself?"

"Ah! More than that, more than that," he answered, with an air of some alarm. "She related to me things – but," he added after a pause, and suddenly changing his manner, "why occupy ourselves with these follies? It was all the biology, without doubt. It goes without saying that it has not my credence. But why are we here, *mon ami*? It has occurred to me to discover the most beautiful thing as you can imagine – a vase with green lizards on it, composed by the great Bernard Palissy. It is in my apartment; let us mount. I go to show it to you."

I followed Simon mechanically; but my thoughts were far from Palissy and his enameled ware, although I, like him, was seeking in the dark a great discovery. This casual mention of the spiritualist, Madame Vulpes, set me on a new track. What if, through communication with more subtle organisms than my own, I could reach at a single bound the goal which perhaps a life of agonizing mental toil would never enable me to attain?

While purchasing the Palissy vase from my friend Simon, I was mentally arranging a visit to Madame Vulpes.

III

TWO EVENINGS after this, thanks to an arrangement by letter and the promise of an ample fee, I found Madame Vulpes awaiting me at her residence alone. She was a coarse-featured woman, with keen and rather cruel dark eyes, and an exceedingly sensual expression about her mouth and under jaw. She received me in perfect silence, in an apartment on the ground floor, very sparsely furnished. In the centre of the room, close to where Mrs. Vulpes sat, there was a common round mahogany table. If I had come for the purpose of sweeping her chimney, the woman could not have looked more indifferent to my appearance. There was no attempt to inspire the visitor with awe. Everything bore a simple and practical aspect. This intercourse with the spiritual world was evidently as familiar an occupation with Mrs. Vulpes as eating her dinner or riding in an omnibus.

"You come for a communication, Mr. Linley?" said the medium, in a dry, businesslike tone of voice.

"By appointment – yes."

"What sort of communication do you want – a written one?"

"Yes, I wish for a written one."

"From any particular spirit?"

"Yes."

"Have you ever known this spirit on this earth?"

"Never. He died long before I was born. I wish merely to obtain from him some information which he ought to be able to give better than any other."

"Will you seat yourself at the table, Mr. Lin-ley," said the medium, "and place your hands upon it?"

I obeyed, Mrs. Vulpes being seated opposite to me, with her hands also on the table. We remained thus for about a minute and a half, when a violent succession of raps came on the table, on the back of my chair, on the floor immediately under my feet, and even on the window-panes. Mrs. Vulpes smiled composedly.

"They are very strong tonight," she remarked. "You are fortunate." She then continued, "Will the spirits communicate with this gentleman?"

Vigorous affirmative.

"Will the particular spirit he desires to speak with communicate?"

A very confused rapping followed this question.

"I know what they mean," said Mrs. Vulpes, addressing herself to me; "they wish you to write down the name of the particular spirit that you desire to converse with. Is that so?" she added, speaking to her invisible guests.

That it was so was evident from the numerous affirmatory responses. While this was going on, I tore a slip from my pocket-book and scribbled a name under the table.

"Will this spirit communicate in writing with this gentleman?" asked the medium once more.

After a moment's pause, her hand seemed to be seized with a violent tremor, shaking so forcibly that the table vibrated. She said that a spirit had seized her hand and would write. I handed her some sheets of paper that were on the table and a pencil. The latter she held loosely in her hand, which presently began to move over the paper with a singular and seemingly involuntary motion. After a few moments had elapsed, she handed me the paper, on which I found written, in a large, uncultivated hand, the words, "He is not here, but has been sent for." A pause of a minute or so ensued, during which Mrs. Vulpes remained perfectly silent, but the raps continued at regular intervals. When the short period I mention had elapsed, the hand of the medium was again seized with its convulsive tremor, and she wrote, under this strange influence, a few words on the paper, which she handed to me. They were as follows:

'I am here. Question me.
'Leeuwenhoek.'

I was astounded. The name was identical with that I had written beneath the table, and carefully kept concealed. Neither was it at all probable that an uncultivated woman like Mrs. Vulpes should know even the name of the great father of microscopies. It may have been biology; but this theory was soon doomed to be destroyed. I wrote on my slip – still concealing it from Mrs. Vulpes – a series of questions which, to avoid tediousness, I shall place with the responses, in the order in which they occurred:

I – Can the microscope be brought to perfection?
Spirit – Yes.
I – Am I destined to accomplish this great task?
Spirit – You are.

I – I wish to know how to proceed to attain this end. For the love which you bear to science, help me!
Spirit – A diamond of one hundred and forty carats, submitted to electro-magnetic currents for a long period, will experience a rearrangement of its atoms inter se and from that stone you will form the universal lens.
I – Will great discoveries result from the use of such a lens?
Spirit – So great that all that has gone before is as nothing.
I – But the refractive power of the diamond is so immense that the image will be formed within the lens. How is that difficulty to be surmounted?
Spirit – Pierce the lens through its axis, and the difficulty is obviated. The image will be formed in the pierced space, which will itself serve as a tube to look through. Now I am called. Goodnight.

I can not at all describe the effect that these extraordinary communications had upon me. I felt completely bewildered. No biological theory could account for the *discovery* of the lens. The medium might, by means of biological *rapport* with my mind, have gone so far as to read my questions and reply to them coherently. But biology could not enable her to discover that magnetic currents would so alter the crystals of the diamond as to remedy its previous defects and admit of its being polished into a perfect lens. Some such theory may have passed through my head, it is true; but if so, I had forgotten it. In my excited condition of mind there was no course left but to become a convert, and it was in a state of the most painful nervous exaltation that I left the medium's house that evening. She accompanied me to the door, hoping that I was satisfied. The raps followed us as we went through the hall, sounding on the balusters, the flooring, and even the lintels of the door. I hastily expressed my satisfaction, and escaped hurriedly into the cool night air. I walked home with but one thought possessing me – how to obtain a diamond of the immense size required. My entire means multiplied a hundred times over would have been inadequate to its purchase. Besides, such stones are rare, and become historical. I could find such only in the regalia of Eastern or European monarchs.

IV

THERE WAS a light in Simon's room as I entered my house. A vague impulse urged me to visit him. As I opened the door of his sitting-room unannounced, he was bending, with his back toward me, over a Carcel lamp, apparently engaged in minutely examining some object which he held in his hands. As I entered, he started suddenly, thrust his hand into his breast pocket, and turned to me with a face crimson with confusion.

"What!" I cried, "poring over the miniature of some fair lady? Well, don't blush so much; I won't ask to see it."

Simon laughed awkwardly enough, but made none of the negative protestations usual on such occasions. He asked me to take a seat.

"Simon," said I, "I have just come from Madame Vulpes."

This time Simon turned as white as a sheet, and seemed stupefied, as if a sudden electric shock had smitten him. He babbled some incoherent words, and went hastily to a small closet where he usually kept his liquors. Although astonished at his emotion, I was too preoccupied with my own idea to pay much attention to anything else.

"You say truly when you call Madame Vulpes a devil of a woman," I continued. "Simon, she told me wonderful things tonight, or rather was the means of telling me wonderful things. Ah! If I could only get a diamond that weighed one hundred and forty carats!"

Scarcely had the sigh with which I uttered this desire died upon my lips when Simon, with the aspect of a wild beast, glared at me savagely, and, rushing to the mantelpiece, where some foreign weapons hung on the wall, caught up a Malay creese, and brandished it furiously before him.

"No!" he cried in French, into which he always broke when excited. "No! You shall not have it! You are perfidious! You have consulted with that demon, and desire my treasure! But I will die first! Me, I am brave! You can not make me fear!"

All this, uttered in a loud voice, trembling with excitement, astounded me. I saw at a glance that I had accidentally trodden upon the edges of Simon's secret, whatever it was. It was necessary to reassure him.

"My dear Simon," I said, "I am entirely at a loss to know what you mean. I went to Madame Vulpes to consult with her on a scientific problem, to the solution of which I discovered that a diamond of the size I just mentioned was necessary. You were never alluded to during the evening, nor, so far as I was concerned, even thought of. What can be the meaning of this outburst? If you happen to have a set of valuable diamonds in your possession, you need fear nothing from me. The diamond which I require you could not possess; or, if you did possess it, you would not be living here."

Something in my tone must have completely reassured him, for his expression immediately changed to a sort of constrained merriment, combined however, with a certain suspicious attention to my movements. He laughed, and said that I must bear with him; that he was at certain moments subject to a species of vertigo, which betrayed itself in incoherent speeches, and that the attacks passed off as rapidly as they came.

He put his weapon aside while making this explanation, and endeavored, with some success, to assume a more cheerful air.

All this did not impose on me in the least. I was too much accustomed to analytical labors to be baffled by so flimsy a veil. I determined to probe the mystery to the bottom.

"Simon," I said gayly, "let us forget all this over a bottle of Burgundy. I have a case of Lausseure's *Clos Vougeot* downstairs, fragrant with the odors and ruddy with the sunlight of the Côte d'Or. Let us have up a couple of bottles. What say you?"

"With all my heart," answered Simon smilingly.

I produced the wine and we seated ourselves to drink. It was of a famous vintage, that of 1848, a year when war and wine throve together, and its pure but powerful juice seemed to impart renewed vitality to the system. By the time we had half finished the second bottle, Simon's head, which I knew was a weak one, had begun to yield, while I remained calm as ever, only that every draught seemed to send a flush of vigor through my limbs. Simon's utterance became more and more indistinct. He took to singing French *chansons* of a not very moral tendency. I rose suddenly from the table just at the conclusion of one of those incoherent verses, and, fixing my eyes on him with a quiet smile, said, "Simon, I have deceived you. I learned your secret this evening. You may as well be frank with me. Mrs. Vulpes – or rather, one of her spirits – told me all."

He started with horror. His intoxication seemed for the moment to fade away, and he made a movement toward the weapon that he had a short time before laid down, I stopped him with my hand.

"Monster!" he cried passionately, "I am ruined! What shall I do? You shall never have it! I swear by my mother!"

"I don't want it," I said; "rest secure, but be frank with me. Tell me all about it."

The drunkenness began to return. He protested with maudlin earnestness that I was entirely mistaken – that I was intoxicated; then asked me to swear eternal secrecy, and promised to disclose the mystery to me. I pledged myself, of course, to all. With an uneasy look in his eyes, and hands unsteady with drink and nervousness, he drew a small case from his breast and opened it. Heavens! How the mild lamplight was shivered into a thousand prismatic arrows as it fell upon a vast rose-diamond that glittered in the case! I was no judge of diamonds, but I saw at a glance that this was a gem of rare size and purity. I looked at Simon with wonder and – must I confess it? – with envy. How could he have obtained this treasure? In reply to my questions, I could just gather from his drunken statements (of which, I fancy, half the incoherence was affected) that he had been superintending a gang of slaves engaged in diamond-washing in Brazil; that he had seen one of them secrete a diamond, but, instead of informing his employers, had quietly watched the negro until he saw him bury his treasure; that he had dug it up and fled with it, but that as yet he was afraid to attempt to dispose of it publicly – so valuable a gem being almost certain to attract too much attention to its owner's antecedents – and he had not been able to discover any of those obscure channels by which such matters are conveyed away safely. He added that, in accordance with oriental practice, he had named his diamond with the fanciful title of 'The Eye of Morning'.

While Simon was relating this to me, I regarded the great diamond attentively. Never had I beheld anything so beautiful. All the glories of light ever imagined or described seemed to pulsate in its crystalline chambers. Its weight, as I learned from Simon, was exactly one hundred and forty carats. Here was an amazing coincidence. The hand of destiny seemed in it. On the very evening when the spirit of Leeuwenhoek communicates to me the great secret of the microscope, the priceless means which he directs me to employ start up within my easy reach! I determined, with the most perfect deliberation, to possess myself of Simon's diamond.

I sat opposite to him while he nodded over his glass, and calmly revolved the whole affair. I did not for an instant contemplate so foolish an act as a common theft, which would of course be discovered, or at least necessitate flight and concealment, all of which must interfere with my scientific plans. There was but one step to be taken – to kill Simon. After all, what was the life of a little peddling Jew in comparison with the interests of science? Human beings are taken every day from the condemned prisons to be experimented on by surgeons. This man, Simon, was by his own confession a criminal, a robber, and I believed on my soul a murderer. He deserved death quite as much as any felon condemned by the laws: why should I not, like government, contrive that his punishment should contribute to the progress of human knowledge?

The means for accomplishing everything I desired lay within my reach. There stood upon the mantelpiece a bottle half full of French laudanum. Simon was so occupied with his diamond, which I had just restored to him, that it was an affair of no difficulty to drug his glass. In a quarter of an hour he was in a profound sleep.

I now opened his waistcoat, took the diamond from the inner pocket in which he had placed it, and removed him to the bed, on which I laid him so that his feet hung down over the edge. I had possessed myself of the Malay creese, which I held in my right hand, while with the other I discovered as accurately as I could by pulsation the exact locality of the heart. It was essential that all the aspects of his death should lead to the surmise of self-murder. I calculated the exact angle at which it was probable that the weapon, if leveled by Simon's own hand, would enter his breast; then with one powerful blow I thrust it up to the hilt in the very spot which I desired to penetrate. A convulsive thrill ran through Simon's limbs. I heard a smothered sound issue from his throat, precisely like the bursting of a large air-bubble sent up by a diver when it reaches the surface of the water; he turned half round on his side, and, as if to assist my plans more effectually, his right hand, moved by some mere spasmodic impulse, clasped the handle of the creese, which it remained holding with extraordinary muscular tenacity. Beyond this there was no apparent struggle. The laudanum, I presume, paralyzed the usual nervous action. He must have died instantly.

There was yet something to be done. To make it certain that all suspicion of the act should be diverted from any inhabitant of the house to Simon himself, it was necessary that the door should be found in the morning *locked on the inside*. How to do this, and afterward escape myself? Not by the window; that was a physical impossibility. Besides, I was determined that the windows *also* should be found bolted. The solution was simple enough. I descended softly to my own room for a peculiar instrument which I had used for holding small slippery substances, such as minute spheres of glass, etc. This instrument was nothing more than a long, slender hand-vise, with a very powerful grip and a considerable leverage, which last was accidentally owing to the shape of the handle. Nothing was simpler than, when the key was in the lock, to seize the end of its stem in this vise, through the keyhole, from the outside, and so lock the door. Previously, however, to doing this, I burned a number of papers on Simon's hearth. Suicides almost always burn papers before they destroy themselves. I also emptied some more laudanum into Simon's glass – having first removed from it all traces of wine – cleaned the other wine-glass, and brought the bottles away with me. If traces of two persons drinking had been found in the room, the question naturally would have arisen, who was the second? Besides, the wine-bottles might have been identified as belonging to me. The laudanum I poured out to account for its presence in his stomach, in case of a *post-mortem* examination. The theory naturally would be that he first intended to poison himself, but, after swallowing a little of the drug, was either disgusted with its taste, or changed his mind from other motives, and chose the dagger. These arrangements made, I walked out, leaving the gas burning, locked the door with my vise, and went to bed.

Simon's death was not discovered until nearly three in the afternoon. The servant, astonished at seeing the gas burning – the light streaming on the dark landing from under the door – peeped through the keyhole and saw Simon on the bed.

She gave the alarm. The door was burst open, and the neighborhood was in a fever of excitement.

Everyone in the house was arrested, myself included. There was an inquest; but no clew to his death beyond that of suicide could be obtained. Curiously enough, he had made several speeches to his friends the preceding week that seemed to point to self-destruction. One gentleman swore that Simon had said in his presence that "he was tired of life." His landlord affirmed that Simon, when paying him his last month's rent, remarked that "he should not pay him rent much longer." All the other evidence corresponded – the door locked inside, the position of the corpse, the burned papers. As I anticipated, no one knew of the possession of the diamond by Simon, so that no motive was suggested for his murder. The jury, after a prolonged examination, brought in the usual verdict, and the neighborhood once more settled down to its accustomed quiet.

V

THE THREE MONTHS succeeding Simon's catastrophe I devoted night and day to my diamond lens. I had constructed a vast galvanic battery, composed of nearly two thousand pairs of plates: a higher power I dared not use, lest the diamond should be calcined. By means of this enormous engine I was enabled to send a powerful current of electricity continually through my great diamond, which it seemed to me gained in lustre every day. At the expiration of a month I commenced the grinding and polishing of the lens, a work of intense toil and exquisite delicacy. The great density of the stone, and the care required to be taken with the curvatures of the surfaces of the lens, rendered the labor the severest and most harassing that I had yet undergone.

At last the eventful moment came; the lens was completed. I stood trembling on the threshold of new worlds. I had the realization of Alexander's famous wish before me. The lens lay on the table, ready to be placed upon its platform. My hand fairly shook as I enveloped a drop of water with a thin coating of oil of turpentine, preparatory to its examination, a process necessary in order to prevent the rapid evaporation of the water. I now placed the drop on a thin slip of glass under the lens, and throwing upon it, by the combined aid of a prism and a mirror, a powerful stream of light, I approached my eye to the minute hole drilled through the axis of the lens. For an instant I saw nothing save what seemed to be an illuminated chaos, a vast, luminous abyss. A pure white light, cloudless and serene, and seemingly limitless as space itself, was my first impression. Gently, and with the greatest care, I depressed the lens a few hairbreadths. The wondrous illumination still continued, but as the lens approached the object a scene of indescribable beauty was unfolded to my view.

I seemed to gaze upon a vast space, the limits of which extended far beyond my vision. An atmosphere of magical luminousness permeated the entire field of view. I was amazed to see no trace of animalculous life. Not a living thing, apparently, inhabited that dazzling expanse. I comprehended instantly that, by the wondrous power of my lens, I had penetrated beyond the grosser particles of aqueous matter, beyond the realms of infusoria and protozoa, down to the original gaseous globule, into whose luminous interior I was gazing as into an almost boundless dome filled with a supernatural radiance.

It was, however, no brilliant void into which I looked. On every side I beheld beautiful inorganic forms, of unknown texture, and colored with the most enchanting hues. These forms presented the appearance of what might be called, for want of a more specific definition, foliated clouds of the highest rarity – that is, they undulated and broke into vegetable formations, and were tinged with splendors compared with which the gilding of our autumn woodlands is as dross compared with gold. Far away into the illimitable distance stretched long avenues of these gaseous forests, dimly transparent, and painted with prismatic hues of unimaginable brilliancy. The pendent branches waved along the fluid glades until every vista seemed to break through half-lucent ranks of many-colored drooping silken pennons. What seemed to be either fruits or flowers, pied with a thousand hues, lustrous and ever-varying, bubbled from the crowns of this fairy foliage. No hills, no lakes, no rivers, no forms animate or inanimate, were to be seen, save those vast auroral copses that floated serenely in the luminous stillness, with leaves and fruits and flowers gleaming with unknown fires, unrealizable by mere imagination.

How strange, I thought, that this sphere should be thus condemned to solitude! I had hoped, at least, to discover some new form of animal life, perhaps of a lower class than any with which we are at present acquainted, but still some living organism. I found my newly discovered world, if I may so speak, a beautiful chromatic desert.

While I was speculating on the singular arrangements of the internal economy of Nature, with which she so frequently splinters into atoms our most compact theories, I thought I beheld a form moving slowly through the glades of one of the prismatic forests. I looked more attentively, and found that I was not mistaken. Words cannot depict the anxiety with which I awaited the nearer approach of this mysterious object. Was it merely some inanimate substance, held in suspense in the attenuated atmosphere of the globule, or was it an animal endowed with vitality and motion? It approached, flitting behind the gauzy, colored veils of cloud-foliage, for seconds dimly revealed, then vanishing. At last the violet pennons that trailed nearest to me vibrated; they were gently pushed aside, and the form floated out into the broad light.

It was a female human shape. When I say human, I mean it possessed the outlines of humanity; but there the analogy ends. Its adorable beauty lifted it illimitable heights beyond the loveliest daughter of Adam.

I cannot, I dare not, attempt to inventory the charms of this divine revelation of perfect beauty. Those eyes of mystic violet, dewy and serene, evade my words. Her long, lustrous hair following her glorious head in a golden wake, like the track sown in heaven by a falling star, seems to quench my most burning phrases with its splendors. If all the bees of Hybla nestled upon my lips, they would still sing but hoarsely the wondrous harmonies of outline that inclosed her form.

She swept out from between the rainbow-curtains of the cloud-trees into the broad sea of light that lay beyond. Her motions were those of some graceful naiad, cleaving, by a mere effort of her will, the clear, unruffled waters that fill the chambers of the sea. She floated forth with the serene grace of a frail bubble ascending through the still atmosphere of a June day. The perfect roundness of her limbs formed suave and enchanting curves. It was like listening to the most spiritual symphony of Beethoven the divine, to watch the harmonious flow of lines. This, indeed was a pleasure cheaply purchased at any price. What cared I if I had waded to the portal of this wonder through another's blood. I would have given my own to enjoy one such moment of intoxication and delight.

Breathless with gazing on this lovely wonder, and forgetful for an instant of everything save her presence, I withdrew my eye from the microscope eagerly. Alas! As my gaze fell on the thin slide that lay beneath my instrument, the bright light from mirror and from prism sparkled on a colorless drop of water! There, in that tiny bead of dew, this beautiful being was forever imprisoned. The planet Neptune was not more distant from me than she. I hastened once more to apply my eye to the microscope.

Animula (let me now call her by that dear name which I subsequently bestowed on her) had changed her position. She had again approached the wondrous forest, and was gazing earnestly upward. Presently one of the trees – as I must call them – unfolded a long ciliary process, with which it seized one of the gleaming fruits that glittered on its summit, and, sweeping slowly down, held it within reach of Animula. The sylph took it in her delicate hand and began to eat. My attention was so entirely absorbed by her that I could not apply myself to the task of determining whether this singular plant was or was not instinct with volition.

I watched her, as she made her repast, with the most profound attention. The suppleness of her motions sent a thrill of delight through my frame; my heart beat madly as she turned her beautiful eyes in the direction of the spot in which I stood. What would I not have given to have had the power to precipitate myself into that luminous ocean and float with her through those grooves of purple and gold! While I was thus breathlessly following her every movement, she suddenly started, seemed to listen for a moment, and then cleaving the brilliant ether in which she was floating, like a flash of light, pierced through the opaline forest and disappeared.

Instantly a series of the most singular sensations attacked me. It seemed as if I had suddenly gone blind. The luminous sphere was still before me, but my daylight had vanished. What caused this sudden disappearance? Had she a lover or a husband? Yes, that was the solution! Some signal from a happy fellow-being had vibrated through the avenues of the forest, and she had obeyed the summons.

The agony of my sensations, as I arrived at this conclusion, startled me. I tried to reject the conviction that my reason forced upon me. I battled against the fatal conclusion – but in vain. It was so. I had no escape from it. I loved an animalcule.

It is true that, thanks to the marvelous power of my microscope, she appeared of human proportions. Instead of presenting the revolting aspect of the coarser creatures, that live and struggle and die, in the more easily resolvable portions of the water-drop, she was fair and delicate and of surpassing beauty. But of what account was all that? Every time that my eye was withdrawn from the instrument it fell on a miserable drop of water, within which, I must be content to know, dwelt all that could make my life lovely.

Could she but see me once! Could I for one moment pierce the mystical walls that so inexorably rose to separate us, and whisper all that filled my soul, I might consent to be satisfied for the rest of my life with the knowledge of her remote sympathy.

It would be something to have established even the faintest personal link to bind us together – to know that at times, when roaming through these enchanted glades, she might think of the wonderful stranger who had broken the monotony of her life with his presence and left a gentle memory in her heart!

But it could not be. No invention of which human intellect was capable could break down the barriers that nature had erected. I might feast my soul upon her wondrous beauty, yet she must always remain ignorant of the adoring eyes that day and night gazed upon her, and, even when closed, beheld her in dreams. With a bitter cry of anguish I fled from the room, and flinging myself on my bed, sobbed myself to sleep like a child.

VI

I AROSE the next morning almost at daybreak, and rushed to my microscope, I trembled as I sought the luminous world in miniature that contained my all. Animula was there. I had left the gas-lamp, surrounded by its moderators, burning when I went to bed the night before. I found the sylph bathing, as it were, with an expression of pleasure animating her features, in the brilliant light which surrounded her. She tossed er lustrous golden hair over her shoulders with innocent coquetry. She lay at full length n the transparent medium, in which she supported herself with ease, and gamboled with the enchanting grace that the nymph Salmacis might have exhibited when she sought to conquer the modest Hermaphroditus. I tried an experiment to satisfy myself f her powers of reflection were developed. I lessened the lamplight considerably. By the dim light that remained, I could see an expression of pain flit across her face. She looked upward suddenly, and her brows contracted. I flooded the stage of the microscope again with a full stream of light, and her whole expression changed. She sprang forward like some some substance deprived of all weight. Her eyes sparkled and her lips moved. Ah! If science had only the means of conducting and reduplicating sounds, as it does rays of light, what carols of happiness would then have entranced my ears! What jubilant hymns to Adonais would have thrilled the illumined air!

I now comprehended how it was that the Count de Cabalis peopled his mystic world with sylphs – beautiful beings whose breath of life was lambent fire, and who sported forever in regions of purest ether and purest light. The Rosicrucian had anticipated the wonder that I had practically realized.

How long this worship of my strange divinity went on thus I scarcely know. I lost all note of time. All day from early dawn, and far into the night, I was to be found peering through that wonderful lens. I saw no one, went nowhere, and scarce allowed myself sufficient time for my meals. My whole life was absorbed in contemplation as rapt as that of any of the Romish saints. Every hour that I gazed upon the divine form strengthened my passion – a passion that was always overshadowed by the maddening conviction that, although I could gaze on her at will, she never, never could behold me!

At length I grew so pale and emaciated, from want of rest and continual brooding over my insane love and its cruel conditions, that I determined to make some effort to wean myself from it. "Come," I said, "this is at best but a fantasy. Your imagination has bestowed on Animula charms which in reality she does not possess. Seclusion from female society has produced this morbid condition of mind. Compare her with the beautiful women of your own world, and this false enchantment will vanish."

I looked over the newspapers by chance. There I beheld the advertisement of a celebrated *danseuse* who appeared nightly at Niblo's. The Signorina Caradolce had the reputation of being the most beautiful as well as the most graceful woman in the world. I instantly dressed and went to the theatre.

The curtain drew up. The usual semicircle of fairies in white muslin were standing on the right toe around the enameled flower-bank of green canvas, on which the belated prince was sleeping. Suddenly a flute is heard. The fairies start. The trees open, the fairies all stand on the left toe, and the queen enters. It was the Signorina. She bounded forward amid thunders of applause, and, lighting on one foot, remained poised in the air. Heavens! Was this the great enchantress that had drawn monarchs at her chariot-wheels? Those heavy, muscular limbs, those thick ankles, those cavernous eyes, that stereotyped smile, those crudely painted cheeks! Where were the vermeil blooms, the liquid, expressive eyes, the harmonious limbs of Animula?

The Signorina danced. What gross, discordant movements! The play of her limbs was all false and artificial. Her bounds were painful athletic efforts; her poses were angular and distressed the eye. I could bear it no longer; with an exclamation of disgust that drew every eye upon me, I rose from my seat in the very middle of the Signorina's *pas-de-fascination* and abruptly quitted the house.

I hastened home to feast my eyes once more on the lovely form of my sylph. I felt th henceforth to combat this passion would be impossible. I applied my eyes to the len Animula was there – but what could have happened? Some terrible change seeme to have taken place during my absence. Some secret grief seemed to cloud the lovel features of her I gazed upon. Her face had grown thin and haggard; her limbs traile heavily; the wondrous lustre of her golden hair had faded. She was ill – ill, and I coul not assist her! I believe at that moment I would have forfeited all claims to my huma birthright if I could only have been dwarfed to the size of an animalcule, and permitte to console her from whom fate had forever divided me.

I racked my brain for the solution of this mystery. What was it that afflicted the sylph She seemed to suffer intense pain. Her features contracted, and she even writhed as if with some internal agony. The wondrous forests appeared also to have lost hal their beauty. Their hues were dim and in some places faded away altogether. I watche Animula for hours with a breaking heart, and she seemed absolutely to wither awa under my very eye. Suddenly I remembered that I had not looked at the water-drop fo several days. In fact, I hated to see it; for it reminded me of the natural barrier between Animula and myself. I hurriedly looked down on the stage of the microscope. The slide was still there – but, great heavens, the water drop had vanished! The awful truth burst upon me; it had evaporated, until it had become so minute as to be invisible to the naked eye; I had been gazing on its last atom, the one that contained Animula – and she was dying!

I rushed again to the front of the lens and looked through. Alas! The last agony had seized her. The rainbow-hued forests had all melted away, and Animula lay struggling feebly in what seemed to be a spot of dim light. Ah! The sight was horrible: the limbs once so round and lovely shriveling up into nothings; the eyes – those eyes that shone like heaven – being quenched into black dust; the lustrous golden hair now lank and discolored. The last throe came. I beheld that final struggle of the blackening form – and I fainted.

When I awoke out of a trance of many hours, I found myself lying amid the wreck of my instrument, myself as shattered in mind and body as it. I crawled feebly to my bed, from which I did not rise for many months.

They say now that I am mad; but they are mistaken. I am poor, for I have neither the heart nor the will to work; all my money is spent, and I live on charity. Young men's associations that love a joke invite me to lecture on optics before them, for which they pay me, and laugh at me while I lecture. "Linley, the mad microscopist," is the name I go by. I suppose that I talk incoherently while I lecture. Who could talk sense when his brain is haunted by such ghastly memories, while ever and anon among the shapes of death I behold the radiant form of my lost Animula!

The Matter Concerning Mr. Symmes and the Hollow World

Michael Penncavage

TO ALL THE WORLD!

I declare the earth is hollow, and habitable within; containing a number of solid concentric spheres, one within the other, and that it is open at the poles 12 or 16 degrees; I pledge my life in support of this truth, and am ready to explore the hollow, if the world will support and aid me in the undertaking.
I have ready for the press, a Treatise on the principles of matter, wherein I show proofs of the above positions, account for various phenomena, and disclose Doctor Darwin's Golden Secret. My terms, are the patronage of this and the new worlds. I dedicate to my Wife and her ten Children. I select Doctor S.L. Mitchill, Sir H. Davy and Baron Alex. de Humboldt, as my protectors. I ask one hundred brave companions, well equipped, to start in the fall season, with Reindeer and sleighs, on the ice of the frozen sea: I engage we find warm and rich land, stocked with thrifty vegetables and animals if not men, on reaching one degree northward of latitude 82; we will return in the succeeding spring.

JOHN CLEVES SYMMES
Of Ohio, Late Captain of Infantry. **(footnote 1)**

* * *

A LOOK of consternation covered Doctor Stewart Mitchill's face as he looked up after reading the leaflet. He folded the paper neatly in half and placed it on the coffee table beside his chair.

"Jonathan, was it *really* necessary to distribute your proclamation as thoroughly as you did?"

Jonathan Cleeves Symmes stood by the window of his study, looking down at the street below, watching the nearby oak shed its remaining leaves in the twilight. He took a deep drag from his pipe and exhaled. The smoke was immediately whisked through the open window. "If that is what it takes for us to obtain the necessary funding, then the answer is *yes*, Stewart."

Howard Davy sat behind Symmes' desk, a snifter of brandy in one hand, cigar in the other. His burly frame filled the leather chair. "A fall start is ambitious, John. Especially when you consider the preparations."

"The least of which is securing an expedition party of the size you noted," added Baron Alex. de Humboldt as he perused Symmes' floor-to-ceiling book collection.

Symmes tapped his pipe against the stone window ledge, watching as the ash sprinkled to ground below. His normally pale cheeks were now flushed. "Is that the reason you called this meeting? To try to talk me out of going? Or perhaps you have changed your mind?"

Howard's mustache rose as he grinned. "No, John. I believe we know *you* far too much to try to talk you out of this. At the same time I think you know *us* all well enough to know that, we do not back down from our promises, nor our friends."

Symmes looked at Davy and nodded. "Of course. Forgive me for being so rash."

"The Hollow Earth exists and awaits our discovery." Stewart answered, crossing his legs. "We must commence preparations. Much work needs to be done."

Davy turned his chair to the immense world map on the wall. "One degree northward of latitude 82," he said, looking to where a red line had been drawn. "It is going to be a bear getting there, gentlemen. A bear indeed."

"If it were easy, Howard, it would have been discovered long ago."

Stewart walked up to the map. "A fertile landscape brimming with vegetation and life, surrounded by ice for hundreds of miles. It is no wonder some of the newspapers revile us as lunatics."

"Which one are you speaking with tomorrow?" asked Davy.

"The *Aurora*," replied Symmes. "It boasts one of the largest circulations in the city. Winning their support will be key in the court of public opinion as well to any private interests that are contemplating funding."

"True," replied Humboldt. "But be prepared. Their staff contains its share of vipers."

Howard pointed to the top of the map. "We are going to have to give considerable discussion concerning the later part of this trip. It is anyone's guess how far we get through the ice with the ship. We might have to travel a large distance with the reindeer."

Symmes grinned. "Do not worry about that, my friend. I made mention of the reindeer to prevent the lenders from thinking I had gone completely insane."

"So we will not be using the animals?"

"That is correct."

"Dogs, then?"

"Let's not get ahead of ourselves. We first need to secure the necessary financial support. Symmes turned and looked back out the window. He looked to his right, to the north.

Even in the twilight the sky seemed foreboding.

* * *

"We appreciate you taking the time to meet with us," said Herbert Bennington, the elder of the two reporters.

Symmes shook each of the men's hands. "I always have time to speak with the men at the *Aurora*. Tell me, is Mr. Walt Whitman still employed there? My previous interview was with him."

"I'm not certain, Mr. Symmes. The *Aurora* employs a great many people," answered Bennington.

William Connolly, the other reporter, removed Symmes' pamphlet from his jacket pocket. "Let us start with the announcement, Mr. Symmes. I'm sure you are aware it has not been well received."

"It is true, Mr. Connelly, that there have been some nay-sayers. But history clearly shows that people who question the norm are often rebuked by those who are scared of change."

"But to say the earth is hollow?" asked Bennington.

"Is no more outlandish than Columbus questioning the earth as flat," replied Symmes.

"But, Mr. Symmes, your comment is a double edged sword. Centuries have passed," challenged Connolly. "Man has become more…more wise. Stories about hollow worlds…"

"Yes?"

"Should be reserved for bedtime fables."

"Let me respond to that with a question, Mr. Connolly. Pluck a hair from your blonde head and cut it in half. Can you tell me what you would find?"

The reporter did not answer.

"How about the insides of your bones, sir? Do you know what they mostly contain?"

"Enlighten me, Mr. Symmes."

"Air. Above all other elements or substances, there exists air."

Bennington wagged his pencil at him. "But to expand that theory to the earth, Mr. Symmes? Isn't that a rather large leap?"

Jonathan clasped his hands together. "I trust you gentlemen know what a bola is?"

The reporters nodded. Symmes continued. "Our planet, like the others in our solar system, are spun in orbit by the pull of the sun, much the same way someone would spin a bola. Likewise, the earth, acting on the gravity of the sun, is spun like a top on its axis. Matter is expelled to the surface as it revolves, thus causing a buildup of air within its core."

"The point is taken, Mr. Symmes. I grant you the notion that air of some quantity exist within the earth's core. But to say there is some sort of livable habitat beneath the ground…?"

"For an answer, let us go back to my previous example, Mr. Bennington. In addition to air there also exist small, concentric circles that are mirror images of the larger one."

"I'm sorry, I'm not following you."

"Imagine the rings on a tree. Smaller images of the outer one. That is what I propose my Hollow World to be. A smaller replica of our own."

"And the access points to these lower levels are what you hope to find in the Arctic?"

"Yes. I believe these openings, which make it possible for light and heat to pass through, are located there. I have obtained numerous accounts from whalers who have reported passing through areas of the Arctic Sea where the water should have been frozen solid."

"I fail to see the correlation between a tepid winter and the existence of a *hollow earth*."

"Mr. Connelly, nothing should be *tepid* in an environment where exposure to the elements can kill a man in minutes. The increased temperatures reported lend further credibility to the Hollow World. Expulsion of heat from within the world below would explain the unnatural temperatures."

"Have you heard of Byron Lentz?" asked Bennington.

"The outspoken physicist," Symmes replied. "And yes, Mr. Bennington, to answer your next question, I am quite aware of his stand regarding my theory."

"Would you like to publicly state your retort?"

"The gentleman, a Harvard man, I believe, is quite entitled to his opinions. Time will tell who is correct."

"So you are firm in your plans to leave in the fall?" he asked.

"Additional funds, both private and public, are being secured. My petition goes to the House of Representatives after the New Year. I fully anticipate their backing."

"What are you requesting?"

"A ship. Large enough to carry my men and equipment."

"And if the government turns you down?"

"Well, Mr. Connelly, I suppose we will just have to wait and see, won't we?"

* * *

The four men crowded around the telegraph like expectant fathers.

"Are you certain it is working properly?" Humboldt leaned over the clerk's chair so much that the operator became alarmed that the machine might get damaged.

"Sirs! I received a telegram a half-hour ago. The machine is fully functional. However, to ensure it continues so I would ask that you please take a step backwards!"

As if on cue, the machine chattered to life and began regurgitating a white ribbon. Symmes gripped his cane in suspense. If the House voted *yes,* they were going; if they voted *no*, his dream was over. The additional private funding had not come about.

The clerk began to read the tape. "*I am pleased to report imperialism is not dead. Vote passed. Requested funds granted. Jim Johnson.*"

Howard let out a whoop of joy. Symmes smiled broadly. His tactic of having his proponents in Congress pitch it as an opportunity for America to expand their territory worked.

The Baron turned to Symmes. "This is cause for celebration. I have a table waiting for us at Delmonicos."

"Really? asked Howard. "And would we still be going if the telegraph was in the negative?"

"No, Mr. Davy. If we were denied funding our punishment would have been my wife's cooking!"

The four men broke into laughter for a moment before Symmes spoke. "Yes. It is most certainly a time to celebrate. But if you can contain your hunger for just a short while longer, there is someplace that I would like to take you."

* * *

The carriage rocked precariously over uneven cobbles. Mitchill's nose wrinkled as he glanced out the window. "Ugh! The smell of rotting fish and dank wood! Why are we at the dockyards, Jonathan?"

"No need to fret." Symmes grabbed his walking stick from against the carriage's velvet interior. "We are here."

The driver slowed and the carriage jostled to a stop. "This horrible road…it feels like we are already out to sea!" commented Davy.

The men stepped out onto the foggy street. "This way, gentlemen," said Symmes as he carefully made his way across the cobbles, his cane in one hand, a lantern in the other.

"Jonathan, did you drag us all the way here just to watch you have a spill?" joked Humboldt.

"Perhaps. But not tonight," answered Symmes as he stopped in front of an entrance to one of the warehouses. Removing a set of keys, he unbolted the door. "If you would follow me."

The three men followed Symmes inside.

Darkness greeted them. It was not until Symmes tuned the lantern to its full exposure that the men saw what the building contained.

Seemingly suspended in midair, and cloaked in shadows was an object the size of a whale.

"Good lord, Symmes!" gasped Stewart. "What is that?"

"A dirigible."

"Really! I had no idea they were so large!" said Howard.

"They aren't," Symmes hooked the lantern onto his cane and held it high in the air, allowing the light to further illuminate areas that had been cloaked in shadow. "It is named, *La Resistance*. And it is one of a kind."

"Who constructed it?" asked Humboldt.

"The pilot – Jacques Pierre Roussoult, a Frenchman who lives in town. The gondola holds eight men and supplies."

"But what..." Davy looked at Symmes incredulously. "You don't actually plan..."

"At the very least we will sail to the Baffin Islands. If the weather permits we might make it as far as the Elizabeth Islands. Regardless, it is certain we will reach a point where ice will be impassable."

"At which point we will continue to travel on land via the reindeer," Davy countered.

"To reach the entrance to the Hollow World it is possible we might have to traverse a large distance of extreme cold. I feel the animals would become overwhelmed."

"And the dirigible wouldn't? I find that hard to believe? Especially with the gases needed to keep it afloat."

"I have been assured it will not be an issue."

Davy turned to Symmes. "You're serious about this?"

"I've already made certain the dirigible can be safely stored on the deck of *The Privateer*."

Stewart chuckled softly. "You never cease to amaze me, Jonathan."

Symmes lowered his cane and unhooked the lantern. His face was lost to the shadows. "I realize this was never part of our original agreement. If any of you had a change of heart, I would understand perfectly."

Davy glanced up at the dirigible. "And let you claim all the glory?"

* * *

"Jonathan, are you certain that you feel well enough to partake on this journey?" Mary had Symmes' leg propped on her lap. Placing her thumbs side-by-side, she began gently massaging his calf. "Hasn't the time come to name a successor? A protegee?"

Symmes' brow flattened as he winced. The pain that had once only been an occasional inconvenience in his knees had gradually metamorphosed into a chronic inflammation throughout his legs. "Soon, Mary. But not yet."

"And why is that? Why must you go? What price glory, Jonathan? Your health? Your life?"

"Don't talk nonsense. I am in command of a 300-ton vessel, a balloon, and ten score of men which include Mitchill, Humboldt, and Davy."

"It wouldn't matter if you had a fleet and ten thousand men under your command You are travelling to the top of the earth, Jonathan! There is a reason why the vas majority of the Arctic remains unexplored!"

Symmes placed his hand against her cheek. "Nothing is going to happen to me, Mary. You are owed a husband, the children a father. You have my word that this mission, whether a success or failure, will be my last. I have every intention of living my remaining days in Hamilton, Ohio."

* * *

"She's a beauty, isn't she?" Davy put his boot up against the dockyard railing and looked out over the water. *The Privateer* was anchored in the harbor, resting comfortably.

Symmes removed a handkerchief from his pocket and dabbed his forehead. "It's days like today that make me feel we will never leave."

"I agree. The summer does not quite want to end. Hard to imagine provisions will begin arriving within the week and that we will be setting sail by month's end."

"Yes. It all seems a bit unreal," replied Symmes as a wave of excitement coursed through his body.

"Is the balloon being prepared?"

"Yes. The talc has been applied to the canvas. It should be ready for storage by the week's end."

"Excellent!"

"Any problems to report regarding the essentials?" asked Symmes. Davy was in charge of supplies.

"Just the muskets. The seller tried to pass off used muskets from the war, claiming they had never been used. I've since found another supplier."

"How many did you acquire?" asked Symmes

"A hundred. As well as fifty side arms."

"A little excessive, no?"

"Next time you see Mitchill, you should thank him. It was he who prevented me from purchasing double."

"I'm sorry. At what point did our mission change from exploration of the Arctic to the invasion of France?"

"If we were traveling to Africa you would have no qualms about the firepower."

"Precisely. But are you expecting the Polar Bears to come armed?"

"The Geographic Society claims the Dark Continent as the last, great unexplored region. I beg to differ." Davy dropped his cigar from the pier.

Symmes watched the wad of tobacco slowly sink below the waves until a dark tide swept in, swallowing it whole.

* * *

Mary was clearly upset as *The Privateer* slipped away from the dock. Symmes waved to her, a confident smile on his face. He continued standing at the stern until she could no longer be distinguished from the others wishing their loved-ones off. His left leg grew numb and if not for railing, he would have collapsed onto the deck.

Leaning against the railing, he began massaging his leg in the manner the doctor instructed. "Tired old man," he murmured as the feeling in his toes returned. He steadied his breathing and wiped the sweat from his brow.

Around him the crew was buzzing in activity. A strong southerly wind had swept in and the mizzen and topgallant sail were being hoisted into position as was the jib. Once the sails were raised, *The Privateer* listed slightly to the port as the sails grappled with the wind.

"Looks like we are under weigh," remarked Mitchill as he approached along the poop rail. "Mother Nature is giving us a bit of a boost."

Symmes felt the wind pass through his shirt, both refreshing him and taking away his self-doubt. "Yes. No turning back now." Taking hold of his cane, he walked off to inspect the balloon.

* * *

"Good morning, Mr. Symmes."

"Good morning, Commander," replied Symmes as he walked up to Captain Stevens. Calm seas and a red sky greeted him as he took a sip of coffee. A landmass could faintly be seen in the distance. "The Okak Islands?"

"Even better. Cape Uivak."

"The southerly wind continues to favor us."

"True, Mr. Symmes. However, our luck may have come to an end."

"How so?"

Stevens motioned to the east.

"Red skies in the morning? Isn't that just superstition?"

"Captains that are not superstitious usually find themselves and their ships on the ocean floor. The weather concerns me. This region is prone to turbulence and flash storms. We will travel at half sail and within sight of land until I am assured the danger is past."

Symmes sighed as he finished his coffee. To slow down after making such great progress was frustrating. But he had little choice. "Very well, Captain."

* * *

The door leading to the deck flung open. "How are we holding up, gentlemen!" yelled Stevens as he poked his head in. A wave crashed behind him, sending spray into the cabin.

Davy wretched up breakfast into the bucket he was grasping. "Not so well."

"Any sign the storm will break?" asked Symmes who was thankful he had not partaken of the meal. He gripped a railing to prevent himself from being thrown from his seat. Only an hour had passed since his conversation with Stevens. What the Captain said could not have been more accurate. The skies had turned from red to gray to brown to black in the matter of minutes. To Stevens' credit, as fast as the weather soured, the crew responded just as quickly. Sails were dropped and bundled. Lines were reigned in. Supplies were secured below. The dirigible was secured with extra tethers. All that remained was to wait below while the skeleton crew on deck kept the vessel in line.

"Not yet. But gales during this season typically pass quickly. If you would excuse me, gentlemen." Slamming the door closed, Stevens returned to the deck.

Symmes looked over at the crew, expecting to see the same worried expression on their faces. Surprisingly, most seemed oblivious to the storm.

Humboldt stood up, groping for one of the crossbeams as the vessel rocked precariously.

"Where are you going?" asked Davy wearily.

"Nature calls at the most inopportune times," he answered as he stumbled away towards the stern.

Symmes looked over at Mitchill. The doctor was clutching a small photograph, lost in thought.

"How did Agatha take it?"

"She told me I was on a fool's mission."

"She might be right," joked Symmes.

"Richard Burton and John Speke search for the source of a *river*, return with questionable proof, and are received in England as heroes. We have solid evidence of another *world*, and are viewed as lunatics."

"Burton and Speke had considerable funding. We have the backing of a country that barely has two coins to rub together."

"And for that we should be put in harm's way?"

"It's just a storm, Stewart. We will be back soon enough."

Mitchill did not respond as he carefully tucked away the photograph.

Symmes wedged himself into a crook and closed his eyes, hoping *somehow* he would be able to doze and make the time go faster. He felt himself starting to nod as a shattering crash rocked through the vessel. Shouts filled the air.

"What in hell is going on?" moaned Davy. *The Privateer* listed to the starboard, corrected itself, then listed again.

The door leading up to the deck swung open. Outside, the rain was still pounding down. "Orders from the Captain! All hands to the bow!" shouted one of the mates. "We're taking on water!"

Like a wild heard of buffalo, the men stampeded away.

Symmes struggled to his feet. "Sit down, Jonathan," moaned Davy. "You will only get in the way. If we are needed they will call," he added, retching again.

A large wave struck portside, causing the ship to rock violently. Symmes flailed out to keep his balance as his weight shifted to his bad leg. He cried out as his knee buckled. Before he could shield himself, his forehead smacked a crossbeam. Darkness followed.

* * *

"Ah, there you are," said Davy. "Awake at last."

A sharp pain seared through Symmes' head as he tried to keep his eyes open.

"That might not be such a good idea." Mitchill was talking. "Keep your eyes closed."

Symmes did as his friend instructed. A cool compress was placed on his temple and the pain receded. Not being able to see, his relied on his other senses. Something was wrong. He was lying on bedding more comfortable than anything *The Privateer* could provide. In addition, the infernal *slosh, slosh* of water lapping against the hull was gone. "Where am I, Stewart?"

"Try to relax, Jonathan. You have been unconscious for almost two days."

Symmes grabbed the cloth and yanked it off. He sat up and immediately regretted it.

"Iqualut. A small village on the Baffin Islands," answered Davy from another part of the room.

"What are we doing here?" asked Symmes as his vision slowly began to take shape.

"An uprooted tree was hurtled at *The Privateer* through the water by the storm surge. The oak struck the bow just below the waterline. A freak occurrence according to Stevens. Fortunately, he was able to contain the damage and prevent the vessel from sinking. He managed to sail *The Privateer* here."

"When are we set to resume?"

"The damage to hull has been sealed with pitch." Davy paused for a moment before answering. "Stevens informed us the ship needs to be removed from the water for proper repairs. The closest port for a ship of its size is St. Johns."

"St. John's! That's back across the Labrador Sea!"

"The Captain says it must be done. The ship, in its current condition, could never withstand the ice."

"Can we obtain another?"

"That was discussed. It doesn't seem likely anywhere north of St. John's." Symmes pounded his fist into his hand. "Damn it! We can not just turn around!"

"Jonathan, there's something else you need to know." said Mitchill. "The accident caused fatalities. Over a dozen men drowned. It pains me greatly to say this, Jonathan..."

Symmes looked around the room. Being so disoriented, he did not realize the fourth member of his quartet was missing. "No!"

"I'm sorry."

Symmes' eyes grew cloudy as he wept for the loss of his longtime friend Baron Alex. de Humboldt.

* * *

A day later Symmes was strong enough to venture out. The village was near the water and Symmes was able to walk to the shore with Davy and Mitchill. Out in the bay *The Privateer* was moored, looking far less magnificent than it once had.

"The Captain wishes to return tomorrow?" asked Symmes.

"Yes. He is going to take his chances. He believes he can reach St. John's without incident." Davy removed a cigar from his pocket and bit the end off. "We can either travel with him or, if you feel your constitution is lacking, we can stay here. I am told a whaler will be passing by in another week and that we can travel south with them."

"And the body?" asked Symmes.

"It will go back with Stevens. I've composed detailed letters for the next of kin in the event we need to stay back," said Mitchill.

"Humboldt would have wanted us to continue."

Davy nodded. "Most certainly."

Symmes scratched his newly formed beard. "I'm going to have Stevens unload the dirigible."

"But why would we want to leave...Jonathan! You can't be serious!"

"It is Jacques Pierre's decision. If he agrees then I will be continuing on."

"Jonathan, it is madness you propose!"

"The basket can hold eight with ample supplies. Roussoult, his two mechanics, and myself are four. Plenty of room for you both. However, I want to be very clear, my friends, that you are under no obligation to accompany me. Think of your families before you make your decision."

"When do you plan to leave, Jonathan?"

"If Roussoult agrees..."

"Of course he is going to say yes," interrupted Mitchill. "That crazy Frenchman would balloon around the globe if he were offered enough money!"

"I leave tomorrow. Take the remainder of today to think about it."

Mitchill and Davy glanced at each other before Davy spoke. "I don't think we'll need that much time, Jonathan. How could we explain ourselves if we returned without you?"

Mitchill added, "We've come much too far to turn around now."

* * *

Roussoult appeared from within the barn as Symmes, Mitchill, Davy, Stevens, and half of *The Privateer's* crew approached. "A glorious day, wouldn't you say so, gentlemen?"

"How go the preparations, Mr. Roussoult?"

"Very well, Mr. Symmes. The supplies are loaded. We are ready to board." Then, to Stevens, "My gratitude, captain, for assisting us."

"We are all quite curious to see this contraption of yours work, Mr. Roussoult."

The six passengers climbed aboard the gondola.

"Captain, would you and your men grab hold of the tethers that are attached to the basket. Grip them tightly, as Francis is going to apply the hot air."

Three men to a tether, the men watched as Francis slowly filled the balloon. Symmes and the others looked on in amazement. He was very familiar with the wonders of air travel, but he knew precious little about the mechanics.

It was not until the balloon was fully inflated that Symmes felt himself rising. "I hope none of you are afraid of heights!" joked Roussoult.

Mitchill looked up at the ceiling with concern. "We must be inches from striking the rafters."

"Nonsense. We have at least a foot of clearance!" Roussoult leaned over the side so much Symmes was certain the rotund Frenchman was going to tumble out. "Captain, if you would gently tug the ropes. It is time for us to escape into the upper air!"

Stevens nodded as the sailors began walking the balloon towards the barn's exit.

Symmes held his breath, worried that any movement would cause the balloon to drift into the barn's rafters.

"Gently, lads!" yelled Stevens. "Careful of the crosswinds - just as if we were back on *The Privateer*."

It took another agonizing minute before the entire balloon was clear of the barn. Satisfied, Roussoult looked over at Symmes, Mitchill, and Davy. "Any last changes of heart, gentlemen?"

The three of them shook their heads. "Good." Then, not bothering to look down, the Frenchman shouted. "Commander, if you would please release the tethers!"

The airship jostled slightly as the crew released the lines. Francis fired the Combustible and the vessel began its ascent.

Symmes heard excited cries from the sailors below. Without thinking he looked out over the gondola. In a matter of moments the balloon had risen considerably. Symmes shut his eyes and turned towards the interior of the basket.

"We are underway, gentlemen!" shouted Roussoult as he walked over to them. "If the winds are in our favor I anticipate passing over the Baffin Islands in several days time. So until then I ask that you make yourselves comfortable and trust me and my men with the operation of *La Resistance*. You will find small, but suitable sleeping quarters below. The winds will become increasingly unpredictable as we approach the Arctic Circle, so I recommend you take full advantage of any favorabilites in the weather."

Symmes viewed his surroundings. As unsettling as traveling on *The Privateer* was, it was nothing compared to the airship, which was little more than an experiment.

* * *

True to his word, several days later Roussoult managed to bring *La Resistance* over the Cumberland Peninsula. "We should be passing over the Artic Circle within the hour." He turned to face them, champagne glass in hand. "A glorious day for our countries. We will soon be traveling over virgin territory."

"To success and fame," said Davy, raising his glass awkwardly due to his thick mitten. "And to you, Captain. We have covered more land in these few days than we ever could have on a ship."

Glasses clinked. The men consumed the contents.

"So, Mr. Symmes, I assume we are almost upon your *Hollow World*?"

"Almost, Captain. We need to venture a little more northward. We must be vigilant for breaks in the ice or similar signs of warmth. Those indicators will lead us, like a compass, to the first of the concentric spheres. We will decide at that point to either to continue in the airship or proceed on foot inside."

Roussoult removed a pipe and bag of snuff. "What do you plan to find in this Hollow World, messieurs? Animals? People?"

"Quite possibly."

Roussoult puffed on his pipe thoughtfully.

* * *

"Eighty-two degrees, Jonathan!" announced Mitchill over the roar of the wind.

Symmes peered out over the gondola with his spyglass. He had been able to master his vertigo and was now able to scan the horizon with confidence. They had been traveling north by northwest and had passed over the Queen Victoria Islands the previous day. Vast expanses of ice and snow greeted them. The entire morning Symmes had scanned the horizon, searching for a sign. Concern filled his mind. Time was running short. The previous two days had been treacherous as the frigid temperatures were making *La Resistance* difficult to operate. The mechanics struggled to keep the balloon functioning properly. Even with the counterweights released the vessel was in danger of becoming too heavy from the ice buildup. He expected Roussoult to announce today that they would need to turn around.

Roussoult barked an order to Francis. It was the first time Symmes had seen concern on the Frenchman's face. Symmes felt the airship descend.

"Captain!" he yelled. "What is wrong?"

"We have too much ice on the rudder, Mr. Symmes!" Roussoult shouted over the roar of the wind. "The balloon needs to be lowered so we can chisel it off." And then, the comment he had been dreading. "We are no longer safe, sir. Once the ice is removed, we will begin our journey back."

Symmes gripped the gondola's railing in frustration. To come so close...

Roussoult carefully lowered *La Resistance* until only several feet separated it from the ground. Gerard unfurled the rope ladder and everyone except Francis descended to the ice. The men began chipping away at the ice, working quickly, aware the winds could become violent at any moment.

After ten minutes of work, Symmes paused to collect his breath. The thinned atmosphere made even the easiest task arduous. He knelt down to take the pressure off his leg. An object in the snow seized his attention. He stared at it for a moment, thinking he was hallucinating.

From beneath the ice a green sprig had surfaced.

"We've found it!" he exclaimed.

The others looked over at him curiously as the wind began to intensify. "The rudder is free!" yelled Roussoult. "Everyone to the blimp!"

Symmes remained where he was, staring at the vegetation in disbelief.

"Mr. Symmes! We must return to the vessel! The wind is increasing and Francis can not keep the dirigible steady for much longer!" shouted the Frenchman.

"No!" hollered Symmes. "We can't leave! Not now! We're here!"

Gerard and Roussoult began climbing the ladder as Davy and Mitchill ran over to Symmes. "Jonathan! We must get back on the ship!" Davy pleaded, grabbing his parka.

Symmes shoved him away. "No! We've found it!"

Mitchill suddenly lunged at him. Using his cane, Symmes struck Mitchill across the side of his head. Before either of them could react, Symmes was striding away.

"I can't keep it steady, gentlemen!" shouted Roussoult.

Davy and Mitchill grabbed the ladder as the ship was propelled upward by the wind. While Roussoult fought for control of *La Resistance*, Francis and Gerard pulled the men inside.

Davy and Mitchill peered over the basket. Between the gusts they could make out Symmes' brown parka. "Jonathan!" they cried. Helpless, they watched as he slowly trotted northward until he was finally lost amidst the snow and ice.

Footnote 1. This is the actual declaration made by John Cleves Symmes, Jr (1780–1829) when announcing his 'Hollow Earth' theory in 1818. The expedition never came to pass, but this story explores what could have happened if it had.

Short Straw

Rebecca Schwarz

"DON'T TELL the trees your name," the wild grasses whispered as they batted their bearded heads against the linen skirt wrapped around Nina's thin hips. Her great grandparents, the first colonists, had brought rice and wheat, barley and rye, and crossed their seeds with the new-world plants. But the grains they produced were inedible. Still, the abandoned grasses persisted, and the wild meadow won a few more inches of ground every year.

She looked up, past the settlement to where the tallest branches of the forest canopy snared the sinking sun. "I have to go," she said.

"If you must go, take us with you," they whispered.

Nina closed her hands capturing two fistfuls of seed heads, pulled them off their stems, and shoved them into her skirt pockets. "There. Happy?"

"No."

Lightheaded from days of excitement and dread, Nina ran up the rutted dirt path toward the settlement's mud and wattle buildings.

Daylight fled from the sky as everyone gathered in the strip of bare earth between the buildings and the carnfruit orchard. Preach stood in the middle, and he graced Nina with an indulgent smile as she joined the gathering. She found Papa who smoothed the loose curls at the nape of her neck by way of greeting. The blade of his hatchet gleamed from where it hung on his belt. Heat radiated off him along with the smell of fresh cut wood. Papa spent his days cutting back the ever-advancing forest saplings. A job no one else wanted.

"Rootless we arrived here, and rootless we remain." Preach held his hands out to them, a dozen family groups, hollow-cheeked and sinewy. "Once every long season, we make the divine sacrifice. We gather tonight to sate our hunger, and to call out the names of those of us who have gone to the orchard. Tonight one of us will join the orchard, so that the devoured may return to sustain us. Flesh for flesh."

Nina looked up past the orchard at the forest towering over them. Every year the great trees encroached. Their roots choked the ground. The orchard's gnarled branches had become brittle in the shade, and the carnfruits that fell into the clearing were pale and flabby. One day the forest would swallow their orchard whole and they would starve, but not today.

Nina's stomach growled. Thin slices of carnfruit sizzled on the griddle over the fire. Everyone sat as plates heaped with food were passed around; fried wood termites, boiled rhizomes topped with a bitter paste made from the carrion flies that hovered around the orchard, and the still sizzling carnfruit. Preach bowed his head. "As we take your bounty into our bodies, we remember that every meal is a communion."

After the feast, Preach stood and took up the carved goblet of pike, the holy drink brewed from the jagged, black leaves that drifted down from the great trees beyond the orchard. All who would draw imbibed. Nina began to shake as the goblet made its way around the circle. Today she was thirteen by the old Sol calendar. She was an adult. This year she would drink – and draw. She hoped her hands would be steady when it was her turn.

People coughed and choked on the liquid, but everyone's face relaxed after a swallow or two. The goblet came to Papa. He raised it to his lips, and bent forward coughing, but his throat never moved. She was sure he hadn't swallowed any. If Preach saw, there would be trouble.

Papa smiled as he handed the goblet to her, but his eyes were hard as stones. The thick, black liquid wobbled as she drew the goblet to her lips. The pike seemed to boil as it raged down her throat. Points of light dappled her vision; someone took the goblet from her as she gasped and sucked in the cool night air.

The orchard began whispering the names of the dead. Celia, Joseph, Bethany, Dan, Jeremy. She listened for Mama's name, even though she'd never heard it. Papa said she never would. She could only remember bits and pieces of Mama; playing with her long, curly hair while riding on her hip as they checked the water collection barrels, the smell of her sweat, the way she would hum an aimless melody in the dark when Nina couldn't sleep.

The faces in the circle wavered in the warm light of the fire as the night filled with the names of those who'd gone to the orchard. The goblet came to her again and she took a second swallow, which burned less. Preach moved around the circle holding a fistful of straws.

She watched the others as they drew out long straws, their faces stretching and drifting in expressions of relief. When they talked it sounded like raindrops plinking in the barrels.

Then Preach stood in front of her. She looked at the bristling crown of stems he held before her and thought of the wild grasses of the meadow. The one she drew out was just long enough to fit in the palm of her hand.

Black holes grew in the faces of the others. A howl filled her ears. It was their voices, she knew, joining together to sing her name. She had drawn the short straw. She would be commended to the orchard.

Everyone rose above her as the hard earth hit her knees. Then Papa yanked her back to her feet and started shouting.

No! She tried to form the word but she couldn't move her mouth. She wasn't afraid. She wanted to go to the orchard, to repay her debt to Papa, Mama, and everyone who had struggled to feed her season after season. She twisted in Papa's iron grip. His voice hammered at Preach who screamed back, their words an unrecognizable slurry shattering the orchard's chorus of names.

Faces crowded in, bright and hollow-eyed in the firelight, twisted in anger.

"I'll go," Nina managed a choked whisper. They would kill Papa or worse, Preach would banish him to the forest. "Let me go!" Preach grabbed Nina's other arm, and Papa's huge fist arrived out of nowhere slamming Preach's jaw so hard he spun like a top before falling to the ground. The blade of Papa's hatchet flashed and the faces fell away.

Papa hoisted Nina over his shoulder. She glimpsed the black silhouettes of their houses and a scrap of the starlit meadow beyond before he plunged into the orchard.

The sticks breaking underfoot sounded like bones snapping. The branches clutched at them and tore at her clothes. The world spun. Her fists unclenched. It was the pike. The drink bestowed a few moments of courage, then demanded sleep.

* * *

She fell through the night and woke when she hit the ground. Papa lay next to her panting in the leaf litter. He groaned and rolled over on his back.

"I can't carry you any further." He wiped jagged leaves off his sweat-soaked forehead.

She sat up in the deep shade, surrounded by the massive trunks of the forest. All was silence except for her blood pulsing a painful beat in her head. The rich, sweet scent of rotting carnfruit dropped in the heart of the orchard was gone, replaced by the bitter odor of the loam she sat on.

"I would have gone to the sacrifice."

"Of course you would have, foolish child."

"I'm not a child! You had no right. Now who will say our names? We'll be forgotten like Uncle Joe and Mama."

"I've forgotten nothing, have you?" He glared. She couldn't remember much. She was only six when Uncle Joe lost his mind and fled, raving into the forest. The next day Mama went in to try to bring him back. "Your mama didn't bring you into this world just to be fed to those damn weeds." Papa sat and pulled off his boots. "Put these on." He tossed them to Nina.

She looked at her bare feet. "I don't want to wear your stupid boots."

"Put them on!" he roared. She flinched and pulled the boots on while Papa studied the enormous trunks. His bare feet sank in to the loam when he stood. He pulled her up, and swept his hand forward in an impatient gesture. "Walk."

She turned and stomped off. The canopy overhead completely obscured the sky leaving the forest floor in murky twilight. It was like waking through vast interior space, as if they'd invaded a sleeping giant's castle. The only other plants she saw were pale ferns and some small patches of tough moss. Blisters formed where Papa's boots knocked against her feet.

Tired, she stopped and turned on Papa bracing for more of his bluster, but his face was drawn and pale. He stumbled to avoid walking into her and sat down hard.

"Where are we going?"

He sat for so long without speaking, she thought he wasn't going to answer her. "Maybe one of the lost missions made it. Maybe there is another settlement – somewhere."

Papa sneered at the stories about the first ship, the one that had crashed in the forest with its xenobotanists and a payload of plants from earth. But the other colonists loved to talk about it, especially when Preach wasn't around. We all wanted to imagine that there was something, and maybe someone, beyond the forest, that there was a *beyond*. Papa told Nina not to believe in fairy tales, said that the astronauts and their missions were history, that mooning over the past didn't put food in anyone's mouths. Fear squeezed her throat. His revised outlook scared her more than anything else. She sat too.

"Try not to touch the ground." He moved his hands up and down his shins, "or anything."

"Why?"

"Just don't."

She pulled her knees up and rested her chin on them. Papa's feet looked strange in the dim light, like polished wood.

"Papa?" She reached out to touch his toes. He jerked his foot back.

"Don't!" He stood awkwardly, stiff-legged – as if his ankles wouldn't move. She stood and looked at the black trunks, everywhere their twisted roots swelled the ground. "Let's keep moving." Papa walked ahead of her with a stumping gait.

Frightened, she followed, keeping her eyes on the woodcutter's hatchet swinging on his belt.

The pulse of her headache from the pike faded, replaced by a low droning. The sound wavered then steadied into a cadence. The voices of the trees were strange, deep and hollow, a vibration rattling through her lungs. The names were unfamiliar.

Nina caught her breath and pointed. "Look!" A figure sat in the leaf litter beyond one of the tree trunks. Lichen rimed the edges of the man's tunic. Bare feet stuck out from the bottoms of his trousers. She ran to him. Papa staggered after her. She studied the gaunt, motionless face, the unseeing eyes and open mouth, all solid wood. The trees had taken him.

"Dead." Papa said. "Look at the wood."

She knelt by the man. The wood was gray as ash with long black cracks.

"Dale," the trees hummed his name.

"Did you know him, Papa?"

Papa knitted his brows. "He disappeared into the forest when I was younger than you." Papa limped away, unconsciously hefting his hatchet like he did whenever he was frustrated.

Each step hurt. Her blisters broke; fluid slicked the insides of Papa's boots. She ignored the pain and trotted after him. They passed more people frozen into gray wood. Some stood, others lay half submerged in the leaf litter as if drowned. The trees chorused their names. Evening arrived; draining away what little light they had, until the massive trunks melted into the darkness.

"Papa, we have to stop," she called after him breathlessly, straining to keep him in sight.

"Did you hear that?"

"What?"

He broke into a stiff-legged run.

"Papa!" She followed his receding white shirt as he staggered from one huddled figure to the next.

Then Nina heard her name: The one that Papa alone had kept alive on his lips all these years.

Papa fell down and pulled himself forward dragging his frozen legs. She ran to him as he wrapped his arms around the figure of a woman sitting cross-legged in the loam, her head tilted up toward where the sky would be.

The trees called down, "Adelaide," brandishing their bitter trophy.

"Adelaide!" Papa wept.

Nina knelt next to Papa and looked at her mother's face. A crack ran through the parched wood from her forehead down across her lips, splitting her chin. Her eyes were blank knots, but Nina recognized the curve of her cheek and the cascading curls of her hair, perfectly rendered in wood.

"Climb up." Papa pushed her onto Mama's lap. Nina pulled her knees to her chest and tried to tug him closer. His wooden legs stretched out behind him. Tears drained into his beard. Her own dropped to soak into Mama's wooden skirts. Exhausted, Nina leaned against the cool, dry wood and closed her eyes.

"Child?" His voice faltered.

"It's okay, Papa." He would never speak her name out here.

"When you were born, your mother said your name the moment she saw you. I was angry at first because she didn't ask me what I thought, but then I looked at you and I could see she was right." Papa smoothed the curls at the nape of Nina's neck. "She gave you your name."

The three of them sat together in the darkness. Nina listened to Papa's breathing and thought of Mama and Papa holding her for the first time in their little room and suddenly wanted to go home. Tears rolled down her cheeks. Somewhere above, the sky stretched from here all the way back to the settlement where everyone she ever knew would be settling down for the night inside their houses made from the saplings Papa had cut.

"Papa?"

"Mmm."

"You punched Preach."

"I surely did."

She giggled. "He squeaked like a cricket."

"I think I've wanted to do that maybe my whole life," he said. She could tell by the sound of his voice that he was smiling.

"I thought the voices in the orchard were our voices." She found a button on his shirt and traced its perfect circle. "That we lived on in the orchard." Silence washed over them again. She huddled in the warmth rising off his neck. "Who will cut the forest back now?"

He heaved a sigh. "I don't know."

She closed her eyes against the darkness and slept.

* * *

Nina woke without opening her eyes. Chilled and stiff, she clung to Mama's carved bodice and tried to claim a few more moments of sleep. Far above, a breeze stirred the branches to a low moan, which resolved into whispered syllables; John, Kelly, Megan, the trees recited the catalog of those they'd murdered. Adelaide, they said.

Her heart began to pound with the urge to say her name, and she knew the trees were getting inside her too. They would pull her name from her mouth, kill her, and add it into their mocking litany.

She opened her eyes. Papa looked back at her with deep brown, fine-grained eyes of still-living wood. His arms, now wrapped around Mama's waist, were already greying. Sometime during the night, he'd torn off the bottom of his shirt and wrapped it around his mouth so that he wouldn't give up his name. She ran her fingers across the warp and weft of the threads, more delicate than anything even he could carve.

"Oh, Papa." Alone, she flung her arms around his hard shoulders and cried on his neck like a child. She looked up at the towering trunks. It could end here. She could just give up her name and stay and it would all be over.

She tore her eyes away from the trees and looked at her legs. Papa's boots had turned to wood where they touched the soft soil. Green, sinuous roots had climbed up them to wind around her calves. She wiggled her feet inside the boots, tried to pry the roots off, but they were strong and growing fast.

She reached around and found Papa's hatchet where it was slung in his belt. The blade broke off in her hand, useless grey wood. She grabbed the handle and pulled. Papa had carved it from carnfruit wood and cured it over a fire until it was black and hard as stone. The handle broke off his belt loop, and she worked it between the flesh of her leg and the roots, ignoring the pain as she pried the grasping tendrils off and yanked her feet out of Papa's boots.

She stretched her toes and ran her hands over the tough skin on the soles of her feet. It felt wonderful to be out of those boots. She looked at the loamy ground, so soft and inviting. Once she started she would have to keep moving. She kissed Mama on the cheek and Papa on the forehead, then stood. Her bare feet tingled pleasantly where they touched the forest floor. There was no path, but many ways. She walked through the trees without looking back. Hungry, thirsty and barefoot, she wouldn't last long, but she'd go as far as she could.

She walked through the day under the constant drone of names. There were fewer and fewer wooden corpses, a record of how far a body could go before succumbing. Dry and swollen, her tongue twitched inside her mouth. If only she could forget her name. It weighed on her – a stone she carried and could not put down and she was so tired. What did it matter if the trees repeated it to each other like a cruel joke, no one would hear it. No! She clamped her lips shut. Her name was hers, a gift they could never understand.

Dizzy with hunger, she walked through afternoon and evening. She kept going after darkness swallowed the trunks, shuffling on stiff legs, until rough bark clapped her face and chest and knocked her to the ground. She got up and staggered on, arms outstretched. She couldn't see anything, couldn't feel her feet or bend her ankles. Another few steps and she tripped over something on the ground. She explored the object with her hands, the supine body of another settler. She curled up on it, digging her fingers into the rotting wood of its shoulders. A castaway clinging to a tiny piece of flotsam in a vast ocean.

* * *

A carrion smell woke her. The sun was up somewhere beyond the trees. Her mouth watered. It smelled like the sweet flesh of the carnfruit. Her feet were deep brown. She touched polished wood of her carved toes.

She stood awkwardly and stumped toward the smell. She was so hungry, empty of everything except for her name. It rattled around inside her. The trees murmured urgently, inviting her to set it free. She hobbled on towards the scent. Bright light filtered between the black trunks here.

A clearing.

She fell to her knees, squinting in the sunlight's glare. Soft moss covered the ground. She crawled toward a stand of enormous flowers. Their wrinkled petals shimmered peach and ochre and brown – human skin tones. Black hair curled out from their fat stems.

Beyond the flowers, crumpled metal glinted. The clothes scattered on the ground didn't look like anything from the settlement. Older, tougher fabric, bleached from years in the sun. A helmet. A space suit, she realized, torn and deflated where the ground had absorbed the body.

She looked up at the petals drinking in the sunlight. The lost mission. A clutch of small trees stood in the very center of the clearing, pink and white blossoms shuddering in the breeze. True fruit trees. Broad-leaved vines smothered the black trunks of the forest. Ferns and short grass carpeted the ground, a thick network of runners under their soft blades. The astronauts and their seeds had survived after all.

Her feet were grey and cracked, her thighs solid wood. She lay down in the shade of the bobbing petals and reached out to clasp the base of the nearest stem. It was warm from the sun, but also from inside. A human warmth. She thought of Mama and Papa embracing deep in the woods. When she was a baby, Papa had carved little figurines from scraps of wood and the memories handed down from his grandparents, a cat, a car, a pair of astronauts in their bulky suits, and their lander. She wondered if they still there, laying in the dark inside the hinged wooden box under her bed. Tears welled in her eyes. Above her, the petals nodded.

She remembered the meadow seeds. They would need moisture to sprout. With stiff fingers, she dug them out of her pockets, opened her cracked lips and put them in her mouth. They tasted like linen and sunlight. And with them resting on her tongue she slept.

As her breathing slowed, a great confusion of voices rose around her, the tree-climbing vines and the ferns chattered in a staccato patois. The young fruit trees, an apple, a cherry, and a fig, were full of questions about the world beyond the clearing, the ancient astronauts from earth were more reticent, content after so long to simply bloom in the sun. When her new friends asked if she had a name, she said, "You can call me Short Straw." She imagined her human name in the little box under her bed, safe among the figures Papa had carved for her so long ago.

The seasons came and went. Nina sank into the rich soil. She learned to drink the sun and eat the dark loam. The grasses she'd carried with her grew from the place where her mouth had been. She bowed to the drenching rain that fell into the clearing and felt the breezes flow through her stems. She told the others about her life in the settlement, about the meadow grasses and the people and how they all loved the sky the same.

As the years passed, the clearing grew into a long swath. The chattering vines climbed the nearest forest trees smothering and silencing them before felling the great trunks. The fruit trees multiplied in the sunlight, raising a spine of young saplings in the center of the open land.

With each season, she released her pollen to the wind and soared up with the sweet flowering scent until one day the wind carried her all the way over the settlement and to the wild meadow beyond.

"I'm here!" she called to the grasses.

"Welcome home," they whispered.

She settled in adding her voice to theirs, whispering to anyone who might be listening, who might be able to hear, that there was something more than the forest beyond the settlement – and that it was coming.

The Road to Cathacara

James C. Simpson

THERE WAS something unusual about the map that rested in the trembling hands of the young student. It was composed of a brittle and yellowed paper that miraculously held together despite its advanced age. At first glance it appeared to be akin to a mythical treasure map, consisting primarily of symbols and crudely drawn geographic locations, but there was writing to be found and that writing was of the most arcane nature. They were written in a language unknown to most but the most ardent scholars and those living were hardly to be trusted as most were committed. There was a rumored maddening effect brought on by such a study and it all related to a word, the only one that was truly discernible on the decaying piece of paper and that was of 'Cathacara.' Was this some lost city? Perhaps, this was some dead civilization that was only seeing light now?

The student knew the name and recognized its import. This was a name that was obscure, yes, but one that had a right to be shunned and feared by those wise enough to understand. It was one of those unholy and dreaded words that was so readily associated with that that most accursed of texts, the book known as the *Necronomicon*. *Cathacara* was its own tome and the student had read whatever excerpts he could gather here and there for it was an obscure and forgotten tome.

He knew that name had been uttered throughout history from Europe to the Americas. It had been found everywhere from colonial America to the trenches of the Great War and beyond. Most of the men who had recounted the story of Cathacara were not long for this world and others were confined and committed for surely they had been insane or driven to madness by what they experienced.

The student was in Germany, deep in the black forest and was alone save for his map and some materials he kept with him on his person. It was a dark overcast day and his vision was not helped by the glowering tall trees which hovered over him, menacing and threateningly. One thing the canopy did do effectively was isolate most of the light rain that fell from the white sky. A chill was in the air and the student pulled his jacket tighter to his person and glanced at the map. It was a crudely drawn thing depicting a forest, the trees appearing like sticks on the paper and a small mountain that lead to what had been the site of some previous carnage. It was here that Cathacara had been seen. That was over 100 years ago and the account was considered by many to be mere ravings of a shell shocked soldier. The man who had told the story was the sole survivor of his company after a brutal massacre that left all his men dead. He was found babbling atop a giant cross claiming that huge glowing red eyes were glaring at him from the soil in No Man's Land. He said that it had been awakened by the blood of so many lives and now was coming for them all. He died in a mental institution before he could live to see the arrival of a Second World War.

Rumors persisted of strange occurrences in that region for some time. After the Second World War, a detailed report was found within the archives of the fallen German government that revealed the results of archaeological and scientific teams to harness something of 'power' from the soil of the site. Some experiments had been made and these extended from Germany to locations on the eastern front that bore what can only be described as 'horrific' results. Tales were told of creatures unimaginable arriving from out of the earth and others told of a red substance similar to blood that had been capable of reanimating the dead.

There was an unofficial search for this location that the student traveled to made by representatives of the Allied nations but reports varied. The Americans scoffed at the existence of such a place, even though the numbers projected by certain expenditures showed that they did indeed invest millions into research for something they did not believe existed. The English knew something of Cathacara. Members of the Office Of Strategic Services gave a chilling report near Koblitz, which mentioned a large archaeological site that was rumored to be replete with masses of the recently dead. It was not linked with any of the death camps. The dead were members of whatever party had been working there. The only signs of traditional death were found among those that had killed themselves, mostly with the aid of their sidearms. The rest had died contorted and in agony, mouths agape and eyes open as if they saw something unspeakable in those final moments before they died. A crater was found lined with the bodies but this was not well made but seemed to rather had been torn from within the earth. The report listed it as being a possible 'sinkhole,' but witnesses to the site claimed otherwise.

The name 'Cathacara' was found etched in blood by one scientist upon a makeshift altar placed in the center of the site, which had a large swastika etched in.

A similar thing had been found in Russia, but that information was suppressed by the Soviets at that time for their own intelligence and was kept secret for several decades. The student had gained access to that report after the fall of that particular government and found that it bore an uncanny resemblance to that presented by the British and the unofficial writings made by the American governments.

The student could see a clearing through the trees and took one more glance at the old map, his hands shivering with the cold dampness of the morning rain and mountain air, and he pocketed the map. He entered a small field, a light breeze causing the grass to sway, the wind giving a lonely howl. The student had wondered to himself why he had come alone. Maybe it was because he was afraid of what others would think of such a venture and he was probably right in that regard. Still, he wanted to know the *truth* and his obsession, for that's certainly what this had been these last few years, had driven him regardless of consequence. When the opportunity came to study abroad he took it without hesitation and promised his professor that he would discover some truth in these 'wild stories' that had so troubled and fascinated him during his stay at the university. He had to find the road to Cathacara.

He walked through the field and felt the rain sting him as it began to increase in volume and the student pulled the brim of his hat over his eyes and wished he had dressed warmer. He saw the mountain ahead of him and the pass. At one time this may have been a well traveled path and one could still sense the grooves of hooves in the dirt.

There were still some wagon ruts to be found and his leg slipped into them once or twice reminding him of how he would 'hobble walk' along the sidewalk as a child, one foot on the street and another on the walk. The dirt had not yet turned to mud and that was something the student was grateful for. He would probably curse himself on the way back but if he found what he was looking for it was doubtful such thoughts would be on his mind.

A tree branched out of a rock at a turn in the pass and that gave the student an opportunity to look over the map once more. He carefully brought out the map and knelt on the ground and looked it over, adjusting his glasses and making sure they were clear and free of raindrops. Despite its reputation as being designed by a madman, the map was well organized. He had been no artist, the soldier who had designed the map, but he knew location and that was apparent. Each drawing had likewise corresponded with both the stories read and the locations thus far. This map was drawn up some time in the late '30s by an American soldier who had been the sole survivor of that awful encounter in 1918. He was asked to show where it took place and drew this map but instructed that only his doctor gain access to view it and not the military. It was an odd stipulation, as the doctor could not discern the imagery either way. However, the army had shown some interest as the man and his map were referenced at various points in the student's study. There was relevancy there even if most choose to ignore it.

The map showed something resembling a small village and then a field with a cross. An 'X' marked the spot like on those fabled treasure maps, except this treasure was surely of a more sinister kind. The student looked ahead and thought of what he might find around the bend and considered turning back for a moment, a queer feeling of childhood fear filling his mind. He quickly dispelled such thoughts as he was a man of science and the rational was what he believed in not the silly superstition of yesteryear.

With grim purpose, the young man tucked the map inside his jacket and stood up and looked up at the threatening sky and could hear the light distance of a rolling thunder. He walked forward and peered around the corner and saw a valley closed in by mountains. Below were the fragments, the remains of what could have been a settlement at one time. Why had this not been more widely documented?

The young man walked down the path and across the jagged rocks and yellow and dead vegetation and toward the remnants of a decaying fence. Beyond that were the outlines of decrepit buildings. Most appeared to have been burnt, others looked like they had collapsed, while others appeared to have been torn asunder. Perhaps, they had been the victim of shelling from the Great War, as the lumber looked blackened and burnt, but the strange formations that appeared in the road suggested something like an earthquake had upset these buildings some time ago. That was a curious observation because this region had never experienced such things.

Most of the area was overgrown with weeds and vines but the plant life all appeared dead despite being exposed to the elements, the rain pouring into the ground from an open sky, the sun able to give ample light. Then the student wondered if sun ever did visit this region? There was a feeling in the air, unique and uncomfortable, that he had remembered but not from anything in nature. It was the feeling of being in a confined and decayed space, chiefly that of a mausoleum. Everything here appeared to be dead.

In the distance, in the field and down the road, he could see the outline of a crooked cross. It appeared to have been the same one that nearly a hundred years before that unfortunate soldier was found quaking in fear and babbling atop of, speaking of demons and the undead risen. He had found protection in the holy symbol but perhaps it was merely to keep his distance from the earth and whatever horror had spilled forth from it.

There was an eerie silence in the air at that moment and the student noticed that there was something missing. There were no animals, no wildlife present. It occurred to him that he had not spied a single grasshopper, ant hill or even a spider's web on his way here. No deer were found running away from his presence, no rabbits hopping by and not even one snake slithered in his path. In the sky he did not spy a single bird nor heard one of their comforting songs. Nothing was alive except for him and the only sound were his footsteps, the light rain on the ground and his own breathing.

He crossed over the field and thought of how many had fallen here and how much blood had been spilled. It was hard to believe that at one time this had been the scene of such absolute carnage. Unlike, other portions of Europe, there was no marker by any government to commemorate the fallen. There were no gravestones in site. Nothing was in the field except for that crooked cross. It was supposed that at one time, this may have been a cemetery and that the cross was adjacent to a church, but whatever became of that site had long since vanished into history.

The one sign that this had indeed been a battle site was the remains of a trench found some meters from the cross. It was all grown in now but there were still some rotten planks to indicate that men had once stood here and looked down 'No Man's Land,' awaiting death or glory. Most would find the former here.

The student peered inside the trench and noticed nothing of interest. If he had the right tools maybe he could scavenge something but the increasing torrents of rain left him cold in more ways than one. He turned around and faced the cross. It stood massive against the white sky, a curious and forgotten shape. It was so out of place here. The wood had splintered and it was a miracle that it was still standing a hundred years later, perhaps longer. The cross was tilted to the right and rusty pieces of iron connected each piece. There was something about the piece that held his attention. He had never been much of a religious man but there was something that kept his gaze and he could not look away.

A chilling wind swept past him and it appeared that the cross creaked and moaned and seemed in a way to speak to the young student who with a trembling hand, reached for the cross.

His hand touched the rotting lumber and as he pressed his palm against the damp wood, a sudden sting made him retract his hand and coddle the pain. He looked at his hand and noticed the very slight mark of a wound and his blood was slowly trickling down his palm and dribbling onto the ground below. He reached for something to cover the wound and accidentally stained the map with his blood. He cursed to himself and went into his knapsack. His blood was soaking into the ground and was not lost with the rain. It slowly sunk into the earth and became absorbed. He did not notice this anomaly and still riffled through his pack, trying to find a first aid kit and a rag, a cloth, something to stop the bleeding.

He was too focused on covering his slowly dripping drops of mortality that he likely didn't notice the slight rumble in the earth nor the distant echo of laughter or the sounds of footsteps. The thunder roared and played into the hand of the owner of this field and shielded it from its intruder.

The young man was bandaging his hand when he noticed the figures in the distance. He noticed a slowly approaching fog and within that fog were the shadows of several people.

They all stood in a solemn line and seemed to be getting closer even if at a snail's pace. He stopped and stood up quickly and adjusted his glasses and could still not be sure if anyone was there.

Something made a sound beneath him. It was a familiar sound and one that he did not expect. It was not just organic, it was a *laugh*. He looked at his feet and stepped lively, leaving his knapsack on the ground and backing away toward the ruined village. There he turned and was met by the grim shadows of an army of men, at least that's what the shapes resembled. He could not see the faces beyond that but they were slowly approaching with the patience of death and they all raised their arms in unison and pointed to the young man and stood and stared. All at once, the fog was a light with the glowing red eyes of the damned and the student could not even emit a scream from his throat.

He removed the map from his jacket, his hands shaking along with the rest of his form. He glanced at the paper in his grasp and looked at horror as the bloodstained map had seemingly *changed*, revealing more arcane symbols of some occult meaning. The location was obscured by the face of something horrible, unspeakable. It was something alien and monstrous and yet so much more horrible because of its very *human* eyes. They were a blood red and the crimson color was painted with his own blood.

Behind him the earth began to split and the rain had increased blocking the man's vision from front and behind and getting darker with each drop until it was the very color as that which flowed in his veins. He slowly turned, the figures in the fog now merely feet away, and noticed that something was coming to greet him from beneath him. It was the owner of the laugh and of the field and the young man's reserve was to race for the cross as if driven to it by some animal instinct. The thing craved more and so did the masses behind it, which were crawling and climbing from the pit. This place was still dead but yet so very much alive now. The man climbed the cross in desperation and as he did more and more blood leaked from his body, from every orifice available, staining his clothes, the rain soaking him with crimson that blurred the boundary between his sinking life and its unwelcome cleansing. He reached the top and screamed and laughed, the combination at odds with itself and lost in the storm and the swirling madness about him. He gazed into the pit and saw the eyes staring up at him and knew what that unfortunate soldier had known a century before and for those last few departing moments, knew him to have not been mad. He had seen Cathacara and the student would soon join the greater majority of those who took the road to Cathacara.

Within a few minutes, the rain stopped suddenly and the storm ceased its violence and all was silent. The fog had fallen back and the shadows and figures had vanished. The earth was open and would remain so for whomever was to pay a visit next.

Upon the ground was an open knapsack and above that, a large crooked cross with a man dangling from it, his blood all but drained, his limbs hanging grotesquely. His eyes were open, his mouth agape.

A crudely drawn map floated through the air and was being delivered by strange winds toward another destination. It no longer bore any sign of blood, at least on the surface. It flew through the air and was being taken to another who would dare pay a visit to the almighty blood god known as Cathacara.

A Map of Illusions

David Sklar

THE FIGURE that walked in the distance might have been a man or a woman, covered completely in black and billowing robes. It could be a traveler needing help or a bandit looking for victims – though the walk was more like a prince or a dignitary. Still, Jibril capped his inkwell and tucked it, with the pen, back into the pouch at his belt. He folded the map – in the desert he did not have to wait for the ink to dry – and tucked it inside his kamis, below where the hairs on his chest had just begun to emerge like sparse grass around the edge of an oasis. And then, having nowhere to run, Jibril stood and waited.

"Jibril Halaam," the stranger spoke, in a voice like a pit with no bottom. The cloth flowed out around him as if blown by a wind from within.

Jibril shivered. "Do I know you?" he asked, hoping not to show the tremor in his voice.

"Your name is unguarded," the stranger answered. "I hear it in the wind."

The nearest village was more than a league away. Jibril knew this; he bore the map pressed against his skin. On the map he had noted every mirage for twenty leagues to the east and north, as he headed into less familiar lands. The illusions Jibril had noted might fool a Crusader or a Turk – but a sorcerer who could pluck his name from the wind? "What do you want with me?" Jibril demanded, breathing sharply.

"You have been making a map of my domain," the stranger responded.

"No, sir," Jibril replied appeasingly. "I swear I have not."

"Do not lie to me, Jibril," the sorcerer commanded. He did not raise his voice, but the tone was stern, and his robes flowed as if a storm twisted underneath.

"It is the truth!" Jibril pleaded. "I have only made maps in the kingdoms ruled by Ṣalāḥ ad-Dīn Yūsuf ibn Ayyūb."

"And this Ṣalāḥ ad-Dīn," the stranger asked, "where is his kingdom?"

"He is the sultan of Egypt and Syria," said Jibril.

The stranger said nothing. His breath flowed through the fabric that wrapped his form.

Jibril reached into his kamis and took out the map. "I can show you on paper," he answered. "On land it is in all directions as far as the eye can see."

"Of course," said the wrapped stranger. "But where the eye cannot see?"

"Begging your pardon," said Jibril, "but what do you mean?

The stranger stood right before him now, and still Jibril saw neither hand nor eye, nor anything but black cloth. Stopping, the stranger sat above the ground, though there was no chair. "It seems a paltry kingdom," the traveler mused, "If he only rules what the eye can see. Surely the land contains shadows and absences, and holes that are too deep to look inside?"

"Of course," Jibril shuddered, wondering if the sorcerer knew what he'd been mapping in the desert. The wind moved the sorcerer's cloak. The cloak, in turn, appeared to move the wind.

"And who rules in those places?" the cloaked stranger asked.

Jibril pondered this a moment. "I do not know."

The stranger said naught, but the wind blew his cloak, and the cloth surface shimmered like sunlight on water.

"Is it you?" Jibril asked, feeling like the ground might swallow him if he fainted.

The answer was barely a movement, less than a nod, but Jibril could not have missed it. The stillness that followed pinned Jibril where he stood, like a moth to a board. Though Jibril could not see his face, the stranger seemed to look beyond the skin and see Jibril's soul like a candle in a cave, its flame fluttering meekly under the wrapped man's breath.

"Why do you wish to map my lands, Jibril?" the stranger asked.

"I swear," Jibril answered, rushing to appease, "I did not know they were yours!"

There was a moment's silence before the other spoke again. "That is not what I asked you."

"I – I was sent by my master," Jibril stammered. "The cartographer Akbar al-Idrisi, to map the mirages in the sultan's lands."

"That also is not what I asked you," the stranger said.

"A map of illusions," Jibril went on, "may help the sultan's armies mislead invaders, if the Crusaders or the Turks should come again. And also, I…I think my master needs a grand project such as this if he should wish to come anywhere close to his father's renown."

The stranger who ruled over darkness and emptiness did not reply. Was silence also a part of his domain?

Jibril did not know how else to reply. The mirages belonged not to Ṣalāḥ ad-Dīn, but instead to this cloth-wrapped stranger, this caliph of unseen places. He understood that now, in some sense of the word, but he could not protest that he had not known – that answer had already fallen flat. "Because the world is vast and wonderful," Jibril blurted out, "and I wish to discover it."

The Caliph of Unseen Places asked, "May I see the map?"

Jibril reached forward, and the wind took the page from his hand. He turned to run after it, but the air current took it around in irregular loops, once, twice, a third time before it circled back to vanish within the Caliph's billowing robes.

Jibril could hear his own heartbeat as the map unfolded beneath the robe. What if the Caliph did not like his work? Or worse, what if the map revealed too much and must be destroyed? Would it be enough to destroy the paper?

At last, the Caliph of Unseen Places spoke: "What is a mirage?"

"You do not know?" Jibril responded, almost forgetting to close his mouth after he spoke.

"Of course," the Caliph said. "But I wish to hear it from you."

So this was a test. Jibril was good at examinations. "Ibn Plato, from Athens, writes that all the world is mirage, a shadow of a reality that is more beautiful and more true. According to Diodorus of Sicily, mirages are caused by stagnant air, catching the shapes of whatever passes through. Ibn Al-Hasan from Basra writes that they are a trick of the eye, caused by the way the light travels in desert heat."

The Caliph of Unseen Places seemed slightly annoyed. "And according to you?"

Jibril took a step backward. "My lord, I am but a mapmaker's apprentice."

The Caliph of Unseen Places rose to his feet.

"I wish I could believe as Plato does," Jibril responded, "that the world we know is but shadows of the ideal. The Brhamins of India speak of something like this as well. But a traveler in the desert will see water where there is none, rather than sand where there is water. This has led many to believe the opposite – that a mirage is what a thirsty and desperate traveler wishes to see."

"Is that what you believe?" the Caliph asked.

"No," Jibril rasped, though his throat was dry. "The mirage I see when I am thirsty is still there if I have a drink."

"Is it movement caught in stagnant air?" the Caliph asked.

"I do not believe so," Jibril replied. "What I see is the shimmer of water, not the shape of a wave."

"So, a trick of the light, then?" the Caliph asked.

"It would seem that way," said Jibril. "Some images change their place with the shifting sand, while others appear at the same time every day in the same place. Both could be a trick of the light, except –"

The Caliph of Unseen Places raised his head almost imperceptibly.

"– there are a few that touch on other senses," Jibril went on. "Three leagues to the east of here, a mirage smells like coriander. South of Aleppo, one sounds like glass chimes."

"I am fond of that one," admitted the Caliph.

"I am, too," Jibril answered, startled at the Caliph's openness. "And on the plains by Ma'arat you can hear the screams of the dying some nights at dusk when the sky turns red."

The Caliph stood suddenly.

"And if neither light nor thirst can explain a mirage," Jibril rushed to finish, "then it must be...it must be something else. A veil over something deeper that men cannot see."

The Caliph stood in silence for a while. Jibril wondered if he was about to speak when the wind blew his cloak, but he said nothing.

The sun beat down on Jibril, and the silence baked within. At last, in the burning desert, Jibril spoke: "I hope my studies have not offended –" he began.

The earth and sky changed colors, so that the sand was blue and the sky was the golds and tans of shifting sands. The caliph's robes billowed like a curtain Jibril could pass through. "Would you like to visit my caliphate, Jibril?" he interrupted.

Near the horizon beyond his left shoulder, Jibril heard a caravan approach, and he wondered what they saw when they looked this way.

Gulliver's Travels
Part I, chapters I–VI

Jonathan Swift

The Publisher to the Reader
[As given in the original edition]

THE AUTHOR of these Travels, Mr. Lemuel Gulliver, is my ancient and intimate friend; there is likewise some relation between us on the mother's side. About three years ago, Mr. Gulliver growing weary of the concourse of curious people coming to him at his house in Redriff, made a small purchase of land, with a convenient house, near Newark, in Nottinghamshire, his native country; where he now lives retired, yet in good esteem among his neighbours.

Although Mr. Gulliver was born in Nottinghamshire, where his father dwelt, yet I have heard him say his family came from Oxfordshire; to confirm which, I have observed in the churchyard at Banbury in that county, several tombs and monuments of the Gullivers.

Before he quitted Redriff, he left the custody of the following papers in my hands, with the liberty to dispose of them as I should think fit. I have carefully perused them three times. The style is very plain and simple; and the only fault I find is, that the author, after the manner of travellers, is a little too circumstantial. There is an air of truth apparent through the whole; and indeed the author was so distinguished for his veracity, that it became a sort of proverb among his neighbours at Redriff, when any one affirmed a thing, to say, it was as true as if Mr. Gulliver had spoken it.

By the advice of several worthy persons, to whom, with the author's permission, I communicated these papers, I now venture to send them into the world, hoping they may be, at least for some time, a better entertainment to our young noblemen, than the common scribbles of politics and party.

This volume would have been at least twice as large, if I had not made bold to strike out innumerable passages relating to the winds and tides, as well as to the variations and bearings in the several voyages, together with the minute descriptions of the management of the ship in storms, in the style of sailors; likewise the account of longitudes and latitudes; wherein I have reason to apprehend, that Mr. Gulliver may be a little dissatisfied. But I was resolved to fit the work as much as possible to the general capacity of readers. However, if my own ignorance in sea affairs shall have led me to commit some mistakes, I alone am answerable for them. And if any traveller hath a curiosity to see the whole work at large, as it came from the hands of the author, I will be ready to gratify him.

As for any further particulars relating to the author, the reader will receive satisfaction from the first pages of the book.

RICHARD SYMPSON.

A Letter from Captain Gulliver to his Cousin Sympson
Written in the Year 1727

I hope you will be ready to own publicly, whenever you shall be called to it, that by your great and frequent urgency you prevailed on me to publish a very loose and uncorrect account of my travels, with directions to hire some young gentleman of either university to put them in order, and correct the style, as my cousin Dampier did, by my advice, in his book called 'A Voyage round the world.' But I do not remember I gave you power to consent that any thing should be omitted, and much less that any thing should be inserted; therefore, as to the latter, I do here renounce every thing of that kind; particularly a paragraph about her majesty Queen Anne, of most pious and glorious memory; although I did reverence and esteem her more than any of human species. But you, or your interpolator, ought to have considered, that it was not my inclination, so was it not decent to praise any animal of our composition before my master Houyhnhnm: And besides, the fact was altogether false; for to my knowledge, being in England during some part of her majesty's reign, she did govern by a chief minister; nay even by two successively, the first whereof was the lord of Godolphin, and the second the lord of Oxford; so that you have made me say the thing that was not. Likewise in the account of the academy of projectors, and several passages of my discourse to my master Houyhnhnm, you have either omitted some material circumstances, or minced or changed them in such a manner, that I do hardly know my own work. When I formerly hinted to you something of this in a letter, you were pleased to answer that you were afraid of giving offence; that people in power were very watchful over the press, and apt not only to interpret, but to punish every thing which looked like an innuendo (as I think you call it). But, pray how could that which I spoke so many years ago, and at about five thousand leagues distance, in another reign, be applied to any of the Yahoos, who now are said to govern the herd; especially at a time when I little thought, or feared, the unhappiness of living under them? Have not I the most reason to complain, when I see these very Yahoos carried by Houyhnhnms in a vehicle, as if they were brutes, and those the rational creatures? And indeed to avoid so monstrous and detestable a sight was one principal motive of my retirement hither. Thus much I thought proper to tell you in relation to yourself, and to the trust I reposed in you.

I do, in the next place, complain of my own great want of judgment, in being prevailed upon by the entreaties and false reasoning of you and some others, very much against my own opinion, to suffer my travels to be published. Pray bring to your mind how often I desired you to consider, when you insisted on the motive of public good, that the Yahoos were a species of animals utterly incapable of amendment by precept or example: and so it has proved; for, instead of seeing a full stop put to all abuses and corruptions, at least in this little island, as I had reason to expect; behold, after above six months warning, I cannot learn that my book has produced one single effect according to my intentions. I desired you would let me know, by a letter, when party and faction were extinguished; judges learned and upright; pleaders honest and modest, with some tincture of common sense, and Smithfield blazing with pyramids of law books; the young nobility's education entirely changed; the physicians banished; the female Yahoos abounding in virtue, honour, truth, and good sense; courts and levees of great ministers thoroughly weeded and swept; wit, merit, and learning rewarded; all disgracers of the press in prose and verse condemned to eat nothing but their own cotton, and quench their thirst with their own ink. These, and a thousand other reformations, I firmly counted upon by your encouragement; as indeed they were plainly deducible from the precepts delivered in my book. And it must be owned, that seven months were a sufficient time to correct every vice and folly to which Yahoos are subject, if their natures had been capable of the least disposition to virtue or wisdom. Yet, so far have you been from answering my expectation in any of your letters; that on the contrary you are loading our carrier every week with libels, and keys, and reflections, and memoirs, and second parts; wherein I see myself accused of reflecting upon great state folk; of degrading human nature (for so they have still the confidence to style it), and of abusing the female sex. I find likewise that the writers of those bundles are not agreed among themselves; for some of them will not allow me to be the author of my own travels; and others make me author of books to which I am wholly a stranger. I find likewise that your printer has been so careless as to confound the times, and mistake the dates, of my several voyages and returns; neither assigning the true year, nor the true month, nor day of the month: and I hear the original manuscript is all destroyed since the publication of my book; neither have I any copy left: however, I have sent you some corrections, which you may insert, if ever there should be a second edition: and yet I cannot stand to them; but shall leave that matter to my judicious and candid readers to adjust it as they please.

I hear some of our sea Yahoos find fault with my sea-language, as not proper in many parts, nor now in use. I cannot help it. In my first voyages, while I was young, I was instructed by the oldest mariners, and learned to speak as they did. But I have since found that the sea Yahoos are apt, like the land ones, to become new-fangled in their words, which the latter change every year; insomuch, as I remember upon each return to my own country their old dialect was so altered, that I could hardly understand the new. And I observe, when any Yahoo comes from London out of curiosity to visit me at my house, we neither of us are able to deliver our conceptions in a manner intelligible to the other.

If the censure of the Yahoos could any way affect me, I should have great reason to complain, that some of them are so bold as to think my book of travels a mere fiction out of mine own brain, and have gone so far as to drop hints, that the Houyhnhnms and Yahoos have no more existence than the inhabitants of Utopia. Indeed I must confess, that as to the people of Lilliput, Brobdingrag (for so the word should have been spelt, and not erroneously Brobdingnag), and Laputa, I have never yet heard of any Yahoo so presumptuous as to dispute their being, or the facts I have related concerning them; because the truth immediately strikes every reader with conviction. And is there less probability in my account of the Houyhnhnms or Yahoos, when it is manifest as to the latter, there are so many thousands even in this country, who only differ from their brother brutes in Houyhnhnmland, because they use a sort of jabber, and do not go naked?

I wrote for their amendment, and not their approbation. The united praise of the whole race would be of less consequence to me, than the neighing of those two degenerate Houyhnhnms I keep in my stable; because from these, degenerate as they are, I still improve in some virtues without any mixture of vice.

Do these miserable animals presume to think, that I am so degenerated as to defend my veracity? Yahoo as I am, it is well known through all Houyhnhnmland, that, by the instructions and example of my illustrious master, I was able in the compass of two years (although I confess with the utmost difficulty) to remove that infernal habit of lying, shuffling, deceiving, and equivocating, so deeply rooted in the very souls of all my species; especially the Europeans.

I have other complaints to make upon this vexatious occasion; but I forbear troubling myself or you any further. I must freely confess, that since my last return, some corruptions of my Yahoo nature have revived in me by conversing with a few of your species, and particularly those of my own family, by an unavoidable necessity; else I should never have attempted so absurd a project as that of reforming the Yahoo race in this kingdom: But I have now done with all such visionary schemes for ever.

April 2, 1727

Part I - A Voyage to Lilliput

Chapter I

MY FATHER had a small estate in Nottinghamshire: I was the third of five sons. He sent me to Emanuel College in Cambridge at fourteen years old, where I resided three years, and applied myself close to my studies; but the charge of maintaining me, although I had a very scanty allowance, being too great for a narrow fortune, I was bound apprentice to Mr. James Bates, an eminent surgeon in London, with whom I continued four years. My father now and then sending me small sums of money, I laid them out in learning navigation, and other parts of the mathematics, useful to those who intend to travel, as I always believed it would be, some time or other, my fortune to do. When I left Mr. Bates, I went down to my father: where, by the assistance of him and my uncle John, and some other relations, I got forty pounds, and a promise of thirty pounds a year to maintain me at Leyden: there I studied physic two years and seven months, knowing it would be useful in long voyages.

Soon after my return from Leyden, I was recommended by my good master, Mr. Bates, to be surgeon to the Swallow, Captain Abraham Pannel, commander; with whom I continued three years and a half, making a voyage or two into the Levant, and some other parts. When I came back I resolved to settle in London; to which Mr. Bates, my master, encouraged me, and by him I was recommended to several patients. I took part of a small house in the Old Jewry; and being advised to alter my condition, I married Mrs. Mary Burton, second daughter to Mr. Edmund Burton, hosier, in Newgate-street, with whom I received four hundred pounds for a portion.

But my good master Bates dying in two years after, and I having few friends, my business began to fail; for my conscience would not suffer me to imitate the bad practice of too many among my brethren. Having therefore consulted with my wife, and some of my acquaintance, I determined to go again to sea. I was surgeon successively in two ships, and made several voyages, for six years, to the East and West Indies, by which I got some addition to my fortune. My hours of leisure I spent in reading the best authors, ancient and modern, being always provided with a good number of books; and when I was ashore, in observing the manners and dispositions of the people, as well as learning their language; wherein I had a great facility, by the strength of my memory.

The last of these voyages not proving very fortunate, I grew weary of the sea, and intended to stay at home with my wife and family. I removed from the Old Jewry to Fetter Lane, and from thence to Wapping, hoping to get business among the sailors; but it would not turn to account. After three years expectation that things would mend, I accepted an advantageous offer from Captain William Prichard, master of the Antelope, who was making a voyage to the South Sea. We set sail from Bristol, May 4, 1699, and our voyage was at first very prosperous.

It would not be proper, for some reasons, to trouble the reader with the particulars of our adventures in those seas; let it suffice to inform him, that in our passage from thence to the East Indies, we were driven by a violent storm to the north-west of Van Diemen's Land. By an observation, we found ourselves in the latitude of 30 degrees 2 minutes south. Twelve of our crew were dead by immoderate labour and ill food; the rest were in a very weak condition. On the 5th of November, which was the beginning of summer in those parts, the weather being very hazy, the seamen spied a rock within half a cable's length of the ship; but the wind was so strong, that we were driven directly upon it, and immediately split. Six of the crew, of whom I was one, having let down the boat into the sea, made a shift to get clear of the ship and the rock. We rowed, by my computation, about three leagues, till we were able to work no longer, being already spent with labour while we were in the ship. We therefore trusted ourselves to the mercy of the waves, and in about half an hour the boat was overset by a sudden flurry from the north. What became of my companions in the boat, as well as of those who escaped on the rock, or were left in the vessel, I cannot tell; but conclude they were all lost.

For my own part, I swam as fortune directed me, and was pushed forward by wind and tide. I often let my legs drop, and could feel no bottom; but when I was almost gone, and able to struggle no longer, I found myself within my depth; and by this time the storm was much abated. The declivity was so small, that I walked near a mile before I got to the shore, which I conjectured was about eight o'clock in the evening. I then advanced forward near half a mile, but could not discover any sign of houses or inhabitants; at least I was in so weak a condition, that I did not observe them. I was extremely tired, and with that, and the heat of the weather, and about half a pint of brandy that I drank as I left the ship, I found myself much inclined to sleep.

I lay down on the grass, which was very short and soft, where I slept sounder than ever I remembered to have done in my life, and, as I reckoned, about nine hours; for when I awaked, it was just day-light. I attempted to rise, but was not able to stir: for, as I happened to lie on my back, I found my arms and legs were strongly fastened on each side to the ground; and my hair, which was long and thick, tied down in the same manner. I likewise felt several slender ligatures across my body, from my arm-pits to my thighs. I could only look upwards; the sun began to grow hot, and the light offended my eyes. I heard a confused noise about me; but in the posture I lay, could see nothing except the sky. In a little time I felt something alive moving on my left leg, which advancing gently forward over my breast, came almost up to my chin; when, bending my eyes downwards as much as I could, I perceived it to be a human creature not six inches high, with a bow and arrow in his hands, and a quiver at his back. In the mean time, I felt at least forty more of the same kind (as I conjectured) following the first. I was in the utmost astonishment, and roared so loud, that they all ran back in a fright; and some of them, as I was afterwards told, were hurt with the falls they got by leaping from my sides upon the ground.

However, they soon returned, and one of them, who ventured so far as to get a full sight of my face, lifting up his hands and eyes by way of admiration, cried out in a shrill but distinct voice, *Hekinah degul*: the others repeated the same words several times, but then I knew not what they meant. I lay all this while, as the reader may believe, in great uneasiness. At length, struggling to get loose, I had the fortune to break the strings, and wrench out the pegs that fastened my left arm to the ground; for, by lifting it up to my face, I discovered the methods they had taken to bind me, and at the same time with a violent pull, which gave me excessive pain, I a little loosened the strings that tied down my hair on the left side, so that I was just able to turn my head about two inches. But the creatures ran off a second time, before I could seize them; whereupon there was a great shout in a very shrill accent, and after it ceased I heard one of them cry aloud *Tolgo phonac*; when in an instant I felt above a hundred arrows discharged on my left hand, which, pricked me like so many needles; and besides, they shot another flight into the air, as we do bombs in Europe, whereof many, I suppose, fell on my body, (though I felt them not), and some on my face, which I immediately covered with my left hand. When this shower of arrows was over, I fell a groaning with grief and pain; and then striving again to get loose, they discharged another volley larger than the first, and some of them attempted with spears to stick me in the sides; but by good luck I had on a buff jerkin, which they could not pierce. I thought it the most prudent method to lie still, and my design was to continue so till night, when, my left hand being already loose, I could easily free myself: and as for the inhabitants, I had reason to believe I might be a match for the greatest army they could bring against me, if they were all of the same size with him that I saw. But fortune disposed otherwise of me.

When the people observed I was quiet, they discharged no more arrows; but, by the noise I heard, I knew their numbers increased; and about four yards from me, over against my right ear, I heard a knocking for above an hour, like that of people at work; when turning my head that way, as well as the pegs and strings would permit me, I saw a stage erected about a foot and a half from the ground, capable of holding four of the inhabitants, with two or three ladders to mount it: from whence one of them, who seemed to be a person of quality, made me a long speech, whereof I understood not one syllable. But I should have mentioned, that before the principal person began his oration, he cried out three times, *Langro dehul san* (these words and the former were afterwards repeated and explained to me); whereupon, immediately, about fifty of the inhabitants came and cut the strings that fastened the left side of my head, which gave me the liberty of turning it to the right, and of observing the person and gesture of him that was to speak. He appeared to be of a middle age, and taller than any of the other three who attended him, whereof one was a page that held up his train, and seemed to be somewhat longer than my middle finger; the other two stood one on each side to support him. He acted every part of an orator, and I could observe many periods of threatenings, and others of promises, pity, and kindness. I answered in a few words, but in the most submissive manner, lifting up my left hand, and both my eyes to the sun, as calling him for a witness; and being almost famished with hunger, having not eaten a morsel for some hours before I left the ship, I found the demands of nature so strong upon me, that I could not forbear showing my impatience (perhaps against the strict rules of decency) by putting my finger frequently to my mouth, to signify that I wanted food. The *hurgo* (for so they call a great lord, as I afterwards learnt) understood me very well. He descended from the stage, and commanded that several ladders should be applied to my sides, on which above a hundred of the inhabitants mounted and walked towards my mouth, laden with baskets full of meat, which had been provided and sent thither by the king's orders, upon the first intelligence he received of me. I observed there was the flesh of several animals, but could not distinguish them by the taste. There were shoulders, legs, and loins, shaped like those of mutton, and very well dressed, but smaller than the wings of a lark. I ate them by two or three at a mouthful, and took three loaves at a time, about the bigness of musket bullets. They supplied me as fast as they could, showing a thousand marks of wonder and astonishment at my bulk and appetite. I then made another sign, that I wanted drink. They found by my eating that a small quantity would not suffice me; and being a most ingenious people, they slung up, with great dexterity, one of their largest hogsheads, then rolled it towards my hand, and beat out the top; I drank it off at a draught, which I might well do, for it did not hold half a pint, and tasted like a small wine of Burgundy, but much more delicious. They brought me a second hogshead, which I drank in the same manner, and made signs for more; but they had none to give me. When I had performed these wonders, they shouted for joy, and danced upon my breast, repeating several times as they did at first, *Hekinah degul*. They made me a sign that I should throw down the two hogsheads, but first warning the people below to stand out of the way, crying aloud, *Borach mevolah*; and when they saw the vessels in the air, there was a universal shout of *Hekinah degul*.

I confess I was often tempted, while they were passing backwards and forwards on my body, to seize forty or fifty of the first that came in my reach, and dash them against the ground. But the remembrance of what I had felt, which probably might not be the worst they could do, and the promise of honour I made them – for so I interpreted my submissive behaviour – soon drove out these imaginations. Besides, I now considered myself as bound by the laws of hospitality, to a people who had treated me with so much expense and magnificence. However, in my thoughts I could not sufficiently wonder at the intrepidity of these diminutive mortals, who durst venture to mount and walk upon my body, while one of my hands was at liberty, without trembling at the very sight of so prodigious a creature as I must appear to them. After some time, when they observed that I made no more demands for meat, there appeared before me a person of high rank from his imperial majesty. His excellency, having mounted on the small of my right leg, advanced forwards up to my face, with about a dozen of his retinue; and producing his credentials under the signet royal, which he applied close to my eyes, spoke about ten minutes without any signs of anger, but with a kind of determinate resolution, often pointing forwards, which, as I afterwards found, was towards the capital city, about half a mile distant; whither it was agreed by his majesty in council that I must be conveyed. I answered in few words, but to no purpose, and made a sign with my hand that was loose, putting it to the other (but over his excellency's head for fear of hurting him or his train) and then to my own head and body, to signify that I desired my liberty. It appeared that he understood me well enough, for he shook his head by way of disapprobation, and held his hand in a posture to show that I must be carried as a prisoner. However, he made other signs to let me understand that I should have meat and drink enough, and very good treatment. Whereupon I once more thought of attempting to break my bonds; but again, when I felt the smart of their arrows upon my face and hands, which were all in blisters, and many of the darts still sticking in them, and observing likewise that the number of my enemies increased, I gave tokens to let them know that they might do with me what they pleased. Upon this, the *hurgo* and his train withdrew, with much civility and cheerful countenances.

Soon after I heard a general shout, with frequent repetitions of the words *Peplom selan*; and I felt great numbers of people on my left side relaxing the cords to such a degree, that I was able to turn upon my right, and to ease myself with making water; which I very plentifully did, to the great astonishment of the people; who, conjecturing by my motion what I was going to do, immediately opened to the right and left on that side, to avoid the torrent, which fell with such noise and violence from me. But before this, they had daubed my face and both my hands with a sort of ointment, very pleasant to the smell, which, in a few minutes, removed all the smart of their arrows. These circumstances, added to the refreshment I had received by their victuals and drink, which were very nourishing, disposed me to sleep. I slept about eight hours, as I was afterwards assured; and it was no wonder, for the physicians, by the emperor's order, had mingled a sleepy potion in the hogsheads of wine.

It seems, that upon the first moment I was discovered sleeping on the ground, after my landing, the emperor had early notice of it by an express; and determined in council, that I should be tied in the manner I have related, (which was done in the night while I slept;) that plenty of meat and drink should be sent to me, and a machine prepared to carry me to the capital city.

This resolution perhaps may appear very bold and dangerous, and I am confident would not be imitated by any prince in Europe on the like occasion. However, in my opinion, it was extremely prudent, as well as generous: for, supposing these people had endeavoured to kill me with their spears and arrows, while I was asleep, I should certainly have awaked with the first sense of smart, which might so far have roused my rage and strength, as to have enabled me to break the strings wherewith I was tied; after which, as they were not able to make resistance, so they could expect no mercy.

These people are most excellent mathematicians, and arrived to a great perfection in mechanics, by the countenance and encouragement of the emperor, who is a renowned patron of learning. This prince has several machines fixed on wheels, for the carriage of trees and other great weights. He often builds his largest men of war, whereof some are nine feet long, in the woods where the timber grows, and has them carried on these engines three or four hundred yards to the sea. Five hundred carpenters and engineers were immediately set at work to prepare the greatest engine they had. It was a frame of wood raised three inches from the ground, about seven feet long, and four wide, moving upon twenty-two wheels. The shout I heard was upon the arrival of this engine, which, it seems, set out in four hours after my landing. It was brought parallel to me, as I lay. But the principal difficulty was to raise and place me in this vehicle. Eighty poles, each of one foot high, were erected for this purpose, and very strong cords, of the bigness of packthread, were fastened by hooks to many bandages, which the workmen had girt round my neck, my hands, my body, and my legs. Nine hundred of the strongest men were employed to draw up these cords, by many pulleys fastened on the poles; and thus, in less than three hours, I was raised and slung into the engine, and there tied fast.

All this I was told; for, while the operation was performing, I lay in a profound sleep, by the force of that soporiferous medicine infused into my liquor. Fifteen hundred of the emperor's largest horses, each about four inches and a half high, were employed to draw me towards the metropolis, which, as I said, was half a mile distant.

About four hours after we began our journey, I awaked by a very ridiculous accident; for the carriage being stopped a while, to adjust something that was out of order, two or three of the young natives had the curiosity to see how I looked when I was asleep; they climbed up into the engine, and advancing very softly to my face, one of them, an officer in the guards, put the sharp end of his half-pike a good way up into my left nostril, which tickled my nose like a straw, and made me sneeze violently; whereupon they stole off unperceived, and it was three weeks before I knew the cause of my waking so suddenly. We made a long march the remaining part of the day, and, rested at night with five hundred guards on each side of me, half with torches, and half with bows and arrows, ready to shoot me if I should offer to stir. The next morning at sun-rise we continued our march, and arrived within two hundred yards of the city gates about noon. The emperor, and all his court, came out to meet us; but his great officers would by no means suffer his majesty to endanger his person by mounting on my body.

At the place where the carriage stopped there stood an ancient temple, esteemed to be the largest in the whole kingdom; which, having been polluted some years before by an unnatural murder, was, according to the zeal of those people, looked upon as profane, and therefore had been applied to common use, and all the ornaments and furniture carried away. In this edifice it was determined I should lodge. The great gate fronting to the north was about four feet high, and almost two feet wide, through which I could easily creep. On each side of the gate was a small window, not above six inches from the ground: into that on the left side, the king's smith conveyed fourscore and eleven chains, like those that hang to a lady's watch in Europe, and almost as large, which were locked to my left leg with six-and-thirty padlocks.

Over against this temple, on the other side of the great highway, at twenty feet distance, there was a turret at least five feet high. Here the emperor ascended, with many principal lords of his court, to have an opportunity of viewing me, as I was told, for I could not see them. It was reckoned that above a hundred thousand inhabitants came out of the town upon the same errand; and, in spite of my guards, I believe there could not be fewer than ten thousand at several times, who mounted my body by the help of ladders. But a proclamation was soon issued, to forbid it upon pain of death. When the workmen found it was impossible for me to break loose, they cut all the strings that bound me; whereupon I rose up, with as melancholy a disposition as ever I had in my life. But the noise and astonishment of the people, at seeing me rise and walk, are not to be expressed. The chains that held my left leg were about two yards long, and gave me not only the liberty of walking backwards and forwards in a semicircle, but, being fixed within four inches of the gate, allowed me to creep in, and lie at my full length in the temple.

Chapter II

WHEN I FOUND myself on my feet, I looked about me, and must confess I never beheld a more entertaining prospect. The country around appeared like a continued garden, and the enclosed fields, which were generally forty feet square, resembled so many beds of flowers. These fields were intermingled with woods of half a stang **(footnote 1)**, and the tallest trees, as I could judge, appeared to be seven feet high. I viewed the town on my left hand, which looked like the painted scene of a city in a theatre.

I had been for some hours extremely pressed by the necessities of nature; which was no wonder, it being almost two days since I had last disburdened myself. I was under great difficulties between urgency and shame. The best expedient I could think of, was to creep into my house, which I accordingly did; and shutting the gate after me, I went as far as the length of my chain would suffer, and discharged my body of that uneasy load. But this was the only time I was ever guilty of so uncleanly an action; for which I cannot but hope the candid reader will give some allowance, after he has maturely and impartially considered my case, and the distress I was in. From this time my constant practice was, as soon as I rose, to perform that business in open air, at the full extent of my chain; and due care was taken every morning before company came, that the offensive matter should be carried off in wheel-barrows, by two servants appointed for that purpose. I would not have dwelt so long upon a circumstance that, perhaps, at first sight, may appear not very momentous, if I had not thought it necessary to justify my character, in point of cleanliness, to the world; which, I am told, some of my maligners have been pleased, upon this and other occasions, to call in question.

When this adventure was at an end, I came back out of my house, having occasion for fresh air. The emperor was already descended from the tower, and advancing on horseback towards me, which had like to have cost him dear; for the beast, though very well trained, yet wholly unused to such a sight, which appeared as if a mountain moved before him, reared up on its hinder feet: but that prince, who is an excellent horseman, kept his seat, till his attendants ran in, and held the bridle, while his majesty had time to dismount. When he alighted, he surveyed me round with great admiration; but kept beyond the length of my chain. He ordered his cooks and butlers, who were already prepared, to give me victuals and drink, which they pushed forward in a sort of vehicles upon wheels, till I could reach them.

I took these vehicles and soon emptied them all; twenty of them were filled with meat, and ten with liquor; each of the former afforded me two or three good mouthfuls; and I emptied the liquor of ten vessels, which was contained in earthen vials, into one vehicle, drinking it off at a draught; and so I did with the rest. The empress, and young princes of the blood of both sexes, attended by many ladies, sat at some distance in their chairs; but upon the accident that happened to the emperor's horse, they alighted, and came near his person, which I am now going to describe. He is taller by almost the breadth of my nail, than any of his court; which alone is enough to strike an awe into the beholders. His features are strong and masculine, with an Austrian lip and arched nose, his complexion olive, his countenance erect, his body and limbs well proportioned, all his motions graceful, and his deportment majestic. He was then past his prime, being twenty-eight years and three quarters old, of which he had reigned about seven in great felicity, and generally victorious. For the better convenience of beholding him, I lay on my side, so that my face was parallel to his, and he stood but three yards off: however, I have had him since many times in my hand, and therefore cannot be deceived in the description. His dress was very plain and simple, and the fashion of it between the Asiatic and the European; but he had on his head a light helmet of gold, adorned with jewels, and a plume on the crest. He held his sword drawn in his hand to defend himself, if I should happen to break loose; it was almost three inches long; the hilt and scabbard were gold enriched with diamonds. His voice was shrill, but very clear and articulate; and I could distinctly hear it when I stood up. The ladies and courtiers were all most magnificently clad; so that the spot they stood upon seemed to resemble a petticoat spread upon the ground, embroidered with figures of gold and silver. His imperial majesty spoke often to me, and I returned answers: but neither of us could understand a syllable. There were several of his priests and lawyers present (as I conjectured by their habits), who were commanded to address themselves to me; and I spoke to them in as many languages as I had the least smattering of, which were High and Low Dutch, Latin, French, Spanish, Italian, and Lingua Franca, but all to no purpose. After about two hours the court retired, and I was left with a strong guard, to prevent the impertinence, and probably the malice of the rabble, who were very impatient to crowd about me as near as they durst; and some of them had the impudence to shoot their arrows at me, as I sat on the ground by the door of my house, whereof one very narrowly missed my left eye. But the colonel ordered six of the ringleaders to be seized, and thought no punishment so proper as to deliver them bound into my hands; which some of his soldiers accordingly did, pushing them forward with the butt-ends of their pikes into my reach. I took them all in my right hand, put five of them into my coat-pocket; and as to the sixth, I made a countenance as if I would eat him alive. The poor man squalled terribly, and the colonel and his officers were in much pain, especially when they saw me take out my penknife: but I soon put them out of fear; for, looking mildly, and immediately cutting the strings he was bound with, I set him gently on the ground, and away he ran. I treated the rest in the same manner, taking them one by one out of my pocket; and I observed both the soldiers and people were highly delighted at this mark of my clemency, which was represented very much to my advantage at court.

Towards night I got with some difficulty into my house, where I lay on the ground, and continued to do so about a fortnight; during which time, the emperor gave orders to have a bed prepared for me. Six hundred beds of the common measure were brought in carriages, and worked up in my house; a hundred and fifty of their beds, sewn together, made up the breadth and length; and these were four double: which, however, kept me but very indifferently from the hardness of the floor, that was of smooth stone. By the same computation, they provided me with sheets, blankets, and coverlets, tolerable enough for one who had been so long inured to hardships.

As the news of my arrival spread through the kingdom, it brought prodigious numbers of rich, idle, and curious people to see me; so that the villages were almost emptied; and great neglect of tillage and household affairs must have ensued, if his imperial majesty had not provided, by several proclamations and orders of state, against this inconveniency. He directed that those who had already beheld me should return home, and not presume to come within fifty yards of my house, without license from the court; whereby the secretaries of state got considerable fees.

In the mean time the emperor held frequent councils, to debate what course should be taken with me; and I was afterwards assured by a particular friend, a person of great quality, who was as much in the secret as any, that the court was under many difficulties concerning me. They apprehended my breaking loose; that my diet would be very expensive, and might cause a famine. Sometimes they determined to starve me;

or at least to shoot me in the face and hands with poisoned arrows, which would soon despatch me; but again they considered, that the stench of so large a carcass might produce a plague in the metropolis, and probably spread through the whole kingdom. In the midst of these consultations, several officers of the army went to the door of the great council-chamber, and two of them being admitted, gave an account of my behaviour to the six criminals above-mentioned; which made so favourable an impression in the breast of his majesty and the whole board, in my behalf, that an imperial commission was issued out, obliging all the villages, nine hundred yards round the city, to deliver in every morning six beeves, forty sheep, and other victuals for my sustenance; together with a proportionable quantity of bread, and wine, and other liquors; for the due payment of which, his majesty gave assignments upon his treasury: – for this prince lives chiefly upon his own demesnes; seldom, except upon great occasions, raising any subsidies upon his subjects, who are bound to attend him in his wars at their own expense. An establishment was also made of six hundred persons to be my domestics, who had board-wages allowed for their maintenance, and tents built for them very conveniently on each side of my door.

It was likewise ordered, that three hundred tailors should make me a suit of clothes, after the fashion of the country; that six of his majesty's greatest scholars should be employed to instruct me in their language; and lastly, that the emperor's horses, and those of the nobility and troops of guards, should be frequently exercised in my sight, to accustom themselves to me. All these orders were duly put in execution; and in about three weeks I made a great progress in learning their language; during which time the emperor frequently honoured me with his visits, and was pleased to assist my masters in teaching me.

We began already to converse together in some sort; and the first words I learnt, were to express my desire 'that he would please give me my liberty;' which I every day repeated on my knees. His answer, as I could comprehend it, was, "that this must be a work of time, not to be thought on without the advice of his council, and that first I must *lumos kelmin pesso desmar lon emposo*;" that is, swear a peace with him and his kingdom. However, that I should be used with all kindness. And he advised me to "acquire, by my patience and discreet behaviour, the good opinion of himself and his subjects." He desired "I would not take it ill, if he gave orders to certain proper officers to search me; for probably I might carry about me several weapons, which must needs be dangerous things, if they answered the bulk of so prodigious a person." I said, "His majesty should be satisfied; for I was ready to strip myself, and turn up my pockets before him." This I delivered part in words, and part in signs. He replied, "that, by the laws of the kingdom, I must be searched by two of his officers; that he knew this could not be done without my consent and assistance; and he had so good an opinion of my generosity and justice, as to trust their persons in my hands; that whatever they took from me, should be returned when I left the country, or paid for at the rate which I would set upon them."

I took up the two officers in my hands, put them first into my coat-pockets, and then into every other pocket about me, except my two fobs, and another secret pocket, which I had no mind should be searched, wherein I had some little necessaries that were of no consequence to any but myself. In one of my fobs there was a silver watch, and in the other a small quantity of gold in a purse. These gentlemen, having pen, ink, and paper, about them, made an exact inventory of every thing they saw; and when they had done, desired I would set them down, that they might deliver it to the emperor. This inventory I afterwards translated into English, and is, word for word, as follows:

> *'Imprimis: In the right coat-pocket of the great man-mountain'* (for so I interpret the words quinbus flestrin,) *'after the strictest search, we found only one great piece of coarse-cloth, large enough to be a foot-cloth for your majesty's chief room of state. In the left pocket we saw a huge silver chest, with a cover of the same metal, which we, the searchers, were not able to lift. We desired it should be opened, and one of us stepping into it, found himself up to the mid leg in a sort of dust, some part whereof flying up to our faces set us both a sneezing for several times together. In his right waistcoat-pocket we found a prodigious bundle of white thin substances, folded one over another, about the bigness of three men, tied with a strong cable, and marked with black figures; which we humbly conceive to be writings, every letter almost half as large as the palm of our hands. In the left there was a sort of engine, from the back of which were extended twenty long poles, resembling the pallisados before your majesty's court: wherewith we conjecture the man-mountain combs his head; for we did not always trouble him with questions, because we found it a great difficulty to make him understand us. In the large pocket, on the right side of his middle cover'* (so I translate the word ranfulo, by which they meant my breeches,) *'we saw a hollow pillar of iron, about the length of a man, fastened to a strong piece of timber larger than the pillar; and upon one side of the pillar, were huge pieces of iron sticking out, cut into strange figures, which we know not what to make of. In the left pocket, another engine of the same kind. In the smaller pocket on the right side, were several round flat pieces of white and red metal, of different bulk; some of the white, which seemed to be silver, were so large and heavy, that my comrade and I could hardly lift them. In the left pocket were two black pillars irregularly shaped: we could not, without difficulty, reach the top of them, as we stood at the bottom of his pocket. One of them was covered, and seemed all of a piece: but at the upper end of the other there appeared a white round substance, about twice the bigness of our heads. Within each of these was enclosed a prodigious plate of steel; which, by our orders, we obliged him to show us, because we apprehended they might be dangerous engines. He took them out of their cases, and told us, that in his own country his practice was to shave his beard with one of these, and cut his meat with the other. There were two pockets which we could not enter: these he called his fobs; they were two large slits cut into the top of his middle cover, but squeezed close by the pressure of his belly. Out of the right fob hung a great silver chain, with a wonderful kind of engine at the bottom. We directed him to draw out whatever was at the end of that chain; which appeared to be a globe, half silver, and half of some transparent metal; for, on the transparent side, we saw certain strange figures circularly drawn, and thought we could touch them, till we found our fingers stopped by the lucid substance. He put this engine into our ears, which made an incessant noise, like that of a water-mill: and we conjecture it is either some unknown animal, or the god that he worships; but we are more inclined to the latter opinion, because he assured us, (if we understood him right, for he expressed himself very imperfectly) that he seldom did any thing without consulting it. He called it his oracle, and said, it pointed out the time for every action of his life. From the left fob he took out a net almost large enough for a fisherman, but contrived to open and shut like a purse,*

and served him for the same use: we found therein several massy pieces of yellow metal, which, if they be real gold, must be of immense value.

'Having thus, in obedience to your majesty's commands, diligently searched all his pockets, we observed a girdle about his waist made of the hide of some prodigious animal, from which, on the left side, hung a sword of the length of five men; and on the right, a bag or pouch divided into two cells, each cell capable of holding three of your majesty's subjects. In one of these cells were several globes, or balls, of a most ponderous metal, about the bigness of our heads, and requiring a strong hand to lift them: the other cell contained a heap of certain black grains, but of no great bulk or weight, for we could hold above fifty of them in the palms of our hands.

'This is an exact inventory of what we found about the body of the man-mountain, who used us with great civility, and due respect to your majesty's commission. Signed and sealed on the fourth day of the eighty-ninth moon of your majesty's auspicious reign.

Clefrin Frelock, Marsi Frelock.'

When this inventory was read over to the emperor, he directed me, although in very gentle terms, to deliver up the several particulars. He first called for my scimitar, which I took out, scabbard and all. In the mean time he ordered three thousand of his choicest troops (who then attended him) to surround me at a distance, with their bows and arrows just ready to discharge; but I did not observe it, for mine eyes were wholly fixed upon his majesty. He then desired me to draw my scimitar, which, although it had got some rust by the sea water, was, in most parts, exceeding bright. I did so, and immediately all the troops gave a shout between terror and surprise; for the sun shone clear, and the reflection dazzled their eyes, as I waved the scimitar to and fro in my hand. His majesty, who is a most magnanimous prince, was less daunted than I could expect: he ordered me to return it into the scabbard, and cast it on the ground as gently as I could, about six feet from the end of my chain. The next thing he demanded was one of the hollow iron pillars; by which he meant my pocket pistols. I drew it out, and at his desire, as well as I could, expressed to him the use of it; and charging it only with powder, which, by the closeness of my pouch, happened to escape wetting in the sea (an inconvenience against which all prudent mariners take special care to provide,) I first cautioned the emperor not to be afraid, and then I let it off in the air. The astonishment here was much greater than at the sight of my scimitar. Hundreds fell down as if they had been struck dead; and even the emperor, although he stood his ground, could not recover himself for some time.

I delivered up both my pistols in the same manner as I had done my scimitar, and then my pouch of powder and bullets; begging him that the former might be kept from fire, for it would kindle with the smallest spark, and blow up his imperial palace into the air. I likewise delivered up my watch, which the emperor was very curious to see, and commanded two of his tallest yeomen of the guards to bear it on a pole upon their shoulders, as draymen in England do a barrel of ale. He was amazed at the continual noise it made, and the motion of the minute-hand, which he could easily discern; for their sight is much more acute than ours: he asked the opinions of his learned men about it, which were various and remote, as the reader may well imagine without my repeating; although indeed I could not very perfectly understand them. I then gave up my silver and copper money, my purse, with nine large pieces of gold, and some smaller ones; my knife and razor, my comb and silver snuff-box, my handkerchief and journal-book.

My scimitar, pistols, and pouch, were conveyed in carriages to his majesty's stores; but the rest of my goods were returned me.

I had as I before observed, one private pocket, which escaped their search, wherein there was a pair of spectacles (which I sometimes use for the weakness of mine eyes,) a pocket perspective, and some other little conveniences; which, being of no consequence to the emperor, I did not think myself bound in honour to discover, and I apprehended they might be lost or spoiled if I ventured them out of my possession.

Footnote 1. A stang is a pole or perch; sixteen feet and a half.

Chapter III

MY GENTLENESS and good behaviour had gained so far on the emperor and his court, and indeed upon the army and people in general, that I began to conceive hopes of getting my liberty in a short time. I took all possible methods to cultivate this favourable disposition. The natives came, by degrees, to be less apprehensive of any danger from me. I would sometimes lie down, and let five or six of them dance on my hand; and at last the boys and girls would venture to come and play at hide-and-seek in my hair. I had now made a good progress in understanding and speaking the language. The emperor had a mind one day to entertain me with several of the country shows, wherein they exceed all nations I have known, both for dexterity and magnificence. I was diverted with none so much as that of the rope-dancers, performed upon a slender white thread, extended about two feet, and twelve inches from the ground. Upon which I shall desire liberty, with the reader's patience, to enlarge a little.

This diversion is only practised by those persons who are candidates for great employments, and high favour at court. They are trained in this art from their youth, and are not always of noble birth, or liberal education. When a great office is vacant, either by death or disgrace (which often happens,) five or six of those candidates petition the emperor to entertain his majesty and the court with a dance on the rope; and whoever jumps the highest, without falling, succeeds in the office.

Very often the chief ministers themselves are commanded to show their skill, and to convince the emperor that they have not lost their faculty. Flimnap, the treasurer, is allowed to cut a caper on the straight rope, at least an inch higher than any other lord in the whole empire. I have seen him do the summerset several times together, upon a trencher fixed on a rope which is no thicker than a common packthread in England. My friend Reldresal, principal secretary for private affairs, is, in my opinion, if I am not partial, the second after the treasurer; the rest of the great officers are much upon a par.

These diversions are often attended with fatal accidents, whereof great numbers are on record. I myself have seen two or three candidates break a limb. But the danger is much greater, when the ministers themselves are commanded to show their dexterity; for, by contending to excel themselves and their fellows, they strain so far that there is hardly one of them who has not received a fall, and some of them two or three. I was assured that, a year or two before my arrival, Flimnap would infallibly have broke his neck, if one of the king's cushions, that accidentally lay on the ground, had not weakened the force of his fall.

There is likewise another diversion, which is only shown before the emperor and empress, and first minister, upon particular occasions. The emperor lays on the table three fine silken threads of six inches long; one is blue, the other red, and the third green. These threads are proposed as prizes for those persons whom the emperor has a mind to distinguish by a peculiar mark of his favour. The ceremony is performed in his majesty's great chamber of state, where the candidates are to undergo a trial of dexterity very different from the former, and such as I have not observed the least resemblance of in any other country of the new or old world. The emperor holds a stick in his hands, both ends parallel to the horizon, while the candidates advancing, one by one, sometimes leap over the stick, sometimes creep under it, backward and forward, several times, according as the stick is advanced or depressed. Sometimes the emperor holds one end of the stick, and his first minister the other; sometimes the minister has it entirely to himself. Whoever performs his part with most agility, and holds out the longest in leaping and creeping, is rewarded with the blue-coloured silk; the red is given to the next, and the green to the third, which they all wear girt twice round about the middle; and you see few great persons about this court who are not adorned with one of these girdles.

The horses of the army, and those of the royal stables, having been daily led before me, were no longer shy, but would come up to my very feet without starting. The riders would leap them over my hand, as I held it on the ground; and one of the emperor's huntsmen, upon a large courser, took my foot, shoe and all; which was indeed a prodigious leap. I had the good fortune to divert the emperor one day after a very extraordinary manner. I desired he would order several sticks of two feet high, and the thickness of an ordinary cane, to be brought me; whereupon his majesty commanded the master of his woods to give directions accordingly; and the next morning six woodmen arrived with as many carriages, drawn by eight horses to each. I took nine of these sticks, and fixing them firmly in the ground in a quadrangular figure, two feet and a half square, I took four other sticks, and tied them parallel at each corner, about two feet from the ground; then I fastened my handkerchief to the nine sticks that stood erect; and extended it on all sides, till it was tight as the top of a drum; and the four parallel sticks, rising about five inches higher than the handkerchief, served as ledges on each side.

When I had finished my work, I desired the emperor to let a troop of his best horses twenty-four in number, come and exercise upon this plain. His majesty approved of the proposal, and I took them up, one by one, in my hands, ready mounted and armed, with the proper officers to exercise them. As soon as they got into order they divided into two parties, performed mock skirmishes, discharged blunt arrows, drew their swords, fled and pursued, attacked and retired, and in short discovered the best military discipline I ever beheld. The parallel sticks secured them and their horses from falling over the stage; and the emperor was so much delighted, that he ordered this entertainment to be repeated several days, and once was pleased to be lifted up and give the word of command; and with great difficulty persuaded even the empress herself to let me hold her in her close chair within two yards of the stage, when she was able to take a full view of the whole performance. It was my good fortune, that no ill accident happened in these entertainments; only once a fiery horse, that belonged to one of the captains, pawing with his hoof, struck a hole in my handkerchief, and his foot slipping, he overthrew his rider and himself; but I immediately relieved them both, and covering the hole with one hand, I set down the troop with the other, in the same manner as I took them up. The horse that fell was strained in the left shoulder, but the rider got no hurt; and I repaired my handkerchief as well as I could: however, I would not trust to the strength of it any more, in such dangerous enterprises.

About two or three days before I was set at liberty, as I was entertaining the court with this kind of feat, there arrived an express to inform his majesty, that some of his subjects, riding near the place where I was first taken up, had seen a great black substance lying on the around, very oddly shaped, extending its edges round, as wide as his majesty's bedchamber, and rising up in the middle as high as a man; that it was no living creature, as they at first apprehended, for it lay on the grass without motion; and some of them had walked round it several times; that, by mounting upon each other's shoulders, they had got to the top, which was flat and even, and, stamping upon it, they found that it was hollow within; that they humbly conceived it might be something belonging to the man-mountain; and if his majesty pleased, they would undertake to bring it with only five horses. I presently knew what they meant, and was glad at heart to receive this intelligence.

It seems, upon my first reaching the shore after our shipwreck, I was in such confusion, that before I came to the place where I went to sleep, my hat, which I had fastened with a string to my head while I was rowing, and had stuck on all the time I was swimming, fell off after I came to land; the string, as I conjecture, breaking by some accident, which I never observed, but thought my hat had been lost at sea. I entreated his imperial majesty to give orders it might be brought to me as soon as possible, describing to him the use and the nature of it: and the next day the waggoners arrived with it, but not in a very good condition; they had bored two holes in the brim, within an inch and half of the edge, and fastened two hooks in the holes; these hooks were tied by a long cord to the harness, and thus my hat was dragged along for above half an English mile; but, the ground in that country being extremely smooth and level, it received less damage than I expected.

Two days after this adventure, the emperor, having ordered that part of his army which quarters in and about his metropolis, to be in readiness, took a fancy of diverting himself in a very singular manner. He desired I would stand like a Colossus, with my legs as far asunder as I conveniently could. He then commanded his general (who was an old experienced leader, and a great patron of mine) to draw up the troops in close order, and march them under me; the foot by twenty-four abreast, and the horse by sixteen, with drums beating, colours flying, and pikes advanced. This body consisted of three thousand foot, and a thousand horse. His majesty gave orders, upon pain of death, that every soldier in his march should observe the strictest decency with regard to my person; which however could not prevent some of the younger officers from turning up their eyes as they passed under me: and, to confess the truth, my breeches were at that time in so ill a condition, that they afforded some opportunities for laughter and admiration.

I had sent so many memorials and petitions for my liberty, that his majesty at length mentioned the matter, first in the cabinet, and then in a full council; where it was opposed by none, except Skyresh Bolgolam, who was pleased, without any provocation, to be my mortal enemy. But it was carried against him by the whole board, and confirmed by the emperor. That minister was *galbet*, or admiral of the realm, very much in his master's confidence, and a person well versed in affairs, but of a morose and sour complexion. However, he was at length persuaded to comply; but prevailed that the articles and conditions upon which I should be set free, and to which I must swear, should be drawn up by himself. These articles were brought to me by Skyresh Bolgolam in person attended by two under-secretaries, and several persons of distinction. After they were read, I was demanded to swear to the performance of them; first in the manner of my own country, and afterwards in the method prescribed by their laws; which was, to hold my right foot in my left hand, and to place the middle finger of my right hand on the crown of my head, and my thumb on the tip of my right ear. But because the reader may be curious to have some idea of the style and manner of expression peculiar to that people, as well as to know the article upon which I recovered my liberty, I have made a translation of the whole instrument, word for word, as near as I was able, which I here offer to the public.

"Golbasto Momarem Evlame Gurdilo Shefin Mully Ully Gue, most mighty Emperor of Lilliput, delight and terror of the universe, whose dominions extend five thousand *blustrugs* (about twelve miles in circumference) to the extremities of the globe; monarch of all monarchs, taller than the sons of men; whose feet press down to the centre, and whose head strikes against the sun; at whose nod the princes of the earth shake their knees; pleasant as the spring, comfortable as the summer, fruitful as autumn, dreadful as winter: his most sublime majesty proposes to the man-mountain, lately arrived at our celestial dominions, the following articles, which, by a solemn oath, he shall be obliged to perform: –

"**1st**, *The man-mountain shall not depart from our dominions, without our license under our great seal.*

"**2nd**, *He shall not presume to come into our metropolis, without our express order; at which time, the inhabitants shall have two hours warning to keep within doors.*

"**3rd**, *The said man-mountain shall confine his walks to our principal high roads, and not offer to walk, or lie down, in a meadow or field of corn.*

"**4th**, *As he walks the said roads, he shall take the utmost care not to trample upon the bodies of any of our loving subjects, their horses, or carriages, nor take any of our subjects into his hands without their own consent.*

"**5th**, *If an express requires extraordinary despatch, the man-mountain shall be obliged to carry, in his pocket, the messenger and horse a six days journey, once in every moon, and return the said messenger back (if so required) safe to our imperial presence.*

"**6th**, *He shall be our ally against our enemies in the island of Blefuscu, and do his utmost to destroy their fleet, which is now preparing to invade us.*

"**7th**, *That the said man-mountain shall, at his times of leisure, be aiding and assisting to our workmen, in helping to raise certain great stones, towards covering the wall of the principal park, and other our royal buildings.*

"**8th**, *That the said man-mountain shall, in two moons' time, deliver in an exact survey of the circumference of our dominions, by a computation of his own paces round the coast.*

"**Lastly**, *That, upon his solemn oath to observe all the above articles, the said man-mountain shall have a daily allowance of meat and drink sufficient for the support of 1724 of our subjects, with free access to our royal person, and other marks of* *our favour. Given at our palace at Belfaborac, the twelfth day of the ninety-first moon of our reign."*

I swore and subscribed to these articles with great cheerfulness and content, although some of them were not so honourable as I could have wished; which proceeded wholly from the malice of Skyresh Bolgolam, the high-admiral: whereupon my chains were immediately unlocked, and I was at full liberty. The emperor himself, in person, did me the honour to be by at the whole ceremony. I made my acknowledgements by prostrating myself at his majesty's feet: but he commanded me to rise; and after many gracious expressions, which, to avoid the censure of vanity, I shall not repeat, he added, "that he hoped I should prove a useful servant, and well deserve all the favours he had already conferred upon me, or might do for the future."

The reader may please to observe, that, in the last article of the recovery of my liberty, the emperor stipulates to allow me a quantity of meat and drink sufficient for the support of 1724 Lilliputians. Some time after, asking a friend at court how they came to fix on that determinate number, he told me that his majesty's mathematicians, having taken the height of my body by the help of a quadrant, and finding it to exceed theirs in the proportion of twelve to one, they concluded from the similarity of their bodies, that mine must contain at least 1724 of theirs, and consequently would require as much food as was necessary to support that number of Lilliputians. By which the reader may conceive an idea of the ingenuity of that people, as well as the prudent and exact economy of so great a prince.

Chapter IV

THE FIRST REQUEST I made, after I had obtained my liberty, was, that I might have license to see Mildendo, the metropolis; which the emperor easily granted me, but with a special charge to do no hurt either to the inhabitants or their houses. The people had notice, by proclamation, of my design to visit the town. The wall which encompassed it is two feet and a half high, and at least eleven inches broad, so that a coach and horses may be driven very safely round it; and it is flanked with strong towers at ten feet distance. I stepped over the great western gate, and passed very gently, and sidling, through the two principal streets, only in my short waistcoat, for fear of damaging the roofs and eaves of the houses with the skirts of my coat.

I walked with the utmost circumspection, to avoid treading on any stragglers who might remain in the streets, although the orders were very strict, that all people should keep in their houses, at their own peril. The garret windows and tops of houses were so crowded with spectators, that I thought in all my travels I had not seen a more populous place. The city is an exact square, each side of the wall being five hundred feet long. The two great streets, which run across and divide it into four quarters, are five feet wide. The lanes and alleys, which I could not enter, but only view them as I passed, are from twelve to eighteen inches. The town is capable of holding five hundred thousand souls: the houses are from three to five stories: the shops and markets well provided.

The emperor's palace is in the centre of the city where the two great streets meet. It is enclosed by a wall of two feet high, and twenty feet distance from the buildings. I had his majesty's permission to step over this wall; and, the space being so wide between that and the palace, I could easily view it on every side. The outward court is a square of forty feet, and includes two other courts: in the inmost are the royal apartments, which I was very desirous to see, but found it extremely difficult; for the great gates, from one square into another, were but eighteen inches high, and seven inches wide. Now the buildings of the outer court were at least five feet high, and it was impossible for me to stride over them without infinite damage to the pile, though the walls were strongly built of hewn stone, and four inches thick. At the same time the emperor had a great desire that I should see the magnificence of his palace; but this I was not able to do till three days after, which I spent in cutting down with my knife some of the largest trees in the royal park, about a hundred yards distant from the city. Of these trees I made two stools, each about three feet high, and strong enough to bear my weight.

The people having received notice a second time, I went again through the city to the palace with my two stools in my hands. When I came to the side of the outer court, I stood upon one stool, and took the other in my hand; this I lifted over the roof, and gently set it down on the space between the first and second court, which was eight feet wide. I then stept over the building very conveniently from one stool to the other, and drew up the first after me with a hooked stick. By this contrivance I got into the inmost court; and, lying down upon my side, I applied my face to the windows of the middle stories, which were left open on purpose, and discovered the most splendid apartments that can be imagined. There I saw the empress and the young princes, in their several lodgings, with their chief attendants about them. Her imperial majesty was pleased to smile very graciously upon me, and gave me out of the window her hand to kiss.

But I shall not anticipate the reader with further descriptions of this kind, because I reserve them for a greater work, which is now almost ready for the press; containing a general description of this empire, from its first erection, through along series of princes; with a particular account of their wars and politics, laws, learning, and religion; their plants and animals; their peculiar manners and customs, with other matters very curious and useful; my chief design at present being only to relate such events and transactions as happened to the public or to myself during a residence of about nine months in that empire.

One morning, about a fortnight after I had obtained my liberty, Reldresal, principal secretary (as they style him) for private affairs, came to my house attended only by one servant. He ordered his coach to wait at a distance, and desired I would give him an hours audience; which I readily consented to, on account of his quality and personal merits, as well as of the many good offices he had done me during my solicitations at court. I offered to lie down that he might the more conveniently reach my ear, but he chose rather to let me hold him in my hand during our conversation.

He began with compliments on my liberty; said "he might pretend to some merit in it;" but, however, added, "that if it had not been for the present situation of things at court, perhaps I might not have obtained it so soon. For," said he, "as flourishing a condition as we may appear to be in to foreigners, we labour under two mighty evils: a violent faction at home, and the danger of an invasion, by a most potent enemy, from abroad. As to the first, you are to understand, that for about seventy moons past there have been two struggling parties in this empire, under the names of *Tramecksan* and *Slamecksan*, from the high and low heels of their shoes, by which they distinguish themselves. It is alleged, indeed, that the high heels are most agreeable to our ancient constitution;

but, however this be, his majesty has determined to make use only of low heels in the administration of the government, and all offices in the gift of the crown, as you cannot but observe; and particularly that his majesty's imperial heels are lower at least by a *drurr* than any of his court (*drurr* is a measure about the fourteenth part of an inch). The animosities between these two parties run so high, that they will neither eat, nor drink, nor talk with each other. We compute the *Tramecksan*, or high heels, to exceed us in number; but the power is wholly on our side.

We apprehend his imperial highness, the heir to the crown, to have some tendency towards the high heels; at least we can plainly discover that one of his heels is higher than the other, which gives him a hobble in his gait. Now, in the midst of these intestine disquiets, we are threatened with an invasion from the island of Blefuscu, which is the other great empire of the universe, almost as large and powerful as this of his majesty. For as to what we have heard you affirm, that there are other kingdoms and states in the world inhabited by human creatures as large as yourself, our philosophers are in much doubt, and would rather conjecture that you dropped from the moon, or one of the stars; because it is certain, that a hundred mortals of your bulk would in a short time destroy all the fruits and cattle of his majesty's dominions: besides, our histories of six thousand moons make no mention of any other regions than the two great empires of Lilliput and Blefuscu. Which two mighty powers have, as I was going to tell you, been engaged in a most obstinate war for six-and-thirty moons past. It began upon the following occasion.

It is allowed on all hands, that the primitive way of breaking eggs, before we eat them, was upon the larger end; but his present majesty's grandfather, while he was a boy, going to eat an egg, and breaking it according to the ancient practice, happened to cut one of his fingers. Whereupon the emperor his father published an edict, commanding all his subjects, upon great penalties, to break the smaller end of their eggs. The people so highly resented this law, that our histories tell us, there have been six rebellions raised on that account; wherein one emperor lost his life, and another his crown. These civil commotions were constantly fomented by the monarchs of Blefuscu; and when they were quelled, the exiles always fled for refuge to that empire. It is computed that eleven thousand persons have at several times suffered death, rather than submit to break their eggs at the smaller end. Many hundred large volumes have been published upon this controversy: but the books of the Big-endians have been long forbidden, and the whole party rendered incapable by law of holding employments.

During the course of these troubles, the emperors of Blefusca did frequently expostulate by their ambassadors, accusing us of making a schism in religion, by offending against a fundamental doctrine of our great prophet Lustrog, in the fifty-fourth chapter of the Blundecral (which is their Alcoran). This, however, is thought to be a mere strain upon the text; for the words are these: 'that all true believers break their eggs at the convenient end.' And which is the convenient end, seems, in my humble opinion to be left to every man's conscience, or at least in the power of the chief magistrate to determine. Now, the Big-endian exiles have found so much credit in the emperor of Blefuscu's court, and so much private assistance and encouragement from their party here at home, that a bloody war has been carried on between the two empires for six-and-thirty moons, with various success; during which time we have lost forty capital ships, and a much a greater number of smaller vessels, together with thirty thousand of our best seamen and soldiers; and the damage received by the enemy is reckoned to be somewhat greater than ours. However, they have now equipped a numerous fleet, and are just preparing to make a descent upon us; and his imperial majesty, placing great confidence in your valour and strength, has commanded me to lay this account of his affairs before you."

I desired the secretary to present my humble duty to the emperor; and to let him know, "that I thought it would not become me, who was a foreigner, to interfere with parties; but I was ready, with the hazard of my life, to defend his person and state against all invaders."

Chapter V

THE EMPIRE of Blefuscu is an island situated to the north-east of Lilliput, from which it is parted only by a channel of eight hundred yards wide. I had not yet seen it, and upon this notice of an intended invasion, I avoided appearing on that side of the coast, for fear of being discovered, by some of the enemy's ships, who had received no intelligence of me; all intercourse between the two empires having been strictly forbidden during the war, upon pain of death, and an embargo laid by our emperor upon all vessels whatsoever. I communicated to his majesty a project I had formed of seizing the enemy's whole fleet; which, as our scouts assured us, lay at anchor in the harbour, ready to sail with the first fair wind. I consulted the most experienced seamen upon the depth of the channel, which they had often plumbed; who told me, that in the middle, at high-water, it was seventy *glumgluffs* deep, which is about six feet of European measure; and the rest of it fifty *glumgluffs* at most.

I walked towards the north-east coast, over against Blefuscu, where, lying down behind a hillock, I took out my small perspective glass, and viewed the enemy's fleet at anchor, consisting of about fifty men of war, and a great number of transports: I then came back to my house, and gave orders (for which I had a warrant) for a great quantity of the strongest cable and bars of iron. The cable was about as thick as packthread and the bars of the length and size of a knitting-needle. I trebled the cable to make it stronger, and for the same reason I twisted three of the iron bars together, bending the extremities into a hook.

Having thus fixed fifty hooks to as many cables, I went back to the north-east coast, and putting off my coat, shoes, and stockings, walked into the sea, in my leathern jerkin, about half an hour before high water. I waded with what haste I could, and swam in the middle about thirty yards, till I felt ground. I arrived at the fleet in less than half an hour. The enemy was so frightened when they saw me, that they leaped out of their ships, and swam to shore, where there could not be fewer than thirty thousand souls. I then took my tackling, and, fastening a hook to the hole at the prow of each, I tied all the cords together at the end. While I was thus employed, the enemy discharged several thousand arrows, many of which stuck in my hands and face, and, beside the excessive smart, gave me much disturbance in my work. My greatest apprehension was for mine eyes, which I should have infallibly lost, if I had not suddenly thought of an expedient. I kept, among other little necessaries, a pair of spectacles in a private pocket, which, as I observed before, had escaped the emperor's searchers. These I took out and fastened as strongly as I could upon my nose, and thus armed, went on boldly with my work, in spite of the enemy's arrows, many of which struck against the glasses of my spectacles, but without any other effect, further than a little to discompose them.

I had now fastened all the hooks, and, taking the knot in my hand, began to pull; but not a ship would stir, for they were all too fast held by their anchors, so that the boldest part of my enterprise remained. I therefore let go the cord, and leaving the looks fixed to the ships, I resolutely cut with my knife the cables that fastened the anchors, receiving about two hundred shots in my face and hands; then I took up the knotted end of the cables, to which my hooks were tied, and with great ease drew fifty of the enemy's largest men of war after me.

The Blefuscudians, who had not the least imagination of what I intended, were at first confounded with astonishment. They had seen me cut the cables, and thought my design was only to let the ships run adrift or fall foul on each other: but when they perceived the whole fleet moving in order, and saw me pulling at the end, they set up such a scream of grief and despair as it is almost impossible to describe or conceive. When I had got out of danger, I stopped awhile to pick out the arrows that stuck in my hands and face; and rubbed on some of the same ointment that was given me at my first arrival, as I have formerly mentioned. I then took off my spectacles, and waiting about an hour, till the tide was a little fallen, I waded through the middle with my cargo, and arrived safe at the royal port of Lilliput.

The emperor and his whole court stood on the shore, expecting the issue of this great adventure. They saw the ships move forward in a large half-moon, but could not discern me, who was up to my breast in water. When I advanced to the middle of the channel, they were yet more in pain, because I was under water to my neck. The emperor concluded me to be drowned, and that the enemy's fleet was approaching in a hostile manner: but he was soon eased of his fears; for the channel growing shallower every step I made, I came in a short time within hearing, and holding up the end of the cable, by which the fleet was fastened, I cried in a loud voice, "Long live the most puissant king of Lilliput!" This great prince received me at my landing with all possible encomiums, and created me a *nardac* upon the spot, which is the highest title of honour among them.

His majesty desired I would take some other opportunity of bringing all the rest of his enemy's ships into his ports. And so unmeasureable is the ambition of princes, that he seemed to think of nothing less than reducing the whole empire of Blefuscu into a province, and governing it, by a viceroy; of destroying the Big-endian exiles, and compelling that people to break the smaller end of their eggs, by which he would remain the sole monarch of the whole world. But I endeavoured to divert him from this design, by many arguments drawn from the topics of policy as well as justice; and I plainly protested, "that I would never be an instrument of bringing a free and brave people into slavery." And, when the matter was debated in council, the wisest part of the ministry were of my opinion.

This open bold declaration of mine was so opposite to the schemes and politics of his imperial majesty, that he could never forgive me. He mentioned it in a very artful manner at council, where I was told that some of the wisest appeared, at least by their silence, to be of my opinion; but others, who were my secret enemies, could not forbear some expressions which, by a side-wind, reflected on me. And from this time began an intrigue between his majesty and a junto of ministers, maliciously bent against me, which broke out in less than two months, and had like to have ended in my utter destruction. Of so little weight are the greatest services to princes, when put into the balance with a refusal to gratify their passions.

About three weeks after this exploit, there arrived a solemn embassy from Blefuscu, with humble offers of a peace, which was soon concluded, upon conditions very advantageous to our emperor, wherewith I shall not trouble the reader. There were six ambassadors, with a train of about five hundred persons, and their entry was very magnificent, suitable to the grandeur of their master, and the importance of their business. When their treaty was finished, wherein I did them several good offices by the credit I now had, or at least appeared to have, at court, their excellencies, who were privately told how much I had been their friend, made me a visit in form. They began with many compliments upon my valour and generosity, invited me to that kingdom in the emperor their master's name, and desired me to show them some proofs of my prodigious strength, of which they had heard so many wonders; wherein I readily obliged them, but shall not trouble the reader with the particulars.

When I had for some time entertained their excellencies, to their infinite satisfaction and surprise, I desired they would do me the honour to present my most humble respects to the emperor their master, the renown of whose virtues had so justly filled the whole world with admiration, and whose royal person I resolved to attend, before I returned to my own country. Accordingly, the next time I had the honour to see our emperor, I desired his general license to wait on the Blefuscudian monarch, which he was pleased to grant me, as I could perceive, in a very cold manner; but could not guess the reason, till I had a whisper from a certain person, "that Flimnap and Bolgolam had represented my intercourse with those ambassadors as a mark of disaffection;" from which I am sure my heart was wholly free. And this was the first time I began to conceive some imperfect idea of courts and ministers.

It is to be observed, that these ambassadors spoke to me, by an interpreter, the languages of both empires differing as much from each other as any two in Europe, and each nation priding itself upon the antiquity, beauty, and energy of their own tongue, with an avowed contempt for that of their neighbour; yet our emperor, standing upon the advantage he had got by the seizure of their fleet, obliged them to deliver their credentials, and make their speech, in the Lilliputian tongue. And it must be confessed, that from the great intercourse of trade and commerce between both realms, from the continual reception of exiles which is mutual among them, and from the custom, in each empire, to send their young nobility and richer gentry to the other, in order to polish themselves by seeing the world, and understanding men and manners; there are few persons of distinction, or merchants, or seamen, who dwell in the maritime parts, but what can hold conversation in both tongues; as I found some weeks after, when I went to pay my respects to the emperor of Blefuscu, which, in the midst of great misfortunes, through the malice of my enemies, proved a very happy adventure to me, as I shall relate in its proper place.

The reader may remember, that when I signed those articles upon which I recovered my liberty, there were some which I disliked, upon account of their being too servile; neither could anything but an extreme necessity have forced me to submit. But being now a *nardac* of the highest rank in that empire, such offices were looked upon as below my dignity, and the emperor (to do him justice), never once mentioned them to me. However, it was not long before I had an opportunity of doing his majesty, at least as I then thought, a most signal service. I was alarmed at midnight with the cries of many hundred people at my door; by which, being suddenly awaked, I was in some kind of terror. I heard the word *Burglum* repeated incessantly: several of the emperor's court, making their way through the crowd, entreated me to come immediately to the palace, where her imperial majesty's apartment was on fire, by the carelessness of a maid of honour, who fell asleep while she was reading a romance.

I got up in an instant; and orders being given to clear the way before me, and it being likewise a moonshine night, I made a shift to get to the palace without trampling on any of the people. I found they had already applied ladders to the walls of the apartment, and were well provided with buckets, but the water was at some distance. These buckets were about the size of large thimbles, and the poor people supplied me with them as fast as they could: but the flame was so violent that they did little good. I might easily have stifled it with my coat, which I unfortunately left behind me for haste, and came away only in my leathern jerkin.

The case seemed wholly desperate and deplorable; and this magnificent palace would have infallibly been burnt down to the ground, if, by a presence of mind unusual to me, I had not suddenly thought of an expedient. I had, the evening before, drunk plentifully of a most delicious wine called *glimigrim*, (the Blefuscudians call it *flunec*, but ours is esteemed the better sort,) which is very diuretic. By the luckiest chance in the world, I had not discharged myself of any part of it. The heat I had contracted by coming very near the flames, and by labouring to quench them, made the wine begin to operate by urine; which I voided in such a quantity, and applied so well to the proper places, that in three minutes the fire was wholly extinguished, and the rest of that noble pile, which had cost so many ages in erecting, preserved from destruction.

It was now day-light, and I returned to my house without waiting to congratulate with the emperor: because, although I had done a very eminent piece of service, yet I could not tell how his majesty might resent the manner by which I had performed it: for, by the fundamental laws of the realm, it is capital in any person, of what quality soever, to make water within the precincts of the palace. But I was a little comforted by a message from his majesty, "that he would give orders to the grand justiciary for passing my pardon in form:" which, however, I could not obtain; and I was privately assured, "that the empress, conceiving the greatest abhorrence of what I had done, removed to the most distant side of the court, firmly resolved that those buildings should never be repaired for her use: and, in the presence of her chief confidents could not forbear vowing revenge."

Chapter VI

ALTHOUGH I INTEND to leave the description of this empire to a particular treatise, yet, in the mean time, I am content to gratify the curious reader with some general ideas. As the common size of the natives is somewhat under six inches high, so there is an exact proportion in all other animals, as well as plants and trees: for instance, the tallest horses and oxen are between four and five inches in height, the sheep an inch and half, more or less: their geese about the bigness of a sparrow, and so the several gradations downwards till you come to the smallest, which to my sight, were almost invisible; but nature has adapted the eyes of the Lilliputians to all objects proper for their view: they see with great exactness, but at no great distance.

And, to show the sharpness of their sight towards objects that are near, I have been much pleased with observing a cook pulling a lark, which was not so large as a common fly; and a young girl threading an invisible needle with invisible silk. Their tallest trees are about seven feet high: I mean some of those in the great royal park, the tops whereof I could but just reach with my fist clenched. The other vegetables are in the same proportion; but this I leave to the reader's imagination.

I shall say but little at present of their learning, which, for many ages, has flourished in all its branches among them: but their manner of writing is very peculiar, being neither from the left to the right, like the Europeans, nor from the right to the left, like the Arabians, nor from up to down, like the Chinese, but aslant, from one corner of the paper to the other, like ladies in England.

They bury their dead with their heads directly downward, because they hold an opinion, that in eleven thousand moons they are all to rise again; in which period the earth (which they conceive to be flat) will turn upside down, and by this means they shall, at their resurrection, be found ready standing on their feet. The learned among them confess the absurdity of this doctrine; but the practice still continues, in compliance to the vulgar.

There are some laws and customs in this empire very peculiar; and if they were not so directly contrary to those of my own dear country, I should be tempted to say a little in their justification. It is only to be wished they were as well executed. The first I shall mention, relates to informers. All crimes against the state, are punished here with the utmost severity; but, if the person accused makes his innocence plainly to appear upon his trial, the accuser is immediately put to an ignominious death; and out of his goods or lands the innocent person is quadruply recompensed for the loss of his time, for the danger he underwent, for the hardship of his imprisonment, and for all the charges he has been at in making his defence; or, if that fund be deficient, it is largely supplied by the crown. The emperor also confers on him some public mark of his favour, and proclamation is made of his innocence through the whole city.

They look upon fraud as a greater crime than theft, and therefore seldom fail to punish it with death; for they allege, that care and vigilance, with a very common understanding, may preserve a man's goods from thieves, but honesty has no defence against superior cunning; and, since it is necessary that there should be a perpetual intercourse of buying and selling, and dealing upon credit, where fraud is permitted and connived at, or has no law to punish it, the honest dealer is always undone, and the knave gets the advantage. I remember, when I was once interceding with the emperor for a criminal who had wronged his master of a great sum of money, which he had received by order and ran away with; and happening to tell his majesty, by way of extenuation, that it was only a breach of trust, the emperor thought it monstrous in me to offer as a defence the greatest aggravation of the crime; and truly I had little to say in return, farther than the common answer, that different nations had different customs; for, I confess, I was heartily ashamed **(footnote 2)**.

Although we usually call reward and punishment the two hinges upon which all government turns, yet I could never observe this maxim to be put in practice by any nation except that of Lilliput. Whoever can there bring sufficient proof, that he has strictly observed the laws of his country for seventy-three moons, has a claim to certain privileges, according to his quality or condition of life, with a proportionable sum of money out of a fund appropriated for that use: he likewise acquires the title of *snilpall*, or legal, which is added to his name, but does not descend to his posterity. And these people thought it a prodigious defect of policy among us, when I told them that our laws were enforced only by penalties, without any mention of reward. It is upon this account that the image of Justice, in their courts of judicature, is formed with six eyes, two before, as many behind, and on each side one, to signify circumspection; with a bag of gold open in her right hand, and a sword sheathed in her left, to show she is more disposed to reward than to punish.

In choosing persons for all employments, they have more regard to good morals than to great abilities; for, since government is necessary to mankind, they believe, that the common size of human understanding is fitted to some station or other; and that Providence never intended to make the management of public affairs a mystery to be comprehended only by a few persons of sublime genius, of which there seldom are three born in an age: but they suppose truth, justice, temperance, and the like, to be in every man's power; the practice of which virtues, assisted by experience and a good intention, would qualify any man for the service of his country, except where a course of study is required. But they thought the want of moral virtues was so far from being supplied by superior endowments of the mind, that employments could never be put into such dangerous hands as those of persons so qualified; and, at least, that the mistakes committed by ignorance, in a virtuous disposition, would never be of such fatal consequence to the public weal, as the practices of a man, whose inclinations led him to be corrupt, and who had great abilities to manage, to multiply, and defend his corruptions.

In like manner, the disbelief of a Divine Providence renders a man incapable of holding any public station; for, since kings avow themselves to be the deputies of Providence, the Lilliputians think nothing can be more absurd than for a prince to employ such men as disown the authority under which he acts.

In relating these and the following laws, I would only be understood to mean the original institutions, and not the most scandalous corruptions, into which these people are fallen by the degenerate nature of man. For, as to that infamous practice of acquiring great employments by dancing on the ropes, or badges of favour and distinction by leaping over sticks and creeping under them, the reader is to observe, that they were first introduced by the grandfather of the emperor now reigning, and grew to the present height by the gradual increase of party and faction.

Ingratitude is among them a capital crime, as we read it to have been in some other countries: for they reason thus; that whoever makes ill returns to his benefactor, must needs be a common enemy to the rest of mankind, from whom he has received no obligation, and therefore such a man is not fit to live.

Their notions relating to the duties of parents and children differ extremely from ours. For, since the conjunction of male and female is founded upon the great law of nature, in order to propagate and continue the species, the Lilliputians will needs have it, that men and women are joined together, like other animals, by the motives of concupiscence; and that their tenderness towards their young proceeds from the like natural principle: for which reason they will never allow that a child is under any obligation to his father for begetting him, or to his mother for bringing him into the world; which, considering the miseries of human life, was neither a benefit in itself, nor intended so by his parents, whose thoughts, in their love encounters, were otherwise employed. Upon these, and the like reasonings, their opinion is, that parents are the last of all others to be trusted with the education of their own children; and therefore they have in every town public nurseries, where all parents, except cottagers and labourers, are obliged to send their infants of both sexes to be reared and educated, when they come to the age of twenty moons, at which time they are supposed to have some rudiments of docility. These schools are of several kinds, suited to different qualities, and both sexes. They have certain professors well skilled in preparing children for such a condition of life as befits the rank of their parents, and their own capacities, as well as inclinations. I shall first say something of the male nurseries, and then of the female.

The nurseries for males of noble or eminent birth, are provided with grave and learned professors, and their several deputies. The clothes and food of the children are plain and simple. They are bred up in the principles of honour, justice, courage, modesty, clemency, religion, and love of their country; they are always employed in some business, except in the times of eating and sleeping, which are very short, and two hours for diversions consisting of bodily exercises. They are dressed by men till four years of age, and then are obliged to dress themselves, although their quality be ever so great; and the women attendant, who are aged proportionably to ours at fifty, perform only the most menial offices. They are never suffered to converse with servants, but go together in smaller or greater numbers to take their diversions, and always in the presence of a professor, or one of his deputies; whereby they avoid those early bad impressions of folly and vice, to which our children are subject. Their parents are suffered to see them only twice a year; the visit is to last but an hour; they are allowed to kiss the child at meeting and parting; but a professor, who always stands by on those occasions, will not suffer them to whisper, or use any fondling expressions, or bring any presents of toys, sweetmeats, and the like.

The pension from each family for the education and entertainment of a child, upon failure of due payment, is levied by the emperor's officers.

The nurseries for children of ordinary gentlemen, merchants, traders, and handicrafts, are managed proportionably after the same manner; only those designed for trades are put out apprentices at eleven years old, whereas those of persons of quality continue in their exercises till fifteen, which answers to twenty-one with us: but the confinement is gradually lessened for the last three years.

In the female nurseries, the young girls of quality are educated much like the males, only they are dressed by orderly servants of their own sex; but always in the presence of a professor or deputy, till they come to dress themselves, which is at five years old. And if it be found that these nurses ever presume to entertain the girls with frightful or foolish stories, or the common follies practised by chambermaids among us, they are publicly whipped thrice about the city, imprisoned for a year, and banished for life to the most desolate part of the country. Thus the young ladies are as much ashamed of being cowards and fools as the men, and despise all personal ornaments, beyond decency and cleanliness: neither did I perceive any difference in their education made by their difference of sex, only that the exercises of the females were not altogether so robust; and that some rules were given them relating to domestic life, and a smaller compass of learning was enjoined them: for their maxim is, that among peoples of quality, a wife should be always a reasonable and agreeable companion, because she cannot always be young. When the girls are twelve years old, which among them is the marriageable age, their parents or guardians take them home, with great expressions of gratitude to the professors, and seldom without tears of the young lady and her companions.

In the nurseries of females of the meaner sort, the children are instructed in all kinds of works proper for their sex, and their several degrees: those intended for apprentices are dismissed at seven years old, the rest are kept to eleven.

The meaner families who have children at these nurseries, are obliged, besides their annual pension, which is as low as possible, to return to the steward of the nursery a small monthly share of their gettings, to be a portion for the child; and therefore all parents are limited in their expenses by the law. For the Lilliputians think nothing can be more unjust, than for people, in subservience to their own appetites, to bring children into the world, and leave the burthen of supporting them on the public. As to persons of quality, they give security to appropriate a certain sum for each child, suitable to their condition; and these funds are always managed with good husbandry and the most exact justice.

The cottagers and labourers keep their children at home, their business being only to till and cultivate the earth, and therefore their education is of little consequence to the public: but the old and diseased among them, are supported by hospitals; for begging is a trade unknown in this empire.

And here it may, perhaps, divert the curious reader, to give some account of my domestics, and my manner of living in this country, during a residence of nine months, and thirteen days. Having a head mechanically turned, and being likewise forced by necessity, I had made for myself a table and chair convenient enough, out of the largest trees in the royal park. Two hundred sempstresses were employed to make me shirts, and linen for my bed and table, all of the strongest and coarsest kind they could get; which, however, they were forced to quilt together in several folds, for the thickest was some degrees finer than lawn. Their linen is usually three inches wide, and three feet make a piece. The sempstresses took my measure as I lay on the ground, one standing at my neck, and another at my mid-leg, with a strong cord extended, that each held by the end, while a third measured the length of the cord with a rule of an inch long. Then they measured my right thumb, and desired no more; for by a mathematical computation, that twice round the thumb is once round the wrist, and so on to the neck and the waist, and by the help of my old shirt, which I displayed on the ground before them for a pattern, they fitted me exactly.

Three hundred tailors were employed in the same manner to make me clothes; but they had another contrivance for taking my measure. I kneeled down, and they raised a ladder from the ground to my neck; upon this ladder one of them mounted, and let fall a plumb-line from my collar to the floor, which just answered the length of my coat: but my waist and arms I measured myself. When my clothes were finished, which was done in my house (for the largest of theirs would not have been able to hold them), they looked like the patch-work made by the ladies in England, only that mine were all of a colour.

I had three hundred cooks to dress my victuals, in little convenient huts built about my house, where they and their families lived, and prepared me two dishes a-piece. I took up twenty waiters in my hand, and placed them on the table: a hundred more attended below on the ground, some with dishes of meat, and some with barrels of wine and other liquors slung on their shoulders; all which the waiters above drew up, as I wanted, in a very ingenious manner, by certain cords, as we draw the bucket up a well in Europe. A dish of their meat was a good mouthful, and a barrel of their liquor a reasonable draught. Their mutton yields to ours, but their beef is excellent. I have had a sirloin so large, that I have been forced to make three bites of it; but this is rare. My servants were astonished to see me eat it, bones and all, as in our country we do the leg of a lark. Their geese and turkeys I usually ate at a mouthful, and I confess hey far exceed ours. Of their smaller fowl I could take up twenty or thirty at the end of my knife.

One day his imperial majesty, being informed of my way of living, desired "that himself and his royal consort, with the young princes of the blood of both sexes, might have the happiness," as he was pleased to call it, "of dining with me." They came accordingly, and I placed them in chairs of state, upon my table, just over against me, with their guards about them. Flimnap, the lord high treasurer, attended there likewise with his white staff; and I observed he often looked on me with a sour countenance, which I would not seem to regard, but ate more than usual, in honour to my dear country, as well as to fill the court with admiration. I have some private reasons to believe, that this visit from his majesty gave Flimnap an opportunity of doing me ill offices to his master. That minister had always been my secret enemy, though he outwardly caressed me more than was usual to the moroseness of his nature. He represented to the emperor "the low condition of his treasury; that he was forced to take up money at a great discount; that exchequer bills would not circulate under nine per cent. below par; that I had cost his majesty above a million and a half of *sprugs*" (their greatest gold coin, about the bigness of a spangle) "and, upon the whole, that it would be advisable in the emperor to take the first fair occasion of dismissing me."

I am here obliged to vindicate the reputation of an excellent lady, who was an innocent sufferer upon my account. The treasurer took a fancy to be jealous of his wife, from the malice of some evil tongues, who informed him that her grace had taken a violent affection for my person; and the court scandal ran for some time, that she once came privately to my lodging. This I solemnly declare to be a most infamous falsehood, without any grounds, further than that her grace was pleased to treat me with all innocent marks of freedom and friendship. I own she came often to my house, but always publicly, nor ever without three more in the coach, who were usually her sister and young daughter, and some particular acquaintance; but this was common to many other ladies of the court. And I still appeal to my servants round, whether they at any time saw a coach at my door, without knowing what persons were in it.

On those occasions, when a servant had given me notice, my custom was to go immediately to the door, and, after paying my respects, to take up the coach and two horses very carefully in my hands (for, if there were six horses, the postillion always unharnessed four,) and place them on a table, where I had fixed a movable rim quite round, of five inches high, to prevent accidents. And I have often had four coaches and horses at once on my table, full of company, while I sat in my chair, leaning my face towards them; and when I was engaged with one set, the coachmen would gently drive the others round my table. I have passed many an afternoon very agreeably in these conversations. But I defy the treasurer, or his two informers (I will name them, and let them make the best of it) Clustril and Drunlo, to prove that any person ever came to me *incognito*, except the secretary Reldresal, who was sent by express command of his imperial majesty, as I have before related.

I should not have dwelt so long upon this particular, if it had not been a point wherein the reputation of a great lady is so nearly concerned, to say nothing of my own; though I then had the honour to be a *nardac*, which the treasurer himself is not; for all the world knows, that he is only a *glumglum*, a title inferior by one degree, as that of a marquis is to a duke in England; yet I allow he preceded me in right of his post. These false informations, which I afterwards came to the knowledge of by an accident not proper to mention, made the treasurer show his lady for some time an ill countenance, and me a worse; and although he was at last undeceived and reconciled to her, yet I lost all credit with him, and found my interest decline very fast with the emperor himself, who was, indeed, too much governed by that favourite.

Footnote 2. An act of parliament has been since passed by which some breaches of trust have been made capital.

The complete and unabridged text is available online, from *flametreepublishing.com/extras*

The Sign in the Moonlight

David Tallerman

YOU WILL HAVE HEARD, no doubt, of the Bergenssen expedition – if only from the manner of its loss. For a short while, that tragedy was deemed significant and remarkable enough to adorn the covers of every major newspaper in the civilised world.

At the time I was in no position to follow such matters. However, in subsequent months I've tracked down many journals from that period. As I write, I can look up at the wall to see a cover of the *New York Times* I've pinned there, dated nineteenth of May 1908, bearing the headline, 'Horror in the Himalayas: Bergenssen five reported lost in avalanche.'

In a sense, I suppose, it's a spirit of morbidity that draws me back to those days upon the mountain and their awful finale, which I failed to witness only by the purest chance. Equally, there's a macabre humour in the thought that to almost all the world I am dead, my body shattered and frozen in the depths of some crevasse. But what draws me most, I think, is the memory of what I saw after I left Bergenssen and the others – that knowledge which is mine uniquely. It's without disrespect to the *Times* that I say they know nothing, nothing whatsoever, of the horror of Mount Kangchenjunga. Likely, there is no one else alive who does.

No rival can rightly be offended when I say that Bergenssen was the finest mountaineer of his generation. No other but that fierce and hardy Swede would have considered an expedition upon Kangchenjunga after the dramatic failure of the first attempt, and the very suspect circumstances of that failure.

I recollect clearly how we spoke of the matter when he first proposed the climb to me. Coincidence had brought us together in a London gentleman's club that I favoured whenever I was in the city on business. His tone was scathing as he cried, "Aleister Crowley, that self-publicising fool? The man's as much a mountaineer as I am Henry Ford."

"You can't deny that Dr. Jacot-Guillarmod knows his business."

"Pah! I'll deny what I like. I doubt if they ever left Darjeeling."

"Then how do you explain the death of Alexis Pache and those three porters?"

Bergenssen furrowed his brows. "Must I explain it? Perhaps what they say about Crowley is true. Perhaps those unfortunates were sacrificed to whatever ghoulish spirits the man had devoted himself to that week. More likely, he plied Pache with alcohol, drugs, or some yet darker vice and the man remained in India to indulge himself. Even if it's true, a better climber would have known the warning signs of an avalanche and avoided it accordingly."

With retrospect, those words seem bitter with irony, but at the time, I was caught up by the Swede's immense self-confidence and courage, which were as infectious as any cold. "Then you really think it's possible? Freshfield and Sella confirmed the findings of the Great Trigonometric Survey – it truly is the third-highest peak on Earth. It would be a grand achievement."

"I believe there's nothing to be lost in the trying."

"Nothing except our lives."

"Well, of course." He grinned, baring perfectly even white teeth. "So are you with me?"

I was violently tempted to agree on the spot. Instead, I prevaricated, knowing in my heart that I was little more than a hobbyist and, in the final analysis, not fitted to such a venture. Bergenssen's dream was a marvellous one, but outside the smoky environs of the club it would evaporate and, though I might think of our conversation with a certain wistfulness, that would soon pass.

I was wrong. That month brought both personal and business misfortunes and, with each fresh trial, my mind called back to Bergenssen and to misty, snow-clad vistas. By the end of February, almost in despair, I wrote a brief note and mailed it immediately. If the offer still stood, then I was in.

Bergenssen's reply came three weeks later, by telegram to my offices. Aside from the date, time and place for our rendezvous it bore only a simple message:

GOOD TO HAVE YOU SIR.

* * *

I won't trouble the reader with facts that can be gleaned elsewhere, and which have no bearing upon the substance of my tale. The details of our preparation are common knowledge, and the names of our three companions may be found from many sources, not least the May obituaries.

Bergenssen – somewhat contradicting his earlier comments to me – thought it wise to follow the route established by Crowley and Jacot-Guillarmod, and if we didn't all agree with his logic then there was no question of debate. He was our leader absolutely, and no one would have suggested the excursion become a democracy.

Therefore, after much prevarication on the part of the local authorities, we began in India, and approached our objective via the Singalila Ridge in West Bengal. From Ghum, we trekked through Jorpakri, Tongly, Sandakphu and Falut, in an unremitting downpour of the most torrential rain I've known.

There's little else to tell of those days, except that Bergenssen travelled under something of a funk, which in turn infected the rest of our party, even down to our squadron of porters. He avoided any questions as to what had put him out of sorts, and so I took it for a mood of grim determination, or perhaps mere consequence of the abysmal weather, leaches, and other hardships.

In any case, we made good progress. We proceeded in short order through Gamotang, whence the work of mountaineering began in earnest, and on through successive camps until – late of an afternoon, with violet hints already softening the robust blue of the Himalayan sky – we came upon camp five.

In my mind's eye I'd expected some place remarkable, befitting the violence that had occurred nearby. In fact, it was nondescript, nothing more than a small mound nestled in the shadow of one minor peak. Strangely, this disappointment didn't so much mitigate my sense of nervous excitement as increase it – as though I'd unconsciously decided to seek elsewhere for the tragic drama the scenery failed to provide.

We were all of us very quiet, however, and Bergenssen seemed practically catatonic, having said not a word all through the afternoon. By the time we'd pitched our tents and retired, the sky was a dark and livid purple that made the snow seem almost black, and my excitement had risen nearly to fever pitch – though I still couldn't say why, or what might possibly relieve it.

Rather than settle down to sleep, I sought out Bergenssen, and was pleased to find him in better cheer than he'd been throughout the day. Without to-do, I said, "This is the point where the Crowley expedition floundered, isn't it? Do you think we're in any danger?"

"If Crowley's to be believed then no, none whatsoever. He blamed the matter entirely on Tartarin and Righi's incompetence, as I'm sure you know."

I detected a note in Bergenssen's tone. "And if he *isn't* to be believed?"

"Well...it's all very strange, you know." He lapsed into silence, and for a while it seemed this cryptic statement would be his last word on the matter. Finally, he continued, "One newspaper claimed that he heard their screams but chose to stay in his tent, drinking tea rather than hurrying to their aid. There was a quote I memorised: 'A mountain accident of this sort is one of the things for which I have no sympathy whatever,' he said. Can you believe that?"

"If there's anything in the rumours about him, I can. They refer to him in certain circles as 'the wickedest man in Britain'. Do you really think it's strange that he'd let his fellows go to their deaths unaided?"

"That? No, that isn't it."

There followed another long pause. These silences unsettled me more than anything because they were so out of keeping with Bergenssen's characteristic bluster. What he eventually said, however, was nearly as unexpected. "You know, I suppose, what Kangchenjunga means?"

I'd passed a few hours in research before we set out. "The Five Treasures of Snows... the natives associate the five peaks with the five repositories of their god."

"Did you know that Crowley claimed the porters were willing to continue – the next morning, that is, after the accident? He said they told him that the spirits of the mountain had been propitiated. One death for every peak."

"But every account reports only four deaths, those of Pache and three of the porters."

Bergenssen looked away, to stare distractedly at the wall of the tent. "Yes. I know."

I sensed that his brief spell of loquacity had come to an end. I bid him goodnight and retired to my own small shelter. Feeling suddenly exhausted, I climbed straight into my sleeping bag and extinguished my lamp.

Yet sleep was not forthcoming. As often happens, bodily tiredness served only to exacerbate the activity of my mind. Outside, the wind ranged between eerie soughing and a penetrating, almost feline screech. Every so often, a crash marked the passage of some loose snow bank into the abyss.

As I lay staring into perfect darkness, I thought upon the rumours I'd heard of Aleister Crowley, tales he seemed to delight in and even propagate. I wondered what succour such a man could hope to find amidst the soul-wrenching desolation and wild beauty of the Himalayas. I imagined myself at the very spot where Crowley had sat, listening as his colleagues were torn from the mountain face, sipping tea as they tumbled down and down toward horrific deaths.

I don't remember falling asleep, but I have vague recollections of dreams in which I was led not by the hardy Bergenssen but by Crowley himself, who beckoned me through the most hazardous of routes, paths he crossed effortlessly only to laugh and caper when I couldn't follow with the same ease.

I remember how I raged at him – and how my cries only made him laugh the harder.

* * *

I woke late. It was that, I suppose, that saved my life.

I transitioned abruptly from deep sleep into wakefulness, and realised the sounds from outside were my colleagues preparing for our departure. Yet I had no urge at all to move. I felt cold beyond belief, and it was more than I could do to control my shivering. Nevertheless, I struggled into my coat and boots, whilst the urge to vomit rose in my gullet.

The moment I stepped outside, Bergenssen rushed over. "My God, man, are you all right? You look like death! Can you stand?"

I struggled to control my thoughts. "I had the malaria," I said. "Last year, in Egypt. I think perhaps it's back." I brushed a palm across my brow, found it clammy. "I'm afraid I'll be going nowhere today."

"Not to worry, old man," Bergenssen said – though in fact, he looked more dejected even than I felt. "It's a poor time for a delay, though."

I couldn't see how this was true. The wind was high, visibility was poor, and in all it promised to be a bad day for mountaineering. When I pointed this out, he said, "Yes, but we have a while yet. I wanted badly to make camp six."

I was startled by the lack of sympathy in his tone. It was a sort of childish spite that made me say, "You should go on. I'll be better soon, I'm sure." Then, beginning to realise how foolishly I was jeopardising myself, I added, "If you rope the worst parts and send someone back in a day or two, I'll be able to catch up."

Bergenssen nodded vigorously. I could see that he very much wanted to believe me. "Yes, I suppose that's the only way. You can manage, can't you? I'd leave one of the porters, you know…"

"Yes?" I said, with sudden hope.

"But we'll need them all at six, you see."

My heart sank. I felt a flush of horror at the thought that the man before me was nothing like the Bergenssen I knew; that no words I could say would move him. "Don't worry," I told him. "What's the worst that can happen to me here?"

So they set out, and I watched until they disappeared. Had I any premonition? I remember being ill at ease, but of course there was the sudden rush of sickness, my half-remembered nightmares, and Bergenssen's uncharacteristic behaviour. With all that, it was easy to dismiss any doubts as fanciful.

Yet very soon I had graver reasons for concern. The weather worsened drastically: the wind rose in a matter of minutes, until soon it was a gale, flinging pirouettes of snow and wailing banshee-like across the cliffs. It wasn't long before I was driven back into my tent, where I huddled, shivering, hoping against hope to hear the sounds of their return.

What I heard instead was the worst thing I could have expected – a colossal crash that seemed to go on for minutes before it subsided into a low muttering.

It could only be an avalanche.

I think I grew feverish then, if I hadn't been already. I know it wasn't long after the avalanche that I convinced myself my companions would not be returning. They were gone, and I was alone.

I shouted and raved for a while. Afterwards, I imagined I'd returned to lucidity. The truth was that my temporary madness had taken a different turn. I was sure I should go outside and start back to camp four, where a portion of our entourage waited with supplies. If I didn't, I would be buried – as Bergenssen and the others had been buried.

I staggered outside. The storm was like nothing I'd seen. Visibility was non-existent, except when a flash of lightning offered brief and violent illumination. Other than that, there was only darkness and snow, mixed inseparably, an ever-shifting funnel that howled around my every step.

Within a minute I'd lost all trace of my tent. On one level, I realised I was as likely to blunder off a cliff as to come anywhere near our last camp, but that realisation did nothing to slow my steps. Increasingly, I was unsure of where I was going, or why. Was something pursuing me? Yes, that was it – now that I thought, I could hear it, hear its measured steps through the bludgeoning of the gale. Was this a thing or a man? Perhaps it was something of both.

I stumbled often and fell more than once, but I seemed to have grown oblivious to pain, or sense, or anything but my fear. I reeled without direction, with no sense of time, unaware even of the storm.

I don't remember finding the valley. All I recollect is a change in the pitch of the wind, a relaxing in the lash of the snow against my back. It seemed quite abrupt. There was light, for the first time in ages. At first, I thought it was artificial. Then I recognised the pallid glow of the moon. It hung low and gigantic, as though I'd scaled a peak that had somehow brought us face to face. The light was sufficient for me to see the crevasse walls to either side – and ahead, the building that rose where those walls met.

I thought it must be a monastery, but it looked as much like a fortress, with four windowless tiers raised on columns, each level roofed in the peculiarly sharp and steep Tibetan style. The wide doors were of plain, black wood, and there was none of the usual ornamentation, except for one detail – the huge, golden pentagram mounted high upon the fourth storey.

At that sight, though I might rationally have assumed myself rescued and safe, my fear redoubled. I managed one more step, before all the strength left my body at once.

I pitched forward. The blackness took me, and – God help me – I was grateful.

* * *

I woke by stages.

For some immeasurable period, I'd been aware of sensations – motion, and later, the cool of water on my brow – but had lacked any understanding of what those feelings meant or how they came to be. I was oblivious to the passage of time. Regardless of whether my eyes were open or closed, they were met by the same ruddy gloom. I was afraid, but in an indistinct way, as one might fear the concept of dying more than the prospect itself. I've no doubt that my fever was still raging, for I remember phases of awful cold and enormous heat.

Eventually, I examined my surroundings with something approaching clarity. I was muddled, the effort of moving my neck made it ache cruelly, and my inner clothes were moist with sweat, but I was lucid enough for curiosity. However, the room I found myself in was very plain. I lay on a low, hard bed, and the only other furnishings were a stool in the opposite corner, a small table beside me, and a narrow brazier. I thought it might be a cell, though there was no indication of a lock on the door. Then I remembered the building I'd seen, and how I'd thought it must be a monastery. The chamber seemed plain enough to be a monk's.

Yet that was strange in itself. If Crowley had been correct then we'd reached to around twenty-five thousand feet; even a conservative estimate placed us at well above twenty-thousand. Such a height was tremendously isolating, too much so for any regular supply or communication from the outside world.

I thought back to the research I'd done before joining with Bergenssen. There'd been one sect in particular who considered Kangchenjunga sacred, and who might very well have built a monastery high amongst its peaks. What were they called? The Kirati, that was it – descendants of an ancient local people, practitioners of a religion rife with shamanism and ancestor-worship. If I remembered rightly, their god was "Tagera Ningwaphuma," called the Supreme Knowledge. Perhaps here, high upon the mountain, I had come upon one of their extreme outposts.

Then I remembered the pentagram above the door. Maybe it wasn't the Kirati after all – or if it was, some even more obscure offshoot cut off from the rest. *Five points*, I thought, *five points for five peaks*, and something in the notion made me shudder.

I climbed unsteadily to my feet. The effort made my head spin, and only a hand outstretched to the wall kept me standing. After a minute, however, the dizziness began to pass. I crossed the stone floor by small steps and tested the door. Sure enough, there was no lock. It swung open freely.

The man who waited outside, who turned at the sound of the door's opening, was swathed in robes of deep crimson. He resembled any other priest of the region, except for two details: his robe was hooded and the hood drawn up, so that I could see only a crude hint of features, and in his hand he gripped a wooden staff which he clearly didn't require for support.

He moved to bar my way. He was smaller than I was, but agile. He said something I didn't understand; it didn't sound like any dialect of Tibetan I'd heard. Something in the words and in his stance made me nervous.

"I'm grateful for your hospitality," I said, "but I won't impose any further." I don't know if I really expected him to understand English. When he evidently didn't, I added in broken Tibetan something to the effect of, "Now I must go."

He pressed closer, with the staff upraised, as if herding me back into my cell. He spoke again, this time more abruptly.

"No," I said, reverting to English. "My friends…on the mountain…" I'd suddenly thought of Bergenssen, and the previously unconsidered possibility that someone might have survived. "Thank you, I must be leaving."

This time he spoke loudly, and waved one hand close to my face as though swatting at an insect.

Suddenly, I felt terribly afraid. I pushed him away. At that, he looked as though he'd shout along the passage for help. In panic, I grabbed for his staff, and had it away from him before he even realised what was happening. He took a swift step back. I swung clumsily. The blow caught his shoulder. In a crouch, he backed off again, and I knew he was preparing to run. I struck again. This time, he slipped backward and his balance went. His head struck the wall with a ghastly slap.

I stood panting for a while, staring down in uncomprehending horror. Finally, I realised the dark trickle pooling between the cobbles was blood. Was he dead? I dared not check. But he wasn't moving, and I could hear no sound of breathing.

It had been an accident.

Or had it?

In either case, how could I explain?

I'd committed an abominable deed. I had killed a man on the most tenuous of grounds. Yet all I felt was fear, so profound that it swallowed every other sensation or possibility, morality included.

I decided I must hide the body. That might forestall any suspicion until I could get out of there. Setting the staff down, I grasped under his shoulders and, with much clumsy effort, managed to manoeuvre him into the room where I'd awoken.

I tried to drag him onto the bed, but the task proved beyond me. I let him flop to the floor instead. As I did so, his hood fell back, and I finally saw his face. He was slim-featured, quite young, and unexceptional – except for the scar on his cheek.

It was a perfect pentagram of whitened skin.

I shuddered with a feeling far worse than fever. Something was terribly wrong here, and in that moment the fact I'd killed a man didn't seem the worst of it. What had I stumbled onto, high upon Kangchenjunga?

If I were under threat and had no means to reason with my captors, if I was already responsible for the death of one of their number, there could be no question but that I'd be safer even in the tempest outside. I returned to the corridor and considered it properly. It was very plain, and so long that I thought it might stretch the entire length of the building. Spaced along its length were other rooms or cells at roughly even intervals. At the far ends were double doors, each pair like those I'd observed from the outside.

It seemed a safe assumption that one set led out to the valley from whence I'd arrived. But which?

I settled on the nearest. In the interest of covertness, and also because its tip was sodden with blood, I abandoned the staff, choosing to support myself against the wall instead. I moved softly, on the very border of panic, convinced I'd be discovered at any instant.

In fact, I reached the doors without incident. After much nervous hesitation, I pushed one slightly open. Only blackness lay beyond. I pushed harder. Crouched low, I eased through the gap.

I was aware of a large space, then of light at its centre, and finally of figures standing within the illumination. Cockroach-like, I scurried through the shadows, hoping for some intense dark to conceal me. I was sure I'd be seen. Yet when I paused to look, the figures were still absorbed.

That calmed me fractionally – enough that I could take in the scene about me. I crouched at the edge of a large, circular chamber cleanly split into halves. The inner portion, where I knelt, was bordered only by plain stone walls. The other, however, presented a series of arches to the most astonishing vista. Evidently we were perched on the very edge of the mountainside, because the view was horizonless and dizzying.

At the centre of the room, directly above the point where the figures were gathered, a narrow well in the domed ceiling let in a beam of scintillating moonlight. Beneath, borne on a low pedestal, sat a large, pentangular dish of crystalline filigree, so delicate and translucent that it might have been carved from ice. So much did it glow and its surface ripple that the dish seemed to have been filled by the rays shining from on high.

I could make no sense of what I saw, except to find it strange and frightening. Nor had I time to consider. Suddenly the figures, who previously had appeared sunken in reverie, began to mill about and to converse in that clipped tongue the monk had employed. I feared I'd been discovered, and tensed instinctively. But none of them were looking in my direction.

It occurred to me they must be wondering after their missing companion, and this was confirmed when a delegation hurried out through the double doors. A minute later came shouts, and a second party followed the first. For a while, there was much activity. I was sure that at any instant one of them would penetrate the shadows and discover me. Yet, though they had time to scour the place, not one seemed to consider that I might have intruded upon their sanctum. Eventually they reconvened, and I allowed myself the faintest release of held breath.

My relief was premature – and hopelessly misjudged.

The gathering split into two factions. Five of the monks surrounded the pentangular dish, whilst the others retreated to form a crescent round it, with the open side in the direction of the doors. Immediately they set up a chant, in a language just as unfamiliar but quite different from the one they'd employed before.

The words played havoc on my nerves, and brought incomprehensible images into my mind – as though I perceived something I couldn't rationally grasp. As the chant heightened, raising towards crescendo, so the slant of moonlight seemed to brighten, and then to pulse. At last, it was as though a column of brilliant, throbbing whiteness fell through the centre of the room. Though this scorched my eyes, it never occurred to me to look away. The dish seemed full almost to overflowing, as though brimming with fluid light.

The five monks assigned to the pentagonal tips, who so far had played no part, lurched abruptly to life as if galvanised. Each grasped his respective point and heaved with all his might. Slowly, the bowl began to tip.

As impossible as I knew it to be, I expected the contents to run out, to splash like mercury over the floor. Instead, just as impossibly, they were projected – in a manner that bore no resemblance to the projection of light. The flow seemed to crawl and seethe through the air. It fell upon the door, where it splashed like thrown paint.

When it settled, a glimmering pentagram hung upon the boards.

I'd barely registered all this when the chant adopted a new tone, shifting register without any loss of intensity. My attention was focused entirely on the doors. They looked soft and unreal under the stamp of fluid moonlight.

They seemed to shudder – once, twice, and a third, most violent, time.

With a force that made wood shiver like paper, they sprang open.

I fell backwards. I think I even cried out. If I did, the sound drew no attention. All thought was devoted to that hideous mantra – which seemed now like a wail of condensed experience, of horrible knowing borne by unfathomable words.

All eyes hung on the open doorway.

I couldn't help but look.

My first thought was of a mirror, so similar was the scene beyond. There was the circular chamber, there the arches opening onto inconceivable space, the pedestal, the figures clustered about it.

Yet almost straight away I perceived a difference. The view through the distant arcade was not the one behind me. Those stark grey pinnacles were unlike any on Earth.

Then it struck me. They weren't of Earth at all.

If they were, what could explain the blue-green orb hung in the sky behind? I knew with absolute certainty that I looked upon a world not my own. More, I felt sure it was our moon, the very same that cast its rays through the ceiling – whose radiation had somehow riven a path through untraversable space.

But if that was true, who were those unshapely forms, robed like their earthly brethren, who turned towards us? They were not men; too tall, too long in limb. A faint and bluish glow ebbed from within their cowls. As they moved towards the door, the shadows flickered jarringly around them. The swish of an arm revealed...what? Not a hand.

They lurched closer, and my heart contracted. I knew that something wholly, inimically inhuman approached. They were almost upon the doorway, and I was frozen. I could only watch – as the foremost reached the brink, tilted its head, as I caught a glimpse of what lay beneath that updrawn hood...

With a cry of horror, I threw myself forward. All I could think to do was hurl myself upon the pentangular dish. I struck it with all my strength. It moved a little, and the moonbeam wavered.

Every one of the creatures turned its stare upon me. Together, they hissed in fury.

I heaved. I thought my bones would break before that dish moved, and still I drove against it. For something so seemingly light, it felt like lead set in concrete. I pushed, without hope, too desperately afraid to stop. At any moment, one of the monks – or, unimaginably worse, one of the moon-beings – would pry me away. I pushed harder, though I thought my tendons must snap. When finally the dish shifted, it was by hardly an inch. I could do no more; I fell back, panting, my back and arms slick with sweat. I'd given my all, and still I'd failed.

Yet somehow, that minute jilt was enough. Free of its axis, the dish tilted, rocked – and fell.

Shattering, it was like ice cascading across the cobbled floor.

Looking back to the entrance, I saw the doors still stood open – but upon that familiar passage I'd arrived by. I sank to my knees, no longer concerned for my safety. Let the monks tear me to pieces if they would. I'd saved my world from something appalling. Even in death, I could take comfort in that.

No hand fell. No blow was struck.

When I eventually dared look up, I understood why. Dust was showering from the ceiling, as though the building were in the grip of a minor earth tremor. An instant later, I felt it, a pulse travelling up through the floor tiles. The pulse became an unrhythmic throb. A block tore loose from the roof and shattered, showering us in fragments. One of the monks screamed and stumbled.

Though I hardly glanced back, I'm sure I was the only one who tried to flee. The monks merely stood, resigned, as their blasphemous temple ruptured around them. Only I ran – darting amongst the falling rubble, certain that at any instant I'd be pulverised. I forgot my weakened state, forgot everything except the hope of night air on my face.

Reaching the second set of double doors, I found them already mangled and half off their hinges. I pressed through the gap this afforded, and still I didn't stop. I kept going until the last rumbling subsided – until the night was utterly still. Only then did I pause to look back.

There was nothing to see but a vast bank of snow, pierced here and there with hints of shattered masonry.

The monastery had been utterly erased.

* * *

You may wonder how I survived to write this record.

I wonder too. I walked, or staggered rather, for some time – hours, days, I can't say. I don't remember how I discovered the remnants of camp four. I came to myself huddled in a tent, with only fragmentary recollections of the intervening time.

I suppose I'd been uncommonly lucky. What had happened, I later discovered, was this: five men died that day on the way to camp six – Bergenssen, our three mountaineering companions, and one of the Sherpas. The rest of the porters turned back immediately, found me gone from camp five and so backtracked to four. Meeting with the party stationed there, they had democratically decided to forget the whole sorry mess and return home. From either idleness or some vestigial loyalty, they'd left both the tents and the supplies.

Thus I found shelter, food, and medicine enough to nurse myself back to health. In the end I felt capable of attempting the downward climb. It was slow progress, but I was in no hurry. In Sandakphu, I learned the truth regarding Bergenssen and the others. It came as no surprise. I carried on, deeper into India. I had some money with me, and access to more. I felt dimly that I could not go home.

I write now from a location I choose not to disclose. I will send this tale to a number of reputable journals, in the hope that one may see fit to print it, whether they believe it or no.

No one should think to seek me out. They won't find me. I've come to realise I have too many unanswered questions weighing on my mind. What had been that impossible passage in the moonlight? What those gangling, unearthly figures? The monastery had been destroyed, its tenants crushed and buried; yet dare I hope that there were no other temples, no other routes between worlds, no acolytes so destitute in soul that they might open them?

And thinking upon that last, one more inescapable question came to my mind: what part in this monstrous affair was played by Aleister Crowley, so-called 'wickedest man in Britain.' Could that wickedness extend to the betrayal of all mankind to something malicious and inhuman?

I have my suspicions.

Now, too, I have a little knowledge; hints to dark and sordid truths, the corrupted fruits of my research. In the course of my search, I have made allies…a very few. The one thing I lack now is proof. When the time should come that I have it, only then will I return – and there shall be a reckoning for the horrors of Kangchenjunga.

Adlivun (The Beneath)

Rachel Verkade

Spring 1911

THE HUNTERS in this village were frustrating enough to make Jonas spit. Bad enough he was trapped out here in this miserable facsimile of civilization without dealing with the half-human savages that called it home, but Dobson and Topham had told him repeatedly that this little coastal village was the best place to go for what he wanted. Jonas shoved his hands deep into the pockets of his fur jacket and drew salt air deep into his lungs. He wanted one thing, and he was determined to get it. Even if he had to deal with this. He hadn't spent the past week on a train to be turned back now.

Sad little huts of wood and metal huddled against the arctic winds. In the distance, a gravel shore stretched out to a blinding expanse of ice, pounded by angry black waves. The only signs of life were a few lonely gulls, wheeling and calling overhead. Jonas crunched his way down the gravel road, barely noticing the ragged clothes hanging on the lines, the weather-beaten walls and sagging roofs of the houses.

The town hall, or so he'd heard, was the best place to go looking for a guide. He'd been told that this was the time of year for hunters, but for whatever reason, he saw that the kayaks were on shore, dry and empty. There were no hides stretched out to be scraped, no meat being dried, no split seal carcasses spilling steam into the air or boiling vats of whale fat tended by heavy-bodied women. He'd seen these things in the villages further south, and seen the photos in the guidebooks, but here all was quiet. Even the Eskimo children, normally running about like gutter rats from house to house, were invisible, not that Jonas missed them. But at least there was no difficulty finding the hall; it was the largest building in the village, built of fine pine boards that had undoubtedly cost much to bring up here. Jonas nodded with approval despite the signs of frost warping the wood, and the smell of vomit wafting from the body slumped against the east wall.

The hall was dim. Jonas imagined it had once smelled of the fresh planks the Americans had brought from down south to give the Eskimos a proper village, but now it stank of dirty bodies swaddled in fur, of bloody meat, and old beer. He could almost taste the grease hanging in the air, caking on his skin and in his hair. Like he'd hoped, the Eskimo men were here, glittering eyes surrounded by greasy hair, thick bodies hunched over tables. Jonas wrinkled his nose, but stepped inside. Dobson and Topham had been up here, and they'd come back with seal skins, soft as silk and shining like silver. Jonas was determined to top them, for once. But to do that…

"Does anyone here speak English?" Jonas said, crossing his arms. He'd been assured that there were English speakers here. Offer enough incentive, Dobson said, and they'll come find you. But the men barely stirred from their tables, their gimlet rat-eyes hardly flickering in Jonas's direction.

"I said, does anyone here speak English?" Jonas snarled. What was wrong with these people? Didn't they understand plain words?

Finally, though, a young man stood up and came towards him. "I speak some." He said, his face flat. "What do you want?"

Finally. Jonas graced the young man with a nod. "I want a hunting guide. My friends have told me this is the best place on the coast to find walrus." He shifted the straps on his shoulder, displaying his handsome rifle. He expected some impressed murmurs, at least a surprised look, but the young man's face was expressionless. "I want a walrus, a bull. I want a fine pair of tusks to bring home." Wouldn't that make Dobson and Topham choke on their brandies? To see him come home with a pair of great walrus tusks, those glorious pieces of creamy ivory mounted over his mantle? How he could regale the guests at his dinner parties with how he conquered the king of the icy seas, how he centered the sight of his rifle on the walrus' great head as it reared from the ice-choked water, its red eyes glittering in the frozen sunlight. Jonas could see it all now.

But the young man was shaking his head, his cheekbones standing harsh in his face. "No. No one will help you here."

Jonas narrowed his eyes. "I can pay." He'd been warned that these backwards people had no concept of money, but he'd brought goods in plenty to exchange. Coffee, sugar, rum, tobacco…anything a primitive hunter might want. "You wouldn't be going out for free. I can…"

But the young man was backing up, raising his hands. "You do not understand. No one here help you. There is no game."

"No game?" Jonas stared. "What do you mean, no game?"

"No animals. There is nothing to hunt."

"That's preposterous. Game is plentiful up here. I've been told you can't walk without tripping over a bloody seal. You can't tell me…"

"No." The young man said with finality. "No animals. Go back."

In frustration, Jonas looked around. The other men had turned away, looking to the walls or looking down, all of them avoiding his eyes. Would none of these foolish people help him? He'd been assured that the walrus were breeding at this time of year, and that the bulls were in the water ripe for the taking. "I have rum. I have tobacco and sugar. I can…"

No one responded. The men continued their quiet conversations around their tables, guttural murmurs hanging like their stink in the air. Baring his teeth, Jonas spat on the floor. "I have goods a-plenty to be shared, but if you all are too foolish to take them…"

No one replied. The men huddled in among the smoke and the grease, and said nothing. Jonas spit another curse. He couldn't stand the dimness, the smell any longer, and he shoved the door open and stormed outside, snarling at the stubbornness of these savage people. No doubt he'd broken one of their godless rules of etiquette, and now no one would talk to him. Jonas's face burned at the thought of going home empty-handed, hearing Dobson and Topham's laughter as they explained some simple tradition he had misinterpreted. They would go with him next time, they'd say, and make sure that he behaved…

"Excuse…you wanted guiding?"

The English was halting, and Jonas turned to see an Eskimo heavily swaddled in fur. It was hard to see anything of his face aside from those near-black eyes they all seemed to have, but from the sounds of his voice he was just a boy. "I did, yes. Is your father a hunter?"

"My father is, yes, but he is dead. I offer myself as guide."

Jonas frowned, but then, children in such savage places grew up quickly. "You are a hunter, then?"

"My husband was, and he taught me very much. I can guide you."

For a moment, Jonas's mind crossed straight to the Greeks, and wondered if these Eskimos had shared their gruesome culture of lying with small boys, but then he looked closer. The skin of the Eskimo's face was smooth, and strands of long, black hair mingled with the fur of the hood. "You're a woman!"

"The woman of our tribe hunt sometimes, when food is scarce, or if she shows great talent." She said, raising her chin in defiance. "I can guide you."

Jonas was stunned. Of course there were women back home who would ride to hounds, or even go out for a pheasant shoot, but this was entirely different. And how would it sound to his friends when he told them who his guide had been? He could hear their mockery now...*Poor Jonas was so lost in the north that he had to hire a mother to look after him.* The greatest tusks ever taken wouldn't spare him the humiliation. It would be like being back at school again.

Jonas started to turn away, but a gloved hand fell upon his shoulder. "No one else will take you. It is me, or no hunt."

Jonas hesitated. He might have thought she was lying, if not for the men he had already spoken to. What would be worse, going back after having been guided by a woman, or going back empty-handed?

"I want a bull walrus," he said, looking down his nose at the fur-clad woman. "I want the tusks, do you understand?"

She nodded. "A bull walrus. I can guide."

Jonas considered. Who was to know just who his guide had been? No one would be there but the two of them. All that mattered was getting his trophies; the rest could be what he wanted it to be, at least as far as his family and friends were concerned. "All right. Two bottles of rum, do we have a deal?"

It was less than he would offer a man, and perhaps she knew that. But whatever the reason, she nodded readily. "That will be fine. My *umiak* is this way. Please follow."

An *umiak* proved to be a moderate-sized boat of bone and sealskin. It rest, upended, on the rocky shore, and Jonas looked at it doubtfully. From what Dobson and Topham had told him, he'd expected a kayak. "Will that thing actually float?"

"The skins are rubbed with seal oil, this keeps the water away." The woman assured him. He was startled by her strength when she lifted one end of the boat. "Please, we must carry it onto the ice."

"Surely we can hire someone..." She was shaking her head, and Jonas sighed. Well, she had reason; if the other villagers were so dead set against being hired as guides, he could only imagine their reaction to being approached as porters. Tugging his leather gloves more firmly onto his hands, Jonas moved to the rear of the boat and bent to take hold and lift. And almost dropped it in surprise at how light it was. He likely would have been able to carry it on his own.

The woman waited for him to adjust before setting off. "My name is Ahnah," she said as they crunched their way across the gravel.

Well, at least he'd found someone with a Christian name. "Jonas Wycliff." He grunted in return, matching his stride to hers. "How long do you think it will take us to find a walrus, Anna?"

"They are travelers at this season. We find them between the shore and the ice. It will not be difficult."

"Excellent." Jonas finally allowed himself a smile. It seemed that at last, he was on his way to his prize. "Do you hunt them often?"

"Usually my husband does the hunting, but I go with him sometimes." Jonas had to catch his footing as they crossed onto the expanse of ice. Anna didn't even pause. "The meat is very good, and the skins and bones are much use." She stopped, abruptly enough that the hull of the boat drove out Jonas's wind. "Here. Now, into the water."

He hadn't realized just how quickly the sea had approached, or just how sudden the divide was. It wasn't like the beaches back home in New England, where rocky sand stretched out to meet shallow, clear water. The ice seemed to suddenly halt, leaving one on the edge of a precipice. The inky black water seemed to have no bottom, and to Jonas's eyes was devoid of life. Standing on this shore, he felt as though he were at the edge of some great, yawning abyss. Were it not for the floating isles of ice he could see in the distance, he could almost believe it.

Anna had lowered the boat to the ice, and pushed it into the water with a low scraping noise. "Come. You can row?"

Jonas bristled, but bit back his first comment. If they couldn't hire someone to help carry the boat, there was no way they'd hire someone to row for them. Anna climbed without fear into the boat's hollow, and, with some trepidation, Jonas followed.

"You have been on the sea before?" Anna asked.

Somehow Jonas didn't think the rowing team at Yale would count with her. "Only on the river. On the sea I travel by steamer." He glanced and sighed internally at her blank look. "A very large boat, driven by burning coal."

"I know what you speak of." Anna said, handing him an oar. "The men from the south come to hunt seals and whales in them."

"Oh." Jonas flushed.

"They are no good for hunting, anyway. The whales and seals learn the sound of water against metal. But the *umiak* is of skin, so to them it sounds as a seal. They will not flee."

Jonas nodded, not without some admiration. Well, these people wouldn't have survived this long without learning some tricks, would they? He dipped his oar into the water, and they began to row.

It was silent out on the ocean, again, not like at home. The few seabirds that were here hung close to shore, and it seemed theirs was the only boat on the water. The only sound were the waves against the tanned hull and the soft dip of the oars into the water. The sound of the arctic wind whistling in Jonas's ears was almost as biting as the cold. Jonas tucked his chin into the collar of his jacket and forced his eyes to stay on Anna's back. He wasn't sure how long it was before he glanced over his shoulder and realized he could no longer see the coastline. The world was now black water and chunks of white ice, with their suddenly small-seeming boat in the middle.

"Did your mother or father speak English, Anna?" Jonas finally said, desperate for any relief to the quiet.

"No." She replied, not looking at him. "My husband learned from traders, and he taught some to me."

"Then, how did you get your name?" Perhaps some missionary had converted her, and she'd chosen to replace her savage name. Jonas had heard of such things.

Now she did pause, and looked over her shoulder at him. "My name is Ahnah. Ah-nah."

When she pronounced the word slowly, Jonas saw his error. So much for real names. "My apologies. I thought you were named Anna."

Ahnah threw back her head and laughed, a surprisingly joyful sound in this desolate place on the lifeless, frozen sea. As Jonas watched, she pushed back her hood, and shining black hair spilled down her back. "Ah-nah. It is a name for a wise woman," she said, regarding him with those strange gimlet eyes.

Jonas smiled, hesitantly. "Anna means 'grace', to my people." There seemed little to be called graceful about the fur-clad woman in front of him, except perhaps for the drift of her hair on the wind.

"Grace." She seemed to consider that, looking out over the dark water. There was nothing to break the silence, not a seabird or a ship's call. He noticed for the first time the marks on her face, black lines down her cheeks and curving around her eyes, streaking down from her lower lip to her chin. Some kind of war paint?

"Are you tattooed?" He asked, surprised, and was surprised again when she smiled.

"I was one of the last girls of my village to have the marks. When the men came to move the village, the priests said it was ugly. They broke the old women's tools, told them they would be punished if they were caught marking girls." It seemed to make her sad, of all things.

"Well, they were right!" Jonas said hotly, but some of his fervor died as Ahnah's black eyes fell on him. "To mutilate young girls in such a way..."

He could see her mouthing the word, 'mutilate', and when understanding came to her eyes her face tightened. "No, not mutilate. It is a sign that a girl is now a woman. A sign of strength and acceptance of the spirit. And they are beautiful." She traced the line around her right eye with one gloved hand, the same loving way Jonas had seen his mother finger a favourite piece of jewelry.

"But," Jonas stammered, "didn't it hurt?"

"Of course," Ahnah nodded. "A great much. It tests how well a woman will have children. That hurts too."

Jonas reddened. He really hadn't planned on being out here dicussing *that*. "Yes, but that's natural. To suffer such pain for marks on your face..."

"Excuse," Ahnah said, regarding him again. "The hunters who come here seeking whales, I have heard them say that they take them for bones, to make corsets. Yes? And this is something a lady wears?"

Jonas's blush deepened. "Well, yes..."

"How does it work?"

Increasingly sure that the woman was somehow mocking him, Jonas shifted in his seat. "Well, it is wrapped around a woman's waist, and then laced as tight as possible and tied tightly."

"Why?"

"For fashion? It does look lovely."

"And it doesn't pain?"

Jonas opened his mouth to say of course not, but then closed it. He remembered his mother's look of relief when she spoke of removing her corset in the evening.

He remembered how faint and pained the ladies he'd courted looked, the stiff way they walked and sat. "…I suppose it does."

Ahnah raised her chin again and smiled. "My marks only hurt once."

There was a moment, and then Jonas laughed. He couldn't help it. "I suppose you have me there." He smiled, tipping the oar towards her. Ahnah laughed as well, shaking her hair behind her in a black banner. She was thin, he realized. He could see her collarbones when she raised her head high, and her cheekbones stood out in contrast to the round-faced people he'd seen elsewhere. "Are you hungry? I have some biscuits." He'd bought them at the train station, but never bothered to eat them.

Ahnah hesitated at first, but accepted, and there were a few moments of quiet as they both ate. The biscuits were stale by now, but at least they were filling, and Jonas tucked the packet back into his pocket. He almost dropped it into the water, but something about that black emptiness still made him nervous.

"Thanks to you," Ahnah nodded, rubbing crumbs from around her mouth. She paused, as though uncertain about her next words, and started to reach for an oar when Jonas saw something over her shoulder. A rippling in the water!

He shouted in excitement, seizing his rifle and socking the butt to his shoulder. The retort seemed to echo almost forever, rippling across the silvery water's surface, up to the empty whiteness of the sky. Ahnah stared at him, her face pale.

Jonas, in the meantime, was cursing. It hadn't been a walrus after all. The animal now bobbing to the surface of the waves, white skin awash with blood, was one of those odd pale whales they had up here. Belugas, that's what they were called. It bobbed in the water like some strange white cork, fins twitching convulsively, black eyes blank. Damn it all, he'd wasted a bullet, and he couldn't even take the skin. "I suppose I got too excited." He sighed, picking up his oar.

"Yes," Ahnah said with no hesitation, turning her back to him.

"Shouldn't we…" Jonas started, but Ahnah shook her head, dipping her oar into the water and beginning to paddle.

Almost three hours later, as Jonas's shoulders were aching, Ahnah finally indicated a stop. "The walrus travel. This is a passage for them. We wait here, and they come." She seemed certain, so Jonas followed her example, drawing his oar from the water and laying it on the floor of the boat. The boat rocked slowly on the waves, and the thump of water against the skin hull pulsed like a heartbeat.

* * *

Despite Ahnah's assurances, Jonas saw no sign that walrus, or any other animal, for that matter, were nearby. He shifted his rifle to his lap and scanned the water, but all he saw was ice and waves. No spouting of whales, no seal barking as it took a breath, not even a gull wheeling overhead. The only sound the thudding of the hull and the endless, eternal grinding of the ice.

Finally, he could stand it no longer. "Why would none of the other hunters come out?"

Ahnah pushed her hair back with a mitten-clad hand. "They fear Sedna."

"Sedna?" Some of the natives had different names for beasts, or so he'd heard. "What is that? An animal?"

"Oh, no." Ahnah regarded him, her hair drifting on the wind. "Sedna is mother to animals."

"What..."

"Long ago," Jonas realized suddenly that he was to hear some savage tale, some pagan myth of the sea, but he resigned himself to it. Anything was better than the silent pulse of the sea. "Long ago." Ahnah said again, her eyes turned to the waves, her hair drifting like seaweed on the breeze. "Sedna was the daughter of a great hunter. She was beautiful, with long, flowing hair as soft as fox fur, and she was proud. So proud that she refused to marry all of the hunters who came to her. Her father became angry, he said that the next man who came, she would marry. But Sedna only laughed.

"But the next man who came was tall and strong. He had a fine bone spear, he had carvings of ivory and shining seal skins. He asked Sedna to be his wife, and her father was pleased. But Sedna still laughed." Ahnah's eyes shone in the dim, yet stunning light that reflected off the water, and Jonas felt a chill despite his layers of fur. Her eyes and hair were the same colour as the void that was the sea. "Her father was angry, and he was tired. He gave Sedna tea which put her to sleep, and while she slept, the hunter carried her away.

"When Sedna woke to her new husband's home, she saw it was grass and stone, a thin nest, and he shed his human skin. Her husband was a raven, and he laughed at her surprise. He said, you are wife now, and you must stay and cook for me. And he left her a salmon to eat, and flew away, and Sedna wept, and angry at her father's trick.

"But Sedna's father somehow knew that his daughter was not happy, and he came in his kayak to Raven's nest. Sedna ran to him, and begged him to take her home, and she climbed in his kayak, and together they set across the sea. Towards home."

The wind seemed to have grown colder, and the sun on the water was dazzling. Jonas blinked hard and forced his eyes to the bottom of the boat.

"But as Sedna and her father paddled away, Raven called a terrible storm on them. The waves were great, the sky roared, and Sedna's father was taken by fear. He called for Raven to forgive him, and in his fear, he threw Sedna into the sea."

Jonas's eyes were drawn to the sides of the boat, to the rims of skin stretched over bone.

"Sedna clung to the side of the kayak and cried for her father to help her. But the fear was to great, and Sedna's father reached for his knife. He did not hear his daughter's cries as he cut at her hands."

The black water, the thudding waves. Blood would be almost invisible in those depths. Was that the crash of ice or the snap of bone? Was that thump the rock of the waves or the impact of a blade?

"Sedna sank to the bottom of the sea, her fingers cut away by her father's blade, and her father went home to mourn her. But Sedna's anger and her pain were great. Her husband deceived her, her father cut her and abandoned her, but they did not know what power Sedna had. Her cut fingers sank into the water, and they became the seals, the walrus, the great fish. Her thumb was last, and it became the whales.

Jonas remembered the pale, dying body of the beluga, its struggles becoming the twitchings of a severed finger, and he choked back on a sudden wave of nausea.

"Sedna huddles in *Adlivun*, the beneath, and her hair tangles around her head, and the animals of her hand still serve her. When she is angry, she calls the animals to her, and tangles them in her hair. They gather to her, and comfort her as her father and husband did not She will not free the animals to the hunters until she is pleased again."

Silence fell with only the steady beat of waves against the skin hull to break it. Jonas felt cold despite the heavy jacket and fur mittens, but he shook his head. A savage tale, to be sure, but weren't all pagan myths? It was no worse than Saturn devouring his children, or the dismemberment of Osiris, or even the severed heads of Bluebeard's wives. A children's story, soon to be lost to legend. But there was something about the story that made Jonas shudder. The image of a woman, nude and rendered gaunt with confinement, squatting like a goblin on the sea bed, her hair a wild and tangled mass about her head. Hair that reached out like the feelers of insects or the legs of spiders, snaring the animals of the water, wrapping them in wiry black cocoons. It was a disturbing image. But this was still a godless land, and there were people here who still believed in such things. Jonas had to remember that. "So the villagers think that this Sedna is keeping the animals away?"

Ahnah nodded. "She has wound the animals in her hair, and she will not let them hunt. The men wait for the..." at this, she paused. "The *Angakkuq*."

An-ga-kuck?" Jonas said doubtfully.

For the first time, Jonas saw frustration on Ahnah's face. "The spirit-man. The one who does the ceremonies."

"The shaman!" Jonas exclaimed, understanding. His voice seemed to echo across the empty water.

"Sha-man." Ahnah said, tasting the word as he had hers. "Yes. He must prepare, and hold a great ceremony, where we beg Sedna for mercy and tell her of the evils we do. Then he will go down to the beneath and comb her hair, and she will release the animals for us to hunt."

Typical pagan foolishness. For this he'd been refused a guide? "So why did you come out?" Jonas sat back in the shifting boat. "If your people are so determined that there aren't any animals and that there's an angry goddess, then why?"

"My husband is gone." She stated, flat and simple, her hair drifting across her face.

That was unexpected. "I'm sorry." Jonas said. "How did he die?"

"Sedna has many laws," Ahnah said, and Jonas wondered how they'd returned to this subject. "She guards her animals carefully. My husband took a seal, but he was impatient. He did not give it water."

"Why would anyone give a seal water?"

Ahnah didn't seem to hear him. "Sedna became angry, and the animals disappeared. All of the hunters stayed in the village. But my husband said that he knew better. He said that Sedna was not there, there was no reason for us all to be hiding."

"Your husband sounds like a wise man," Jonas nodded. He wished her husband was the one he was dealing with now.

"No, you do not understand." Ahnah said stubbornly. "He said that we should go and hunt, because Sedna was not real. And he went out in his kayak before the rest of the village woke. He said to me he would bring home a fat seal, that we would have meat. But he did not come back. Sedna took him."

That image again, of the hair-wrapped cocoon, but this time the bundle was the shape of a man, and writhed with the struggles of the drowning. And somewhere below the tangled mass, the goblin woman bared her teeth in a smile.

Jonas shuddered, and then shook himself. *Pull yourself together, man!* "It must have been a terrible loss for you."

Ahnah nodded slowly, her hair drifting in front of her face. "I miss him very much, my husband. But he angered Sedna." She was twirling the ends of her hair around her finger, a gesture Jonas usually found endearing in women. Now he found himself watching how the thin black strands bit into her flesh, the way her finger was so quickly tangled and constricted by the strands. A thin trickle of sweat down his back made him shiver.

"Ahnah, why did you bring me out here?" He found himself asking through numb lips.

She looked at him, her eyes glittering like glass shards through the curtain of her hair. "Sedna took my husband because he does not believe. And you do not believe, do you?"

The image of a woman squatting, naked and toadlike, her hair an impenetrable bramble. A man struggled with hair around his throat, his screams turned to a stream of silver bubbles. "No." Jonas said.

"Just so," Ahnah nodded. "He did not believe, and he broke her laws. I did not stop him, though I knew better. And now, for that, our village is hungry. We are thin bones, because of my husband's sin." Strands of her black hair snapped off as she tugged her hand free, and they fell like spider's legs across the back of her hand. "You do not believe, as my husband did not. I bring you to show that I understand my sin and his. Sedna will understand and be happy again."

Jonas would never know if she had not noticed his rifle, if she'd forgotten he had it, or if it simply had not occurred to her that he would use it. But when she lunged at him, a bone knife in her hand, there was no surprise in her black eyes at the retort. No surprise at the scarlet blood spilling from the hole in her throat to mat in the fur of her jacket. If anything, there was a calmness about her. Wind hissed and gurgled through her wound. Her teeth, smeared with blood, shone through the tangle of her hair, but her eyes were blank and calm. Such a calmness that it didn't seem at all strange when she seized the oars and held them tight to her chest as she fell overboard.

Jonas scrambled for the oars, plunging his hand into the black, ice-choked water. It soaked straight through his fur and leather gloves, and there was a blinding moment of exhilaration before the pain began. Cursing, he jerked back and stuffed his dripping hand underneath his jacket. His fingers felt as though they were being stabbed with tiny needles of ice. They throbbed and pulsed in the soaked leather, the heat from his body barely reaching them. Clenching his hand close to him, he leaned over the side of the boat, hoping against hope that he would see the oars floating nearby.

As he'd thought before, the blood was lost, drawn into the sea and become part of it. The sea had swallowed the oars, but Ahnah floated there, face to the empty sky. Her lips had peeled back from her teeth, and already frost was clouding her eyes, ice choking the exposed hole in her throat. Her hair had tangled and matted across her face in the fall, and was stiffening with ice, hanging like a net as she drifted in the void

Jonas huddled back in the boat, shuddering. He tried madly to recall if anyone knew where he was. He'd deliberately avoided talking to anyone after he'd met Ahnah, and none of the villagers had seen them going out…the conductor on the train back at the station knew where he was going and why, but not the specifics….

Jonas's heart turned as icy as his fingers. No one knew where he was. They hadn't even brought any food, aside from those long-ago biscuits. He had come out here with a madwoman, and now…

A madwoman? Then where are the oars?

Sank, clearly. They must have.

Driftwood sank? Really?

Jonas bit his lower lip as shudders racked his body, clenching his wet hand into painful spasms. Ahnah's corpse bobbed like a corpse, only the gleam of her teeth visible through the heavy black mat of her hair. Frost was blossoming on her skin, and on the dark fur of her hood…

Dark? Was it so dark before?

Her hair was so tangled in it that he couldn't be sure, and the water, the black, black water…

The pulsing thud of the waves against the hull droned on, almost drowning out the faint scratching noise, like of a tiny creature at a hole. And it wasn't until Jonas felt the distant tickle on his ankle that he truly understood.

Numb with cold and understanding, Jonas curled in the bottom of the boat as the thousands upon thousands of black hairs pressed through the pores of the sealskins and wound their way around him.

Journey to the Centre of the Earth

Chapters XXX–XXXIX

Jules Verne

[Publisher's Note: At this point in the story the three adventurers – Professor Lidenbrock, his nephew Axel, and their guide Hans – have descended into the bowels of the earth through a volcanic crater in Iceland. Down there, Axel became separated from the group, but was able to communicate with them through the walls in the 'whispering gallery'. He wakes to find them reunited in a vast underground cavern; the following chapters detail the wonders they behold.]

Chapter XXX
A New Mare Internum

AT FIRST I could hardly see anything. My eyes, unaccustomed to the light, quickly closed. When I was able to reopen them, I stood more stupefied even than surprised.

"The sea!" I cried.

"Yes," my uncle replied, "the Liedenbrock Sea; and I don't suppose any other discoverer will ever dispute my claim to name it after myself as its first discoverer."

A vast sheet of water, the commencement of a lake or an ocean, spread far away beyond the range of the eye, reminding me forcibly of that open sea which drew from Xenophon's ten thousand Greeks, after their long retreat, the simultaneous cry, "Thalatta! Thalatta!" The sea! The sea! The deeply indented shore was lined with a breadth of fine shining sand, softly lapped by the waves, and strewn with the small shells which had been inhabited by the first of created beings. The waves broke on this shore with the hollow echoing murmur peculiar to vast enclosed spaces. A light foam flew over the waves before the breath of a moderate breeze, and some of the spray fell upon my face. On this slightly inclining shore, about a hundred fathoms from the limit of the waves, came down the foot of a huge wall of vast cliffs, which rose majestically to an enormous height. Some of these, dividing the beach with their sharp spurs, formed capes and promontories, worn away by the ceaseless action of the surf. Farther on the eye discerned their massive outline sharply defined against the hazy distant horizon.

It was quite an ocean, with the irregular shores of earth, but desert and frightfully wild in appearance.

If my eyes were able to range afar over this great sea, it was because a peculiar light brought to view every detail of it. It was not the light of the sun, with his dazzling shafts of brightness and the splendour of his rays; nor was it the pale and uncertain shimmer of the moonbeams, the dim reflection of a nobler body of light. No; the illuminating power of this light, its trembling diffusiveness, its bright, clear whiteness, and its low temperature, showed that it must be of electric origin. It was like an aurora borealis, a continuous cosmical phenomenon, filling a cavern of sufficient extent to contain an ocean.

The vault that spanned the space above, the sky, if it could be called so, seemed composed of vast plains of cloud, shifting and variable vapours, which by their condensation must at certain times fall in torrents of rain. I should have thought that under so powerful a pressure of the atmosphere there could be no evaporation; and yet, under a law unknown to me, there were broad tracts of vapour suspended in the air. But then 'the weather was fine.' The play of the electric light produced singular effects upon the upper strata of cloud. Deep shadows reposed upon their lower wreaths; and often, between two separated fields of cloud, there glided down a ray of unspeakable lustre. But it was not solar light, and there was no heat. The general effect was sad, supremely melancholy. Instead of the shining firmament, spangled with its innumerable stars, shining singly or in clusters, I felt that all these subdued and shaded lights were ribbed in by vast walls of granite, which seemed to overpower me with their weight, and that all this space, great as it was, would not be enough for the march of the humblest of satellites.

Then I remembered the theory of an English captain, who likened the earth to a vast hollow sphere, in the interior of which the air became luminous because of the vast pressure that weighed upon it; while two stars, Pluto and Proserpine, rolled within upon the circuit of their mysterious orbits.

We were in reality shut up inside an immeasurable excavation. Its width could not be estimated, since the shore ran widening as far as eye could reach, nor could its length, for the dim horizon bounded the new. As for its height, it must have been several leagues. Where this vault rested upon its granite base no eye could tell; but there was a cloud hanging far above, the height of which we estimated at 12,000 feet, a greater height than that of any terrestrial vapour, and no doubt due to the great density of the air.

The word cavern does not convey any idea of this immense space; words of human tongue are inadequate to describe the discoveries of him who ventures into the deep abysses of earth.

Besides I could not tell upon what geological theory to account for the existence of such an excavation. Had the cooling of the globe produced it? I knew of celebrated caverns from the descriptions of travellers, but had never heard of any of such dimensions as this.

If the grotto of Guachara, in Colombia, visited by Humboldt, had not given up the whole of the secret of its depth to the philosopher, who investigated it to the depth of 2,500 feet, it probably did not extend much farther. The immense mammoth cave in Kentucky is of gigantic proportions, since its vaulted roof rises five hundred feet **(footnote 1)** above the level of an unfathomable lake and travellers have explored its ramifications to the extent of forty miles. But what were these cavities compared to that in which I stood with wonder and admiration, with its sky of luminous vapours, its bursts of electric light, and a vast sea filling its bed? My imagination fell powerless before such immensity.

I gazed upon these wonders in silence. Words failed me to express my feelings. I felt as if I was in some distant planet Uranus or Neptune – and in the presence of phenomena of which my terrestrial experience gave me no cognisance. For such novel sensations, new words were wanted; and my imagination failed to supply them. I gazed, I thought, I admired, with a stupefaction mingled with a certain amount of fear.

The unforeseen nature of this spectacle brought back the colour to my cheeks. I was under a new course of treatment with the aid of astonishment, and my convalescence was promoted by this novel system of therapeutics; besides, the dense and breezy air invigorated me, supplying more oxygen to my lungs.

It will be easily conceived that after an imprisonment of forty seven days in a narrow gallery it was the height of physical enjoyment to breathe a moist air impregnated with saline particles.

I was delighted to leave my dark grotto. My uncle, already familiar with these wonders, had ceased to feel surprise.

"You feel strong enough to walk a little way now?" he asked.

"Yes, certainly; and nothing could be more delightful."

"Well, take my arm, Axel, and let us follow the windings of the shore."

I eagerly accepted, and we began to coast along this new sea. On the left huge pyramids of rock, piled one upon another, produced a prodigious titanic effect. Down their sides flowed numberless waterfalls, which went on their way in brawling but pellucid streams. A few light vapours, leaping from rock to rock, denoted the place of hot springs; and streams flowed softly down to the common basin, gliding down the gentle slopes with a softer murmur.

Amongst these streams I recognised our faithful travelling companion, the Hansbach, coming to lose its little volume quietly in the mighty sea, just as if it had done nothing else since the beginning of the world.

"We shall see it no more," I said, with a sigh.

"What matters," replied the philosopher, "whether this or another serves to guide us?"

I thought him rather ungrateful.

But at that moment my attention was drawn to an unexpected sight. At a distance of five hundred paces, at the turn of a high promontory, appeared a high, tufted, dense forest. It was composed of trees of moderate height, formed like umbrellas, with exact geometrical outlines. The currents of wind seemed to have had no effect upon their shape, and in the midst of the windy blasts they stood unmoved and firm, just like a clump of petrified cedars.

I hastened forward. I could not give any name to these singular creations. Were they some of the two hundred thousand species of vegetables known hitherto, and did they claim a place of their own in the lacustrine flora? No; when we arrived under their shade my surprise turned into admiration. There stood before me productions of earth, but of gigantic stature, which my uncle immediately named.

"It is only a forest of mushrooms," said he.

And he was right. Imagine the large development attained by these plants, which prefer a warm, moist climate. I knew that the *Lycopodon giganteum* attains, according to Bulliard, a circumference of eight or nine feet; but here were pale mushrooms, thirty to forty feet high, and crowned with a cap of equal diameter. There they stood in thousands. No light could penetrate between their huge cones, and complete darkness reigned beneath those giants; they formed settlements of domes placed in close array like the round, thatched roofs of a central African city.

Yet I wanted to penetrate farther underneath, though a chill fell upon me as soon as I came under those cellular vaults. For half an hour we wandered from side to side in the damp shades, and it was a comfortable and pleasant change to arrive once more upon the sea shore.

But the subterranean vegetation was not confined to these fungi. Farther on rose groups of tall trees of colourless foliage and easy to recognise. They were lowly shrubs of earth, here attaining gigantic size; lycopodiums, a hundred feet high; the huge sigillaria, found in our coal mines; tree ferns, as tall as our fir-trees in northern latitudes; lepidodendra, with cylindrical forked stems, terminated by long leaves, and bristling with rough hairs like those of the cactus.

"Wonderful, magnificent, splendid!" cried my uncle. "Here is the entire flora of the second period of the world – the transition period. These, humble garden plants with us, were tall trees in the early ages. Look, Axel, and admire it all. Never had botanist such a feast as this!"

"You are right, my uncle. Providence seems to have preserved in this immense conservatory the antediluvian plants which the wisdom of philosophers has so sagaciously put together again."

"It is a conservatory, Axel; but is it not also a menagerie?"

"Surely not a menagerie!"

"Yes; no doubt of it. Look at that dust under your feet; see the bones scattered on the ground."

"So there are!" I cried; "bones of extinct animals."

I had rushed upon these remains, formed of indestructible phosphates of lime, and without hesitation I named these monstrous bones, which lay scattered about like decayed trunks of trees.

"Here is the lower jaw of a mastodon," **(footnote 2)** I said. "These are the molar teeth of the deinotherium; this femur must have belonged to the greatest of those beasts, the megatherium. It certainly is a menagerie, for these remains were not brought here by a deluge. The animals to which they belonged roamed on the shores of this subterranean sea, under the shade of those arborescent trees. Here are entire skeletons. And yet I cannot understand the appearance of these quadrupeds in a granite cavern."

"Why?"

"Because animal life existed upon the earth only in the secondary period, when a sediment of soil had been deposited by the rivers, and taken the place of the incandescent rocks of the primitive period."

"Well, Axel, there is a very simple answer to your objection that this soil is alluvial."

"What! At such a depth below the surface of the earth?"

"No doubt; and there is a geological explanation of the fact. At a certain period the earth consisted only of an elastic crust or bark, alternately acted on by forces from above or below, according to the laws of attraction and gravitation. Probably there were subsidences of the outer crust, when a portion of the sedimentary deposits was carried down sudden openings."

"That may be," I replied; "but if there have been creatures now extinct in these underground regions, why may not some of those monsters be now roaming through these gloomy forests, or hidden behind the steep crags?"

And as this unpleasant notion got hold of me, I surveyed with anxious scrutiny the open spaces before me; but no living creature appeared upon the barren strand.

I felt rather tired, and went to sit down at the end of a promontory, at the foot of which the waves came and beat themselves into spray. Thence my eye could sweep every part of the bay; within its extremity a little harbour was formed between the pyramidal cliffs, where the still waters slept untouched by the boisterous winds. A brig and two or three schooners might have moored within it in safety. I almost fancied I should presently see some ship issue from it, full sail, and take to the open sea under the southern breeze.

But this illusion lasted a very short time. We were the only living creatures in this subterranean world. When the wind lulled, a deeper silence than that of the deserts fell upon the arid, naked rocks, and weighed upon the surface of the ocean. I then desired to pierce the distant haze, and to rend asunder the mysterious curtain that hung across the horizon. Anxious queries arose to my lips. Where did that sea terminate? Where did it lead to? Should we ever know anything about its opposite shores?

My uncle made no doubt about it at all; I both desired and feared.

After spending an hour in the contemplation of this marvellous spectacle, we returned to the shore to regain the grotto, and I fell asleep in the midst of the strangest thoughts.

Footnote 1. One hundred and twenty. (Tr.)
Footnote 2. These animals belonged to a late geological period, the Pliocene, just before the glacial epoch, and therefore could have no connection with the carboniferous vegetation. (Tr.)

Chapter XXXI
Preparations for a Voyage of Discovery

THE NEXT MORNING I awoke feeling perfectly well. I thought a bathe would do me good, and I went to plunge for a few minutes into the waters of this mediterranean sea, for assuredly it better deserved this name than any other sea.

I came back to breakfast with a good appetite. Hans was a good caterer for our little household; he had water and fire at his disposal, so that he was able to vary our bill of fare now and then. For dessert he gave us a few cups of coffee, and never was coffee so delicious.

"Now," said my uncle, "now is the time for high tide, and we must not lose the opportunity to study this phenomenon."

"What! The tide!" I cried. "Can the influence of the sun and moon be felt down here?"

"Why not? Are not all bodies subject throughout their mass to the power of universal attraction? This mass of water cannot escape the general law. And in spite of the heavy atmospheric pressure on the surface, you will see it rise like the Atlantic itself."

At the same moment we reached the sand on the shore, and the waves were by slow degrees encroaching on the shore.

"Here is the tide rising," I cried.

"Yes, Axel; and judging by these ridges of foam, you may observe that the sea will rise about twelve feet."

"This is wonderful," I said.

"No; it is quite natural."

"You may say so, uncle; but to me it is most extraordinary, and I can hardly believe my eyes. Who would ever have imagined, under this terrestrial crust, an ocean with ebbing and flowing tides, with winds and storms?"

"Well," replied my uncle, "is there any scientific reason against it?"

"No; I see none, as soon as the theory of central heat is given up." "So then, thus far," he answered, "the theory of Sir Humphry Davy is confirmed."

"Evidently it is; and now there is no reason why there should not be seas and continents in the interior of the earth."

"No doubt," said my uncle; "and inhabited too."

"To be sure," said I; "and why should not these waters yield to us fishes of unknown species?"

"At any rate," he replied, "we have not seen any yet."

"Well, let us make some lines, and see if the bait will draw here as it does in sublunary regions."

"We will try, Axel, for we must penetrate all secrets of these newly discovered regions."

"But where are we, uncle? For I have not yet asked you that question, and your instruments must be able to furnish the answer."

"Horizontally, three hundred and fifty leagues from Iceland."

"So much as that?"

"I am sure of not being a mile out of my reckoning."

"And does the compass still show south-east?"

"Yes; with a westerly deviation of nineteen degrees forty-five minutes, just as above ground. As for its dip, a curious fact is coming to light, which I have observed carefully: that the needle, instead of dipping towards the pole as in the northern hemisphere, on the contrary, rises from it."

"Would you then conclude," I said, "that the magnetic pole is somewhere between the surface of the globe and the point where we are?"

"Exactly so; and it is likely enough that if we were to reach the spot beneath the polar regions, about that seventy-first degree where Sir James Ross has discovered the magnetic pole to be situated, we should see the needle point straight up. Therefore that mysterious centre of attraction is at no great depth."

I remarked: "It is so; and here is a fact which science has scarcely suspected."

"Science, my lad, has been built upon many errors; but they are errors which it was good to fall into, for they led to the truth."

"What depth have we now reached?"

"We are thirty-five leagues below the surface."

"So," I said, examining the map, "the Highlands of Scotland are over our heads, and the Grampians are raising their rugged summits above us."

"Yes," answered the Professor laughing. "It is rather a heavy weight to bear, but a solid arch spans over our heads. The great Architect has built it of the best materials; and never could man have given it so wide a stretch. What are the finest arches of bridges and the arcades of cathedrals, compared with this far reaching vault, with a radius of three leagues, beneath which a wide and tempest-tossed ocean may flow at its ease?"

"Oh, I am not afraid that it will fall down upon my head. But now what are your plans? Are you not thinking of returning to the surface now?"

"Return! No, indeed! We will continue our journey, everything having gone on well so far."

"But how are we to get down below this liquid surface?"

"Oh, I am not going to dive head foremost. But if all oceans are properly speaking but lakes, since they are encompassed by land, of course this internal sea will be surrounded by a coast of granite, and on the opposite shores we shall find fresh passages opening."

"How long do you suppose this sea to be?"

"Thirty or forty leagues; so that we have no time to lose, and we shall set sail tomorrow."

I looked about for a ship.

"Set sail, shall we? But I should like to see my boat first."

"It will not be a boat at all, but a good, well-made raft."

"Why," I said, "a raft would be just as hard to make as a boat, and I don't see –"

"I know you don't see; but you might hear if you would listen. Don't you hear the hammer at work? Hans is already busy at it."

"What, has he already felled the trees?"

"Oh, the trees were already down. Come, and you will see for yourself."

After half an hour's walking, on the other side of the promontory which formed the little natural harbour, I perceived Hans at work. In a few more steps I was at his side. To my great surprise a half-finished raft was already lying on the sand, made of a peculiar kind of wood, and a great number of planks, straight and bent, and of frames, were covering the ground, enough almost for a little fleet.

"Uncle, what wood is this?" I cried.

"It is fir, pine, or birch, and other northern coniferae, mineralised by the action of the sea. It is called surturbrand, a variety of brown coal or lignite, found chiefly in Iceland."

"But surely, then, like other fossil wood, it must be as hard as stone, and cannot float?"

"Sometimes that may happen; some of these woods become true anthracites; but others, such as this, have only gone through the first stage of fossil transformation. Just look," added my uncle, throwing into the sea one of those precious waifs.

The bit of wood, after disappearing, returned to the surface and oscillated to and fro with the waves.

"Are you convinced?" said my uncle.

"I am quite convinced, although it is incredible!"

By next evening, thanks to the industry and skill of our guide, the raft was made. It was ten feet by five; the planks of surturbrand, braced strongly together with cords, presented an even surface, and when launched this improvised vessel floated easily upon the waves of the Liedenbrock Sea.

Chapter XXXII
Wonders of the Deep

ON THE 13th of August we awoke early. We were now to begin to adopt a mode of travelling both more expeditious and less fatiguing than hitherto.

A mast was made of two poles spliced together, a yard was made of a third, a blanket borrowed from our coverings made a tolerable sail. There was no want of cordage for the rigging, and everything was well and firmly made.

The provisions, the baggage, the instruments, the guns, and a good quantity of fresh water from the rocks around, all found their proper places on board; and at six the Professor gave the signal to embark. Hans had fitted up a rudder to steer his vessel. He took the tiller, and unmoored; the sail was set, and we were soon afloat. At the moment of leaving the harbour, my uncle, who was tenaciously fond of naming his new discoveries, wanted to give it a name, and proposed mine amongst others.

"But I have a better to propose," I said: "Grauben. Let it be called Port Gräuben; it will look very well upon the map."

"Port Gräuben let it be then."

And so the cherished remembrance of my Virlandaise became associated with our adventurous expedition.

The wind was from the north-west. We went with it at a high rate of speed. The dense atmosphere acted with great force and impelled us swiftly on.

In an hour my uncle had been able to estimate our progress. At this rate, he said, we shall make thirty leagues in twenty-four hours, and we shall soon come in sight of the opposite shore.

I made no answer, but went and sat forward. The northern shore was already beginning to dip under the horizon. The eastern and western strands spread wide as if to bid us farewell. Before our eyes lay far and wide a vast sea; shadows of great clouds swept heavily over its silver-grey surface; the glistening bluish rays of electric light, here and there reflected by the dancing drops of spray, shot out little sheaves of light from the track we left in our rear. Soon we entirely lost sight of land; no object was left for the eye to judge by, and but for the frothy track of the raft, I might have thought we were standing still.

About twelve, immense shoals of seaweeds came in sight. I was aware of the great powers of vegetation that characterise these plants, which grow at a depth of twelve thousand feet, reproduce themselves under a pressure of four hundred atmospheres, and sometimes form barriers strong enough to impede the course of a ship. But never, I think, were such seaweeds as those which we saw floating in immense waving lines upon the sea of Liedenbrock.

Our raft skirted the whole length of the fuci, three or four thousand feet long, undulating like vast serpents beyond the reach of sight; I found some amusement in tracing these endless waves, always thinking I should come to the end of them, and for hours my patience was vying with my surprise.

What natural force could have produced such plants, and what must have been the appearance of the earth in the first ages of its formation, when, under the action of heat and moisture, the vegetable kingdom alone was developing on its surface?

Evening came, and, as on the previous day, I perceived no change in the luminous condition of the air. It was a constant condition, the permanency of which might be relied upon.

After supper I laid myself down at the foot of the mast, and fell asleep in the midst of fantastic reveries.

Hans, keeping fast by the helm, let the raft run on, which, after all, needed no steering, the wind blowing directly aft.

Since our departure from Port Gräuben, Professor Liedenbrock had entrusted the log to my care; I was to register every observation, make entries of interesting phenomena, the direction of the wind, the rate of sailing, the way we made – in a word, every particular of our singular voyage.

I shall therefore reproduce here these daily notes, written, so to speak, as the course of events directed, in order to furnish an exact narrative of our passage.

Friday, August 14. – Wind steady, N.W. The raft makes rapid way in a direct line. Coast thirty leagues to leeward. Nothing in sight before us. Intensity of light the same. Weather fine; that is to say, that the clouds are flying high, are light, and bathed in a white atmosphere resembling silver in a state of fusion. Therm. 89° Fahr.

At noon Hans prepared a hook at the end of a line. He baited it with a small piece of meat and flung it into the sea. For two hours nothing was caught. Are these waters, then, bare of inhabitants? No, there's a pull at the line. Hans draws it in and brings out a struggling fish.

"A sturgeon," I cried; "a small sturgeon."

The Professor eyes the creature attentively, and his opinion differs from mine.

The head of this fish was flat, but rounded in front, and the anterior part of its body was plated with bony, angular scales; it had no teeth, its pectoral fins were large, and of tail there was none. The animal belonged to the same order as the sturgeon, but differed from that fish in many essential particulars. After a short examination my uncle pronounced his opinion.

"This fish belongs to an extinct family, of which only fossil traces are found in the devonian formations."

"What!" I cried. "Have we taken alive an inhabitant of the seas of primitive ages?"

"Yes; and you will observe that these fossil fishes have no identity with any living species. To have in one's possession a living specimen is a happy event for a naturalist."

"But to what family does it belong?"

"It is of the order of ganoids, of the family of the cephalaspidae; and a species of pterichthys. But this one displays a peculiarity confined to all fishes that inhabit subterranean waters. It is blind, and not only blind, but actually has no eyes at all."

I looked: nothing could be more certain. But supposing it might be a solitary case, we baited afresh, and threw out our line. Surely this ocean is well peopled with fish, for in another couple of hours we took a large quantity of pterichthydes, as well as of others belonging to the extinct family of the dipterides, but of which my uncle could not tell the species; none had organs of sight. This unhoped-for catch recruited our stock of provisions.

Thus it is evident that this sea contains none but species known to us in their fossil state, in which fishes as well as reptiles are the less perfectly and completely organised the farther back their date of creation.

Perhaps we may yet meet with some of those saurians which science has reconstructed out of a bit of bone or cartilage. I took up the telescope and scanned the whole horizon, and found it everywhere a desert sea. We are far away removed from the shores.

I gaze upward in the air. Why should not some of the strange birds restored by the immortal Cuvier again flap their 'sail-broad vans' in this dense and heavy atmosphere? There are sufficient fish for their support. I survey the whole space that stretches overhead; it is as desert as the shore was.

Still my imagination carried me away amongst the wonderful speculations of palaeontology. Though awake I fell into a dream. I thought I could see floating on the surface of the waters enormous chelonia, pre-adamite tortoises, resembling floating islands. Over the dimly lighted strand there trod the huge mammals of the first ages of the world, the leptotherium (slender beast), found in the caverns of Brazil; the merycotherium (ruminating beast), found in the 'drift' of iceclad Siberia. Farther on, the pachydermatous lophiodon (crested toothed), a gigantic tapir, hides behind the rocks to dispute its prey with the anoplotherium (unarmed beast), a strange creature, which seemed a compound of horse, rhinoceros, camel, and hippopotamus. The colossal mastodon (nipple-toothed) twists and untwists his trunk, and brays and pounds with his huge tusks the fragments of rock that cover the shore; whilst the megatherium (huge beast), buttressed upon his enormous hinder paws, grubs in the soil, awaking the sonorous echoes of the granite rocks with his tremendous roarings. Higher up, the protopitheca – the first monkey that appeared on the globe – is climbing up the steep ascents. Higher yet, the pterodactyle (wing-fingered) darts in irregular zigzags to and fro in the heavy air. In the uppermost regions of the air immense birds, more powerful than the cassowary, and larger than the ostrich, spread their vast breadth of wings and strike with their heads the granite vault that bounds the sky.

All this fossil world rises to life again in my vivid imagination. I return to the scriptural periods or ages of the world, conventionally called 'days,' long before the appearance of man, when the unfinished world was as yet unfitted for his support. Then my dream backed even farther still into the ages before the creation of living beings. The mammals disappear, then the birds vanish, then the reptiles of the secondary period, and finally the fish, the crustaceans, molluscs, and articulated beings. Then the zoophytes of the transition period also return to nothing. I am the only living thing in the world: all life is concentrated in my beating heart alone. There are no more seasons; climates are no more; the heat of the globe continually increases and neutralises that of the sun. Vegetation becomes accelerated. I glide like a shade amongst arborescent ferns, treading with unsteady feet the coloured marls and the particoloured clays; I lean for support against the trunks of immense conifers; I lie in the shade of sphenophylla (wedge-leaved), asterophylla (star-leaved), and lycopods, a hundred feet high.

Ages seem no more than days! I am passed, against my will, in retrograde order, through the long series of terrestrial changes. Plants disappear; granite rocks soften; intense heat converts solid bodies into thick fluids; the waters again cover the face of the earth; they boil, they rise in whirling eddies of steam; white and ghastly mists wrap round the shifting forms of the earth, which by imperceptible degrees dissolves into a gaseous mass, glowing fiery red and white, as large and as shining as the sun.

And I myself am floating with wild caprice in the midst of this nebulous mass of fourteen hundred thousand times the volume of the earth into which it will one day be condensed, and carried forward amongst the planetary bodies. My body is no longer firm and terrestrial; it is resolved into its constituent atoms, subtilised, volatilised. Sublimed into imponderable vapour, I mingle and am lost in the endless foods of those vast globular volumes of vaporous mists, which roll upon their flaming orbits through infinite space.

But is it not a dream? Whither is it carrying me? My feverish hand has vainly attempted to describe upon paper its strange and wonderful details. I have forgotten everything that surrounds me. The Professor, the guide, the raft – are all gone out of my ken. An illusion has laid hold upon me.

"What is the matter?" my uncle breaks in.

My staring eyes are fixed vacantly upon him.

"Take care, Axel, or you will fall overboard."

At that moment I felt the sinewy hand of Hans seizing me vigorously. But for him, carried away by my dream, I should have thrown myself into the sea. "Is he mad?" cried the Professor.

"What is it all about?" at last I cried, returning to myself.

"Do you feel ill?" my uncle asked.

"No; but I have had a strange hallucination; it is over now. Is all going on right?"

"Yes, it is a fair wind and a fine sea; we are sailing rapidly along, and if I am not out in my reckoning, we shall soon land."

At these words I rose and gazed round upon the horizon, still everywhere bounded by clouds alone.

Chapter XXXIII
A Battle Of Monsters

SATURDAY, AUGUST 15. – The sea unbroken all round. No land in sight. The horizon seems extremely distant.

My head is still stupefied with the vivid reality of my dream.

My uncle has had no dreams, but he is out of temper. He examines the horizon all round with his glass, and folds his arms with the air of an injured man.

I remark that Professor Liedenbrock has a tendency to relapse into an impatient mood, and I make a note of it in my log. All my danger and sufferings were needed to strike a spark of human feeling out of him; but now that I am well his nature has resumed its sway. And yet, what cause was there for anger? Is not the voyage prospering as favourably as possible under the circumstances? Is not the raft spinning along with marvellous speed?

"You seem anxious, my uncle," I said, seeing him continually with his glass to his eye.

"Anxious! No, not at all."

"Impatient, then?"

"One might be, with less reason than now."

"Yet we are going very fast."

"What does that signify? I am not complaining that the rate is slow, but that the sea is so wide."

I then remembered that the Professor, before starting, had estimated the length of this underground sea at thirty leagues. Now we had made three times the distance, yet still the southern coast was not in sight.

"We are not descending as we ought to be," the Professor declares. "We are losing time, and the fact is, I have not come all this way to take a little sail upon a pond on a raft."

He called this sea a pond, and our long voyage, taking a little sail!

"But," I remarked, "since we have followed the road that Saknussemm has shown us –"

"That is just the question. Have we followed that road? Did Saknussemm meet this sheet of water? Did he cross it? Has not the stream that we followed led us altogether astray?"

"At any rate we cannot feel sorry to have come so far. This prospect is magnificent, and –"

"But I don't care for prospects. I came with an object, and I mean to attain it. Therefore don't talk to me about views and prospects."

I take this as my answer, and I leave the Professor to bite his lips with impatience. At six in the evening Hans asks for his wages, and his three rix dollars are counted out to him.

Sunday, August 16. – Nothing new. Weather unchanged. The wind freshens. On awaking, my first thought was to observe the intensity of the light. I was possessed with an apprehension lest the electric light should grow dim, or fail altogether. But there seemed no reason to fear. The shadow of the raft was clearly outlined upon the surface of the waves.

Truly this sea is of infinite width. It must be as wide as the Mediterranean or the Atlantic – and why not?

My uncle took soundings several times. He tied the heaviest of our pickaxes to a long rope which he let down two hundred fathoms. No bottom yet; and we had some difficulty in hauling up our plummet.

But when the pick was shipped again, Hans pointed out on its surface deep prints as if it had been violently compressed between two hard bodies.

I looked at the hunter.

"*Tänder,*" said he.

I could not understand him, and turned to my uncle who was entirely absorbed in his calculations. I had rather not disturb him while he is quiet. I return to the Icelander. He by a snapping motion of his jaws conveys his ideas to me.

"Teeth!" I cried, considering the iron bar with more attention.

Yes, indeed, those are the marks of teeth imprinted upon the metal! The jaws which they arm must be possessed of amazing strength. Is there some monster beneath us belonging to the extinct races, more voracious than the shark, more fearful in vastness than the whale? I could not take my eyes off this indented iron bar. Surely will my last night's dream be realised?

These thoughts agitated me all day, and my imagination scarcely calmed down after several hours' sleep.

Monday, August 17. – I am trying to recall the peculiar instincts of the monsters of the pre-adamite world, who, coming next in succession after the molluscs, the crustaceans and le fishes, preceded the animals of mammalian race upon the earth. The world then belonged to reptiles. Those monsters held the mastery in the seas of the secondary period. They possessed a perfect organisation, gigantic proportions, prodigious strength. The saurians of our day, the alligators and the crocodiles, are but feeble reproductions of their forefathers of primitive ages.

I shudder as I recall these monsters to my remembrance. No human eye has ever beheld them living. They burdened this earth a thousand ages before man appeared, but their fossil remains, found in the argillaceous limestone called by the English the lias, have enabled their colossal structure to be perfectly built up again and anatomically ascertained.

I saw at the Hamburg museum the skeleton of one of these creatures thirty feet in length. Am I then fated – I, a denizen of earth – to be placed face to face with these representatives of long extinct families? No; surely it cannot be! Yet the deep marks of conical teeth upon the iron pick are certainly those of the crocodile.

My eyes are fearfully bent upon the sea. I dread to see one of these monsters darting forth from its submarine caverns. I suppose Professor Liedenbrock was of my opinion too, and even shared my fears, for after having examined the pick, his eyes traversed the ocean from side to side. What a very bad notion that was of his, I thought to myself, to take soundings just here! He has disturbed some monstrous beast in its remote den, and if we are not attacked on our voyage –

I look at our guns and see that they are all right. My uncle notices it, and looks on approvingly.

Already widely disturbed regions on the surface of the water indicate some commotion below. The danger is approaching. We must be on the look out.

Tuesday, August 18. – Evening came, or rather the time came when sleep weighs down the weary eyelids, for there is no night here, and the ceaseless light wearies the eyes with its persistency just as if we were sailing under an arctic sun. Hans was at the helm. During his watch I slept.

Two hours afterwards a terrible shock awoke me. The raft was heaved up on a watery mountain and pitched down again, at a distance of twenty fathoms.

"What is the matter?" shouted my uncle. "Have we struck land?"

Hans pointed with his finger at a dark mass six hundred yards away, rising and falling alternately with heavy plunges. I looked and cried:

"It is an enormous porpoise."

"Yes," replied my uncle, "and there is a sea lizard of vast size."

"And farther on a monstrous crocodile. Look at its vast jaws and its rows of teeth! It is diving down!"

"There's a whale, a whale!" cried the Professor. "I can see its great fins. See how he is throwing out air and water through his blowers."

And in fact two liquid columns were rising to a considerable height above the sea. We stood amazed, thunderstruck, at the presence of such a herd of marine monsters. They were of supernatural dimensions; the smallest of them would have crunched our raft, crew and all, at one snap of its huge jaws.

Hans wants to tack to get away from this dangerous neighbourhood; but he sees on the other hand enemies not less terrible; a tortoise forty feet long, and a serpent of thirty, lifting its fearful head and gleaming eyes above the flood.

Flight was out of the question now. The reptiles rose; they wheeled around our little raft with a rapidity greater than that of express trains. They described around us gradually narrowing circles. I took up my rifle. But what could a ball do against the scaly armour with which these enormous beasts were clad?

We stood dumb with fear. They approach us close: on one side the crocodile, on the other the serpent. The remainder of the sea monsters have disappeared. I prepare to fire. Hans stops me by a gesture. The two monsters pass within a hundred and fifty yards of the raft, and hurl themselves the one upon the other, with a fury which prevents them from seeing us.

At three hundred yards from us the battle was fought. We could distinctly observe the two monsters engaged in deadly conflict. But it now seems to me as if the other animals were taking part in the fray – the porpoise, the whale, the lizard, the tortoise. Every moment I seem to see one or other of them. I point them to the Icelander. He shakes his head negatively.

"*Tva,*" says he.

"What two? Does he mean that there are only two animals?"

"He is right," said my uncle, whose glass has never left his eye.

"Surely you must be mistaken," I cried.

"No: the first of those monsters has a porpoise's snout, a lizard's head, a crocodile's teeth; and hence our mistake. It is the ichthyosaurus (the fish lizard), the most terrible of the ancient monsters of the deep."

"And the other?"

"The other is a plesiosaurus (almost lizard), a serpent, armoured with the carapace and the paddles of a turtle; he is the dreadful enemy of the other."

Hans had spoken truly. Two monsters only were creating all this commotion; and before my eyes are two reptiles of the primitive world. I can distinguish the eye of the ichthyosaurus glowing like a red-hot coal, and as large as a man's head. Nature has endowed it with an optical apparatus of extreme power, and capable of resisting the pressure of the great volume of water in the depths it inhabits. It has been appropriately called the saurian whale, for it has both the swiftness and the rapid movements of this monster of our own day. This one is not less than a hundred feet long, and I can judge of its size when it sweeps over the waters the vertical coils of its tail. Its jaw is enormous, and according to naturalists it is armed with no less than one hundred and eighty-two teeth.

The plesiosaurus, a serpent with a cylindrical body and a short tail, has four flappers or paddles to act like oars. Its body is entirely covered with a thick armour of scales, and its neck, as flexible as a swan's, rises thirty feet above the waves.

Those huge creatures attacked each other with the greatest animosity. They heaved around them liquid mountains, which rolled even to our raft and rocked it perilously. Twenty times we were near capsizing. Hissings of prodigious force are heard. The two beasts are fast locked together; I cannot distinguish the one from the other. The probable rage of the conqueror inspires us with intense fear.

One hour, two hours, pass away. The struggle continues with unabated ferocity. The combatants alternately approach and recede from our raft. We remain motionless, ready to fire. Suddenly the ichthyosaurus and the plesiosaurus disappear below, leaving a whirlpool eddying in the water. Several minutes pass by while the fight goes on under water.

All at once an enormous head is darted up, the head of the plesiosaurus. The monster is wounded to death. I no longer see his scaly armour. Only his long neck shoots up, drops again, coils and uncoils, droops, lashes the waters like a gigantic whip, and writhes like a worm that you tread on. The water is splashed for a long way around. The spray almost blinds us. But soon the reptile's agony draws to an end; its movements become fainter, its contortions cease to be so violent, and the long serpentine form lies a lifeless log on the labouring deep.

As for the ichthyosaurus – has he returned to his submarine cavern? Or will he reappear on the surface of the sea?

Chapter XXXIV
The Great Geyser

WEDNESDAY, AUGUST 19. – Fortunately the wind blows violently, and has enabled us to flee from the scene of the late terrible struggle. Hans keeps at his post at the helm. My uncle, whom the absorbing incidents of the combat had drawn away from his contemplations, began again to look impatiently around him.

The voyage resumes its uniform tenor, which I don't care to break with a repetition of such events as yesterday's.

Thursday, August 20. – Wind N.N.E., unsteady and fitful. Temperature high. Rate three and a half leagues an hour.

About noon a distant noise is heard. I note the fact without being able to explain it. It is a continuous roar.

"In the distance," says the Professor, "there is a rock or islet, against which the sea is breaking."

Hans climbs up the mast, but sees no breakers. The ocean' is smooth and unbroken to its farthest limit.

Three hours pass away. The roarings seem to proceed from a very distant waterfall.

I remark upon this to my uncle, who replies doubtfully: "Yes, I am convinced that I am right." Are we, then, speeding forward to some cataract which will cast us down an abyss? This method of getting on may please the Professor, because it is vertical; but for my part I prefer the more ordinary modes of horizontal progression.

At any rate, some leagues to the windward there must be some noisy phenomenon, for now the roarings are heard with increasing loudness. Do they proceed from the sky or the ocean?

I look up to the atmospheric vapours, and try to fathom their depths. The sky is calm and motionless. The clouds have reached the utmost limit of the lofty vault, and there lie still bathed in the bright glare of the electric light. It is not there that we must seek for the cause of this phenomenon. Then I examine the horizon, which is unbroken and clear of all mist. There is no change in its aspect. But if this noise arises from a fall, a cataract, if all this ocean flows away headlong into a lower basin yet, if that deafening roar is produced by a mass of falling water, the current must needs accelerate, and its increasing speed will give me the measure of the peril that threatens us. I consult the current: there is none. I throw an empty bottle into the sea: it lies still.

About four Hans rises, lays hold of the mast, climbs to its top. Thence his eye sweeps a large area of sea, and it is fixed upon a point. His countenance exhibits no surprise, but his eye is immovably steady.

"He sees something," says my uncle.

"I believe he does."

Hans comes down, then stretches his arm to the south, saying:

"*Dere nere!*"

"Down there?" repeated my uncle.

Then, seizing his glass, he gazes attentively for a minute, which seems to me an age.

"Yes, yes!" he cried. "I see a vast inverted cone rising from the surface."

"Is it another sea beast?"

"Perhaps it is."

"Then let us steer farther westward, for we know something of the danger of coming across monsters of that sort."

"Let us go straight on," replied my uncle.

I appealed to Hans. He maintained his course inflexibly.

Yet, if at our present distance from the animal, a distance of twelve leagues at the least, the column of water driven through its blowers may be distinctly seen, it must needs be of vast size. The commonest prudence would counsel immediate flight; but we did not come so far to be prudent.

Imprudently, therefore, we pursue our way. The nearer we approach, the higher mounts the jet of water. What monster can possibly fill itself with such a quantity of water, and spurt it up so continuously?

At eight in the evening we are not two leagues distant from it. Its body – dusky, enormous, hillocky – lies spread upon the sea like an islet. Is it illusion or fear? Its length seems to me a couple of thousand yards. What can be this cetacean, which neither Cuvier nor Blumenbach knew anything about? It lies motionless, as if asleep; the sea seems unable to move it in the least; it is the waves that undulate upon its sides. The column of water thrown up to a height of five hundred feet falls in rain with a deafening uproar.

And here are we scudding like lunatics before the wind, to get near to a monster that a hundred whales a day would not satisfy!

Terror seizes upon me. I refuse to go further. I will cut the halliards if necessary! I am in open mutiny against the Professor, who vouchsafes no answer.

Suddenly Hans rises, and pointing with his finger at the menacing object, he says:

"*Holm.*"

"An island!" cries my uncle.

"That's not an island!" I cried sceptically.

"It's nothing else," shouted the Professor, with a loud laugh.

"But that column of water?"

"*Geyser,*" said Hans.

"No doubt it is a geyser, like those in Iceland."

At first I protest against being so widely mistaken as to have taken an island for a marine monster. But the evidence is against me, and I have to confess my error. It is nothing worse than a natural phenomenon.

As we approach nearer the dimensions of the liquid column become magnificent. The islet resembles, with a most deceiving likeness, an enormous cetacean, whose head dominates the waves at a height of twenty yards. The geyser, a word meaning 'fury,' rises majestically from its extremity. Deep and heavy explosions are heard from time to time, when the enormous jet, possessed with more furious violence, shakes its plumy crest, and springs with a bound till it reaches the lowest stratum of the clouds. It stands alone. No steam vents, no hot springs surround it, and all the volcanic power of the region is concentrated here. Sparks of electric fire mingle with the dazzling sheaf of lighted fluid, every drop of which refracts the prismatic colours.

"Let us land," said the Professor.

"But we must carefully avoid this waterspout, which would sink our raft in a moment."

Hans, steering with his usual skill, brought us to the other extremity of the islet.

I leaped up on the rock; my uncle lightly followed, while our hunter remained at his post, like a man too wise ever to be astonished.

We walked upon granite mingled with siliceous tufa. The soil shivers and shakes under our feet, like the sides of an overheated boiler filled with steam struggling to get loose. We come in sight of a small central basin, out of which the geyser springs. I plunge a register thermometer into the boiling water. It marks an intense heat of 325°, which is far above the boiling point; therefore this water issues from an ardent furnace, which is not at all in harmony with Professor Liedenbrock's theories. I cannot help making the remark.

"Well," he replied, "how does that make against my doctrine?"

"Oh, nothing at all," I said, seeing that I was going in opposition to immovable obstinacy.

Still I am constrained to confess that hitherto we have been wonderfully favoured, and that for some reason unknown to myself we have accomplished our journey under singularly favourable conditions of temperature. But it seems manifest to me that some day we shall reach a region where the central heat attains its highest limits, and goes beyond a point that can be registered by our thermometers.

"That is what we shall see." So says the Professor, who, having named this volcanic islet after his nephew, gives the signal to embark again.

For some minutes I am still contemplating the geyser. I notice that it throws up its column of water with variable force: sometimes sending it to a great height, then gain to a lower, which I attribute to the variable pressure of the steam accumulated in s reservoir.

At last we leave the island, rounding away past the low rocks on its southern shore. Ians has taken advantage of the halt to refit his rudder.

But before going any farther I make a few observations, to calculate the distance we ıave gone over, and note them in my journal. We have crossed two hundred and seventy eagues of sea since leaving Port Gräuben; and we are six hundred and twenty leagues rom Iceland, under England **(footnote 3)**.

Footnote 3. This distance carries the travellers as far as under the Pyrenees if the league measures three miles. (Tr.)

Chapter XXXV
An Electric Storm

FRIDAY, AUGUST 21. – On the morrow the magnificent geyser has disappeared. The wind has risen, and has rapidly carried us away from Axel Island. The roarings become lost in the distance.

The weather – if we may use that term – will change before long. The atmosphere is charged with vapours, pervaded with the electricity generated by the evaporation of saline waters. The clouds are sinking lower, and assume an olive hue. The electric light can scarcely penetrate through the dense curtain which has dropped over the theatre on which the battle of the elements is about to be waged.

I feel peculiar sensations, like many creatures on earth at the approach of violent atmospheric changes. The heavily voluted cumulus clouds lower gloomily and threateningly; they wear that implacable look which I have sometimes noticed at the outbreak of a great storm. The air is heavy; the sea is calm.

In the distance the clouds resemble great bales of cotton, piled up in picturesque disorder. By degrees they dilate, and gain in huge size what they lose in number. Such is their ponderous weight that they cannot rise from the horizon; but, obeying an impulse from higher currents, their dense consistency slowly yields. The gloom upon them deepens; and they soon present to our view a ponderous mass of almost level surface. From time to time a fleecy tuft of mist, with yet some gleaming light left upon it, drops down upon the dense floor of grey, and loses itself in the opaque and impenetrable mass.

The atmosphere is evidently charged and surcharged with electricity. My whole body is saturated; my hair bristles just as when you stand upon an insulated stool under the action of an electrical machine. It seems to me as if my companions, the moment they touched me, would receive a severe shock like that from an electric eel.

At ten in the morning the symptoms of storm become aggravated. The wind never lulls but to acquire increased strength; the vast bank of heavy clouds is a huge reservoir of fearful windy gusts and rushing storms.

I am loth to believe these atmospheric menaces, and yet I cannot help muttering:

"Here's some very bad weather coming on."

The Professor made no answer. His temper is awful, to judge from the working of his features, as he sees this vast length of ocean unrolling before him to an indefinite extent. He can only spare time to shrug his shoulders viciously.

"There's a heavy storm coming on," I cried, pointing towards the horizon. "Those clouds seem as if they were going to crush the sea."

A deep silence falls on all around. The lately roaring winds are hushed into a dead calm; nature seems to breathe no more, and to be sinking into the stillness of death. On the mast already I see the light play of a lambent St. Elmo's fire; the outstretched sail catches not a breath of wind, and hangs like a sheet of lead. The rudder stands motionless in a sluggish, waveless sea. But if we have now ceased to advance why do we yet leave that sail loose, which at the first shock of the tempest may capsize us in a moment?

"Let us reef the sail and cut the mast down!" I cried. "That will be safest."

"No, no! Never!" shouted my impetuous uncle. "Never! Let the wind catch us if it will! What I want is to get the least glimpse of rock or shore, even if our raft should be smashed into shivers!"

The words were hardly out of his mouth when a sudden change took place in the southern sky. The piled-up vapours condense into water; and the air, put into violent action to supply the vacuum left by the condensation of the mists, rouses itself into a whirlwind. It rushes on from the farthest recesses of the vast cavern. The darkness deepens; scarcely can I jot down a few hurried notes. The helm makes a bound. My uncle falls full length; I creep close to him. He has laid a firm hold upon a rope, and appears to watch with grim satisfaction this awful display of elemental strife.

Hans stirs not. His long hair blown by the pelting storm, and laid flat across his immovable countenance, makes him a strange figure; for the end of each lock of loose flowing hair is tipped with little luminous radiations. This frightful mask of electric sparks suggests to me, even in this dizzy excitement, a comparison with pre-adamite man, the contemporary of the ichthyosaurus and the megatherium **(footnote 4)**.

The mast yet holds firm. The sail stretches tight like a bubble ready to burst. The raft flies at a rate that I cannot reckon, but not so fast as the foaming clouds of spray which it dashes from side to side in its headlong speed.

"The sail! The sail!" I cry, motioning to lower it.

"No!" replies my uncle.

"*Nej!*" repeats Hans, leisurely shaking his head.

But now the rain forms a rushing cataract in front of that horizon toward which we are running with such maddening speed. But before it has reached us the rain cloud parts asunder, the sea boils, and the electric fires are brought into violent action by a mighty chemical power that descends from the higher regions. The most vivid flashes of lightning are mingled with the violent crash of continuous thunder. Ceaseless fiery arrows dart in and out amongst the flying thunder-clouds; the vaporous mass soon glows with incandescent heat; hailstones rattle fiercely down, and as they dash upon our iron tools they too emit gleams and flashes of lurid light. The heaving waves resemble fiery volcanic hills, each belching forth its own interior flames, and every crest is plumed with dancing fire. My eyes fail under the dazzling light, my ears are stunned with the incessant crash of thunder. I must be bound to the mast, which bows like a reed before the mighty strength of the storm.

(Here my notes become vague and indistinct. I have only been able to find a few which I seem to have jotted down almost unconsciously. But their very brevity and their obscurity reveal the intensity of the excitement which dominated me, and describe the actual position even better than my memory could do.)

Sunday, August 23. – Where are we? Driven forward with a swiftness that cannot be measured.

The night was fearful; no abatement of the storm. The din and uproar are incessant; our ears are bleeding; to exchange a word is impossible.

The lightning flashes with intense brilliancy, and never seems to cease for a moment. Zigzag streams of bluish white fire dash down upon the sea and rebound, and then take an upward flight till they strike the granite vault that overarches our heads. Suppose that solid roof should crumble down upon our heads! Other flashes with incessant play cross their vivid fires, while others again roll themselves into balls of living fire which explode like bombshells, but the music of which scarcely-adds to the din of the battle strife that almost deprives us of our senses of hearing and sight; the limit of intense loudness has been passed within which the human ear can distinguish one sound from another. If all the powder magazines in the world were to explode at once, we should hear no more than we do now.

From the under surface of the clouds there are continual emissions of lurid light; electric matter is in continual evolution from their component molecules; the gaseous elements of the air need to be slaked with moisture; for innumerable columns of water rush upwards into the air and fall back again in white foam.

Whither are we flying? My uncle lies full length across the raft.

The heat increases. I refer to the thermometer; it indicates ...(the figure is obliterated).

Monday, August 24. – Will there be an end to it? Is the atmospheric condition, having once reached this density, to become final?

We are prostrated and worn out with fatigue. But Hans is as usual. The raft bears on still to the south-east. We have made two hundred leagues since we left Axel Island.

At noon the violence of the storm redoubles. We are obliged to secure as fast as possible every article that belongs to our cargo. Each of us is lashed to some part of the raft. The waves rise above our heads.

For three days we have never been able to make each other hear a word. Our mouths open, our lips move, but not a word can be heard. We cannot even make ourselves heard by approaching our mouth close to the ear.

My uncle has drawn nearer to me. He has uttered a few words. They seem to be 'We are lost'; but I am not sure.

At last I write down the words: "Let us lower the sail."

He nods his consent.

Scarcely has he lifted his head again before a ball of fire has bounded over the waves and lighted on board our raft. Mast and sail flew up in an instant together, and I saw them carried up to prodigious height, resembling in appearance a pterodactyle, one of those strong birds of the infant world.

We lay there, our blood running cold with unspeakable terror. The fireball, half of it white, half azure blue, and the size of a ten-inch shell, moved slowly about the raft, but revolving on its own axis with astonishing velocity, as if whipped round by the force of the whirlwind. Here it comes, there it glides, now it is up the ragged stump of the mast, thence it lightly leaps on the provision bag, descends with a light bound, and just skims the powder magazine. Horrible! we shall be blown up; but no, the dazzling disk of mysterious light nimbly leaps aside; it approaches Hans, who fixes his blue eye upon it steadily; it threatens the head of my uncle, who falls upon his knees with his head down to avoid it. And now my turn comes; pale and trembling under the blinding splendour and the melting heat, it drops at my feet, spinning silently round upon the deck; I try to move my foot away, but cannot.

A suffocating smell of nitrogen fills the air, it enters the throat, it fills the lungs We suffer stifling pains.

Why am I unable to move my foot? Is it riveted to the planks? Alas! the fall upon our fated raft of this electric globe has magnetised every iron article on board. The instruments, the tools, our guns, are clashing and clanking violently in their collisions with each other; the nails of my boots cling tenaciously to a plate of iron let into the timbers, and I cannot draw my foot away from the spot. At last by a violent effort I release myself at the instant when the ball in its gyrations was about to seize upon it, and carry me off my feet....

Ah! What a flood of intense and dazzling light! the globe has burst, and we are deluged with tongues of fire!

Then all the light disappears. I could just see my uncle at full length on the raft, and Hans still at his helm and spitting fire under the action of the electricity which has saturated him.

But where are we going to? Where?

* * *

Tuesday, August 25. – I recover from a long swoon. The storm continues to roar and rage; the lightnings dash hither and thither, like broods of fiery serpents filling all the air. Are we still under the sea? Yes, we are borne at incalculable speed. We have been carried under England, under the channel, under France, perhaps under the whole of Europe.

* * *

A fresh noise is heard! Surely it is the sea breaking upon the rocks! But then...

Footnote 4. Rather of the mammoth and the mastodon. (Tr.)

Chapter XXXVI
Calm Philosophic Discussions

HERE I END what I may call my log, happily saved from the wreck, and I resume my narrative as before.

What happened when the raft was dashed upon the rocks is more than I can tell. I felt myself hurled into the waves; and if I escaped from death, and if my body was not torn over the sharp edges of the rocks, it was because the powerful arm of Hans came to my rescue.

The brave Icelander carried me out of the reach of the waves, over a burning sand where I found myself by the side of my uncle.

Then he returned to the rocks, against which the furious waves were beating, to save what he could. I was unable to speak. I was shattered with fatigue and excitement; I wanted a whole hour to recover even a little.

But a deluge of rain was still falling, though with that violence which generally denotes the near cessation of a storm. A few overhanging rocks afforded us some shelter from the storm. Hans prepared some food, which I could not touch; and each of us, exhausted with three sleepless nights, fell into a broken and painful sleep.

The next day the weather was splendid. The sky and the sea had sunk into sudden repose. Every trace of the awful storm had disappeared. The exhilarating voice of the Professor fell upon my ears as I awoke; he was ominously cheerful.

"Well, my boy," he cried, "have you slept well?"

Would not any one have thought that we were still in our cheerful little house on the Königstrasse and that I was only just coming down to breakfast, and that I was to be married to Gräuben that day?

Alas! If the tempest had but sent the raft a little more east, we should have passed under Germany, under my beloved town of Hamburg, under the very street where dwelt all that I loved most in the world. Then only forty leagues would have separated us! But they were forty leagues perpendicular of solid granite wall, and in reality we were a thousand leagues asunder!

All these painful reflections rapidly crossed my mind before I could answer my uncle's question.

"Well, now," he repeated, "won't you tell me how you have slept?"

"Oh, very well," I said. "I am only a little knocked up, but I shall soon be better."

"Oh," says my uncle, "that's nothing to signify. You are only a little bit tired."

"But you, uncle, you seem in very good spirits this morning."

"Delighted, my boy, delighted. We have got there."

"To our journey's end?"

"No; but we have got to the end of that endless sea. Now we shall go by land, and really begin to go down! Down! Down!"

"But, my dear uncle, do let me ask you one question."

"Of course, Axel."

"How about returning?"

"Returning? Why, you are talking about the return before the arrival."

"No, I only want to know how that is to be managed."

"In the simplest way possible. When we have reached the centre of the globe, either we shall find some new way to get back, or we shall come back like decent folks the way we came. I feel pleased at the thought that it is sure not to be shut against us."

"But then we shall have to refit the raft."

"Of course."

"Then, as to provisions, have we enough to last?"

"Yes; to be sure we have. Hans is a clever fellow, and I am sure he must have saved a large part of our cargo. But still let us go and make sure."

We left this grotto which lay open to every wind. At the same time I cherished a trembling hope which was a fear as well. It seemed to me impossible that the terrible wreck of the raft should not have destroyed everything on board. On my arrival on the shore I found Hans surrounded by an assemblage of articles all arranged in good order. My uncle shook hands with him with a lively gratitude. This man, with almost superhuman devotion, had been at work all the while that we were asleep, and had saved the most precious of the articles at the risk of his life.

Not that we had suffered no losses. For instance, our firearms; but we might do without them. Our stock of powder had remained uninjured after having risked blowing up during the storm.

"Well," cried the Professor, "as we have no guns we cannot hunt, that's all."

"Yes, but how about the instruments?"

"Here is the aneroid, the most useful of all, and for which I would have given all the others. By means of it I can calculate the depth and know when we have reached the centre; without it we might very likely go beyond, and come out at the antipodes!"

Such high spirits as these were rather too strong.

"But where is the compass? I asked.

"Here it is, upon this rock, in perfect condition, as well as the thermometers and the chronometer. The hunter is a splendid fellow."

There was no denying it. We had all our instruments. As for tools and appliances, there they all lay on the ground – ladders, ropes, picks, spades, etc.

Still there was the question of provisions to be settled, and I asked – "How are we off for provisions?"

The boxes containing these were in a line upon the shore, in a perfect state of preservation; for the most part the sea had spared them, and what with biscuits, salt meat, spirits, and salt fish, we might reckon on four months' supply.

"Four months!" cried the Professor. "We have time to go and to return; and with what is left I will give a grand dinner to my friends at the Johannaeum."

I ought by this time to have been quite accustomed to my uncle's ways; yet there was always something fresh about him to astonish me.

"Now," said he, "we will replenish our supply of water with the rain which the storm has left in all these granite basins; therefore we shall have no reason to fear anything from thirst. As for the raft, I will recommend Hans to do his best to repair it, although I don't expect it will be of any further use to us."

"How so?" I cried.

"An idea of my own, my lad. I don't think we shall come out by the way that we went in."

I stared at the Professor with a good deal of mistrust. I asked, was he not touched in the brain? And yet there was method in his madness.

"And now let us go to breakfast," said he.

I followed him to a headland, after he had given his instructions to the hunter. There preserved meat, biscuit, and tea made us an excellent meal, one of the best I ever remember. Hunger, the fresh air, the calm quiet weather, after the commotions we had gone through, all contributed to give me a good appetite.

Whilst breakfasting I took the opportunity to put to my uncle the question where we were now.

"That seems to me," I said, "rather difficult to make out."

"Yes, it is difficult," he said, "to calculate exactly; perhaps even impossible, since during these three stormy days I have been unable to keep any account of the rate or direction of the raft; but still we may get an approximation."

"The last observation," I remarked, "was made on the island, when the geyser was –"

"You mean Axel Island. Don't decline the honour of having given your name to the first island ever discovered in the central parts of the globe."

"Well," said I, "let it be Axel Island. Then we had cleared two hundred and seventy leagues of sea, and we were six hundred leagues from Iceland."

"Very well," answered my uncle; "let us start from that point and count four days' storm, during which our rate cannot have been less than eighty leagues in the twenty-four hours."

"That is right; and this would make three hundred leagues more."

"Yes, and the Liedenbrock sea would be six hundred leagues from shore to shore. Surely, Axel, it may vie in size with the Mediterranean itself."

"Especially," I replied, "if it happens that we have only crossed it in its narrowest part. And it is a curious circumstance," I added, "that if my computations are right, and we are nine hundred leagues from Rejkiavik, we have now the Mediterranean above our head."

"That is a good long way, my friend. But whether we are under Turkey or the Atlantic depends very much upon the question in what direction we have been moving. Perhaps we have deviated."

"No, I think not. Our course has been the same all along, and I believe this shore is south-east of Port Gräuben."

"Well," replied my uncle, "we may easily ascertain this by consulting the compass. Let us go and see what it says."

The Professor moved towards the rock upon which Hans had laid down the instruments. He was gay and full of spirits; he rubbed his hands, he studied his attitudes. I followed him, curious to know if I was right in my estimate. As soon as we had arrived at the rock my uncle took the compass, laid it horizontally, and questioned the needle, which, after a few oscillations, presently assumed a fixed position. My uncle looked, and looked, and looked again. He rubbed his eyes, and then turned to me thunderstruck with some unexpected discovery.

"What is the matter?" I asked.

He motioned to me to look. An exclamation of astonishment burst from me. The north pole of the needle was turned to what we supposed to be the south. It pointed to the shore instead of to the open sea! I shook the box, examined it again, it was in perfect condition. In whatever position I placed the box the needle pertinaciously returned to this unexpected quarter. Therefore there seemed no reason to doubt that during the storm there had been a sudden change of wind unperceived by us, which had brought our raft back to the shore which we thought we had left so long a distance behind us.

Chapter XXXVII
The Liedenbrock Museum of Geology

HOW SHALL I describe the strange series of passions which in succession shook the breast of Professor Liedenbrock? First stupefaction, then incredulity, lastly a downright burst of rage. Never had I seen the man so put out of countenance and so disturbed. The fatigues of our passage across, the dangers met, had all to be begun over again. We had gone backwards instead of forwards!

But my uncle rapidly recovered himself.

"Aha! Will fate play tricks upon me? Will the elements lay plots against me? Shall fire, air, and water make a combined attack against me? Well, they shall know what a determined man can do. I will not yield. I will not stir a single foot backwards, and it will be seen whether man or nature is to have the upper hand!"

Erect upon the rock, angry and threatening, Otto Liedenbrock was a rather grotesque fierce parody upon the fierce Achilles defying the lightning. But I thought it my duty to interpose and attempt to lay some restraint upon this unmeasured fanaticism.

"Just listen to me," I said firmly. "Ambition must have a limit somewhere; we cannot perform impossibilities; we are not at all fit for another sea voyage; who would dream of undertaking a voyage of five hundred leagues upon a heap of rotten planks, with a blanket in rags for a sail, a stick for a mast, and fierce winds in our teeth? We cannot steer; we shall be buffeted by the tempests, and we should be fools and madmen to attempt to cross a second time."

I was able to develop this series of unanswerable reasons for ten minutes without interruption; not that the Professor was paying any respectful attention to his nephew's arguments, but because he was deaf to all my eloquence.

"To the raft!" he shouted.

Such was his only reply. It was no use for me to entreat, supplicate, get angry, or do anything else in the way of opposition; it would only have been opposing a will harder than the granite rock.

Hans was finishing the repairs of the raft. One would have thought that this strange being was guessing at my uncle's intentions. With a few more pieces of surturbrand he had refitted our vessel. A sail already hung from the new mast, and the wind was playing in its waving folds.

The Professor said a few words to the guide, and immediately he put everything on board and arranged every necessary for our departure. The air was clear – and the north-west wind blew steadily.

What could I do? Could I stand against the two? It was impossible? If Hans had but taken my side! But no, it was not to be. The Icelander seemed to have renounced all will of his own and made a vow to forget and deny himself. I could get nothing out of a servant so feudalised, as it were, to his master. My only course was to proceed.

I was therefore going with as much resignation as I could find to resume my accustomed place on the raft, when my uncle laid his hand upon my shoulder.

"We shall not sail until tomorrow," he said.

I made a movement intended to express resignation.

"I must neglect nothing," he said; "and since my fate has driven me on this part of the coast, I will not leave it until I have examined it."

To understand what followed, it must be borne in mind that, through circumstances hereafter to be explained, we were not really where the Professor supposed we were. In fact we were not upon the north shore of the sea.

"Now let us start upon fresh discoveries," I said.

And leaving Hans to his work we started off together. The space between the water and the foot of the cliffs was considerable. It took half an hour to bring us to the wall of rock. We trampled under our feet numberless shells of all the forms and sizes which existed in the earliest ages of the world. I also saw immense carapaces more than fifteen feet in diameter. They had been the coverings of those gigantic glyptodons or armadilloes of the pleiocene period, of which the modern tortoise is but a miniature representative **(footnote 5)**. The soil was besides this scattered with stony fragments, boulders rounded by water action, and ridged up in successive lines. I was therefore led to the conclusion that at one time the sea must have covered the ground on which we were treading. On the loose and scattered rocks, now out of the reach of the highest tides, the waves had left manifest traces of their power to wear their way in the hardest stone.

This might up to a certain point explain the existence of an ocean forty leagues beneath the surface of the globe. But in my opinion this liquid mass would be lost by degrees farther and farther within the interior of the earth, and it certainly had its origin in the waters of the ocean overhead, which had made their way hither through some fissure. Yet it must be believed that that fissure is now closed, and that all this cavern or immense reservoir was filled in a very short time. Perhaps even this water, subjected to the fierce action of central heat, had partly been resolved into vapour. This would explain the existence of those clouds suspended over our heads and the development of that electricity which raised such tempests within the bowels of the earth.

This theory of the phenomena we had witnessed seemed satisfactory to me; for however great and stupendous the phenomena of nature, fixed physical laws will or may always explain them.

We were therefore walking upon sedimentary soil, the deposits of the waters of former ages. The Professor was carefully examining every little fissure in the rocks. Wherever he saw a hole he always wanted to know the depth of it. To him this was important.

We had traversed the shores of the Liedenbrock sea for a mile when we observed a sudden change in the appearance of the soil. It seemed upset, contorted, and convulsed by a violent upheaval of the lower strata. In many places depressions or elevations gave witness to some tremendous power effecting the dislocation of strata.

We moved with difficulty across these granite fissures and chasms mingled with silex, crystals of quartz, and alluvial deposits, when a field, nay, more than a field, a vast plain, of bleached bones lay spread before us. It seemed like an immense cemetery, where the remains of twenty ages mingled their dust together. Huge mounds of bony fragments rose stage after stage in the distance. They undulated away to the limits of the horizon, and melted in the distance in a faint haze. There within three square miles were accumulated the materials for a complete history of the animal life of ages, a history scarcely outlined in the too recent strata of the inhabited world.

But an impatient curiosity impelled our steps; crackling and rattling, our feet were trampling on the remains of prehistoric animals and interesting fossils, the possession of which is a matter of rivalry and contention between the museums of great cities. A thousand Cuviers could never have reconstructed the organic remains deposited in this magnificent and unparalleled collection.

I stood amazed. My uncle had uplifted his long arms to the vault which was our sky; his mouth gaping wide, his eyes flashing behind his shining spectacles, his head balancing with an up-and-down motion, his whole attitude denoted unlimited astonishment. Here he stood facing an immense collection of scattered leptotheria, mericotheria, lophiodia, anoplotheria, megatheria, mastodons, protopithecae, pterodactyles, and all sorts of extinct monsters here assembled together for his special satisfaction. Fancy an enthusiastic bibliomaniac suddenly brought into the midst of the famous Alexandrian library burnt by Omar and restored by a miracle from its ashes! Just such a crazed enthusiast was my uncle, Professor Liedenbrock.

But more was to come, when, with a rush through clouds of bone dust, he laid his hand upon a bare skull, and cried with a voice trembling with excitement:

"Axel! Axel! A human head!"

"A human skull?" I cried, no less astonished.

"Yes, nephew. Aha! M. Milne-Edwards! Ah! M. de Quatrefages, how I wish you were standing here at the side of Otto Liedenbrock!"

Footnote 5. The glyptodon and armadillo are mammalian; the tortoise is a chelonian, a reptile, distinct classes of the animal kingdom; therefore the latter cannot be a representative of the former. (Tr.)

Chapter XXXVIII
The Professor in his Chair Again

TO UNDERSTAND this apostrophe of my uncle's, made to absent French savants, it will be necessary to allude to an event of high importance in a palaeontological point of view, which had occurred a little while before our departure.

On the 28th of March, 1863, some excavators working under the direction of M. Boucher de Perthes, in the stone quarries of Moulin Quignon, near Abbeville, in the department of Somme, found a human jawbone fourteen feet beneath the surface. It was the first fossil of this nature that had ever been brought to light. Not far distant were found stone hatchets and flint arrow-heads stained and encased by lapse of time with a uniform coat of rust.

The noise of this discovery was very great, not in France alone, but in England and in Germany. Several savants of the French Institute, and amongst them MM. Milne-Edwards and de Quatrefages, saw at once the importance of this discovery, proved to demonstration the genuineness of the bone in question, and became the most ardent defendants in what the English called this 'trial of a jawbone.' To the geologists of the United Kingdom, who believed in the certainty of the fact – Messrs. Falconer, Busk, Carpenter, and others – scientific Germans were soon joined, and amongst them the forwardest, the most fiery, and the most enthusiastic, was my uncle Liedenbrock.

Therefore the genuineness of a fossil human relic of the quaternary period seemed to be incontestably proved and admitted.

It is true that this theory met with a most obstinate opponent in M. Elie de Beaumont. This high authority maintained that the soil of Moulin Quignon was not diluvial at all, but was of much more recent formation; and, agreeing in that with Cuvier, he refused to admit that the human species could be contemporary with the animals of the quaternary period. My uncle Liedenbrock, along with the great body of the geologists, had maintained his ground, disputed, and argued, until M. Elie de Beaumont stood almost alone in his opinion.

We knew all these details, but we were not aware that since our departure the question had advanced to farther stages. Other similar maxillaries, though belonging to individuals of various types and different nations, were found in the loose grey soil of certain grottoes in France, Switzerland, and Belgium, as well as weapons, tools, earthen utensils, bones of children and adults. The existence therefore of man in the quaternary period seemed to become daily more certain.

Nor was this all. Fresh discoveries of remains in the pleiocene formation had emboldened other geologists to refer back the human species to a higher antiquity still. It is true that these remains were not human bones, but objects bearing the traces of his handiwork, such as fossil leg-bones of animals, sculptured and carved evidently by the hand of man.

Thus, at one bound, the record of the existence of man receded far back into the history of the ages past; he was a predecessor of the mastodon; he was a contemporary of the southern elephant; he lived a hundred thousand years ago, when, according to geologists, the pleiocene formation was in progress.

Such then was the state of palaeontological science, and what we knew of it was sufficient to explain our behaviour in the presence of this stupendous Golgotha. Any one may now understand the frenzied excitement of my uncle, when, twenty yards farther on, he found himself face to face with a primitive man!

It was a perfectly recognisable human body. Had some particular soil, like that of the cemetery St. Michel, at Bordeaux, preserved it thus for so many ages? It might be so. But this dried corpse, with its parchment-like skin drawn tightly over the bony frame, the limbs still preserving their shape, sound teeth, abundant hair, and finger and toe nails of frightful length, this desiccated mummy startled us by appearing just as it had lived countless ages ago. I stood mute before this apparition of remote antiquity. My uncle, usually so garrulous, was struck dumb likewise. We raised the body. We stood it up against a rock. It seemed to stare at us out of its empty orbits. We sounded with our knuckles his hollow frame.

After some moments' silence the Professor was himself again. Otto Liedenbrock, yielding to his nature, forgot all the circumstances of our eventful journey, forgot where we were standing, forgot the vaulted cavern which contained us. No doubt he was in mind back again in his Johannaeum, holding forth to his pupils, for he assumed his learned air; and addressing himself to an imaginary audience, he proceeded thus:

"Gentlemen, I have the honour to introduce to you a man of the quaternary or post-tertiary system. Eminent geologists have denied his existence, others no less eminent have affirmed it. The St. Thomases of palaeontology, if they were here, might now touch him with their fingers, and would be obliged to acknowledge their error. I am quite aware that science has to be on its guard with discoveries of this kind. I know what capital enterprising individuals like Barnum have made out of fossil men. I have heard the tale of the kneepan of Ajax, the pretended body of Orestes claimed to have been found by the Spartans, and of the body of Asterius, ten cubits long, of which Pausanias speaks. I have read the reports of the skeleton of Trapani, found in the fourteenth century, and which was at the time identified as that of Polyphemus; and the history of the giant unearthed in the sixteenth century near Palermo. You know as well as I do, gentlemen, the analysis made at Lucerne in 1577 of those huge bones which the celebrated Dr. Felix Plater affirmed to be those of a giant nineteen feet high. I have gone through the treatises of Cassanion, and all those memoirs, pamphlets, answers, and rejoinders published respecting the skeleton of Teutobochus, the invader of Gaul, dug out of a sandpit in the Dauphiné, in 1613. In the eighteenth century I would have stood up for Scheuchzer's pre-adamite man against Peter Campet. I have perused a writing, entitled Gigan –"

Here my uncle's unfortunate infirmity met him – that of being unable in public to pronounce hard words.

"The pamphlet entitled Gigan –"

He could get no further.

"Giganteo –"

It was not to be done. The unlucky word would not come out. At the Johannaeum there would have been a laugh.

"Gigantosteologie," at last the Professor burst out, between two words which I shall not record here.

Then rushing on with renewed vigour, and with great animation:

"Yes, gentlemen, I know all these things, and more. I know that Cuvier and Blumenbach have recognised in these bones nothing more remarkable than the bones of the mammoth and other mammals of the post-tertiary period. But in the presence of this specimen to doubt would be to insult science. There stands the body! You may see it, touch it. It is not a mere skeleton; it is an entire body, preserved for a purely anthropological end and purpose."

I was good enough not to contradict this startling assertion.

"If I could only wash it in a solution of sulphuric acid," pursued my uncle, "I should be able to clear it from all the earthy particles and the shells which are incrusted about it. But I do not possess that valuable solvent. Yet, such as it is, the body shall tell us its own wonderful story."

Here the Professor laid hold of the fossil skeleton, and handled it with the skill of a dexterous showman.

"You see," he said, "that it is not six feet long, and that we are still separated by a long interval from the pretended race of giants. As for the family to which it belongs, it is evidently Caucasian. It is the white race, our own. The skull of this fossil is a regular oval, or rather ovoid. It exhibits no prominent cheekbones, no projecting jaws. It presents no appearance of that prognathism which diminishes the facial angle **(footnote 6)**. Measure that angle. It is nearly ninety degrees. But I will go further in my deductions, and I will affirm that this specimen of the human family is of the Japhetic race, which has since spread from the Indies to the Atlantic. Don't smile, gentlemen."

Nobody was smiling; but the learned Professor was frequently disturbed by the broad smiles provoked by his learned eccentricities.

"Yes," he pursued with animation, "this is a fossil man, the contemporary of the mastodons whose remains fill this amphitheatre. But if you ask me how he came there, how those strata on which he lay slipped down into this enormous hollow in the globe, I confess I cannot answer that question. No doubt in the post-tertiary period considerable commotions were still disturbing the crust of the earth. The long-continued cooling of the globe produced chasms, fissures, clefts, and faults, into which, very probably, portions of the upper earth may have fallen. I make no rash assertions; but there is the man surrounded by his own works, by hatchets, by flint arrow-heads, which are the characteristics of the stone age. And unless he came here, like myself, as a tourist on a visit and as a pioneer of science, I can entertain no doubt of the authenticity of his remote origin."

The Professor ceased to speak, and the audience broke out into loud and unanimous applause. For of course my uncle was right, and wiser men than his nephew would have had some trouble to refute his statements.

Another remarkable thing. This fossil body was not the only one in this immense catacomb. We came upon other bodies at every step amongst this mortal dust, and my uncle might select the most curious of these specimens to demolish the incredulity of sceptics.

In fact it was a wonderful spectacle, that of these generations of men and animals commingled in a common cemetery. Then one very serious question arose presently which we scarcely dared to suggest. Had all those creatures slided through a great fissure in the crust of the earth, down to the shores of the Liedenbrock sea, when they were dead and turning to dust, or had they lived and grown and died here in this subterranean world under a false sky, just like inhabitants of the upper earth? Until the present time we had seen alive only marine monsters and fishes. Might not some living man, some native of the abyss, be yet a wanderer below on this desert strand?

Footnote 6. The facial angle is formed by two lines, one touching the brow and the front teeth, the other from the orifice of the ear to the lower line of the nostrils. The greater this angle, the higher intelligence denoted by the formation of the skull. Prognathism is that projection of the jaw-bones which sharpens or lessons this angle, and which is illustrated in the negro countenance and in the lowest savages.

Chapter XXXIX
Forest Scenery Illuminated By Electricity

FOR ANOTHER half hour we trod upon a pavement of bones. We pushed on, impelled by our burning curiosity. What other marvels did this cavern contain? What new treasures lay here for science to unfold? I was prepared for any surprise, my imagination was ready for any astonishment however astounding.

We had long lost sight of the sea shore behind the hills of bones. The rash Professor, careless of losing his way, hurried me forward. We advanced in silence, bathed in luminous electric fluid. By some phenomenon which I am unable to explain, it lighted up all sides of every object equally. Such was its diffusiveness, there being no central point from which the light emanated, that shadows no longer existed. You might have thought yourself under the rays of a vertical sun in a tropical region at noonday and the height of summer. No vapour was visible. The rocks, the distant mountains, a few isolated clumps of forest trees in the distance, presented a weird and wonderful aspect under these totally new conditions of a universal diffusion of light. We were like Hoffmann's shadowless man.

After walking a mile we reached the outskirts of a vast forest, but not one of those forests of fungi which bordered Port Gräuben.

Here was the vegetation of the tertiary period in its fullest blaze of magnificence. Tall palms, belonging to species no longer living, splendid palmacites, firs, yews, cypress trees, thujas, representatives of the conifers, were linked together by a tangled network of long climbing plants. A soft carpet of moss and hepaticas luxuriously clothed the soil. A few sparkling streams ran almost in silence under what would have been the shade of the trees, but that there was no shadow. On their banks grew tree-ferns similar to those we grow in hothouses. But a remarkable feature was the total absence of colour in all those trees, shrubs, and plants, growing without the life-giving heat and light of the sun. Everything seemed mixed-up and confounded in one uniform silver grey or light brown tint like that of fading and faded leaves. Not a green leaf anywhere, and the flowers – which were abundant enough in the tertiary period, which first gave birth to flowers – looked like brown-paper flowers, without colour or scent.

My uncle Liedenbrock ventured to penetrate under this colossal grove. I followed him, not without fear. Since nature had here provided vegetable nourishment, why should not the terrible mammals be there too? I perceived in the broad clearings left by fallen trees, decayed with age, leguminose plants, acerineae, rubiceae and many other eatable shrubs, dear to ruminant animals at every period. Then I observed, mingled together in confusion, trees of countries far apart on the surface of the globe. The oak and the palm were growing side by side, the Australian eucalyptus leaned against the Norwegian pine, the birch-tree of the north mingled its foliage with New Zealand kauris. It was enough to distract the most ingenious classifier of terrestrial botany.

Suddenly I halted. I drew back my uncle.

The diffused light revealed the smallest object in the dense and distant thickets. I had thought I saw – no! I did see, with my own eyes, vast colossal forms moving amongst the trees. They were gigantic animals; it was a herd of mastodons – not fossil remains, but living and resembling those the bones of which were found in the marshes of Ohio in 1801. I saw those huge elephants whose long, flexible trunks were grouting and turning up the soil under the trees like a legion of serpents. I could hear the crashing noise of their long ivory tusks boring into the old decaying trunks. The boughs cracked, and the leaves torn away by cartloads went down the cavernous throats of the vast brutes.

So, then, the dream in which I had had a vision of the prehistoric world, of the tertiary and post-tertiary periods, was now realised. And there we were alone, in the bowels of the earth, at the mercy of its wild inhabitants!

My uncle was gazing with intense and eager interest.

"Come on!" said he, seizing my arm. "Forward! Forward!"

"No, I will not!" I cried. "We have no firearms. What could we do in the midst of a herd of these four-footed giants? Come away, uncle – come! No human being may with safety dare the anger of these monstrous beasts."

"No human creature?" replied my uncle in a lower voice. "You are wrong, Axel. Look, look down there! I fancy I see a living creature similar to ourselves: it is a man!"

I looked, shaking my head incredulously. But though at first I was unbelieving I had to yield to the evidence of my senses.

In fact, at a distance of a quarter of a mile, leaning against the trunk of a gigantic kauri, stood a human being, the Proteus of those subterranean regions, a new son of Neptune, watching this countless herd of mastodons.

Immanis pecoris custos, immanior ipse **(footnote 7)**.

Yes, truly, huger still himself. It was no longer a fossil being like him whose dried remains we had easily lifted up in the field of bones; it was a giant, able to control those monsters. In stature he was at least twelve feet high. His head, huge and unshapely as a buffalo's, was half hidden in the thick and tangled growth of his unkempt hair. It most resembled the mane of the primitive elephant. In his hand he wielded with ease an enormous bough, a staff worthy of this shepherd of the geologic period.

We stood petrified and speechless with amazement. But he might see us! We must fly!

"Come, do come!" I said to my uncle, who for once allowed himself to be persuaded.

In another quarter of an hour our nimble heels had carried us beyond the reach of this horrible monster.

And yet, now that I can reflect quietly, now that my spirit has grown calm again, now that months have slipped by since this strange and supernatural meeting, what am I to think? what am I to believe? I must conclude that it was impossible that our senses had been deceived, that our eyes did not see what we supposed they saw. No human being lives in this subterranean world; no generation of men dwells in those inferior caverns of the globe, unknown to and unconnected with the inhabitants of its surface. It is absurd to believe it!

I had rather admit that it may have been some animal whose structure resembled the human, some ape or baboon of the early geological ages, some protopitheca, or some mesopitheca, some early or middle ape like that discovered by Mr. Lartet in the bone cave of Sansau. But this creature surpassed in stature all the measurements known in modern palaeontology. But that a man, a living man, and therefore whole generations doubtless besides, should be buried there in the bowels of the earth, is impossible.

However, we had left behind us the luminous forest, dumb with astonishment, overwhelmed and struck down with a terror which amounted to stupefaction. We kept running on for fear the horrible monster might be on our track. It was a flight, a fall, like that fearful pulling and dragging which is peculiar to nightmare. Instinctively we got back to the Liedenbrock sea, and I cannot say into what vagaries my mind would not have carried me but for a circumstance which brought me back to practical matters.

Although I was certain that we were now treading upon a soil not hitherto touched by our feet, I often perceived groups of rocks which reminded me of those about Port Gräuben. Besides, this seemed to confirm the indications of the needle, and to show that we had against our will returned to the north of the Liedenbrock sea. Occasionally we felt quite convinced. Brooks and waterfalls were tumbling everywhere from the projections in the rocks. I thought I recognised the bed of surturbrand, our faithful Hansbach, and the grotto in which I had recovered life and consciousness. Then a few paces farther on, the arrangement of the cliffs, the appearance of an unrecognised stream, or the strange outline of a rock, came to throw me again into doubt.

I communicated my doubts to my uncle. Like myself, he hesitated; he could recognise nothing again amidst this monotonous scene.

"Evidently," said I, "we have not landed again at our original starting point, but the storm has carried us a little higher, and if we follow the shore we shall find Port Gräuben."

"If that is the case it will be useless to continue our exploration, and we had better return to our raft. But, Axel, are you not mistaken?"

"It is difficult to speak decidedly, uncle, for all these rocks are so very much alike. Yet I think I recognise the promontory at the foot of which Hans constructed our launch. We must be very near the little port, if indeed this is not it," I added, examining a creek which I thought I recognised.

"No, Axel, we should at least find our own traces and I see nothing –"

"But I do see," I cried, darting upon an object lying on the sand.

And I showed my uncle a rusty dagger which I had just picked up.

"Come," said he, "had you this weapon with you?"

"I! No, certainly! But you, perhaps –"

"Not that I am aware," said the Professor. "I have never had this object in my possession."

"Well, this is strange!"

"No, Axel, it is very simple. The Icelanders often wear arms of this kind. This must have belonged to Hans, and he has lost it."

I shook my head. Hans had never had an object like this in his possession.

"Did it not belong to some pre-adamite warrior?" I cried, "to some living man, contemporary with the huge cattle-driver? But no. This is not a relic of the stone age. It is not even of the iron age. This blade is steel –"

My uncle stopped me abruptly on my way to a dissertation which would have taken me a long way, and said coolly:

"Be calm, Axel, and reasonable. This dagger belongs to the sixteenth century; it is a poniard, such as gentlemen carried in their belts to give the *coup de grace*. Its origin is Spanish. It was never either yours, or mine, or the hunter's, nor did it belong to any of those human beings who may or may not inhabit this inner world. See, it was never jagged like this by cutting men's throats; its blade is coated with a rust neither a day, nor a year, nor a hundred years old."

The Professor was getting excited according to his wont, and was allowing his imagination to run away with him.

"Axel, we are on the way towards the grand discovery. This blade has been left on the strand for from one to three hundred years, and has blunted its edge upon the rocks that fringe this subterranean sea!"

"But it has not come alone. It has not twisted itself out of shape; some one has been here before us!

"Yes – a man has."

"And who was that man?"

"A man who has engraved his name somewhere with that dagger. That man wanted once more to mark the way to the centre of the earth. Let us look about: look about!"

And, wonderfully interested, we peered all along the high wall, peeping into every fissure which might open out into a gallery.

And so we arrived at a place where the shore was much narrowed. Here the sea came to lap the foot of the steep cliff, leaving a passage no wider than a couple of yards. Between two boldly projecting rocks appeared the mouth of a dark tunnel.

There, upon a granite slab, appeared two mysterious graven letters, half eaten away by time. They were the initials of the bold and daring traveller:

[Runic initials appear here]

"A.S.," shouted my uncle. "Arne Saknussemm! Arne Saknussemm everywhere!"

Footnote 7. "The shepherd of gigantic herds, and huger still himself."

The complete and unabridged text is available online, from *flametreepublishing.com/extras*

The Lady of the Lost Valley

John Walters

THE HEAT and filth of India was an inconvenience that I could endure, but the savagery of Afghanistan drained the vitality clean out of me. To convalesce I sought the hills of Kashmir. Traveling as I was at the sufferance of the British Raj, I registered with the local authorities at Shrinagar before I boarded the narrow-gauge train that would take me into the mountains.

In the dusty first-class carriage I was alone but for a staid gentleman in a gray suit and bowler hat. He was trim and fit, with dark brown hair and sideburns that curled into his thick moustache. It was hard to guess his age, but easy to guess his financial standing by the cut of his clothes and the quality of his luggage.

When I entered I proffered my hand. "Harvey Ashtree. I'm a reporter for the *San Francisco Sun*."

"Clarence Redcliff. Bank of England." After which he returned to his newspaper without another glance in my direction.

Being exhausted in mind and spirit, I would have been content with Redcliff's sealed lips, but for one peculiarity which piqued my curiosity. He had a large leather pouch, which he kept beside him at all times: he napped with it under his head, he carried it with him to the bathroom, and he tucked it beneath his arm as he read or gazed out the window. Not unusual, you might say, considering that the land we traversed was rife with thievery. But whenever he would pay for something, he would pull a thick wallet from his inside coat pocket, and would not touch the pouch at all.

What, therefore, if not money, did he keep in it? Diamonds, rubies, sapphires, or some other precious jewels? Deeds to land? Gold? Artifacts? Or perhaps he was not as he appeared; perhaps he was a spy and was concealing government secrets.

Insatiable curiosity was one of my worst personal faults but greatest professional virtues. I had forsaken my homeland, my parents, many comforts and conveniences, even my fiancé, for a chance at a posting as foreign correspondent. In the past year I had endured fever, diarrhea, and scabies, I had got caught in monsoon floods and riots, I had been robbed at knifepoint and shot at on battlefields. I was not about to pass up a potentially interesting story because of a stuffy British gentleman's reticence.

Eventually I could think of nothing else but the pouch and what it contained.

Searching for a clue, I attempted to engage him in conversation.

Night had blotted out the Indian countryside, and the only lights were the brilliant stars overhead and the flickering torches and cooking fires of villages we passed through. It is at such times, listening to the monotonous clacking of the train's wheels on the track, that a man might feel a sense of isolation more heavily than usual, and be more lugubrious and therefore crave companionship more than he is normally apt to.

"How far are you going?" I began.

"Hmm?" He lowered the newspaper a few centimeters, so that his disapproving eyes appeared over the edge of the page.

Not to be deterred, I repeated my question.

"To the end of the line," he said, and returned the newspaper to its former position.

"I have considered doing so myself," I said. "Have you been this way before? Do you know what to expect?"

Slowly he lowered the paper again. "There is nothing there. Nothing. Not even a hotel. You would be wise to get off sooner."

"If you don't mind my asking, if nothing is there, why are you going?"

He frowned, put down his paper, and headed for the lavatory.

In his flustered annoyance he had left the leather pouch behind.

I glanced at the lavatory door, then at the pouch. I leaned back and closed my eyes, then opened them again. I reached for the book I had been reading, a volume of Kipling's stories, but did not pick it up.

I could think of nothing but the unknown contents of the pouch. I knew I had no right to look, but I might never get another chance.

I moved over to his seat, feeling guilty but determined. While trying to maintain an air of innocence I watched the door, while at the same time I was slowly unzipping the pouch.

My heart pounding, I peered inside, frowned, furtively glanced at the door, and looked again more closely.

I had expected to find something of inestimable value. Instead, there were a few crumbs of what appeared to be stale cake.

I rubbed some between my fingers, took a tiny nibble. It tasted bittersweet and slightly earthy.

Zipping the pouch shut, I quickly crossed back to my seat, picked up my book, and pretended to read.

A moment later Mr. Redcliff reappeared. When he saw his pouch where he had left it, safe and sound, he was obviously relieved. He cast a suspicious glance in my direction, but I feigned obliviousness. Then he returned, with the pouch, to his ablutions.

* * *

I think that I have never seen such a splendid sunrise as the one I saw that early morning as the train wound slowly upward through the foothills toward the distant snow-capped Himalayan peaks. Rose, salmon and yellow bled across the clouds and splashed onto the distant peaks. The colors seemed to form splendid paintings in the sky that rivaled the masters. Then everything seemed bathed in golden haze. When that dissipated, the blue of the sky, emerald of the hills and rainbow colors of the wildflowers leapt into my eyes and gently massaged and soothed them. Redcliff seemed to have calmed down and was as absorbed in the beauty of the countryside as I was.

Occasionally the train stopped at tiny villages where a few peasants clad in lungis and worn sweaters would clamber off, but no one would board.

The end of the line was a barren cement platform. The nearby stationmaster's office, a stone hut from which most of the overlying plaster had eroded away, appeared to have been deserted for a long time.

Dew sparkled on deep green grass shot with purple and white flowers.

On the road a line of ox carts and about two-dozen Indians dressed in festive clothing were waiting. The women wore blue, green, or gold saris; the men wore white, red, or light brown suits. Several carried thick garlands of flowers. As the train pulled in with a loud hiss and exhalation of steam, they all laughed and pointed, obviously waiting for someone.

A tall thin Indian man with a large beak-like nose and a seemingly perpetual smile was the first to mount the platform. He spread his arms and cried, "Mr. Redcliff! I am so pleased to see you!" He turned to the others. "Look! He is here. He is really here. Isn't it wonderful?"

Redcliff, luggage in hand, slowly stepped down. I followed him. "What are you doing?" he whispered. "Can't you see there's nothing for you here?"

I shrugged. "I've found wherever I go there's always a local willing to rent a room."

"You're making a mistake. Turn around and go back while you can."

"Why?"

But the tall man had noticed me. "Look! Mr. Redcliff has brought a friend. Welcome!" He bowed, and shook first Redcliff's hand, then my own. "My name is Ashok Banergee. I am at your service."

A woman in a gold sari had climbed the steps behind Banergee.

Once I saw her I saw nothing else.

The first thing I noticed was her hair. It was three times the length of her body. Two other women in green saris carried the thick black tresses behind her.

But her eyes – her eyes were even more astonishing. They were the color of autumn: golden brown. They gazed upon me with insight, compassion, and tenderness.

And her smile: it was a slight smile, but spoke of confidence and control.

"Is she not magnificent?" Banergee said. "And see how her hair has grown since you were last here. Does it not shine splendidly?"

Her expression and her smile did not change, as if accepting such complements was her due. She turned and left the platform, followed by her ladies-in-waiting. In the back of one of the ox-carts deep pillows had been arranged; she sat down, and one of the ladies opened a yellow parasol and handed it to her.

"Come," said Banergee. "Let us be going. You must accept our hospitality, Mr...."

"This is Mr. Ashtree, from San Francisco," Redcliff said. "But he is not staying. He was just going to get back on the train."

Banergee expressed astonishment. "An American! You must join us, Mr. Ashtree. Surely you can spare a few days."

"I would be delighted," I said.

Redcliff frowned.

"Wonderful, wonderful! You can both ride with me."

"How did you know I was coming?" Redcliff asked.

"*She* knew. She was certain of it. I must admit I had my doubts. But we traveled all night, and here you are. She was right. She is always right. I will never doubt her again."

"Did she receive a telephone or telegraph message?" I asked.

"We have no such things. She just *knew*."

"Extraordinary," I said.

"Indubitably," replied Banergee, and patted my shoulder, as a teacher might encourage a pupil who pleases him.

All day we were bumped and jolted in the back of the carts as the oxen plodded slowly higher and higher into the hills. Redcliff was tight-lipped; Banergee bored us with incessant nonsensical small talk. We stopped for lunch in a meadow beside a crystal-clear stream. Blankets were spread and food enough for a small army was laid out: chapattis, rice, curries, vegetables, fruit, biscuits, cookies, cakes, and so on. Everyone laughed and chatted as if at a party.

In late afternoon we climbed down from the carts and lit torches.

"Alas," said Banergee, "the oxen can go no farther. Now we must walk. But it is not far, and the air is cool and refreshing, is it not?"

So as the sun disappeared in an amber blaze and more stars appeared overhead than I have ever seen in my life, we trudged up the hillside. The single line of torches looked like a luminescent snake slithering along in the blackness.

After we had been walking for two or three hours, and my legs felt like lead and my chest ached with every breath, the torches ahead of us suddenly seemed to vanish.

"What happened?" I asked.

"We have almost arrived," said Banergee. "You will see."

We reached a narrow defile, a gap between two hills scarcely wide enough for one person to pass through.

"During the day this opening is all but invisible unless you are right on top of it," Banergee said. "I myself, when I first came, stumbled upon it by accident, as did most of the others here. As did your Mr. Redcliff."

"Is that so?" I said.

"It most assuredly is," Banergee replied. "Few have been led here as you are now."

"Then I am privileged."

"It is an auspicious occasion," Banergee agreed.

The solid rock on either side was damp and mossy in places. The torchlight cast long grotesque shadows. Far above was the star-strewn night sky.

The passage opened into a long valley. I could smell the sap of evergreens, and hear the chuckle of mountain streams. Much was in darkness, but the torches of those ahead of us curled down a trail, and far in the distance were the lights of a cluster of cottages.

"Beautiful, is it not?" said Banergee. "I first saw the valley in the light of day; it is far more impressive then. But still, the night has its own charm."

The wonder of the moment blocked my throat so that I could not answer. Mythical Shangri-La came to mind. I wondered if I might wake up on a blood-splashed battlefield in Afghanistan: it was too perfect to be true.

By the time we reached the cottages, which were built of stone and wood and – wonder of wonders – illuminated by electricity, I was too tired to follow much of Banergee's lengthy explanation of how they managed to carry the generator and a supply of diesel to run it up the mountain and into the valley. I was shown to a small room with a comfortable bed and thick quilt, and almost at once fell into a deep sleep.

Sometime before dawn I awakened in darkness and absolute silence. Feeling the urge to urinate, I pulled on my boots and jacket (I had not taken off the rest of my clothes) and stepped outdoors. After relieving myself, I noticed that firelight still glowed from within a larger building that had the appearance of a community hall.

I thought to warm myself by the fireplace for a time, as my sleep had left me. But first I wanted to be sure I wouldn't disturb anyone, so I peered through a window.

It was one long room, with a huge stone fireplace at one end. Candelabras were placed at intervals to give more light. All around the sides were couches, armchairs, and pillows on which sat everyone I had met on the journey up and several others that were strangers to me. Redcliff and Banergee sat side by side near the fire. Everyone was staring at the ceiling or the flickering lights on the walls. I could have thought they were all statues; nobody moved.

Nobody, that is, except one person.

The light reflected on her sari. Her hair was piled on her shoulders, and arranged in large loops on her left arm. She walked slowly from person to person, stepping carefully over legs and around furniture, always with that mystical, benevolent smile. She paused before each one and waved her right hand over their head, as if blessing them.

When she came opposite my window she looked me in the eye. Perhaps the smile increased slightly, perhaps not. Her gaze seemed to probe deeply into my mind and heart. She motioned to an empty chair, obviously inviting me inside to join them.

I backed away and returned to my room, where I lay awake a long time in the dark.

* * *

When I woke up in the late morning, I was not sure whether what I had seen was real or a dream.

The valley, in daylight, was very beautiful.

The cluster of buildings sat on a level area midway up one of the green slopes. The hillside was terraced for cultivation. Far below a river sped over large boulders. Stands of dark evergreens mottled the bright meadow grass. Towering over the valley's end were the snow-capped peaks of the Himalayas.

All was quiet but for the whisper of the wind and the flowing river. I assumed that everyone was asleep after the night's festivities.

But then I heard Banergee's voice. "Ah! Mr. Ashtree! You have risen. We can share breakfast."

He led me to the kitchen, where he quickly prepared chapattis and eggs. "Tea? Or would you prefer coffee?"

"Tea is fine. I have learned to adapt."

"Very wise of you. This tea is exquisitely flavored. I have added cardamom, cinnamon, and various other spices."

I sipped the muddy brew. "It's good," I said, though in truth it was a bit heavy for my tastes.

When we were finished Banergee said, "You must allow me to show you around."

He led me farther up the valley. The narrow path went first through a small forest, then up a grassy slope to a point where the walls of the two sides of the valley met and were too steep to climb.

"This is the heart of the valley," he said. "Look."

Along the edges of the rock grew a pale yellow fungus.

"It looks like some kind of mushroom," I said.

"When I first stumbled upon this valley I thought I must have been the first to have ever seen it," Banergee said. "I was in the employ of a party of climbers and had got lost.

I had not eaten in days. I wandered until I came to this very place and found these plants. Hoping that they were not poisonous, I ate my fill. Afterwards I discovered that I was not the first person to come. *She* was already here. She came strolling across the meadow, smiling her beautiful smile. Her hair was not as long as it is now, of course; it was scarcely past her shoulders. Once I saw her I could not think of leaving. Afterwards, others came, and we built our tiny village."

"And you have never felt the urge to leave?"

Banergee assumed a serious expression. "Mr. Ashtree, these mushrooms bestow life, and strength, and a sense of the splendor of creation upon those who consume them. Yet, alas, I was not wholly wrong when I suspected poison. Once you take the first bite you must periodically have more, or you will experience intense pain and eventual death. Your friend Mr. Redcliff tried to leave by taking a supply with him, but as you see he was forced to return."

My thoughts raced back to that moment of curiosity when I had opened Redcliff's pouch and tasted the bittersweet fragment. A sense of dread and shame caused my scalp to tingle and my face to flush.

Banergee looked closely at me. "You yourself have ingested it, have you not?"

"Only a tiny bit – a few crumbs. Surely that would not…"

"Yes! She told me that you had. She *knew*. She is never wrong."

"Who is she?"

"Why, Mr. Ashtree, she owns this valley. It belongs to her. We are here at her sufferance. But she is exceedingly magnanimous; she has never turned anyone away."

"I cannot stay."

"Mr. Redcliff said the same, and as you can see…"

"My situation is different."

"But you are our brother now; we are your family."

In a daze I stumbled back down the hill.

I found Redcliff sipping tea in the kitchen. "Why didn't you tell me what was going on here?" I asked.

"I tried to warn you; you wouldn't listen."

"But you were carrying such a dangerous substance so openly."

His eyes narrowed. "I thought you had stolen some. So now you have found yourself in a fix, have you? But life here is not so bad once you get used to it."

"Is that why you tried to get away?"

He sighed. "Back in London I have a wife and three children, and I did not want to be separated from them. I should have taken the stuff for analysis, tried to find a cure, but a sense of guilt prevented me. The guilt is a part of the curse, I suppose."

"The curse?"

"Well, I guess it's a curse or a blessing, depending on how you look at it. It does seem to bestow longevity and good health. The rest of those here seem content enough with their fate."

"We can leave again, you and I, and take a good quantity with us. We can have it examined; I'm sure a cure can be found."

He sighed again, and shook his head. "The more you take, the more your resistance fades. I don't think I would be able to leave again."

"I'll go. If I succeed, I'll come back for you."

"You have tasted of the elixir of life, and found that it has turned and bit you. Relax and accept the inevitable. Have some tea."

But I was in no mood to yield to his little charade.

I had the urge to make my escape at once, but when I stepped outside I heard a rumble of thunder and saw that dark clouds with flickers of lightning had gathered in the east.

I returned to my room, lay on my bed, and ruminated.

A mild pain stabbed my stomach. Then I felt nauseated, as if I had eaten spoiled food. As the thunder outside grew louder and rain began to drum on the roof, the pains increased in frequency and intensity.

An almost uncontrollable urge came over me to eat some more of the mushrooms. I didn't want to fight it; I wanted to relax, to give in, to enjoy the little bit of paradise that was being offered to me. I found myself wondering if there would be another gathering tonight, and imagined myself sitting in the midst of the others in a haze of contentment.

At the same time a voice deep within was screaming at me to resist.

And so I spent the afternoon tossing on my bed, warring with myself.

At twilight the storm passed, the pain lessoned, and I stepped outside to watch the crimson of the sunset fade from the clouds and darkness fill the valley.

From somewhere the generator coughed and began to hum, and lights came on.

Then I saw *her*. Her gold sari reflected the lights. Her attendants walked behind her, carrying her hair.

She stopped, beckoned to me, then entered the large building.

Others followed her.

I wanted to go too. I wanted to kill the voice telling me not to. *She* was calling me. Not with words, but somehow, in my mind.

Who was she? I had never heard her speak, and did not know her name.

Suddenly a great fear of her gripped my heart. Was she even human? And if she was not, was she angel or demon? Was she some kind of strange spider whose nest was in this faraway place, and was I now condemned to be bound more and more tightly to her web of illusion until I was no longer aware of what was happening to me?

Could I break the spell? And if so, how?

Her power seemed bound up with the mushrooms. Therefore the only way to break the spell would be to destroy them. I had only eaten a minute quantity; perhaps I could survive without them.

And what of the others? Would the fly prefer to fall forever asleep, without ever realizing what has happened to it, or would it prefer to awaken to the horror of its situation with the hope, however faint, of struggling free and escaping?

I could not answer for all flies – only for myself.

It was not difficult to locate the room where the generator was kept; the throb of its engine guided me. The diesel was kept in large cans; I managed to carry two, and at the same time hold a long pitch-pine torch under my arm.

I struggled through the forest and up the slope to where the mushrooms grew. Banergee had taken pains to explain to me that this was the *only* place they grew, emphasizing the sacredness of this part of the valley. There was sure to be some down in the village, certainly at least in the room where the others had gathered. Perhaps they kept a further supply on hand somewhere else too. But this was the source, and if I cut off the source sooner or later there would be none left.

First I studied the area to ascertain where they grew, then I planted the flickering torch in the ground a safe distance away and began to splash the sour-smelling diesel over the mushrooms.

A sense of foreboding caused me to turn.

She was there, standing at the edge of the torchlight. Her hair was loose all around her, trailing away behind. A slight breeze caused it to shimmer.

Her golden brown eyes gazed at me steadily. Her expression did not change. She did not plead, nor did she rage.

It occurred to me that she was powerless to stop me.

I picked up the torch.

She raised her right hand, and closed it loosely into a fist.

A sharp pain in my stomach caused me to double over. I dropped the torch; it guttered feebly.

She rubbed her fingers against her thumb. It felt as if my bowels were being crushed in ground glass. I gasped, and cried out.

The wind picked up. She seemed to grow, and her features darkened in the fading torchlight. Her long manicured fingernails became talons. Her mouth opened: fangs were within. Her hair writhed like snakes.

In the back of my mind there was the thought that all this would be over and everything would be all right if I would just go back down and join the others.

I felt I was drifting in a void, unsure of what to do. As if sensing my hesitancy, she eased her grip.

I grabbed the torch and threw it. For a moment nothing seemed to happen, then flames erupted with a loud whoosh.

Her hair and her sari caught fire; blisters popped up on her face. Wreathed in fire, her eyes showed incredulity at my betrayal. She fell to her knees, then the conflagration consumed her.

Slowly I rose and staggered down the path clutching my stomach. Sometimes I had to stop because of the pain; sometimes I lost the path and found myself against a sheer wall, or at the edge of a chasm.

On the way I formulated a simple plan: I would grab Redcliff from their midst and help him make it back to civilization and his wife and children, and then I would return with the authorities to help the others.

When I reached the village I did not stop to knock; I opened the door and rushed into the room. All had gathered. They held the pale yellow pieces of mushroom in their hands like bread at a communion ceremony.

I spotted Redcliff near the fireplace and took a few steps in his direction.

Then I realized *she* was there, looking as fresh as ever, her hair piled on her shoulders and looped on her left arm, the firelight behind forming a halo around her. She looked at me with her usual confident and compassionate expression and beckoned to me, pointing to an empty chair.

I tried to steel myself from her overtures and remember my plan.

But my attention was drawn to her face. So benevolent. So seraphic. She was still willing to give me her benediction.

I suddenly felt overcome with remorse. Tears filled my eyes. I fell at her feet and begged her forgiveness.

"Is she not wonderful?" Banergee whispered. "Oh, is she not magnificent?"

* * *

There was no condemnation for what I had done. Indeed, it was never spoken of. The supply of mushroom that remained was apportioned evenly to all, myself included, at the nightly gatherings, at which she continued to officiate as she had always done. When I received a full dosage I was transported to a place that, if not paradise, was at least a simulation of it. I realized why the others had stayed here: not out of obligation or fear, but out of love. I was content with that; it was enough.

And finally, when we had shared the last bits, we awaited the end.

Perhaps someone will enter this valley someday and discover this manuscript. If so, I want to make it clear that above all, this is a love story.

Remember her.

In the Abyss

H.G. Wells

THE LIEUTENANT stood in front of the steel sphere and gnawed a piece of pine splinter. "What do you think of it, Steevens?" he asked.

"It's an idea," said Steevens, in the tone of one who keeps an open mind.

"I believe it will smash – flat," said the lieutenant.

"He seems to have calculated it all out pretty well," said Steevens, still impartial.

"But think of the pressure," said the lieutenant. "At the surface of the water it's fourteen pounds to the inch, thirty feet down it's double that; sixty, treble; ninety, four times; nine hundred, forty times; five thousand, three hundred – that's a mile – it's two hundred and forty times fourteen pounds; that's – let's see – thirty hundredweight – a ton and a half, Steevens; *a ton and a half* to the square inch. And the ocean where he's going is five miles deep. That's seven and a half" –

"Sounds a lot," said Steevens, "but it's jolly thick steel."

The lieutenant made no answer, but resumed his pine splinter. The object of their conversation was a huge ball of steel, having an exterior diameter of perhaps nine feet. It looked like the shot for some Titanic piece of artillery. It was elaborately nested in a monstrous scaffolding built into the framework of the vessel, and the gigantic spars that were presently to sling it overboard gave the stern of the ship an appearance that had raised the curiosity of every decent sailor who had sighted it, from the Pool of London to the Tropic of Capricorn. In two places, one above the other, the steel gave place to a couple of circular windows of enormously thick glass, and one of these, set in a steel frame of great solidity, was now partially unscrewed. Both the men had seen the interior of this globe for the first time that morning. It was elaborately padded with air cushions, with little studs sunk between bulging pillows to work the simple mechanism of the affair. Everything was elaborately padded, even the Myers apparatus which was to absorb carbonic acid and replace the oxygen inspired by its tenant, when he had crept in by the glass manhole, and had been screwed in. It was so elaborately padded that a man might have been fired from a gun in it with perfect safety. And it had need to be, for presently a man was to crawl in through that glass manhole, to be screwed up tightly, and to be flung overboard, and to sink down – down – down, for five miles, even as the lieutenant said. It had taken the strongest hold of his imagination; it made him a bore at mess; and he found Steevens, the new arrival aboard, a godsend to talk to about it, over and over again.

"It's my opinion," said the lieutenant, "that that glass will simply bend in and bulge and smash, under a pressure of that sort. Daubrée has made rocks run like water under big pressures – and, you mark my words" –

"If the glass did break in," said Steevens, "what then?"

"The water would shoot in like a jet of iron. Have you ever felt a straight jet of high pressure water? It would hit as hard as a bullet. It would simply smash him and flatten him. It would tear down his throat, and into his lungs; it would blow in his ears" –

"What a detailed imagination you have!" protested Steevens, who saw things vividly.

"It's a simple statement of the inevitable," said the lieutenant.

"And the globe?"

"Would just give out a few little bubbles, and it would settle down comfortably against the day of judgment, among the oozes and the bottom clay – with poor Elstead spread over his own smashed cushions like butter over bread."

He repeated this sentence as though he liked it very much. "Like butter over bread," he said.

"Having a look at the jigger?" said a voice, and Elstead stood behind them, spick and span in white, with a cigarette between his teeth, and his eyes smiling out of the shadow of his ample hat-brim. "What's that about bread and butter, Weybridge? Grumbling as usual about the insufficient pay of naval officers? It won't be more than a day now before I start. We are to get the slings ready today. This clean sky and gentle swell is just the kind of thing for swinging off a dozen tons of lead and iron; isn't it?"

"It won't affect you much," said Weybridge.

"No. Seventy or eighty feet down, and I shall be there in a dozen seconds, there's not a particle moving, though the wind shriek itself hoarse up above, and the water lifts halfway to the clouds. No. Down there." – He moved to the side of the ship and the other two followed him. All three leant forward on their elbows and stared down into the yellow-green water.

"*Peace*," said Elstead, finishing his thought aloud.

"Are you dead certain that clockwork will act?" asked Weybridge presently.

"It has worked thirty-five times," said Elstead. "It's bound to work."

"But if it doesn't?"

"Why shouldn't it?"

"I wouldn't go down in that confounded thing," said Weybridge, "for twenty thousand pounds."

"Cheerful chap you are," said Elstead, and spat sociably at a bubble below.

"I don't understand yet how you mean to work the thing," said Steevens.

"In the first place, I'm screwed into the sphere," said Elstead, "and when I've turned the electric light off and on three times to show I'm cheerful, I'm swung out over the stern by that crane, with all those big lead sinkers slung below me. The top lead weight has a roller carrying a hundred fathoms of strong cord rolled up, and that's all that joins the sinkers to the sphere, except the slings that will be cut when the affair is dropped. We use cord rather than wire rope because it's easier to cut and more buoyant – necessary points, as you will see.

"Through each of these lead weights you notice there is a hole, and an iron rod will be run through that and will project six feet on the lower side. If that rod is rammed up from below, it knocks up a lever and sets the clockwork in motion at the side of the cylinder on which the cord winds.

"Very well. The whole affair is lowered gently into the water, and the slings are cut. The sphere floats, – with the air in it, it's lighter than water, – but the lead weights go down straight and the cord runs out. When the cord is all paid out, the sphere will go down too, pulled down by the cord."

"But why the cord?" asked Steevens. "Why not fasten the weights directly to the sphere?"

"Because of the smash down below. The whole affair will go rushing down, mile after mile, at a headlong pace at last. It would be knocked to pieces on the bottom if it wasn't for that cord. But the weights will hit the bottom, and directly they do, the buoyancy of the sphere will come into play. It will go on sinking slower and slower; come to a stop at last, and then begin to float upward again.

"That's where the clockwork comes in. Directly the weights smash against the sea bottom, the rod will be knocked through and will kick up the clockwork, and the cord will be rewound on the reel. I shall be lugged down to the sea bottom. There I shall stay for half an hour, with the electric light on, looking about me. Then the clockwork will release a spring knife, the cord will be cut, and up I shall rush again, like a soda-water bubble. The cord itself will help the flotation."

"And if you should chance to hit a ship?" said Weybridge.

"I should come up at such a pace, I should go clean through it," said Elstead, "like a cannon ball. You needn't worry about that."

"And suppose some nimble crustacean should wriggle into your clockwork" –

"It would be a pressing sort of invitation for me to stop," said Elstead, turning his back on the water and staring at the sphere.

* * *

They had swung Elstead overboard by eleven o'clock. The day was serenely bright and calm, with the horizon lost in haze. The electric glare in the little upper compartment beamed cheerfully three times. Then they let him down slowly to the surface of the water, and a sailor in the stern chains hung ready to cut the tackle that held the lead weights and the sphere together. The globe, which had looked so large on deck, looked the smallest thing conceivable under the stern of the ship. It rolled a little, and its two dark windows, which floated uppermost, seemed like eyes turned up in round wonderment at the people who crowded the rail. A voice wondered how Elstead liked the rolling. "Are you ready?" sang out the commander. "Ay, ay, sir!" "Then let her go!"

The rope of the tackle tightened against the blade and was cut, and an eddy rolled over the globe in a grotesquely helpless fashion. Someone waved a handkerchief, someone else tried an ineffectual cheer, a middy was counting slowly, "Eight, nine, ten!" Another roll, then with a jerk and a splash the thing righted itself.

It seemed to be stationary for a moment, to grow rapidly smaller, and then the water closed over it, and it became visible, enlarged by refraction and dimmer, below the surface. Before one could count three it had disappeared. There was a flicker of white light far down in the water, that diminished to a speck and vanished. Then there was nothing but a depth of water going down into blackness, through which a shark was swimming.

Then suddenly the screw of the cruiser began to rotate, the water was crickled, the shark disappeared in a wrinkled confusion, and a torrent of foam rushed across the crystalline clearness that had swallowed up Elstead. "What's the idea?" said one A.B. to another.

"We're going to lay off about a couple of miles, 'fear he should hit us when he comes up," said his mate.

The ship steamed slowly to her new position. Aboard her almost everyone who was unoccupied remained watching the breathing swell into which the sphere had sunk. For the next half-hour it is doubtful if a word was spoken that did not bear directly or indirectly on Elstead. The December sun was now high in the sky, and the heat very considerable.

"He'll be cold enough down there," said Weybridge. "They say that below a certain depth sea water's always just about freezing."

"Where'll he come up?" asked Steevens. "I've lost my bearings."

"That's the spot," said the commander, who prided himself on his omniscience. He extended a precise finger south-eastward. "And this, I reckon, is pretty nearly the moment," he said. "He's been thirty-five minutes."

"How long does it take to reach the bottom of the ocean?" asked Steevens.

"For a depth of five miles, and reckoning – as we did – an acceleration of two feet per second, both ways, is just about three-quarters of a minute."

"Then he's overdue," said Weybridge.

"Pretty nearly," said the commander. "I suppose it takes a few minutes for that cord of his to wind in."

"I forgot that," said Weybridge, evidently relieved.

And then began the suspense. A minute slowly dragged itself out, and no sphere shot out of the water. Another followed, and nothing broke the low oily swell. The sailors explained to one another that little point about the winding-in of the cord. The rigging was dotted with expectant faces. "Come up, Elstead!" called one hairy-chested salt impatiently, and the others caught it up, and shouted as though they were waiting for the curtain of a theatre to rise.

The commander glanced irritably at them.

"Of course, if the acceleration's less than two," he said, "he'll be all the longer. We aren't absolutely certain that was the proper figure. I'm no slavish believer in calculations."

Steevens agreed concisely. No one on the quarter-deck spoke for a couple of minutes. Then Steevens' watchcase clicked.

When, twenty-one minutes after, the sun reached the zenith, they were still waiting for the globe to reappear, and not a man aboard had dared to whisper that hope was dead. It was Weybridge who first gave expression to that realisation. He spoke while the sound of eight bells still hung in the air. "I always distrusted that window," he said quite suddenly to Steevens.

"Good God!" said Steevens; "you don't think –?"

"Well!" said Weybridge, and left the rest to his imagination.

"I'm no great believer in calculations myself," said the commander dubiously, "so that I'm not altogether hopeless yet." And at midnight the gunboat was steaming slowly in a spiral round the spot where the globe had sunk, and the white beam of the electric light fled and halted and swept discontentedly onward again over the waste of phosphorescent waters under the little stars.

"If his window hasn't burst and smashed him," said Weybridge, "then it's a cursed sight worse, for his clockwork has gone wrong, and he's alive now, five miles under our feet, down there in the cold and dark, anchored in that little bubble of his, where never a ray of light has shone or a human being lived, since the waters were gathered together. He's there without food, feeling hungry and thirsty and scared, wondering whether he'll starve or stifle. Which will it be? The Myers apparatus is running out, I suppose. How long do they last?"

"Good heavens!" he exclaimed; "What little things we are! What daring little devils! Down there, miles and miles of water – all water, and all this empty water about us and this sky. Gulfs!" He threw his hands out, and as he did so, a little white streak swept noiselessly up the sky, travelled more slowly, stopped, became a motionless dot, as though a new star had fallen up into the sky. Then it went sliding back again and lost itself amidst the reflections of the stars and the white haze of the sea's phosphorescence.

At the sight he stopped, arm extended and mouth open. He shut his mouth, opened it again, and waved his arms with an impatient gesture. Then he turned, shouted "El-stead ahoy!" to the first watch, and went at a run to Lindley and the search-light. "I saw him," he said. "Starboard there! His light's on, and he's just shot out of the water. Bring the light round. We ought to see him drifting, when he lifts on the swell."

But they never picked up the explorer until dawn. Then they almost ran him down. The crane was swung out and a boat's crew hooked the chain to the sphere. When they had shipped the sphere, they unscrewed the manhole and peered into the darkness of the interior (for the electric light chamber was intended to illuminate the water about the sphere, and was shut off entirely from its general cavity).

The air was very hot within the cavity, and the india rubber at the lip of the manhole was soft. There was no answer to their eager questions and no sound of movement within. Elstead seemed to be lying motionless, crumpled up in the bottom of the globe. The ship's doctor crawled in and lifted him out to the men outside. For a moment or so they did not know whether Elstead was alive or dead. His face, in the yellow light of the ship's lamps, glistened with perspiration. They carried him down to his own cabin.

He was not dead, they found, but in a state of absolute nervous collapse, and besides cruelly bruised. For some days he had to lie perfectly still. It was a week before he could tell his experiences.

Almost his first words were that he was going down again. The sphere would have to be altered, he said, in order to allow him to throw off the cord if need be, and that was all. He had had the most marvellous experience. "You thought I should find nothing but ooze," he said. "You laughed at my explorations, and I've discovered a new world!" He told his story in disconnected fragments, and chiefly from the wrong end, so that it is impossible to re-tell it in his words. But what follows is the narrative of his experience.

It began atrociously, he said. Before the cord ran out, the thing kept rolling over. He felt like a frog in a football. He could see nothing but the crane and the sky overhead, with an occasional glimpse of the people on the ship's rail. He couldn't tell a bit which way the thing would roll next. Suddenly he would find his feet going up, and try to step, and over he went rolling, head over heels, and just anyhow, on the padding. Any other shape would have been more comfortable, but no other shape was to be relied upon under the huge pressure of the nethermost abyss.

Suddenly the swaying ceased; the globe righted, and when he had picked himself up, he saw the water all about him greeny-blue, with an attenuated light filtering down from above, and a shoal of little floating things went rushing up past him, as it seemed to him, towards the light. And even as he looked, it grew darker and darker, until the water above was as dark as the midnight sky, albeit of a greener shade, and the water below black. And little transparent things in the water developed a faint glint of luminosity, and shot past him in faint greenish streaks.

And the feeling of falling! It was just like the start of a lift, he said, only it kept on. One has to imagine what that means, that keeping on. It was then of all times that

Elstead repented of his adventure. He saw the chances against him in an altogether new light. He thought of the big cuttlefish people knew to exist in the middle waters, the kind of things they find half digested in whales at times, or floating dead and rotten and half eaten by fish. Suppose one caught hold and wouldn't let go. And had the clockwork really been sufficiently tested? But whether he wanted to go on or to go back mattered not the slightest now.

In fifty seconds everything was as black as night outside, except where the beam from his light struck through the waters, and picked out every now and then some fish or scrap of sinking matter. They flashed by too fast for him to see what they were. Once he thinks he passed a shark. And then the sphere began to get hot by friction against the water. They had underestimated this, it seems.

The first thing he noticed was that he was perspiring, and then he heard a hissing growing louder under his feet, and saw a lot of little bubbles – very little bubbles they were – rushing upward like a fan through the water outside. Steam! He felt the window, and it was hot. He turned on the minute glow-lamp that lit his own cavity, looked at the padded watch by the studs, and saw he had been travelling now for two minutes. It came into his head that the window would crack through the conflict of temperatures, for he knew the bottom water is very near freezing.

Then suddenly the floor of the sphere seemed to press against his feet, the rush of bubbles outside grew slower and slower, and the hissing diminished. The sphere rolled a little. The window had not cracked, nothing had given, and he knew that the dangers of sinking, at any rate, were over.

In another minute or so he would be on the floor of the abyss. He thought, he said, of Steevens and Weybridge and the rest of them five miles overhead, higher to him than the very highest clouds that ever floated over land are to us, steaming slowly and staring down and wondering what had happened to him.

He peered out of the window. There were no more bubbles now, and the hissing had stopped. Outside there was a heavy blackness – as black as black velvet – except where the electric light pierced the empty water and showed the colour of it – a yellow-green. Then three things like shapes of fire swam into sight, following each other through the water. Whether they were little and near or big and far off he could not tell.

Each was outlined in a bluish light almost as bright as the lights of a fishing smack, a light which seemed to be smoking greatly, and all along the sides of them were specks of this, like the lighter portholes of a ship. Their phosphorescence seemed to go out as they came into the radiance of his lamp, and he saw then that they were little fish of some strange sort, with huge heads, vast eyes, and dwindling bodies and tails. Their eyes were turned towards him, and he judged they were following him down. He supposed they were attracted by his glare.

Presently others of the same sort joined them. As he went on down, he noticed that the water became of a pallid colour, and that little specks twinkled in his ray like motes in a sunbeam. This was probably due to the clouds of ooze and mud that the impact of his leaden sinkers had disturbed.

By the time he was drawn down to the lead weights he was in a dense fog of white that his electric light failed altogether to pierce for more than a few yards, and many minutes elapsed before the hanging sheets of sediment subsided to any extent. Then, lit by his light and by the transient phosphorescence of a distant shoal of fishes, he was able to see under the huge blackness of the super-incumbent water an undulating expanse of greyish-white ooze, broken here and there by tangled thickets of a growth of sea lilies, waving hungry tentacles in the air.

Farther away were the graceful, translucent outlines of a group of gigantic sponges. About this floor there were scattered a number of bristling flattish tufts of rich purple and black, which he decided must be some sort of sea-urchin, and small, large-eyed or blind things having a curious resemblance, some to woodlice, and others to lobsters, crawled sluggishly across the track of the light and vanished into the obscurity again, leaving furrowed trails behind them.

Then suddenly the hovering swarm of little fishes veered about and came towards him as a flight of starlings might do. They passed over him like a phosphorescent snow, and then he saw behind them some larger creature advancing towards the sphere.

At first he could see it only dimly, a faintly moving figure remotely suggestive of a walking man, and then it came into the spray of light that the lamp shot out. As the glare struck it, it shut its eyes, dazzled. He stared in rigid astonishment.

It was a strange vertebrated animal. Its dark purple head was dimly suggestive of a chameleon, but it had such a high forehead and such a braincase as no reptile ever displayed before; the vertical pitch of its face gave it a most extraordinary resemblance to a human being.

Two large and protruding eyes projected from sockets in chameleon fashion, and it had a broad reptilian mouth with horny lips beneath its little nostrils. In the position of the ears were two huge gill-covers, and out of these floated a branching tree of coralline filaments, almost like the tree-like gills that very young rays and sharks possess.

But the humanity of the face was not the most extraordinary thing about the creature. It was a biped; its almost globular body was poised on a tripod of two frog-like legs and a long thick tail, and its fore limbs, which grotesquely caricatured the human hand, much as a frog's do, carried a long shaft of bone, tipped with copper. The colour of the creature was variegated; its head, hands, and legs were purple; but its skin, which hung loosely upon it, even as clothes might do, was a phosphorescent grey. And it stood there blinded by the light.

At last this unknown creature of the abyss blinked its eyes open, and, shading them with its disengaged hand, opened its mouth and gave vent to a shouting noise, articulate almost as speech might be, that penetrated even the steel case and padded jacket of the sphere. How a shouting may be accomplished without lungs Elstead does not profess to explain. It then moved sideways out of the glare into the mystery of shadow that bordered it on either side, and Elstead felt rather than saw that it was coming towards him. Fancying the light had attracted it, he turned the switch that cut off the current. In another moment something soft dabbed upon the steel, and the globe swayed.

Then the shouting was repeated, and it seemed to him that a distant echo answered it. The dabbing recurred, and the globe swayed and ground against the spindle over which the wire was rolled. He stood in the blackness and peered out into the everlasting night of the abyss. And presently he saw, very faint and remote, other phosphorescent quasi-human forms hurrying towards him.

Hardly knowing what he did, he felt about in his swaying prison for the stud of the exterior electric light, and came by accident against his own small glow-lamp in its padded recess. The sphere twisted, and then threw him down; he heard shouts like shouts of surprise, and when he rose to his feet, he saw two pairs of stalked eyes peering into the lower window and reflecting his light.

In another moment hands were dabbing vigorously at his steel casing, and there was a sound, horrible enough in his position, of the metal protection of the clockwork being vigorously hammered. That, indeed, sent his heart into his mouth, for if these strange creatures succeeded in stopping that, his release would never occur. Scarcely had he thought as much when he felt the sphere sway violently, and the floor of it press hard against his feet. He turned off the small glow-lamp that lit the interior, and sent the ray of the large light in the separate compartment out into the water. The sea-floor and the man-like creatures had disappeared, and a couple of fish chasing each other dropped suddenly by the window.

He thought at once that these strange denizens of the deep sea had broken the rope, and that he had escaped. He drove up faster and faster, and then stopped with a jerk that sent him flying against the padded roof of his prison. For half a minute, perhaps, he was too astonished to think.

Then he felt that the sphere was spinning slowly, and rocking, and it seemed to him that it was also being drawn through the water. By crouching close to the window, he managed to make his weight effective and roll that part of the sphere downward, but he could see nothing save the pale ray of his light striking down ineffectively into the darkness. It occurred to him that he would see more if he turned the lamp off, and allowed his eyes to grow accustomed to the profound obscurity.

In this he was wise. After some minutes the velvety blackness became a translucent blackness, and then, far away, and as faint as the zodiacal light of an English summer evening, he saw shapes moving below. He judged these creatures had detached his cable, and were towing him along the sea bottom.

And then he saw something faint and remote across the undulations of the submarine plain, a broad horizon of pale luminosity that extended this way and that way as far as the range of his little window permitted him to see. To this he was being towed, as a balloon might be towed by men out of the open country into a town. He approached it very slowly, and very slowly the dim irradiation was gathered together into more definite shapes.

It was nearly five o'clock before he came over this luminous area, and by that time he could make out an arrangement suggestive of streets and houses grouped about a vast roofless erection that was grotesquely suggestive of a ruined abbey. It was spread out like a map below him. The houses were all roofless enclosures of walls, and their substance being, as he afterwards saw, of phosphorescent bones, gave the place an appearance as if it were built of drowned moonshine.

Among the inner caves of the place waving trees of crinoid stretched their tentacles, and tall, slender, glassy sponges shot like shining minarets and lilies of filmy light out of the general glow of the city. In the open spaces of the place he could see a stirring movement as of crowds of people, but he was too many fathoms above them to distinguish the individuals in those crowds.

Then slowly they pulled him down, and as they did so, the details of the place crept slowly upon his apprehension. He saw that the courses of the cloudy buildings were marked out with beaded lines of round objects, and then he perceived that at several points below him, in broad open spaces, were forms like the encrusted shapes of ships.

Slowly and surely he was drawn down, and the forms below him became brighter, clearer, more distinct. He was being pulled down, he perceived, towards the large building in the centre of the town, and he could catch a glimpse ever and again of the multitudinous forms that were lugging at his cord. He was astonished to see that the rigging of one of the ships, which formed such a prominent feature of the place, was crowded with a host of gesticulating figures regarding him, and then the walls of the great building rose about him silently, and hid the city from his eyes.

And such walls they were, of water-logged wood, and twisted wire-rope, and iron spars, and copper, and the bones and skulls of dead men. The skulls ran in zigzag lines and spirals and fantastic curves over the building; and in and out of their eye-sockets, and over the whole surface of the place, lurked and played a multitude of silvery little fishes.

Suddenly his ears were filled with a low shouting and a noise like the violent blowing of horns, and this gave place to a fantastic chant. Down the sphere sank, past the huge pointed windows, through which he saw vaguely a great number of these strange, ghostlike people regarding him, and at last he came to rest, as it seemed, on a kind of altar that stood in the centre of the place.

And now he was at such a level that he could see these strange people of the abyss plainly once more. To his astonishment, he perceived that they were prostrating themselves before him, all save one, dressed as it seemed in a robe of placoid scales, and crowned with a luminous diadem, who stood with his reptilian mouth opening and shutting, as though he led the chanting of the worshippers.

A curious impulse made Elstead turn on his small glow-lamp again, so that he became visible to these creatures of the abyss, albeit the glare made them disappear forthwith into night. At this sudden sight of him, the chanting gave place to a tumult of exultant shouts; and Elstead, being anxious to watch them, turned his light off again, and vanished from before their eyes. But for a time he was too blind to make out what they were doing, and when at last he could distinguish them, they were kneeling again. And thus they continued worshipping him, without rest or intermission, for the space of three hours.

Most circumstantial was Elstead's account of this astounding city and its people, these people of perpetual night, who have never seen sun or moon or stars, green vegetation, nor any living, air-breathing creatures, who know nothing of fire, nor any light but the phosphorescent light of living things.

Startling as is his story, it is yet more startling to find that scientific men, of such eminence as Adams and Jenkins, find nothing incredible in it. They tell me they see no reason why intelligent, water-breathing, vertebrated creatures, inured to a low temperature and enormous pressure, and of such a heavy structure, that neither alive nor dead would they float, might not live upon the bottom of the deep sea, and quite unsuspected by us, descendants like ourselves of the great Theriomorpha of the New Red Sandstone age.

We should be known to them, however, as strange, meteoric creatures, wont to fall catastrophically dead out of the mysterious blackness of their watery sky. And not only we ourselves, but our ships, our metals, our appliances, would come raining down out of the night. Sometimes sinking things would smite down and crush them, as if it were the judgment of some unseen power above, and sometimes would come things of the utmost rarity or utility, or shapes of inspiring suggestion. One can understand, perhaps, something of their behaviour at the descent of a living man, if one thinks what a barbaric people might do, to whom an enhaloed, shining creature came suddenly out of the sky.

At one time or another Elstead probably told the officers of the *Ptarmigan* every detail of his strange twelve hours in the abyss. That he also intended to write them down is certain, but he never did, and so unhappily we have to piece together the discrepant fragments of his story from the reminiscences of Commander Simmons, Weybridge, Steevens, Lindley, and the others.

We see the thing darkly in fragmentary glimpses – the huge ghostly building, the bowing, chanting people, with their dark chameleon-like heads and faintly luminous clothing, and Elstead, with his light turned on again, vainly trying to convey to their minds that the cord by which the sphere was held was to be severed. Minute after minute slipped away, and Elstead, looking at his watch, was horrified to find that he had oxygen only for four hours more. But the chant in his honour kept on as remorselessly as if it was the marching song of his approaching death.

The manner of his release he does not understand, but to judge by the end of cord that hung from the sphere, it had been cut through by rubbing against the edge of the altar. Abruptly the sphere rolled over, and he swept up, out of their world, as an ethereal creature clothed in a vacuum would sweep through our own atmosphere back to its native ether again. He must have torn out of their sight as a hydrogen bubble hastens upward from our air. A strange ascension it must have seemed to them.

The sphere rushed up with even greater velocity than, when weighted with the lead sinkers, it had rushed down. It became exceedingly hot. It drove up with the windows uppermost, and he remembers the torrent of bubbles frothing against the glass. Every moment he expected this to fly. Then suddenly something like a huge wheel seemed to be released in his head, the padded compartment began spinning about him, and he fainted. His next recollection was of his cabin, and of the doctor's voice.

But that is the substance of the extraordinary story that Elstead related in fragments to the officers of the *Ptarmigan*. He promised to write it all down at a later date. His mind was chiefly occupied with the improvement of his apparatus, which was effected at Rio.

It remains only to tell that on February 2, 1896, he made his second descent into the ocean abyss, with the improvements his first experience suggested. What happened we shall probably never know. He never returned. The *Ptarmigan* beat about over the point of his submersion, seeking him in vain for thirteen days. Then she returned to Rio, and the news was telegraphed to his friends. So the matter remains for the present. But it is hardly probable that no further attempt will be made to verify his strange story of these hitherto unsuspected cities of the deep sea.

The Country of the Blind

H.G. Wells

THREE HUNDRED MILES and more from Chimborazo, one hundred from the snows of Cotopaxi, in the wildest wastes of Ecuador's Andes, there lies that mysterious mountain valley, cut off from the world of men, the Country of the Blind. Long years ago that valley lay so far open to the world that men might come at last through frightful gorges and over an icy pass into its equable meadows; and thither indeed men came, a family or so of Peruvian half-breeds fleeing from the lust and tyranny of an evil Spanish ruler. Then came the stupendous outbreak of Mindobamba, when it was night in Quito for seventeen days, and the water was boiling at Yaguachi and all the fish floating dying even as far as Guayaquil; everywhere along the Pacific slopes there were land-slips and swift thawings and sudden floods, and one whole side of the old Arauca crest slipped and came down in thunder, and cut off the Country of the Blind for ever from the exploring feet of men. But one of these early settlers had chanced to be on the hither side of the gorges when the world had so terribly shaken itself, and he perforce had to forget his wife and his child and all the friends and possessions he had left up there, and start life over again in the lower world. He started it again but ill, blindness overtook him, and he died of punishment in the mines; but the story he told begot a legend that lingers along the length of the Cordilleras of the Andes to this day.

He told of his reason for venturing back from that fastness, into which he had first been carried lashed to a llama, beside a vast bale of gear, when he was a child. The valley, he said, had in it all that the heart of man could desire – sweet water, pasture, and even climate, slopes of rich brown soil with tangles of a shrub that bore an excellent fruit, and on one side great hanging forests of pine that held the avalanches high. Far overhead, on three sides, vast cliffs of grey-green rock were capped by cliffs of ice; but the glacier stream came not to them but flowed away by the farther slopes, and only now and then huge ice masses fell on the valley side. In this valley it neither rained nor snowed, but the abundant springs gave a rich green pasture, that irrigation would spread over all the valley space. The settlers did well indeed there. Their beasts did well and multiplied, and but one thing marred their happiness. Yet it was enough to mar it greatly. A strange disease had come upon them, and had made all the children born to them there – and indeed, several older children also – blind. It was to seek some charm or antidote against this plague of blindness that he had with fatigue and danger and difficulty returned down the gorge. In those days, in such cases, men did not think of germs and infections but of sins; and it seemed to him that the reason of this affliction must lie in the negligence of these priestless immigrants to set up a shrine so soon as they entered the valley. He wanted a shrine – a handsome, cheap, effectual shrine – to be erected in the valley; he wanted relics and such-like potent things of faith, blessed objects and mysterious medals and prayers. In his wallet he had a bar of native silver for which he would not account; he insisted there was none in the valley with something of the insistence of an inexpert liar. They had all clubbed their money and ornaments together, having little need for such treasure up there, he said, to buy them holy help against their ill. I figure this dim-eyed young mountaineer, sunburnt, gaunt, and anxious, hat-brim clutched feverishly, a man all unused to the ways of the lower world, telling this story to some keen-eyed, attentive priest before the great convulsion; I can picture him presently seeking to return with pious and infallible remedies against that trouble, and the infinite dismay with which he must have faced the tumbled vastness where the gorge had once come out. But the rest of his story of mischances is lost to me, save that I know of his evil death after several years. Poor stray from that remoteness! The stream that had once made the gorge now bursts from the mouth of a rocky cave, and the legend his poor, ill-told story set going developed into the legend of a race of blind men somewhere 'over there' one may still hear today.

And amidst the little population of that now isolated and forgotten valley the disease ran its course. The old became groping and purblind, the young saw but dimly, and the children that were born to them saw never at all. But life was very easy in that snow-rimmed basin, lost to all the world, with neither thorns nor briars, with no evil insects nor any beasts save the gentle breed of llamas they had lugged and thrust and followed up the beds of the shrunken rivers in the gorges up which they had come. The seeing had become purblind so gradually that they scarcely noted their loss. They guided the sightless youngsters hither and thither until they knew the whole Valley marvellously, and when at last sight died out among them the race lived on. They had even time to adapt themselves to the blind control of fire, which they made carefully in stoves of stone. They were a simple strain of people at the first, unlettered, only slightly touched with the Spanish civilisation, but with something of a tradition of the arts of old Peru and of its lost philosophy. Generation followed generation. They forgot many things; they devised many things. Their tradition of the greater world they came from became mythical in colour and uncertain. In all things save sight they were strong and able, and presently the chance of birth and heredity sent one who had an original mind and who could talk and persuade among them, and then afterwards another. These two passed, leaving their effects, and the little community grew in numbers and in understanding, and met and settled social and economic problems that arose. Generation followed generation. Generation followed generation. There came a time when a child was born who was fifteen generations from that ancestor who went out of the valley with a bar of silver to seek God's aid, and who never returned. Thereabouts it chanced that a man came into this community from the outer world. And this is the story of that man.

He was a mountaineer from the country near Quito, a man who had been down to the sea and had seen the world, a reader of books in an original way, an acute and enterprising man, and he was taken on by a party of Englishmen who had come out to Ecuador to climb mountains, to replace one of their three Swiss guides who had fallen ill. He climbed here and he climbed there, and then came the attempt on Parascotopetl, the Matterhorn of the Andes, in which he was lost to the outer world. The story of the accident has been written a dozen times. Pointer's narrative is the best. He tells how the little party worked their difficult and almost vertical way up to the very foot of the last and greatest precipice, and how they built a night shelter amidst the snow upon a little shelf of rock, and, with a touch of real dramatic power, how presently they found Nunez had gone from them. They shouted, and there was no reply; shouted and whistled, and for the rest of that night they slept no more.

As the morning broke they saw the traces of his fall. It seems impossible he could have uttered a sound. He had slipped eastward towards the unknown side of the mountain; far below he had struck a steep slope of snow, and ploughed his way down it in the midst of a snow avalanche. His track went straight to the edge of a frightful precipice, and beyond that everything was hidden. Far, far below, and hazy with distance, they could see trees rising out of a narrow, shut-in valley – the lost Country of the Blind. But they did not know it was the lost Country of the Blind, nor distinguish it in any way from any other narrow streak of upland valley. Unnerved by this disaster, they abandoned their attempt in the afternoon, and Pointer was called away to the war before he could make another attack. To this day Parascotopetl lifts an unconquered crest, and Pointer's shelter crumbles unvisited amidst the snows.

And the man who fell survived.

At the end of the slope he fell a thousand feet, and came down in the midst of a cloud of snow upon a snow slope even steeper than the one above. Down this he was whirled, stunned and insensible, but without a bone broken in his body; and then at last came to gentler slopes, and at last rolled out and lay still, buried amidst a softening heap of the white masses that had accompanied and saved him. He came to himself with a dim fancy that he was ill in bed; then realised his position with a mountaineer's intelligence, and worked himself loose and, after a rest or so, out until he saw the stars. He rested flat upon his chest for a space, wondering where he was and what had happened to him. He explored his limbs, and discovered that several of his buttons were gone and his coat turned over his head. His knife had gone from his pocket and his hat was lost, though he had tied it under his chin. He recalled that he had been looking for loose stones to raise his piece of the shelter wall. His ice-axe had disappeared.

He decided he must have fallen, and looked up to see, exaggerated by the ghastly light of the rising moon, the tremendous flight he had taken. For a while he lay, gazing blankly at that vast pale cliff towering above, rising moment by moment out of a subsiding tide of darkness. Its phantasmal, mysterious beauty held him for a space, and then he was seized with a paroxysm of sobbing laughter...

After a great interval of time he became aware that he was near the lower edge of the snow. Below, down what was now a moonlit and practicable slope, he saw the dark and broken appearance of rock-strewn turf. He struggled to his feet, aching in every joint and limb, got down painfully from the heaped loose snow about him, went downward until he was on the turf, and there dropped rather than lay beside a boulder, drank deep from the flask in his inner pocket, and instantly fell asleep...

He was awakened by the singing of birds in the trees far below.

He sat up and perceived he was on a little alp at the foot of a vast precipice, that was grooved by the gully down which he and his snow had come. Over against him another wall of rock reared itself against the sky. The gorge between these precipices ran east and west and was full of the morning sunlight, which lit to the westward the mass of fallen mountain that closed the descending gorge. Below him it seemed there was a precipice equally steep, but behind the snow in the gully he found a sort of chimney-cleft dripping with snow-water down which a desperate man might venture. He found it easier than it seemed, and came at last to another desolate alp, and then after a rock climb of no particular difficulty to a steep slope of trees. He took his bearings and turned his face up the gorge, for he saw it opened out above upon green meadows, among which he now glimpsed quite distinctly a cluster of stone huts of unfamiliar fashion. At times his progress was like clambering along the face of a wall, and after a time the rising sun ceased to strike along the gorge, the voices of the singing birds died away, and the air grew cold and dark about him. But the distant valley with its houses was all the brighter for that. He came presently to talus, and among the rocks he noted – for he was an observant man – an unfamiliar fern that seemed to clutch out of the crevices with intense green hands. He picked a frond or so and gnawed its stalk and found it helpful.

About midday he came at last out of the throat of the gorge into the plain and the sunlight. He was stiff and weary; he sat down in the shadow of a rock, filled up his flask with water from a spring and drank it down, and remained for a time resting before he went on to the houses.

They were very strange to his eyes, and indeed the whole aspect of that valley became, as he regarded it, queerer and more unfamiliar. The greater part of its surface was lush green meadow, starred with many beautiful flowers, irrigated with extraordinary care, and bearing evidence of systematic cropping piece by piece. High up and ringing the valley about was a wall, and what appeared to be a circumferential water-channel, from which the little trickles of water that fed the meadow plants came, and on the higher slopes above this flocks of llamas cropped the scanty herbage. Sheds, apparently shelters or feeding-places for the llamas, stood against the boundary wall here and there. The irrigation streams ran together into a main channel down the centre of the valley, and this was enclosed on either side by a wall breast high. This gave a singularly urban quality to this secluded place, a quality that was greatly enhanced by the fact that a number of paths paved with black and white stones, and each with a curious little kerb at the side, ran hither and thither in an orderly manner. The houses of the central village were quite unlike the casual and higgledy-piggledy agglomeration of the mountain villages he knew; they stood in a continuous row on either side of a central street of astonishing cleanness; here and there their particoloured facade was pierced by a door, and not a solitary window broke their even frontage. They were particoloured with extraordinary irregularity, smeared with a sort of plaster that was sometimes grey, sometimes drab, sometimes slate-coloured or dark brown; and it was the sight of this wild plastering first brought the word 'blind' into the thoughts of the explorer. "The good man who did that," he thought, "must have been as blind as a bat."

He descended a steep place, and so came to the wall and channel that ran about the valley, near where the latter spouted out its surplus contents into the deeps of the gorge in a thin and wavering thread of cascade. He could now see a number of men and women resting on piled heaps of grass, as if taking a siesta, in the remoter part of the meadow, and nearer the village a number of recumbent children, and then nearer at hand three men carrying pails on yokes along a little path that ran from the encircling wall towards the houses. These latter were clad in garments of llama cloth and boots and belts of leather, and they wore caps of cloth with back and ear flaps. They followed one another in single file, walking slowly and yawning as they walked, like men who have been up all night. There was something so reassuringly prosperous and respectable in their bearing that after a moment's hesitation Nunez stood forward as conspicuously as possible upon his rock, and gave vent to a mighty shout that echoed round the valley.

The three men stopped, and moved their heads as though they were looking about them. They turned their faces this way and that, and Nunez gesticulated with freedom.

But they did not appear to see him for all his gestures, and after a time, directing themselves towards the mountains far away to the right, they shouted as if in answer. Nunez bawled again, and then once more, and as he gestured ineffectually the word 'blind' came up to the top of his thoughts. "The fools must be blind," he said.

When at last, after much shouting and wrath, Nunez crossed the stream by a little bridge, came through a gate in the wall, and approached them, he was sure that they were blind. He was sure that this was the Country of the Blind of which the legends told. Conviction had sprung upon him, and a sense of great and rather enviable adventure. The three stood side by side, not looking at him, but with their ears directed towards him, judging him by his unfamiliar steps. They stood close together like men a little afraid, and he could see their eyelids closed and sunken, as though the very balls beneath had shrunk away. There was an expression near awe on their faces.

"A man," one said, in hardly recognisable Spanish – "a man it is – a man or a spirit – coming down from the rocks."

But Nunez advanced with the confident steps of a youth who enters upon life. All the old stories of the lost valley and the Country of the Blind had come back to his mind, and through his thoughts ran this old proverb, as if it were a refrain –

'In the Country of the Blind the One-eyed Man is King.'

'In the Country of the Blind the One-eyed Man is King.'

And very civilly he gave them greeting. He talked to them and used his eyes.

"Where does he come from, brother Pedro?" asked one.

"Down out of the rocks."

"Over the mountains I come," said Nunez, "out of the country beyond there – where men can see. From near Bogota, where there are a hundred thousands of people, and where the city passes out of sight."

"Sight?" muttered Pedro. "Sight?"

"He comes," said the second blind man, "out of the rocks."

The cloth of their coats Nunez saw was curiously fashioned, each with a different sort of stitching.

They startled him by a simultaneous movement towards him, each with a hand outstretched. He stepped back from the advance of these spread fingers.

"Come hither," said the third blind man, following his motion and clutching him neatly.

And they held Nunez and felt him over, saying no word further until they had done so.

"Carefully," he cried, with a finger in his eye, and found they thought that organ, with its fluttering lids, a queer thing in him. They went over it again.

"A strange creature, Correa," said the one called Pedro. "Feel the coarseness of his hair. Like a llama's hair."

"Rough he is as the rocks that begot him," said Correa, investigating Nunez's unshaven chin with a soft and slightly moist hand. "Perhaps he will grow finer." Nunez struggled a little under their examination, but they gripped him firm.

"Carefully," he said again.

"He speaks," said the third man. "Certainly he is a man."

"Ugh!" said Pedro, at the roughness of his coat.

"And you have come into the world?" asked Pedro.

"*Out* of the world. Over mountains and glaciers; right over above there, half-way to the sun. Out of the great big world that goes down, twelve days' journey to the sea."

They scarcely seemed to heed him. "Our fathers have told us men may be made by the forces of Nature," said Correa. "It is the warmth of things and moisture, and rottenness – rottenness."

"Let us lead him to the elders," said Pedro.

"Shout first," said Correa, "lest the children be afraid...This is a marvellous occasion."

So they shouted, and Pedro went first and took Nunez by the hand to lead him to the houses.

He drew his hand away. "I can see," he said.

"See?" said Correa.

"Yes, see," said Nunez, turning towards him, and stumbled against Pedro's pail.

"His senses are still imperfect," said the third blind man. "He stumbles, and talks unmeaning words. Lead him by the hand."

"As you will," said Nunez, and was led along, laughing.

It seemed they knew nothing of sight.

Well, all in good time he would teach them.

He heard people shouting, and saw a number of figures gathering together in the middle roadway of the village.

He found it tax his nerve and patience more than he had anticipated, that first encounter with the population of the Country of the Blind. The place seemed larger as he drew near to it, and the smeared plasterings queerer, and a crowd of children and men and women (the women and girls, he was pleased to note, had some of them quite sweet faces, for all that their eyes were shut and sunken) came about him, holding on to him, touching him with soft, sensitive hands, smelling at him, and listening at every word he spoke. Some of the maidens and children, however, kept aloof as if afraid, and indeed his voice seemed coarse and rude beside their softer notes. They mobbed him. His three guides kept close to him with an effect of proprietorship, and said again and again, "A wild man out of the rock."

"Bogota," he said. "Bogota. Over the mountain crests."

"A wild man – using wild words," said Pedro. "Did you hear that – *Bogota*? His mind is hardly formed yet. He has only the beginnings of speech."

A little boy nipped his hand. "Bogota!" he said mockingly.

"Ay! A city to your village. I come from the great world – where men have eyes and see."

"His name's Bogota," they said.

"He stumbled," said Correa, "stumbled twice as we came hither."

"Bring him to the elders."

And they thrust him suddenly through a doorway into a room as black as pitch, save at the end there faintly glowed a fire. The crowd closed in behind him and shut out all but the faintest glimmer of day, and before he could arrest himself he had fallen headlong over the feet of a seated man. His arm, outflung, struck the face of someone else as he went down; he felt the soft impact of features and heard a cry of anger, and for a moment he struggled against a number of hands that clutched him. It was a one-sided fight. An inkling of the situation came to him, and he lay quiet.

"I fell down," he said; "I couldn't see in this pitchy darkness."

There was a pause as if the unseen persons about him tried to understand his words. Then the voice of Correa said: "He is but newly formed. He stumbles as he walks and mingles words that mean nothing with his speech."

Others also said things about him that he heard or understood imperfectly.

"May I sit up?" he asked, in a pause. "I will not struggle against you again."

They consulted and let him rise.

The voice of an older man began to question him, and Nunez found himself trying to explain the great world out of which he had fallen, and the sky and mountains and sight and such-like marvels, to these elders who sat in darkness in the Country of the Blind. And they would believe and understand nothing whatever he told them, a thing quite outside his expectation. They would not even understand many of his words. For fourteen generations these people had been blind and cut off from all the seeing world; the names for all the things of sight had faded and changed; the story of the outer world was faded and changed to a child's story; and they had ceased to concern themselves with anything beyond the rocky slopes above their circling wall. Blind men of genius had arisen among them and questioned the shreds of belief and tradition they had brought with them from their seeing days, and had dismissed all these things as idle fancies, and replaced them with new and saner explanations. Much of their imagination had shrivelled with their eyes, and they had made for themselves new imaginations with their ever more sensitive ears and finger-tips. Slowly Nunez realised this; that his expectation of wonder and reverence at his origin and his gifts was not to be borne out; and after his poor attempt to explain sight to them had been set aside as the confused version of a new-made being describing the marvels of his incoherent sensations, he subsided, a little dashed, into listening to their instruction. And the eldest of the blind men explained to him life and philosophy and religion, how that the world (meaning their valley) had been first an empty hollow in the rocks, and then had come, first, inanimate things without the gift of touch, and llamas and a few other creatures that had little sense, and then men, and at last angels, whom one could hear singing and making fluttering sounds, but whom no one could touch at all, which puzzled Nunez greatly until he thought of the birds.

He went on to tell Nunez how this time had been divided into the warm and the cold, which are the blind equivalents of day and night, and how it was good to sleep in the warm and work during the cold, so that now, but for his advent, the whole town of the blind would have been asleep. He said Nunez must have been specially created to learn and serve the wisdom, they had acquired, and that for all his mental incoherency and stumbling behaviour he must have courage, and do his best to learn, and at that all the people in the doorway murmured encouragingly. He said the night – for the blind call their day night – was now far gone, and it behoved every one to go back to sleep. He asked Nunez if he knew how to sleep, and Nunez said he did, but that before sleep he wanted food.

They brought him food – llama's milk in a bowl, and rough salted bread – and led him into a lonely place, to eat out of their hearing, and afterwards to slumber until the chill of the mountain evening roused them to begin their day again. But Nunez slumbered not at all.

Instead, he sat up in the place where they had left him, resting his limbs and turning the unanticipated circumstances of his arrival over and over in his mind.

Every now and then he laughed, sometimes with amusement, and sometimes with indignation.

"Unformed mind!" he said. "Got no senses yet! They little know they've been insulting their heaven-sent king and master. I see I must bring them to reason. Let me think – let me think."

He was still thinking when the sun set.

Nunez had an eye for all beautiful things, and it seemed to him that the glow upon the snowfields and glaciers that rose about the valley on every side was the most beautiful thing he had ever seen. His eyes went from that inaccessible glory to the village and irrigated fields, fast sinking into the twilight, and suddenly a wave of emotion took him, and he thanked God from the bottom of his heart that the power of sight had been given him.

He heard a voice calling to him from out of the village. "Ya ho there, Bogota! Come hither!"

At that he stood up smiling. He would show these people once and for all what sight would do for a man. They would seek him, but not find him.

"You move not, Bogota," said the voice.

He laughed noiselessly, and made two stealthy steps aside from the path.

"Trample not on the grass, Bogota; that is not allowed."

Nunez had scarcely heard the sound he made himself. He stopped amazed.

The owner of the voice came running up the piebald path towards him.

He stepped back into the pathway. "Here I am," he said.

"Why did you not come when I called you?" said the blind man. "Must you be led like a child? Cannot you hear the path as you walk?"

Nunez laughed. "I can see it," he said.

"There is no such word as *see*," said the blind man, after a pause. "Cease this folly, and follow the sound of my feet."

Nunez followed, a little annoyed.

"My time will come," he said.

"You'll learn," the blind man answered. "There is much to learn in the world."

"Has no one told you, 'In the Country of the Blind the One-eyed Man is King'?"

"What is blind?" asked the blind man carelessly over his shoulder.

Four days passed, and the fifth found the King of the Blind still incognito, as a clumsy and useless stranger among his subjects.

It was, he found, much more difficult to proclaim himself than he had supposed, and in the meantime, while he meditated his *coup d'état,* he did what he was told and learnt the manners and customs of the Country of the Blind. He found working and going about at night a particularly irksome thing, and he decided that that should be the first thing he would change.

They led a simple, laborious life, these people, with all the elements of virtue and happiness, as these things can be understood by men. They toiled, but not oppressively; they had food and clothing sufficient for their needs; they had days and seasons of rest; they made much of music and singing, and there was love among them, and little children.

It was marvellous with what confidence and precision they went about their ordered world. Everything, you see, had been made to fit their needs; each of the radiating paths of the valley area had a constant angle to the others, and was distinguished by a special notch upon its kerbing; all obstacles and irregularities of path or meadow had long since been cleared away; all their methods and procedure arose naturally from their special needs. Their senses had become marvellously acute; they could hear and judge the slightest gesture of a man a dozen paces away – could hear the very beating of his heart. Intonation had long replaced expression with them, and touches gesture, and their work with hoe and spade and fork was as free and confident as garden work can be. Their sense of smell was extraordinarily fine; they could distinguish individual differences as readily as a dog can, and they went about the tending of the llamas, who lived among the rocks above and came to the wall for food and shelter, with ease and confidence. It was only when at last Nunez sought to assert himself that he found how easy and confident their movements could be.

He rebelled only after he had tried persuasion.

He tried at first on several occasions to tell them of sight. "Look you here, you people," he said. "There are things you do not understand in me."

Once or twice one or two of them attended to him; they sat with faces downcast and ears turned intelligently towards him, and he did his best to tell them what it was to see. Among his hearers was a girl, with eyelids less red and sunken than the others, so that one could almost fancy she was hiding eyes, whom especially he hoped to persuade. He spoke of the beauties of sight, of watching the mountains, of the sky and the sunrise, and they heard him with amused incredulity that presently became condemnatory. They told him there were indeed no mountains at all, but that the end of the rocks where the llamas grazed was indeed the end of the world; thence sprang a cavernous roof of the universe, from which the dew and the avalanches fell; and when he maintained stoutly the world had neither end nor roof such as they supposed, they said his thoughts were wicked. So far as he could describe sky and clouds and stars to them it seemed to them a hideous void, a terrible blankness in the place of the smooth roof to things in which they believed – it was an article of faith with them that the cavern roof was exquisitely smooth to the touch. He saw that in some manner he shocked them, and gave up that aspect of the matter altogether, and tried to show them the practical value of sight. One morning he saw Pedro in the path called Seventeen and coming towards the central houses, but still too far off for hearing or scent, and he told them as much. "In a little while," he prophesied, "Pedro will be here." An old man remarked that Pedro had no business on path Seventeen, and then, as if in confirmation, that individual as he drew near turned and went transversely into path Ten, and so back with nimble paces towards the outer wall. They mocked Nunez when Pedro did not arrive, and afterwards, when he asked Pedro questions to clear his character, Pedro denied and outfaced him, and was afterwards hostile to him.

Then he induced them to let him go a long way up the sloping meadows towards the wall with one complacent individual, and to him he promised to describe all that happened among the houses. He noted certain goings and comings, but the things that really seemed to signify to these people happened inside of or behind the windowless houses – the only things they took note of to test him by – and of these he could see or tell nothing; and it was after the failure of this attempt, and the ridicule they could not repress, that he resorted to force. He thought of seizing a spade and suddenly smiting one or two of them to earth, and so in fair combat showing the advantage of eyes. He went so far with that resolution as to seize his spade, and then he discovered a new thing about himself, and that was that it was impossible for him to hit a blind man in cold blood.

He hesitated, and found them all aware that he had snatched up the spade. They stood alert, with their heads on one side, and bent ears towards him for what he would do next.

"Put that spade down," said one, and he felt a sort of helpless horror. He came near obedience.

Then he thrust one backwards against a house wall, and fled past him and out of the village.

He went athwart one of their meadows, leaving a track of trampled grass behind his feet, and presently sat down by the side of one of their ways. He felt something of the buoyancy that comes to all men in the beginning of a fight, but more perplexity. He began to realise that you cannot even fight happily with creatures who stand upon a different mental basis to yourself. Far away he saw a number of men carrying spades and sticks come out of the street of houses, and advance in a spreading line along the several paths towards him. They advanced slowly, speaking frequently to one another, and ever and again the whole cordon would halt and sniff the air and listen.

The first time they did this Nunez laughed. But afterwards he did not laugh.

One struck his trail in the meadow grass, and came stooping and feeling his way along it.

For five minutes he watched the slow extension of the cordon, and then his vague disposition to do something forthwith became frantic. He stood up, went a pace or so towards the circumferential wall, turned, and went back a little way. There they all stood in a crescent, still and listening.

He also stood still, gripping his spade very tightly in both hands. Should he charge them?

The pulse in his ears ran into the rhythm of 'In the Country of the Blind the One-eyed Man is King!'

Should he charge them?

He looked back at the high and unclimbable wall behind – unclimbable because of its smooth plastering, but withal pierced with many little doors, and at the approaching line of seekers. Behind these others were now coming out of the street of houses.

Should he charge them?

"Bogota!" called one. "Bogota! Where are you?"

He gripped his spade still tighter, and advanced down the meadows towards the place of habitations, and directly he moved they converged upon him. "I'll hit them if they touch me," he swore; "by Heaven, I will. I'll hit." He called aloud, "Look here, I'm going to do what I like in this valley. Do you hear? I'm going to do what I like and go where I like!"

They were moving in upon him quickly, groping, yet moving rapidly. It was like playing blind man's buff, with everyone blindfolded except one. "Get hold of him!" cried one. He found himself in the arc of a loose curve of pursuers. He felt suddenly he must be active and resolute.

"You don't understand," he cried in a voice that was meant to be great and resolute, and which broke. "You are blind, and I can see. Leave me alone!"

"Bogota! Put down that spade, and come off the grass!"

The last order, grotesque in its urban familiarity, produced a gust of anger.

"I'll hurt you," he said, sobbing with emotion. "By Heaven, I'll hurt you. Leave me alone!"

He began to run, not knowing clearly where to run. He ran from the nearest blind man, because it was a horror to hit him. He stopped, and then made a dash to escape from their closing ranks. He made for where a gap was wide, and the men on either side, with a quick perception of the approach of his paces, rushed in on one another. He sprang forward, and then saw he must be caught, and *swish*! The spade had struck.

He felt the soft thud of hand and arm, and the man was down with a yell of pain, and he was through.

Through! And then he was close to the street of houses again, and blind men, whirling spades and stakes, were running with a sort of reasoned swiftness hither and thither.

He heard steps behind him just in time, and found a tall man rushing forward and swiping at the sound of him. He lost his nerve, hurled his spade a yard wide at his antagonist, and whirled about and fled, fairly yelling as he dodged another.

He was panic-stricken. He ran furiously to and fro, dodging when there was no need to dodge, and in his anxiety to see on every side of him at once, stumbling. For a moment he was down and they heard his fall. Far away in the circumferential wall a little doorway looked like heaven, and he set off in a wild rush for it. He did not even look round at his pursuers until it was gained, and he had stumbled across the bridge, clambered a little way among the rocks, to the surprise and dismay of a young llama, who went leaping out of sight, and lay down sobbing for breath.

And so his *coup d'état* came to an end.

He stayed outside the wall of the valley of the Blind for two nights and days without food or shelter, and meditated upon the unexpected. During these meditations he repeated very frequently and always with a profounder note of derision the exploded proverb: "In the Country of the Blind the One-Eyed Man is King." He thought chiefly of ways of fighting and conquering these people, and it grew clear that for him no practicable way was possible. He had no weapons, and now it would be hard to get one.

The canker of civilisation had got to him even in Bogota, and he could not find it in himself to go down and assassinate a blind man. Of course, if he did that, he might then dictate terms on the threat of assassinating them all. But – sooner or later he must sleep!…

He tried also to find food among the pine trees, to be comfortable under pine boughs while the frost fell at night, and – with less confidence – to catch a llama by artifice in order to try to kill it – perhaps by hammering it with a stone – and so finally, perhaps, to eat some of it. But the llamas had a doubt of him and regarded him with distrustful brown eyes, and spat when he drew near. Fear came on him the second day and fits of shivering. Finally he crawled down to the wall of the Country of the Blind and tried to make terms. He crawled along by the stream, shouting, until two blind men came out to the gate and talked to him.

"I was mad," he said. "But I was only newly made."

They said that was better.

He told them he was wiser now, and repented of all he had done.

Then he wept without intention, for he was very weak and ill now, and they took that as a favourable sign.

They asked him if he still thought he could '*see*'

"No," he said. "That was folly. The word means nothing – less than nothing!"

They asked him what was overhead.

"About ten times ten the height of a man there is a roof above the world – of rock – and very, very smooth."…He burst again into hysterical tears. "Before you ask me any more, give me some food or I shall die."

He expected dire punishments, but these blind people were capable of toleration. They regarded his rebellion as but one more proof of his general idiocy and inferiority; and after they had whipped him they appointed him to do the simplest and heaviest work they had for anyone to do, and he, seeing no other way of living, did submissively what he was told.

He was ill for some days, and they nursed him kindly. That refined his submission. But they insisted on his lying in the dark, and that was a great misery. And blind philosophers came and talked to him of the wicked levity of his mind, and reproved him so impressively for his doubts about the lid of rock that covered their cosmic casserole that he almost doubted whether indeed he was not the victim of hallucination in not seeing it overhead.

So Nunez became a citizen of the Country of the Blind, and these people ceased to be a generalised people and became individualities and familiar to him, while the world beyond the mountains became more and more remote and unreal. There was Yacob, his master, a kindly man when not annoyed; there was Pedro, Yacob's nephew; and there was Medina-saroté, who was the youngest daughter of Yacob. She was little esteemed in the world of the blind, because she had a clear-cut face, and lacked that satisfying, glossy smoothness that is the blind man's ideal of feminine beauty; but Nunez thought her beautiful at first, and presently the most beautiful thing in the whole creation. Her closed eyelids were not sunken and red after the common way of the valley, but lay as though they might open again at any moment; and she had long eyelashes, which were considered a grave disfigurement. And her voice was strong, and did not satisfy the acute hearing of the valley swains. So that she had no lover.

There came a time when Nunez thought that, could he win her, he would be resigned to live in the valley for all the rest of his days.

He watched her; he sought opportunities of doing her little services, and presently he found that she observed him. Once at a rest-day gathering they sat side by side in the dim starlight, and the music was sweet. His hand came upon hers and he dared to clasp it. Then very tenderly she returned his pressure. And one day, as they were at their meal in the darkness, he felt her hand very softly seeking him, and as it chanced the fire leapt then and he saw the tenderness of her face.

He sought to speak to her.

He went to her one day when she was sitting in the summer moonlight spinning. The light made her a thing of silver and mystery. He sat down at her feet and told her he loved her, and told her how beautiful she seemed to him. He had a lover's voice, he spoke with a tender reverence that came near to awe, and she had never before been touched by adoration. She made him no definite answer, but it was clear his words pleased her.

After that he talked to her whenever he could take an opportunity. The valley became the world for him, and the world beyond the mountains where men lived in sunlight seemed no more than a fairy tale he would some day pour into her ears. Very tentatively and timidly he spoke to her of sight.

Sight seemed to her the most poetical of fancies, and she listened to his description of the stars and the mountains and her own sweet white-lit beauty as though it was a guilty indulgence. She did not believe, she could only half understand, but she was mysteriously delighted, and it seemed to him that she completely understood.

His love lost its awe and took courage. Presently he was for demanding her of Yacob and the elders in marriage, but she became fearful and delayed. And it was one of her elder sisters who first told Yacob that Medina-saroté and Nunez were in love.

There was from the first very great opposition to the marriage of Nunez and Medina-saroté; not so much because they valued her as because they held him as a being apart, an idiot, incompetent thing below the permissible level of a man. Her sisters opposed it bitterly as bringing discredit on them all; and old Yacob, though he had formed a sort of liking for his clumsy, obedient serf, shook his head and said the thing could not be. The young men were all angry at the idea of corrupting the race, and one went so far as to revile and strike Nunez. He struck back. Then for the first time he found an advantage in seeing, even by twilight, and after that fight was over no one was disposed to raise a hand against him. But they still found his marriage impossible.

Old Yacob had a tenderness for his last little daughter, and was grieved to have her weep upon his shoulder.

"You see, my dear, he's an idiot. He has delusions; he can't do anything right."

"I know," wept Medina-saroté. "But he's better than he was. He's getting better. And he's strong, dear father, and kind – stronger and kinder than any I other man in the world. And he loves me – and, father, I love him."

Old Yacob was greatly distressed to find her inconsolable, and, besides – what made it more distressing – he liked Nunez for many things. So he went and sat in the windowless council-chamber with the other elders and watched the trend of the talk, and said, at the proper time, "He's better than he was. Very likely, some day, we shall find him as sane as ourselves."

Then afterwards one of the elders, who thought deeply, had an idea. He was the great doctor among these people, their medicine-man, and he had a very philosophical and inventive mind, and the idea of curing Nunez of his peculiarities appealed to him. One day when Yacob was present he returned to the topic of Nunez.

"I have examined Bogota," he said, "and the case is clearer to me. I think very probably he might be cured."

"That is what I have always hoped," said old Yacob.

"His brain is affected," said the blind doctor.

The elders murmured assent.

"Now, *what* affects it?"

"Ah!" said old Yacob.

"*This*," said the doctor, answering his own question. "Those queer things that are called the eyes, and which exist to make an agreeable soft depression in the face, are diseased, in the case of Bogota, in such a way as to affect his brain. They are greatly distended, he has eyelashes, and his eyelids move, and consequently his brain is in a state of constant irritation and distraction."

"Yes?" said old Yacob. "Yes?"

"And I think I may say with reasonable certainty that, in order to cure him completely, all that we need do is a simple and easy surgical operation – namely, to remove these irritant bodies."

"And then he will be sane?"

"Then he will be perfectly sane, and a quite admirable citizen."

"Thank Heaven for science!" said old Yacob, and went forth at once to tell Nunez of his happy hopes.

But Nunez's manner of receiving the good news struck him as being cold and disappointing.

"One might think," he said, "from the tone you take, that you did not care for my daughter."

It was Medina-saroté who persuaded Nunez to face the blind surgeons.

"*You* do not want me," he said, "to lose my gift of sight?"

She shook her head.

"My world is sight."

Her head drooped lower.

"There are the beautiful things, the beautiful little things – the flowers, the lichens among the rocks, the lightness and softness on a piece of fur, the far sky with its drifting down of clouds, the sunsets and the stars. And there is *you*. For you alone it is good to have sight, to see your sweet, serene face, your kindly lips, your dear, beautiful hands folded together...It is these eyes of mine you won, these eyes that hold me to you, that these idiots seek. Instead, I must touch you, hear you, and never see you again. I must come under that roof of rock and stone and darkness, that horrible roof under which your imagination stoops...No; you would not have me do that?"

A disagreeable doubt had arisen in him. He stopped, and left the thing a question.

"I wish," she said, "sometimes –" she paused.

"Yes," said he, a little apprehensively.

"I wish sometimes – you would not talk like that."

"Like what?"

"I know it's pretty – it's your imagination. I love it, but *now* –"

He felt cold. "*Now*?" he said faintly.

She sat quite still.

"You mean – you think – I should be better, better perhaps –"

He was realising things very swiftly. He felt anger, indeed, anger at the dull course of fate, but also sympathy for her lack of understanding – a sympathy near akin to pity.

"*Dear*," he said, and he could see by her whiteness how intensely her spirit pressed against the things she could not say. He put his arms about her, he kissed her ear, and they sat for a time in silence.

"If I were to consent to this?" he said at last, in a voice that was very gentle.

She flung her arms about him, weeping wildly. "Oh, if you would," she sobbed, "if only you would!"

* * *

For a week before the operation that was to raise him from his servitude and inferiority to the level of a blind citizen, Nunez knew nothing of sleep, and all through the warm sunlit hours, while the others slumbered happily, he sat brooding or wandered aimlessly, trying to bring his mind to bear on his dilemma. He had given his answer, he had given his consent, and still he was not sure. And at last work-time was over, the sun rose in splendour over the golden crests, and his last day of vision began for him. He had a few minutes with Medina-saroté before she went apart to sleep.

"Tomorrow," he said, "I shall see no more."

"Dear heart!" she answered, and pressed his hands with all her strength.

"They will hurt you but little," she said; "and you are going through this pain – you are going through it, dear lover, for *me*...Dear, if a woman's heart and life can do it, I will repay you. My dearest one, my dearest with the tender voice, I will repay."

He was drenched in pity for himself and her.

He held her in his arms, and pressed his lips to hers, and looked on her sweet face for the last time. "Good-bye!" he whispered at that dear sight, "good-bye!"

And then in silence he turned away from her.

She could hear his slow retreating footsteps, and something in the rhythm of them threw her into a passion of weeping.

He had fully meant to go to a lonely place where the meadows were beautiful with white narcissus, and there remain until the hour of his sacrifice should come, but as he went he lifted up his eyes and saw the morning, the morning like an angel in golden armour, marching down the steeps…

It seemed to him that before this splendour he, and this blind world in the valley, and his love, and all, were no more than a pit of sin.

He did not turn aside as he had meant to do, but went on, and passed through the wall of the circumference and out upon the rocks, and his eyes were always upon the sunlit ice and snow.

He saw their infinite beauty, and his imagination soared over them to the things beyond he was now to resign for ever.

He thought of that great free world he was parted from, the world that was his own, and he had a vision of those further slopes, distance beyond distance, with Bogota, a place of multitudinous stirring beauty, a glory by day, a luminous mystery by night, a place of palaces and fountains and statues and white houses, lying beautifully in the middle distance. He thought how for a day or so one might come down through passes, drawing ever nearer and nearer to its busy streets and ways. He thought of the river journey, day by day, from great Bogota to the still vaster world beyond, through towns and villages, forest and desert places, the rushing river day by day, until its banks receded and the big steamers came splashing by, and one had reached the sea – the limitless sea, with its thousand islands, its thousands of islands, and its ships seen dimly far away in their incessant journeyings round and about that greater world. And there, unpent by mountains, one saw the sky – the sky, not such a disc as one saw it here, but an arch of immeasurable blue, a deep of deeps in which the circling stars were floating…

His eyes scrutinised the great curtain of the mountains with a keener inquiry.

For example, if one went so, up that gully and to that chimney there, then one might come out high among those stunted pines that ran round in a sort of shelf and rose still higher and higher as it passed above the gorge. And then? That talus might be managed. Thence perhaps a climb might be found to take him up to the precipice that came below the snow; and if that chimney failed, then another farther to the east might serve his purpose better. And then? Then one would be out upon the amber-lit snow there, and half-way up to the crest of those beautiful desolations.

He glanced back at the village, then turned right round and regarded it steadfastly.

He thought of Medina-saroté, and she had become small and remote.

He turned again towards the mountain wall, down which the day had come to him.

Then very circumspectly he began to climb.

When sunset came he was no longer climbing, but he was far and high. He had been higher, but he was still very high. His clothes were torn, his limbs were blood-stained, he was bruised in many places, but he lay as if he were at his ease, and there was a smile on his face.

From where he rested the valley seemed as if it were in a pit and nearly a mile below. Already it was dim with haze and shadow, though the mountain summits around him were things of light and fire. The mountain summits around him were things of light and fire, and the little details of the rocks near at hand were drenched with subtle beauty –

a vein of green mineral piercing the grey, the flash of crystal faces here and there, a minute, minutely-beautiful orange lichen close beside his face. There were deep mysterious shadows in the gorge, blue deepening into purple, and purple into a luminous darkness, and overhead was the illimitable vastness of the sky. But he heeded these things no longer, but lay quite inactive there, smiling as if he were satisfied merely to have escaped from the valley of the Blind in which he had thought to be King.

The glow of the sunset passed, and the night came, and still he lay peacefully contented under the cold clear stars.

THE END

Biographies & Sources

Mike Adamson
An Echo of Gondwana
(First Publication)
Mike Adamson holds a PhD in archaeology from Flinders University of South Australia, where he has both studied and taught for some 24 years. Born in England, his family emigrated in 1971, and after early aspirations in art and writing Mike secured degrees in marine biology and archaeology. He has taught with Australia's Colleges of Tertiary and Further Education, and is a passionate photographer, master-level hobbyist and journalist for international magazines. Recently, Mike rediscovered a passion for speculative fiction and has placed some 20 stories with magazines and anthologies to date. His interests embrace science fiction, fantasy, horror, historical and military fields.

Sarah L. Byrne
Tears of the Gods
(Originally Published on *The Future Fire*, 2014)
Sarah L. Byrne is a writer and scientific editor in London, UK. Her short speculative fiction has appeared in various publications, including *Daily Science Fiction* and *Nature*, and been performed live at a Liars' League event in London; and her scientific non-fiction has been published in *Chemistry World* and *The Scientist*. She has also worked as an editor on various scientific and medical journals, on subjects ranging from molecular biology to psychiatry – material which provides unending inspiration for her fiction.

Thomas Canfield
The Temple of the Cat
(First Publication)
Thomas Canfield resides in the mountains of western North Carolina, USA, where he recently encountered the exotic Eastern Hellbender, North America's largest salamander. A good twenty inches from stem to stern, the Hellbender is an attention-grabbing sight, sufficiently ugly to give even the most intrepid soul pause. Thomas has had recent tales in *Silent Screams*, *Third Flatiron*, *Big Pulp*, *Helios Q.*, *Kzine* and *Space & Time*. His phobias run to politicians, lawyers and TV pitchmen. He likes dogs and beer.

Arthur Conan Doyle
The Lost World (chapters VII–X)
(Originally Published in *The Strand Magazine*, 1912)
Arthur Conan Doyle (1859–1930) was born in Edinburgh, Scotland. As a medical student Doyle was so impressed by his professor's powers of deduction that he was inspired to create the illustrious and much-loved figure Sherlock Holmes. However, he became increasingly interested in spiritualism and the supernatural, leaving him keen to explore fantastical elements in his stories. Doyle's vibrant and remarkable characters have breathed life into all of his stories, engaging readers throughout the decades. His novel

The Lost World, in which living prehistoric animals are discovered, is a classic of the Lost World genre, and the first to introduce the character Professor Challenger.

Ronald D. Ferguson
Wolf Brother's Song
(First Publication)
Ronald D. Ferguson is a full time writer who gave up teaching college mathematics and writing college textbooks because fiction is more fun. He prefers writing science fiction and fantasy or peculiar mishmashes of the two. He lives near the shadow of the Alamo with his wife and a rescue dog named Cash. His short fiction has appeared in *Nature: Future*, *Daily Science Fiction*, *The Universe Annex*, NewMyths.com, *Compelling Science Fiction*, *Deep Magic*, and elsewhere. See www.ronalddferguson.com and amazon.com/Ronald-D.-Ferguson/e/B001KDIDPU.

Kevin M. Folliard
Baryonyx Crossing
(First Publication)
Kevin M. Folliard is a Chicagoland fiction writer with a degree in English and creative writing from the University of Illinois in Urbana Champaign. His published fiction includes scary stories collections *Christmas Terror Tales* and *Valentine Terror Tales*, and adventure novels such as *Jake Carter & the Nightmare Gallery*, *Violet Black & the Curse of Camp Coldwater*, and *Jimmy Chimaera & the Temple of Champions*. Folliard's work has been collected by Nosetouch Press, *Double Feature Magazine*, Frith Books, Parsec Ink, and more. You can learn more about his writing at www.kevinfolliard.com.

Charlotte Perkins Gilman
Herland (chapters I–II)
(Originally Published in *The Forerunner*, 1915)
Celebrated feminist writer Charlotte Perkins Gilman (1860–1935) was born in Hartford, Connecticut. She is perhaps best remembered as the author of the short story 'The Yellow Wallpaper', which details a woman's descent into madness after she is cooped up in a misguided attempt to restore her to health. The story was a clear indicator of Gilman's views on the restraints of women and related to her own treatment for postpartum depression. She is also notable for having written the utopian novel *Herland*, in which three men stumble across a society composed entirely of women. Gilman's writings are not only engrossing in their own right, but also continue to spark discussion about gender and society.

H. Rider Haggard
King Solomon's Mines (chapters VIII–XIII)
(Originally Published by Cassell & Company, 1885)
Sir Henry Rider Haggard (1856–1925) was born in Norfolk, England. Best-known for his adventure novels set in exotic locations, Haggard is considered a pioneer in the Lost World literary genre. He spent some years in South Africa, after which he wrote his most famous novel *King Solomon's Mines*, which was the first English adventure novel set in Africa. Later on in his life Haggard was appointed as a Knight Bachelor and Knight Commander for his services to the British Empire.

Sara M. Harvey

The Shell-Spire

(First Publication)

Sara M. Harvey lives and writes fantasy and horror in (and sometimes about) Nashville, Tennessee. She is also a costume historian, theatrical costume designer, and art history and fashion teacher. She has three spoiled-rotten dogs, one awesome daughter, and one feisty son; her husband falls somewhere in between. Sara's fiction has appeared in various anthologies such as *Steam-Powered: Lesbian Steampunk Stories*, *Upside Down: Inverted Tropes in Storytelling*, and *Submerged*. Her novel-length fiction includes *A Year and a Day*, *Seven Times a Woman*, *Music City*, and *The Blood of Angels* trilogy. She tweets @saraphina_marie, wastes too much time on facebook.com/saramharvey, and needs to update her website saramharvey.com.

Robert E. Howard

The Lost Race

(Originally Published in *Weird Tales,* 1927)

Robert Ervin Howard (1906–36) was born in Peaster, Texas. He is responsible for forming the subgenre within fantasy known as 'Sword and Sorcery', establishing him as a pulp fiction writer. Being a very intellectual and athletic man, Howard wrote within the genres of westerns, boxing, historical and horror fiction as well, and created the famous pulp hero Conan the Cimmerian. Howard will perhaps always be known best for his association with the pulp magazine *Weird Tales*, in which he published many stories of an adventure, horror and fantasy nature.

Rudyard Kipling

The Man Who Would Be King

(Originally Published in *The Phantom 'Rickshaw and Other Tales,* A.H. Wheeler, 1888)

English writer and poet Rudyard Kipling (1865–1936) was born in Bombay, India. He was educated in England but returned to India in his youth which would inspire many of his later writings, most famously seen in *The Jungle Book*. He would later return to England and after travelling the United States he settled in Vermont, America. He was awarded the Nobel Prize for Literature in 1907, which made him the first English-language writer to receive the accolade. His narrative style is inventive, an engaging commentary on imperialism, making it no surprise that his works of fiction and poetry have become classics.

H.P. Lovecraft

At the Mountains of Madness

(Originally Published in *Astounding Stories,* 1936)

Master of weird fiction Howard Phillips Lovecraft (1890–1937) was born in Providence, Rhode Island. Featuring unknown and otherworldly creatures, his stories were one of the first to mix science fiction with horror. Plagued by nightmares from an early age, he was inspired to write his dark and strange fantasy tales; and the isolation he must have experienced from suffering frequent illnesses, can be felt as a prominent theme in his work. Lovecraft inspired many other authors, and his most famous story 'The Call of Cthulhu' has gone on to influence many aspects of popular culture.

K.G. McAbee
In Ice Entombed
(First Publication)
K.G. McAbee writes science fiction, fantasy, horror, steampunk, mystery and pulp. She's a member of Sisters in Crime, The Wolfe Pack and International Thriller Writers, and her work has won the Black Orchid, the Dream Realm and other awards, plus an honorable mention in Writers of the Future. She lives in a 200-year-old log cabin in the woods of upstate South Carolina with her gorgeous husband and rejoices in an unholy passion for 1950s science fiction movies, preferably with giant bugs, and old horror movies, preferably with Peter Cushing, Boris Karloff or Christopher Lee.

A. Merritt
The Face in the Abyss (chapters I–V)
(Originally Published in *Argosy All-Story Weekly*, 1923)
Abraham Merritt (1884–1943) was born in Beverly, New Jersey. A writer of speculative fiction as well as an inductee to the Science Fiction and Fantasy Hall of Fame, Merritt wrote characteristic pulp fiction themes of lost civilizations, monsters and treacherous villains. Many of his short stories and novels were published in *Argosy All-Story Weekly.* His most famous novels are perhaps *Burn Witch Burn*, *The Ship Ishtar* and *Dwellers in the Mirage*. His writing was known for its excessive descriptive detail as well as the immense creativity of the alternative worlds he created.

James De Mille
A Strange Manuscript Found in a Copper Cylinder (chapters I–VI)
(Originally Published by Harper & Brothers, 1888)
James De Mille (1833–80) was born the son of a merchant in Saint John, New Brunswick, and was one of the few renowned Canadian authors of the nineteenth century. The majority of his works took a humorous and satirical approach to popular fiction, including mystery and adventure stories, and were much-influenced by his travels in Italy. In addition to teaching at Acadia and Dalhousie, he suffered from severe debt brought by the failure of his book business in 1856. After his death, *A Strange Manuscript Found in a Copper Cylinder* – which has now become his most admired work – was serialized in *Harper's Weekly*. Whilst this story was written before the publication of Rider Haggard's *She* and *King's Solomon's Mines*, it was published after them, and so may have been unfairly viewed at the time as being derivative .

Fitz-James O'Brien
The Diamond Lens
(Originally Published in *Atlantic Monthly*, 1858)
Born in County Cork in Ireland, Fitz-James O'Brien (1828–62) was an Irish-American poet and writer deeply involved in the genre of Gothic fiction, and an early writer in the science fiction movement. He was the son of a lawyer and first worked in London as a journalist before moving to New York City to begin writing. Amongst his most famous short stories are 'The Wondersmith' and 'The Diamond Lens'. O'Brien died after being wounded in the American Civil War, and H.P. Lovecraft said that O'Brien's tragically young death 'undoubtedly deprived us of some masterful tales of strangeness and terror'.

Michael Penncavage
The Matter Concerning Mr. Symmes and the Hollow World
(Originally Published in Issue 117 of *Space and Time Magazine*, 2012)
The expedition proposed by John Cleves Symmes, Jr in 1818 serves as the inspiration for this story by Michael Penncavage. His other stories include 'The Cost of Doing Business', which won the Derringer Award for best mystery, and 'The Converts', which was recently filmed as a short movie. Another story of his has also been adapted as a play. Michael's fiction can can be found in over 95 magazines and anthologies from 7 different countries such as *Alfred Hitchcock Mystery Magazine* (USA), *Here and Now* (England), *Tenebres* (France), *Crime Factory* (Australia), *Reaktor* (Estonia), *Speculative Mystery* (South Africa), and *Visionarium* (Austria).

Adam Roberts
Foreword: Lost Worlds Short Stories
Adam Roberts is a writer and academic with a passion for science fiction. He is the author of sixteen SF novels, most recently *The Thing Itself* (Gollancz 2015). He is also the author of *The Palgrave History of Science Fiction* (2nd edition: Palgrave 2016). He lives a little west of London, UK, with his wife and two children.

Rebecca Schwarz
Short Straw
(First Publication)
Rebecca Schwarz lives in Austin, Texas with her husband, two daughters, and an ever-changing menagerie of house pets. By day, she is a mild-mannered editorial assistant for a scientific journal; by night she writes speculative fiction. Her work has appeared in *Interzone*, *Daily Science Fiction*, Flash Fiction Online, PodCastle, and *Bourbon Penn*. She is the current director of the ArmadillCon Writers' Workshop, and when not otherwise occupied, is working on her first novel. You can read about her writing life at www.curiousworlds.blogspot.com and find her on Twitter @curiousworlds.

James C. Simpson
The Road to Cathacara
(First Publication)
James C. Simpson is a mysterious recluse from the wild mountains of Pennsylvania. He has had a lifelong fascination with the macabre, being particularly keen on the Gothic masters. Among his favorites are Mary Shelley, Bram Stoker, Edgar Allan Poe, H.P. Lovecraft, Arthur Machen, Algernon Blackwood, E.F. Benson, and Ambrose Bierce. When he is not writing a new tale of terror, he often finds himself enjoying the solitude of nature or the darkened realm of the cinema. He has been published several times, including in the anthologies *Luna's Children: Stranger Worlds*, *Legends Of Sleepy Hollow*, *Miskatonic Dreams*, and *Undead Of Winter*, among others.

David Sklar
A Map of Illusions
(First Publication, with an abbreviated version having appeared in the 2015 Art and Words show in Fort Worth, Texas)
David Sklar grew up in Michigan, where the Michipeshu nibbled his toes on the days Lake Superior was feeling frisky. A Rhysling nominee and a past winner of the

Julia Moore Award for Bad Verse, he has more than 100 published works, including fiction in *Nightmare* and *Strange Horizons*, poetry in *Ladybug* and *Stone Telling*, and humour in *Knights of The Dinner Table* and McSweeney's Internet Tendency. David lives with his wife, their two barbarians, and a secondhand familiar in a cliffside cottage in Northern New Jersey, where he almost supports his family as a freelance writer and editor.

Jonathan Swift
Gulliver's Travels (part I, chapters I–VI)
(Originally Published by Benjamin Motte, 1726)
Jonathan Swift (1667–1745), born in Dublin, Ireland, was perhaps the greatest prose satirist in the English language. His unique 'Swiftian' prose style, mixing irony, light-hearted humour and biting ridicule, inspired such later writers as John Ruskin and George Orwell. Unlike other satirists, his prose remained largely free of embellishments, rhetoric and affectations, and he opted instead for a plainer, common form. He is best known for his story *Gulliver's Travels*, and his hyperbolic essay 'A Modest Proposal.' Most of Swift's prose and poetry was published pseudonymously while he worked for the church in Ireland, and as a political pamphleteer during the Whig-Tory conflict in England.

David Tallerman
The Sign in the Moonlight
(Originally Published in *Nightmare Magazine*, 2013)
David Tallerman is the author of the YA fantasy series *The Black River Chronicles*, which began in late 2016 with *Level One*, the *Tales of Easie Damasco* series, and the Tor.com novella *Patchwerk*. His comics work includes the absurdist steampunk graphic novel *Endangered Weapon B: Mechanimal Science* and the Rosarium miniseries *C21st Gods*. David's short stories have appeared in around 80 markets, including *Clarkesworld*, *Nightmare*, *Alfred Hitchcock Mystery Magazine* and *Beneath Ceaseless Skies*. A number of his best dark fantasy and horror stories were included in his debut collection *The Sign in the Moonlight and Other Stories*. He can be found online at davidtallerman.co.uk.

Rachel Verkade
Adlivun (The Beneath)
(First Publication)
Rachel Verkade is a Canadian who somehow ended up living in the UK, possibly because that's where her husband was born. Her fiction has previously been published in *Under the Bed*, *Romance Magazine*, *69 Flavors of Paranoia*, 365 Tomorrows, Pseudopod, *On the Premises*, *The New Accelerator*, and the anthology *Enter the Apocalypse*. Her poetry has been featured in *Liminality* and the anthology *Corpse Roads*, and her reviews and essays can be found at *The Escapist* and *The Future Fire*. She currently lives in Kent with her husband, three cats, and a homicidal parrot.

Jules Verne
Journey to the Centre of the Earth (chapters XXX–XXXIX)
(Originally Published in French by Pierre Jules-Hetzel, 1864; Originally Published in English by Griffith and Farran, 1871)
Jules Verne (1828–1905) was born in Nantes, France. As a novelist, poet and playwright, he wrote adventure novels and had a big impact on the science fiction genre. Along with H.G. Wells, Verne is considered to be one of the founding fathers of science fiction. His most famous adventure novels formed the series *Voyages Extraordinaires*, and include *Journey to the Centre of the Earth* and *Twenty Thousand Leagues Under the Sea*. His works continue to be popular today, and Verne ranks as the most translated science fiction author to date, with his works often reprinted and adapted for film.

John Walters
The Lady of the Lost Valley
(Originally Published in *Fear or Be Feared: Fantasies*, 2012)
John Walters is an American writer, a graduate of Clarion West and member of Science Fiction Writers of America, who recently returned to the United States after living abroad for many years in India, Bangladesh, Italy, and Greece. He writes science fiction and fantasy, thrillers, mainstream fiction, and memoirs of his wanderings around the world. He currently lives in Seattle, Washington, with two of his five sons, precariously eking out a living as a fulltime freelance writer. You can find his blog at: www.johnwalterswriter.com.

H.G. Wells
In the Abyss
(Originally Published in *Pearson's Magazine,* 1896)
The Country of the Blind
(Originally Published in *The Strand Magazine*, 1904)
Herbert George Wells (1866–1946) was born in Kent, England. Novelist, journalist, social reformer and historian, Wells is one of the greatest science fiction writers of all time and, along with Jules Verne, is sometimes referred to as a 'founding father' of the genre. With Aldous Huxley and, later, George Orwell, he defined the adventurous, social concern of early speculative fiction where the human condition was played out on a greater stage. Wells created over 50 novels, including his famous works *The Time Machine*, *The Invisible Man*, *The Island of Dr. Moreau* and *The War of the Worlds*, as well as a fantastic array of short stories.